# Prophecy's Final Price

## Book 3 of the Graves of Good and Evil

A.B.B. Olson

# Prophecy's Final Price

## A.B.B.OLSON

### COPYRIGHT 2016 A.B.B.OLSON

ISBN:0997257229    Soft Cover        978-0-997257229

To my brother Mattbat
Who has listened to me babble about this since I was three.
And my parents, David and Rita,
Who wanted a farmer...and got a writer.
Thanks for standing by me all this time.

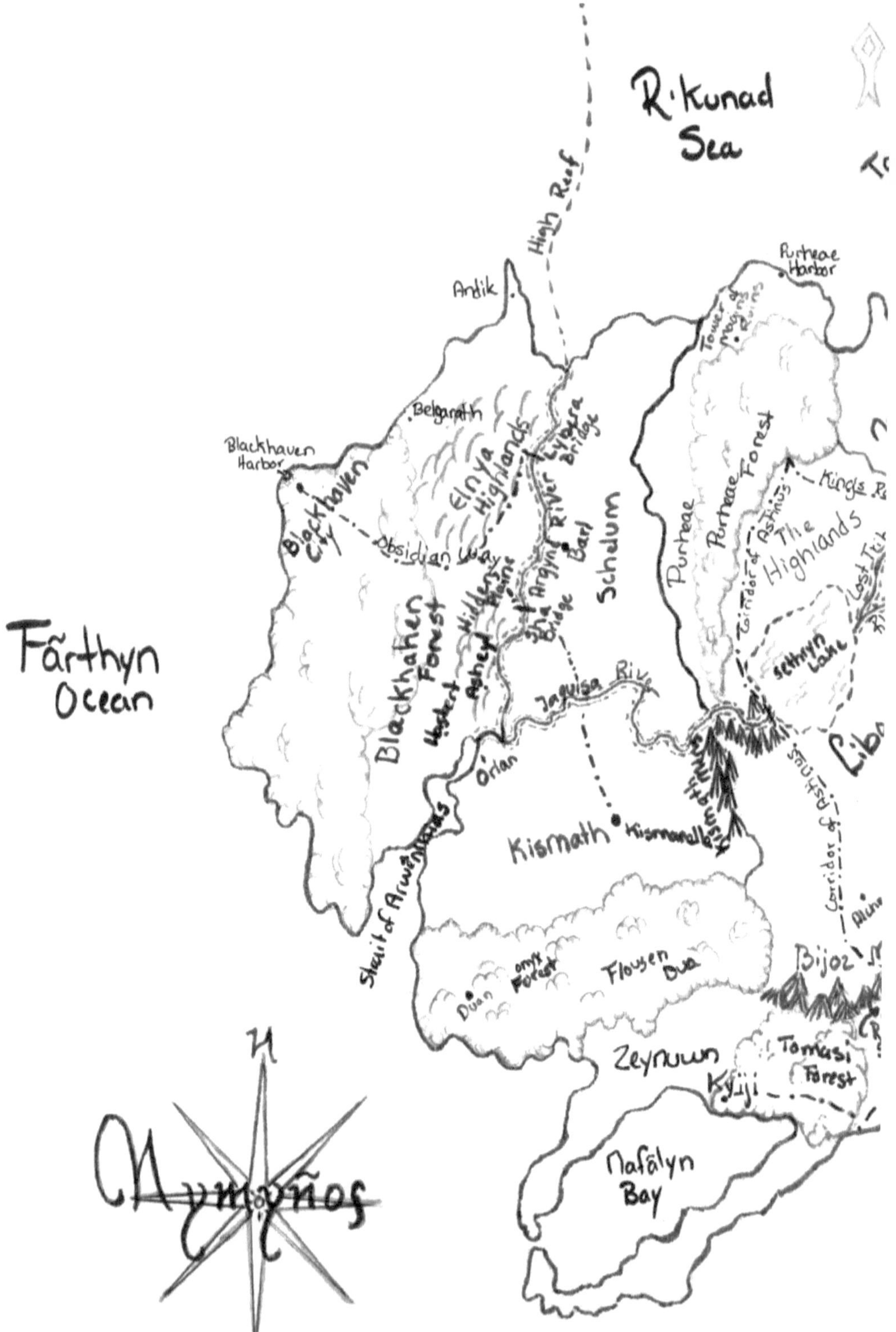

R'kunad Sea
High Reef
Andik
Purheae Harbor
Tower of Magus Ruins
Belgarath
Blackhaven Harbor
Blackhaven City
Elnya Highlands
Lyayra Bridge
Argyn River
Barl
Schelum
Obsidian Way
Purheae
Purheae Forest
Corridor of Asthius
The Highlands
Kings R
Sethryn Lake
Fãrthyn Ocean
Blackhahen Forest
Hidden Ravine
Ashey
Sha Bridge
Jaguisa Riv
Orlan
Kismath
Kismanelle
Kismath Mtns
Corridor of Asthius
Strait of Arwen
Onyx Forest
Flousen Dua
Duan
Bijoz
Zeynuwn
Tomasi Forest
Kyjji
Nafãlyn Bay
N
Nymyños

Zaedio

Norman's Reef

Nestra

Althirim

Thimble River

Longman's Ford

Dushvata

Seaduens

Arnen

Silver Stone River

Florwen Hune

Amaden

White Forest

Fandis Forest

Karus Kiver

Ivory River

Forest of Ullor Lands

Kajgenja

Kajgen Lake

Driad

Aethid

Kiros Deadlands

Klokhet

Fãrthyn Ocean

Assassin's Forest

Trohasa Forest

Anutn

Plains of Prado

shulan Thulare

Arsenhis

Bragminis City

Forest & Clashmoor

Cyres

Helum

Talenias

Mt. Asterb

Kiyb

Ruins of Irisandri

Fãrthyn Ocean

Legend
꘏꘏ Forest    ≅≋ River    — Border
⋀ mountain    ·—·—· Road    ᷧᷧ Hills

CONTENTS:

# Prologue

The night was dark and full of screams, the piteous cries of people in dire agony. Tonora moved through them like an angel, a beacon of beauty and light amongst the horror-stricken village. But her face was not serene like a heavenly being. It was savage and torn, angry tears burning on her cheeks. A splotch of blood glistened on her temple, but the elf paid her injury no heed. Instead she knelt down next to a gasping young boy, his face brutally slashed, one pointed ear hanging off to the side.

"Breathe now, it will be okay," Tonora whispered, white light expanding from her fingertips.

The boy squirmed beneath her, mewling sadly, but despite her efforts only a small number of superficial cuts went away. Tonora sobbed desperately, shaking her hands as though she might force the healing power to finally manifest itself in the way it did for everyone else. She alone of her entire clan could not heal, could not really do anything, though she was their leader.

"You do not have the necessary skill required to heal that boy, Queen Tonora," said a low voice behind the elf and she pivoted on her heels.

A young man, *man*, stood there with his hands folded peacefully at his waist. He looked upon her devastated face with a knowing kindness that sent furious chills down the female's spine. She stood in a rush, her white and green gown fluttering about her with the movement.

"How dare you show your face here, human? Have you come to gloat over the massacre your people wrought? Have you come to finish the job?" Tonora demanded harshly, spreading herself out in order to shield the boy behind her.

"No, I am not your enemy, Queen Tonora. I have long argued with my fellow humans to stop this mad war against your people, to stop the slaughter of innocents in the name of research. My name is Astinus Seer."

Tonora's lip curled nastily. "I know of you. You reside in the blasted tower of murderers and rapists. You do not deserve life."

"Are you one to make such damnation?" Astinus asked, raising his chin a fraction. "How does that judgment make you any better than Roluf Gwemhead, or Quorn Jester, the Magins who sit on the council with me? Do you have the right to say a life is not worthy?"

Tonora sucked in an angry breath. "I have never demanded a life be taken so that I may know how that life could have gone on for millennia. I have never taken a life that did not try to take mine, or someone else's."

"No, you have not, and therefore I say you are not my enemy, nor am I yours. I reside there because it is where I belong, with my fellow Men. Allow me to speak to you with civility."

"What would you say?" the elf queen replied, trying to control her burning ire.

Astinus gazed around at the few surviving elves moving about the village, kneeling over their fallen comrades and healing those who could be. "Might we speak somewhere less overheard?"

Tonora let out a gusty sigh and gestured to a small hut that had not been burned to the ground like so many others. Once inside, Astinus turned to her with a grave countenance.

"Your kin, indeed all elves, have within them great power, the strength to heal not only broken bodies but plants as well, returning a lightning-struck tree to life, for instance. I have watched you for many years, watched you struggle with your failure to replicate this ability."

"If you have come here only to insult me, I shall end your life," Tonora interrupted angrily.

"I do not insult you, I promise," Astinus said calmly, smiling sadly. "Though you may wish that I had, in the end. You are different, my lady, than any of your people. You cannot heal because you are not like them, you do not have the same power. You have... Maginic power."

"I am not a Magin!" Tonora snarled, leaping forward in her fury.

Astinus shook his head, backing away from the fierce elf. "No, you are not. I only said you have Maginic power. You cannot be a Magin because you have not manifested as such. Magins can be detected by other Magins, and you have never been, and you're an elf. As I said, you are something different. You have within you only a destructive power, which is why you cannot heal anything more than a scrape. You are, for lack of a better term, a War Magin. That is why your attempts to heal always are accompanied by a light, while your kinsmen's are not."

"How do you know this?"

"I have seen it. The true reason I am here is to relate to you a vision I had."

"Then relate it and be gone. Your presence here is making me ill," Tonora snapped, sitting down on a short bench.

Astinus chuckled softly. "Have it your way. You have a great destiny before you, Queen Tonora. There is a human king to the east who has discovered a way of breeding elf, man, and goblin together to create a super race. The Eseirik, he calls them. However, they are the precursor to another race, one that has not yet been formed. They will be your kin, captured inside the tormented bodies of demons, shadows of their former selves. If not stopped, this demon race will slowly consume the entire elven population, obliterating them completely. There will not be a single elf left on all of Nymyños.

"They will be the slaves of death itself, kept on a leash wielded by a cruel and sadistic human tyrant. They will be used to herd all the non-humans into slavery or doom. They will corrupt the land, turning it into a choking, dying place, reminiscent of Serenyi. You know of Serenyi, do you not?"

Tonora nodded shortly. "My mother was a child on the boat that landed at Zeynuwn."

"Then you know the horrors of the last year of the continent. The rivers turned to muck, the mountains erupted in fire, grass wilted and broke into dust, the sun itself paled, turned gray. It will happen again, for it is a condition brought on by despair, evil, and all around misuse of the earth. But you can stop it. You, Queen Tonora, can free the slaves of death."

Tonora eyed him warily. "And how am I supposed to do this?"

"I am not sure. The vision did not seem complete, as though something may change it. Prophecy is not a stable magic. Every vision is susceptible to the nuances of the people it affects. One small choice can utterly change, even reverse, a prophecy."

"So everything you say could be a waste of time, then."

Astinus shook his head. "I believe it to be of utmost importance. I have here the prophecy as I Saw it."

He handed the elf a scrap of parchment and allowed her the time to read it. Tonora's face did not change at all.

"A blanket of ash upon the ground, a shadow of evil, and a beam of hope, both flickering across the grayness. Powers too great to be measured or contained erupt from the two, warring, neither giving ground. In the background flit the million souls that hinge on the defeat or victory of either one."

Astinus nodded as he accepted the paper back.

"A bunch of vagaries and guesses," Tonora sighed. "I do not understand how you could have gotten what you just told me from that bit of nonsense."

"This is the tangible prophecy," the Seer explained. "What I Saw was much more detailed. I saw you, your soul and blood at least, within that beam of hope, and I saw the tormented figures of the slaves of death amongst the million souls. You must make your choice, Queen Tonora, I have given you all I can."

"Which is not a lot," Tonora replied as they stood and left the hut. "It does not help my people."

Astinus shook his head. "Not now, not from the devastation my colleagues have, and will continue to wreak upon them, it does not. But in the future—a future I will probably not be around to see, it will. Please, Queen Tonora, do not forget my words tonight in your justifiable hatred of Men. Do not doom your people because you cannot trust in me. Please, I have never wished ill on the Elves."

Tonora looked at him oddly, surprised by his most desperate words yet. "I will not forget them, Seer Astinus."

"Then I have done what I came to do. Goodbye, and good luck, Tonora."

"Go west," the elf queen said as he began to walk back the way he had arrived. "That way, you will be caught by my soldiers and killed. Go west and circle back to your flaming tower."

Astinus nodded and followed her advice, knowing how much it cost her to spare the life of a human. He arrived back at the Tower of Magins near dawn, and climbed wearily to his room. Veries Gurgen bounded by him at one point, giving him a dazzling smile as she read a letter, probably from Teral Shedaerd, her lover who was off with Roluf gathering more Magins. Veries was quite large now, nearing the end of her pregnancy. Astinus rolled his shoulders and cricked his neck, looking forward to a long slumber in his bed.

Years passed, and everyone got older and harder, the war became so violent one could hardly walk outside without seeing blood sprayed on some tree trunk, or a dying elf attempting to escape while soldiers laughed at their efforts. The Magins were now in Triads, divided amongst each other, bickering and plotting becoming more and more evident. Veries no longer smiled, her son was growing, his powers less than she had hoped for, though she still loved him. Teral rarely acknowledged her, though he did dote on the boy, Temas. Astinus watched the proceedings with increasingly sad eyes, especially because his visions were getting darker and more clouded with doubt and fear.

He had not gone to see Tonora again, though he knew she was still out there, fighting side by side with her people. He never heard reports of her using her power, however, and that simultaneously relieved and worried him. What if she never used it? Would she be able to do as she was prophesied to do? Relief because if the Magins knew of her power, they would certainly destroy her.

However, a new terror had cropped up, the Magins' Fifteen Stones, one of which had been used to create new Magins, half-Magins, though they were considered half only because they were not born with their powers. Some of them had strength that eclipsed many of the pure-Magins. It was a dark time for all of them.

Astinus stood staring out his window one night when he saw one of these half-Magins sneak into the forest, and he watched for a long time, tense.

Then the young man snuck back, hours later. Astinus watched as nearly every night the same young man flitted between the tower and forest. Finally, curiosity and worry getting the best of him, the now old Seer crept out after the boy. He kept a safe distance, and he was taken completely by surprise when the half-Magin ducked into one of the hidden elfin villages. Astinus carefully followed, and found himself leaving the small cluster of huts behind, moving through the forest once more.

A while later, he stopped and crouched in the deep shadows of a large oak, watching as the young man turned about in a clearing, apparently waiting for something. Then, to Astinus's utter shock, Tonora stepped into the small clearing, a look of tenderness on her exquisite face.

"Aeryn," she breathed and rushed into his arms.

They embraced for a short while and then the elf queen broke away. "Nomaq is doing much better, thanks to you. Everyone is baffled by it, but they take it in stride. What would have happened had you not healed her, I do not know."

"I would never have met you, Nora, which would make the world an empty place indeed."

Tonora smiled brilliantly and the couple embraced once more, but this time they shed their clothes and joined. Though Astinus was now in his seventies, nearly twenty years since he had seen her last, Tonora was as beautiful and youthful as she had been. It felt indecent to watch the coupling, but he could not tear his eyes away, for the portent of it was grave. He watched as the stunning elf became awash in ecstasy and the young man bit down on her shoulder, obviously overcome with pleasure and love. Then they lay still, breathing deep and murmuring quietly.

Astinus turned and crept away, his mind reeling all the way back to the tower. Several days later the young half-Magin Aeryn was killed for treason, caught as he was creeping into the forest, and the Seer wept.

Another several years passed before any change came. And then one day a young creature appeared in the hands of the guards, a half-elf who had been found wandering along the border of Maginic lands. Jair by name, the young male sneered and snarled as he was brought before Gwemheoad and the council. Astinus was there, nearly blind with cataracts, his skin paper-thin and yellow with jaundice. The boy suddenly jerked free of his captors and red light lashed out his fingers, stunning the entire room. His magic had blasted a hole through the wall, and dust and debris now filtered through the room.

"He's a Magin!" someone cried, and Jair went still, crouched like some feral animal.

Roluf Gwemheoad looked positively hungry, albeit surprised, as he came down to face the boy.

"Where did you come from?"

"I am from the wind, and the stars, and the moons," the half-elf replied haughtily, staring the exalted Magin in the eye.

Gwemheoad smiled. "Give him a room, and enroll him in our studies. I see great things in his future."

Not long after that, Astinus called his old friend Veries to his room and passed her his key, speaking the last words of his life.

"The moon heiress shall free the slaves of death."

Tonora turned around with a gasp when she heard someone enter the small clearing behind her. Her heart thudded slowly as she stared at the male behind her. She knew him, had seen him lurking around corners, watching her.

"Jesper...what are you doing here?" she asked quietly, studying his manic eyes.

"Tonora," he said in his deep, seething voice. "I have loved you unceasingly for so long and yet you deny me. Will you deny me once more? I know of your affair with that tower heathen. Who do you think tipped the guards off?"

"Why would you do such a thing? You claim to love me. Is not true love simply a desire to make that person happy? I loved Aeryn with all my heart, Jesper! And he loved me! *Why* would you do such a thing?"

Jesper shuffled forward, his head cocked to one side. "He was tainting you! Can you not see that? I freed you from his vile grasp!"

Tonora's face shone with tears and she resisted the urge to strike the other elf down. "He was kind, he saved Nomaq's life at risk to his own! You monster!"

"No, no... I am no monster, Tonora. He was spilling his vile seed into you. And then you birthed that half-elf, that abomination you call your son. I will cleanse you of him with my love. It is pure and true. Come, lie in the grass and I shall free you."

"Get away from me!" Tonora hissed, flicking a blade up into her hand and backing away from Jesper's desperate clutching. "Stay back!"

"Come. Let me free you!"

She shrieked as the male leapt onto her, his fingers clawing at her body. Tonora managed to get the knife up and slashed it across Jesper's cheek, but he was so strong. So very strong.

He wrested the knife from her hands and threw her to the ground where she tried to crawl away, but the male wrenched her back. Tonora sucked in a desperate breath and tried to cry out, but he crushed his hand to her windpipe, cutting off her air. His cold fingers tore away her belt and fumbled with her skirts, yanking them up around her waist.

"No! Jesper! Please!" Tonora wheezed as he pawed at her undergarments.

"I am going to free you," he muttered over and over again.

Tonora, desperate, lurched to the side and grabbed up the knife once more. She jabbed it toward his head, but he caught her wrist. They struggled for a few agonizing seconds and then Tonora's arms gave out. The knife twisted as she let go, and it plunged downward into her chest, slammed all the way to the hilt by the momentum of Jesper's hands. Tonora's body went rigid and she began to tremble, mewling sobs escaping from her throat.

"No! No Tonora!" Jesper cried as he fell backward from the blood blossoming on her chest. Hot tears splashed down his face as he watched her struggle in the throes of death.

Tonora closed her eyes and remembered Astinus's desperate words. She remembered all the deaths, all the pain, all the loss. With a final breath, she opened her eyes and stared upward at the moons, pleading to them that they would watch over her people. Her throat worked a bit longer, and then her sight darkened and she sighed.

"Free them," she whispered.

Jesper watched in horror as her body went lax and her head lolled to one side, staring at him with empty, accusing eyes. Then a convulsion wracked her form and lifted her spine from the ground. A blue light bloomed out of her mouth, writhing and pulsing gently. He moved forward, wondering, hoping. Perhaps she was alive. But her back slumped again and she lay too still. The light hovered for a moment and then began to move about like an abandoned child, searching desperately for its home. Jesper reached out a shaking finger and touched it. It pulsed and moved away.

He looked upward, studying the moons Tonora had prayed to. He looked to the ball of light. "Up. Go up," he told it.

The blue light quivered for a moment longer and then shot upward into the dark sky. Jesper watched it in awe, and then he fell back in astonishment when it seemed to impact the very sky. When the startling display of fireworks ended, there in the night sky hung what appeared to be a new moon. A blue moon. Jesper fled, leaving Tonora's body in the small clearing to be found later by her grief-stricken kinsmen.

Jair sat in his small cell of a room, staring at the opposite wall. The Tower was abuzz with speculation as to what had caused the midnight show of bursting stars and the emergence of a new moon. Some were convinced it was a new world, created in a shower of energy and space. Others argued for a more religious explanation. Alone, Jair knew the truth and was enraged by what he knew to be his mother's death. He had felt it, like a twisting in his heart as her life was stolen from her. He did not know his father, though he had heard stories of him, but Jair remembered his mother.

She had been beautiful and fierce, more powerful than most of the Magins in the Tower. She had not used her power often, only in secret, but he had known. He could sense it within her. Furious, Jair raked his hands back through his shaggy auburn hair. It was cut short, just long enough to cover the points on his half-elven ears. He could feel that same power within himself, now, roiling and seething like a ball of frozen fire in his gut. He stalked out of his room, hands clawed with power-induced contraction. He encountered the twisted Buftren Julyt striding down the corridor, his dark purple coat flaring out behind him as he stomped along.

The Third Magin registered him with slow surprise, the lethargic act his very last. Jair lifted a red-wreathed hand and clenched it. Julyt's throat crumpled inward and the man fell to his knees as blood spurted from his ragged flesh.

Jair rounded a corner and found himself facing three of his peers, human students of the Magins. One of them opened his mouth, a cruel smirk on his lips, but the half-blood swept his hands out in front of him and the three fell still as magic sliced through their middles. As the bodies slid apart, Jair stepped over them, already forming his next Weave.

Shelan Turwen and Vurn Seratinaine were the next to fall, the Eleventh and Twelfth Magins died screaming as the young Magin tore their flesh from their bodies. The first to give him a fight was Cerin Maorn. The violent Thirteenth bared his teeth and slashed his arm down when Jair lashed out at him, but his Weave was blocked. Cerin growled and brown light expanded out of his body, warping toward Jair, but the half-blood spread his fingers and thin red lines razored through the brown wall that would trap him. Cerin grunted, and then screamed as the red lines sliced into his body.

Jair was disgusted. Four of the supposed great Magins were dead at his hand and not one of them had presented a challenge. Halfway through the Tower, Jair encountered his friend Temas, son of Veries and Teral. Temas looked shaken, his face pale and his eyes wide.

"Jair! Something's happening! Father said Buftren is dead, probably others! Someone is killing us!"

"Step aside, Temas," Jair said quietly, his power pulsing within him.

Temas's face fell and he swallowed. He was not strong enough to sense what Jair was holding, but he could see the red dancing about his hands. "It's you, isn't it? You killed Buftren. Why?"

"This Tower murders my people, murdered my mother. I will not suffer them to live any longer."

"Not all of them, Jair, please. Please, my parents..."

"Tell Veries to run."

"My...my father, Jair?" Temas reached toward him, a begging look in his normally arrogant eyes.

The half-elf snarled, but he couldn't ignore the expression on his only true friend's face. "I will allow the Third Triad to live, if they flee right now. Tell them!"

Temas stumbled away, scrabbling at the wall as he used it to keep his feet. Jair allowed him only a moment's head start then began walking down the corridor after him. Behind him grew an increasingly bloody trail as he viciously and efficiently took the lives of the Magins and their students. He had not encountered one of the Fifteen since Cerin, however, and was growing impatient. Jair was nearing the center of the Tower now, a few levels above ground. He could hear the heavy footsteps of people running; their screams and ragged breaths as they searched like frantic mice for a way out. He barred it. A crowd was beginning to grow before him, students and Magins crammed into the corridor, unwilling to come any nearer to him. For those more powerful, Jair would be wreathed in an aura of red power, by far more than most of them could ever dream of holding.

There was a commotion and the crowd squeezed against the wall to allow three figures through. Tayrn Verla, Hylen Vertin, and Quorn Jester stepped forward, wreathed in gold, blue, and yellow. Jair shifted, spreading his feet and opening his fists so that his fingers spread around condensed orbs of red.

"Stand down, boy," Tayrn said, his voice firm.

Jair studied the three men. Tayrn was his biggest threat; a big man in a black knee-length coat, he was extremely strong, and experienced. Hylen was middling; a skirt-chaser and more concerned with his looks than with Weaving. Quorn would be a gnat in comparison, but the man had spent his entire time at the Tower learning how to cause pain. Jair shifted his Weaves, splitting them into dozens of different strands, each writhing and coiling, waiting to be released. Tayrn's eyes flicked down at his hands and his face tightened.

"Don't do this, Jair. You won't like the outcome."

"Bleed him and get it over with, Verla," Quorn spat, his reedy voice bored.

"Do not push me, Quorn," Tayrn responded quietly, his eyes steady on Jair.

"You know what I can do, Second," Jair said to the big man. "You know what I am capable of, and that I have the motive to do it. I cannot allow the genocide of my people to continue."

"Your people?" Hylen scoffed, folding his arms. "Your people are a miserable infection on this land, writhing in the mud like beasts. Their queen is a filthy whore who spreads her legs for anyone she thinks might give them mercy."

Jair's hand shot forward and half a dozen Weaves unfurled from it, wrapping around Hylen. "Their queen was my mother, and she was murdered last night because of you and your Triads. I am their king, now." He clenched his hand and the Weaves tightened on Hylen, slicing through his blue shield as if it were paper. The man didn't even scream as he was diced to pieces by razor thin Weaves.

Quorn howled, but Jair spun and shot out his other hand, releasing a handful of what looked like red eggs. The magic slammed into the man's chest and shoulders, and where they touched, blood blossomed from gaping holes. Quorn went down and Jair twisted to avoid Tayrn's golden scythe. The Weave dissipated as it missed, but a score of fine wires expanded out from Tayrn's hands, twisting as they sought Jair. The half-elf tried to block the wires, but his magic simply fell apart as soon as it approached, so instead he threw himself to the side and jerked his hand up. The ceiling rumbled and then collapsed, smashing into the frightened crowd and throwing Tayrn to the ground.

The wires flickered out and Jair rolled, scooting away on his back, hands held out between his knees.

The Second Magin roared as a bar of undulating red light blasted into him, but he managed to sweep it aside before it could do anything more than redden his skin. The return Weave picked Jair up and slammed him into the wall, then the floor, then the other wall. As soon as he dropped, Jair clasped his palms together, spread his fingers, and screamed in release as a jet of pure power shot out of him and pinned Tayrn to the rubble. The man bellowed and his legs kicked, but Jair advanced, holding his hands out in front of him. Tayrn began to convulse, then his skin blackened and he shrieked, clawing at his own chest. Jair let his hands fall and the red light faded away. All that remained of Tayrn was a faintly human-shaped pile of char.

Jair could hear the pleas and cries of the people on the other side of the rubble, but he paid them no heed. He walked back into the center of the corridor, closed his eyes, and took a deep breath. He sucked in every ounce of power he could maintain until he could feel the very fiber of his being begin to shake with the strain. Then he drew more until the ground around him trembled, shards of shattered stone danced along the floor, some even rose up to hang in the air.

Jair sent his power outward, seeking the cracks in the stone, the beating hearts, the joints of bone. He sought out Roluf Gwemheoad, standing in his room preparing to face his rogue student. Satisfied Jair stilled his magic, and for a moment everything hung suspended, immobile and silent. Then the half-elf let out a roar and punched his hands downward, sending fire and spirit along every tendril of power.

The stone walls around him exploded outward with concussive force. Fire roared around the air in a vortex, ruffling Jair's hair as he stood at the center of the maelstrom. The tower itself was blown to pieces; Magins, their guards, and their families were blasted away, some simply dissolving as the magic screamed through the air. Jair watched in wretched anger as those few survivors fled into the forest, which now was bent back away from the wreckage as though it too wanted to flee. The grounds were completely covered in blood, squishing unpleasantly beneath the feet of the terrified people. When he finally let the power go, lashing away from him like a whip; silence fell.

Jair searched around the devastation until he found a chair that had survived, and swallowed, tears falling down his face as he thought of his beautiful mother, laying cold and dead on the ground. He was exhausted. Weariness dragged at him like the hands of the dead but after a while he stood and searched the deserted grounds for the remains of Gwemheoad's room. The man himself was lying splayed on the ground, his robes torn away, along with most of his flesh. Jair moved slowly over the area until he found the objects he had been looking for. A polished wooden box, protected by a strong Weave, broke open easily enough for him, and inside was a blue silk bag bulging with fifteen stones. Another box opened to reveal two pendants of identical size, though polar opposite in purpose. Jair lifted them and put them about his neck, sighing.

Then he found a twisted wooden staff that Reatun Fall had made, something to channel the power of the magical reservoir he had created, the Cyree. With some effort, Jair found the remains of the Stepping Chamber. Luck favored him, and the small blue splotch that indicated the Cyree pond was still intact. Carefully, Jair Wove the necessary pattern that was needed to activate the map, using the very last ounce of his strength. A tiny portal opened, barely large enough to fit a hand through, showing a small amount of too-still water. Jair pushed the Staff through the hole and watched it sink to the bottom, then released the Weave. Then he too went into the forest.

After several days of searching, he found them; the remnants of the elves and other faery folk that lived within. He brought them to the tower, showed them they were free, and there they set up their new home, dragging away the bodies and using the rubble to build their homes. In the center stood the jagged ruins of the Tower of Magins, a stub of what once had been there. Jair fell for the most beautiful of all the maidens, and he loved her so greatly that she eventually allowed him to court her. A few years later they were married, and Nomaq, the child his father had saved long ago, though he did not know it, gave birth to Amram, great grandfather of Dietirin, father of Tlonna, who unbeknownst to everyone, would take up the mantle meant for her ancestor Tonora, and pay the final price for it.

Here is the conclusion to the Aftermath.

# Chapter 1
## Continue Onward

Sodo took a deep breath, rolled his shoulders, and bent back over the worktable, frowning. He squinted his normal eye and widened his tainted one, hoping to see something different in the formula. It swirled innocently before him, undulating veins of red suspended within the clear viscous material called Nytrynhimmel. Sodo sucked in another breath and pushed his face even closer to the beaker. There was something... there!

The alchemist jumped backward in shock and victory, letting out a cry of triumph. "Naphitha!" he shouted, turning about to grin at his human fiancée.

Miazie scowled at him. "Naphitha? Sodo, if you are going to yell random words at me, I would appreciate it if they are ones I understand."

Sodo grinned brighter. "It is the chemical that makes this so different from Nytrynhimmel. It burns brighter, hotter, faster, and is incredibly difficult to put out. I think Tlonna and Losolin did the only thing possible to do so."

The Belau glanced at the concoction, barely seeing it. "Is that the red?"

The smile on her beloved's face slid away, leaving her rather worried. "No, that is blood, well..." he paused, thinking. "It is a cocktail of blood, naphitha, and some sort of Weave."

Now Miazie looked disturbed. "Sithian was able to make a Weave that sustained liquid as volatile as this?"

Sodo shook his head. "It is not sustaining it really, just augmenting it. It is more like a temperature gage. See, Nytrynhimmel ignites through friction, which can be caused by the simple act of throwing it against something. Then, by the time the Nytrynhimmel is burning merrily, the heat is intense enough to light the cocktail. It then bursts, creating a devastating and long-lasting explosion. The fires out in the forest were so hard to put out because they were not feeding per say, but rather continuously igniting."

"It's all rather advanced, isn't it?" Miazie asked, coming to stand next to her lover.

"Frighteningly so," Sodo concurred, nodding. "I am more curious about how they got the recipe for Nytrynhimmel, though."

Miazie shrugged and went back to her journal. "Sithian has more resources at his side than we ever thought possible. The time for pondering is long gone, my love, now is the time for decisive action."

Tlonna leaned against the crenellation, staring eastward as she had for two days straight. Somewhere out there was her son, and she had to believe, Aidyn. Yayènia stood next to her, picking at her boot heel with a knife, trying to remove a stubbornly wedged stone.

"Tell me again why we are standing here rather than racing after our friend?" the queen demanded quietly, feeling lost and helpless.

Yayènia sighed and gave up on the stone. She turned to her sister with a grim expression. "Because Aidyn can take care of himself, and we have to take care of our people. We no longer have the security of an heir, we have only one advisor, and a select few trustworthy folk to guard your reckless life."

"But he may need our help. You cannot know the agony I felt through him. Never in all my life have I believed I was going to die so acutely. The pain was...immeasurable. I tell you, had you all not connected with me, I would have been torn apart."

"As I said, we are here to guard you from yourself," Yayènia muttered, recalling the vivid torment that had washed through her as soon as she touched Aladorn's hand. "Perhaps you should trap Losolin in your room for a couple of days and make an heir, solve one of our problems."

Tlonna did not respond to her sister's weak attempt at humor. Instead she sighed rather dolefully and slumped further against the wall. "Sithian said there was something Aidyn was keeping from me. Something that could undo him."

Yayènia shrugged with one shoulder. "We all have secrets, why should the assassin be any different? He probably has more than all of us. Midian thought the truth of my parentage would undo you, but it did not. The Rahlans have skewed versions of what can shake a person to the core."

"Perhaps," Tlonna conceded after a moment of silence. "But it bothers me that the connection is gone, and it bothers me that Sithian would say such a thing. Why? If he was going to capture Aidyn, why say that? To what purpose? And why capture him at all? He must know that Aidyn will never give up any information, and what information do we have that is so vital? He seems to know everything already."

The High Commander shrugged again. "Questions we do not have answers for, and probably will not have until Aidyn is returned to us."

"If."

"Do not be so cynical. If you doubt him, then he will never come back," Yayènia shot back. "Believe in your heart and in your mind that he will survive to escape, and then he will. We have already discovered that our strength can be sent to him across the miles. Why not our thoughts as well?"

"Since when do you believe in such things?"

The older elf shook her head. "Since I heard your voice in the dark, yours and Suneelo's, begging me to come back. Whispers in the blackness." Yayènia touched her throat, where a pinkish raised scar swept from either side, a constant reminder. "I would not have found the strength to heal had I not believed someone was waiting for me on the other side."

Tlonna was watching her sister, her eyes shaded and faraway. The white pupils contracted as a shaft of sunlight hit her face, illuminating the soft curves of the queen's visage. "I miss him."

"We all do," Yayènia replied quietly, "we all do."

Tears began rolling down Tlonna's face, silent and warm. The elf did not make a sound as she turned once more to gaze out over the forest; hoping, wishing...doubting her friend was still alive.

Losolin sat next to Suneelo in the map room as Ghealan and Aladorn leaned over the table, pointing and arguing about likely places to set up defenses throughout Blackhaven Kingdom. Even after so long of being in constant company the two were still unsure of each other. They had ridden together as Warriors of the Shadow once, an exclusive band of mercenaries that considered desertion, for whatever reason, equal to treason. Ghealan had deserted when he met Erdwyf, and Aladorn still mistrusted him for it.

The wiat's face was drawn and tinged with gray, deep circles about his eyes for lack of rest. Even an elf can only take so much before the body begins to demand such things. Worry and fear for his brother kept him from even sitting down for more than a few minutes, so he paced. The dark elf's finger shook as he pointed at Sethryn Lake.

"I still say we should start here," he muttered, his voice weak.

"It is not our responsibility to go that far from our land to set up defensive points," Ghealan countered yet again.

"Remind me again what it is that we did at Alchemian, then?" Aladorn snapped, his dull green eyes glaring.

"That was different," the Second Commander replied stubbornly, though he knew it was not.

Losolin intervened finally, having grown tired of the argument. "Why do you say we should begin the fight at the Sethryn?"

Aladorn turned to the king. "Unless the humans want to risk running into the Purheae Forest, then their only path would be to come straight through the aisle between the forest and the Kismath Mountains. It would take away the advantage of their numbers. You have seen it many times, Losolin. It is less than half a mile wide, with the river between. We will have every advantage."

Losolin looked at his brother, who shrugged, distracted. "The forest is no longer haunted," the king reminded his dark friend.

"I know that, they do not," Aladorn contradicted immediately.

Ghealan shook his head and dropped into a chair. "I still say it is not in our best interest to run halfway across the bloody continent to fight an army that would, and has, willingly come to our gates."

"Do not forget that your wife sits at the head of the country the Zaedicans plowed through on their way to Alchemian. What is to stop them from doing so again?" Suneelo suddenly said, his voice savage.

"I forget nothing!" Ghealan shouted back, "but we cannot afford to leave our own borders undefended! What if they come by sea again?"

"With what ships?" the captain retorted, as riled and weary as everyone else. "The merchant vessels, and the scout ship sent out awhile back said that there were fifty-two ships sitting in the port at Zaedic. Thirty-nine ships were sunk or defeated at the harbor, and Alexander and his corsairs burned eight. That leaves five ships. If they come at us with that, my harbor guards can easily take them down, especially if Master Jamìn raises the chain. They will not risk an attack by sea again."

"Can you guarantee that, Suneelo? What I have seen so far is that we cannot predict our enemy, for they are far too unstable for such a thing. I would not risk the city on a few dozen harbor guards for the sake of the other kingdoms."

"What does it make us if we ask for help from the provinces during one battle, and stand aside during another? Blackhaven remains one of the strongest kingdoms in all of Nymyños, particularly now that Demetrius is dead. If we forsake our fellow lands, then we forsake our honor, and our righteousness," Losolin said stiffly, shaking his head. "We will speak of this with Tlonna and Yayènia when they get in, and with them we shall make our decision."

Tlonna and Yayènia arrived at the castle within the hour, emotionally drained, physically fatigued. The sisters walked slowly, speaking quietly with heads bowed. Losolin and Suneelo met them at the top of the fourth floor stairs, looking equally weary.

"Aladorn says he wants to begin setting up defenses on the edge of the Sethryn, and let Sithian's men crash against us there, in the narrows between the Kismath Mountains and Purheae Forest," Suneelo informed the females as they turned back toward the map room.

"And Ghealan advises staying here, fortifying the walls and standing strong behind them," Losolin finished.

"He would," Yayènia nodded, looking glum. "He has never been one for aggressive battle fighting. Let me guess, he says it is not our responsibility to run across half the bloody continent in order to defend countries when our own is in danger?"

"Aye," Losolin nodded. "And he has a point, I know it, but still it does not sit well with me."

The foursome stepped inside the map room to find Aladorn and Ghealan standing with their backs to each other, glaring at opposite walls. Tlonna sighed in a fatigued sort of way.

"Where on the Sethryn would you advise setting up defenses?" she asked, taking her customary seat just behind the tiled image of Blackhaven at the head of the table.

Nymyños spread out before her, the thin peninsulas of Zeynuwn nearly reaching the edge of one side, the horns of Blackhaven and Seaduens the other. A new table, the size of a couch table was placed across the room, was situated directly between the two horns of the Elven nations, the island kingdom of Zaedic tiling the top. The small, rather random table was both a large joke and matter of principle. Suneelo walked over to it and sat on the edge, folding his arms across his chest.

Aladorn walked over and pressed his tawny finger to the westernmost edge of the lake. "Here, right on the Corridor of Astinus. It has served us well in the past, it would do so again. We set up trenches for the archers, murder holes, pitch ditches, even security mounds, and the bastards would not have a chance. If they force a retreat, we lure them into the Kismath range, set up avalanches and the like, and stop them there. Have a whole string of planned retreats if necessary, run southwest into Kismath, perhaps dig in at Kismanelle."

"The city was overrun sixty odd years ago, what makes you think it would be worth digging in at all?" Ghealan snapped, turning about. "I was there, Aladorn; Yayènia and I both were. We watched the city burn to the ground."

"As you said, it was sixty some years ago. That is more than half a human's lifespan. Do you not think they might rebuild, or at least set up a village somewhere near? Kismanelle was built where it was because it sat atop the plateau, away from the frozen tundra, the marshes, easily defendable against goblins. Why would they stay away after all this time?" the wiat shot back, angry.

Ghealan made to answer but Yayènia cut him short. "They would not return to that place, Aladorn," she said gently. "The streets and walls were stained with the blood of their neighbors and family. Every home and shop was put to flame and burned to the ground. Every stone building was smashed and torn down. The wall was the only thing left standing, and that only partially. It was a place of terror and death, no one who remembers that siege would ever willingly return to stay."

"So you too advise against my plan?" the dark elf asked, sounding defeated.

Yayènia lifted her eyebrows. "Not at all. I rather like it, actually. Perhaps we can call to Furntil Eldrout again, get his warriors to join us once more."

"Nia!" Ghealan grunted, surprised and affronted. "How can you agree with this when our own city is in great need of our protection?"

"By remembering that in doing this we do protect our city, Lan. If we keep the main force at bay, making sure they sustain heavy losses, then they will never again step foot within Blackhaven borders. If we stop them there, even if we are pushed back to Kismath, then we will have stopped them for good. Every battle, every loss and every gain since the time Aderiaen began his assent to power has been in order to reach this point." Yayènia's eyes went distant as she began to see with clairvoyance the goal she had fought for so long to attain. "Every swing of our swords and every shot with our bows have been to reach this final battle, this great crashing of good versus evil. I say we fight until it is over, until the ground runs red with the blood of our enemies and the skies turn black with the carrion birds as they wheel above the rotting corpses of those who would drive us from our homes."

Tlonna and everyone in the room gazed at the warrior, moved by her passionate words. Her fist was clenched on the table, her entire body straining forward in eagerness.

"I must think on this. Give me one day, and I shall have your answer. I will take no more council on this matter, unless I ask explicitly for it, so do not think to sway me either way. You are dismissed," the queen said after a moment, startling everyone.

"What about my brother?" shouted Aladorn, finally releasing his pent up fury and despair, throwing his arms in the air. "Are you going to just let him die?"

Tlonna pivoted slowly, her chest heaving. The others in the room watched between them, their eyes flicking back and forth, waiting. The wiat glared at his queen, verdant eyes flashing.

"Do not think Aidyn ever slips my mind, Aladorn. I cannot sleep because whenever I close my eyes I see the vision that assaulted me when we contacted him. When I am in silence I hear his screams. There is nothing more we can do at this moment."

The dark elf's ire melted from him, leaving him with shoulders slumped and face ashen. "I just got him back."

"I know. He...he means a lot to me too, Al," Tlonna said quietly, stepping out of the room.

Yayènia left the room after her sister, watching the queen's receding back before heading off to her own office. A small, cool hand wrapped about her bicep, squeezing gently. Turning, she frowned down at Miazie, who looked pale and distraught.

"What is it?"

"Sodo has figured out the chemicals that induced the fires. It is...very disturbing."

"How so?" the warrior asked, turning fully to face the human, her arms crossed, studded vambraces level with the Belau's chin.

"He calls it naphitha... it's a chemical that bursts into flame on contact with heat, and is impossible to douse."

"If it is impossible to douse, how did Tlonna and Losolin do it?" Yayènia demanded, losing her patience.

Miazie let out a gusty sigh. "If you would stop interrupting me I will tell you! Sodo says the only thing that could possibly put out a naphitha concoction is what they did, with magic, healing magic to be precise. Tlonna nearly drained Losolin by using his power with hers, but it saved the entire forest. Without that, it would have gone on until the entire region was an inferno. It is part blood, and part Maginic Weave. The cocktail is also part Nytrynhimmel."

"That is what we used at Alchemian, is it not? How does Sithian have it?"

The woman shrugged, at a loss. "That is what bothers Sodo so much. If Sithian's forces have access to the alchemists, why did we even fight that battle? Was it all for naught?"

Yayènia's hand automatically went up to her throat, where the scar from Midian's blade rose from her flesh. "No. We slaughtered their troops, destroyed their morale, killed Midian for good, and showed them we will not stand their presence here in Nymyños. If nothing else, we did that."

Miazie still looked perturbed, for which the elf could not blame her. Then her hands went to her belly in a very odd fashion. "What do we do? What did Tlonna say? Are we to follow after, or wait for them to come back?"

"She said she needs to think, and she will tell us tomorrow," Yayènia said, narrowing her gaze at the woman, who seemed oblivious to her suspicion. "As far as what we do...we wait. Tlonna and Losolin's display deeply unnerved the enemy, it is the reason they fled, I am sure. Sithian saw that he had no chance against either of them, especially not both, and ran for his life. He has Aidyn, so he has a chip against us, but he is a fool if he thinks he will get anything from him. The assassin has been through more resistance training than all of us put together, and that is no small amount. I say have Sodo write to his guild mates, see what they have to say, if there have been any disappearances, or strange behavior in the camp. We cannot talk to Tlonna again today, she made that much clear, but I will speak with Losolin, let him know what you have told me. And Miazie," Yayènia said as the human began to turn away, "do not tell anyone what you know. Not yet."

"Of course," the Belau returned and hastened off back to her suite, where Sodo was still puzzling over the presence of naphitha.

Losolin listened as Yayènia repeated Miazie's concerns to him, fiddling with a letter opener on the table while Suneelo lounged against the windowsill. The three of them were still in the map room, Aladorn and Ghealan having stormed off to their respective apartments. Ghealan had taken to staying at his suite in the castle, not caring to return to his empty manor house, with the memories of Erdwyf and Jaryikin lurking in every room.

"Are they positive?" the king asked when his sister had finished speaking.

"She looked and sounded to be so, and I am sure Miazie would not say such a thing without doing her best to prove it first," Yayènia replied, nodding.

Losolin sighed, dropped the letter opener and looked at his brother. "What are we going to do? Enemies in every corner, friends dropping like diseased cows, kingdoms being shaken to their very foundations. I fear the future."

Suneelo shook his head, glancing between his young sibling and his wife. "Do not fear the inevitable. Embrace it, challenge it, fight it, but do not fear it. That way lurks only madness."

The king gazed at the captain in appreciation. "You sound so wise. Some days you make me feel a fool, young and inexperienced."

The other male snorted quietly. "I am old, and you are no fool. Young yes, fool, not so much. When you hit five hundred then you can begin complaining about age."

Yayènia gave her husband a knowing smile and sat down next to Losolin. "You are not alone in your fear, little brother," she said gently. "We are all uncertain, and despite my dear husband's words, we are all frightened of it. It is the unknown that makes us shiver, and the future is always unknown, no matter how many prophecies you read. Just remember that you are not alone."

Losolin patted her hand, and they delved into a discussion about what Tlonna would say the next day.

The hours passed swiftly, and Tlonna found herself pacing, hating the decision she had come to, knowing it would cause pain. She did not keep track of the time, and when she finally stopped to look out her balcony door, she found that dawn was creeping through the air. The elf strode over and yanked open the door to let in the cool morning breeze, which dangerously ruffled the papers on her desk. She eyed them with distaste, half-hoping they would fly out of her office. She watched the castle awaken from her perch on the fourth floor, watched the early risers strolling about the pillared bridges and walkways, some arcing above the courtyard, others winding through it. She closed her eyes as the morning herald echoed through the city, the quick rapping of the drums, the tolling of the bells, and the blaring of the horns. It was quick and simple, meant simply to awaken the sleepers. She thought it beautiful.

Tlonna shut and locked her door, needing the time to gather her thoughts and courage for what she was about to ask her family, or demand of them if necessary. Her heart thudded slowly against her chest, warning her of the probable reaction from her sister and brother-in-law. The queen picked up a quill and fumbled with it, staring blankly at her paper-littered desk. She knew not how long she sat there, but the sun was well into the sky when the embossed silver handle on her door wiggled as someone grabbed it.

"Loni?" called Losolin, his voice quiet. "Everyone is in the map room."

Taking a steadying, deep breath, Tlonna lifted herself from her chair and unlocked the door. Her husband's deep blue eyes met hers with a knowing stare, the dark bronze of his lashes casting sweeping shadows against his brow.

"Whatever it is you are planning...know I will do my best to support you."

The Magin Queen smiled and placed her hand on his cheek. "I hope you do not regret that, when I am finished."

"I do too," Losolin muttered as he followed his wife to the room.

They were all there, Yayènia and Suneelo, Miazie and Sodo, Aladorn and Ghealan. They all looked up as Tlonna and Losolin entered, each with varying degrees of suspicion. The queen gently pushed her husband into a chair and then stood at the head of the long table, all eyes on her.

"I have thought over all of your suggestions as far as what to do about Sithian's troops. I ask you now to hear me out completely before commenting."

Her council's expressions all turned nervous and worried, but they stayed silent. Tlonna took a deep breath and pressed her knuckles to the worn tabletop. "We will meet them at Sethryn Lake."

Ghealan's eyes flared but he kept his mouth closed, his arms folded across his broad chest.

"However, not all of us will be going. Losolin, Ghealan, and Suneelo will march with the army, while Yayènia, Aladorn, and I will remain here to wait for Aidyn, and to take care of some things that cannot be left for others to do. When these things are taken care of, we will ride to the battlefront and join in. I however, will not be staying there. Things are coming into play and I must take heed. The time has come for answers. I will no longer sit back and wonder."

Yayènia's expression was one of pure mutiny. "Never before have the troops of Blackhaven gone into battle without their High Commander. What you ask of me is...treachery! Cowardice! You ask that I forswear myself so that you can take care of things here? That is what Miazie is here for, and the whole bleeding city council!"

"I ask that you remain at my side, your queen's side, while she answers the call of duty."

"Duty? You throw that word in my face like a curse!" Yayènia shrieked, her rage so great she shot up out of her chair. "You break not only tradition but the morale of the soldiers, they march because they march behind me! That is the way it has been for thousands of years! The Blackhaven Militia marches behind its High Commander!"

Tlonna took her sister's tirade in stride, not letting the absolute rage get to her. She was frozen against the response of her commands, now. Losolin too looked unhappy, but he remained quiet. Suneelo looked away.

"Why? What things are you going to take care of?" he asked, his voice calm as usual, but those closest to him heard the tremor of anger.

"Four years ago I was given three gifts from Andramaky, the Cyree. The first was *Isten shä Talchin*, the Staff of Cyree," the Magin patted the staff that was strapped to her back at all times. "The second was a cloak, also given to Miazie and Losolin to help shield us from unwanted eyes, and to protect us from dire elements. The third was a sword made of ivory, a virgin blade, wrought from the bones of the earth itself. I know not what creature gave its ivory in order to make the blade, but I know it was a sacrifice of great cost. Only I can lift it."

"She gave you four gifts, Tlonna," Miazie interceded quietly. When everyone turned to the Belau, she gestured at her friend. "She tossed you into the Cyree itself, giving you the ability to see beyond what was there. Your vision changes whenever you Weave, we have all seen it. Even though your pupils remain white, they still elongate and the iris changes. You never speak of it, but we have all seen it."

Tlonna closed her eyes for a moment, hating them. "It is true. When I use my power I see things differently. Sometimes the color is washed away so that I can see objects better, and sometimes I can see just as well at night as I can during the day. But only when I am Weaving."

"To what purpose?" Ghealan asked, not looking at her.

The queen shrugged. "I do not yet know. Ever since Purheae I can see more. I can see auras and shifts in the faintest of light. It is hard to keep my eyes open."

"And what point do you think staying behind will serve? You have not found the answers in four years, how do you expect to find them in a few weeks?" Yayènia snarled, pacing.

Suneelo reached out and grabbed her elbow as she went by, jerking her to a halt. She sneered down at him, but stayed still as he gave her a warning look.

Tlonna shrugged again. "That is not why I want to stay here, Nia. First of all, I want to wait as long as possible for Aidyn to return. Second, I need to wait for the messengers from Flousen Dua to return; I cannot send them off and not be here when they arrive. And third, I need to find out what happened to Eyin Thorn and his people."

With her logic thrown in their faces, no one could argue against her decision, though Yayènia still looked furious. "Keep Ghealan here and let me go! Why do you need me?"

"Because Ghealan is here to see the war through to the end, and you have a duty to protect your queen at all costs, no matter what injury you must take to your grossly inflated pride!" Tlonna shouted, her patience worn out.

The room went deathly quiet as the sisters seethed at each other, their shoulders heaving with each breath. Finally Yayènia tossed her arm out of Suneelo's restraining grasp. "As you command, my queen," she growled and stomped out of the room.

Tlonna took yet another deep breath and turned to the rest of her friends and family. "I know this is hard for all of you, and trust me, it is not easy for me, but it is what I think is for the best. I have too often forsaken reason for passion and ended up with the blood of thousands upon my hands. I will hear your arguments now."

No one spoke as they each looked at her with weary eyes, ready for the fight to be over. Losolin finally cleared his throat and scooted closer to the table. "What would you have us do at Sethryn?"

Tlonna gave him a small, grateful smile. "I want every able-bodied soldier marching with you in one week's time. Once you reach the lake, set up what Aladorn at first suggested, trenches and traps. I am sending the engineer Matthias Goss and his companion Lukan along with you. They will help you devise shields and the like to protect our people. Hold Sithian's troops there until you must retreat, then head southwest into the Kismath range, if necessary. Suneelo, I want most of your guards to stay behind, protect the city and the outlying towns and villages. How many do you have?"

The Captain of the Guard answered immediately, his eyes alight with a sudden fever of battle. "Nine hundred and eighty-six. They are split into several different areas. Two hundred and twelve wall guards, one hundred and thirty-two castle guards, three hundred and sixty-two forest guards, in patrols of six, and two hundred and eighty city guards."

Tlonna nodded, impressed. "Split the castle guards in half and send equal companies to Belgarath, Andik, Hastert, and Mardyn. Send them with the same decrees of protection that we extended with the initial siege."

Suneelo nodded his concurrence and began dividing up the companies right there. Ghealan frowned at her. "That will leave only sixty-six guards inside the castle grounds."

"I know, but the castle is in the center of the city. It is also the most defendable," Tlonna replied and stood. "Any other questions? I am to meet with Daphne in the treasury."

"Do you think Sithian will try anything during the winter?" Sodo asked, speaking for the first time.

The queen shrugged. "He learned a harsh lesson, but he is still a child. I cannot say for sure what exactly he will do so far as that."

"It would be to our advantage if he did," Ghealan ventured, twisting a scrap piece of parchment in his large hands.

"Then drive him to it, Lan. Force him to confront us on our terms rather than his. Drag him out of his comfort zone and destroy his sense of invincibility."

"That is what I do," the warrior snarled at the twisted paper.

Tlonna nodded once and left the room, needing to get away.

# Chapter 2
## Questions and Demands

Deep in the Liberated Lands in the center of Nymyños rose a large plateau known as Anutch. What once had been a steady kingdom was now a barren wasteland of burnt building and withering crops, but it teemed with men. Soldiers and mercenaries from Zaedic and Talenias, and the far Scattered Isles up north were setting up more permanent residences, nursing wounds from the most recent battle and trying to get the terrifying images from their minds. Several woke in the night, screaming as they relived the devastation wrought by the Magin Queen Everwood as she disintegrated an entire company of their comrades. Or they woke in shivers, remembering the concussive thunder and sticky rain that had knocked them to the ground, drowning out the fire that was supposed to be immune to water. Their eyes were often drawn toward the center of the camp, where their king held his greatest prize, and that too filled them with terror. In that tiny tent less than ten square feet in area sat a chair.

Harshly bound to the chair was Aidyn Sestuns, Master Assassin for the Throne of Blackhaven. Clotted strings of blood hung quivering from his mouth and nose, clinging to his bare chest, which was so bruised the soft tan skin beneath was barely visible. The muscles on his thighs stood out against his black leather pants, straining with the awkward angle at which his legs were tied, dried blood crusting the area in which he had taken a piece of shrapnel. The jagged piece of unidentifiable metal had been harshly yanked out by Sithian, but there had been no other tending done to it. His deltoids were over-extended as his arms crisscrossed each other, tied to the opposite sides of the chair back.

Breath rattled out of his chest as he struggled to stay alert. Aidyn spat, trying to clear away the bloody coagulations that stubbornly clung to his lips. The glob landed on the toe of a boot that had just entered the tiny space. A backhanded slap cracked his already sore neck, rocking the chair over onto two legs. Settling his weight, the dark elf righted the chair and glared up through bruised eyes at Sithian, who was using a Weave to clean off his footwear.

"It has been five days, Assassin. I don't think they are coming for you."

"Believe what you wish boy," Aidyn replied in a coarse voice. "If they come, they will not come for me. They will come for you."

Sithian, King of Zaedic and son of Tlonna, smirked, setting his boot on the chair between Aidyn's legs. He leaned forward, folding his arms across his knee and staring directly into the elf's emerald eyes.

"Should we begin again?" he asked pleasantly, sliding his foot right up against his captive's groin, pressing hard.

The elf did not blink as he felt the first painful waves roll up from his genitals. He barely felt it now, so immense was the pain that he knew was coming. Sithian removed his boot and walked around behind Aidyn, sliding his fine-boned hand across the bruised chest. His fingers suddenly clenched on the elf's shoulders, close to the neck, and Weaves the color of the early dawn sky dug into him, forcing his muscles to go rigid.

A few moments later blood began to squish through Aidyn's clenched teeth, and roll from his nose. A bloody tear squeezed out of his eye, directly above the curving, arrow-shaped scars on his cheek.

"Tell me where she got her powers!" Sithian screamed, as he had for the last several days. "How did she attain them? What does she know of the prophecy?"

Aidyn rocked forward, trying to get his shoulders free of the evil grasp. At least when Sithian had done it directly into his mouth or neck he had gone unconscious almost immediately. This way he stayed cognizant, unable to slip away. The Magin released the elf and knelt down in front of him, his eyes wide with false sadness.

"You don't have to endure this, Aidyn. You could just tell me the answers to the questions I ask you, and you would be free. I know how much it hurts you. I do."

The dark elf's chest heaved as he turned his head to spit out more blood. "Do you honestly think that after so long I would tell you? What would be the point of enduring this if I was going to just give up?"

Sithian smiled with one side of his mouth. He straightened his back and pressed his cold, dry lips to the scars on Aidyn's cheek. The elf grunted in revulsion, and then his right eye went blind as a swirling blackness enveloped it, making him shiver.

"When I found out that Athelias had sent the Eseirik after you and your friends, I saw an opportunity. Oh, I knew they would fail, of course, but I figured I would make it worthwhile. I gave them a weapon with two triangular blades that were coated in an insidious poison and a Weave. I knew that Tlonna would send someone after the hybrids, such a threat could not be allowed to remain, after all. And who would she send? Her immortal sister, or her murderous shadow? Either way I won. They allow me to give you pain. I can control you through agony. Slowly, I will consume you until you are literally begging at my feet for a reprieve."

"You cannot control me, boy. I have suffered pain you cannot even begin to fathom. Believe me, nothing you do will break me," Aidyn breathed, moving his chin away from Sithian's cold fingers.

Sithian chuckled, trailing his fingers down the assassin's neck. "So stubborn, poor creature. I don't have to make it bloody. I could do it so that your body would not be visibly affected at all. You are so beautiful, it is almost a shame," he crooned, his lips close to the delicately pointed elf ear, running his fingers through the blood on the elf's cheek, "but I do so love blood. The smell, the feel, the *taste*...there's nothing like it."

Aidyn moved his head away from Sithian's caressing touch, watching through his peripheral as the boy rubbed his crimson fingers together. He touched the blood to his lips, his sapphire eyes closing in pleasure. Then suddenly the hand Aidyn could not see clamped hard on his side, sending shivering waves of burning ice up into his ribcage.

"I do hope you survive long enough for me to reveal what I know to my mother. What I know about you, and her. It would be such a shame for you not to be there."

"Whatever you think you know," Aidyn wheezed, trying to regain his senses, "it is not going to do the damage you need it to."

"We shall see," Sithian murmured as he gathered Aidyn's hair in his fist and almost gently flipped it over his shoulder, revealing the back of his neck, "we shall see."

Night fell swiftly as Aidyn stared out of the opening in his tent, the sliver revealing to him, as always, the two guards who were quite unnecessary. He had tried since they had arrived at Anutch to loosen the knots on his arms and legs, but had so far been unsuccessful. His wrists and ankles were bloody and raw from the constant strain, his fingernails torn, his joints aching. For the first time in his long life, he felt despair. He missed his friends and his family, and he wanted only to die.

He closed his eyes and let his head drop backward, stretching the cramped muscles in his neck. He let the memory come, though it had only been five days, it felt like months, years, since it had happened. He remembered the overwhelming presence of Tlonna washing through him, her anger and fury and fear, seeing through her eyes. He remembered the lessening of the pain, and then in increments it lessened further. First the vengeful soul of his long-lost brother swept through him, giving him strength, and then the stubborn will of Yayènia, the quiet determination of Suneelo, the angry defiance of Ghealan, and the furious healing power of Losolin. They had all come to him, somehow spanning the distance, filling his body and mind with their strength and love.

It had deeply unnerved him, having that many consciousnesses sweeping through him, but it had completely unhinged Sithian. Aidyn's mouth twitched upward in a smile as he remembered the frantic terror writ on the face of the half-blood. They had spoken, all of them, though the assassin was sure that they had been Tlonna's words, spoken in Parlêthian, the language of the elves, the damning promise.

We are coming.

But they had not come yet, and he was dying.

Yayènia was waiting outside the door of Tlonna's office when she came back after the meeting. Before the queen could even open her mouth to speak, the warrior grabbed her elbow and tossed her roughly into the room. Tlonna's hip jarred agonizingly against the vine-carved edge of her desk. She righted slowly, having never actually been at the receiving end of Yayènia's vicious temper. Before she could turn, the weapons-master's armored hand shot out and struck her across the shoulder, hard enough to make the muscle knot painfully.

Tlonna winced against the expected blow to follow, her eyes squeezed shut. It did not come, so she cracked her eyes open to stare at Yayènia. She was livid, her chest heaving with each gasping breath.

"I spend years getting those soldiers into form, spend months individually training companies so that they will have confidence when they go into battle, and then you yank me away? They will break when they realize I have abandoned them, and why not? I ask them to fight, yet I do not? I ask them to die, yet I do not even lift a weapon? I ask them to protect their homeland, yet I am expected to sit here and do nothing while you *wait?*"

"I wonder if it is a lack of confidence in yourself or your soldiers that causes you to think you are needed to win every battle," Tlonna noted dryly, surreptitiously rubbing her throbbing hip. "Have you done such a lousy job at training them that all their practice will go out of their heads if they do not see you?"

Rage ignited even hotter in Yayènia's face as she clenched her hands at her sides, suppressing the urge to draw steel. "You do not know what you demand!"

"I know exactly what I demand, High Commander!" Tlonna shouted back, keeping a rein on her own considerable power. "Why is it such a burden to stand at my side at this time? I told you we would eventually make it to the battle lines, though I do not know when. You are always saying that you must guard me. What has changed?"

"You ask me to betray one oath for another!" Yayènia cried, her expression turning from one of wrath to desperation. "How am I to choose between loyalty to my soldiers and loyalty to the throne? They are supposed to be one and the same! I am your guard, yes, but I am not your shadow! That is Aidyn and Suneelo! Yet you send him out, my husband, to stand in my place while I stand in his! How is that right? He is not the High Commander of the Blackhaven Militia, Tlonna, I am! Ghealan is no longer bound to us, and his heart is no longer here. You send males out to do my job, the job I have done for the past three hundred years! You are supposed to be the symbol of purity in this battle! The one who gives us hope and reason to fight!"

"I cannot be a symbol of purity. Just look at my eyes."

Yayènia did indeed look her sister in the eye, staring into the white pupils that saw too much, and sneered. "What lives inside you does not change who you are. You are strong enough to defeat this evil, and you will see this damnable prophecy through to the end."

"At which point I die," Tlonna breathed, knowing that Yayènia would immediately deny the words.

Instead, the warrior dropped her gaze and then her face took on a cruel expression. "We shall see, Astinus did not know who he was messing with when he Saw that prophecy. He did not count on me, Suneelo, Losolin, Aladorn, Ghealan, and Aidyn. He made a grave mistake with that. You will live to pay for the crimes you have committed against those who stand at your side."

Tlonna let out a sniff of laughter. "Very true." She sighed, looking at her sister's furious face. "I ask this of you because you are one I trust implicitly with my life. With Aidyn gone, I have but one infallible protector, and I need you," Tlonna said, her voice thick with emotion. "Every moment is an agonizing struggle because a part of me is missing, the part that was bonded to Aidyn, the part that was ripped away, and I feel empty. I cannot sleep for the sickness in my heart and mind. I am tainted, Yayènia, and I cannot cleanse myself. Always Jair is there, within my mind, whispering insidious desires of murder and revenge. All of them, whispering constantly, even in my sleep I hear them, begging for the blood of all but a few. How can I stay on a path of truth and justice, when these damned souls murmur in my head at all times. I need you to keep me on this side of sanity for as long as you can."

"I am not one to guard sanity, Tlonna. I walk a gray line between reason and madness as it is. How am I to guard yours when I do not have a full grasp on my own?" Yayènia asked, tears welling in her own eyes. "I do not have the strength for the both of us. Every night Suneelo has to tell me who I am because in my dreams I forget. I stabbed him once, believing he was Arakis, the man who owned me when I was but a child. He held me as a cried, screaming bloody revenge on the bastard who tore away my innocence. Always we have been but a battlefield away, and now you send him halfway across the continent? How can you be so cruel?"

Tlonna sat on her desk, looking out of the balcony window. "By experiencing the cruelty myself. Remember I send Losolin along with him. Trust in them, as you told me to trust in Aidyn. They will survive, as they have all these years."

"This is a war like none we have ever seen, all of us, and we have seen a lot," the warrior said after a moment. "Magic and steel crosses without hesitation, alliances are made and broken every time we turn around, assassins and spies run rampant across the nations...how do you know what to expect? It is my profession and yet I find myself befuddled by it all."

Tlonna sighed, crossing her arms. "The opposing side is led by my flesh and blood, wrought from the twisted desires of my greatest enemy, torn from my womb with greedy fingers. Every thought in that boy's head is there because of me. How could I not know?"

"But he is even crazier than his father, unpredictable at best!"

The Magin shook her head. "No, you just have to think of it this way. Sithian wants me dead, why?"

Yayènia shrugged, looking indifferent.

"Because I offend him. I killed his father; I stand against everything he stands for. I made his entire kingdom dependant on mine by allowing trade, therefore opening doors for his enslaved populace to realize what they were missing, allowing them to realize that he was not doing the best thing for them. I weakened his image in the eyes of peasants. Like his father, that is the same as openly insulting him. It does not sit well on arrogant shoulders. And, he knows I am more powerful by far. That is the salt in the wound. He was bred to be the most powerful Magin of all time, but he has been thwarted in that as well. Losolin is nearly his equal, though he cannot do the damage Sithian and I can. My being alive insults him, and like the child he is, he will do his best to get his revenge."

Tlonna stood and walked around her desk, scanning the bookshelf behind it. When she found the title she wanted, the elf pulled it out and opened it, placing the rather thin volume on the desk. Yayènia frowned down at the pages as her sister turned them.

"This is a book entitled *The Just and Inherit Right of Man's Revenge.*"

"I have never heard of it."

The queen shook her head slightly. "You would not have, for it was written by Hadian Rahlan, and was kept in the castle at Zaedic. It was Sithian's favorite read."

"How did you get it?"

"I asked Alexander to retrieve it for me," Tlonna replied, smiling at the memory of the corsair Commodore. It had been a long time since she had seen the ragtag bunch of grimy sailors, and she missed them.

"Why?" Yayènia asked, not smiling.

"Because it explains Sithian's behavior. Listen.

*'It is the god-given right that Man should rule both Elf and Dwarf, for it is we who have been given the correct amount of passion and patience to take such a burden. For too long have we been held back by the vicious tyranny of the dwarves, and the*

---

*haughty disdain of the elves, and it is upon us now to take up sword and axe and cut down these arrogant races. It is our destiny to swarm across the land like a purge, taking no surrender of the lesser peoples, turning them into slaves as we have, according to legend, so long been held. My ancestors spoke of great abuse at the hands of the giant elves that storm the land. Now I say, take up your arms and teach them their proper place! The god of man, the One God, has so divined that it is our right to be the masters over all. Sweep away the weak, the dangerous, and the unholy, and bring upon the ages a new reign! This can only be achieved by one of pure heart and bravery, for no coward can make the decisions to massacre the ancient folk and their heathen beliefs. They will never convert, so, with the will of the One God, we shall destroy them until the land is ablaze in righteous humans, masters of the pagans, and then, at long last, Man will sleep soundly in his bed, knowing the balance of the world has been set right.'"*

Yayènia's mouth opened in horror. "It preaches slavery and obeisance to one rule, one god. That is the dogma that ignited the War of Monotheism! That is what Sithian wants?"

"I do not believe he cares much about the religious aspect of it, but yes, he wants all non-human creatures to bow before him in abject fealty. He believes himself to be that one human pure of heart and bravery. Midian gave him this book when he took Sithian from me, Kelus told me. Sithian carried it with him, slept with it, read it over and over again. It is all like that, bigotry and esoteric ranting, frightening in its single-mindedness. Hadian Rahlan wanted one thing only, much as Midian and Sithian, the absolute control of all the 'worthy' people, in other words, humans. They are all connected in their hatred of the elves and dwarves, and every faery creature in between. Sithian hates us all the more because he is half tainted, in his mind. He considers himself holy because he sacrificed part of his humanism to have the strength to fight us."

"But that is insane! Midian raped you, and that is why the three children were half-bloods. It has nothing to do with holiness or self-sacrifice!" Yayènia gasped, disgusted.

"Sithian realizes that, but he does not allow the people to know. Haydyn told me they were considered gods whenever they went into Zaedic's towns and villages. He said that their word was law, no matter what it was. Once Sithian saw a young woman walking down the street with her husband, and commanded her to please him. The husband was restrained by guards while Sithian raped her in the middle of the street. No one did anything because he was Sithian Rahlan; he was a god amongst slaves."

The warrior looked ill, her lips twisted into a repulsed sneer. "What causes such evil to ensnare people like that?"

Tlonna shrugged, closing the thin book. "Different ways of life."

"And what do you plan to do whilst your restraining husband is away?" Yayènia asked, suddenly suspicious.

The Magin Queen's white-pupil eyes came up slowly to meet her sister's, and in them swirled the deadliest of all magic, a promise of righteous vengeance. The warrior nearly gasped when she saw a flicker of light dance across Tlonna's reflective pupil, sparking when it hit the pearly blue iris.

"I am going back to the Cyree."

"What! But you said you had to stay here!"

"That is why I need you with me. I need to get the Cyree, and it is a dangerous place."

"How do you plan to do this without anyone finding out?"

"I will tell Miazie and Sodo, and they will remain here as stewards of the throne. They are not warriors, and will be of little use on the battlefield. Are you in agreement?"

Yayènia stared at the younger elf before her, taken completely off-guard. "You are mad," she whispered, shaking her head.

Tlonna shrugged one shoulder. "Only way I can handle the whispers," she replied blandly.

"Why did you not say this was your plan all along? Why not stop me earlier?"

"Those things needed to be said, and now we can move on. Are you with me?"

Yayènia sucked in a deep breath and held it as she ran the possible scenarios through her mind, her eyes flicking around the office. Finally, she expelled the breath and nodded. "As always, though I believe it to be madness. When do we leave?"

"The day after the army marches out."

"And how do we get there without being spotted by the army?"

Tlonna grinned, but there was no humor in it. "I will leave that to you. Plan for three."

"Three?"

"Why do you think I had Aladorn stay as well? I also plan on searching for Aidyn's whereabouts. He must be somewhere in the Liberated Lands with Sithian, because anyone who saw him would probably recognize him, or know someone who would. We would hear something."

"It has only been a week, Tlonna. It could very easily take more time than that for word to reach us. Aladorn will not be so willing to leave the one place he knows his brother would aim for."

The queen shook her head. "Aladorn is driving himself mental pacing about the city. We will be doing something assertive in order to find Aidyn, rather than just waiting."

Yayènia sighed, brushing an armored hand across her brow to sweep stray strands of blonde hair back from her face. "Do you have an idea about where he might be?"

"You are the High Commander, surely you have figured it out by now."

When the warrior frowned and shook her head in denial, Tlonna half-smiled. "Where did the Zaedican force hole up during the battle at Alchemian?"

Yayènia nearly knocked herself unconscious when she slapped her gauntlet to her forehead in self-disgust. "Anutch!"

"Anutch," Tlonna said, grinning maliciously.

The commander was quiet for a bit, and then her conversation with Miazie danced into her thoughts. "Miazie is pregnant," she said.

Tlonna's face exhibited utter surprise. "She told you?"

Yayènia shook her head. "No, but who else puts their hands on their belly in a protective gesture other than pregnant people? Erdwyf did it all the time."

"I wonder if she has told Sodo yet."

"I do not know. I think she just found out."

Tlonna frowned thoughtfully, rubbing her chin. "Do we say anything to her?"

Yayènia gave her an incredulous look. "Why are you asking me? I know nothing about this sort of thing! I found out Erdwyf was pregnant through her parents' old servant."

"Mmm... I suppose I could always say something. I feel as though she and I have been drifting apart since we went to Kajgenia. She was my only friend there for a while, and a good one at that."

Yayènia nodded. "She is a good person, Tlonna. You should not let her drift too far."

The queen returned the nod. "I know."

"What of their wedding? When is that supposed to happen?"

"I do not know. They said they wanted it to be soon, but not intrusive on the war. Personally I think the war is intrusive on their wedding, but that is just my opinion, I suppose," Tlonna muttered, flopping down in her chair.

Yayènia rested her hip against the large desk. "I could always scare her into it."

Tlonna chuckled, shaking her head. "You could, but then she might pop her baby out too early."

The warrior laughed and crossed her arms. "I want to do something to her. She is still so nervous around me, even after Purheae."

The queen lifted one shoulder in a shrug. "Just do not frighten the wits, or the baby, out of her, please."

"Will do," Yayènia agreed and made to leave. At the door, she paused and turned back to her sister. "Tlonna, whatever it is that you think you still need to be good enough, you do not need it. I really hope you realize that."

"Thank you, Yayènia," Tlonna said quietly as the commander stepped out of her office.

Yayènia strode down the corridor to Miazie's office and banged on the door with her gauntlet. There was a mild shriek from within, and then the obvious sound of hurried movements. After a moment or two, a shaking voice bid entrance, so Yayènia wrenched the door open and stomped inside, putting a very dangerous look on her face.

"Yayènia!" Miazie squeaked, sitting very stiffly in her chair.

Sodo was leaning against her bookcase, his arresting face a little too flushed to be normal. He lifted the eyebrow above his black eye in a questioning dare. Yayènia slammed the door behind her and leaned heavily on her knuckles on Miazie's desk. The only sound was the wood groaning in protest as the elf pressed on it, hard. The human looked petrified, her back ramrod straight and her eyes wide and unblinking.

"What can I do for you?"

"Do you have any idea how much trouble you are in with Tlonna?" Yayènia snarled, leaning ever closer to the Belau.

"Why?" she whimpered, shrinking in her chair.

"What secret have you been keeping from your friends, Miazie?"

"S-secret?"

"Yes, it lives within you, and yet you refrain from telling your queen about it?"

Now Sodo looked concerned, and Miazie utterly frozen with terror. The Alchemist moved to stand behind her chair and pinned Yayènia with a defiant glare.

"What are you talking about, Yayènia?"

"Have you even told him, yet?"

Miazie's throat moved as she swallowed, still unsure of what the warrior was talking about. When she looked as though she were seconds away from fainting, Yayènia straightened and grinned, taking both people by surprise.

"How far along are you?"

The absolute change in tone and atmosphere seemed to completely unbalance the poor human. Sodo's face lit up in a triumphant grin and he ran his hand down the back of Miazie's long, raven hair.

"How did you know?" he asked, unable to contain his smile.

Yayènia waved her hand in the air. "I know people," she lied.

Sodo chuckled, and answered for his fiancée. "Nearly three months, we think."

Miazie sucked in several deep breaths as she tried to get her emotions under control and then sagged back in her chair. "Spirits, Nia, you nearly scared me to death."

"That was the point."

"Why?"

"Because I still make you nervous, and I should not."

The human looked chagrinned. "Oh, well, that is completely your fault. If you were not so damn good with those weapons of yours, and your temper, I would probably not want to piss myself every time you go off on a tirade."

"Please do not piss yourself on my behalf," Yayènia said dryly.

# Chapter 3
### Break Away

"What do you think? I rather like the way they look, don't you?" said a loud voice, waking Aidyn from his light slumber.

He jerked his head up and blinked at Sithian, who stood before him with his arms spread wide. Aidyn stared at him a moment before realizing that the Magin was wearing his weapons, and his *ärdyz* shirt. Fury erupted inside the elf and he let out a roar that frightened Sithian, who had become confidant in the assassin's debilitation.

Aidyn's muscles bunched and he strained forward, snarling. The chair creaked and groaned, but held. Sithian chortled, dropping his hands to the hilts of the scimitars. "I am not used to fighting with two equal sized blades, but in the end I will have you to teach me."

"I will never teach you anything," the dark elf grunted.

"No? Is that anything like what you said about your most desperate desires? Or your first love, what was her name...Rahna? You will eventually tell me everything, you can't resist much longer. You're dying."

"I never told you that," Aidyn rasped, straining.

Sithian blinked in mock surprise. "No? 'Please Rahna...do not leave...please, I will find a way to make it work. Please...please. No Tlonna, we must not continue this. You are to be married to Herrich, and I can only give you this night.' You said it all, assassin, how many lovers has she had? Is that where she gets her power? From the seed of males?"

"You are a greater fool than I thought if you believe that," Aidyn replied, attempting to laugh. "Her power comes from her heart and soul, Sithian, a purity that you will never attain. Did you not realize that when your own brother was stronger than you? There was a reason Haydyn could best you. It was his heart."

"Lies!" Sithian shrieked, backhanding Aidyn. "Filthy lies!"

He drew the left scimitar and brandished it at the dark elf. Rage ignited within Aidyn as he stared down at the point of his own blade. All the enticements Sithian had crooned at him, the insults, the molestations, and the threats came crashing down on him, roiling through his mind like a hurricane, leaving a wake of fury. Then the eye passed, and a dead calm overcame the assassin. With a splintering crack, the chair exploded into pieces. Aidyn leapt upward, an animalistic bellow erupting from his lungs. His limbs trembled with the strain of moving after so long in a stationary position, but the elf hardly noticed. Pieces of splintered wood whipped about him, still attached by the lengths of rough cord. He crashed into the king as Sithian rushed from the tent in terror, breaking through the shield that had been placed around the tiny prison. His skin was seared in the effort, but Aidyn did not feel the pain. His arms locked around Sithian's waist and he lifted him high, bits of chair flying about.

The guards in the camp rushed to their king's aid but were stopped by the secondary shield Sithian had placed around the vicinity of the tent. The two night guards of the elf's prison were long abed, and the few soldiers staring in shock on the other side of the shield could only watch as Aidyn slammed the younger male into the ground so hard Sithian's body left an impression in the earth. Groaning, the Magin rolled away from the enraged elf, desperately trying to gather his wits in order to Weave. As Aidyn came for him, Sithian was able to get his hands on his knife and, as the elf moved close, he buried it deep in his thigh, trying to buy himself time.

The assassin flinched but did not slow, his body and mind already used to much more severe agony. Sithian grabbed Aidyn's legs and brought the badly injured elf down to the ground, where they struggled in a violent brawl. The king was too preoccupied to Weave, so he settled for grappling with killer. Eventually, he felt Aidyn's weakened hands slide awkwardly and he Wove a shield around his fist. He slammed the hand hard into the assassin's head, knocking him over.

Aidyn's vision sparked when he felt Sithian's fist clobber him, but as he went flying he reached out and grabbed Sithian by the hair, taking him along for the short ride. The king once again lost the ability to Weave his magic as the elf repeatedly slammed his fist into his face, shattering his nose and a good portion of his jaw. Sithian gurgled as he choked on his own blood, struggling desperately to fend off the furious assassin. Darkness edged in along his eyes and he gave up, too weak. Dropping the fistful of hair, Aidyn reached down and quickly removed his effects from the barely conscious king, keeping his boot hard on his throat, removing it only so that he could strip off his shirt and put it on himself. He positioned his weapons in their proper place on his body and knelt down beside Tlonna's son.

He grabbed Sithian's hands and twisted sharply, effectively shattering the wrist bones and ripping the tendons, rendering the Magin's hands completely useless. Sithian screamed in agony, blood spraying from his mouth as he was brutally wrenched back into consciousness. He writhed about on the ground as he pulled in his crumpled hands and held them to his chest. Drawing a curved dagger from his boot, the assassin pressed the tip to the back of his enemy's head and shoved it upward, driving the blade deep into Sithian's brain. The Magin went limp and the assassin looked out at the infuriated and awestruck guards still watching from a few yards away. He knew that Sithian would be alive in a few hours, resurrected by the pendant about his neck, but when he tried to pull the talisman off it violently lashed out, knocking Aidyn backward. He returned and yanked the blade out of Sithian's head and set it to his throat, intending to cut his head off, but the pendant threw him backward again, leaving him a little stunned. Rolling onto his feet, he accepted the futility of attempting again, and readied to leave.

The dark elf took a few steps back and then sprinted toward the shield Weave. He connected with it hard but his momentum propelled him through, though this time he left a smear of blood along the respective edges of the hole he created. He spun through the air and landed hard on his shoulder. He watched as the hole disappeared, causing his blood to create an odd wing shape as it came together. The guards stared at him in horror, and then fled. Aidyn wanted so badly to rest for a few minutes, but he knew the alarm would go up immediately so he clambered to his feet. His one consolation was that no one would be able to reach Sithian until he removed the shield Weave, which would not be for a very long time.

The assassin limped away, moving as fast as he could. His head throbbed and his vision was dim, but he ignored it and kept going, slipping and sliding as his muscles tried to give out, blood hemorrhaging out of his numerous wounds. As Aidyn came near to the edge of the plateau where the remains of a gate stood guarded by half a dozen men, the elf slipped into the new stables. The horses whickered at him, and he found one to his liking. Not bothering with tack, Aidyn pulled himself onto the chestnut gelding and galloped out of the stable, twisting his hands in the mane in order to keep his seat.

The guards shouted in warning, leveling their bows and spears, but the elf bent low over the horse's back and barreled right through them. He cried out as a barbed arrow slammed into his back, just below his shoulder blade, but he kept atop the horse, galloping him all the way down the winding trail that led to the grasslands of the Liberated Lands. Once there he gave the horse his head, and clung in desperation to him, and to life.

# Chapter 9
## A Bitter Reunion

Tlonna and Yayènia were outside the gate several days after the meeting with their companions, examining the damage to the gate and surrounding walls and towers. The army was readying to leave the next day, and the queen wanted the wall repairs contracted by then.

The two sisters listened to the chief architect of the city, a taller-than-average dwarf named Malkrin. He tugged at his yellow beard and pointed with his other hand at a large crack running from the top of a crenellation to about halfway down the wall.

"That'll need ta be replaced completely. Get enough masons in 'ere ta do it and it'll take about a week. Then 'ave yer Magins come in an' seal it up nice like the rest o' the wall. Not a 'ard job, but a lengthy one."

Tlonna nodded. "Give it priority, then, if you will. I also want the towers fortified, perhaps even added on to."

Malkrin nodded, making a note on his ledger. He moved over a few yards, pointing again, "And if ye look o'er 'ere," he began, but Yayènia shushed him, waving her arm in the air.

"Tlonna, did you hear that?" she asked in a whisper, looking into the forest.

Tlonna frowned, following her sister's gaze, and shook her head. "Hear what?"

Yayènia's eyes narrowed and she walked off into the woods, drawing her longblade. Tlonna motioned to Malkrin to stay where he was and followed the warrior, drawing her own sword. Together they moved swiftly and silently through the forest, following Yayènia's super keen sense of hearing. She twisted and turned through the trees, sometimes leaving the road altogether.

Suddenly the High Commander stopped short and then pushed Tlonna into the deep shadows of a massive *kairhotuss* tree, its heavy limbs nearly touching the ground. The queen's breath came fast as she waited in suspense, wondering what in the world could be roaming about her woods in a manner that would cause alert to the warrior.

It was then that she heard the faint, dragging footsteps. Several moments later, Aidyn limped into view, barely upright, blood running freely from a dozen wounds, with more dried and caked all over, and the flesh on his upper arms scraped raw and scabbed over.

"Aidyn!" Tlonna cried and rushed out to aid the weakened elf, tears rushing down her face.

Yayènia stood before them, her mouth open in utter shock. "Aidyn?"

"'Lonna..." he mumbled, and then fell forward.

The queen lunged and caught him as he fell, his eyes fluttering weakly. She went to the ground with him, laying him out. "Aidyn?"

The dark elf let his head fall back and he groaned as Tlonna shook her head, pressing her free hand to one of the many wounds in an effort to stop the bleeding. The assassin's lips were wet with blood, and he forced his eyes open. "Tlonna," he breathed, fumbling for her hand.

"He should not be bleeding this much, not with the healing that has taken place in several different places," Yayènia whispered, standing beside her sister.

"These wounds are magic, they will not ever truly heal without magical aid," Tlonna replied, her voice nasally from emotion. "We need Losolin."

The assassin's shallow, rattling breath quickened for a moment and he opened his eyes, which were clouded in pain.

"Aidyn," the queen wept, meeting his magnificent, emerald gaze. "Please...do not leave me."

"I have not betrayed you, but I needed to see you before..." he whispered, managing a weak smile.

"What? Aidyn, no, no, please. You cannot leave me, I love you, I need you...please, do not say that!"

The assassin's eyes closed and his head lolled onto her shoulder, and for one panic-stricken moment Tlonna believed him gone, but then another shallow breath lifted his chest and she relaxed a little. Yayènia thunked down onto the ground on the other side of Aidyn, her face wet with tears, such a rare sight it nearly sent Tlonna into hysterics.

"Is he...?" the warrior asked, lifting a hand as though to touch the dark elf but let it fall without finishing the motion.

"No, unconscious. We need to get him back to the city." Tlonna replied, cradling her friend.

Yayènia nodded, looking around for a way to get her friend back without compounding his grievous injuries.

"If Aidyn dies, I will not make it."

"He will not die. He is more indestructible than me," the High Commander said adamantly, sitting back on her heels. "I will make a stretcher, if you stay here and promise me not to move at all."

Tlonna nodded and swallowed, shifting to make Aidyn's position a bit more comfortable. Bending over, she pressed her lips to his mouth, tasting his blood, smearing it across her cheek when she rubbed it against his. She kissed him again, tears splashing from her eyes to wash away a fraction of the blood on his face. His scent, that intoxicating light aroma of ginger and cloves and pure masculinity, though tainted by the metallic smell of blood, filled her nostrils and she relaxed further, knowing deep within that he would be all right. Slowly, Tlonna withdrew from the one-sided kiss and sat up, staring down at his beautiful face for a long, long time.

"Tlonna," Yayènia said quietly, nudging her, having returned with materials to make a stretcher.

When the Magin looked at her sister, she blinked to find the warrior's fingers inches from her face. Yayènia's thumb pressed against her lips and slid across before moving back. When Tlonna frowned at her in confusion, she held up her thumb to show the blood she had wiped away.

"No need to go around looking like a blood-sucker."

"I..."

Yayènia smiled sadly. "I know. He is your closest friend."

"Yes, he is."

In silence, the warrior lashed together a litter and then helped Tlonna logroll the dark elf onto it. Together they moved quickly back toward the city, sprinting soundlessly over the leafy road. Malkrin gave a start when the two elves reappeared with the unconscious Aidyn, and he stared at them as they passed. They reached Aladorn and Suneelo who were speaking with several of the gate guards.

Aladorn's face went gray when he saw whom it was they carried and nearly went to his knees as they lost all strength.

"Where was he?" he asked in a voice trembling so bad his words were rather garbled.

"Shuffling through the forest. I do not know where he came from, but we need to get him to the hospital wing immediately," Tlonna replied, gesturing with her end of the stretcher.

Aladorn became silent, running beside them until they reached the castle. When they reached the steps, instead of waiting for the females to adjust to the slant, he picked Aidyn up and cradled his little brother in his arms, aware of the blood trickling down his skin from where Aidyn's temple rested against his neck. He swallowed back his fear, and sprinted up the steps.

Aidyn had yet to relate his battle with the Eseirik, but the wiat knew that he had been close to death when he had gone to Kajgenia, and only augmented his injuries trying to save Demetrius. From what Tristan had told them of the dark elf's condition, they were all surprised Aidyn had survived at all. Now he was just as wounded, two terribly deep injuries in his thighs bleeding profusely, not helped by the fact that he had walked on them. His arms were shredded, and his face torn in several places. A broken shaft of wood protruded from his back and blood stained nearly every visible inch of him, bruises riddled his arms and throat. When they reached the castle, Tlonna sent servants off to find Losolin and Ghealan.

Soon they were all crowded in the infirmary as one of the healers took custody of the injured assassin. They waited impatiently as Aidyn was stripped and his wounds taken stock. After what seemed an interminably long wait, the healer moved out from behind the privacy screen and faced them, his expression strained.

"He will live," he told the gathered elves, "but he will not be able to fight for some time. He has a stab wound in his right thigh, and it nearly sliced the muscle in half, and an older laceration in his left thigh. The injuries on his face and head are mostly superficial, as are the burns on his arms, but he has several broken ribs, and he has lost a lot of blood. The arrow in his back was stopped by the shoulder blade but tore a lot of muscle in that area. He must have exerted himself mightily after escaping whatever he escaped, for the wounds all show signs of delayed healing."

"You said mostly superficial, what of the ones that are not?" Aladorn demanded quickly, barely letting the healer finish.

"He took a massive blow to the head, perhaps even two; such blunt trauma can often lead to severe if not fatal depressions against the brain. I don't believe he will be adversely affected, but I am going to have to pull that part of his skull back into place."

"I will do it," Losolin said automatically.

"Can you?" Tlonna asked, noting the exhaustion in her husband's face. He had been in and out of infirmaries all week long, doing what he could for those injured in the recent battle, hardly resting, that and preparing for the battle to come.

"I can do it, but nothing else. I have gone beyond my limits this week," the king replied morosely.

"It is a very delicate area, my lord," the healer said, also worried.

"I am aware," Losolin stated quietly and moved around the screen to Aidyn's bed.

The assassin lay stretched out on a bed, his clothes and weapons stripped from him, and a white blanket pulled up to his chin. Blood had bloomed in several spots on the white linen, and his pillow was crimson. Losolin's heart skipped a few beats as he gazed down at his friend. Acutely aware of his failing strength, the Magin gently placed his hands on Aidyn's head, surrounding the concaved area with his thumbs and forefingers.

Green light pulsed out from between his fingers and sank into the assassin's head. Slowly, so as not to create more problems, Losolin used his magic to push the shattered piece of skull back into place and fuse it whole once again. As soon as his magic found no more injury in the area, it receded back into the king's body, the whole process taking several minutes, and depleting his already overused power. Losolin stayed conscious long enough to see Aidyn's eyelids flicker weakly before he collapsed from pure exhaustion.

The others heard Losolin fall and rushed around to find him on his knees, his head and arms resting on Aidyn's bed near the assassin's elbow. Tlonna moved to her husband and gently lifted him up. Suneelo took him from her and held him much as Aladorn had carried his own brother. The wiat was now standing next to Aidyn's bed, gazing down at the sleeping assassin, his brother's blood caked down his throat and hands.

The healer gently prodded the entire group out of the infirmary with promises that they could visit tomorrow. When he turned back to Aidyn, he sucked in a deep breath, well aware of the fact that he had just taken on a very great responsibility.

A few hours later the dark elf woke, startling into consciousness with a jerk, grimacing as pain lanced through his battered body.

"Welcome back, Lord Aidyn," the healer said, noticing the assassin's alertness.

"Where am I? I saw Tlonna and Yayènia...where are they?" he asked immediately, as always disregarding his own pain.

"They are both resting; you are home, Lord Aidyn, in the hospital wing of Blackhaven Castle. You must rest now. You are safe."

"What are my injuries?"

The healer sat back from checking the elf's thigh wound and sighed. "You had blunt force trauma to your skull, and would have died were it not for King Losolin. You have two grievous lacerations in your thighs, one exposing the femur, you have several burns, cuts, bruises, and five broken ribs, and an arrow wound in your back. There are burns around your neck, shoulders, and face along with magically induced searing of the flesh. You lost a lot of blood, even for your race. You were very near death. From what I can tell, during your internment, you were being..." the young man hesitated, not sure how the elf would take the explanation.

"What? What did he do to me?"

"You were being alternately burned and frozen from the inside out. The only reason you survived is because there was a magical barrier around your organs protecting them."

"It was Losolin," Aidyn murmured, recalling the healing that had blasted through him. "How can you tell all this? What is your name? You are too young to be this knowledgeable."

"My name is Braden, and my father was a healer. He taught me everything he knew. I can tell about the magic because it left visible traces, sort of like translucent gauze all through your body. When King Losolin healed you, the last of the magic faded away, as it was no longer needed. It receded back into him, and knocked him out."

Aidyn took the news stoically. "How soon can I be out of here?"

Braden shook his head. "Everyone hates this place," he muttered. "You cannot leave this bed for two weeks, and it will be another six before you can fight anything more than a fly. No arguments and no leniency. I will not have the death of the greatest assassin and warrior ever to live on my shoulders."

"I am not the greatest of anything," Aidyn snapped, infuriated by the dismal news of his incapacitation. "And there is a war going on! I cannot lay here during a siege!"

"You can and you will. I will get it ordered by the king and queen if I must," the young man said, hardly threatened by the angry elf. "If you ever want to fight again, or even walk upright, you will follow my orders to the letter. Is that clear?"

Aidyn glared at the adamant human, and then nodded shortly, giving his assent. He winced when the healer slapped his shoulder.

"Just be grateful you're not a human. These kinds of wounds, if not immediately fatal, will take a man out for months at least, perhaps forever, and never truly heal. Take it at ease as well that the siege was lifted the same day you were captured. The army prepares to march even now to chase the Zaedicans and their allies into the sea. They depart tomorrow"

The dark elf dropped his head back onto his pillow and stared at the obsidian ceiling above him, saying nothing. He felt useless and trapped.

Tlonna rolled away from Losolin, trying not to disturb her exhausted husband. He had barely stirred since the infirmary, and Suneelo had carried him all the way to their bed. When the captain had left, Tlonna had undressed him and pulled the covers over the king, and had not slept a wink since. Worry for both him and Aidyn kept her mind reeling, unable to come to terms with their predicaments. Though Losolin's strength would return in full by morning, he would push himself just as hard the next day, and the next, and the next, until he either died from exhaustion or was no longer needed. She worried about what he would do as soon as he was out of her sight.

As far as Aidyn went, Tlonna loved him dearly, perhaps a little too much, always hurting for him and his struggles. The assassin kept running into crucibles that nearly took him down, usually at the behest of someone other than himself. His body was being ravaged and not given the necessary time to heal, his mind likewise battered. The queen felt responsible for his dire situation, knowing that Aidyn would always, no matter what the cost, step in front of her to preserve her life.

Her relief at seeing him alive was deeply dimmed by the horrible anguish he was in now. She could not imagine the sort of brutality he must have endured at the hands of Sithian, her own son. Tlonna sat on the edge of the bed and hugged herself, shivering with the enormity of the future and the present. Her eyes closed and she leaned forward, forcing herself not to cry.

Though she knew there was something more in Aidyn's heart than he shared, Tlonna felt as though she knew him better than anyone alive. Her father and Demetrius had known him for a very long time, but they were both gone now. Despair washed over her in waves, causing her to suck in great, shaking breaths in order to calm herself.

The siege and every event leading up to it seemed purposeless, seemed to be aimed only at causing chaos and anarchy throughout the world. Nothing made sense, and only fear seemed to be constant. It was a nagging doubt, an uncertain shadow lurking in everybody's soul. The Everwood Queen trembled in fear.

Yayènia was standing outside the door to infirmary before the healers even woke, long before dawn. When Braden unlocked the door, he seemed surprised to see her.

"High Commander?"

"How is he?" she demanded without preamble as she pushed by the healer and into the large room.

"Resting. High Commander, you really should not be here. Lord Aidyn needs to rest if he is ever to regain his health."

"Shut your mouth," Yayènia snarled, trying to find the assassin amongst the other sleeping forms in the room. "Where is he?"

Braden sighed, accepting defeat. He had been present those years ago when Yayènia had escaped from Midian's grasp, had dropped three stories from broken arms and shattered her kneecaps upon landing. He had been there when she'd wrenched her broken body out of the slings and walked on those destroyed legs in order to save her husband. He was not going to fight her stubbornness. "He is in one of the private rooms, at his request. Follow me, if you are determined to bother him."

Yayènia glared at the back of the human's head as she followed him deeper into the infirmary, through a wide hall, and into a circular room with doors lining the wall. Braden unlocked one and stepped aside, impatiently gesturing for the female to enter.

Aidyn opened his eyes when he heard the door open, and he managed a small smile when Yayènia strode in, looking wrathful as always.

"Such a pretty sight in the morning," he croaked, trying to sit up and failing.

"Ah, Aidyn," Yayènia breathed. She dragged a chair close to the bed and sat. "How are you feeling?"

"Useless."

The warrior chuckled as she clasped his tawny hand in hers and examined the contrast in their skin. The assassin also looked down at their fingers and shook his head at the alternating brown against white. Yayènia brought his hand up to her lips and kissed his bruised knuckles, surprising him.

"You will never be useless," she said quietly, "far from it. I think..." the female paused, uncomfortable with what she was about to say. "I think you are incredible, wonderful, exceptionally kind, and brave. Tlonna could never have a better protector, and I know you love her. Do not deny it, for it is no bad thing, and I want you to know that I am sorry you never had a chance to be with her."

Aidyn stared at the warrior for a long time, quite unsure of what to say. Finally, he swallowed and looked away. "I did."

Yayènia frowned. "What?"

"Once, long ago, I lay with her. Dietirin asked me to because he knew I...he knew, and it was her birthday, the forty-fifth. She does not remember it, but Miazie does. It is one of the memories she retains." Aidyn sighed hopelessly. "I have pushed it away from my thoughts since she and Losolin found each other, but now it is all I can think about. I remember it as though it was yesterday, and I ache as I have never before."

"What of Rahna?" Yayènia asked, not at all surprised by the news.

The assassin closed his eyes and dropped his head against the pillow. "Rahna had been dead a century already."

"I know, but I thought you loved her yet, her memory. It is uncommon for one of our kind to find love more than once every few centuries, if that."

"I did. I do...but this is different, always has been. With Rahna it was a burning passion that left me breathless with desire and lust. More primal and juvenile. With Tlonna, it is something deeper, lodged within my heart, refusing to let go. Every time I look at her I ache, though I am happy for her and Losolin and would never think of tearing them apart. I do not know what to do. I never wished for this, I wanted to cling hopelessly to the memory of Rahna and die with my fidelity intact."

"It is not unfaithful to love someone, especially after another has been gone for centuries, Aidyn. I am not going to say you should foster your love for my sister, but do not try to push it away for the wrong reasons. We are elf-kind, it is our purpose in life to love, no matter what the consequences or the pain that it can bring."

Aidyn squeezed his eyes shut and took a deep, shuddering breath. "Oh that I had told her the truth that night, Nia!"

Yayènia frowned at his desperate expression, though he could not see her. "What did you tell her?"

"After we had lain together I told her I would always be a friend; there if she needed me, but otherwise I would stay away from her in all forms but professional. She cried, begged me to renege, even tried to seduce me back into bed for one more tryst, but I denied her. Always I denied her. When Constancias's attempt to marry Tlonna off to Herrich Lostug fell through, even Dietirin asked if I would become her consort. Ah, what a fool I was! And Sithian knows, somehow. He claims I told him, but I do not remember it."

Yayènia watched helplessly as her friend dug his fingers into his battered face, his back arching slightly with both mental and physical agony. She saw a tear slide down his cheek, catch on the black scars, and disappear. Unable to take the sight any longer the weapons-master gripped both his strong wrists in her hands, pulled them away from his face, and crushed her lips to his.

Aidyn stiffened in shock as Yayènia kissed him, her hands holding his arms out wide in steel grips. She kissed him for a long time, and quite passionately, even releasing his hands to frame his face. The assassin was unsure of what he was supposed to do, so he simply lay there, pinned to the bed by her lips. But after a while he found himself kissing her back out of sheer brazen instinct. After an impossibly long time, Yayènia broke off, a little breathless but unashamed. The male stared up at her in bewilderment, unconsciously licking his lips, her taste still lingering.

"What was that about?" he managed finally, huskily.

Yayènia swallowed, a little shaken by her own action, and the fact that she wanted to straddle the assassin and find out if the rumors were true. "I am Tlonna's sister, and I can do what she cannot."

"You are married as well," Aidyn muttered, narrowing his eyes in confusion.

"Yes, and there is no one else for me other than Suneelo, but I know that our marriage, and trust, will not be ruffled by something as simple as a kiss, especially when it involves someone as honorable and trustworthy as you," Yayènia replied curtly. "Besides," she shrugged, "we are all old. What is a kiss between friends when we have hundreds of years behind us?"

Aidyn shook his head in disbelief. "True, but it is still dangerous. I do not have the control over my emotions and lust I used to have."

"No," Yayènia said, sitting once more, "you have more."

"How is that?"

"Everything has come back to you, stronger perhaps than before and yet you still remain Tlonna's truest friend. Were I you, I certainly could not hold myself back so well."

Aidyn finally succeeded in sitting up, grimacing all the while. "It has been so hard, Yayènia, so painful."

"I do not doubt it."

"Should I tell Losolin?"

The High Commander frowned in thought. "No. I think that for the time being you should keep this to yourself. Who else knows?"

"Miazie, Sithian as I said, and perhaps Aladorn."

"Perhaps?"

Aidyn let out an amused, aggravated huff. "For seven hundred years we were separated, slowly forgetting the other, but somehow he understands me better than anyone ever did. He can read my face like a book."

Yayènia smiled at his exasperated tone. "Suneelo is the same way with me. Speaking of whom, I need to find and confess to."

"You will tell him?"

"Of course. If I keep it a secret then it becomes a sin and a lie," she lifted her eyebrow at him. "But I may as well make it worth the explanation." She stood and bent down to grab the startled dark elf once more.

This time Aidyn did not hold back, knowing she did it for him, and his fingers dug into her shoulders as he pulled her closer. Yayènia closed her eyes and for a moment let her mind fall hopelessly into Aidyn's passion. When her heart began to beat faster with desire, she pulled away, knowing that in another moment she would be ripping his clothes off. Aidyn's chest was heaving and he slid backward in his bed, breathless.

"There goes any hope of sleep for the next few days," he muttered finally, but Yayènia was already gone.

The next dawn arrived too fast for everyone else, but as the clarion calls of horns blew through the morning air, people looked up at the brightening sky with a final hope in their eyes. Mothers, wives, children, all manner of friends and family embraced as their soldiers marched out of their homes, some for the last time. They lined up on the main thoroughfare through all of Blackhaven, Obsidian Way, lines ten deep, stretching from the gate to halfway through the city.

Losolin, Ghealan, and Suneelo mounted their horses and rode to the head of the army. Tlonna, Yayènia, Aladorn, Miazie, and Sodo rode with them, dismounting once they reached the gate. Masons, mainly comprised of dwarves, crawled all over the wall and towers, swiftly rigged scaffolding framing the spindly-looking spires. The front lines of soldiers stared upward with glittering eyes; their identical, short-plumed silver helmets flashing in the early morning light.

Tyre and Aselios, the two human recruits from the original force Tlonna and Losolin had put together, sat proudly beside Captains Sargotarh and Orthak, black and silver cloaks of office drifting slightly on the breeze. Behind them were Bryce and Erich, the men from Talenias, also resplendent in their black and silver cloaks. Tlonna gave them each a proud smile, which they all returned, and then she turned to her husband.

"Losolin, know that every night we are apart I will dream of you," she murmured, pressing her palm against his cheek.

He cupped her hand in his, his dark eyes sparkling with moisture as he gazed upon her. "I love you with every fiber of my being, Tlonna. Promise me we will look upon each other again."

Fear gathered in the Magin Queen's chest, hardening into a writhing ball, but she held it back with resolve. "We will, my heart. We will. Remember what I said last night?"

Losolin half-smiled, remembering quite vividly the actions of the night before, not so much the words, but he knew of which ones she spoke. "As long as we love, we cannot be defeated," he whispered. It was one of the oldest elfin proverbs, and swiftly becoming their mantra.

"And that as long as we both survive, I will always find you, no matter what the cost. You are my life."

"As you are mine," the king replied, kissing her knuckles.

Damning protocol, Tlonna threw her arms around her husband and pressed her lips to his, trying to convey every emotion into a single kiss. His strong hands held her close, tightening briefly before they released her waist. Breathing deep to keep herself from crying, Tlonna stepped away just in time to see Yayènia and Suneelo sharing a similar moment, while Ghealan stared off to the east with a morose expression.

Once they had all embraced and said goodbye, the three males to head the army remounted and signaled for the drummers to begin the cadence. As the first rattling rhythm shattered the early morning quiet, Tlonna lifted her hand in the air, eliciting a roar of loyalty and love from the gathered soldiers. Yayènia yanked her longblade out and stabbed the sky above, opening her mouth in a battle cry. The thunderous roar grew even louder, shaking the very earth itself. Even Aladorn could not help the slow grin that spread across his face at the sight of the cheering and stomping Blackhavenites. Finally Losolin lifted his sword and pointed it forward, signaling the march.

It took nearly an hour for the last line of wagons to pass beneath the gate once Losolin, Ghealan, and Suneelo had ridden through. Tlonna and Yayènia dropped their arms in exhaustion, giving each other sympathizing glances. Aladorn leaned between two crenellations, his shoulder blades sticking up into the air.

"What now?" he asked dully, all excitement drained from him once more.

Tlonna shook her head. "I was planning on taking you with Yayènia and me to the Cyree, with the task of searching for Aidyn, but now that he has returned..."

"You were going to leave the kingdom? You were going to go look for him?" the wiat asked sharply, turning about.

"Yes. And I am still going to leave, though you now have the choice to stay behind with your brother, which I would advise, or you may come with us. We are going to travel hard and fast to the Cleshnoe and try to find some answers at the pond."

Aladorn stared at her, his verdant eyes unreadable. "How long?"

When Tlonna looked to Yayènia, the warrior stepped forward. "The route we are taking is a difficult one. We will be taking Sha Bridge and then turning south into Kismath. We will stay close to the river until the troops come into sight, and then we will veer further south and head through the tundra of Kismath. I estimate two weeks one way."

The male looked ill. "You would take Tlonna, our queen, along that route? Are you crazy?"

"Absolutely," Yayènia shot back, her eyes fierce. "With just the two or three of us, we will be able to slip through without hazard. And if we do run into goblins or the like, well, that is my purpose."

"When do you leave?"

"Tonight," Tlonna said quietly.

"What of Aidyn? And what if something happens to you? How do I explain it to Losolin, much less the kingdom?"

"Aidyn has you. He is back, he is safe, there is nothing more we can do for him at this time. As for something happening to me, do not count on it, Aladorn. I am not so easy to kill, especially these days."

The dark elf let out a frustrated sigh. "You ask a lot of me, Tlonna. You seem to be asking a lot of everyone."

Yayènia grunted in agreement, but said nothing more. Finally he looked away. "I cannot leave him now. He is not in good shape, and I cannot leave him like this."

Tlonna laid a comforting hand on his shoulder. "I know, and I would never command you to do so. I will go to him now and inform him of my plan so that he too can yell at me."

Aladorn smiled a little at that, and then followed the two sisters down the stairs to where their horses stood waiting. Takîreaes and Udu snapped at each other, trying to gain dominance over the other. Aladorn's dun mare stood nervously beside Takîreaes, flicking her tail in annoyance. They mounted and headed back toward the castle just as the sun crested the tallest canopy of the massive *kairhotuss* tree in the center courtyard.

Tlonna entered the hospital wing alone, telling her persistent castle guards to stay outside. Braden met her with a bow and then shook his head.

"Your highness, he is not healing. I thought that perhaps his injuries were in such a state because of the extremity of his escape, but now I believe it be a combination of that, and a lack of caring. He is not allowing his body to heal the way elves do. He is keeping that energy from doing anything, so his body cannot do what is necessary."

"Why would he do that?" Tlonna demanded, concerned.

"Perhaps it is his form of *El shä Rók*, believing that he failed in his duty, or it is something deeper that I cannot fathom. Whatever it is, he is dying my lady, and I can do nothing to prevent it."

Fear and fury warred for a moment within Tlonna, but the anger quickly won out. She stormed past the startled healer and into the private room.

"What do you think you are doing?" she shouted at her friend as she burst into his room.

The dark elf cracked his eyes open and then closed them again, turning his head away from her. "Let me rest, Tlonna," he muttered.

"You have rested long enough," the queen spat, disgusted. "Stop feeling sorry for yourself and begin the healing process. What is wrong with you?"

Aidyn opened his eyes again and glared at her. "I am nearly eight hundred years old. Perhaps I have lived too long and this is what I get for it."

Tlonna sneered. "That is ridiculous and you know it. You have centuries left if you so choose, Aidyn, and I do not know why you are so miserable, but you need to stop. I cannot live in this world without you."

"There is nothing more in me, just...leave me lying here. I do not care and I cannot see a path on which to begin again."

The Magin sat on the edge of his bed; her anger sapped by his words. She grabbed his foot, wiggling it a bit. "Remember who you are, my friend, and do not let your soul and your courage be lost to the rapids of despair. You fought a great battle and came out victorious. You have suffered, and you have lost all throughout your life, but have you not also gained so much? What of Aladorn, your lost brother, now found? Losolin, Suneelo, and Ghealan, who count you among their closest friends? Of me, who calls you best friend and more? We are the path, but it is up to you to take it."

The assassin turned his gaze away, ashamed. "It is hard to care after so long, Tlonna, and it is wrong that it is so. When I escaped Sithian, I stole a horse. I rode it death, Tlonna. I, *an elf*, rode a horse to death because I did not care about it. But what can I do? My heart feels empty and I fight only because that is what I am good at, what I have always done."

"What do you wish to do?"

"I do not regret my life, or dislike my profession because I believe in it, but...have I missed something crucial? I think sometimes that if I had been willing to give up the College, Rahna would still be alive. Even if she was not mine, she would be alive."

"You do not know that. No one can determine the fate of a life once it is gone, and you cannot know that your job brought on her demise. To do so would be extremely foolish and rather egotistical. Nothing you do or once did can affect the destiny of another being. It is their choices, their desires that do so. You can only change yours."

"I believe quite the opposite," Aidyn muttered, still looking away. "My destiny, and yours, and everyone's is altered by other people. We make choices depending on how it will affect others, and so it was my choice to remain a killer, and she died for it."

"After all these years, you still love her so?" Tlonna asked softly, surprised and humbled.

The assassin finally looked at her, albeit through narrowed eyes. "I always will, but it is not the love of desire. It is the love of a memory and the pain of loss. My heart belongs to another and has for many years," he whispered, his eyes sliding away once more.

Tlonna frowned at him, wondering. "Does she know?"

Aidyn chuckled in spite of himself, amused by her obliviousness. "Not a clue, and I shall never tell her."

"Why ever not?"

"Because our friendship would shatter and I could not bear the loss. And she belongs to another who is her true soul mate."

"How can she be with her soul mate if you love her and she is not with you? She must be blind and dumb, in which case she is not worthy of you anyway," Tlonna replied acidly, indignant that her friend suffered for another.

The dark elf was coughing now, hard enough to shake the bed. Alarmed, the queen jumped to her feet and prepared to call for a healer. Aidyn finally got his laughter under control and watched with sparkling eyes as Tlonna moved closer to him, her strange eyes concerned.

"I have only seen humans do that for such a long time. Aidyn, are you going to be okay?"

"I will be just fine, but tell me of what has happened in my absence."

"A lot," Tlonna replied, never knowing that his humor was at her expense, and proceeded to tell him of the vicious fight once he had been taken, the fire, and subsequent break of the siege. "The army left just now," she concluded.

"You are not with it?" Aidyn asked, startled.

"No. Ghealan, Suneelo, and Losolin are riding out with it; Yayènia and I are going on a separate mission."

The assassin shook his head. "I cannot believe Yayènia was willing to stay behind, even it if is for a week or so."

Here Tlonna hesitated, unsure of how to proceed. "Yayènia and I are not...we are not staying here. We leave tonight for the Cleshnoe Forest."

"What!" Aidyn snapped, shocked. "Why?"

"To seek answers. Aladorn was to come with us, and look for you, but now that you have returned he has elected to stay behind and be at your side. I wish I could do so as well, but there are questions that need answers, and I do not have the luxury of time."

"What of Miazie and Sodo?"

Tlonna smiled faintly. "Miazie is to rule as regent in my and Losolin's absence. Sodo has succeeded in separating the chemicals that induced the fire, and is looking closely at how to replicate it.

Miazie and he are engaged to be married, and so preparations are being made for when we all return. And she is pregnant, so travel for her is forbidden."

"They are waiting until after the war to do it? That is rather unusual, is it not, particularly for humans?"

"They did not want to rush it, and they wanted everyone to be present. They have great faith in our ability to win. And with the two engineers traveling with the soldiers, hopes are raised even more."

"What will they be making?" Aidyn asked, intrigued.

The female shrugged. "I know not, and perhaps that is best. I told them I do not want a war machine, but we shall see."

"It sounds as though everyone is moving along just fine, then. So much has happened in the what, two weeks, I have been gone."

"Indeed, but I can tell you it was a sad and desperate time, none of us slept well, and I believe Aladorn did not sleep at all."

"He looked quite exhausted when he came and visited me yesterday morning after Yayènia. I told him not to kill himself for me, and he nearly hit me, I think."

"As he should have," Tlonna said sharply. She shifted suddenly, thinking of something else. "Aidyn...what happened to the bond?"

The assassin's bandaged hand came up immediately to press against his heart. "It is still there, I think, but it is cloaked somehow, so that you would not feel the pain I was experiencing."

"Was it that bad?" the female asked in a timid voice.

Aidyn closed his eyes again, reliving every agonizing moment. "Tlonna, when I was in training I was locked in a tiny room for six months and beaten every day, brutally tortured, brought to within an inch of my life, I even drowned twice, and it was nothing compared to what Sithian did to me. He very nearly had me. I apparently told him things, but I do not recall it. Nothing truly important, but secrets of my life I have kept quiet from all but a few. I have never wished to die so fervently."

"Oh, Aidyn, I am so sorry. Sorry I brought this pain upon you, that I did nothing to stop it. Can you ever forgive me?" Tlonna asked, her voice keening with sorrow.

The dark elf grabbed her hand and held it to his chest, against his heart. "Nothing you could ever do would need forgiveness, Tlonna. What you did that first day, linking with everyone else and coming to me...it gave me the strength and courage to survive. I would have been lost were it not for that. Every time I thought I was about to break, I remembered your voice echoing through the air, I heard the threat, and I found the strength to live another day. I felt Aladorn, Yayènia, Ghealan, Suneelo, and Losolin as well, but your presence was overwhelming in its comfort and strength. Losolin's magic healed and protected me, but it was your magic that kept me truly alive."

"Then why are you allowing yourself to die now?" she asked quietly, flattening her hand against his bruised chest, feeling the slow, faint beat of his heart.

"Because now that I am home I see the pain I caused everyone, and I do not like it."

"Well get over it," Tlonna teased gently, bending down to kiss his forehead, resisting the urge to move lower to his mouth. "I must ready to leave, but know that I love you."

Aidyn nodded and weakly lay back on his pillow, closing his eyes in weariness as Tlonna departed. "As I do you," he murmured once she was gone.

# Chapter 5
## Two Figures in the Snow

Tlonna ran her finger over the threading of her new pack, her old one having been tossed out by her maid with a sharp word of what is and what is not proper for a queen to have. It was made of strong, supple un-dyed leather, and sewn together with black leather stitches. Tlonna had told the seamstress expressively not to put any symbols on it, and she had obliged. She quickly opened her wardrobe and pulled wide the bottom cubby, in which she hid her traveling clothes. They had been washed and mended, and there were some new garments as well, but both Carlotta and Mattie, her lady-in-waiting and couturier, had looked scandalized when she had asked for them back. Now they were hidden in case one of the women, or both, ever got the courage to throw them out.

Tlonna sat on her heels and pulled out the clothing, running her hands over the material, memories washing through her. There was her pink tunic from the Zaedican elf Syntyche, along with the gray britches, and her worn black leather pants, her three black tunics, and two pairs of tight, fawn-colored cotton pants. The new garments consisted of two sets of gray and blue traveling outfits, and one black set. The elf hastily folded them into her pack, and then tossed in her undergarments. She drew tight the drawstring, and shoved the carved bone through the enforced ring to secure the top. Then she tied on her sleeping roll, strapped on a bundle of faggots for firewood, and shoved in her traveling kit, complete with sewing items, stitches, poultices, wax and seal, a flint and tinderbox, and more.

There was a knock on the door and she froze, worried one of her maids might catch her in the act of packing. The story they were filtering through the castle was that she and Yayènia were riding to the outposts within the kingdom to speak with the guards at each. Aladorn was sending birds to the posts with orders for them to acknowledge that the two females had been there if they were questioned.

Tlonna relaxed when Yayènia quietly announced herself, and then entered. She appraised her sister's pack with a professional eye, and said nothing.

"What is it?" the queen asked, closing the side pocket with her kit inside.

"Aladorn just sent the birds. Our tack is ready in the stables, and is being cleaned and inspected for faults. Udu and Takîreaes are being bathed, curried, and shod as we speak, and food is being packed into the saddle bags."

"How long until everything is in order?"

Yayènia shrugged. "An hour, no more. I was thinking we might actually stop at the outpost near Sha Bridge just to make our story a little more believable."

Tlonna nodded. "That would be fine. Can you think of anything else we might need?"

"Yule is just around the corner, so the temperatures will be freezing, we will have to be prepared for the Kismathian winter, which is brutal. Do you have winter clothing?"

"Oh yes, I learned that lesson already. What does the city do for Yule? Will it be a problem that we will be gone?"

Yayènia shrugged again. "We may be back for it. There is a big celebration, just like at Samhain, but the clothing is classic, not costume, and both the largest *kairhotuss* trees in the central courtyard and in the city square are lit with colored candles and draped in bits of cloth from the citizens. There is a day of reflection, when no one works, and a night of dreams, where everyone forgets the woes of life and remembers the laughter and the love. On the day of Yule, gifts are exchanged, and the people rejoice, or at least that is what they are supposed to do."

"I hope we are back for it, then," Tlonna said wistfully, smiling. "Anything else we need to bring?"

The warrior shook her head. "Warm blankets, clothing, and cloaks, and we should be good."

"Then we are set. What are you going to do in the meantime?"

"Relax," Yayènia replied, and headed for the library.

An hour and a half later, Yayènia and Tlonna were riding out of the gate with the sun at their backs. As soon as they were out of sight of the wall, they let their stallions run. Blackhaven Forest whipped by them in a blur, the pounding hooves giving flight to fallen leaves and debris. A few hours later, they heard the army in front of them and slowed, wanting so badly to run up and join them. Instead,

Yayènia led the way off the road and into the trees. By the time the sun was beginning to fall, they were nearing the edge of the forest, and had slowed to a trot.

"The guard post is another hour from here, and Sha Bridge a little more," Yayènia said, pointing east-southeast. "We should stop for a few minutes, check the tower and meet with the guards, make sure they have no complaints, and then we can be on our way."

"What if they have complaints?" Tlonna asked, taking the Staff of Cyree off her back and lashing it to Takîreaes's pommel.

The High Commander snorted. "We tell them to get over it."

"How very diplomatic," the queen wryly replied as her sister took the lead.

"Indeed," the warrior said, and took off once more.

They reached the outpost just before sundown, and rode right up to the stone base. The guard tower was made of black-streaked granite blocks with a slender, spiraling staircase hugging the side. Unlike the obsidian walls and castle of the city, these towers were not magically reinforced, and so their stone had to be naturally strong and reliable.

Tlonna looked up at the soaring tower and blinked when she saw half a dozen arrows pointing down at her head. "You would threaten your queen and high commander?"

The arrows did not move or slacken. "Prove yourself," came the threatening reply.

Yayènia dropped her cowl back with a sigh and stared upward, not flinching from the barbed missiles aimed at her face. "*Kresno klamen zephyr afle yesten...*" she began.

"*Nyn flounen re, ib qre, nyn flounen syn,*" the speaker replied automatically and the bows slackened and went away.

"When the silver streak comes, do not flee or hide, do not hope?" Tlonna asked, translating the Parlêthian words.

"It is a code so that soldiers will know friendlies in enemy territory, or on suspicious ground," Yayènia explained as she dismounted Udu.

Tlonna nodded in understanding as she too dismounted. The High Commander led the way up the winding stairs and into the tower itself. They were high up, nearly eighty feet from the ground, once inside the guardroom. There were chairs and a table on which lay several cards, dice, and coins, called spikes, the standard metal currency throughout Nymyños, though each coin was marked with the original kingdom's emblem. A tankard of beer also sat on the table, half empty. Yayènia eyed it with a critical gaze, and then turned a piercing look on the men.

"Anything to report, Watchmen?"

The six soldiers glanced at each other and then shook their heads in unison. "Nothing to report, High Commander er'Tiena. There has been no movement in our area for a good long time. Our birds are getting fat."

Tlonna looked at the small wire cage hanging from the rafters and lifted a brow. Three pigeons cooed down at her, looking fat and sleepy as they ruffled their feathers.

"I see. No complaints, then?"

Again the soldiers looked at each other, shuffling their feet. Finally one of them spoke when Yayènia sighed loudly. "Is it true Lord Aidyn was captured? Did Sithian Rahlan really defeat him?"

Tlonna turned slowly on her heel to stare at her sister, shocked that the remote watchtower was privy to such information.

Yayènia frowned. "How do you know about that?"

"A passerby mentioned it, High Commander. Is it true?"

"Lord Aidyn is perfectly fine, and in Blackhaven City. You should not listen to rumors, Watchman. What did this passerby say?" the warrior replied immediately, frowning.

"Just that the Master Assassin had been defeated while protecting the queen," the guard glanced at Tlonna with a slight bow of his head, "and that no one knew where he was. We sent out a watch-note to all the sentry towers in this region."

Yayènia pinched the bridge of her nose, squeezing her eyes shut in irritation. "Aidyn is fine. Get me a quill and parchment so I can rescind the notice."

As the soldiers complied, Tlonna wandered over to the door and stepped out onto the balcony that encircled the tower. The railing came up to her hips, and she leaned against it, looking out over the great canopy of the Blackhaven Forest. Less than a mile away it ended, giving way to the narrow strip of the Noyv Meadowland, and then to the Hidden Plains, where the tribal Plains Elves lived.

The queen surveyed her land with a swelling heart, her eyes sweeping the dark landscape with unbridled joy. She was smiling when a soldier stepped up next to her.

"I take the first watch every morning, and I never fail to be touched by the sunrise flaming up over the trees. It is beautiful, my queen. A true masterpiece of nature."

Tlonna turned to the man and smiled down at him. "I am glad you think so. It brings my heart joy to look upon it. Have your months of service been tedious?"

He shrugged. "I fought at Alchemian, and I fought in the raid nine years ago. I have seen enough violence for the balance of my life, and then some. This post suits me. Few come this way, and only assassins coming to and from the College ever cause any stir. Not bad stir, mind you, but they always stop and tell us of their adventures. They are the ones who told us of Lord Aidyn."

"Do you know where the College of Assassins lies?" Tlonna asked, surprised the man knew anything about them, and that the assassins stopped at the outpost.

"Somewhere in that direction," he said, waving his hand directly west. "They never tell us, but considering the fact that they always come from or head off in that direction, that is what I would assume. We figure it would be certain death to go after them just to find out where a building is."

"It would indeed," Tlonna commented dryly, smiling.

The soldier nodded in earnest, grinning back at her. She was discussing the layout of the land with him when Yayènia stepped out onto the balcony.

"The birds are off to the towers to end this foolishness. It is time we are off."

Tlonna bowed her head to the surprised soldier and followed her sister back through the tower and down to their horses. "I am surprised that the guards care so much for Aidyn that they would take it upon themselves to send out a watch-note."

Yayènia shook her head. "Everyone cares about Aidyn. He is a hero of Blackhaven even if he will not admit it. As an assassin he has helped to make the world a brighter place, and as a guardian of the bloodline of Ewôsdírn he has protected our rulers from the threat of our enemies and meddling, corrupt politicians. His death would devastate the nation, and until this blasted war is over, people will watch him and hope for a lifting of the darkness."

"When will it end?" the Magin asked quietly, partly to herself.

"When evil no longer touches the land, and people are no longer afraid of the shadows," Yayènia replied cryptically, urging Udu into an easy trot.

The evening and the land passed swiftly until they reached Sha Bridge. The Argynd River was flowing sluggish and low, but both elves knew the current beneath the chunks of ice that careened down the way was swift and deadly. Sha Bridge was flanked by two slender towers, on top of which fluttered pennants of Blackhaven, though they were in sad shape. Tlonna frowned at the towers, trying to see the door.

"There is no way in or out," Yayènia said quietly, seeing the frown. "Soldiers were put inside, and then the base was sealed up so that no enemy could get inside. The soldiers died up there, never having the chance to survive."

"Why? Who commissioned such a thing?"

"Queen Gredeil, your...our grandmother, during the last years of the War of Monotheism. Fanatics were sweeping across the land, burning every village in sight, screaming to their god that it was what he willed. Gredeil ordered towers like these to be built all over the kingdom, and soldiers were sacrificed to them. It is the only time in history the Blackhaven Militia revolted against the throne."

"What happened to the rest of the towers?" Tlonna asked, amazed she had never heard of any of this, at least that she could remember.

Yayènia squinted up at one of the faded banners. "Once Dietirin took the throne, he ordered stairs to be built for each one, and a door. They are now the outpost towers, like the one we visited today. These were left this way as a reminder of the cost of such things. Dietirin never liked throwing lives away, even if it did mean a cleaner or faster end to things. I say we camp here tonight, and head into the human territories tomorrow. I would like to breathe clean air for one more night."

Tlonna blinked at the sudden switching of topics. She glanced at the rising moons, blue Tonora first as always, the red moon not quite visible. "As you wish. It has been a long day."

As they set up camp, pitching Yayènia's smallish military tent, Tlonna kept glancing at the towers, wondering if the spirits of the men who had died there lingered. She decided she did not want to find out.

Later, as they were sitting by the fire, their dinner consumed and cleaned away, the queen and the commander gazed blankly at each other, each lost in private thoughts.

Tlonna danced a small blue and yellow flame over her knuckles, her mind elsewhere. "Nia, what do you think the difference is between dreams and reality?"

The warrior's eyes focused on her sister and she blinked slowly. "What?"

The flame grew larger until it was the size of the Magin's palm. She tossed it between her hands, rolling it about with lazy motions. "When we dream, we are lost in a world of our imagination's making, and the influence of others often leads to strange encounters and dialogue. Is it a different perception of the things we truly want in life, or are they hopes and wishes that we fear would come true, but secretly desire anyway?"

Yayènia frowned as the yellow and blue ball of flame danced before her eyes. "I do not know. My dreams usually involve rather odd things, like sentient chairs or talking animals. I certainly do not wish for those things in my life. Imagine, a chair that thought."

Tlonna's lips quirked into a half-smile at the notion. "I will not share mine, for they are more often than not nightmares that leave me breathless and shivering with sweat. But I find myself wondering more and more what makes us do such things in our sleep. Why do we think in our most restive state?"

"Perhaps, only in our dreams can we truly be ourselves. I would love to live in a world where the only thing I had to worry about is what the chair I am sitting on thinks of my rear-end. I rarely dream of battle, and that is what I do for a living. Sure I have nightmares, I wake screaming from the horrors of my past, but when they are innocent dreams, they really are...ridiculously harmless," Yayènia replied softly.

The queen smiled at the thought again and she doused the flame. "In another life, were I not stuck in this position, I think I would like to be a mystic, reading the stars and deciphering things that have no true impact on life, but make it that much more appealing and worthwhile. What about you?"

There was silence for a long time while the warrior thought of an answer, her ice blue eyes looking off into the distance. "I would have been a musician, had Yenji not sold me. Baroness, yes, but I would have been a musician. Did you know Suneelo plays the piano?"

Tlonna's eyebrows twitched in surprise. "I did not. What would you play?"

Yayènia smiled. "I play the flute, but I would like to learn the viola, and the drums. Suneelo tried to teach me the piano, but I do not have the hands for it, too small." She held up her hands with fingers spread to illustrate her point.

"I did not know you played the flute."

"Nobody other than Suneelo does, and now you."

"I would like to hear you play sometime."

Yayènia smiled again and leaned backward into the tent so that only her legs were sticking out. When she reemerged, she was holding a slender wooden case. Inside was a flute carved from the wood of a *kairhotuss* tree.

"They make the purest sound," the warrior explained as her sister stared in utter shock. "Usually they are made from clay or rosewood, but *kairhotuss* makes the most beautiful sound." When she put the instrument to her lips and blew a few lingering notes, the air seemed to calm and quiet around them.

As Yayènia played, moving from one clarion note to the next, Tlonna felt her body soften and relax, the tension of the last few months draining out of her. When she looked at her sister, the warrior had her eyes closed as her fingers danced along the carven length of the flute. Looking closely, Tlonna saw that intricate swirls were etched into the ivory wood, leaping and flowing like the notes they symbolized.

Suddenly everything seemed less demanding, and she took a deep breath, her eyes closing. The spirits, rather than mutter at her in their indecipherable language, hummed along in a harmonious choir while Jair quieted to listen. It was the most at peace she had been in years, and tears welled in her closed eyes at the sheer beauty of it. Yayènia played for what seemed like hours, though it may have been only a few minutes.

When the music stopped, Tlonna let out a contented sigh and forced herself to open her eyes. Yayènia had her head down and the flute in her lap, idly fiddling with the keyholes. Her shoulders were hunched forward in a protective stance.

"That was beautiful," the Magin whispered, unwilling to make too much noise. "Yayènia, I never knew."

The warrior looked up with wide eyes. "You cannot tell anyone. If they knew..."

"What? Why would it be bad?"

"My credibility would be absolutely shattered, Tlonna! No one wants to follow a flute-playing pansy into battle; they want a vicious, iron-hard fighter."

"And playing the flute makes you a pansy? What of Suneelo, who plays the piano? Does that make him a weakling? Or Aidyn who plays the lute, and is learning the guitar?"

"Aidyn knows the lute? What is a guitar?"

Tlonna nodded. "I caught him playing once, a year or so back. He thought the door was locked to one of the smaller common rooms, and I heard the music and walked in on him. He was mortified."

Yayènia frowned. "What is a guitar?"

"A thinner version of the lute, with more strings. Some human just invented it. There was an elf playing it at the Samhain ball."

"I never thought Aidyn of all people would care about music. I wonder where he learned."

"Where did you learn?"

The older female blanched slightly and looked away, the murky shadow of memory lurking in her eyes. "Arakis made me learn when I was his wife. I had to sit in his room and play all night long while he and one of the other wives fornicated. If I hit a sour note he made me join in, and sometimes he would just sit and watch. If I did not participate, he would beat one of the servants. I learned to never hit a sour note."

"I am so sorry," Tlonna breathed, moving over to sit next to her tortured sister. "I wish he were still alive so I could strip him of all ranks and titles and force him to work in the most demeaning vocation. Then, when he got too old to work, I would hang him in a public execution."

Yayènia made a gurgling sound in her throat and laid her head on Tlonna's shoulder. "I wish he were alive too, then."

They were awake and mounted before dawn broke across the horizon. Sha Bridge lifted them above the raging Argynd, its low railing glistening with frosted dew and moisture from the river. Takîreaes and Udu stepped carefully on the black-striated granite, testing their weight before moving on. The two stallions tossed their heads and flicked their tails, uneasy at the slippery surface.

Yayènia sat rigidly, her hands tight on the reins, though they sat unguided in her lap. Udu's hooves slipped a little when he hit a patch of solid ice and she let out a squeaky yelp, her eyes tightly closed. Tlonna trusted Takîreaes as he picked his careful way across the bridge, and she swayed loosely in the saddle. She was astonished by her sister's actions, but said nothing, knowing Yayènia would likely be humiliated and offended if she did.

It took several minutes to cross Sha Bridge, and even when the thicker air and less-clean atmosphere of the human realm greeted the two elves, they let out a sigh of relief.

"It is amazing how easy it is to forget the corruption of the other lands," Tlonna muttered as she wiped the back of her hand across her mouth.

Yayènia made a grunting noise of consent and urged Udu onward, veering slightly south. "There is a ford a few hours from here, and that is where we should cross into Kismath. It is the only crossing on this side of the province."

"No bridge?" Tlonna asked in bewilderment.

The warrior tugged on her braid as she shook her head. Tlonna realized with a little surprise that her helmet was hanging from her saddle. "The Kismathians never built one. The ruling house always said it was an unnecessary blight upon the earth, and that if one could not cross through a river, one had no business going above it."

"They seem a strange people," the queen replied, frowning in thought.

"You have no idea. They were beautiful people, as far as humans go, but not quite right in the head, I do not think. They worshipped animals and sacrificed them to the gods, I am not quite sure what their religion was called, but it certainly angered the monotheists."

"Sure," Tlonna said, sounding very understanding, which Yayènia knew she was not.

"Anyway, they never built a bridge, and always made the trading caravans, emissaries, anyone who ever came to Kismath cross at the ford or go through the twisting, deadly pass in the Kismath

Range. It was horrible for everyone else, and many died in the crossings every year, but still the Kismathians refused to build even a footbridge, even a ferry crossing. It angered nearly every province. Only Blackhaven and Flousen Dua never tried to force the issue, but they did encourage it. Of course, the Duani elves can just walk to Kismath. The border on that side is made up by the Onyx Forest, and the thing that protects them is simply the harsh terrain of the Kismath tundra."

"So why did Flousen Dua refrain from coming to Kismath's aid during the war?" Tlonna asked, surprised her sister knew so much about the kingdom.

Yayènia gave her a long-suffering glance. "Flousen Dua, like Blackhaven, was suffering from a severe depletion of their population. Do not forget that the entire kingdom is elven, unlike Blackhaven. They lost nearly half their population in the span of two hundred years, which is a pretty small amount of time when talking about our people. They simply could not afford to send aid out when they were already suffering."

"What I want to know is how the Darkwights were able to move about the elven communities and no one ever saw them. How did they convert so many elves without anyone figuring it out?" Tlonna asked, her voice breathy with honest frustration.

The commander shrugged. "Think about it. It takes one demon to convert one elf. Once that elf is turned, he can then turn another, and another. Sodo said that from what he could tell of his attack only one of them was doing the transformation. The others were there to help hold him down, and that he was so debilitated he could not even cry out. Darkwights are elves, so they have the same strength as us, naturally. If he is good enough, one demon could take one elf, as I said. Once there were two of them, they could each take two, or one, whichever they ran across. After they are turned, they are not going to go running back to the elves, are they? They are going to join the gang. No one would know what was happening. Any elf who saw a Darkwight would think, there is a Darkwight, not, there is an elf turned into a demon, until it was too late. It makes sense, really."

"I thought warriors are supposed to be all brawn and no brain?" Tlonna replied, teasing.

Yayènia glowered at her for a second and then chuckled. "I thought queens were supposed to be all fluff and no stuff."

They laughed, and let the horses have their heads. The two stallions let loose, stretching their muscular bodies and bellowing with joy. Takîreaes's slightly leaner build allowed him to take the lead early on, but Udu's stamina never flagged. They reached the Jaquisa River by noon.

"The ford is a little further west, I think," Yayènia said, shading her eyes against the uncommonly bright winter sun.

Snow flurries whirled around them, coating the ground in a light blanket. Tlonna brushed the white flakes from Takîreaes's sable mane and nodded. "Lead the way, then."

It took them another half hour to find the ford, and they dismounted in unhappiness. The Jaquisa raged just as much as the Argynd, fed as they were by the Fàrthyn Ocean from the Strait of Arwênlhias. Though the Jaquisa River was much narrower than the broad Argynd, it was rumored to be many times deeper.

"Can we cross?" Tlonna asked, eyeing the rushing water in doubt.

"It will be hard going, but we should be able to make it fine. Tie up all your things so that it does not hang down, and take off your shoes."

"It is going to be freezing!"

Yayènia grimaced as she followed her own orders. "Yes it is, but we are elves. We will not die from the cold."

"I think I would have pushed for a bridge," Tlonna muttered as she stripped off her boots and tied them to the pommel of Takîreaes's saddle.

Together the two females made their way into the frigid water, wincing as it sluiced up against their ankles like razor blades. The stallions whickered in distaste, but followed their people into the river. Tlonna shrieked when she stepped into a hole and dropped to her thighs into the icy water. She clutched at her stirrup, holding on with a death grip. Yayènia had her hand on Udu's pommel as she let him guide the way, her muscles rigid with fear and cold.

Tlonna shivered uncontrollably, making the steam that lifted from her body quiver. Takîreaes snorted at her and kept moving forward, determined not to let Udu win.

A high wave came at them, sloshing against the horses' flanks and dousing the elves to the waist. Yayènia let out a dismayed howl and nearly bounced against her stallion in her disgust of all things wet.

Tlonna's heart was beating fast as she struggled to keep her footing on the brittle, slippery rocks below. She thanked whatever spirits were listening that she was an elf, and would not die from this experience, or suffer from frostbite or illness.

At one point Yayènia let out a yelp as Udu's hoof slipped and he went down to his front knees, whinnying in fear. The warrior was now soaked from head to foot, her face pale red against the cold as she trembled. It took them nearly an hour to make the crossing, both of them frozen cold and wet, the horses shivering uncontrollably. Once they reached the shore of Kismath and found a protected spot within the shadow of a few massive boulders, Tlonna barely waited for her sister to dump some wood on the ground before pointing her finger at it.

A massive flame erupted from her hand and bit into damp wood, ignoring the fact that it was wet. They quickly took care of the stallions, making sure to check any scrapes they had retrieved from the crossing, and to remove all frost from their coats. Then they slumped down next to each other in several blankets and shivered until they were slightly warmer.

"That was miserable," Yayènia said after a minute, pulling away and wrapping another blanket around her own body. "If I ever suggest crossing a river that does not have a bridge, would you please stop me?"

Tlonna chuckled morosely, pulling her blanket tighter. "If I ever get the idea in my head to try to avoid our own army would you please stop me?"

Yayènia snorted and poked the fire. She finally dragged her pack over and flipped it open, yanking out a pot. She got to her feet with a dramatic groan and trudged the several yards to the river. There she hunkered down and dunked the pot into the water. She returned and hooked the pot onto the steel cooking tripod Tlonna had put over the fire.

"What do we have for this night?"

The warrior gave her sister a mischievous grin. "What did you catch?"

Tlonna huffed. "I am the queen! I do not hunt!"

There was a moment of stunned silence and then Yayènia burst out laughing, doubling over as Tlonna tried to hold a straight face. Before long she too was laughing at her own nonsense. Yayènia shook her head as her laughter faded away and pulled her pack close again.

"We have rabbit left from yesterday, enough to make a stew." The older elf lifted a package of treated leaves and tossed it at her sister.

Tlonna caught it and opened it to reveal the roasted hare inside. She set it to the side and reached inside her own pack to grab a canteen. She jiggled it at Yayènia. "From the palace cellar."

The commander grabbed at it, letting out a lusty growl. "Ladies are not supposed to drink, Tlonna, soldiers are."

The queen laughed as she relinquished the skin. "I believe it is cognac."

"You believe? You should know."

Tlonna shrugged. "I just grabbed what I could before Laurent kicked me out. He is a mean cook."

"He is not afraid of me, which has always been a bit of a challenge to me. The day I can frighten him, he will cook me biscuits and gravy whenever I want for as long as he is head chef."

"Biscuits and gravy? Of all the dishes in the world, you choose that one?"

Yayènia smiled with nostalgia. "We made it a lot when I was with Ghealan. I acquired a great fondness for it."

"All right, all right," Tlonna said, laughter bubbling in her voice.

Their light chatter continued as they cooked dinner, still rubbing the cold from their limbs. Once the stew was simmering happily, Tlonna took a deep breath.

"Where do we go from here, Nia? Anything I need to know about?"

The warrior's face fell. "Kismath is a dangerous place, even for us. The constant rain and snow is bad enough, but then you have the wind snagging the icicles and tossing them about at fatal speeds. I have seen a man take one through the head like a flaming sword. The only way to avoid the danger is to take shelter during the ice storms, which can last for hours, even days if they are truly bad."

"We will not have to. I can shield us individually so we will have independence, but the ice will not reach us."

Yayènia shrugged, not entirely convinced. "Then there is the temperature itself. We will have to be extra careful because we are here in the dead of winter. Traveling at night will be absolutely impossible."

Tlonna sighed. "Anything else?"

"Goblins, and possibly some indigenous people who came back after the war to try and remake their lives. Nothing I am too worried about, to be honest. I fear the earthen enemies. We will simply have to be ready for anything."

Those solemn words ended the conversation, and Tlonna got up to wash the cooking pot. Still chilled they checked the horses, and then bedded down in their tent, pressing their backs together for shared warmth.

They passed through the relatively flat landscape for two days before running into the first real trouble. Yayènia's head jerked up when the keening started, very faint but piercing nonetheless. Snow was billowing around them as they trotted across the frozen land. Tlonna saw her sister's reaction and stopped Takîreaes, looking around.

"What is it?" she asked, her voice muffled by the wind and her thick cowl. She wore her slippery black cloak from the Cyree beneath her fur mantle, and it kept her warm enough.

"Ice storm," Yayènia replied, shouting over the howl. "We need to either find shelter or try out your shield."

"You sound doubtful!"

The wind was picking up quickly, screaming through the large boulders and stunted trees. The elves now had to yell to be heard, and even then, it was difficult to hear. Yayènia made a careless gesture as her sister began to Weave, lights coalescing through her fingers as though she had a bubble of water before her. Suddenly there were two bubbles bobbing in the air, their edges barely discernible, faint colors catching when the weak sun hit the edges. Tlonna threw one at Yayènia and brought the other toward her chest. Takîreaes snorted as the air around him grew suddenly warm and dry.

Yayènia and Udu both tensed in surprise as the same thing happened around them, the whipping snow slamming against the shield but melting immediately after.

"Nice!" the warrior shouted, making Tlonna wince.

"The shields are connected, so you do not have to yell at me," the Magin replied dryly.

Yayènia looked sheepish for a second and then disturbed. "This is odd, I must say. I can hear you better than if we were next to each other in a room."

"That is because these shields occupy the same space, they are just separated with a Weave of spirit. They are made from the same original Weave, which makes them the same," she added when her sister looked ill.

"So why not use this shield all day? We could travel much easier if we were not freezing the whole time."

Tlonna shook her head in denial. "I cannot hold it constantly. It takes a good deal of energy to hold up a shield for one person for a few hours, much less two. I can do it, but not all day."

Yayènia didn't bother to continue the conversation, knowing that what she wanted now, for Tlonna to drop the shield and find shelter, would not happen. She grimaced at the barely visible barrier bobbing a few inches in front of Udu's nose, flinching once as the first flying icicle shattered against the shield.

# Chapter 6
## Renewal

Aidyn blinked several times, trying to focus his vision as he sat up. He groggily clutched the side of his head. Though Losolin had fixed the serious wound the assassin still suffered from terrible headaches. As he pressed his bare feet to the chilly obsidian floor of his tiny hospital room, he winced as a thousand shocks streaked up his leg, but they faded quickly and he was able to stand. He cricked his neck and twisted his torso, stretching out the cramped muscles.

The dark elf carefully stepped over to the chair shoved into the corner and picked up a loose pair of cotton pants and the same style shirt. Grimacing, Aidyn slipped them on and walked out of the room. Braden saw him and hurried over.

"I know I said you could leave today, but I worry that you will push yourself too far and not allow the rest of the healing to take place."

Aidyn braced himself against an empty bedrail and sighed. "I will not be pushing anything, Braden. I have been pushed too far in recent times, and I do not like the feeling. Take comfort in that."

"Hardly. Do you want help to your suite?"

The assassin scowled at him. "Allow me to retain some dignity, boy! You have me walking about in pajamas!"

"They're not pajamas, they are unrestrictive clothes that will not stick to any of your injuries, and will not constrict against them. If I see you in that creepy, light-elusive, painted-on outfit you normally wear, I will rescind your freedom and you will be strapped to your bed until you are completely healed, down to the smallest bruise. Is that clear?"

Aidyn's glower smoldered. "Creepy? *Painted-on?*"

Braden was not the least bit cowed. "When clothing forces my gaze to slip by it, I define them as creepy. Aidyn, when you wear them, I can see your leg muscles flex. That kind of restriction will be detrimental to your recovery."

"My pants are leather! They have nothing to do with the *ärdyz* illusion!" the elf protested, disturbed by the human's observance of his legs.

"I do not care what they are made of; they are too tight for you right now. Obey my rules, or suffer the consequences. Trust me; it will not be worth it."

Aidyn seethed down at the healer for a moment longer, and then nodded. "Have it your way."

Braden's face lit up into a bright grin. "Thank you! Now go on. I believe your brother is waiting outside for you."

"What?"

"Commander Aladorn was informed of your release, and I would predict he is waiting outside the door right now."

Aidyn sighed in resignation and moved toward the infirmary wing. His movements were careful, and though he did not limp he walked slower than normal. As predicted, Aladorn was pacing out in the hall.

"Ah, little brother, I am glad to see you up," the wiat said heartily when Aidyn appeared. Noting the uncomfortable way the assassin moved, he frowned. "Are you still hurting?"

"Where are my weapons? And my clothes?" Aidyn asked, tugging at the loose cotton items that covered his slender body, and ignoring the question.

"In your room, under lock and key. You are not supposed to put them on yet."

"Braden!" the assassin growled, but he moved away from the hospital, toward the stairs.

Aladorn fell in beside him, half-smiling. "I have checked on your things every day to make sure they were not disturbed by the maids. Can you make it up the stairs?"

The younger dark elf eyed his brother in disgust. "Of course I can," he scoffed and lifted his bare foot to prove the point. A jolt of pain shot down through his right leg, radiating from the stab wound in his thigh. He winced but managed to keep his balance.

Aladorn rolled his eyes and grabbed his brother's elbow, holding him steady. Aidyn's face was gray with pain and shame as he hobbled up the two flights of stairs to his suite. He was breathless by the time they made it, and he collapsed into one of his chairs as soon as Aladorn let go.

"Are you sure you are supposed to be out of bed?" the wiat asked, sitting next to the assassin.

"Braden said I could leave. I am not supposed to do anything for another week though," Aidyn admitted, picking at a loose thread on his trousers. "I feel naked."

"You are less naked now than you usually are. Spirits, Aidyn, those pants of yours...I am surprised you can get them on."

The assassin smirked. "Braden said the same thing. Why does everyone stare at my legs?"

"I am not sure it is your legs they are staring at, little brother."

Again the killer's lips lifted into a naughty smile. "Your clothing is not the loosest," he said, gesturing at the wiat's snug black britches, which were made of flexible wool.

Aladorn returned the smirk. "I can disappear if I so choose."

"So can I."

The wiat snorted a laugh, accepting his brother's words as true. "What do you plan on doing for the next week?"

Aidyn's face fell as he shrugged one bruised shoulder. "I do not yet know. Tlonna and Yayènia left already, and my bond with her is gone. When you all came to me through that connection I felt all of your fear and worry. I somehow managed to cut it off or mask it, I am not sure what. If I knew where she was, I would go after her."

"Yayènia is leading her through Kismath."

"I know, but Kismath is a big province, and there are several different ways they could have gone."

Once again Aladorn conceded the point.

"What are you supposed to be doing?" Aidyn asked, noticing the way Aladorn fidgeted, restless.

"I am to patrol the harbor and the wall, ensure the repairs are going as planned and make sure we did not miss anything."

"You sound thrilled."

"I should be with the army, marching toward battle and yet I am here, walking the walls and talking to stubborn dwarves about their contracts," the wiat admitted angrily, folding his arms across his broad chest.

Aidyn frowned as he stood along with his brother. "I know how you feel. Are you going to ride out to the battle when Tlonna and Yayènia return?"

"I sure as hell plan on it," the older elf snapped. "What are you going to do?"

Shrugging, the assassin tried to hook his thumbs around his scimitar hilts, realized too late they were not there, and wound up making an awkward thrusting motion with his arms. "Library," he growled, and limped off.

Aladorn watched him go with swelling pain in his heart.

The army moved quickly for its size, reaching the Purheaen border within a week and setting up camp on the edge of Lake Sethryn.

"Our first stand will be here," Losolin said, pointing at their current spot on the map spread over the table. "If we get pushed back, we will retreat here," he traced a line into the Kismath Mountains, stopping about halfway through. "I have soldiers setting up traps even now, securing the only pass through them."

"If we retreat there, then won't the army just march onward toward Blackhaven? The path will be clear," Orthak said, frowning.

"No, they are not here to attack the city; they are here to kill us. And we are not leaving the way clear. The Silvers will be blocking the way, but I honestly do not see why we would ever retreat. This is a good, defensible spot," the king replied, shaking his head.

Appreciative chuckles and glances passed amongst those gathered, but it did not last long. The numbers they faced were several times larger than any other force they had encountered before. The approaching army made the one that had attacked Alchemian seem small, and even then they had been outnumbered by the thousands.

"And then what?" Sargotarh asked, leaning back in his chair, feet propped on the table. "What would be the next move?"

Losolin smiled grimly. "We move deeper into the frigid plains of Kismath. We will have cold weather gear cached there for when we arrive. *If* we arrive. The enemy will not be prepared for such a thing."

"The winter nearly destroyed them at Alchemian, what makes you think they won't be prepared for such a thing this time?" Orthak asked, always the one to point out flaws even if he did not believe them to be a problem.

"We cannot know for sure, but our information says these are inexperienced men from warm-climate areas. The Seadueni elves have not seen snowfall in a century, and the remaining Talenians are too little a number to make a difference. They are the only ones with experience in freezing temperatures."

"Perhaps they will inform the rest of the army of the cold," Sargotarh said dryly, a knowing smile on his lips.

Losolin returned the smile. "The day Seaduens elves listen to humans will be the day I become a dark elf. And Sithian's men are no better. They are untrained, unruly, and most do not speak an intelligent language."

Suneelo sat forward, glancing at Ghealan who remained back in his chair, arms folded. "If we get pushed back through Kismath, our next camp will be at Kismanelle, taking root in the remains of the city. Once there, we can see what defenses can be laid, and where our next stand will be, if needed."

"Are we honestly preparing for such a rout?" Sargotarh asked, alarmed.

The Captain of the Guard shrugged. "We must be prepared for every event. Remember who we are fighting."

The reminder that they were going up against Sithian Rahlan, son of Tlonna and Midian, leader of the most reckless army in the world silenced many of the doubts. They were in for a long fight.

# Chapter 7
## Kismath

Yayènia yawned loudly, covering her mouth with the back of her hand. Tlonna glared at her as she yawned seconds later. They were two days into their journey across the frigid tundra of Kismath, and so far Tlonna's shields had kept them safe from the fatal ice storms. The two elves were walking their horses, giving the stallions a little rest. Snow was built in drifts up to their thighs, so they were practically digging their way across the landscape. The hardy pine trees that dotted the land in small groves offered little shelter at night, so they had spent the previous night in a snow cave. Tlonna was sincerely grateful that her sister had learned such tricks in her tenure as a soldier.

"Kismanelle is about four more hours away, and the far border another two days. Tlonna, are you sure you want to see the city?"

The queen nodded as she pushed her hands out in front of her, clearing away a drift that stood taller than her head. "I need to see it with my own eyes."

The warrior sighed in resignation and continued on her way, tugging Udu along behind. It took them six hours to reach the abandoned city because of the snow and wind. Memories flashed through Yayènia as they approached the decimated walls, making her mind flinch. Her face, however, betrayed nothing of her feelings with the expression Tlonna was quickly starting to call her Ice Face.

The Magin slid off Takîreaes once they stood between two blackened piles of rubble that the commander said were once the gate towers. Before them lay the snow- and windswept main street, littered with rubble, frozen carcasses, and discarded weapons. Tlonna hitched Takîreaes to a post as Yayènia dismounted.

"This was once called the Street of Maln, and now it is a thoroughfare of the dead," Yayènia said in her expressionless voice, coming to stand beside her sister. "I remember standing in about this same spot once the battle was over, and watching the city burn around me. There was no one left alive. Ghealan and I just stood here, helpless."

"The bodies are still here, undisturbed. I wonder why that is?" Tlonna pondered as she strode down the frozen, silent street.

"This place is cursed. Even the animals can feel it. They will not come into this city for anything. Notice there are no birds on the eaves, no dogs in the streets, not even rats in the alleys. This is a place of death and death alone."

"You sound almost frightened," Tlonna remarked dryly, knowing that her sister was not even close to the word.

Yayènia chortled quietly, her teeth glinting in the dreary sunlight. "Respectful, is more like it. I am experiencing a strange bout of nightmarish recollection. The screams echo in the shadows of every building, the cries of anguish, the pleas and the prayers that fell on empty ears, the curses and furies that only angered the opposition. Every person I watched die here walks with us, whispering their promises of vengeance and betrayal." The warrior's voice was hushed and breathless, the air before her lips frosting with each syllable. "We stood away, knowing that if we came to the rescue, we would only add to the carnage. None of us would have made it out alive, not that it mattered in the end."

"What do you mean?"

"We came here to rescue the royal family and as many citizens as we could. We left with less than a dozen people, and half of our soldiers. The king and queen were slaughtered when they ran back to the city, and most of their people were dead long before we even arrived. It was a total loss, and to this day, the agonizing failure keeps me awake at night. I know Ghealan suffers the same."

"It was not your fault. You did what you could, Nia."

The commander's face twitched in annoyance. "I know that. Unfortunately, not all the Kismathians who died knew that. They cursed us with their last breaths, screaming their injustice."

Tlonna did not reply, instead staring up at the remains of the castle wall that stood atop a hill in the center of the city. It was a blockish affair, with four square towers at each corner, and smaller towers dotting the lengths. Three of the four larger towers were missing their tops, and most of their sides. The fourth was still whole, but was beginning to crumble to one side. The castle itself, once the two elves picked their way inside the shattered remnants of the gate, was in shambles. It was a square horseshoe shape, with two long wings set at ninety-degree angles from the entry wing. The massive double doors that had once led to the grand entryway hung at awkward angles from one hinge apiece. From what they could see from where they stood on the frozen cobblestone way, the interior of the castle had been put to flame.

Frozen bodies cluttered the courtyard, most in contorted postures of severe agony, both mental and physical. Some had horrid burns on their desiccated flesh, others were missing pieces and parts, many had both. A single arras hung stiffly from the left castle turret. The colors were faded and bled out, but Tlonna could discern the violet and black that were once the proud colors of Kismath. The black strike of lightning was faded near to brown, and seemed to mock the dead people below.

Yayènia shoved aside one door and held it open so Tlonna could walk through. Inside the castle were the same colored tapestries and runners, the bolt of lightning spaced evenly throughout. The gray granite walls were dark with frozen soot and grime. Dark stains splashed against the stone were often accompanied by a slumped corpse or random body part. The absolute wreckage surprised Tlonna with its pure disarray and violence. Even though a hundred years had passed, the freezing cold temperature had kept the bodies in a semi-cryogenic state, their flesh dried and desiccated, but still whole.

Tlonna's eyes were wet with tears as she walked amongst the terrified dead. Yayènia was a silent guardian at her back, her boot heels thumping quietly on the icy floor. They walked through the first floor quickly, and then ascended to the second. The castle was made up of three floors, and though it was much smaller than the behemoth of Blackhaven, Castle Kismath had been grand. The second floor was reached by a central staircase that was several yards wide, a purple and black carpet covering nearly the entire thing. Tlonna ran her fingers over the freezing granite baluster as she walked along the open corridor, her eyes scanning every inch of the building.

"What do you want with this place?" Yayènia finally asked, her voice tired.

"I need justification for this war, Nia. Aderiaen slaughtered the Kismathians, and razed their kingdom. Midian tried to do the same thing to us, and now Sithian wants to do it to all of Nymyños. It has to stop, but I cannot just say that what they did here was wrong and go after them for it. I needed to see it with my own eyes, touch it and smell it. This was a grave injustice, and all the Kismathians ever did wrong was stand up against the Rahlans. Whom would I be if I simply sent my people to die in a cause not wholly honorable? This way I can say I have seen the devastation visited upon innocent people by this tyrannical family, and I can declare war with my integrity intact."

"You fear your people would not agree with your choice to go after Sithian's hordes?" Yayènia asked in disbelief.

"No, I fear that I would not agree with it. It is a terrible burden to demand this of people. I needed to see the wreckage myself."

"Are we actually going to the Cyree, or was that a lie?"

"No, I need to return there, but I needed to stop here as well. Do you know where Jaryn and Sybilla are?"

Yayènia took a deep breath and then nodded. "Third floor. Follow me."

Tlonna did as she was told, trailing behind her sister as they returned to the wide staircase and went up the second flight. The third floor was wider than the others were and the doors more widely spaced. Here and there were frozen women with their rigid skirts bundled up around their waists, looks of utter terror and shame stamped on their faces.

"If you were here after the battle..." the queen began, but the commander cut her off, her voice unusually curt.

"There were living people to worry about, the dead do not suffer. Do not accuse me and my warriors of leaving the women exposed when we were trying to ensure the survival of those who were suffering."

"Yayènia, I just-"

"The entire place was on fire, my soldiers were already weary and several were wounded, but they followed Lan and me in without hesitation. Most of the rescued had to be carried out, and we did not have the numbers or the time to stop and pull down the skirts of a hundred raped and dead women."

Tlonna fell silent, not wanting to elicit another outburst from her volatile sister. They were at the end of the north wing of the castle now, and the hallway was quite grand, even with all the devastation. The ceiling was frescoed in images of human triumphs, and walls adorned in the stuffed heads of large and small game, weapons, heraldry, and mirrors, the latter of which were mostly shattered. Gilded tables and chairs lined the wide corridor, their black and purple cushions slashed and faded, frosted over.

Yayènia came to an extravagantly tall door and pushed on the gold knob, swinging the portal wide open. She walked into the royal suite without hesitation, her memory of over a century serving her well. The warrior stepped through the shattered frame of a balcony door and held her arm out, once again wearing her Ice Face. Tlonna let out an involuntary gasp of horror. King Jaryn and Queen Sybilla's bodies were stripped naked and skewered with enough spears to keep them upright even in death. Their severed heads were nailed to the wall with giant iron stakes, their expressions pure agony.

Their fine garments were piled at their feet and covered in frozen feces, urine, and blood. Tlonna's stomach heaved and she had to press her lips together in order to keep from losing control. She did not ask why Yayènia had left them like this. She did not want to hear the answer.

"Have you had enough of your justification, yet?" the weapons-master asked quietly, her arms folded across her chest.

Tlonna, not trusting to open her mouth, nodded. She started to follow Yayènia off the balcony and then stopped. She took off her black and silver cloak with its embroidered Tree of Blackhaven, and draped it over the two naked bodies. Then she Wove a shield around it and tied it off, so that the wind and snow could never remove it. Feeling slightly better, the Magin Queen followed her High Commander sister out of the room, back through the castle, and out of city itself. Takîreaes and Udu seemed well rested and ready for another hard trek as their riders mounted up. Tlonna felt sick as the city slowly receded behind them.

Tlonna and Yayènia were silent. Neither could think of anything useful to say, and so they said nothing. The journey across the frozen plateau upon which the city of Kismanelle sat was slow but steady as the weather remained calm with only the occasional billow of snowy wind. For the next day and a half they remained mostly quiet, reflecting on the horrors of what they had seen and remembered. Their reminiscence persisted until they began to descend from the tundra into the marshland.

Yayènia pulled Udu up and looked over at her sister. "From here until we reach the border we are in goblin territory. They will most likely stay away from us, as they fear elves and horses, but some will probably think they can overwhelm us and attack. They will pose no true threat, but goblins are nasty tricksters. We will not be able to stop and camp at night."

Tlonna shrugged. "Whatever needs to be done I will do it. Lead on, High Commander."

Yayènia sighed and shook her head, but she urged her stallion into an easy trot. Takîreaes snorted and followed him, tossing his mane of sable hair. It took them less than an hour to get to the very bottom of the plateau and into the marshland. Steam rose up off the ground in oily, curling wisps. The unpleasant air smelled of rot and stale water, the cloying scent of fish underlying it all. Tlonna made a face, wishing for once she did not have the heightened senses of both elf and Magin. Yayènia tied a bandana over her nose and mouth and then handed one to the queen.

"They are treated with the extract of apples to ward off the stench of the marshes," she said as Tlonna sniffed the kerchief in surprise.

"Smart," she murmured, tying it around her head.

Yayènia's eyes crinkled above her cloth mask. "I have my moments. Now, there are only a few dry trails through this place, and if I remember correctly we are one the widest one. However, we may have to get wet now and again."

Tlonna sighed. "Wonderful."

The warrior chortled as she swayed with Udu's easy stride. Tlonna glowered at the back of her head for the better part of the day, but when darkness fell, her sister turned with a different look in her eyes.

"Night is the time of the goblins, Tlonna. Get out a torch."

The Magin shook her head. "I can do better. Give me your hand."

Yayènia twisted and leaned back in the saddle so that she could touch her fingers to the queen's. A tingling warmth spread up her arm and across her chest. She gasped in alarm when light began expanding from her very flesh.

"What did you do?" she demanded, looking back at her sister.

Tlonna was glowing brightly, so much so in fact that she had an aura of light surrounding her for several feet. "It is a Weave of fire and spirit, Nia. You look the same as I do, and it will not waste valuable wood and oil. It is a sustaining Weave so it will only fade once there is a brighter light to contend with, such as the sun."

Yayènia made a face but she turned back around and resumed the ride, her eyes searching the wide expanse of light for movement. It was amazing that it did not blind her to the darkness outside the ring of light, for she could still see the clumps of brown marsh weed and the movements of the fish in the dark water. Though it made her uneasy, the warrior had to admit that her sister's magic was by far better than a sight-limiting torch. The goblins would be petrified of them now.

The night passed without incident, and as soon as the sun was up above the horizon the warm glow emanating from the sisters faded away, leaving them chilled and strangely despondent.

"Aftereffect, I am afraid," Tlonna called after a few moments of uneasy silence.

Yayènia's shoulders lifted unevenly in a resigned shrug, but she said nothing. The Magin Queen chuckled quietly to herself. They slogged along for the rest of the day, resting only briefly to allow the horses to eat and drink while they stretched tired muscles and nibbled on strips of salted beef and pork.

"Best stuff," Yayènia muttered as she tore off a piece of the dry meat. "Lightweight, travels well, keeps for a long time...we used to eat this all the time when I was roaming with Ghealan and the Warriors."

Tlonna grimaced as she chewed on the rubbery meat. "Let me guess, this is a remnant of the stuff you had back then?"

The commander laughed, her eyebrows lifting in mock confirmation. "Do you not like it?"

"Mmm...it is wonderful food, to be sure. Dry, stringy, leathery. What is not to like?"

Again Yayènia laughed, ripping off another chunk. "I enjoy it. You can hunt for goblin meat if it does not satisfy you."

"I would rather eat marsh weed," Tlonna replied in good humor, petting Takîreaes's nose.

The stallion reached down and yanked the strip of meat from her hands, chewing contentedly.

"Hey! You are not supposed to eat meat," she reprimanded him, shaking her finger at his nose.

Yayènia grunted. "He is a warhorse. They always get bits of flesh and muscle during a battle. It is only natural they would not have an aversion to eating it at other times. Particularly salted beef. Delicious."

"You are mad," Tlonna snorted, climbing onto Takîreaes's saddle. "Without a doubt mad."

The warrior shrugged as she mounted as well. "Someone has to be in order to muck about with you all the time. Bloody menace."

Tlonna burst out laughing, the grumpiness in the warrior's voice so overdone she couldn't help her amusement. Yayènia looked back at her and grinned, enjoying the banter.

# Chapter 8

## Suspicions

Aladorn knocked on Miazie's office door, waiting impatiently for the reply. When it came, he strode into the room and planted his feet. The Belau looked up with a quizzical expression.

"What do you want, Al?"

"Did you sign an order for the south wall to be left alone?"

The High Advisor cocked an eyebrow. "Yes. Do you have a problem with that?"

The wiat stared down at her in disbelief. "Several, in fact! Tlonna signed the original orders for the entire wall to be looked at, not just parts, and the south wall needs some repairs!"

"Aladorn, Sithian's men did not even get to the south wall before they ran off. What damage is there was done long before this battle. And I'm sure Tlonna just skimmed the contract before signing it. If she had seen the amount of repairs being suggested, she would have never have signed it. The treasury just does not have the money to back all of it and stay afloat. Don't forget we are still in this war. We can't spend all of our money now."

"I forget nothing, Miazie, but Tlonna is our queen! If she signs an order, it is meant to be followed to the letter. You do not have the power to rescind her orders, or overwrite her signature. The wall is key to Blackhaven City's survival! You know nothing of battle, so you think an enemy is going to come at you from the same angle every time. They do not. They come at you from every angle, seeking a weakness, probing for any fault. The south wall is that weakness."

"I am not going to pull that contract again. It can be taken care of later, but not now. How is Aidyn?"

Aladorn scowled at her. "You are not going to get away with this. Miazie, this is outrageous. Your reasoning is broken."

"Your edict is broken. Do not forget that Tlonna left me in charge in her stead. That gives me all the power of a regent."

"You tread on dangerous ground, woman. You are precariously close to sounding like a usurper."

Miazie's mouth dropped open in offense. "How dare you, Aladorn! Get out of my office, right now! Get out!"

The wiat folded his arms and glared at her, unmoving. "Not until you rescind the order and have the south wall put back on the roster."

"I told you we do not have the funds for such a thing."

"Fine. I will speak with Daphne and get her opinion on that. I would suggest you rethink your responsibilities, and the hazard you pose by using Tlonna and Losolin's power without reason."

Miazie seethed at the door once Aladorn had gone, her chest rising with every angry breath. After a minute or so, she tugged on a slender rope to summon her aide, Liv.

"Yes High Advisor?" the woman asked as she dipped into a low curtsey.

The Belau eyed the woman with a critical gaze. She was slender and short, her young face plain but not unattractive. Her black and silver livery dress draped over her form like a robe.

"Summon Martin Crotes immediately, and let him know I would not appreciate his dallying."

"Right away, High Advisor. Anything else?"

"Yes, when he arrives you are to make sure no one comes near this door, including Master Sodo. Is that clear?"

Liv nodded as she curtseyed again. "Absolutely, High Advisor."

When she was alone once more, Miazie undid the top three buttons of her square-cut dress, revealing a good portion of her breasts, and rigged another so that it was halfway undone. She pulled out a few of the pins that were holding up her hair, combed her fingers through the raven lengths to smooth them, and took a deep breath as she looked down. Her breasts filled the free space given by the open neckline and she grunted in satisfaction. The distraction would serve her well.

Several minutes later Martin entered her office, his pompous face filled with disinterest. That is until his eyes landed on Miazie's open cleavage. Sparks lit up in his eyes and he bowed low.

"Lady Miazie, I am honored you would call on me. What is it I can do for you?"

Miazie leaned back in her chair, allowing him a good view. "Have any of your spies returned? It has been a long time since you sent them out."

The man was not looking at her face when he answered. "Not yet, but information gathering requires a lot of time. My men will return no later than Lamat, however."

"Have you attained any useful information at all, then?" the Belau asked, her eyes boring into his forehead.

Her tone and words made him glance up at last. "I have, but I was under the impression I am to give it to either Queen Tlonna or King Losolin alone."

Miazie smiled faintly, absently running a finger along the top of her collarbone. She took a deep breath. "They are both gone from the city as you know, but the need for information does not stop with their absence. Do you really believe they have the time to sit down with men who are little more than wealthy pimps and cons? Your only value is your network of spies, Master Crotes. Do not set yourself above that."

Anger flashed across the man's face but he schooled it immediately. "I am a nobleman by birth, Lady Miazie, and a landowner."

"You are a whoremaster and a crook," Miazie shot back, sitting forward. "However, you do have value to me."

"How's that?"

She let out a dramatic sigh. "It is not easy being of influence in the company of elves, Master Crotes, surely you realize that. I have worked long and hard to obtain the connections I now have. But it comes with a price." She leaned farther out, breathing deep at the same time, forcing the button she had rigged to pop open.

Martin's eyes widened and he shifted in his chair, licking his lips. Miazie was in serious danger of falling out of her dress. She pretended not to notice anything and leaned back with a heavy sigh.

"I am afraid my own passions have gone by the wayside. Did you know that I was once the crown princess of Anutch?"

"I did. I once visited there. You were just about to turn thirteen, I believe."

Miazie smiled, pretend joy lighting her face. Inside, she was disgusted and had to keep reminding herself of the reason of her charade. "I think I remember that." She closed her eyes and appeared to recollect. "Oh, yes, I do. You were there on business, I believe. You were very dashing in your blue coat."

Martin looked immensely pleased with himself. The Belau recalled the gossip among the palace women that he was quite sought after as a bedmate if Aidyn wouldn't give them the time of day, which he rarely did.

"Very good memory, High Advisor."

"Thank you. You know, Martin," she drawled his name, smiling softly, "I have always thought you were handsome."

"Aren't you engaged to that elf scholar?"

"He's an alchemist, and yes, but he's an elf...and it is an arrangement. Relations between Alchemian and Blackhaven, you see."

"I do. So...what is it you desire of me?" Martin asked, his ardor visible.

"Can you not guess?" Miazie replied coyly, trailing her finger between her breasts.

The man was across the desk in a flash, his hands and lips hot on her throat and chest. Miazie squeezed her eyes shut and swallowed, pretending great zeal. When his hand slipped up the skirt of her dress, she forced herself to keep her legs pliant, and when he touched her, she affected a moan.

Her hands ripped at his belt and then squeezed him tightly. His fingers exploring her already and she was sitting low in her chair, one foot braced against her desk. Miazie's breath was coming fast for real now, but it was not passion that elicited it. Martin groaned as her hand caressed him, keeping him stiff and quivering.

"You know what I need to hear?" Miazie murmured in his ear as his lips bent to suckle her breast.

"Anything, anything you want."

"Have your spies heard anything about plans for Blackhaven?"

"Some. The transition in Talenias was not as smooth as it appeared to be. There are groups of," he paused to kiss her collarbone, "Cleicks and loyalists amassing south of Helum. They plan to move on Blackhaven at the beginning of the year and will cause absolute havoc."

Miazie kept his mind focused on her body as he talked, heedless of what he said. "And there is some sort of discourse in Seaduens. Haven't quite figured it out yet," he stopped to kiss her neck some more. When he lifted his head, his eyes were glazed.

"The Lostugs want revenge," he murmured, trying to peel her dress down.

"What sort of revenge?"

"Don't know, but they're furious. Half the family's dead thanks to the Ewôsdírns."

Miazie rubbed her thumb along the side of his organ, causing him to gasp. "Is there anyone else your spies go to other than you?"

"Danner McKay," Martin said immediately and then squealed in shock.

Miazie's grip on him had tightened severely, and she had jerked up. His hand flailed out of her skirt as he reeled backward. The Belau released him and tipped her desk over with her braced foot. As she had planned, the woman heard Liv shouting frantically, fumbling with the key to her office door. Martin had fallen over, his pants tangling up around his ankles. Miazie grabbed her katan, the one Damon had commissioned for her years ago, and stabbed him.

The man screamed as the blade pierced his heart. He squirmed about on the carpet for a few seconds and then fell still, blood pooling out from his chest. Liv finally succeeded in unlocking the door and shot inside. She screamed in fright and swooned in the doorway. Miazie glanced down at her, unsurprised, and buttoned her dress.

Guards appeared seconds later, brandishing weapons. They took a quick scan of the scene and bowed to her. "What happened High Advisor?"

"This man tried to push himself on me, and I stabbed him for it. Would you please get one of your men to take Liv to the infirmary, and remove him from my office?"

"Of course. Are you well?"

Miazie nodded, knowing she looked the part of the attacked lady with her hair in disarray and her dress twisted. Her plan had worked well, but she had not counted on Aidyn. The assassin limped into view around the corner, his emerald eyes taking in her appearance with little emotion.

"Lord Aidyn," the guards murmured, bowing as they carried the two people away.

The dark elf did not say anything as he looked at her. Finally Miazie let out an angry huff.

"What?"

"Sodo will not be pleased."

"Sodo will not be pleased about what?"

Aidyn lifted an eyebrow. "You seduced Crotes so that he would tell you what he knows, and then killed him for it. Trust me, Miazie, I knew the man. He was a lecherous cur, but he would never rape a woman. You, on the other hand, seem to be losing your grip on what is right and what is wrong."

Miazie was dumbfounded that he had deduced her long thought-out plan by just observing the scene for a few seconds. "That...He would never have said anything about what he knew, Aidyn."

"Oh, I know that, but why kill him?"

"Do you honestly believe he would stay silent if I had let him live?" the Belau asked in astonishment. "In order to let him live, I would've had to allow him to have me. I could not let that happen."

"I do believe he would stay silent. Everyone knows you are engaged to Sodo. He would not risk his life for a few days of bragging rights. As I said, I knew the man."

"What would you have done in my place? You and I both know he would not have fingers, toes, or a penis. You would have dismembered him in the first hour, and then once you were satisfied he had told you everything, he would have been hanged. I did it my way."

"You just murdered a man, Miazie! How can you justify that?"

"And how many have you murdered, Aidyn?"

The dark elf's eyes dilated angrily. "I do not take the lives of people who have done little to no harm. Everyone I have killed has tried or succeeded at taking a life, whether mine or someone else's. Martin Crotes was a crooked man, but to my knowledge, which is extensive, he never harmed another person. What you just did is inexcusable."

"What are you going to do, Aidyn? Put me on trial? Torture me? Assassinate me?" Miazie snarled. "I just eliminated a threat; got the name of his successor, and soon we will have control over his network of spies. Are you telling me I have done wrong?"

"It does not matter why you did the deed, only that you took a life without cause. And I should expose you, but instead I will wait until Tlonna or Losolin return, and let them deal with it. Until then, know that I am going to be watching you, and if I see you pull another trick like this; know that I will break you before you have a chance to scream."

"I never knew you thought of me as an enemy, Aidyn."

"I never knew you were a murderer, Miazie."

"I'm not."

The assassin turned to go, but he looked at her over his shoulder. "Martin Crotes would beg to differ."

Miazie watched him shuffle off with a sick feeling in her stomach. Her intentions had been good, her need to know if there were any plots against the throne greater than her wish to have unstained hands. But still, Aidyn's look of utter disgust made her want to crawl under a rock and hide in shame.

She was still sitting at her righted desk several hours later when the door opened. She looked up, expecting Sodo. Her fiancé did not stand in the door, but one of her personal messengers. Tlonna had given her the heady right to choose their livery, as long as the black and silver of Blackhaven was somewhere in the design. Miazie had chosen her own signet, the one she had picked up in an Arseninis stationary. It was an open book with three arcing stars above, and she had the symbol depicted in green thread down the sleeves and hems of her messengers. Their pants were a fitted black trouser, and their tunics an almost whimsical affair of layered black chiffon. The buttons on the stiff collar and cuffs were silver, and their shiny black boots were tooled with silver. A green silk cummerbund completed the uniform, and everyone seemed to admire them. Tlonna had smiled her agreement when Miazie had put forth the design.

The messenger now standing in her office wore the outfit with pride, his back straight, chest puffed out as he bowed from the waist. "High Advisor Miazie, I have a proposal from Count Iranyo Tod. He said he wished for you to review it and see to its dismissal or acceptance as soon as possible."

Miazie frowned as the young man handed her the sealed leather envelope. "I did not know we were accepting law proposals this late in the year."

The messenger bowed again. "I know little of law, High Advisor, and less of politics."

"You help shape law and politics with every message you run for me. Never underestimate the power of a single word or suggestion, Danny. Without messengers, people of authority would not be able to pull the strings that keep kingdoms on their feet. Remember that."

"I will, High Advisor."

"Good. You are dismissed."

"Thank you High Advisor."

Miazie watched Danny slip from her office before breaking the seal of yellow wax and flipping open the envelope. The proposed bill was short and quite to the point, written most likely by Iranyo's underappreciated scribe.

*Proposal 913*

*Dictated by Iranyo Tod, Count of Merchants of the Kingdom of Blackhaven Forest*

*Due to the increased demand for all services put forth by the various merchants, guilds, and independent vendors by the citizens and officiates of Blackhaven City, the need for reform has risen. I call for the increase of Merchant Tax to be taken from either the portion that goes directly to the sellers themselves, or else from the sum given to the Treasury of the Crown, as the majority of sellers have refused to raise their prices to the amount needed. The percentage need be at least thirty-five, from the original twenty in order to cover the amount of supply in demand.*

*Solicited on this day, the 29th of Resen, Year 547 of the 8th Age.*

Miazie rubbed her temples, still vastly upset by the proceedings of the day. Iranyo was asking a lot. The way the law sat now, as set down by Queen Sha two millennia ago, the merchant received fifty percent of all proceeds, the crown thirty, and the Merchant Guild twenty. The guild was responsible for the city warehouses, their staff, and keeping track of trade agreements. A select few guild masters brought any issues to Iranyo, and he then brought them to Tlonna, Losolin, or Miazie for review if needed.

The Belau ran the numbers quickly in her head. Under the old law, an item sold for fifty geld would net twenty-five for the merchant, ten for the guild, and fifteen for the crown. Under the proposal, the guild would end up with seventeen-fifty, and the seller the same amount while the crown cut the loss with seven-fifty, or the crown would keep their sum of fifteen while the seller netted the same as the guild, seventeen-fifty.

No merchant would be happy with that, she knew, but the treasury was sorely depleted and the taxes were low to allow the hassled citizens to get back on their feet. Neither end could afford the cut, but neither could the Merchant's Guild keep supplying quality items at the same rate as two millennia before while everyone else raised their prices. Miazie squeezed her hands against the side of her head. She went to ring the bell to summon Liv, and then remembered the woman was still in the infirmary. Sighing, the Belau stood and strode out of her office, passing the small room on the left side of her door that housed her messengers when they were in, during normal castle hours.

Praying Daphne would still be in her own office, Miazie hurried down the wide corridor lined with closed and locked doors, turned a corner, and headed down a shorter hallway. The doors to Aladorn, Ghealan, and Yayènia's offices were all shut, but she noticed a light coming from under the wiat's. His office, like hers, was newly given. She had vacated her old room and moved into those that had belonged to Erdwyf. Her old office was smaller, and did not have the adjacent rooms Erdwyf's did. As High Advisor, she enjoyed such pleasantries as messengers and an aide. Liv's office had once been Feorien's.

Knocking, Miazie waited until Aladorn's voice bade her enter. He looked up at her with surprise. "I heard what happened. A bit reckless for you, is it not?"

"I did what I believed necessary. Unfortunately, I put too little faith in the man, according to your brother, but what's done is done and I still feel as though I did what I felt necessary."

Aladorn grunted but did not seem to have issue with her actions as Aidyn did. "Did you need something? Have you come to rescind your order on the wall?"

"No, I thought you spoke with Daphne about it."

"I did. She is looking into the expenses. What do you want, then?"

Miazie ran a hand back through her hair. She had taken out all the combs after the fiasco with Martin. "Iranyo Tod just sent me an amendment he wants passed. I could use your input."

"Why mine? I am no politician or lawyer."

"No, but you were a great help to Tyular when you lived there, and I could use some advice. The proposal is practical, but it will make only one party out of three happy."

"Then do not pass it. As standing regent you can veto an amendment, or put it into play," the wiat said, revealing that he knew much more about political law than he let on.

Miazie sighed. "I know that, but I do not want to make a rash decision on this. I am going to have Daphne look at it too."

Aladorn frowned. "That woman works hard, and a lot. Is this something you really need her help on?"

"More like her advice. I want her input as much as yours. I'm not Tlonna, I cannot pass a law without someone yelling at me for making the wrong choice."

"Wisely said. Too bad you did not listen to your own knowledge earlier."

"All right, Aladorn, I get it. Now will you please look this over?" she handed him the bill, and he took it in his tawny hand.

As he read, Miazie watched his brow furrow. She fondly remembered their one night together, and was intrigued by how much he resembled his brother. Aladorn did not have the raw beauty of Aidyn, but he was gorgeous. He set the parchment down and was silent for a long time. "Either way, the guild gets the geld, and the others suffer a large cut."

"So what do you say?"

"Split the difference between the treasury and the merchants, if you decide to let it pass. And I would give the guild thirty, not thirty-five. Every amendment like this, proposed by the sect that stands to profit, is going to give them a buffer for profit. Most likely, they need only twenty-five or thirty percent, but decided to see what they could get away with. If we do agree to give them only a five percent raise, they will holler with injustice and we will not hear the end of it for many years."

Miazie grunted as she took the bill back. "You are a surprising man, Aladorn Sestuns."

"Not really a man, but fine."

She let out a short laugh. "Either way, you proved yourself capable as any man I've been with."

The wiat's eyes narrowed as he stared at her. He too remembered their one night together years ago at an inn in Arseninis. "I beg to differ."

Miazie grinned mischievously. "All right, much more capable than any man, but I have to say Sodo has you beat."

Aladorn barked a laugh, unable to keep it back. "Your potions master is young. Give him time and he may reach my level. You are just fuddled from your time with the human, Damon."

The Belau could not reply, she was giggling too hard at the ridiculousness of their conversation. Even the dark elf was laughing without restraint now, shaking his head.

"Get out of my office before you make me lose all my self-control," he chortled at last, giving her a light shove in the shoulder.

"All right, but you better watch it, Al. I see a lot of ladies mooning after you and that *snide* little brother of yours. Don't let them all down."

"I have heard Aidyn described as many things...snide would be a first. Why are you so irked with him? He has had a hard time recently. He aches from the inside out. Give him a break, would you?"

Miazie's mirth faded. "I know that, but he was rather nasty to me today."

"You killed a man, perhaps not an innocent man, but not an evil one. Besides, slaughter is his territory; he does not like people stepping into his profession."

"He and I always got along. Now I think he may loathe me."

Aladorn smiled faintly. "Aidyn is touchy, and his feelings are quite raw right now. Ever since he was touched by the Eseirik's weapon he has felt peoples' darker intentions much clearer. Give him time to adjust, and you will come to see what a selfless, gentle person he can be. Besides, according to the rumors, he would make even me seem like a novice in bed. Perhaps you should try him before you off and marry your alchemist. Then you would really come to see his inner self."

Miazie blushed crimson as the memory she had of him and Tlonna came rushing to the fore. She'd already experience his talent and suffered a miserable night for it. Aladorn mistook the blush and leaned back, tapping his glass pen against his thigh.

"You have already had him, then?"

"No!" she blurted, too quickly.

The wiat's eyebrow rose to give her a look of surprised interest. "Perhaps you tried, and were rejected?"

Miazie snorted so hard it hurt her throat. "Not that either. It is impossible to explain, so I will not even try. Suffice it to say I have never lain with Aidyn, nor do I intend to. I love Sodo, and he is the only one for me."

"All right, have it your way. I will get the story eventually."

"Yeah," Miazie muttered as she left his office to give the treasurer a visit. "I'm sure you will."

Daphne gave her a look of such incredulity that the High Advisor took a step back. "First Aladorn wishes me to see if we actually have the funds to repair the south wall, and now you want me to see if we have the funds to support some ludicrous amendment? You do realize that other than Ayona, I am the only person in this entire city that works with the treasury?"

Miazie frowned. "What does Ayona do for you?"

The treasurer returned the look. "She's a scribe, what do you think she does for me? She writes the tallies."

The Belau held up her hands in a surrender pose. "All right, Daphne, I'm sorry, but I simply wanted your advice on what to do."

Daphne ripped the bill from Miazie's hand and quickly scanned it. Her brow drew down in an even deeper scowl. She held it out again and allowed the advisor to tuck it back into her belt.

"Come, I want to show you something," the woman said, striding out of her office.

The two women crossed the fourth floor of the castle and stood outside a small, unobtrusive door. Daphne pulled out three different keys and slid them into the three holes on the door. She turned each a different degree, and then stepped inside one of the few rooms Miazie had never been in, the Blackhaven Treasury.

"This is where all of our funds sit," Daphne said, holding out an arm.

The room was a massive vaulted affair with only one window, which was so slender Miazie would have a problem sticking her arm out of it, and a few circular skylights. The floor was completely bare, the obsidian blocks shining like black water in the narrow shaft of late evening light streaming through the window. Giant ironbound crates stood lined up all along the walls, each completely enclosed.

"I don't understand," Miazie said, looking about for the piles of geld she had expected to see. Her father's holding had been an unorganized mess of gold, silver, and copper spikes piled on the floor.

"Each of these crates is designated to a certain category, such as gold spikes, or priceless artifacts. Only Tlonna, Losolin, and I know the combinations to every one of them. Some of my aides know the combination to get into the transfer boxes, but none of the holding crates."

"Transfer boxes?"

Daphne sighed and led the way to one of the massive crates. It stood several inches above Miazie's head. The treasurer leaned in so she couldn't see her hands, fiddled with a lock, and then stepped back. A narrow door opened into the side of the crate. Miazie and Daphne stepped inside, and the Belau gasped in surprise and amazement.

Copper coins filled nearly the entire box, but there was a thick sheet of glass between the narrow space in which the two women stood. A slot little more than a hand's width was cut into the glass and frosted to protect from cuts. A tray jutted out from the opening, and copper spikes pushed up against a sliding glass window that stopped them from spilling into the tray.

"How do you prevent theft?"

Daphne shrugged. "I trust every one of my aides, else I would not have hired them. And," she added when Miazie looked doubtful," each crate sits on a scale that is accurate to within an ounce. I know the average weight of each spike, and I check the scales each morning and night to ensure that what I have charted to be taken out or put in matches with the calculated weight."

"Ingenious," Miazie breathed. "Absolutely magnificent."

"Thank you."

"You did this? You made these?"

Again the treasurer shrugged. "I did not make them, but I designed them. My father was an inventor, he loved to make new things and improve old things. My mother was Keeper of the Treasury before me, and my grandfather before her. Since King Dietirin was crowned in eighty-nine-eighty-seven, my family has been the treasurers."

"That is a long legacy," Miazie breathed, completely stunned.

"Five hundred and sixty years," Daphne said, nodding.

"Then your child will carry on the tradition?"

The woman smiled sadly. "I have no children, nor a husband. But I brought you here for a reason. I wanted you to see just how the kingdom sits. In a year, we average an income of one million, four hundred and eighteen thousand, nine hundred and twenty-five geld. Almost fifty thousand of that goes towards just the upper branches of the military, including Yayènia er'Tiena and Lord Aidyn. Between you and me though, neither the Tienas, Ghealan, nor Aidyn have taken any pay for over nine years, their choice. A little over twenty thousand of the treasury goes to the city council, and us," she gestured between herself and Miazie. "The castle staff and messengers equal about twelve thousand five hundred, leaving an average of about one million, three hundred and thirty-five thousand geld to run the city on. That includes but is not limited to any repairs, streets, military barracks, though admittedly the Tienas do pay for a lot of that out of their own coffers, and industry costs, such as shipbuilding. Usually, we end up with a buffer of about five thousand a year, which generally goes up a slight amount each year, of course," Daphne took a deep breath as she guided Miazie out of the transfer box.

"However, we are a city recovering from a nine-year occupation, and a subsequent siege, of which we are still off and fighting. For those nine years, we had no income, only expenses. And we just finished the reconstruction of all the major parts of the city."

"So you're saying we have no geld."

"What I'm saying is we need every copper spike we can get right now. We have less than twenty thousand in this room, excluding assets, which the throne will never consent to sell, because I will not allow it. Right now, trade is booming very well, but not enough to save us immediately. We cannot afford that bill right now any more than we can afford the repairs to the south wall. Unfortunately, the repairs are not something that can wait on us having the available sums," she pinned Miazie with a stern look before continuing. "This kingdom, this city in particular, is balancing on a very fine point right now. We have a great façade, because most everything we have is paid for, but we are in a crisis. What is going to happen, I cannot say. I just know the numbers don't look good."

Miazie huffed out a breath and placed her hands on her hips. "Iranyo will not accept a complete veto."

Daphne shook her head. "I doubt it."

"So, what do I do?"

"You're the High Advisor, Miazie, not me. But, what I would suggest is the same as Aladorn. Split the costs between the vendors and the treasury. It's a painful but not mortal blow to the coffers. One we might survive."

Miazie hung her head and let out a soft chuckle. "I don't know how Tlonna and Losolin do it. I really don't."

Daphne led the way out of the treasury. "There is a reason we are their aides, Miazie, and not the other way around. Tlonna was groomed for this nearly all her life, and a long life she has. The king is sharper than Yayènia's sword, and has a mind for mathematics as well. He caught onto the economics quicker than Tlonna. Spirits, quicker than me to be honest."

The Belau nodded as she turned to head back to her office. "I thank you for showing me the treasury, and for the advice. It has opened my eyes."

"I certainly hope so. Have a good night, Miazie."

"You as well, Daphne," she replied and watched the tall woman stride back to her own office.

Miazie sighed and read the amendment one more time, hoping she wasn't about to make a large mistake. Something gnawed at her, a worry that she couldn't quite pin down, like an itch that was not in the spot you think it is when you go to scratch it. She was still standing a few feet away from the treasury door when someone snuck up behind her and wrapped their arms about her middle.

Squealing in fright and surprise, Miazie flung her limbs out in every direction, struggling mightily in the iron arms that held her. Her captor was laughing.

"Stop squirming, Miazie, you are going to hurt yourself."

"Sodo!"

The alchemist set her down and stood grinning down at her like a fool. "Hello."

The Belau tried to glare up at him, but couldn't keep it on her face. "I thought I told you not to do that anymore! You are going to give me a heart attack!"

Sodo shook his head, still grinning. "You should not make yourself so easy to spook. Sometimes I worry that you might be blind, or deaf."

"No, I'm human, and you're an elf. You're silent, and I don't have super hearing. I swear, being around you is one way to feel inadequate."

Sodo's grin faded. "Never say that, Miazie, never that. You are my everything, you make me whole. I am the inadequate one for making you feel less than you are. I want to make you feel like a queen."

"You know, had I not left with Tlonna I would be a queen."

Sodo brushed the wild strands of black hair back from her face. "And I would never have met you."

Miazie grabbed his hand as it started to pull away and held it to her face. "Sodo, I did a terrible thing today."

The elf's face became completely still and emotionless. "I heard. You seduced Martin Crotes into giving you information he would never have told you otherwise, and then you killed him."

"What you must think of me..."

"I think you are brave, and courageous, and little reckless, but in your heart you are good and kind, and I believe that anything you do is with good intentions. Miazie, I love you, and nothing you do will ever change that. My heart is yours to do with as you wish."

The words left her feeling a little breathless, and she leaned into him. "Do you think Aidyn will ever forgive me?"

Sodo was silent for a minute as he thought, his hands holding tight to her back. "I think Aidyn has a lot to figure out right now, and what you did probably shocked him more than anything. He will need some time, but being who and what he is, I am sure there is nothing to forgive except perhaps a little jealousy that you took Martin's life, and not him."

"Do you really believe that?"

The alchemist pulled away and held her at arms' length. "I do. Aidyn is an assassin, but a genuinely kind person with a terrible background and an even worse present. Give him time to come around, and you will have your friend back."

Miazie wrapped her arms around Sodo's slender waist and pressed herself to him, wishing as she always did that she was worthy of his love. Her face was level with his sternum, she felt like a child in his arms. Sodo's body pulled away as he bent down to kiss her gently, his lips smiling as he did so.

"You worry too much. We elves live too long to worry about such petty things as squabbles. Come, it is late and I am tired. I helped Tarsin in class today. He wanted me to explain the more subtle workings of the Liberated Lands."

"I hope you didn't reveal all the secrets," Miazie murmured, holding his hand as they walked.

"Never. There has to be some mystery left I suppose."

They strode back to her office, where she locked away the troublesome amendment, tidied up a bit, and then retired to their apartment. Miazie combed out her tangled locks while Sodo undressed and slid into a hot bath.

"Do you think I will ever be as good as Erdwyf?"

"What are you talking about? You are doing fine, love, give yourself some credit. Erdwyf only made it seem easy because she had been doing it for three hundred years or so. You will get there, I promise."

Miazie snorted. "Three hundred years, Sodo? I'll be lucky if I get sixty years."

Water splashed as he dropped his hand and glowered at her, his wet hair sticking to his face. "Do not say that. Remember what the healer said? You will live much longer than the average human because of your...memories."

She rolled her eyes and dropped her dress to the floor. Stepping into the large tub with her fiancé, she rubbed her hands against his knees, which he drew up to allow her more room.

"Will you want to be with me when I'm bent with age, wrinkled and covered in liver spots?"

Sodo captured her hands and brought her closer to him. He wrapped her legs about his waist, sighing with contentment. "I will love you until the day I die, no matter how you look, and my soul will love you for all eternity. We will be in Summerland together, Miazie, I swear it."

Miazie rested her head against his wet shoulder, breathing in his scent that could not be washed away, as they made love. Her fingers gripped his biceps, and she lost herself in his arms.

# Chapter 9
## Idle

Losolin let out a loud breath as he leaned back in the creaky chair, his shoulders thumping against it dangerously hard. The back made a threatening sound of cracking, but the king ignored it as he rubbed both hands over his face.

"You are sure?" he groaned between his fingers, his eyes shut.

"Positive. They are just sitting there, milling about like ants. It is like the boy has no idea what to do now that he is here," Sargotarh grumbled, swinging one long leg over a chair and straddling it. "His general, Orlando, has been seen a few times rampaging through the camp like a bull, screaming orders that are ignored, beating the soldiers senseless because of it. Sithian has an iron hand controlling all his men, and his general is furious about it. I do not know why he is stalling, but we have not seen a single battle movement since we arrived."

"What is he waiting for?" Suneelo muttered, sitting to the right of his brother. "Surely he is not going to sit there for us to attack."

"You have to remember that if you put all extraordinary circumstances aside, Sithian is barely five years old. His cognitive ability to reason is hindered by his father's impatience. Midian taught him his way of ruling, absolute control. Why do you think Sithian and Rhiannan stayed out of the fighting at Alchemian?" Losolin said, linking his hands to cradle the back of his head.

When the two others just stared at him, he sighed. "They did not know how to fight! Look at how easily Sithian dispatched his sister...Tlonna said they all had incredible power, so how did one kill the other without too much consequence? They know nothing of tactical fighting. They know cutthroat actions and radical massacre. Now that he has had a taste of real warfare, Sithian is frightened by his own ineptitude and is keeping a leash on his troops because he is trying to figure out how to beat us. He knows our army is one of the best, perhaps *the* best, in all the land, and his is not. He has numbers against us, but we have the advantage of skill and training. He knows that now."

"But this fellow Orlando obviously knows battle. He is a warrior, King Losolin, that much I can tell," Sargotarh countered, looking a little befuddled.

"He is a war monger and a brute, but knows little of organized warfare. Look at how quickly they fled from our walls. We sliced through them like a hot knife through butter, but they still had thousands to throw against us. Why retreat? Because they are scared, and unsure."

Suneelo leaned forward and hunched against the table, his expression dark. "So what? We would lose the advantage we came here for in the first place if we go around the lake to get at them, but they are not moving either. Do we just sit here until all the humans die of old age and people forget what we are fighting about?"

Losolin shook his head. "No, they will come to us, but not for a while if what Sargotarh says is accurate. Sithian is as impatient as his father."

"And as dangerous as his mother," Suneelo pointed out, lifting his eyebrows at his brother.

"I cannot deny that," the Magin conceded with a small smile. "Or his aunt."

Confusion danced across the captain's face for a second, and clouded Sargotarh's, and then realization dawned on them both.

"I never thought of it that way," Suneelo gasped, his eyes widening. "That means I am that brat's uncle!"

Losolin nodded slightly, knowing exactly how his brother felt. "Where is Ghealan? I thought he was supposed to be back by now."

Sargotarh nodded. "He was on his way but one of the Silvers called to him and he went off to talk to him."

"Which one?" Suneelo asked, frowning slightly. In Yayènia's absence, he was in charge of the *Zephyr Leifen*, though they did a fair job of keeping themselves in line.

The Captain of Cavalry scrunched up his face as he tried to remember. "It was a human, male. I am not sure who, but he had short, spiky, dark hair."

"That would be Dane. He is one of the best spearman I have ever seen, including elves. The man is a master," Suneelo said, folding his arms across his chest. "I wonder what he wanted."

"I do not know, did not look very urgent though."

Losolin sighed as the two went on to talk about the Silvers, and the oddness of having them around and not Yayènia. He knew Suneelo missed his wife, just as he missed Tlonna. In fact, everyone seemed to miss Yayènia. The regular soldiers, officers included, looked a bit lost and forlorn without their hot-blooded commander among them. Losolin wondered how she was taking the absence of her army. Before too long his thoughts were on Tlonna. What was she doing, and how she was coping with all the loss, and Aidyn's violent fall? He knew without a doubt she was not sitting in Blackhaven just to wait for a few messengers. Most likely she was off in the countryside looking for more answers, and finding ones she did not need or want. He hoped she had at least stayed within the kingdom.

"What do you think?"

Losolin blinked, his thoughts fading away as his brother poked him in the shoulder with a hard finger. "What?"

"What do you think about setting up a more permanent defense between the forest, the lake, and the mountains? Sar suggests building a wall."

The king looked at Sargotarh, who was resting his hands on the back of the chair, and his chin on top of his hands. He looked like nothing more than a young, wide-eyed elf waiting for an answer from an indulgent parent. Losolin had to remind himself that he had seen the same wide-eyed elf stab the curved dagger at his belt into the belly of a man, and yank it upward to tear him in half, his face spattered with blood.

"What would we build it with, and how fast? Besides, it would block eastern Nymyños from the west, and no one would like that," Losolin said after a moment.

"It would have a gate," Sargotarh muttered, his chin still atop his knuckles. "And there is plenty of dying trees up in the mountains. We could send the humans up to cut them down, and have the dwarves and elves construct the wall. At first, we would dig the trench while the Men are up in the mountains. We need a trench anyway, why not eventually fill it with a wall?"

"It is sound advice, *bruun*. We are going to need strong defenses if we are to stand at all."

"I do not want to be here long enough to justify a wall."

"But they are just sitting there! How long are we supposed to do the same, until we become complacent and they can run over us when we are not looking?" Suneelo argued, sweeping his hand over the table as if to illustrate the army being knocked over.

Losolin sat forward, his chair creaking and shifting slowly to the side. "I do not like the idea of shutting off the only true pass to West Nymyños without the input of the others. Tyular, Barukh, Tristan, and Erdwyf might not look favorably upon it."

"You are worried about what Erdwyf might think?" the king's brother scoffed, his expression incredulous. "And the others? They are our friends, not just other leaders, Losolin, your friends, to be exact. Send them letters if you must; but we have no time to wait for a response. Make the decision and command it tonight."

Losolin sighed as he squeezed his eyes shut, wishing he could just go home and hold Tlonna in his arms. He needed to see her. "Fine. I will have an answer for you in an hour or so. I am going to take a ride."

Sargotarh and Suneelo shared a look as he got up and shoved at the shabby chair. Two legs flew away from the seat, and the back simply fell off. The seat and its remaining two legs fell forward, pitifully slow, to land with a quiet thud on the ground.

"I am King of Blackhaven, and that is the best seat they can find? Even when I was poor I had better furniture," Losolin muttered, stalking from the tent.

Neñyos frisked beneath him, eager for a run. Losolin kept him reined in tight, however, for the landscape at the foothills of the Kismath Mountains was treacherous. Below him raged the Jaquisa River, large chunks of ice floating past like barges. Directly ahead of him was the shadowy presence of the Purheae Forest. Though he knew it was relatively safe, the soldiers closest to it seemed on edge. His army spread out like a silver, black, and blue snake, stretching between the forest, across the narrow strip of land that arced over the river. The natural bridge forced the water to tunnel its way through the earth, where it fell from the other side in what he had recently learned was called the Elnoris Falls, and butted up against the foothills.

Losolin looked outward with a mix of pride and trepidation. Soon, too soon, his people would be fighting for their lives, pressed by the gargantuan horde of murdering mercenaries brought to the land by Sithian Rahlan. Over half of them were new recruits, but seasoned in the battle that had taken place at the walls of Blackhaven. The others were veterans from the reclamation of the city who had marched across the entire breadth of Nymyños on the single word of Tlonna and himself, and had integrated themselves into Blackhaven society. They had fought the Seadueni Elves when Stoffnias had barred their way, though admittedly not well, and then had become the stabilizing force in the recovery of the city. A good six thousand were also veterans of Alchemian.

Yes, he thought, there were a great many battle-hardened people down there, tired of the constant fighting just as he was. But they fought because they knew that as long as they stood free, Zaedic and her allies would never let them be. Losolin sighed as he eyed the line Sargotarh had suggested for the wall. He could see the elf's reasoning, but a part of him did not like the idea of walling off the entire western part of the continent, even if it did have a flaming gate.

It would wind its way from a cliff inside Purheae, about a mile in from the border all the way into the Kismaths, with a gate along the only pass through the mountains, and one between the forest and the river. It would be of lumber harvested from the deadwood in the mountains.

Losolin liked Sargotarh, it was quite impossible not to, what with his wide-eyed exuberance, but he seemed almost indifferent to the rest of the world. He cared only for Blackhaven, and its people. Losolin had asked Suneelo about the Captain of Cavalry, thinking him strangely happy for being what he was. His brother had snorted.

"Sar is four hundred and eighty years old, single and free as a bird. He was born in, and has fought for, the city all his life. His parents were murdered while he was in training, when he was twenty-three, and he never once looked back after the funeral. He finds his happiness in the knowledge that he kills evil people. He was trained by Aidyn, once. Long ago."

Losolin had been silent after that, and had since taken on a new perspective of the elf. His life of service meant that he was knowledgeable and loyal, and probably wealthy beyond his dreams. All the elfin leaders were, having accumulated quite the savings over their long lives. He had only recently discovered that Yayènia and Suneelo brought in an annual income of nearly thirteen and a half thousand geld, which was exorbitantly high, as far as he could tell. The kingdom, after all, only brought in just under a million in a year, before expenses. He sighed, wishing his mind would shut up for once.

# Chapter 10
## A Pain in the Heart

Aidyn was laying across his bed; his legs sprawled to either side so his booted feet nearly hung off the edge. His hands were idly playing with his hair as he stared up at the thick curtain above his bed. His eyes strayed to the portrait of Rahna for a moment and then went back to the idle examination of his bed curtain. His thoughts, however, were treading the dangerous path of Tlonna, and he was letting them. Ever since he had lost the connection with her because of the twisting of magics within him, Aidyn had felt a little forlorn and desperate. He didn't feel as powerful as he once had, or as invincible. He greatly missed the feeling. He also missed knowing where she was, and if she was okay. It bothered him not to know.

The assassin had been moping about the castle for several days now, his recovery well on its way, wishing he could do something useful. Aladorn had his hands full with running the entirety of the military arms left in Blackhaven City, and Sodo was busy with the Academy, and Miazie. Ever since her escapade into his professional territory she had been on edge with everyone, and hopelessly distracted by her looming wedding. Aidyn lifted one hand and dropped it to his belly, absently feeling the ridges of muscle that were present even in his indolent position. Even through his loose shirt, every time he moved slightly he could feel the muscles bunch and slide. Despite that fact, he felt old and ugly, scarred and ruined.

Aidyn was losing himself in a haze of self-loathing and pity when his door burst open and someone called his name. Not bothering to get up, the dark elf lifted his head and frowned. The person, a female, moved through his front room and then knocked on his bedroom door.

"What?"

"Can I come in?" she asked, sounding frightened and hesitant.

Aidyn's frown deepened as he considered Miazie's presence in his apartment. "It is open."

He watched the door handle tilt and slowly the human revealed herself. She looked unsettled at seeing him in such a position. He did not care.

"I'm sorry to bother you."

"I am very busy at the moment," Aidyn replied, sarcastic as he laid his head back down.

Miazie's faint chuckle brought him little relief at her presence. He still refused to get up. He scowled at the curtain above his head when the mattress tilted and she crawled onto his bed. The human settled herself next to him, her knees resting across his outstretched left leg, her head a foot away on the next pillow. She looked disturbed.

"Well this is unusual," Aidyn finally said, turning his head so that he could look at her out of his left eye.

Miazie did not reply for a while, completely ignoring the fact that she was laying on his bed, across his leg, and on his pillow. In fact it was the pillow he usually slept on. He scowled.

"I'm sorry to bother you."

"You already said that. What are you bothering me for?"

She sucked in a deep, shaky breath and let it out in a huff. "I've had a...vision."

Aidyn simply waited for her to elaborate, ignoring the weight of her legs on his, adamantly refusing to move at all.

"I saw you, Tlonna, and Yayènia in Purheae, traveling through the forest with great need."

"How refreshing. Why do you need to lay on me to tell me this?"

Miazie lifted herself up onto one elbow and stabbed him with a glare. He realized her eyes were nearly the same color as his, though quite a bit lighter. "You are taking up the entire bed. And besides," she slapped her hand to his lower belly, making him jump in surprise and a little pain. He was not all the way healed, after all. "You are not old or ugly or ruined, maybe a little scarred but who says that's a bad thing?"

"What are you talking about?" Aidyn said loudly, deeply bothered that she would say such a thing when he had just been thinking it.

Miazie's hand yanked at his shirt, ripping it out of his belt and lifting it up to his upper ribs, and then straddled him. The assassin tried to sit up but she dug her nails into his torso and held him there with the threat of scratching him across his stitches.

"What in the gods' names are you doing?" he breathed, holding himself up by his elbows.

"You need to listen to me. Your connection to Tlonna is not lost; you have simply hidden your heart from her. You were afraid she would come after you, so when she connected her mind and the others' to yours, you let it shield not only your injuries, but your emotions as well. Release that barricade and you will find her again."

"How in the nine bloody hells do you know about all this?" he whispered, suddenly and ridiculously afraid of the tiny human.

Miazie sighed and slid her hand up his hairless, rigid abdomen until her palm rested against his chest, right above his heart. Aidyn swallowed, their gazes locked.

"I was once in love with you, Aidyn, did you know that?"

He shook his head, petrified.

"I was, and I still think you are perfect in nearly every way, but you are a fool. I know how you feel about Tlonna, so don't try to argue with me. I...heard your thoughts..."

Aidyn continued to stare at her, unable to speak or look away, her hand cool against his warm flesh. Her fingers flexed against his pectoral, her pinky idly moving across his nipple.

"I was just sitting at my desk, reading, and suddenly your thoughts were in my head, as though they were my own. You know I retain the memory of your night with Tlonna?"

"Yes," he wheezed, his voice coarse with emotion.

"I think that, because I have such a pivotal memory of you, I am partially connected to you as I am Losolin and Tlonna. I can sometimes hear their thoughts, though I did not realize it until very recently. I always believed them to be my imagination. Now, I know differently, and I understand more. You guard yourself so tightly my friend, that you are shutting out even your own heart. You must let go of your fear and realize that while you repress your emotions about Tlonna, you will never regain the connection. As long as you keep your mind shielded, she will be lost to you."

"She is already lost to me."

"As a lover, as a wife, yes, but as a friend, no. She loves you Aidyn, don't you understand that? She always has, always will. You are her balance. There is something...something I need to tell you, but you must not reveal it to anyone, especially Tlonna or Losolin. Is that clear?"

"What is it?"

Miazie took a steadying breath and leaned forward, pushing him back until she could loom over him as she never could if they were standing. Her hand pressed hard against his chest, feeling every slow beat of his heart.

"You are the Lover."

"What?"

"You are the one named in the Prophecy as the Lover who will Rule. I don't yet know what you will rule, but I know it is you. I don't know how or why, I just do. I saw it when I saw that Sithian was going to be the reason Tlonna dies, not Midian. You are Tlonna's first physical lover, her first love, and you loved her first. You are three times over what the prophecy demands."

"What about Losolin? Are you saying he does not love her? If you think that you are absolutely mad."

"No, of course not," the Belau scoffed, removing her hand to wave it in dismissal. "Losolin loves her more than life itself, he proved that at Purheae, but he was not her first. He is her foundation, yes, but he is not named in the prophecy. Please accept this, Aidyn, or all is lost. Please."

The assassin pushed his shirt down and finally succeeded in sitting up, causing Miazie to scoot down his body so she was sitting on his thighs rather than his hips. "First Yayènia and now you. Would you females just leave me alone with my problems? I am older than the two of you combined, and then some. I think I can handle my relationships without the input of starry-eyed brides."

"Would you call Yayènia a starry-eyed bride to her face?"

"Yes! And then I would point out Suneelo just to prove it! Get out of my room, woman!"

Miazie shook her head. "Not until you accept Tlonna back into your heart."

Aidyn seriously had to control his fist from walloping her across the face. She was sitting on his knees now, her hands resting on his thighs. He looked away, unable to stare at her without a violent urge rushing to the fore.

"Oh yeah, beating me to a pulp would fix everything," she said, her voice condescending.

"Stop it! Get out of my head!" Aidyn yelled, throwing his arms about in frustration.

"You stop being a ridiculous child! You say you are so much older than I am, act like it! And I don't need to hear your thoughts to see your intentions! Your expressions say it all!" Miazie returned in kind.

Aidyn's rage ignited like a pitch ditch. He grabbed her by the shoulders and shoved her down on his bed, reversing their position. He put his lips very near to hers.

"You have no idea what I have been through, Miazie. You cannot even begin to comprehend the pain, or the loss! If I choose to have a selfish moment and wallow in the agony of losing everyone I have ever cared about in this world, then I will have one, and you can keep your damnable opinions to yourself. I did not ask for this! I did not say to the gods that I wanted to live a life of constant rejection and fear and loss! Get it out of your puny human mind that you can understand it, and get out of my bloody mind!"

Tears glistened in Miazie's eyes, and when she blinked they rushed onto her cheeks and dripped onto his duvet. His fingers were iron against her shoulder, and she was thankful he had not grabbed her throat instead. She could already feel the bruises forming. His face was so close, she could feel his breath on her lips. She found herself wanting to lift her mouth to his, even terrified as she was. What power did he have that made females lose their heads around him?

"Aidyn, please, I do not say these things to hurt you. I want to help you. I don't like seeing you suffer for something you don't need to suffer for. Please believe me."

The assassin's face was a mask of stone, betraying nothing of what he was feeling inside. After a moment of dead silence, he released her shoulder with a shove. Even against his soft mattress it hurt from the sheer anger in the motion, but she kept her lips shut against the cry of the pain that welled in her throat. Miazie stayed there, afraid to move. Aidyn was looking at the corner of his bed; his shoulders slumped inward, apparently having forgotten her presence though he was still atop her.

"You do not know the feeling..." he muttered after a while and slid off his bed, his boots thumping to the obsidian floor.

She stared at his trim form as he tore at the cotton shirt covering him. It shredded against his fingers, ripping across his muscled and scarred back as though it were made of the weakest lace. Miazie's breath caught as she saw the tracks of stitches and newly healed wounds covering his entire torso. The worst one went from his hipbone all the way up at a slant to touch his shoulder blade, a hundred little stitches looking like a crooked seam.

"Oh, Aidyn!" she breathed, horrified.

The elf turned on her with blazing emerald eyes, his face slightly deranged. His fingers twitched, the rags of his shirt hanging from each hand. He dropped them in disgust and went for the waistband of his baggy pants. Miazie had to force herself to turn her eyes away as he kicked off his boots and yanked at the loose trousers.

"What are you doing?" she asked, staring determinedly at the foot of his bed.

"I am tired of being the source of people's pity. They can pity themselves. Close your eyes if you are so bashful though I know you have seen it all before," he muttered, walking around the four-poster toward his wardrobe.

Miazie did as he suggested, but he moved so quickly she still caught a seductive glance of his toned, ravaged body. She swallowed, thinking of Sodo in desperation. The Belau heard rummaging in the wardrobe and hazarded a look. Aidyn was kneeling at the base, struggling with a lock that must be nearly as old as he, though in much worse shape. His spine pressed against his flesh, extensor muscles gliding beneath it. Miazie had to tear her eyes away from the dimples on his lower back. When he tossed the key to the side and simply yanked at the poor thing, it shattered like glass, throwing bits of iron about the room, making Miazie flinch.

He tossed the remains of the lock on top with the key and gingerly opened the lid. Inside seemed blacker than night, a darkness deeper than anything she had ever seen before. Miazie thought for a moment that he had some sort of sinister magic hidden in the chest, and then he pulled out a lump of it. It was his *ärdyz* clothing.

Aidyn sighed in something akin to ecstasy as the tunic slithered over his torso. He stood and Miazie squeezed her eyes shut once more. When she opened them a few moments later, he was yanking on the laces of his pants, which were so skintight it didn't really matter that she had closed her eyes. For the first time she realized they were made of supple leather, oiled to a sheen that did little to distract the eye.

"Stop staring, Miazie." His voice startled her so much she blushed crimson. "You have seen me before. Hell, you have experienced what so many others pretend to have experienced with me. What is your issue?"

"The difference between your...cotton garments and your...garb is quite stunning."

"As it is meant to be. Get off of my bed."

The simmering anger in his voice had her obeying immediately, and suddenly she knew a small portion of the fear his victims must experience when they realize he had come for them.

"What are you going to do? Braden says you are not supposed to be doing anything extraneous for at least another month."

Aidyn's eyes narrowed in warning. "Stop checking with Braden about my condition. If you want to know how I feel, ask me," he grabbed his belt off a hook in the wall and snapped it in place, stabbing the two halves of his custom-built belt buckle together with unnecessary force.

He grabbed his baldric and slid it over his shoulder, linking it to his belt. Miazie swallowed in unrestrained anxiety as he lifted his scimitars off their stand and shoved them into their scabbards, and followed them with his longblade. Standing in his full assassin's garb after several weeks, he looked positively alarming. Aidyn eyed her with suspicion when he picked up his tension blade and its sheath and slid it into place, quickly strapping on his vambrace before she could figure out how it worked.

"I thought you could read my mind."

The Belau looked away. "Only when you are not guarding it from me. What are you going to do?"

"Tlonna is my charge, my ward, if you will. Tell me where she has gone and I will follow."

"No."

Aidyn's face hardened even further, turning him into a cold, beautiful, expressionless statue. "Where did she and Yayènia go?"

"I'm not telling you."

Without another word, the assassin walked out of his room, stopped for a second in the front room, and then out of his apartment completely. Miazie stood by his bed feeling unimportant and completely stunned. As her mind started working again, she rushed after him, noticing as she did that his pack, which he always kept ready, was missing from its usual place by the door. Panic seized her and she sprinted down the hall, searching for the dangerous assassin.

"Aidyn!" she shouted, her voice echoing down the tall corridor.

People stuck their heads out of doors or stopped in their wandering to stare at her, some with concern. Miazie cursed and ran in the most likely direction.

"Aidyn!"

"Miazie, what is going on?" Aladorn asked as he came up beside her halfway down the hall.

"Your brother is a psycho! You have to stop him!" the Belau shrieked, clutching at the wiat's shirt in desperation.

"Why? What is he going to do?" the elf covered her hands with his, calming them.

"He's going after Tlonna and Yayènia!"

The dark elf frowned down at her. "So?"

"Aladorn, he's not healed yet! He still has stitches in him! They will need to be taken out, and I know he can't take out the ones in his back on his own. Those wounds were caused by magic, which means they will take much longer to heal than any injury caused by steel, and he's not ready to be gallivanting all over the bloody continent. He's going to kill himself! He doesn't even know where they are!"

The wiat studied her face for a second before prying her fingers off his shirt. "If Sodo were heading into certain danger, and you were in pain but well enough to walk, would go after him?"

"Well of course I would, but that's—"

Aladorn silenced her with a look. His dark eyebrows lifted as he stared down at her, his hands still holding hers. They looked so small and pale in contrast to the elf's, she abruptly felt very fragile.

"Let him go, Miazie, otherwise he will never heal."

"But what if he never finds her? What if...what if he gets hurt?"

The wiat snorted quietly and dropped her hands. "We are talking about Aidyn, here, not you. If he gets hurt he will fix himself up as best as he can, and continue onward. I am his brother, do you think if I were truly concerned I would be standing here talking to you?"

"Well...no."

"Then stop panting and go back to your room. Sodo is glaring at me."

Miazie looked down the hallway to find her fiancé leaning against the door to their apartment, his arms folded and his face set into a careful expression of nonchalance. She sighed and shook her head in exasperation.

"You elves are going to be the death of me," she grumbled.

"Quite the contrary, I believe. Now go on. I will take care of my *little* brother."

"What will you do?"

Aladorn shrugged, verdant eyes looking over her head to the far wall. "Make sure he has everything he needs, I suppose."

"You should stop him."

"How? Miazie, you know as well as I that no one can best him in a fight, which is what it would come down to if I truly tried to stop him from going. I will delay him for a while, perhaps, but in the end he will leave."

"I just hope this isn't the end of him."

Aladorn closed his eyes against the pain of the thought. "I do not think he survived all he has just to die like this. Go on."

Aidyn jerked to a stop when Aladorn's hand clamped on his shoulder.

"Would my suggestion to stay another week fall on deaf ears?"

The assassin chuckled once and turned to face his sibling. "I suppose it would depend on your reasoning."

Relief that he was at least willing to listen allowed Aladorn's chest to loosen. "You are going to need help removing the stitches in your back, otherwise your skin will close up over them and we will have to cut you open to get them out, resulting in new stitches." The look that said the assassin couldn't care less about how many stitches he would need had Aladorn moving quickly on. "And I could use your help in dealing with the death duties of Martin Crotes."

"Is that not Miazie's job?"

The wiat sighed. "Because she is the one who killed him, she is not allowed to be involved with anything concerning his affairs."

Aidyn made a face. "That woman is going to get herself in some serious trouble one of these days, and we are not going to be able to get her out."

"You will get no argument from me on that," Aladorn snorted. "But...please, I beg you to stay at least until your stitches can be removed?"

The assassin huffed and then swung his pack into Aladorn's stomach. The wiat grunted as he took the heavy bag from his brother.

"Fine, but you can carry that back to my room."

Aladorn shouldered the bag and followed Aidyn back up the three flights of stairs to his apartment. "What were you going to do, by the way?"

"You did not know?" the warrior asked, completely stymied.

The wiat shrugged. "It did not make any difference. I just want you to stay here for another week."

Aidyn let out a short laugh. "Either you are lying to me, or you are too protective. Either way, you do not come out looking good."

Aladorn's brow lifted as he tossed the pack against the wall. "But I got my way. Now I do not have to spend my nights fretting about you lying out in the cold, frozen to death."

"You only get a week, and that is only if Braden insists it will be that long before he will take out my sutures."

The older dark elf shrugged again. "I will take what I can get. Are you allowed to be wearing those now?"

Aidyn folded his arms across his chest, his eyes narrowing. "You can keep me here a little longer, but if you try to force me to wear those thrice-damned cotton things Healers call clothes, I will have to hurt you."

"All right, no cotton garments, I surrender."

"Lord Aladorn!"

The brothers turned to stare at messenger who was standing nervously in the open door of Aidyn's apartment. He was shaking so hard the rolled parchment in his hand was getting wrinkles.

"What is it?"

"A letter came in from the aerie."

"The aerie? Who from?"

The messenger shrugged. "I don't know, sir, it has no seal."

Frowning, Aladorn took the message from the boy and unrolled it. "*Kalise!*" he swore, and then reread the note.

"What is it?" Aidyn demanded, yanking the parchment from his brother's fingers.

"Stoffnias has a company of soldiers in Purheae. Eyin and his people are prisoners in their own home. Nebet'thu must have arrived just before they did. No wonder there was no warning when the bastards came through," the wiat explained quickly, watching as the assassin read.

"We need to send them aid. It looks as though the guards Suneelo sent down to patrol their borders were destroyed," Aidyn said, ignoring the still frightened messenger standing in his doorway.

"Send who, Aidyn? We have few enough soldiers left here in the city with most everyone off to fight the war. We cannot afford to deplete our forces anymore."

"I will go."

"No."

The assassin shoved by his brother, going for his pack. The messenger went sheet white and fainted when Aidyn got within a few feet of him.

"Damn," he muttered. "Take care of that, will you? I am sorry Al, I must go. You know it."

The wiat picked up the unconscious boy and slung him over his shoulder. "But what about your stitches?"

Aidyn sniffed in dismissal. "A few stitches are a cheap enough price to pay for the lives of dozens. I will send word when the matter is taken care of."

"Aidyn! You could die!"

"I should have died a long time ago, Aladorn. This time will be no different."

"Please, let me send...I will send to Losolin. They are closer anyway."

"No, Al. He has enough to deal with as it is," Aidyn paused halfway down the hall to lay a comforting hand on his brother's free shoulder. "This is my job, *bruun*, I swore by the Honor of Assassins to step in the line of danger, protect the defenseless, and be brave in the face of evil. I am not just a blade in the shadow."

"I know that, but you are also not invincible."

Aidyn smiled a quiet smile to himself, his gaze turning inward. "I do not need to be. I will see you later, Aladorn."

"Aidyn..."

"I know, Al. I do to."

Aladorn swallowed back his fear and his protestations as he watched his little brother jog down the stairs he had just convinced him to return from. Feeling oddly saddened, he hitched the comatose messenger further up his shoulder and took him to the infirmary, where he had to face the wrath of Braden, Aidyn's Healer.

Whäd whinnied at the assassin as he walked into the stables. "Ready for another go, love?" he asked, running his hands into her splotchy mane.

The stable hand quickly saddled her and soon he was riding out, feeling every step of the way, despite his horse's smooth gait.

# Chapter 11
## The Other Elves

Aidyn arrived in Purheae several days later, feeling as though he had been beaten every day since he had left. He gritted his teeth against the discomfort and urged Whäd onward into the province. He passed over several bridges, trying to remember where Erdwyf had marked Eyin's vicinity on a map in the Map Room. Of all the places in Nymyños, he knew Purheae the least, having always avoided the blighted land. It was late one night when he climbed up onto a tall hill and stood looking out over the forest. In the distance, several miles away, he saw the faint glow of a large fire.

Finally having a bearing, Aidyn went back down to Whäd and angled her in the right direction. He hit the forest less than an hour later and plunged into the tangled depths without pause. He finally had to dismount and lead his horse on foot. Aidyn walked for several more hours, listening with his sensitive ears for any sound other than the low clicking and grumbling of the hostile forest. A few times he had to frighten off a curious creature, and once he had to draw his sword to ward off a hulking beast that tried to scare him into its trap.

When dawn broke against the dense canopy of the trees Aidyn stepped into a clearing and found himself facing a clapboard wall. Patting Whäd's nose and putting a finger to his lips in warning, the assassin walked back a couple feet and then ran at the wall. His booted feet caught purchase for a few steps as he ran up the wall, sufficient to get him high enough to wrap his fingers about the top edge. With a grimace against the pulling sting of his old sutures, Aidyn lifted his body up and over the wall, dropping in silence to the ground. To his surprise, a young human child was staring at him with her mouth open in complete shock.

He crouched and gestured with one hand, hoping he was being friendly enough. The girl walked toward him, her eyes and mouth still wide open.

"Hello," he whispered in the common language, Hindarün.

"Yer pretty," she giggled, touching his face with her small hand.

"So are you. Will you be my friend and take me to King Eyin or Nebet'thu?"

The girl turned shy and nodded, looking away. "The white elf is pretty too, but not like you."

Feeling smug, Aidyn stood and whistled softly for Whäd to stay where she was. She returned a quiet snort. Gesturing, the assassin followed the child into the village, where people stopped and stared, most in absolute terror, as he walked by. Some screamed. By the time he was halfway through the center, he had caused enough of a commotion that both Eyin Thorn and Nebet'thu were heading toward him, along with Meradyn.

The young king had a new crown on his head, a thin, studded iron band with two marvelous horns twisting up from above his eyebrows. Though they were only a few inches tall, they gave the human quite the presence. The three met Aidyn by a walled well, each staring at him in varying degrees of surprise. Nebet'thu finally came forward with his hand extended.

"Aidyn."

"Neb."

"You received my letter, then?"

The assassin nodded. "Unfortunately, the army is off fighting a war, and the city guard is cut nearly in half. I am your relief."

"I cannot think of anyone better suited. You know King Eyin, and Commander Meradyn."

"Aye. Greetings from Blackhaven."

Eyin started to bow, but Meradyn stopped him, bowing in his place. "How did you get in here? What are you doing with Marcia?"

Aidyn glanced down at the girl, who was still staring at him with her thumb in her mouth. "I came over the wall. Marcia watched me, and agreed to bring me to you."

"All right, Marcia, go on now. I'm sure your mother is petrified by now," Eyin said to the child, who reluctantly left Aidyn's side. "So...can you help us?"

"If you can help me."

Three sets of eyes narrowed in suspicion.

"Do you have a healer here?"

Eyin nodded, still glowering at him. "Why? Are you harmed?"

"You could say that. I need to have a few stitches removed. I...spent some time in enemy hands and then left Blackhaven a bit too early to come here. The healer?"

"Right this way," the king said, all suspicion draining from his face.

The four of them walked to one of the larger yurts that ringed the center area, and entered without knocking. Two women started in fright as Aidyn straightened beside Nebet'thu once ducking through the human-sized doorway.

"King Eyin!"

"Aidyn here needs some stitches removed."

"At once King Eyin!" the young woman said, eyeing the assassin in fear and amazement. "Would you reveal them, sir?"

Aidyn took a deep breath and quickly removed his various weapons and his vambraces. When he pulled his shirt over his head, there was a collective gasp of horror from everyone in the yurt. The stitches, as Aladorn had warned, were now partially grown over with half-healed flesh. The healers looked ill.

"Spirits, Aidyn! Who in the nine hells got a hold of you?" Nebet'thu asked, eyeing the injuries with revulsion.

"Sithian."

"*Leif.*"

"Would you please...sit...sir?" the young woman finally asked, swallowing.

Aidyn obliged her and sat on the edge of one of the beds. The scissors in her hand trembled, and he cursed silently. He spent the next hour gritting his teeth as she dug into his skin, trying to find all of the nearly three hundred stitches decorating his body. The worst was the one running from his hip to his shoulder, and the deep laceration in his thigh. The bed he was sitting on was splattered with blood, as was the floor between his feet.

Eyin, Meradyn, and Nebet'thu stayed with him the whole time, asking him questions and telling him of their situation. Stoffnias's soldiers had arrived less than a day after Nebet'thu, and had quickly and mercilessly slaughtered the other villages. The only reason the Stone Hunters had been saved was that Eyin, Neb, and Meradyn had met them on the outskirts of the village. The plains elf had threatened them with vicious retribution from his people, while Eyin warned them of the implications of murdering him now that he was known and accepted by all the kings of the east, and by Tlonna and Losolin. Meradyn had snarled at them. Now the company of twenty-four elven warriors was camped a quarter of a mile away from the village, with sentries patrolling the entire area.

Aidyn told them of Whäd and Eyin sent someone to retrieve her. When the healer finished snipping at him, she dropped the bloody scissors and picked up a clean towel.

"You'll need new stitches, my lord," she said in the thick accent of the Purheaens as she dabbed at the blood coursing down his body.

"I think not. Just give me a few towels soaked in hot water and balsam."

The young woman looked affronted, but went to do his bidding. While she was gone, Nebet'thu leaned forward.

"What of the siege? What happened?"

Aidyn told them of the violent battle at the wall, including his capture. "Once I was taken, I do not know what happened other than the bastards set the forest ablaze, and Tlonna and Losolin retaliated with magic, sending them into a retreat. Now they are set up at the border of your land, between the Kismath Mountains and Sethryn Lake in an effort to take the fighting away from populated areas and give them a bit of a territorial advantage."

"Is there anything we can do?" Meradyn asked, looking furious.

"You are held here by two dozen Seadueni soldiers, Commander, there is little you could do to help in the battle now raging."

"But—"

"Your people have been massacred to within an inch of extinction. You need to focus on protecting and rebuilding your home, not throwing your lives away in a misguided attempt to prove your bravery and your commitment to the Nymyñosian Alliance. Everyone knows of both, you do not need to prove it, at least until you have the means to do so," Aidyn said, cutting the young man off.

The healer reappeared holding a stack of steaming towels and the assassin sighed. He took the stack from her and began wiping away the blood, which had begun to dry against his skin. Lying back on the bed, he pressed the towels against his limbs and his torso, closing his eyes in relief.

The three others watched him in concern. Gathering his courage, Eyin leaned forward and gently poked his finger into Aidyn's muscled shoulder, making sure he was still awake, and alive. The elf opened one eye and peered at him, amused.

"What can you do to help us in this state?" the young man asked quietly.

Aidyn snorted. "I am not in a *state*, King Eyin. I will kill the Seadueni thugs squatting on your doorstep, and then I will return to Blackhaven."

"When?"

"In a few days, when I have had time to observe their behavior and get an accurate account of their skills."

"But they are not doing anything. How can you get an account if they are not fighting?" Meradyn asked, scowling in confusion.

"A person's every move is an observable thing. How they walk, how they stand, how they recline," Aidyn gestured at his own stretched out body, "how they gesture with their hands. They can tell the story of how a person will react in a situation if you are observant enough to notice. A true warrior always moves with a grace and a surety of their own making, a compilation if you will, of their individual muscle movements and memory. Each body has an individual way of moving, though the foundation is much the same, an entity adjusts to the millions of quirks in its own body. With me?"

"So, even though you and I will complete the same action, in a similar fashion, we don't do it the same?" the young fighter summed hesitantly.

"Precisely. There are varying degrees of how each muscle, tendon, and bone moves within each body. Therefore, there are varying degrees of how each person moves. I can tell how a person fights by watching even their most simple of movements. Your king here is a brawler, depending more on brute strength and momentum than on any refined tactic, as evidenced by his blunt movements, the way his hands rests on the palm alone, not the fingers."

Eyin blanched and removed his hands from his knees, but Aidyn moved on without pausing. "Nebet'thu is a highly detail-oriented fighter, each motion is thought out seconds before he completes them, already knowing what the outcome will be. You can tell by the way his fingers individually touch things, running over them with a swift precision that tells him everything he needs to know in a heartbeat."

Neb lifted an eyebrow at the assassin, not at all surprised by his assessment. He had been trained to fight since early childhood. Aidyn hooked his emerald stare onto Meradyn. "You are between them, more on the side of brawler, but more refined because of the lessons you received from Yayènia. Look at the way you sit, half off the edge, ready for a brawl, yet relaxed and observant at the same time. Your hands are still, too still. Your stiffness tells me you are unsure of your status in this room. You know I could defeat you in seconds, even wounded as I am, and you show it. Most people go too still when I am around, or High Commander Yayènia."

Silence filled the yurt, punctuated only by the day-to-day sounds coming from outside. Aidyn lifted his hand and adjusted a balsam-soaked rag on his side.

"As I said, I will observe them for a few days, and then I will take them out. You may come with me if you so choose, to learn how I see things."

"Oh yes, Lord Aidyn, I would appreciate that very much. When will you be ready?"

The dark elf shook his head. "I need to rest for a few hours, and then I will go out. Is there a place I can stay while I am here?"

Eyin sat back, eyeing Meradyn with the suspicion of adolescents. He turned to Aidyn after a moment and nodded. "You can stay with Nebet'thu. I believe his yurt has another bed in it."

"It does," Neb confirmed slowly, looking a bit unhappy with the outcome.

Aidyn sent him what he hoped was a reassuring smile. The plains elf did not look reassured. "Then if you do not mind I will rest here for a bit, and then put my things away before I go out. Meradyn, I will expect you to be clothed simply, and ready for a fight if needed."

"I will be, Lord Aidyn."

The dark elf nodded and settled in to allow the balsam to work on his battered body. A few hours later, when the sun was directly overhead, he dressed carefully, which made the healers blush all over again. He hissed as the wound in his thigh pulled with the leather, but did not reopen. He left his *ärdyz* tunic unlaced, but snapped his belt and baldric on anyway. Stamping into his boots, Aidyn grabbed up his pack and followed the healers' instructions to Neb's yurt.

It was identical to all the others but for the fact that it had no decoration on the outside from living there year after year. He knocked on the door, barely waiting for the reply before stepping inside. It was one circular room with two beds, a table, two chairs, and a fire pit in the center. Nebet'thu's bed was the one closest to the door, and looked as pristine as the one against the far side, under the window.

"Sorry about this," Aidyn muttered as he dropped his bag at the foot of the unused bed.

Neb shrugged, looking up from the book that held his attention. "The only reason I got my own yurt in the first place is because everyone was terrified of me. No one wanted to share with the tall elf. Now you are here, and you make me look almost normal."

"Their attitude has not improved since you arrived?" the dark elf asked, not really surprised.

"They have gotten used to me, and trust me a little more, it will take longer with you I am afraid. You have several inches on me, are a dark elf, and a famous assassin."

"They know of me?"

Neb shrugged again. "Eyin, Meradyn, Jorunson, and Marc talked about their adventures in Blackhaven. These people know about you, Tlonna, Losolin, your brother, Miazie...everyone."

Aidyn frowned. "I suppose that is to be expected. Have you seen the Seadueni at all since the day they arrived?"

"Some. They come into the village to steal supplies when they need them, or want them. They tried to take a few of the women, but I stopped that, with Mer's help. You should not underestimate the young man, Aidyn. He has great potential."

"I know that, but potential or not he has yet to see true battle. I would like to see him reach that potential, not die before he has the chance."

The tribal elf conceded with a nod. "These are not Stoffnias's best soldiers, but they are not slouches either. They truly did massacre the other two villages, left nothing but bloody smears on the trees, and smoking piles of ash on the ground. I do not think they took captives, but I am not completely positive."

Aidyn shook his head. "Seadueni rarely take captives. They will take females for a little sport, but discard their bodies within a week, and not hide the fact. Do not worry, I will take care of them."

"You are so sure?"

"Completely. I do not know if you heard, but I wiped out an entire den of trained assassins some weeks ago. There were twenty-one of them, hybrid creatures called Eseirik. None survived."

"Is that were you got those?" Nebet'thu asked, pointing at his own cheek.

"Aye. I did not say I was unharmed, but none of them survived. I do not worry about two dozen regular soldiers, especially two dozen Seadueni soldiers."

Nebet'thu smiled grimly. "I suppose they should be the ones worrying."

"I suppose."

Meradyn was nearly bouncing out of his skin with excitement when Aidyn stepped out of Nebet'thu's home. He now had his *ärdyz* laced and his weapons were in perfect position. His inky cloak billowed in the forest breeze, lifted by even the gentlest of winds. The human was in brown and green clothing, the trim done in light tan and his boots supple dark leather. He held his arms out to his sides and twisted a bit, waiting for comment.

Aidyn lifted an eyebrow. "Did you make it yourself?" he asked, hiding his smile

Meradyn didn't know if he was being complimented or insulted so he settled for silence. In truth, the elf knew the boy's clothing would do well to hide him in the tangled terrain of Purheae.

"Are you ready? Let me see your weapon."

Meradyn pushed his heavy wool cloak back and drew his sword. It was a simple thing, with a solid wooden hilt, a double-edged straight blade with twin runners. The crossguard was carved in the relief of a stag's horns, and curved upward nearly parallel with the blade, and the hilt itself was the beast's head. Aidyn took the sword and swung it about, splitting the air with a high whine. He held it in various positions, testing the balance and weight, slid the edge across the back of his arm to test the keenness, adding a scratch to his vambrace, and then snapped his knee into the flat of the blade.

Meradyn and several other people who were watching gasped in fright, thinking the blade would shatter. Though it vibrated violently with the force of Aidyn's blow, it held firm.

"Good blade. Give my compliments to your blacksmith," the elf said, handing the human back his sword. "Come on."

Aidyn headed out immediately, going for the simple door in the clapboard wall. Meradyn placed his weapon back in its sheath, humbled, and hurried after.

"Can you teach me how to be like you?" he asked once he had caught up.

"Do you have six hundred years?"

Meradyn didn't reply to that. "Nebet'thu said I have great ability, and High Commander Yayènia said the same thing. You know what she calls me?"

"*Leatran*," Aidyn replied without emotion. "Quicksilver."

"That's right. Do you think I'm faster than you?"

The dark elf's laughter burst out of him before he could stop it. "No, Meradyn, I do not," he finally managed. "I have seven centuries on you, son. Not if you trained all your life would you be faster than me. I do not say these things to be arrogant, or cruel, I say them so that you will not underestimate your enemies and get yourself killed. What you lack in speed and strength, against elven warriors at least, you must make up for in quick thinking and agility."

"But elves are the most agile people alive!"

"No, we are mostly just big and fast. I am agile, like Neb, like Yayènia, Tlonna, Losolin, Ghealan, Aladorn, all of us...but we are all trained masters. Most soldiers, even elven ones, know brute force and a small amount of skill. You, Meradyn, have the opportunity to learn from us. Do not miss your chance by trying to *be* us."

Meradyn fell silent for a while, traipsing along with the assassin as he mused over his words. Finally, he pointed off to the side.

"Their camp is right over here."

Aidyn adjusted his course and slowed, gesturing for Meradyn to remain quiet. The human needed no reminder. They came upon a small rise and looked down, standing at the edge of the thick tangle of trees. Below was a small clearing, large enough to house two dozen tents, and one larger. Because the steamy forest protected its inhabitants from the worst of the winter weather, most of the tents had their flaps open to allow for fresh air. Fair elves lounged about, idly playing with their weapons and armor. They all had the light color hair of Seadueni elves, rather than the whole range of blondes, brunettes, reds, and blacks of Blackhaven and Flousen Dua.

From his position, Aidyn could just pick out their features. He lay flat on his stomach, with a nervous Meradyn beside him.

"Damn."

"What?" Meradyn whispered, shooting a worried look at his companion.

"Merbon."

"What?"

"Merbon Alswaith, nasty bugger. No wonder none of your people survived. He revels in bloodshed."

"You know him?"

Aidyn was silent for a bit, wondering if he should tell the young man the truth. At last he sighed in resignation. "Yes, I know him. In fact, I know most of those males down there. See that one?"

He pointed at a too-thin elf bending over a fire, stirring a pot. Meradyn nodded.

"He may be skinny, but he is so fast you do not see him until his blade is in your gut. This," Aidyn pulled his sleeve down to reveal a faint scar across his shoulder, "is from him."

"He cut you?"

"*Aiya*, and has only one testicle and eight fingers left to prove it."

"You cut off only one?" Meradyn asked, a bit of laughter in his whispered words.

The dark elf nodded. "He got in my way, but was not my target. I was going after a sergeant named Malick who had raped and murdered four Kajgenian women. See how lightly his fingers move, how rapidly he stirs that pot?"

The human squinted, trying to see. "Not really, no. But why does it matter?"

"As I explained earlier, every movement is a testament to ability. His fingers, the ones he has left, are very light on the spoon, ready for anything. That one over there," again Aidyn pointed, this time selecting an elf with light bronze hair and a gigantic broadsword on his back, "his name is Spy."

"Spy?" Meradyn snorted quietly, deeply amused.

"Short for Spyler, but appropriate because he has incredible eyesight, above and beyond even the average elf. There are others I have fought down there, many who would know me on sight, perhaps even the sound of my voice, but they are not important. The only one who matters is Merbon. He is a vicious fighter, more prone to sadistic evisceration than swift killing. He and those with him are members of an elite squad of mercenaries known as the White Hand Warriors. They are paid by the throne to do the dirty work the Lostugs do not want the rest of the kingdoms to blame them for."

"I've heard of them before...wasn't someone in Blackhaven once a member?"

Aidyn smiled faintly. "King Losolin, several years ago. He did not know himself, having been fed false memories of his childhood and earlier life. It is where he honed the rather...astonishing skill he has today. Merbon and his ilk are often granted positions of authority in the kingdom. In Seaduens, soldiers and particularly warriors are given power over the regular citizens, and are allowed great privilege and immunity. An officer in the army has more power than well over half the population."

"That seems an ill way to run a country," Meradyn murmured, glowering down at the unconcerned elves.

"It is, which is why Seaduens has always been an enemy to the rest of Nymyños. Even when I was born, nearly eight hundred years ago, the place was considered a lost cause in the peaceful union that was Nymyños. The War of Monotheism was dying down you see, and the people were not looking for a fight. Seaduens refused to let up on their harsh laws, and their border patrol simply butchered anyone who came within sight that was not accompanied by a flag-bearing entourage. Even in times of peace they were a thorn in the side of Nymyños. Now, Queen Tlonna is determined to wipe their atrocious rule off the face of the earth and replace it with a more benevolent, constructive rule."

"She is?"

Aidyn made a face. "Well, she will be, eventually. Right now she is more concerned with the immediate threat of Sithian and his hordes."

"But Stoffnias is part of that, isn't he?"

"Yes."

"Then I'm confused."

The elf chuckled quietly, shaking his head. "We all are, Meradyn. Now be quiet and I will teach you some of what I know."

The two lay side by side on their stomachs for several hours, watching and discussing. They returned three more times over as many days, going to different positions in order to see the setup of the whole camp. When they returned on the fourth day Aidyn had been in the Stone Hunters' village, he was ready to take out the squad.

Nebet'thu continued to work with Meradyn, Eyin, and the other young men of the village who were interested in learning to fight. Meradyn was by far the best, and Aidyn agreed to spar with him once in a while. The fights never lasted more than a few minutes, even with the assassin barely putting in an effort.

"Remember what Yayènia told you!" Aidyn instructed, sweeping his waster at Meradyn's exposed belly. "Protect and attack at the same time!"

The young man parried the whistling wooden blade, knocking it away from his core, but Aidyn reversed his swing quickly and jabbed it backward, thwacking it into Meradyn's shoulder. It was not a killing blow, but numbed the human's arm so much he dropped his stick and stumbled back, grappling for another weapon. He yanked a wooden dagger out of his belt and threw it at Aidyn in desperation. The elf swept his sword down and deflected the flying blade, forcing it to fly wildly in another direction. It hit Eyin in the back of the head.

The king turned from where he was speaking with Nebet'thu to glare at the two duelers, but they were paying him no heed.

"Everything is a weapon!" Aidyn shouted at the panicked Meradyn.

The young man lurched to the side as the elf's waster came screaming down so that it missed by less than an inch. He slammed into Aidyn's thighs, which would have been a human's lower belly, and took him down in a tumble of limbs. The assassin grunted as his still-sore body hit the ground, but he was focused on Meradyn's flailing extremities.

"Mer!" Eyin called, surprised by the turn of events.

Nebet'thu was watching in high amusement as Aidyn wrestled with a human who was three-quarters his size. The dark elf jerked his elbow into the soft area beneath Meradyn's jaw, stunning him for a moment, and then slammed his knee upward. The poor boy let out a high-pitched shriek and tumbled off Aidyn, holding his crotch and groaning. The elf stood and brushed himself off, his breath frosting in the air before him.

Meradyn writhed on the ground, his eyes closed. A bruise was forming on his chin already, blood trickling from between his lips.

"Low, Aidyn, low."

"He needs to learn," the assassin replied to Neb's assessment. "Otherwise a sore scrotum will be the least of his problems."

The plains elf shook his head but didn't argue, knowing the truth of the other's words. "So, when do you go after the Seadueni?"

"This evening. I am going to prepare."

Nebet'thu watched the assassin stride away. The plains elf tossed the village's practice weapons in the small bucket they used to keep them in, and then turned to help a bloodless Meradyn to his feet.

# Chapter 12
## Illusionist

Aidyn dressed carefully, meticulously, his clothing so black it seemed to elude light. Though night is not a true black, the *ärdyz* deception worked better than any dark blue or gray ever could. He made sure nothing was free to jingle as he walked, and nothing loose to flutter in the wind. Eyin was waiting for him as he stepped from the yurt, his movements sharp and nervous.

"Do you really think you can kill them all?" the human asked.

"No," the assassin replied, "I know I can. How is Meradyn?"

"He's...recovering. And there are twenty-five of them! Please allow me to aid you in some way!" Eyin begged, clutching at the elf's arm.

Aidyn sighed. "Leave me be King of Purheae. This is my job, let me do it."

The young man muttered under his breath, but he stepped away from the killer. "Good luck, then."

The assassin sniffed derisively and strode into the forest. He drew level with the edge of the trees minutes later, standing in the deepening shadows of late dusk. Three elves were directly across from him, standing at watch. The first one went down silently, a throwing knife buried in his throat. As his companions turned, Aidyn sprinted to the left, his right hand letting loose another dagger. The target fell as the dark elf drew his longblade, rolled to avoid a punch, and severed the third elf's hamstrings. After kicking in the male's face, Aidyn retrieved his daggers and moved on.

He had taken less than five steps when he heard a soft movement to his right. Leaping backward, Aidyn swung his blade in an arc parallel to the ground, slicing the throat of the fourth sentry. He hit the ground and rolled, coming back to his feet in one motion. Looking carefully about, the assassin waited. When no attack was forthcoming he moved off to the left, gliding through the sentry lines like a ghost, dispatching them easily. Finally, seven guards later, Aidyn stood looking into the camp from a direction he and Meradyn had seen from farther away. He could see Merbon clearly, sitting at ease before the large fire. Around him were seventeen more elves, fully armored in Seaduens garb. Aidyn shrugged slightly, feeling the silky black material slide over his skin. It was armor enough.

The assassin surveyed the camp for a while longer, choosing his routes, numbering his targets. Spyler and Torsin, the skinny one, would die first and second. Merbon would die last. He would savor his death as only an assassin could. Aidyn's stomach fluttered with excitement. From where he stood he let his eyes wander across the rocky terrain, solidifying his path. A moment later he was moving, half crouched as the light failed and cast him in dusky shadows, an illusion of movement.

As soon as he was at the edge of the firelight, Aidyn drew his longblade and dove into camp, alarming everyone. He was already in the center when an attack finally came. As planned, he took down a completely stunned Spy first, and then a snarling Torsin. The third died seconds later, and the assassin crouched down, letting his rear enemy stab his front enemy with a spear, and vice versa. Leaning out from between the dying elves Aidyn kicked the haft up, snapping it in two. Two more rushing soldiers impaled themselves on the ends, slamming into them before they could stop.

He rolled, scooting to the side when a soldier appeared out of the smoke, swinging another spear. Aidyn grabbed the end, just behind the head and yanked hard, pulling his assailant off balance. The elf stumbled into a fire, screaming and writhing as he burned. Now armed with a spear and sword, the assassin dove into a cluster of oncoming Seadueni. Swinging around hard, he swept the spearhead across the faces of those in front, and then took down the next row with his sword.

The fight was over before he knew it, and Aidyn was standing before a panicking Merbon, whom he knocked to the ground.

"What do you want Aidyn?" the captain breathed, scooting back on his elbows.

"Your life," the assassin said as he slammed a long knife into Merbon's knee to pin him in place.

The elf screamed for a good long time and tried to pull out the weapon, but Aidyn stopped him. When he finally stopped screaming, he lay back panting, glaring at the dark elf.

"Who sent you?"

Aidyn crouched down and cocked his head to the side. "I do not believe, Captain Merbon, that you are in a position to be asking questions."

"Who sent you?"

"Is it not obvious? I came on my own. You Seadueni piss me off, plundering, murdering, and cavorting about like drunken humans all in the name of your corrupt system. You attacked allies of Blackhaven Forest, never a good idea, and then you squatted here once your allies were driven from the walls of Blackhaven City. You were told to leave, held off by a plains elf, a twenty-three year old king, and his like-aged commander. If the warning did you little good, the fact that you were pushed back by those three should have told you to leave."

"You mean they called you here?"

"No one calls me anywhere, Merbon. Perhaps it was the previous affronts you and your ilk did to me that was the deciding factor in my wishing your death. You, Spy, Torsin, Paerin over there," Aidyn gestured to the crispy elf in the fire, "you all gave me scars three hundred years ago when I went after Malick. I am simply returning the favor."

"Three hundred years Aidyn, which was a long time ago!" Merbon shouted in disbelief.

"All right, perhaps I killed all your stupid soldiers because they obliterated two villages full of innocent people without cause, and held a third captive. You were the heading force of that, so you are going to die too."

"You would risk your life for a few hundred barbarians?"

"First of all," Aidyn began, sitting back on his heels, "I was not risking my life because you and your soldiers were not a threat to me. And second, our definitions of barbarism are wildly different. For instance, what I considered barbaric is the routine slaughter of innocent people, while you consider that sport. You consider my retribution against the murderers of the innocent barbaric, while I consider it justice."

"Stoffnias will not let this stand!" Merbon shrieked, writhing about in a final attempt to free himself.

The assassin sneered, and then shoved the spear he was still holding into his chest. He waited until the Seadueni stopped twitching before dropping the haft. Standing up, he felt the sudden burn of injuries that adrenaline masked. He rolled his shoulders and walked from the campsite. There was a laceration on his thigh below the older one, he noted, and two on his right shoulder, ironically on either side of the ancient scar Torsin had given him. Aidyn scratched at the scars on his face, remembering the last time he had gone head-to-head with more than twenty enemies. This time around had been effortless in comparison.

He passed the dead sentries, and continued on to the village. When he strode into the main area, everyone came rushing out of their yurts. Eyin appeared at the back, and the people separated to let him through. The human was obviously relieved.

"Did you doubt me that much, King Eyin?" Aidyn asked, grinning lopsidedly.

"They are all dead?" the king asked, looking startled now.

"That is what I was sent in to do, was it not?" the elf replied, raising his eyebrows. "Yes, they are all dead, including Captain Merbon. He was the last."

Eyin smiled and let out a breath. "Thank Gagu. Do you have wounds that need tending? Do you need anything?"

"Thank me, not some disinterested and uninvolved god, and I have a few cuts, yes," Aidyn snapped, turning for Nebet'thu's yurt.

Several women rushed after him, waving about their kits. The first one to the door he allowed in, and shut out the rest.

"I am perfectly able to tend to myself, madam."

She blinked at him with round hazel eyes. She was rather gentle looking, and simple, and not the same one who had tended him when he had arrived.

"I know, Lord Aidyn, but a warrior should never have to. You saved us all, and for that we owe you this much at least."

The elf sat down on the bed and looked at her, raising his chin in contemplation. "True, but I would never expect it. Spirits know such payment is rarely freely given."

"This is not the way it should be. Where are you hurt?" she said, turning to her healing kit.

Silently, Aidyn removed his shirt, and then his pants. Though he still wore his breechclout, there was little left to the imagination and when the girl turned around again she blushed crimson and gasped.

"What is your name?" Aidyn asked as he sat down again and examined the cut on his thigh. It was relatively deep, and blood was beginning to clot along the edge.

The puckered scar from Sithian's dagger ran from the middle of his thigh on the side, to the top. The new injury went from his knee and ended almost in the dead center of the old one, creating a lopsided 'T' shape on his leg. He frowned at it.

"Elizabeth, Lord Aidyn, please straighten your leg."

"Why, Elizabeth, are you embarrassed about seeing my body? As a healer, surely you have seen naked men."

"Oh, I have...but none such as you," she replied quietly, bending over his leg. "My mother used to tell me stories about elves. I never believed them until Nebet'thu rode into the village, and then you."

"Why would you not believe them? We are people, just like humans or dwarves," Aidyn argued, leaning back on his elbows.

Elizabeth shrugged, still working on his thigh. Her fingers were small and deft, and they slid over his skin with a cool touch. "You seemed too wondrous to be true. Even now, my eyes can't quite understand what they're seeing."

"How do you mean?"

She looked up and crimson stained her cheeks once more. "You're so beautiful, so perfect. I bet your wife is the most beautiful person on earth."

Aidyn grinned. "I do not have a wife, Elizabeth, and the most beautiful person on earth is Queen Tlonna, who is already married."

"Oh...I just thought..."

"I know what you thought, and I know what you want, but I am not going to lay with you. You are too young, even for a human, and I would destroy you for every man who came into your life," Aidyn replied softly.

Elizabeth nodded and went back to work. Aidyn let his head drop between his shoulders, stretching his neck. When he felt her fingers leave his thigh, he sat up once more, leaning forward so she could work on the wounds on his shoulder.

She cleaned them thoroughly and wrapped them in clean white gauze, and before she stood, Elizabeth pressed her lips to his shoulder, just below the wrap. "You really are beautiful, you know that," she said quietly. "And I'm not as young as you think."

Aidyn merely smiled, and watched her leave the yurt. He lay back and closed his eyes, letting the weariness drift him off to sleep. In the morning, he dressed and shoved Neb's shoulder to wake him. The hunter had come in a few minutes after Aidyn had fallen asleep and had not wanted to disturb the assassin, so his clothes were piled on the floor beside his bed, and were now being stood on by the dark elf.

The elf squinted up at him, sleep clouding his light-colored eyes. "Have a little fun with the healer last night?"

"What? No."

The hunter frowned. "She left the yurt all flushed and pouting. I thought that was your trademark."

"No, that is what my rejection looks like. My job is done here, now. I am leaving," the assassin replied, feeling restless.

Neb shook his head as he sat up. He pulled a clean shirt out of the chest by his bed and put it on. "You really do not like being away from her, do you?"

"Who?" Aidyn snapped, rubbing at his bandaged thigh.

"Tlonna. Every time you are away from her you get all...twitchy and annoyed. What is she to you?"

The dark elf was staring at him, emerald eyes wide with shock. "She is a friend, and my ward. And how do you know how I am when she is away?"

"I thought Yayènia was Tlonna's personal guard," Neb replied, ignoring the other's question.

"Yayènia is High Commander. I am the Assassin for the Throne of Blackhaven, and when I am not on missions, which is often, I am Tlonna's shadow," Aidyn replied, caught off guard.

Neb eyed him suspiciously, and then shrugged. "Well, you will be home soon, and you can get back to her."

"How do you know how I am when we are apart?" Aidyn demanded, not about to let the fairer elf off the hook.

"All right, I do not, but others have told me. Aladorn and I talked a lot on the way to Blackhaven City from Asheyl, and he told me a little of how you two have been acting. If I were not so sure of Tlonna and Losolin's fidelity to each other, I would think you were her lover."

Aidyn nearly hit the plains elf, but resisted. "We have a lot of history, Nebet'thu, and our friendship is solid. She is a popular target, I am her protector. Clear?"

Neb put his hands up as if in surrender. "Fine, fine, Aidyn. I was just making an observation. So...when do *I* get to go home?"

The dark elf shrugged. "I do not know. I would say the boys need more instruction, though."

The plains elf folded his arms and sighed. "I want to go home, see my wife—"

"Who you hated last summer," Aidyn muttered.

"... and breathe clean air," Nebet'thu finished, glowering at the taller male. "Eesa and I have made amends."

"How nice. I have no power to send you home, I am afraid," the assassin shot back without missing a beat, dragging a hand back through his raven hair to get it out of his face.

Several strands stubbornly fell back as soon as he lifted his hand, and he huffed, which lifted a few away for a second more. Nebet'thu watched him, one eyebrow lifted.

"Problems?"

"A few!" Aidyn said acidly, turning away. "Where is Eyin?"

"In his yurt, I would think."

The dark elf stomped out of the small house, aggravated. He found the largest yurt, which was actually three yurts put together, and walked inside without knocking. Eyin was shirtless, gritting his teeth as an old man held what looked like a pick and hammer to his shoulder. Black lines of dye mingled with blood on his arm as the elder pounded at his flesh. Aidyn cocked his head in order to see the design, interested.

It was a blocky black spiral with thick lines of red forming a serpentine equal-armed cross through it. The red was completely finished, and the elder was working in the black. It looked to be an immensely painful experience.

"What is this?" Aidyn asked the sweating king.

"My mark as leader of the tribe," Eyin said through clenched teeth. "The elders say it is an ancient tradition, one that has been nearly lost to us. The square spiral is a symbol of the eternity of nature and cultural malleability, and the crossbars represent the separation between this life and the next, fluidity. It has been found on several stones in the forest, carved by ancients, and only recently deciphered."

"So why get it as a mark?"

Eyin could not reply for a while as the elder began tapping harder as he crossed over a red line. When he finished, Eyin lifted his other arm and used it to wipe the sweat from his brow.

"It is a symbol of hope and strength for my people, as I am supposed to be. The elders say it is a good thing to connect the spirit of the Purheaens to the body of their king."

"Ah," Aidyn said, watching the old man as he worked.

After a long time, the elder backed away from Eyin's bleeding arm and dropped his tools into a bowl of water. The young king winced as he moved his arm into a different position, having held it in stasis for an hour. The tattoo was complete.

"How long has it taken?"

Eyin took a towel from the old man and pressed it against his shoulder. "The cross took two weeks. The spiral yesterday and today."

"You are stronger than you appear. That looked quite painful."

"Painful is an understatement. What can I do for you, my friend?" Eyin replied, standing and stretching, favoring his left a little.

"My job here is done, I need to leave immediately."

"You do?"

"Yes, unless you need my presence for something more," Aidyn confirmed, sticking his thumbs through his belt and leaning back on his heels.

The human looked upset that he was leaving, and appeared to be desperately searching his mind for a reason to have him stay. Finally he took a deep breath. "No, I do not. Will Master Nebet'thu be leaving with you?"

"No. He will stay until summoned back by King Losolin or Queen Tlonna. Unless you wish him to leave, I suppose."

"No! I do not! He is teaching us a lot! Please don't take him away!"

"All right! Calm down, Eyin, as I said, he will stay until summoned," Aidyn promised, taken aback by the frantic upswing in emotion.

"I am sorry, but fear for my people has driven me to desperation. Master Nebet'thu has already improved the skill of every fighter here. I wish you would stay as well, but I understand your desire to return."

The elf studied the young human for a moment and then turned away. "I may be returning soon, with Queen Tlonna and High Commander Yayènia, anyway. I cannot guarantee anything, but I will give you that hope."

"Why?"

"I am not sure, but Lady Miazie has said they must come here," the assassin said as he stepped to the door.

Eyin looked confused. "Well, I hope they do because I need to speak with her as it is."

Aidyn nodded and jogged down the three steps to the ground. Meradyn was sparring with two other boys, their wooden wasters cracking against each other with surprising strength. The elf watched them for a moment, analyzing, before stepping inside of their ring. Surprise and alarm registered on all their faces, but they could not stop their weapons fast enough. Aidyn, however, could. Two of them slammed against his blocking, vambrace-covered arm, and the third connected with the heel of his boot as he kicked out and threw it off.

The entire lower half of Meradyn's face was brown and yellow with a bruise, his lower lip swollen to twice its normal size. He gave Aidyn a stubborn look of defiance.

"You all have good form, no doubt thanks to the instruction of Nebet'thu, but you are moving too swiftly for your skill level. Going too fast is just as bad as going too slow. Perfect your moves, and then move up in speed, perfect it again, and so on, until you are at maximum control and speed. Here, start again," Aidyn said, tossing the practice weapons off his arm and allowing the boys to adjust themselves.

He pulled out his scimitar and mimicked their stance, smiling at their looks of reverence. "Move slowly now, go!"

They watched him, imitating his movements a split second later, trying to keep their balance and concentration. Meradyn's weapon moved after his the fastest, and the steadiest. The two other boys did their best, and Aidyn was not disappointed.

"Good, now faster."

He worked with them for another hour, speeding up the routine each time they seemed to have it under control. Then he let them try it with his weapons, which were much heavier than their wooden practice blades. Meradyn held his longsword in trembling fingers, while his friends gaped at the scimitars in their hands.

Nebet'thu had joined Aidyn earlier, and now stood by the assassin watching in reluctant appreciation. The silver weapons flashed in the morning air, swirling bits of snow about as it filtered through the trees. Meradyn moved with good balance, adjusting to the weight of the longsword as he spun through the formations. The two others were less successful. One lost his grip on the scimitar and sent it flipping through the air, and the other moved too fast and lodged the blade into the side of a tree.

Aidyn leapt upward to catch the spinning scimitar before it skewered someone and slammed it back into its sheath. Nebet'thu yanked the other out of the tree and handed it to the dark elf. Meradyn finished the routine and stood panting with exertion, the longsword pointed down to the ground.

"Well, perhaps you should wait a bit longer on letting them have real weapons," Aidyn chortled, taking his sword away from the tired commander.

Neb laughed and nodded. "I agree. You have shown these boys something today, though, that is for sure. I do not think they will believe themselves warriors for a long time, now."

"Good, because they are not. Keep working with them, Nebet'thu, and perhaps I will return sooner than you want to help once more."

"Do as you must, Aidyn, do as you must," the tribal elf chuckled and waved off the assassin, who was already walking away.

# Chapter 13
## History and Memory

Yayènia yawned as she stretched and wished she were still in bed. Tlonna copied her, glaring in indignation.

"Stop that," she muttered once she could talk again.

"You are the one who insisted we get up," the commander grumbled back, as she idly scratched Udu's neck.

"We are near to the place where it all came together for me. Where I learned the truth of who I was, where Miazie broke the memory Weave," Tlonna said, looking around.

She and Yayènia were less than a day away from the Cleshnoe Forest. Once out of Kismath they had ridden fast and hard across the Liberated Lands, hugging the gentle foothills of the Bijoz Mountains. Riding less than a mile north of where the Battle of Alchemian had taken place, they had kept a straight path through the hills in order to avoid the memories. Snow was drifting up in places, slowing their progress a bit but not enough to hinder them. They were now inadvertently mirroring the path Aidyn had taken to hunt down the Eseirik.

Yayènia was bored from the lack of action and so kept pulling out her swords just to hold them in her hands as they rode. Good practice, she called it. Tlonna envied her sister's ability to balance so perfectly in the saddle of a running warhorse while holding two heavy katans out to the side. She did not, however, envy her the sore arms at night.

Tlonna had requested that the warrior play her flute nearly every night but had been denied all but a few times because of the chilly air and the soreness of Yayènia's arms. Though she had tried to play the instrument a few times, the Magin seemed incapable of making her embouchure tight enough to produce anything more than a squeaky rush of air. Yayènia had laughed at her, taken back her flute, and proceeded to make the most beautiful music Tlonna had ever heard. There was much to be envious about.

When they finally reached the forest Tlonna's heart seemed to thicken in her chest. Memories washed over her as she saw herself, Losolin, and Miazie struggling through the trees, desperate for help and knowledge. Yayènia allowed Tlonna to take the lead as they ducked under the quiet foliage of the wintry forest. Red-capped cardinals and white-coated foxes watched them with wary eyes as they went by.

"What do you suppose that is?" the warrior asked a while later, pointing at an odd, pillar-like stone jutting up from the ground.

It was quite large and carved all over with strange, archaic symbols, faded with time and broken by lichen. The clearing all around it was empty of all sorts of plants, except for a short grass, brown with the season.

"I do not know, we did not encounter it on our way through here the first time," Tlonna replied, impressed by the size and oddness of the monolith. "But depending on how far we are from the border of Talenias, I believe we are close to where the Cyree lies. I can feel it, almost like a thinning of the air."

Yayènia shrugged off her pack and handed it to her sister. Without a word of explanation she removed her various belts and sprang up onto a tree. Like a creature born to climb she rushed up the trunk and into the bare canopy, her cleated boots catching hold and propelling her upward. Tlonna stared after her, shaking her head. After a minute or so Yayènia reappeared and slid down the tree. She landed on the ground with a light thud, and bent to retrieve her things.

She gestured off to the southeast. "Talenias is about another hour from here. There appears to be a low plateau running from the Bijozs into the forest, with a river running atop it. It stops about five or six miles directly west."

"That would be where the Cyree is, then," Tlonna said as she handed her sister her pack.

They gathered up the grazing horses and set off once more. The sun was winking gold through the branches by the time they found the serene waterfall and pool that made up the magical Cyree. This time there was no shimmering Andramaky waiting for them, but Tlonna felt as though the Cyree's sacrificial elf-presence lingered.

"This is it, huh?" Yayènia said, dismounting and looking about, her hands on her hips.

"This is it," Tlonna confirmed, kneeling by the edge of the water.

A pervading sense of ancient power filled her lungs as she breathed deeply, her eyes closing in rapture. Last time she had been here she had been in a trance held by the Cyree, and then frightened out of her wits by the proceeding events. Now she took the time to soak in the immortal ambience of the place, her magic purring in ecstasy as it reveled in the purity of power. It cocooned her mind, easing the constant pressure of her colossal power.

Yayènia dropped her belongings on the ground and flopped down next to them to stretch out her slender legs. Tlonna ignored her, lost in the pulsing rhythm of magic. Jair crooned in satisfaction at the spirits who sang to her, their voices ranging from the deepest bass to the highest soprano.

Tears splashed down her face as she swayed with the melodies undulating within her to mingle with the still waters of the Cyree.

Aidyn ran Whäd hard, pushing her to near exhaustion. They sped between the dark and quiet battles lines of both Blackhaven and Zaedic, the assassin using every trick he had to remain undetected as he thundered by. Even so, a Blackhaven sentry noticed him and shot off an arrow, shouted a warning, and missed Whäd's rump by several yards. A call went up, but by the time the guards found his trail Aidyn was long gone.

Though he could not feel Tlonna anymore, he was fairly certain he knew where she was headed. Gathered from her and Losolin's account of their journey years before, and from Tlonna's sudden obsession with places of history and power, he figured she was off to the Cyree pond.

His urgency was fueled not only by his desire to tell her and Yayènia of Miazie's vision, but of the simple longing to see her. He passed by Anutch, his insides churning, and hurried onward into the Plains of Arada. The weather was worse than it had been the first time he had gone through this winter and the long grasses rattled like old bones as the icy wind taunted them. Whäd snorted in displeasure as flying snow slapped at her nose and stiffened her tail.

Aidyn bent low over her neck and glared through the whiteness, his hood pulled low over his face to ward off the biting chill. The forest came as a surprise. The trees blocked most of the wind and the blinding snow almost immediately, the calming sentinels standing tall against the rampaging blizzard. Aidyn sighed in relief, pulled out a comb, and tried to unfreeze his hair. Once they were deep enough into the forest he dismounted and curried Whäd, removing the frost from her coat and mane. A day later he found tracks. He followed them, relieved by their freshness. When he came upon the stone monolith, he stopped, irresistibly drawn to the place that was of such importance to him.

When he was but a week old, Aidyn's family had been chased from their home in Talenias. His father, at Aladorn's desperate bidding, had taken the infant Aidyn and fled to this place where they were to wait for the rest of the family. They had never come, and it had taken Aladorn and Aidyn seven hundred and eighty years to find each other. Their father, Bailan, had carved into the pillar in hopes that his wife and two older sons would find it.

The grown assassin knelt by the monolith, his tawny fingers running gently over the ancient stone. No one knew or remembered who had erected the pillar, not even the oldest elves in the land, and few even knew of its existence any more. Aidyn searched for a few seconds and then his heart thudded to a slow stop. There, just below his thumb was the carving his long-deceased father had left in desperation. It was a circle with two opposing claw-like appendages jutting from the sides, the same symbol Aidyn had adopted as his emblem, and was on the hilts of his weapons, his belt buckle, even the clasps on his vambraces. Beneath the symbol was a rough Parlêthian 'B', which stood for Blackhaven, where Bailan had taken Aidyn.

It was rounded out now, softened by age and weather, but it still brought tears to the assassin's eyes. His forehead hit the frigid stone and he sobbed as he never had before, the long-hidden emotions wracking over his hunched form. He could not remember his mother's face, or that of his brother Aolan, but Aladorn's quiet words of them washed through his mind like memories themselves.

For a long time he knelt at the monolith, belatedly letting the premature and violent separation of him and his family strike at his heart. He had been too young to understand the implications of the separation and by the time he was old enough to appreciate it he was a hardened assassin with blood already on his hands. It hurt. When he at last sat back and wiped his face clean, Aidyn snorted at his own reaction. It was ridiculous that so much time had passed and yet he had never cried over them, and it chose now to hit him hard. He was old, having lived as full a life as possible, and now he sobbed like a mentally disturbed child.

With a sigh full of disgust and scorn, Aidyn remounted a placid Whäd and turned her about, searching the ground for tracks. He found them, and felt a bit discomfited when he realized the two females had gone right by the monolith, even slowed to study it before moving on.

With a click to his horse, Aidyn moved her onward. Grumbling to himself, he shook his head to dispel the last dredges of emotion from his mind.

Yayènia lounged against a tree, her knees drawn up to her chest as she watched Tlonna grovel at the side of the creepy pond. The staff across her back glowed in eerie reverence and the black cloak about her shoulders sat perfectly still, as though a part of the earth itself. From her angle it even appeared to meld to the ground. Finally, after nearly an hour Tlonna stood and walked to where her sister sat.

"We will stay the night. There is something I must do and you cannot come with me."

"Why not?"

"Because anyone who touches the waters of the Cyree can never leave its presence."

"But you were in it, and you left," Yayènia argued, angry about such a command.

"Because I am the Magin Queen, and my powers come from this well of magic. It and I are linked in the way a mother and child are connected."

Yayènia got to her feet and glared into Tlonna's altered eyes. After a moment, she nodded. "Do what you must, but if you make me regret this I will make you pay."

"I have no doubt," Tlonna replied quietly as she began to remove her belongings.

"What are you doing?" the warrior asked, alarmed as her sister took off her two cloaks, and started undoing her belt.

"I do not want to have to swim with all of my clothes on. Will you keep them warm and dry for me? I will be cold coming out."

"You are going to swim in it?"

"Sort of. I need to get to the bottom, where I can breathe."

"What!?"

"It is not a pool of true water, Yayènia. The top layer is only an illusion, though a rather physical one. It is pure magic beneath, power in its rawest form."

"You are mad, but who am I to judge?"

"Indeed. Here," Tlonna muttered, and handed the commander her boots.

Once she was completely naked the Magin Queen shivered to the edge of the pool and then dove in. The water hit her like an icy blast, a hundred times colder than the wild rapids of the Jaquisa River, but smooth and slick like oil. Forcing her rigid limbs to move, Tlonna swam downward a few more strokes, and felt the water begin to change. The pressure lessened, and the bitter chill ebbed. The farther down she went the easier it became. By the time she was at the bottom it was a pleasantly warm temperature, and she could breathe, even though it was uncomfortable to do so. Looking about, Tlonna found what she had suspected would be there.

The elf walked into the narrow opening, and found herself in a different world. The air rushed by her in bubbles as she moved, her hair lifted off her shoulders to float on its own, raised as though by a wind. Tlonna filled her body with magic, causing the change of her eyes to come, though she did not Weave. To do so would mean death even for her.

As her eyes changed, so did her vision, and therefore the walls of the cave she now stood in. There were three massive drawings on the walls; primitive yet detailed enough to illustrate the point. Tlonna stared at herself, or who she assumed was her, depicted as a female figure bathed in light that stood across a great void, a male figure surrounded by blood opposite. As her vision changed, the aura of light turned to an aura of darkness, the blood to darkness, and the void to light. Tlonna lifted a finger and ran it gently across the façade of the wall, and the power of prophecy lifted from the ancient ink to swirl about her.

Another drawing showed her crouching in the center of a feral storm, her hands lifting the Staff of Cyree above her head in a wild gesture of triumph. The staff turned to a bolt of lightning when her sight shifted. The third image was the most disturbing of all, with her once more in the center but accompanied by a male different from the one in the first drawing, his hands toward the sky. A white rod lifted from the ground between them, and a massive wall kept hundreds upon thousands of people away as it roiled about them. With the change, she and the male switched places.

Tlonna gasped, frightened by the images as much as the meaning behind them. Her heart thundered against her chest, desperate to escape its cage. There, amidst the purest form of magic, the very well of power, Tlonna felt true fear of the future.

# Chapter 19
## The Deadly Truth

Sithian rubbed the back of his neck, and grimaced as he felt the rough scar at the base of his skull where the bastard dark elf had stabbed him. He leaned forward as Orlando, general of his forces, explained the position of the Blackhaven line.

"They are stretched out here, weakened by their lack of numbers. If we drove through them here, we would be able to completely surround them in minutes, wipe them from the face of the earth," he said, gesturing with a thick finger.

Sithian glared at him, disgusted by his bulky appearance, how his bulging muscles glistened with an ever-present sheen of sweat. "I said I do not want to attack. You will do as I say, or suffer the consequences."

"Why not, King Sithian? They are just sitting there, same as us. We are giving them time to call on their allies who ring this entire continent. Our forces are tapped out; we have nowhere else to draw upon! Please forgive my questioning of your orders, but my lord, it doesn't make any sense!"

"I will make them come to me. A ruler does not go to his subjects, they come to him. These people are my slaves, doing my bidding whether or not they realize it yet."

Orlando tried to keep his expression from showing his abject disgust and disbelief, but Sithian noticed the struggle anyway. The disturbed Magin shot up out of his chair and clutched at his tangle of raven hair.

"I am the bringer of righteous revenge of Man, Orlando! I am the tainted victim, given life in order to cleanse this land of the foul presence of faery creatures, the elves, the dwarves, the sprytes, dryads, and every other one that stains the face of the world. My father knew this, it is why he took my mother and brought me to life. He knew I would have to be cursed in order to have the strength to do as I must. Don't you see? Why do you question this?"

"I am only a soldier, my lord, I am sorry I have upset you. Perhaps I should call for Learia?"

"What?" Sithian hissed, turning slowly to stare at his general.

"Your wife, the queen? Should I send for her?"

It took a moment for the words to penetrate the thick fog of madness within Sithian's mind, but when they did he grinned. "Yes, yes send her to me. I need to release my tension. Too bad your wife is dead. I'm sure you could use some release."

Orlando bowed. "Your sister, my wife, was killed in the course of duty, King Sithian, I know that."

"Yes, yes she was. She couldn't even scream, which was a bit of a pity, I suppose, considering. I wonder if she screamed when the dark elf slew her body."

"I wouldn't know, your highness," Orlando growled as he stormed out of the tent. He found Learia sitting in her smallish tent, humming to herself as she rubbed her belly with oil.

"He wants you," the general said, eyeing her body. "But he's raving. You must watch yourself more than usual this time. He is getting stronger, but so is the madness."

"He may be fit and vital, Orlando, but you have the experience that excites me," the queen crooned, taking his hand and pressing it to her breast.

"He would have me executed if he even suspected our affair, Learia, this is too dangerous."

The young woman smiled coyly and drew his hand down to cup her between the legs. "This child is yours, I know it. Sithian does not have the strength of seed needed to make a baby. Our son will grow into a strong, powerful man, and he will kill Sithian and take his place. Our child will be king, and you and I will be at the top of the world. Know that every time Sithian moves within me, I am with you in my heart."

Orlando resisted the warmth of her womanhood and pulled his hand away. "Please, you must go to him. I do not want you hurt because you lingered. He is becoming more and more unstable by the day. Now he thinks he is some great martyr, sent to save the human race. His ambitions are well placed, but his mind is gone. I do not want his insanity directed at you."

Learia smiled again and kissed the muscular man, her true love. "I will go."

As she walked through the corridor of tents, the queen mused on her life. Rhiannan had found her when she was just barely a woman, pure and untouched by any man. Sithian had shown her kindness and passion for only a few weeks before turning away and becoming distant and cold. After the defeat at Alchemian, the half-breed king had become even more introverted and hostile, even murdering his own sister after forcing her to marry Orlando. It was when Rhiannan had been declared dead that Learia had gone to the general. At first it was simply a duty, a queen to a mourning general. She had made sure he had everything he needed and they had developed a friendship. Then Sithian had gone away for a few weeks to visit a Nymyñosian cohort, and Learia had gone to Orlando in the night. They had made love and found love that night.

Their relationship had been secret to even their closest servants, and then she had become pregnant. As soon as Sithian had returned home, Learia had lured him into bed and suffered his abusive lust in order to protect herself, her child, and Orlando. She claimed it was that night that Sithian had seeded her, but it was a lie.

Learia hurried into Sithian's tent and cleared her throat. The half-breed turned to her, and as always her breath was taken away. Not by his stunning, cold beauty or his hard, slender body, but by the madness raging in his eyes. It was impossible not to be physically attracted to him, as her body often pointed out, but his violent insanity often culled that lusty desire.

"Learia."

"Sithian."

"How do you fare?"

The young queen smiled gently. "Well, my lord. Our child grows daily. He is kicking, now. Would you like to feel him?"

Sithian's eyes darted to her belly, which was expanding in the fourth month of her pregnancy. "Tell me again which time it was you believe it to have been conceived."

A flutter of alarm tightened Learia's heart, but she remained outwardly calm and loving, wondering if her deranged husband could now read minds. "I believe it to be the night you returned from your trip to Seaduens. I had missed you so much during your absence, and to have you in my arms once more was a pleasure I do not take for granted. It was a night of such passion, Sithian, it must be the one."

"Perhaps. Can you still be entered?"

Sithian's crude questions no longer bothered her, so she undid the laces on her loose gown and dropped it to the floor in answer. He barely waited for her to step away from the clothes before picking her up and slamming her onto his desk. The various quills, papers, weights, and other items jabbed into her back, but she didn't care. Sithian undressed and was soon atop her, gasping as he relieved his tension within her.

His mouth was on her, not gentle as it had once been during the early days of their marriage, but rough as his teeth snipped at her flesh, sometimes drawing blood. Learia moaned beneath him in feigned ecstasy, arching her back as he neared his peak, and pretended to join him in is ecstasy. His perspiration dripped onto her chest and neck as he finished, gasping not her name, but senseless words of madness. Learia tried to wrap her arms around his neck to bring him close in a parody of love, but his hand suddenly gripped her throat, his teeth bared in a vicious snarl.

Frightened, Learia tried to breathe, but what little air she managed to suck in was stolen by terror when undulating ribbons of dark blue magic rose before her eyes.

"You shouldn't lie to me, Learia. I can *see* inside your mind."

"Please...Sithian...I can't—"

"Shut up!" the young half-breed hissed, bending down to press his cheek against hers. "Or I will kill you without looking into your mind to find out if you are innocent or not."

"For...what?"

"Treachery, adultery, whoring, whatever you want to call it. Four months ago I was in Seaduens, and you were not! Four months ago I was riding a Seadueni duchess as she screamed my name in pleasure! You were in Zaedic!"

Learia began to gag as her mouth filled with saliva but she could not swallow. She shook her head in denial, but Sithian's hand pressed even harder against her throat and her vision began to darken.

"You have betrayed me!"

Tears coursed from her face, hot and fast. She shook her head again, clutching at his slender, impossibly strong wrist.

"Tell me who, and I will spare you the pain of delving into your mind, whore!"

Again Learia shook her head, not in denial but in a final desperate act to get some air. Her body had begun to tingle unpleasantly. Sithian's cheek twitched and his magic clawed into her face, leaving trails of bitter cold beneath her flesh. She saw herself gasping beneath Orlando as the big man moved within her. Try as she might, Learia could not close the memory off, and she looked beyond the image to Sithian's face.

For a moment it reflected emotions that were true, not twisted by insanity. Betrayal, sadness, and a childish hurt showed her the honest beauty of his face, the man he could have been, the man his elven mother would have wanted. And then the rage swept it all away. Learia screamed out in agony as a terrible, searing pain erupted in her belly. She looked down, gasping as Sithian's hand finally released her throat, to see his knife driven into her stomach. He yanked it out and stabbed it in again, and again, ripping apart her insides, murdering her and her unborn child. Orlando's child.

"Perfidious tramp! Treacherous snake! Vile seductress!" Sithian shouted, viciously stabbing her.

Learia's last vision was of his tortured face as she fell away, the wounded hurt of a person betrayed, and the unchecked fury of a person unbalanced.

Sithian stood over the bloody corpse of his wife for a long time, his breathing harsh and ragged. The knife dripped hot blood onto his foot, but he did not notice it. He saw again and again his wife writhing beneath the muscled body of his trusted general. With a curse, he tossed the knife onto her disloyal belly, yanked a heavy robe over his shoulders, and pulled on his discarded pants. Sithian shoved his arms through the sleeves and stormed from the tent, heedless of the blood that stained the front of him. His guards exchanged looks, but he ignored them as they fell into step behind him.

"Orlando!"

The big man appeared in the entrance of his tent, his face losing all color when he took in Sithian's appearance. "Yes, King Sithian?"

"It appears my wife was unfaithful. Do not worry for me, she is dead. Would you please remove her from my tent?"

"Of...of course, my lord. Do you know who she was...unfaithful with?" Orlando stammered, horror rising in his eyes.

Sithian barely caught the wicked smile from betraying him, but catch it he did. Instead he woefully shook his head. "No, my friend, she kept that secret from me. I am sure that if you heard anything about it, you would bring it to me immediately?"

"Yes, my lord, of course I would."

"I knew it, General. Please hurry with the body. I do not like the smell of blood on my personal things."

Orlando's eyes unwillingly flashed to the blood splattered all over his king's body, but wisely said nothing. He bowed his acquiescence and hurried off, his shoulders slumped. Sithian watched him go with burning eyes.

He turned to his guards, who were silent sentinels at his back. "I am going back to Zaedic for a time. Gather my things and prepare for the journey. We will not be staying long, but I need to find another wife who will bear my child, and I need to check on a few things."

One of the guards bowed low and hurried off to do his king's bidding while the other stayed put, unwilling to leave his king unguarded. Sithian eyed him, wondering if he too was a sneaking traitor, but shrugged it off. If he was, he would kill him. Eventually, he would kill them all.

Aidyn dismounted a ways away from the clearing. He could see Yayènia through the trees, but not Tlonna. The warrior was stirring a pot of what smelled like stew as she hummed in a distracted way. He was about to announce himself when a soft splash came from the still waters of the pond a few yards from Yayènia. She looked up, her hand going to her left katan, but then Tlonna's head broke the surface and the Magin gasped in a breath.

Aidyn's entire body went rigid with shock as she swam to the edge of the pond and crawled out, stark naked and glistening with water. Cursing silently to himself, he tried to tear his eyes away from her glorious beauty, but was unable. He watched her jog over to Yayènia who held out a thick blanket, and he watched her huddle in it, obviously freezing. The male bit his lip, attempting to control his body as he finally succeeded in tearing his gaze away. He wiped his sweating palms on his shirt and sucked in great breaths, turning away from the two females to stare into the forest.

Finally, he got himself under control and mounted Whäd, not wanting to look as though he had been standing there the whole time. He waited for several more minutes, and then moved her forward.

Tlonna was shivering so bad she could hardly keep her seat, but Yayènia's fire-warmed blanket and hot stew were doing wonders.

"Does this have that salted beef in it?" she asked, chewing on a rubbery piece of meat.

"Yes indeed. Everything does, as far as I am concerned," the warrior replied happily, blowing on her spoon to cool it down.

Tlonna shook her head, which was quite unnecessary because of her shivering, but she felt better for it. After a few minutes of quiet, her sister gave her the look she had been dreading.

"So, what did you see down there?"

The Magin Queen ate a few more bites and then sighed. She ran a hand over the thick brown blanket and wondered where to begin.

"There were drawings down in a cave at the bottom. Three of them, about as tall as I am. Not very ornate, but well done. They are very old, as old as the Cyree itself, for they were drawn by Astinus the Seer. It is actually quite amazing, for as aged as they are they are in good condition."

"Tlonna," Yayènia said in warning.

"All right, they are images of prophecy, the rawest form of prophecy that is not seen in the prophet's own head. As I said, there are three of them, all include me, and my opposite."

"Your opposite?"

Tlonna nodded, trying to explain that which she only knew in her heart. She was spared having to explain when a rider burst out of the forest. She and Yayènia shot to their feet in surprise, reaching for weapons.

Too late the Magin realized she was wearing only a blanket, which with her movements slid from her shoulders to puddle at her feet. Magic roared to the fore, the deadliest weapon she could muster. Yayènia let out a cry of recognition, and lowered her katans.

Tlonna blinked up at Aidyn, sitting tall and rigid on the back of his beautiful mare. His emerald gaze seemed tormented as he stared at the ground between her and Yayènia. He finally, slowly, brought his eyes up to her face and held them there. Without warning Tlonna felt a shocking jolt of pain in her chest, a breathtaking punch of air that took her to her knees. At the same time Aidyn let out a surprised grunt and clutched at his chest, his eyes going wide. Yayènia shouted at them both, confused and frightened by their actions.

Gasping for air Tlonna huddled on the ground, shivering not only from the cold against her exposed flesh, but from the burning agony in her heart.

The bond was back and stronger than ever before.

Aidyn slid off Whäd and his knees nearly buckled. The horse snorted at him, turning a judging blue eye his way. He reached up to give her a reassuring pat, but found himself clutching at her for strength instead. The overwhelming sense of Tlonna nearly knocked him over. He shuddered, trying to keep back the tears that streamed down his face. How much time went by while he stood with his face buried in Whäd's neck, he did not know.

When a warm hand reached up to touch his shoulder, Aidyn nearly lost control and struck out, but he checked himself just in time. He turned to see Tlonna standing next to him, thankfully covered again. Without a word she wrapped her arms around his ribcage and embraced him, trembling uncontrollably. He held her close, and inhaled the scent of clean water and the faint fragrance of wildflowers.

"Tlonna," he breathed, pressing his cheek to her sodden, frozen hair.

"Oh, Aidyn," she mewled back at him, her face buried in his shoulder.

"I have missed you," the assassin whispered, putting more emphases in the words than he meant to.

"As I have you, my reckless, blessed friend. How can you stand it?"

Aidyn frowned at the ground, not sure what she meant. Then he realized she must feel the physical pain he was enduring, though it barely registered on a conscious level anymore.

"I do not feel it, Tlonna, not anymore. I am beyond that level of pain now. Please, try to block it away. I do not want you to suffer for me."

"I will try. What...what are you doing here? How did you find us?" she replied, pulling away a little to look up at him.

Aidyn was unable to meet her gaze so he lifted his eyes above her head, where he was greeted with Yayènia's knowing stare. He dropped his eyes to the ground.

"I came from Purheae. Nebet'thu sent a letter of distress to Blackhaven three weeks ago. Stoffnias had a squad of his soldiers holding Eyin's village hostage. They massacred the other two beforehand. Eyin, Meradyn, and Nebet'thu stopped them from entering the Stone Hunters' village, but they could not make them leave."

Tlonna's face was ashen with fury and fear. "What happened?"

Aidyn lifted an eyebrow in sarcastic surprise. "I killed them, what do you think?"

"You killed them all? How many?"

"Twenty four, and their leader, Merbon, so twenty-five. Several of them have encountered me before so they were a little taken aback when I appeared in their midst."

"You killed Merbon?" Yayènia asked, her voice laced with envy. "I always wanted to take that worm's life."

"Well, trust me he died badly and screaming injustice," the assassin replied coldly, a malicious smile twisting his features into a mask of vengeance that would have made Tlonna take a step back were she not so glad to have him in her arms and in her heart.

"Who else was with him?" Yayènia pried, desperate to hear of her enemies' demise.

"Spy, Torsin, and Paerin, probably a few others I did not take the time to notice."

The female's features lit up with the glorious fires of redemption. "You killed Paerin?"

"Actually, a fire killed him. He had the misfortune of being at the end of his own spear when I got a hold of it."

"Brilliant!" Yayènia shrieked and pushed past Tlonna to embrace Aidyn in a rib-cracking hug.

The two fighters continued to exchange thrilled words about the demise of so many of their personal foes for a few minutes. Tlonna finally sighed loudly to interrupt them.

Aidyn grinned up at her, looking happier than he had in a very long time, and then stepped away from Yayènia, who was clutching his arms and giggling.

"How did you find us?"

The assassin shrugged. "I knew where you were headed, and I know this area quite well. It was not hard to find, that and you did not hide your trail at all."

"You tracked us?" Yayènia frowned up at him as she led the way back to the campfire.

"Once I got nearer to this place."

"This is the Cyree, a place of pure magic," Tlonna said, sweeping her arm out to include the pond, waterfall, and the narrow strip of land between the trees and the water. "This is where all magic returns one it is grounded from the body of a Magin."

When both Yayènia and Aidyn gave her blank looks, she sighed. "When I use my power, I usually do not use it all, but it lingers within my body. If I do nothing, it will sit below my skin, and apparently makes me glow. Because I do not like to glow, I ground it, push it from my body and release it into the air. It then sinks back into the earth, like water on parched ground, and makes its way back here. At the bottom of the Cyree pond is where it all coalesces. Every Magin who grounds their power sends it here, though not consciously. It is like an underground river, constantly flowing, moving in a circle to return to its home waters."

"So...magic only exists because of this pond?" Aidyn asked, confused.

"No," Tlonna said, shaking her head, "magic existed long before this place did, for magic has always existed. It is like the space above us, immortal, all that is and was. It has no intentions, it simply is. But the first Magins created the Cyree pond, and Cyree the guardian who no longer subsists in order to bring control to magic. Before the Cyree, power simply floated about, wreaking havoc all over the world. When they contained it here, the strange incidences stopped."

"What incidences?" Yayènia muttered, having never heard any of this.

Tlonna gave her a small, amused smile. "Explosions destroying towns. Babies being born with extra limbs, or not enough. Crops withering for no reason, people bursting into flame unexpectedly. Random happenings that no one could explain, so they shook their fists at the skies and damned the gods, or those with strange pastimes. People with magical abilities who did not know that was what their problem was. Understand?"

Both warriors nodded, feeling a little put off.

"Well, once the Magins, Tayrn Verla and Reatun Fall, in particular, completed the Cyree, the magic-born havoc ceased, at last having a place to call home, in essence. Because it is pure, anyone who touches it automatically becomes a part of it, for the magic takes anything impure and morphs it to its state. It cannot allow a pure form of itself to wander out in the world, and begin the cycle of devastation anew."

"Why would someone who had touched the Cyree begin the cycle again? How would that happen? Does not every Magin use its flow to Weave? Is that not releasing it into the world?" Yayènia countered, frowning at the still pond with its silent waterfall.

"We do, but the magic comes up through energy fields all around us, the very earth and air itself courses through our bodies and then manifests itself through the threads of power we call upon. Each Weave consists of an element, Fire, Earth, Air, Water, and Spirit, which comes from below the surface of the earth. As the power comes up through our bodies, and morphs into the elemental thread, it changes, taking on the personal aspects of the Magin. That is why each Magin has an individual color to their power."

"But I have seen more than one with red or black magic, a few green, even two browns," Aidyn said, completely befuddled now.

Tlonna offered a quiet smile of understanding. "Yes, but each of those colors, while similar, is indeed unique. Have you ever noticed how Losolin's magic comes out with striations of darker green twisting about, whereas mine, when it was only white, came out pure white?"

"We always thought that had to do with the amount of power you were capable of summoning," Yayènia muttered, folding her arms as she poked the fire.

"It has nothing to do with strength, and everything to do with character and intention. Losolin's power is mostly a healing magic, but he can do some pretty destructive stuff with it when he is angry or fearful. I, on the other hand, can only destroy, and my intentions are usually focused on angry justice. If you remember, both Haydyn and Midian had black magic?"

Aidyn and Yayènia nodded, staring at each other as Tlonna dressed and then sat and wrapped the blanket over her shoulders once more.

"Though in Midian it made sense, Haydyn had a good heart, and good intentions for nearly everything he did. So why did he have the same cruel looking power?"

Yayènia shrugged weakly. "Because he had an evil father?"

"Then Sithian and Rhiannan would have had the same black strength. It was because of the sadness in his heart. The darker a power is, the more mournful the soul that wields it."

"But...but Midian!" the commander stammered, disbelieving.

"Midian knew himself to be utterly alone, and he carried within him a great sadness for it. He never showed it to anyone, but I was forced to look into his eyes day after day, and there, beneath that cruel, warped anger was a misery more profound than anything I have ever seen," Tlonna replied softly, her mind's eye far away, seeing the tortured man's haunted gaze glaring at her from behind an icy, perfect façade. "Everyone, from the gentlest to the most vicious yearns to be loved by someone or something. Midian wanted to be loved by his people, believing as he did that he was delivering them from the cruelty of a nation where lived races that were superior to theirs, if only because of their longer existence. He wanted to be loved by his slaves, by his captives, but most of all by his people."

"Then why is yours so light?" Aidyn asked, knowing intimately the grief in Tlonna's own heart.

Tlonna was silent for a bit, looking at the ground between her feet, contemplating the assassin's loaded question. She knew the answer, but she did not know how to explain it without terrifying her two closest friends. Finally, she took a deep breath and lifted her gaze to the fire.

"My power is white for the same reason I can submerge myself in the Cyree and not become leashed to it. I am...not really a Magin. I am something else."

"What?" Aidyn's utter was just above a whisper, the silky smoothness of his voice lifting on the air like a sigh of wind.

Tlonna continued to stare into the fire, focusing on a white-hot ember deep in the center. "I am a Magin, but more than that. I am a channel. Magic flows through me like a sieve. I can hear the spirits at all times along with Jair's shade, which I absorbed in Purheae, because like the Cyree, I am a pure form of power. If you were able to see the bottom of the pond you would see streaks of white running through the viscous form of magic like ink dropped into a glass of water. The whiteness is the absence of all influence from a third party. I do not draw my power from within myself; I draw it directly from here. If I were to be the vessel for all the magic I control, I would cease to be, dissolved by the pure essence of power.

"There is a reserve of magic within me, of course, that which I was born with, but the great amount of it that you see me wield during battle is coming directly from here, streaming through my body, not from it. In that way I am not a Magin, because all Magins hold within them their full amount of power at all times. When they Weave, the second it leaves their touch it is being replaced, so that they are constantly full. If they exhaust themselves, it is because their bodies cannot take the strain anymore, the magic is still all there. When they finish, there is a vestige of power lingering in their hands that needs to be grounded, given back, otherwise they are like a too-full cup, overflowing with power, and it will spill out of them uncontrolled. I too have to ground myself because as I draw from here, it flows through my body, up through my center, and when I stop it does not drain back down, it simply sits there, waiting to be used. That is why I glow when I do not ground it out. That power is an unhealthy amount to carry within a body, even an elven body. If I did not let it go, the magic would eventually begin to dissolve my very flesh and bone."

Yayènia and Aidyn sat staring at her with nearly identical blank expressions. Finally her sister spoke, her words carefully chosen.

"So, what is the limit of your strength? At which point would you simply not be able to do anything further?"

Tlonna thought again how to phrase her answer before replying. "I am not strong enough to level the entire kingdom of Blackhaven in a single blow, but I could take out the city and probably half the forest before I was torn apart by the magic. I could do that in less than five minutes and not a single person within that two hundred mile radius would have more than dust as their remains. The people on the fringes of it would most likely suffer pulverized bones, seared flesh, and their heads would probably explode. Belgarath and Asheyl would suffer massive headaches and a few broken limbs. Andik would feel a concussion in the earth, but not suffer for it. I would not even be a pile of dust on the ground."

Again stunned silence fell as the two gaped at her in utter astonishment, never expecting such an answer. Again it was Yayènia who broke it.

"I did not know magic was so complicated. I thought Magins just had it within them, like blood, and if they used too much of it, they died, like blood loss."

"We do."

"Yes, but I did not know it went back into the earth, to converge here, just to be used again, over and over like water. And I always believed the colors to be dictated by strength and personality,

A.B.B. Olson

not intention. And...I never thought it could be strong enough to wipe out thousands of people like that, literally wipe them from the face of the earth. I knew it was powerful, and could be used as a weapon, but I did not think it was capable of that much destruction."

Tlonna looked up at her, finally removing her gaze from the fire. Yayènia was staring straight at her, the icy blue of her irises steady and fearless, simply concerned.

"Magic is the very force of this world, Yayènia, it is the basis of all religion, the scapegoat for uneducated people's problems, and the very essence of life. We breathe it in even now, and we expel it back into the air with each exhale. Our minds are inebriated with it, our souls languishing in it. It infuses everything."

"But you said it was all contained in the pond!" Aidyn argued, a scowl of confusion on his face, his finger pointed at the Cyree.

"There is more than one type of magic, my friends. That is what I am saying. There is the tangible force that Yayènia and I use, though in different capacities, and then there is the invisible, unnoticed magic of emotion and intent."

"What?" both warriors said at once, straightening their backs as they stared at her.

"Have you never felt the prickling at the back of your neck as a sense of danger? Or the sour, dry taste of fear on your tongue? Or the intoxicating, heady sense of authority lightening your very body? Have you never experienced the rushing, warming sense of love driving you to do something reckless and exciting? Or the godlike sense of strength you get while in a frightened or angry rampage? What do you think that is?"

"Emotion, feelings," Yayènia muttered as she hunched back down.

"It is a form of magic. It is just as capable of destroying a town as my type. I need you to understand that. Emotion is the strongest catalyst of reaction there is. It lacks the reason of calculated magic, but not the potency. Brandon Stynbek had no magic, but he managed to nullify the defiant strength of the entire Dwarven nation, and put the whole of the Elven nation into slavery and imprisonment. How do you think he did that?"

Tlonna waited for a second, but knew no response was coming. "He used his emotion, coupled with his ability to manipulate the emotion of others, to perform great deeds. Though they were terrible and wrong he moved people to great extremes using only words. I think that this is very important to understand in this battle. Emotion is the driving force behind this war."

"Be that as it may," Aidyn began, shifting on his cold seat, "the soldiers driven before Sithian and his savagery have lost what reasoning they may have had. They lust now only for blood and women, so what difference does it make?"

Tlonna shrugged, the tense mood broken. "I just wanted you to know that this magic," she gestured at the Cyree, "is not the only one in the world, and not the only thing to be feared."

Yayènia sat up, and arched her back to stretch it. She slanted a look at Aidyn. "What are you doing here? Certainly you did not traverse the width of Nymyños, through what is currently hostile territory, to let us know Purheae had been taken hostage and is now free."

The assassin got up and motioned to Whäd, who walked closer, trailing her reins on the frosty ground. He began to remove her tack as he spoke.

"Miazie...she killed Martin Crotes."

"What!?" Tlonna and Yayènia both yelped, their surprise evident.

"He was withholding information, secret plots discovered by his spies, and so she killed him for it."

"Apparently she has been hanging around with you two a little more than she should," Tlonna said dryly. "Anything else I need to know about?"

"*Aiya*, the Merchant's Guild is trying to pass an amendment that would increase their profits by ten percent, taking it from the throne and the individual sellers. Miazie is battling that right now. And...she had a vision."

"A vision?" the queen asked, pinching the bridge of her nose as a creeping headache threatened her calm.

"Yes, she saw the three of us wandering through Purheae Forest."

"That is it? Just us three walking through the trees? Nothing more detailed?" Yayènia pressed when Tlonna remained silent.

Aidyn shook his head as he began currying Whäd's flanks. "That was it."

"How helpful. So that is why you came? Because she saw that?"

The assassin glanced at the warrior, slightly frowning. "Partly, and I figured I was already this close, I might as well meet up with you."

"Aidyn, you were in Purheae!"

"Which is much closer than Blackhaven, Nia. Why are you so upset I am here?"

Yayènia huffed and relented. "I am not upset. I am just curious."

Tlonna watched their exchange with interest, considering the many crucibles their friendship had been through. It was not easy to remain close with someone who had driven a sword through your belly, no matter how defensive the move was. She noticed a slight tension between them that seemed to disappear entirely at times, like when they had been reveling in the Seadueni deaths. Now it was back, sitting among them like a fourth person.

Once Aidyn had finished taking care of his magnificent piebald mare, tethering her with Udu and Takîreaes, he reclaimed his seat. He gratefully accepted the bowl of steaming stew Tlonna handed him and crouched over its warmth. Yayènia waited for him to take a bite before turning to her sister.

"How do you know all this? Last I heard, you and Losolin had not recovered your memories, because Miazie has them, along with many of your earlier years. Years of study and experience. How do you know so much about magic when you are still relatively new to it?"

The queen picked up her discarded bowl and eyed it critically. It was still steaming. She sucked air in to try and soothe it as she took a bite, not wanting to swallow the blistering food just yet. Yayènia's ice blue eyes were fixed on her face, her own bowl settled between her knees, ignored. Finally Tlonna was able to swallow without too much harm, wondering how Aidyn didn't seem bothered by it, and let out a breath.

"You are correct in saying I still do not remember most of my childhood, or my years at the Academy and so on. I have, however, been reclaiming that knowledge by more archaic means."

"How?" the warrior demanded, suspicious.

"Reading," Tlonna replied wryly with a smiled at her sister's irritated glower. "I have been reading the books I read those many years ago. But, as for what I know about magic, I have been reading Father's books."

"Dietirin wrote a book?" Yayènia gasped, forgetting as always that he was her father as well.

"Several, in fact," Tlonna confirmed, daring another bite. "He was over a thousand years old, and had been trained by his father Damian in the ways of magic. He knew nearly all there was to know, and he wrote it all down. From the simplest meditation methods to the most complex, deadly Weaves. Even though he could not perform the things I can, he knew how to do them. He is the one who introduced me to the magic of emotion. He understood that without an underlying foundation of belief and sentiment nothing true could ever be accomplished, including Maginic Weaving. He spoke about Aidyn in that regard."

The assassin nearly swallowed his spoon in surprise, coughing violently as he choked on it.

"What?" he wheezed, his eyes watering.

Tlonna smirked at him. "He said that 'my closest friend and protector, Aidyn Sestuns, can perform amazing feats of strength, stealth, and acrobatics that even I cannot fathom, nor come close to executing with my rather considerable power. He comports himself with a well-earned pride and dignity, coupled with his singular ferocity, and twists this combination into the deadly force that is his body. I have seen him in a fatal rage, which allowed him to put his fist through a dwarf's head, shattering the very skull within like glass. Only through a pure, seething fury could this be accomplished, even with his incredible physique. This is the magic of emotion, the undeniable strength of passion.'

"The entire book is like that, using both of you, and Ghealan as examples of magical emotion, though Aidyn is by far the most used," Tlonna said, trying to hide her smile at the assassin's stunned expression.

"He talks about me too?" Yayènia asked, sounding for a moment like a needy child.

"Yes, he talks about how you seem to slip away from injury even while you are blinded by anger. He calls it your 'void of fury', where all you feel and see is anger and threats."

"I remember that day," Aidyn muttered as he studied his fist. "The dwarf's name was Froloh, and he had just killed his wife and child in a fit of drunken anger. Dietirin and I tracked him down and I hit him in the face. At first I thought I had missed, because my fist was out in the open, and then I realized it was covered in blood, brains, and hair. His head literally exploded from the force of my punch. Dietirin was ill for a week and would not speak to me."

Tlonna gave him a quiet smile. She reached across the gap between them to grip his hand in hers. "He loved you Aidyn, you know that?"

The dark elf nodded silently. He gave her hand a little squeeze and then let it go so he could finish his stew. Yayènia was also silent, reflecting on what Tlonna had told her. Together, the three of them contemplated the mysteries of the elf that had been Dietirin, father and friend to two of them, best friend to the other. Finally, Tlonna finished her meal and cleaned out her bowl using water from her canteen.

She went over to visit the horses for a bit, scratching poor Whäd's nose as she was being nuzzled by both stallions. She combed her fingers through Takîreaes's long sable mane as he put aside his affections for the new female to bury his nose in Tlonna's shoulder, huffing loudly. The elf laughed softly and gently kneaded his impressive muscles. The stallion nipped at her hip, hoping for a treat.

"You be nice to Whäd, she is not your lady, though a fine little one you two would make," Tlonna murmured to him, smiling broadly.

Udu nudged her from across Whäd's back, wanting attention. She scratched his jaw and nose, running her palm across the gray splotch on his velvety nose. When the horses were finally satisfied with her attention and went back to their eating and teasing, Tlonna wandered back to Yayènia and Aidyn, who were discussing Miazie's erratic behavior. She groaned quietly as she sat down, feeling the ache of her swim earlier.

Aidyn glanced at her, his emerald eyes flashing in the firelight, and seemed to check her for injury. Tlonna gave him a look of utter innocence, pleased with his presence, and his apparent full recovery. Though she could hardly believe the pain she felt from him, it did not seem to bother him at all. Their night passed with uneventful conversation and firelight.

Tlonna yawned and rolled herself up even tighter in her sleeping roll, flexing her toes as a slight chillness crept inside her and

Yayènia's tent. She felt safer than she had in a long time, with her deadly sister's back pressed against hers, and Aidyn just a few feet away in his own tent. There seemed a palpable sense of security blanketed around her, and she smiled in the darkness. Even though she ached for Losolin's arms around her, Tlonna was content enough feeling Aidyn's presence through the bond.

She longed to have the same link with her husband, but knew it would never work as Losolin did not have the same oath bound ties as Aidyn. Though he did not seem to know, or at least acknowledge the fact, there was magic in the Honor of Assassins, a visceral force that linked his intention to his soul. Tlonna wondered vaguely if it had anything to do with the three identical scars slashing across his palms, the trinity of cuts given him when he swore the oaths, and again when he became Master. Yawning again, the Magin tried to shut off her racing, wandering mind. It was a long time before she got to sleep, her last conscious thoughts about Losolin, and hoped he was safe.

# Chapter 15

## The Final Battle Begins

Losolin sat atop a rigid Neñyos, staring out across the wide expanse of field. There had been disturbing news of late, a mysterious rider galloping through the battlefield in the middle of the night, and Sithian leaving behind his general. Though he knew the boy was unstable, Losolin had a hard time seeing anyone abandon their troops. Suneelo and Ghealan were equally baffled by Sithian's behavior, scowling in confusion when the report came in. The king had learned to greatly appreciate the scouts and spies, never before having the opportunity to use them.

Losolin turned to the left when Ghealan rode up next to him, looking as daunting as ever in his armor.

"How long?" he asked the giant elf, unsettled by his quiet.

Ghealan continued to watch the growing plume of dust as he considered his answer. Finally he drew his sword and braced it against his thigh.

"They are here."

Losolin frowned at the distant cloud. "But it is far away!"

"No, they are here."

The Magin opened his mouth to reply but it was drowned out by a sudden roar. Thousands of screaming men poured over the crest of the ridge a quarter mile away, brandishing their weapons in menace. Their slow and quiet approach had been hidden by the running cavalry behind. Cavalry, Losolin now believed, that was running in a large circle to raise a dust cloud that would fool them.

Losolin and Ghealan snapped hard on the reins of their horses to urge them into a gallop. With the enemy hot on their tails, the warhorses bellowed and tugged at their bits, wanting their heads. The two elves reached the line of ready phalanx elves, their fine-boned faces set into a line of dangerous sneers, ready and willing to clash against the oncoming horde.

Ghealan yanked his big stallion around, pulling him in a hard circle so that he could face the advancing enemy. The horse reared up and nearly pirouetted in order to obey his person's command. Losolin spurred Neñyos onward through the opening aisle in the soldiers, swinging his sword above his head to rouse his soldiers. They responded with a cheer that shook the very ground as they stamped their feet and bellowed as only battle-hardened warriors can.

The king finally found his brother and Orthak, the dwarf Captain of Infantry, standing amid the *Zephyr Leifen.* The silver-cloaked fighters bowed low when he dismounted and patted a heaving Neñyos on the neck.

"It looks to be nearly their entire force, probably seventy percent on foot with few archers," he said briefly to Suneelo and Orthak.

The dwarf tugged on his beard and huffed, his feet spread as he thought. "I wonder what that boy said to Orlando when he left. Certainly he wouldn't say 'throw all my troops into a pitched battle against 'em just to see what comes', would he?"

Losolin shrugged. "Sithian is on a slippery slope of insanity. Tlonna thinks he was driven insane while he was still very young by Midian's cruel rearing. Then, having been on his own for quite some time he never had anyone to correct him. Now he is a child playing with fire, and he is spreading it everywhere with his carelessness."

Orthak grunted, "I still don't think he would have been happy with this."

Suneelo clapped the dwarf on the back. "Well, since I do not care whether or not he is happy, I say take what gifts are given us without complaint!"

Orthak ripped his axe out of his belt and lifted it high in the air. He swung it about with abandon as he howled. The Silvers all grinned their ominous smiles and followed the dwarf's example. Losolin stood amidst a circle of completely mad warriors. There was a ripple through the lines standing in front of them and seconds later the angry sounds of fighting ripped through the air. Suneelo grabbed his brother's arm and shoved him back a few steps, out of the ring of Silvers and away from Orthak.

Losolin glowered at him. "What? Do you expect me to stand to the side and let my people die while I do nothing?"

"Of course not," Suneelo scoffed, "but I would prefer you not get torn apart by them."

He pointed at the silver-cloaked warriors who had all drawn steel and were linking elbows. It was a strange sight to see, elf linking with dwarf, dwarf with human, spryte with elf, and so on until it was a large circle with Orthak in the center. Their gauntleted hands grabbed onto a strange ring Losolin had never noticed before that anchored their linked arm to their free bicep. It was the most confusing formation the king had ever seen. One of the regular cavalry soldiers mounted up and looked to Orthak, who nodded. The soldier slapped his sword hard against his horse's withers and sent it into a panicked run. The roiling army split like a curtain, wide enough to allow the ring of Silvers through.

Suddenly the purpose became clear to Losolin. As soon as they reached the battlefront they started running to the side, spinning in a great circle. The Zaedicans were slaughtered as the wheeling ring of sharpened steel cleaved through the ranks, unstoppable because no soldier knew who to fight. An opponent was before him only for a split second before the next one came running in to finish him off. Losolin stared in shocked awe, never considering such a move even possible.

Orthak ran in the center like a living pivot and smashed in the heads of any foe who somehow slipped between the spinning warriors, or who was simply trampled underfoot. Suneelo gestured to the now distant ring as the army closed back in.

"Yayènia is usually in the center, a position they like to call the spoke. They usually get so sore and beaten from this move that they cannot fight for a day or two after, because of the tremendous strain they put on their arms, but I have never seen it fail."

"Why did they do it now? We are not desperate yet."

Suneelo smiled. "Why should we wait to become desperate before taking out great numbers of the enemy with a single devastating move? Why should we save all our tricks for the last?"

Losolin shrugged his acceptance of the logic. "Why did they not do it at Alchemian?"

"The landscape was too rough. If even one of them trips, the entire ring can go down. I have seen it happen when they practice. Nia will set up obstacle courses for them to run through, and I once saw someone trip, and the entire line shattered and whipped about, still linked. There were several broken bones, mostly elbow and shoulder joints that were shattered. There was also a time I saw one of them trip, and the two on either side caught him and held him up in time, carrying him until he got his feet back under him, still 'fighting'."

"Impressive."

"They are not considered the elite fighting squad of Nymyños for no reason, Losolin. You have to remember that each one of those warriors has been personally selected and trained by Yayènia. She has no tolerance for the word failure or impossible. She will try the craziest thing because it just might work, things other people are too terrified, or logical, to even consider thinking about. She thought up this move, which she calls the wheel and spoke for obvious reasons, and tried it out the next day. It took her more than three years to figure out a possible way to do it, and ten for it to become what it is now. They had the ring attached to their bicep about halfway through the process, and only within the last two has it developed well enough for any real use."

"How so?" Losolin asked, intrigued.

Suneelo grabbed his own bicep and twisted his hand about. "There is a thick band of steel on their arms, padded with leather so it does not cause burning or freezing, and that band has another laid on the inside, not attached, just around it and oiled so that it can spin. The ring is attached to that movable piece which allows their sword arms and linked arms the ability to move a little more. Often times, before they added the second band, they would come back with broken fingers, wrists, even broken humerus bones."

Losolin grunted his appreciation of the technology and turned to watch the milling mass of people in front of him. "When do you think we will get to fight?"

The captain chuckled. "Soon enough, I suppose."

His words proved too true. Minutes later the line broke as a strong charge drove right through the Blackhaven soldiers. The enemy pushed them to the side and went straight for the king and his brother. Guards popped out of nowhere to form a protective circle around Losolin, their blades crossing to form giant Xs. The Magin tightened his grip on the hilt of his sword. He wanted to reserve all his power for healing when the time came rather than expend his energy fighting with his relatively weak destructive powers. Suneelo shouted orders as he searched for Ghealan in the press of bodies.

The snarling visages of the Zaedican force sneered through the gaps between the guards and tried desperately to get at their target. The guards were holding them back with little effort as they advanced their phalanx formation and sliced the enemy to ribbons. Screams arose all around the tight group though Losolin had no way to tell whether the cries were from his people or the invaders.

The press of Zaedicans lightened with each heave from the guards, many of them simply being shoved down and trampled. Losolin had no choice but to move with them as the ring around him advanced. Suneelo seemed on edge as he walked slowly beside him as they were moved along. The brothers stood shoulder to shoulder, turning as they watched the battle rage around them.

Soon enough the attack was driven back, but the battle did not ease up. Suneelo slipped out of the ring of his guards and disappeared into the melee, his slender sword flashing in the sunlight. Snow was turning to muddy, bloody slush as Losolin stood within his protective circle and hated it. Then suddenly a surprised wedge of men crashed through the ring of guards, caroming into the king. The wild look on their faces told Losolin that he had not been their intended target, but they were not disappointed.

He ducked under the savage swing of the closest man, spun lightly on the ball of his foot, and sliced his sword across the exposed belly of the man. He had to dance back a few steps to avoid the crazy slashing of a war axe wielded by a brutishly large man, and then he dashed forward. He used his slender build and lighter form to dart in the opposite direction of the heavy swing. The man died gargling steel, his yellowed eyes wide with surprise at such an end. Losolin yanked his sword out of the man's throat, spun to meet the next attacker, but found instead one of his guards standing a few feet in front of him, gaping in shock at his king's actions.

Losolin looked around to find that his protectors had immediately turned to the threat that had bulldozed through them and dispatched them without too much fuss. All the guards were eyeing him in new regard.

"I was a peasant and a soldier long before I was king, remember," he said to them all, lifting an eyebrow as he cleaned off his sword.

As one the guards bowed and turned away once again to protect their not so helpless ruler. The battle dragged on for several hours, with Losolin moving slowly in his steel ring. Suneelo popped in every so often to give him reports, and to check on him. At one point Losolin grabbed his brother's elbow and hauled him back.

"Here is an idea. Why not I go out, and you stay here and be the poor defenseless noble standing uselessly in the middle of a ring of guards?"

Suneelo scowled at him. "You are King Losolin. I am Captain Suneelo. Our titles say why."

"I am perfectly capable of fighting, Suneelo! Let me out of here!" Losolin shouted and brandished his sword in the air.

The captain adamantly refused to let his brother out of the ring of guards, and then slipped between two of them as he went to rejoin the fight. Losolin fumed at the back of a broad-shouldered human who stood directly in front of him. He was still fuming as a foot of steel erupted from between the shoulder blades of the man, startling him so much he stumbled back. All around his guards began struggling, fighting with a yet unseen foe. Losolin waited as calmly as he could, hopelessly wishing he could get to the broad human to heal him, but another guard had stepped in to fill the spot and was straddling the body with his booted feet.

Then that guard fell, a morning star buried in his skull, to leave the path open to Losolin. He swore in revulsion as black-cloaked Darkwights filled his vision. The demons had not revealed themselves until now, and he had believed they had all deserted Sithian's cause. Apparently he had been wrong.

"Peassant elf king," one of them hissed, swinging his giant morning star.

"Demon."

The twisted creature hissed and came for him, the air whistled between the large spikes on the deadly weapon as it sailed through the air. Losolin ducked low to avoid the crushing blow by mere inches, and then skittered to the side, yanked out a throwing dagger and tossed it hard. The small blade buried itself into the hip of the demon, which caused it to stumble. Losolin took the opening as it came, kicking his boot heel into the exposed face of the Darkwight, and followed it with his sword.

Others came in, barely hindered by the valiant effort of the guards. Losolin danced back again to assess his options. Four of the demons stood before him, holding a variety of weapons. He knew from experience they were deadly warriors as well as wickedly strong and fast. Two held curved elfish swords, possibly from when they had once been elves, and the other two held a club and spear. They all came for him at once. Losolin dodged the club as he decided death by sword was better than being clobbered. He groped for another throwing knife, but he did not have time to get it out. A boot smashed into his fist, knocking the blade from his hand, and perhaps breaking a knuckle or two. The Magin ignored the pain and brought his vambraced forearm up to block a stab from the spear and sent the weapon up high over his head. He kicked into the groin of the wielder and snatched the spear as it thunked down to his shoulder. Losolin twisted his grip on it, yanked it from the Darkwight's hand. He jerked the spear back and then forward again, and smacked it into the face of the creature. He turned just in time to avoid being skewered by one of the swords, twisting his ribs away from the blow.

The club sailed an inch away from his ear, smashing hard onto his right shoulder, numbing his entire sword arm. He held onto his weapon with tenacity though, and backed up as he searched for an opening. A wall of black velvet was all he saw. Frustrated, the Magin lashed out with his power and sent a bolt of crackling green lightning into the club-wielding demon. It howled and shrieked and dropped its weapon to claw at its body. The Darkwight stumbled back, fell, and started twitching on the ground as lightning scorched up his spine.

Losolin did not watch the spectacle as he was already engaged with the three others. He kicked out at one of the swords as it came in from the side as he slashed down to parry the other. The spear came at him from the other side, which he avoided by jerking his belly back just in time. He hopped once to regain his balance and then smashed his fist into the face of the demon right in front of him. It reeled back, clutching its shattered nose. Losolin snarled in defiance and punched it again, this time driving bone up into the brain. The Darkwight dropped like a sack of potatoes as the king dove backward to avoid the slashing weapons that came at him from the side. He stabbed his blade into the toe of the last sword wielder and then brought it up with a vicious yank to cleave the demon's face in two. The spear finally caught him but it glanced off his armor and dove harmlessly to the side. Again Losolin grabbed it and pulled hard, yanking the Darkwight forward. He brought his knee up into the demon's chin. Blood sprayed as the blackened tongue was bitten in half. His sword sheared through flesh and bone to explode out of the creature's back and severed the spine.

Panting, Losolin looked around at his guards who were still fighting the more regular soldiers. Several lay on the bloody, cold ground, and many of them writhed in the throes of death. Immediately the king sheathed his sword and went to his knees, hands already glowing. He healed a young man with a gaping hole in his chest, and several older guards with shattered bones or hemorrhaging wounds. The two soldiers he had watched go down were long dead, one missing half his head.

Getting to his feet along with the grateful and breathless guards, Losolin turned to those still fighting. He saw one get his side ripped open by a jagged axe, and went to him as he began to fall. The elf's glowing hand caught the soldier and pushed him upright as his other ripped out his sword and stabbed the enemy before him. The guard's face went from pale to flushed as the pain receded and his wound closed.

"My lord!" he gasped, eyes wide with awe.

"I need you alive, my friend," Losolin said and smiled as he steadied the young man.

The guard nodded emphatically and set his feet wide to wait for the next attack with renewed vigor. The Magin wandered around the ring, healing those with even the most minor of injuries, knowing they had received them in the duty of protecting him. They all panted their thanks as he moved on. Losolin felt a shift in the fighting and put a hand on an elf next to him.

"What is it?" he asked, pulling himself up on the slightly taller guard.

"Looks like they are retreating, King Losolin," the warrior replied softly. "Here come the Silvers."

Losolin peered out at the thinning ranks of soldiers as they chased after the retreating enemy. But they could only go out so far before they had to turn back. And indeed the silver-cloaked warriors were returning, Orthak and Ghealan at their head. The Magin frowned at the conspicuous absence of his brother.

The commander casually glanced at the carnage on the ground. "They are in full retreat, Losolin. I do not know what they hoped to accomplish, but I do not believe they succeeded in it. The losses on our side were remarkably small considering how much vaster their force is."

Losolin nodded. "Where is Suneelo? And Sargotarh?"

Ghealan nodded to the right. "Sar is dispatching a few mercenaries that decided to surrender, and Neel is off yelling at the infantry that let the crush break through them."

The Magin breathed a sigh of relief. He looked to Orthak. "How did the wheel and spoke fare?"

The dwarf patted his gory axe. "We took 'em by surprise, and we took 'em down. I think we took out a solid thousand. We had to break and fight solitary on the way back through because we ran into their cavalry. We lost Max, but he went down with five of the enemy, so he died a beautiful death I can assure ya. Laren has his body."

Losolin looked at the miniscule elf who had a body draped over his shoulder. Laren's dainty face was somber as he clutched his fallen comrade. The king had heard that the elf was half tree-elf, though no one would ever ask the warrior. Not even Yayènia knew.

"He will be given a burial of honor tonight, unless he had a death request," Losolin finally said as he turned back to Orthak.

The dwarf shook his head. "He didn't have any family, far's I know. I say give him a warrior's pyre."

"It shall be done. Thank you my friend," the king replied and gestured to Laren.

After the pyre for Max and the larger, lower pyres for the rest of the dead were beginning to die down, Losolin convened with his officers, a much smaller group than the one that had been at Alchemian. Ghealan, Suneelo, Sargotarh, and Orthak watched him as he paced, their faces closed and somber.

"Why did they attack today?" he asked yet again of the males who knew more about war than he ever would.

Ghealan finally leaned forward, the heel of his boot digging a trench in the ground as he spoke quietly. "The Seaduens Militant was not among the numbers that attacked. They are still back in the camp, though a separate camp to be sure. They are holding back, waiting for the invaders to weaken us enough and then they will ride in and take us out. Their tactics are deadly. They have entire companies that will do the wheel and spoke move, though on a much greater scale."

"Is that where Yayènia got the idea?" Losolin asked the commander.

"No, they got it from her. Stoffnias saw her and the Silvers practicing it and stole the move. Fortunately for us, we know the counter-move to it, they do not," Ghealan said, now moving his toe over the trench to smooth it out. "But it matters not. What does is what are we going to do when they decide to join the battle?"

"Who says they're going to? They hate humans more than they hate us," Orthak muttered. He folded his thick arms across his middle as he frowned at his companions. "Maybe they're just sittin' back to watch us tear each other apart, and pick up the spoils. Those Seadueni thugs are not beyond such a thing."

Losolin shook his head. "You are right, they are not, but I do not think that is what they are doing. I think they are waiting for the reason Ghealan says. So, what do we do? You all are the military minds of the millennia, not me!"

Suneelo gave him an odd look. "Yayènia is the military mind of the millennia, not us. Lan is the next best thing, though."

Ghealan sighed heavily as he braced his forearms on his knees. "What we need is a good raid to shock them out of their passiveness. Send the Silvers in with another five hundred soldiers in the middle of the night to set their camp aflame."

"Do we send them to the Zaedican camp, or the Seadueni?" Losolin asked, liking the idea.

"Seaduens has entered this war wrongly. It is time they were taught a lesson," the commander said, his voice harsh with condemnation. "Send them a nightmare."

"When?"

Ghealan and Suneelo shared a look. "Tonight."

"But they just lost Max," Losolin argued. "Will they not grieve?"

"How do you think warriors grieve, Lord Losolin? They take revenge on those who cause it," Sargotarh said, the words all the more disturbing because of his innocent features.

"All right, do it. Who will lead them?"

"I will," Sargotarh replied immediately, standing and stretching his back. "I lost a good friend today. I plan to take many of theirs."

Losolin nodded his agreement and the elf walked out of the tent to gather the warriors. He turned to the others. "Who was his friend?"

"Max," Suneelo said softly. "He trained him from childhood when his parents were stricken with fever and died. Sar thought of him as his son, but when Max got older and they fought side by side, their bond turned from father and son to brothers."

Losolin nodded in the silence. A sudden thought struck him as the others began to get up. "What about the wheel and spoke? The Silvers will be too exhausted and sore to fight so soon."

Orthak shook his head. "Trust me, Lord Losolin, the ache does not really set in until the next day. That and the fires of revenge will burn even that away tonight. They will be fine."

The king felt his own exhaustion setting in, not only from the fighting he had done but also from the extensive healing he had done during and after the battle. He yawned but tried to hide it behind his hand. Suneelo gave him a little push.

"Sleepy so soon little brother?"

"Respect your king," Losolin muttered, twisting his torso to stretch out his sore muscles.

Suneelo snorted loudly. "Whatever. Get to bed and rest. We need your strength to last."

"Did you know Ghealan calls you Neel?" the Magin asked suddenly. He had never heard the nickname before.

"Yes," the captain drawled, eyeing him. "Three hundred years of friendship often leads to shortened names."

"No one shortens my name."

"What, do you want us to call you Los, or Lin? How about Oso?"

Losolin smiled at his brother's tease. "All right, all right. What about Aidyn?"

"What about him?"

"What is his nickname?"

Suneelo smirked. "You would have to ask him. He threatened us all with bodily harm if we continued calling him it, and if we ever told anyone what it was."

"You and who else? What was it?" Losolin asked, absurdly eager for such unimportant talk.

"Lan, Nia, Erd, Dietirin, and myself."

When he realized his brother was not going to tell him, Losolin dropped the subject, determined to get it out of Aidyn when next he saw the assassin. It must have been bad.

"Do you think this raid will be successful?" he finally asked as they reached his tent.

Suneelo's shoulders went rigid for a second and then slumped slightly. He shook his blond head. "I do not know. With Yayènia, they are one smooth group. Without her, they are not as flawless as usual. This is the first battle they have ever fought without her. She may not always fight with them, but she is always around which gives them great confidence and determination to prove themselves worthy. I am not saying they are slacking in her absence, but they do not feel as invincible."

"You did not answer my question," Losolin murmured when his brother fell silent.

Suneelo looked uncomfortable for a moment. "Max should not have died today. He was one of the best human fighters I have ever seen in my life. He defeated me in hand-to-hand combat once; hit me in the face so hard I woke up in hospital several hours later. Nia chewed both our heads off for good long time. But other than her, no one else has ever beaten me in hand-to-hand, including Sar, who trained Max, and was trained by Aidyn. It will work, but we will have too many casualties on our side. It may be that three of them die, but three is too many when talking about a group of forty-odd fighters.

"You must remember that they are going up against elven warriors, not human or demon. The Seadueni will be surprised at first but they will retaliate quickly, and they will recognize the silver cloaks. That will infuriate them beyond reason."

"That could be a good thing," Losolin argued. "Fighters lacking reason lack focus and make mistakes."

Suneelo nodded. "Absolutely, but what it takes away in focus it replaces with strength. A human Silver going against a raging elf will have a hard time keeping his limbs intact. But I do not see the future. Perhaps I am being grim and unhelpful and this night will go off without a hitch."

Losolin smiled faintly as he began stripping off his armor. "Perhaps. Get some rest Suneelo. You will need it tomorrow."

The brothers said goodnight, and the king went to sleep with worries on his mind. The nightmares permitted little rest.

# Chapter 16
## The Divinely Deluded

The haunting melody filtered through the trees like a soft wind. Tlonna was drawn to it, her soul brought to a surrender-like peace. Suddenly they broke upon a clearing littered with benches, aged tents, a large blackened pole, and an altar of sorts covered in candles and oils. Nearly a dozen people gaped at them, their wretched-looking bodies covered in tattered rags.

Yayènia and Aidyn shared an odd look, their hands going for their respective twin blades.

Aidyn's voice came out quiet and cold, sending shivers up Tlonna's spine. It was the voice of the Master Assassin.

"Monotheists. Kill them."

Tlonna cried out in horror as her two guardians went for the people, who scattered. By the time her order of 'stop!' came out, both elves had humans on the end of their blades. Yayènia gave her an incredulous look.

"Tlonna, these people are vile," she spat, shaking her right katan to rid it of the gargling human.

"How so? They seem perfectly innocent to me, bringing harm to no one."

Aidyn kicked a cowering man out his way as he stalked to the blackened pole. "This thing is used to burn people alive, polytheists mainly, but other monotheists as well, those who do not follow their particular sect of religion. These are the people who clutter every city, decrying every faith but their own, damning every soul who does not convert. They chase people down in the streets, demanding that they be heard."

"Their belief is that all people were created by this One God, and that we are hopelessly wicked souls unable to do anything worthwhile without it being a selfish and therefore evil act," Yayènia put in, glaring at the people before her.

"You say that every Monotheist is a cretin who deserves only death?"

Aidyn shook his head while Yayènia chewed on her lip, apparently in contemplation. The assassin slanted a look at her. "No.

Their religion is not evil, it is a religion like any other, a philosophy of great and noble ideals. The practitioners however, are very divided. There are two factions: the Reformed, and the Justified. The Reformed are regular people who go to their temples, pray or whatever it is that they do, and continue on with their lives with a sense of faith and good intentions. It is the Justified who caused the War of Monotheism, and who to this day create havoc and unrest. These people here are Justified Monotheists, these are the cretins who deserve only death. These are the people who kill for their god, though I doubt it is what he would wish."

Tlonna gestured to one man who seemed less cowed than all the rest. "Get up. Is what they say true?"

The man got to his feet and adjusted his filthy toga over his bony frame. "All people are equal in this life, no better than the lowest person. We were all created by the One True God, creator of all things, protector of all pure souls. Every man able to work and earn should give all he can to those who can't. No single person should profit, for that proves him greedy and selfish. All must give to the whole. All must suffer as one."

"And this pole?" Tlonna asked quietly.

"Fire is the only way to purge a tainted soul. Only once the corrupt flesh has burned away can the Creator take the freed soul."

A spark of indignation and anger flickered to life in Tlonna. "So you say the very nature of a person is evil? That we are born wicked?"

The monotheist beamed at her. "Yes! Only through a lifetime of service to others can the soul be redeemed. The One True God is flawless, perfect in every way, infallible."

"If he created everything..." Tlonna began, catching a long-suffering look as it passed between Aidyn and Yayènia, "then he would be the creator of evil, too, yes?"

The man paused, looking unsure for a moment. He glanced at his fellows who watched him with rapturous gazes. An expression of enlightenment crossed his haggard face.

"No, that is the nature of man, or elf," he added the last with a gesture to the three of them.

"Then he is not infallible. He created something inherently bad, something so irredeemably nefarious that none of us are capable of perfection."

He grasped at a single word. "Not irredeemable! Through selfless service or released by righteous fire one can be taken into His benevolent embrace."

"Through groveling slavery you mean."

"No. Is it slavery to bring every person to the same plane of opportunity?"

Tlonna snorted. "If we were all equal to the lowest form of being, then we would eventually end up as slavish, moronic, useless heaps of flesh and bone. I doubt that is what your god would want for his creations. I would think he would want for his children to strive to be the best possible person they could be, and if they had the means to help others, then to do so. Blind slavery is not proof of faith. In fact you should not have to *prove* your faith. It should be strong enough in your heart that it can take doubt and not need to be pushed on others in order to validate it. If you do want to prove it to others, do it by living your life for yourself, and those you care about.

"Prove it by being a genuine person of integrity. By being an honorable and hard working person who cares and loves his kith and kin with a ferocity equal to the hatred of your enemies. As for opportunity, we are all given the same opportunity in life. We are all born the same, born with the same limbs and minds. Some of us may be born in better wealth than others, but I have known peasants who have risen to be kings, and kings who have fallen to become peasants. Life is life, and yours is only yours. You must stand up and live it as you see fit, not as some dogmatic creed tells you to. To do so is to be a coward unfit to stand on your own two feet."

The man and his fellow monotheists were sheet white and trembling in the face of Tlonna's righteous tirade. Yayènia glowered down at the scraggly woman who cowered at her feet. She nudged the woman with her boot.

"How many have you put to death?" she demanded and pointed with her sword at the pole.

The monotheist licked her lips, her watery eyes darting about in fear. Yayènia's scowl deepened and she lifted her left sword in a threatening manner.

"Five! Five!" she shrieked and fell onto her face, weeping.

Aidyn simply looked at the man to his left.

"Eight."

As the people began confessing their numbers, the leader straightened his back. "The words you speak are blasphemous treachery! You are beautiful so you have never suffered. You know nothing of pain and sacrifice! You are a creature of opportunity and privilege! You care nothing of the troubles of others! You are evil and cruel, unjust in your damnation of our pure souls. There is a man invading corrupt Nymyños this very moment who understands this. He strives to strike down those who believe themselves mighty and great. He will bring an era of hope and equality to this god-forsaken land. He will strike you down as his forefathers did the heretic kingdoms of the west. You will learn your place in the world of God."

Tlonna's eyes were stone as they bored into the man who, despite the vehemence of his words, shrank before her. "You believe Sithian to be your savior?"

"You are unfit to utter his name!"

Tlonna's fist hit the man square in the jaw, hard enough to shatter teeth and bone alike. She stalked over to where his body had landed to straddle his waist with her booted feet.

"I gave birth to that monster, you depraved, deluded fool. No god, whether singular or in a pantheon, would sanction what that child does. He is a wicked monster, devoid of any true emotion of faith or love. He cares not for your religion. He cares only for his own wants and needs, which consist of rape, torture, and conquest. He has murdered his brother and sister, and hundreds more besides. He brought war to this land, which was previously peaceful and relatively safe from evil. If you believe him to be your messiah, I will give you the same fate he is destined for."

The man lay writhing on the ground, clutching at his ruined face and staring up at her with terror-filled eyes. Aidyn and Yayènia stood silent and still, watching as their queen's rage grew until magic crackled up around her in a flickering aura. The other monotheists cowered against the ground, weeping and crying out for mercy. Tlonna's shoulders and chest heaved as she fumed down at the man.

"You wish to suffer the same as Sithian and his horde of mercenaries? You believe them righteous in their cause?"

The man sobbed in agony, his hands and neck covered in glistening ruby blood. He managed a nod.

"Equality is our only hope!" he wheezed through his shattered mouth.

Tlonna's control snapped and she slammed her boot into his crotch. She pointed a finger at his face and white, black, and blue magic shot out of it to explode into him. The man shrieked once and then lay still, half his face blown away. The Magin Queen turned slowly and stepped over the body and looked over at Yayènia and Aidyn.

"Finish them off."

The two set about their work without comment to dispatch the misled fools who killed in the name of their god. Tlonna walked away from the clearing to find the horses, whom they had left tethered to a tree when they had first heard the music. Yayènia found the source of the music in the hands of two of the monotheists. A simple clay flute and a small dulcimer. She shook her head at the insanity of it all and glanced up to see Aidyn slide his scimitars across the throat of the last monotheist, the only non-human of the group. A dwarf, though he had apparently shaved off his beard, or had it shaved off for him.

Tlonna waited by the horses while the task was finished and remained silent when her two protectors returned, splattered with blood. They mounted up and rode away, not speaking.

# Chapter 17
## Unexpected Fingers

The trio rode quickly and stopped to rest only for short amounts of time. Winter's fury was in full force now and snow whipped about with abandon. Tlonna wondered why she was always traveling in the snow. At least it was the right color.

Yayènia and Aidyn had said nothing about their encounter with the monotheists, keeping their thoughts to themselves. Tlonna rode in front of them now, not wanting to see their shared looks of worry and resignation. They reached the sight of battle three days later, arriving with the crows and vultures and the fading sun that cast the bloodied ground in a mockingly golden color.

The three hastened by, heading straight for the Blackhaven lines. Tlonna was absolutely stunned at the sight of the wall, small and barely started as it was. She made a beeline for the soldiers working on it and reined Takîreaes in barely a foot away. The soldiers went for their weapons, and then realized who it was they were about to draw steel on.

"Queen Tlonna! High Commander! Lord Aidyn!" they shouted as one as they went into the military bow.

"Where is King Losolin?" Tlonna demanded, barely acknowledging the soldiers' salute.

"In camp, my lady. The command tent is marked with the standard of Blackhaven, your standard, and the Tiena Badger."

"Thank you," she said and rode off, Aidyn and Yayènia close behind.

The camp was large but orderly, clean and quiet for its size. Yayènia looked on in pride, her back stiff in the saddle as she acknowledged the surprised, gleeful hails sent her way by soldiers. They found the command tent and dismounted, handed their reins to very surprised guards. Tlonna ducked inside before they could be announced.

Losolin stood over a table shaking his head, his big hands splayed flat against a map as Orthak said something about troops being stationed in the mountains to the south. They all looked up when the tent lightened with the newcomers' entrance.

Suneelo and Losolin gaped at their wives and Aidyn, their mouths open and eyes unblinking.

Without preamble, Tlonna pointed to the outside of the tent. "Why in all the nine bloody hells is there a wall being built in the middle of the flaming continent?"

Losolin was so taken aback that he straightened to his full height of seven-foot-five, his arms at his sides. "If we have to guard every bit of this frontier, then we would be spread far too thin. If an attack came, they would plow right through us and this whole thing would be over."

Tlonna dropped her arm and stared at him. "What do the other monarchs say about it?"

The king looked uncomfortable. "We did not have time to wait for their replies. I sent out letters explaining, but we could not risk delay. They will understand, Tlonna. It will not be a permanent fixture, anyway. What are you three doing here?"

Yayènia stepped away from her sister and went to her husband. She grabbed his head and pulled it down to her mouth so she could passionately kiss him. Suneelo's hands, which had gone stiff with surprise, bent to her waist and pulled her close, reveling in her presence. Tlonna blinked at them once and then turned back to her own spouse. Losolin looked upset as he stared back at her.

"Yayènia and I were in the Cleshnoe, which is where Aidyn found us. He had gone to Purheae because of a letter of distress from Nebet'thu, and then came to find us."

"Purheae? What were you doing in the Cleshnoe?"

"I went back to the Cyree. Stoffnias had a company of soldiers holding Eyin and his people hostage after wiping out the other two villages. Losolin, what is going on here?"

The king, plainly trying to ignore the embracing couple to his right, stepped closer to his wife. "Sithian is gone, Tlonna. He left the camp several days back, after nearly a week of little action, and as soon as he left, they attacked. The Seadueni are sitting behind their lines, waiting for something. We sent in a raid, which went off like clockwork, but the captured Seadueni are not talking. We have lost three *Zephyr Leifen*, and over a thousand soldiers to date. They outnumber us five to one, if not more."

Tlonna felt faint and she pressed a hand to her breast in a vain effort to still her pounding heart. Losolin turned to Aidyn, who was standing by her side.

"I am glad to see you have recovered. You look well."

The assassin smiled. "I have, apparently in no small amount to you. I owe you my life, Losolin."

The king shook his head. "No, you never have and never will. I am glad you found her."

"She is no small amount of excitement that is for sure."

Losolin chuckled quietly and then turned back to his wife. "I have missed you."

Tlonna suddenly felt awful as she heard Yayènia and Suneelo break apart and begin to speak softly to one another, their fingers twined together. She lowered her head and slumped her shoulders.

"I am a terrible wife," she muttered.

Losolin's cool fingers lifted her chin and he kissed her softly, chastely. "Never. I understand you, Loni, I do. I love you."

Tlonna repeated the devotion and then hugged him, pressing her body tight against his, mindful of his armor. Sargotarh, Orthak, and Ghealan still stood silently by and studied the ground. The tent became very quiet for a moment and then Yayènia stepped away from Suneelo, not at all bashful about her passionate display of affection.

"So, what have you males done to my army? Three of my Silvers are dead, and a thousand soldiers. Tell me why."

Ghealan folded his arms and glared at her. "You know how important a leader's presence is to an army. You know why, Yayènia. Max, Jory, and Phoebus died because they did not have the savage need to be invincible for you. They do not fight for themselves, they fight for you. Without you here they feel lost, abandoned."

"Do not blame her for my command, Ghealan!" Tlonna snapped, angered by the elf's accusations. "If you must lay blame somewhere, lay it on me. Otherwise keep your finger pointing to yourself. It is useless and degrading."

The male stared down at her, not at all cowed by his queen. "Tlonna, you know how badly we are outnumbered. Our soldiers fight for you, and for Yayènia, but neither of you have been here. What do you expect?"

"I expect training and passion to override the want of someone's presence. I expect my people to want to defend their homeland and freedom without me telling them to do so. I expect my officers, my friends, to lead them with same resolute determination I would. Your petty excuses and weak logic have lost soldiers their lives," Tlonna's hand swept out to encompass them all, bitter and angry. "I am not staying here, we must move on to finish another goal, and when we do ride out I expect things to change. I understand the difficulty you are having, but we faced this in Alchemian, and we drove them back time and again."

"You are leaving again? When? Where to?" Losolin asked, grabbing her arm.

Tlonna looked him in the face and nearly drowned in the oceanic pools of his eyes. "I do not know when, but soon. Yayènia, Aidyn, and I must go to Purheae. I do not know why, but Miazie had a vision and I feel the need to heed it."

The king sucked in a deep breath and nodded his understanding. Aidyn stepped up to face Suneelo. "You should know that your guards do not have very good night vision. I passed by here about a week ago, and they shot at me, but missed by several yards."

"That was you?" Losolin exclaimed, staring at the dark elf in exasperation. "We had panicky soldiers for days because of that!"

Aidyn shrugged. "I was in a hurry."

Everyone groaned in disbelief. The assassin was unperturbed. Tlonna sighed and shook her head. "I am exhausted. Where is your tent?"

Losolin took her hand and kissed it. "I will show you. Dismissed everyone. We will reconvene at dawn."

As everyone departed Tlonna followed her husband through the aisles of tents and wagons in the dark. The feel of his hand in hers filled her with an unexpected sense of joy and comfort. She saw Yayènia and Suneelo duck into a large tent and smiled, happy that they too could be together. Aidyn, she noticed, was following them, as always a deadly shadow. Losolin held open the flap of their new field tent, a two-room, three-peaked contraption with a hole in the top for smoke to exit. Losolin had set up their cot, which was big enough for the two of them, in the farthest corner, and put the brazier in the same room. His pack was leaning against the thick canvas wall, still full. She dropped hers next to it. Aidyn had disappeared.

"You have not yet unpacked?"

Losolin glanced at the bag and shrugged. "Seemed pointless."

He began removing his armor and placing it on the stand that guarded the entrance to the pseudo bedroom. Tlonna sat in the only chair and began undoing her boots, sighing with relief as she wiggled her toes. A scratch moved the flap of the tent and Losolin bade the person enter. It was a servant.

"Would you like me to light the brazier, King Losolin?"

"No need," Tlonna muttered and lit the small iron hearth with a thought.

The servant started in fright and then bowed respectfully. "Would you like me to bring your dinner in?"

"Yes, that would be fine," Losolin replied in a tired voice, struggling to reach around and unbuckle the strap that held his cuirass in place.

Tlonna stretched her freed toes and stood, going to help him as the servant departed with another bow. She pushed his straining hand away and pulled loose the leather. When the cuirass opened and allowed Losolin to remove it, Tlonna saw the wrinkles in his shirt from where the metal and leather had pressed against it. Blood was caked into the gray silk in several places, thin lines that appeared to be more from the armor digging into his skin from heavy blows than actual edged steel.

Tlonna bent to unbuckle the greaves from his calves, even though he didn't need the help. Here too the leather of his pants was creased and pressed against his leg. Losolin let out a groan as he slid off his boots and finally stood without any metal or heavy leather on him. He picked up his plumed helmet and set it atop the stand, completing the panoply.

He turned to her, but she pushed his reaching arms away. Losolin watched as she tugged his shirt out of his belt and then untied the laces. She kissed the flesh as it was revealed. When Tlonna pushed the open shirt off his shoulders and down his arms, she gasped at what she saw. His beautiful torso was battered, bruised, and bloody. Many of the injuries looked old and untended, some of them fresh and untended.

"Losolin, why have you not had a healer attend you?"

He pulled her gently searching hands away and held them out to the side. "There are many who need the healers' attention more than I do. I will heal quickly, the humans do not. Do not worry for me."

The flap moved again with a questioning scratch and again Losolin bade the servant to enter. He bore two covered plates of food, but nearly dropped them when his gaze fell on the abused upper body of his king. The man quickly set the plates down on the only table, which sat just outside the separating flap of the two rooms, and bowed.

"I will send for a healer, King Losolin."

"No, do not. These are just scratches. Go on now, you have others to attend."

"As you wish, my lord."

When the servant was gone, Tlonna tugged at Losolin's belt, pulling the excess length out of its knot and unbuckling it.

"Are you going to make me eat naked?" he teased as she yanked the leather away with a slithering snap.

Tlonna shook her head. "You have lost weight. Everything is tightened against you."

"You are one to speak."

She sent him a quick frown. "That is different. Sit."

Losolin sat on the cot when she gently pushed him. Tlonna retrieved the covered plates and handed him one. They ate quickly, barely tasting the steaming rice and beans. The fire was now crackling merrily in its iron prison. It sent dancing shadows about the inside of the otherwise dark tent and made Losolin's wounded skin seem more hale.

"It is different this time around," Losolin unexpectedly said into the quiet. "I remember being tired and sore at Alchemian, I remember bruises, but I do not remember being in actual pain just from wearing my armor. Every time I put it on it is like a new torture, one designed specifically for me. My arms and legs burn with the exhaustion of carrying its weight, my back screams when I bend down, my neck and shoulders never seem to relax fully. It is a hellish nightmare that never ends. For days when we first arrived there was nothing to do but sit and wait. I yearned for something to happen. Now...all I want is a break. But there is none. There is no time for rejuvenation."

Tlonna ran her fingers through his hair, which didn't appear to have been washed in days. "I have never seen you look so weary. Losolin, you must not do this to yourself."

"What choice do I have, Tlonna? Without you and Yayènia here, the soldiers need a leader. Ghealan has lost all passion. He just does his job and barely speaks. He certainly does not charge up his men like he used to. Suneelo, Sargotarh, Orthak, and Yaedin, the Silver, do an amazing job, but it is just not enough. I have to push myself hard for their sake."

"I know I am the last person to be telling you this, but what good will it do them if you die? Losolin, we are elves, not gods. We can die from abuse just as much as the next person, it just takes longer."

"You are flaming right. You are the last person who is allowed to tell me that," Losolin muttered and pushed her hand away.

Tlonna's heart sank and her stomach began to feel queasy. She had never before seen her husband so withdrawn from her. She mindlessly finished the meal and then turned to him. He glanced at her from his peripheral and shook his head.

"What?"

"Losolin, please. Tell me what is wrong. Do not hide yourself from me."

The king's lips thinned as he inhaled sharply, obviously frustrated. "What in the nine bloody hells were you doing at the Cyree? Did you not get enough of your seeking answers in Purheae? For the love of the gods, Tlonna, what if something had happened? Did anyone know where you were?"

"Aladorn and Aidyn, Miazie and Sodo of course. I would never go off on a journey without telling someone, Losolin. I did not tell any of you who were leaving because you would have tried to stop me. I could not allow that. You needed to have your mind focused on this task, not worrying about mine."

"I always worry about you, whether you are by my side or not, Tlonna. You may not put great stock in your life, but to me it is everything. Were something to happen to you, I would die. I would physically die, damn it!"

"You would not die, Losolin, unless you did something stupid."

The male sharply shook his head. "You...you are so aggravating sometimes! Do you not care about anything anymore? Stab me thrice and drown me, Tlonna, you have to accept that people love you, and your nonchalance about self-sacrifice is painful! It is as if you care naught for us or what you do to us. Is that it?"

"Of course not, but I see no other option so rather than dwell on it I have tried to get over it and move on, to make a difference while I still can. Damn it Losolin I am terrified! Do you think I am perfectly fine with it? I am scared and it takes everything I have within me not to run away and hide for the rest of my life! I just got my life back, I do not want it to end now, but if it has to then I am going to do everything I can to leave this world a brighter place! Do you understand now? I do not talk about it, I do not debate it because if I think about it I begin to lose my will!"

Tears splashed hot and angry down Tlonna's face and she furiously wiped them away. She got to her feet and walked over to stand before the brazier, her arms wrapped around herself. It was a full minute before she felt his arms encompass her.

Losolin buried his face in the back of her neck and squeezed his eyes shut but two stubborn tears fought their way through his lids anyway. He could feel her shaking and tightened his embrace, trying to convey his love through sheer presence.

"Share your burden with me, my heart. That is my purpose. Trust in me."

Tlonna leaned back into his chest and sucked in a deep breath. "I will. But for tonight can we just be together? Please?"

Losolin kissed the back of her head and rumbled his agreement. They set the empty plates outside for the servant to retrieve when he made his next round, and hurried back inside the warm inner room. Tlonna undid her own belt as Losolin pulled a bag of sand out from beneath the brazier and tossed it under the thick coverlet on the cot.

As she un-tucked her tunic, Tlonna realized how comfortable the bed looked. It was a wide cot, covered in a downy mattress and dressed in black and silver bedclothes. Even the pillows had cases on them, silver affairs with black embroidery on the edges.

"Fancy," she muttered when Losolin turned to her as she untied her pants.

The king's eyes flared with desire and he pointed to the bed. "Get in."

Tlonna knew the look and did as he bid, leaving her unlaced pants on. She let out a pleased moan as she slid between the warm blankets and writhed in joy. Losolin kicked out of his breeches and stood gloriously tall and naked before her, albeit thinner and beaten.

Tlonna felt her heart begin to race as she gazed on the sight of her husband. The male lifted the very bottom of the blankets, wrapped his hand around her ankles, and gave a little tug. She felt her pants slide down a few inches and stop just below her hips. He tugged harder, pulling them down further to her thighs. Tlonna rocked her hips gently to help him as he yanked. Finally her pants flew from her feet and he dropped them unceremoniously on the ground. He ran his hands up her shapely calves, caressing the smooth flesh with his fingers.

Shivers ran up Tlonna's spine as his lips followed. He crawled beneath the blankets, sealing in the warmth. His mouth reached her thighs and then her hips, taking in everything. Her body taut with lust and love, Tlonna reached for his arms, grabbed his triceps and pulled him up to her. Their lips met with a frenzied need as their bodies joined, fitting so perfectly Tlonna was, as always, convinced that they had been made for each other.

After a while their skin began to glisten with perspiration and the fire welled upward. Tlonna, cognizant of the fact that guards and neighboring tents would see the blazing light, lifted her hand, Weaving air away to weaken the fire. Losolin's mouth was hot on her neck and jaw. His naturally streaked blond hair fell from his shoulders to veil their faces, mingling with her own locks on the pillow.

Little more than an hour later Tlonna's back arched as she clutched at Losolin's shoulders, her thighs and hips straining upward to press against him. When they at last lay still and sated, Tlonna felt hot tears splash down her face as she held him in her arms, pulling him close. Losolin trapped one of her legs between his and slid his arm around her back to lock her in place while the other one pillowed her head. His dark eyes glittered in the faint light as they searched her face.

"I missed you so much," he whispered, his body utterly spent.

"And I you. You are a much better bedmate than Yayènia."

Losolin's laughter filled her with joy as it shook his whole body. It was deep and masculine, as husky as his voice. "I hope so," he finally muttered, kissing the tip of her nose.

She wrinkled it as she made a face. "Did you know she talks in her sleep?"

"Yeah?"

Tlonna nodded, burying her face in his armpit. "She says the funniest things. A couple nights ago she said, 'you broke my toe and stole my cat'. I have no idea what she was dreaming about, but it must have been interesting."

Again Losolin's quiet laughter filled the tent. He rolled onto his back and pulled her along for the ride. His warm body was quickly lulling her to sleep. Tlonna could feel him against her hip and she reached down to gently stroke it. Losolin's laughter cut off with a gasp.

"None of that, now," he panted. "Tlonna, love, I am so spent."

"Mm..." she murmured, barely aware. "I love you too."

Losolin let out a heavy breath as her hand fell limp to his side and she succumbed to sleep. He was vividly reminded of the time she had fallen asleep much like this, though she had been soaking wet, and they had not remembered each other. She had promised to guard his dreams. He had dreamed of her.

Morning came swift and freezing. Losolin woke with a start to find Tlonna cuddled against his side and shivering slightly in the cold morning air. The fire had gone out, and somehow the blankets had moved to a slant, exposing her naked back. He quickly yanked them up to cover her, but she woke with the movement.

"Good morning," she whispered, pressing her frosty lips to his shoulder.

"Morning," he replied, trying to wake himself up enough to move.

Cursing Sithian, winter, the sun, and everything in between, Losolin finally found the energy to roll out of bed. He gasped as his naked flesh was assaulted by the bitter chill. He had gotten used to sleeping in whatever clothing he had been wearing the day previous, and now he remembered why. Shivering even as his body began to steam, the king bent to his pack and pulled out clothes for the day. He grabbed a cloak and wrapped it about his waist.

Losolin poked his head out of the tent, glaring through the still-dark morning. He found a large pebble and threw it at the lit tent that housed the servants who attended him and the officers. A head appeared in the opening, red with cold.

"Yes, King Losolin?"

"Will you bring in some water for a wash?" he asked, realizing that the poor humans must be absolutely freezing.

The servant nodded, unable to get a confirmation through his chattering teeth, and disappeared back inside. Losolin skipped back inside, trying to keep his feet away from the brittle ground as much as possible, and sat on the edge of the cot. Tlonna was now shivering hard, so much she shook the cot as she tried to sit up.

"Spirits!" she wheezed, clutching the blankets to her naked body.

With a flick of her hand, she relit the brazier. Losolin crouched to toss another bit of firewood inside, and then rejoined her on the bed. A few minutes later two servants appeared with hipbaths and rolled them in on small carts.

"We'll be right back with wood to heat it, your majesties."

Tlonna shook her head. "I can do it. Get back inside before you get frostbite."

The servants bowed their appreciation and rushed off. The queen dipped a shaking finger in each tub of water and moments later each was steaming. Losolin handed her a washcloth and watched in rapture as she stepped into the bath and began washing off the residue from daily existence and the dirt of travel.

Tearing his gaze away from her glistening body, Losolin got to the task of cleaning himself. The water was soon pink from the dried blood he scrubbed off. Once clean, the couple dried and dressed, shivering less as the tent began to warm. Unfortunately, they had to meet with the others in the command tent. As Tlonna helped Losolin don his armor, she kissed each part before she covered it up, claiming it would keep him safe. Once finished, they embraced, their lips meeting one more time before the day began.

As they walked outside, hand in hand, Aidyn stepped out of his black tent and stretched in the predawn light. He had pitched the tent in the small space between theirs and Ghealan's. In spite of the cold, he still wore his leather pants, and his *ärdyz* tunic. The only concession to the weather he had made was to wear both his black and white cloak. His raven hair and tawny skin looked lustrous against the snow. He gave them a small smile and joined them as they walked the short distance to the big tent. No one else had arrived yet. The assassin stacked wood in the two braziers and stepped aside so the Magins could light them. He bundled his cloaks about his trim body and sat, shivering a little.

"I did not think you were ever affected by anything," Tlonna teased softly as she took a seat beside him.

Losolin claimed the place on her right, still clutching her hand.

Aidyn rolled his emerald eyes. "It is just a show to make you two feel better."

Both high elves chuckled at his jibe, but Losolin suddenly fixed him with a suspicious stare. The assassin stared back, unsure what was expected of him.

"What was the nickname the others used to call you?"

The dark elf had not been expecting that question, so he gaped for a bit as he gathered his wits. "Who mentioned it?"

"I heard Ghealan call Suneelo 'Neel', and asked if anyone else had a cognomen I did not know about. He said you did, but refused to tell me for fear of bodily harm."

"Smart boy," Aidyn said emphatically, indicating he had no intention of revealing the offending name.

Tlonna nudged him with her elbow. "Tell us."

"No."

"Please?"

"No."

"Then I guess everyone will have to find out that you play the lute."

Losolin chuckled, but Aidyn's mouth dropped open at the threat of blackmail. "You would not."

"I would."

The assassin's expression was one of disbelieving betrayal. He was silent for a good long time, pouting. Finally he sighed. "Fingers."

"What?" Tlonna and Losolin choked at the same time.

Aidyn lifted his hands and waggled his fingers at them. They were long and slender, tapered like an artist's. Tlonna had never noticed, but he had the most beautiful fingers she had ever seen. A momentary vision of those fingers running over her body shocked her, but she hastily shut out the thought and realized Losolin was laughing so hard he could hardly get his breath.

"Fingers?" he wheezed, shaking his head in hilarity. "At least everyone else's was just a shortening of their names!"

Aidyn sneered at him. "Oh, all right...Wheezy."

Tlonna's laugh burst out of her before she could stop it. It was then that everyone else decided to show up, perplexed at their amusement. Losolin had his head on the table, his shoulders quivering as he sniggered.

The assassin was shaking his head, a smile playing at the edges of his lips. Tlonna was giggling, leaning back in her chair as she clutched at her stomach.

"What is going on?" Suneelo asked as he eyed the three with suspicion.

"F-Fingers!" Losolin laughed, his voice muffled by the table.

Yayènia, Ghealan, and Suneelo all burst out laughing as Aidyn threw his hands up in the air in defeat. Sargotarh and Orthak shared a glance, confused. Losolin finally sat up and wiped the tears of mirth from his face.

"I was expecting something like Aidy or something. Not Fingers!" he chortled, shaking his head.

"All right, all right, are you finished?" Aidyn grumped and smacked the back of Losolin's head.

Yayènia sat next to Aidyn. "I like that! Aidy."

"Ah, no," the dark elf moaned and give her a plaintive look. "It took me eighty years to shed Fingers, and now this."

"Get over it," Ghealan said as he sat down. He placed his well-worn helmet on the table before him and combed his fingers through the plume.

"But it does not shorten my name. What use is it?" Aidyn asked, desperate not to be pinned with a new sobriquet.

"It makes you blush," Yayènia said coyly as she nudged him in the ribs. "That is reason enough. You blush so prettily."

"Can we get on with the purpose of this meeting, please! Is there not a war going on?" he said loudly. He shoved the warrior hard enough to make her chair tip.

Losolin snickered again. "As you wish. Fingers."

The laughter erupted all over again. It took a long time for them to settle down enough to get to the task of running the battle.

# Chapter 18
## New Developments

The air was bitterly cold, the ground frozen and covered in winking frost. It was an unusually harsh season for Zaedic. The fields lay fallow, the people wrapped in scarves and cloaks as they hurried through the streets. The season that on the continent south of Zaedic brought such joy and cheer produced only strife and hunger to the island nation. They seldom ventured from their homes and did so only to open their businesses in the vain hope that someone might actually buy something that day, or to stand on the docks and watch the empty horizon, waiting for the day when the white ships would return. Over half the population had been forcefully drafted into the army, which had left the city and all the outlying villages weak and destitute.

Their king had returned but he had not spoken to them, so they stood on the harbor and waited in the bitter chill, the winter wind the only sound.

Sithian stood before his father's tomb and stared blankly at the stone visage of the dead Magin. In his hand rested the Resurrection Pendant, the pearlescent surface a façade that belied its strength. His thumb ran absently over its embossed star, the chain swayed slightly in the cold breeze from where it hung between his fingers. He had always wondered why the symbol was the same as his mother's personal emblem until he'd found the journal Gwemheoad had kept. The log had been recovered just days after the destruction of the Tower of Magins by one of the First Magin's illegitimate sons, who later became the founder of the Rahlan line. His daughter was Inabes, who married the first Sithian.

The journal had stated that Gwemheoad had discovered the prophecy Astinus had Seen about the Slaves of Death before he died. After convincing Veries Gurgen to show him the Seer's chronicle, Gwemheoad had inscribed the two pendants with the symbols the Seer had sketched into the margins having seen them in his vision.

Sithian shook his head. Then the bastard Jair had taken them after destroying the Tower and all the Magins within it, and thus they had been passed down through the Ewôsdírn line for generations after.

It was natural that such powerful talismans would have an impact on the upstart elven family, so much so that they made the two symbols integral to the kingdom itself. The tree became their emblem, strengthened by the fact that the nation was housed in the great forest, and the star and sun became the symbol for the heir-apparent. Now it was just Tlonna's symbol for so many people associated it to the blasted Everwood, which admittedly was why Astinus had probably Seen it in the first place.

Sithian shook his head again and turned his attention back to the tomb before him. Such a waste it had been to bring his father back from the dead. He had hoped that Midian's amplified strength would be enough to defeat at least one of Tlonna's minions, but the bitch Yayènia had somehow survived. Even turning Rhiannan into a doppelganger of the female warrior had failed to kill anyone of importance. Sure the traitor Kelus was dead, and Haydyn, but they had simply been nuisances, not real threats. Aidyn had managed to defeat her and had fully recovered from the wounds he'd received. Sithian glowered at his father's crypt. Every attempt to tear apart the rock-solid loyalty of Tlonna's little support group had failed miserably. It was insulting and aggravating. They just kept healing. For a moment the young king believed his cause to be a lost one, until he remembered that he had one more advantage over the *Magin Queen*. There was a traitor in their midst, a puppet of the Rahlan family for over two decades, and Sithian held the strings. He chuckled for the first time in days but it soon faded.

Sithian's mind was tortured and his thoughts raced, unable to come to any conclusions. His wife lay buried not ten feet away, dead by his hand but her by her own choice. He was the last of his family, the last of his kind. And still, across the R'Kunad, his mother faced off against his enormous army. Her and everyone he considered an enemy to him and his cause. His cause. He grunted to himself. Everyone had a different idea of what *his cause* was, but only he knew the truth. Some believed he was simply carrying on his father's and grandfather's plan to overtake Nymyños, and others thought he was on a religious crusade to destroy polytheistic nations once and for all. Still more were of the opinion that he was trying to wipe out the elves. In truth, he didn't care at all about religion or ruling Nymyños. He barely cared about the elves either, but that was the idea he fueled the most because it was a common point of dissention among humans. In truth, he just wanted to kill his mother and every single one of her blasted followers. He wanted access to her power so he could control the kings of the Twelve Kingdoms, or however many were left after Midian's campaign through them. He wanted to be able to pitch them against one another and watch them kill each other. Sithian didn't care if Nymyños fell into unchecked anarchy, he wanted the continent to burn. He wanted all those fools who blindly followed Tlonna *bloody* Ewôsdírn to burn in the deepest ninth hell. She was root of all evil, the catalyst for the fall of the House of Rahlan. It was because of her that Zaedic now had paved roads, even a small library, and he cursed her for it.

No longer was there a deep revulsion of the mainlanders in the Zaedicans. They no longer saw them as power-hungry revolutionists who kept their vast wealth and knowledge deep within vaults. No, his people saw the Nymyñosians as benevolent caregivers, spreaders of peace and education, and now they detested him for keeping it from them.

If Midian were alive, he would have found a way to slip by the army blocking the way through Nymyños and slaughter Blackhaven Kingdom once more, or at least the city. But the king was dead, and only his twenty-one year old half-blood son remained. Sithian looked down at the pendant in his hand, felt the power it held within its unambiguous shape.

Silently, the young king dropped the pendant in the frozen grass and walked away from his father's tomb.

Inside his quiet, chilly palace, Sithian found that his seneschal had done as ordered. A few young women were lined up in a row, looking frightened. These women were different, but he barely cared. He stared at their bodies, stripped of all clothing. His sapphire eyes roamed over their hips, judging their childbearing possibilities, and then moved to their faces. They were all of an age with him, native islanders, shivering in the unusual cold.

Sithian dismissed the brunettes; they reminded him of Learia, and then the ones with black hair, who reminded him of his sister. Only two remained now, a sumptuous blonde with light green eyes, and a rare ginger with wide blue eyes. They stared at him, their flesh trembling in the chilly air. Rhiannan's words floated back to him from the past.

*"You demand and demand, never giving thought to the consequences or the prices. You are foolish in your greed, and someday you will lament your decisions!"*

She had been right. He did lament his decision. Learia had been an unfaithful tramp. He decided he would give these two women a choice.

"I am in need of a new wife. The last one was a whore and died for it. Would either of you consider yourselves to be whores?"

Both women shook their heads in denial. Sithian paced before them.

"Have either of you been with a man before?"

The blonde woman lifted her hand, hesitant. "Once, King Sithian. I was raped in the street."

"Did you enjoy it?"

"No, King Sithian."

"Too bad," the king murmured as he walked by her, completely unaware that he had been the one to rape her. "Sex is a glorious thing, you know. It is the ultimate joining of two people, the most carnal, animal need we have. Some even say sex is the route to the gods. What do you two think?"

The redhead bit her lip. "I would not know, my lord, but if you say it is glorious, then I believe you."

"I have never known real sex, so I too must take your word for it," the blonde replied, lifting one shoulder.

Sithian liked them. He liked them a lot. But Tlonna was blonde.

"What is your name," he asked the redhead.

"Isolde Hart," she said and curtseyed as she did so.

"Isolde. What would you say to my proposal of marriage? You would be queen, with responsibilities in the kingdom and my bed. Are you agreeable?"

The blonde appeared relieved, and he turned his back on her to focus solely on Isolde.

"I accept, King Sithian."

"Excellent. The wedding will be day after tomorrow. You have two days to prepare."

Sithian left the women standing in the large hall, striding away as his servants rushed inside to take care of the details. He didn't care what happened to the blonde. He grinned for the first time in a long time as he went up to his office.

The wedding took place with more gusto than the previous one. Isolde's dress had been tailored within two days, rather than simply found as Learia's had been. After the ceremony there was a feast. The people of Zaedic gaped at the inside of the castle, dressed in what they considered their finery. It was the first time in living memory any of them had been invited to such a thing.

As far as Sithian was concerned, he simply wanted to get the woman up to his bed and consummate the marriage. During the dinner, he slid a hand between her legs and pressed his hand against her sensitive areas through the silk and taffeta of her skirt. She gasped and blanched at the same time.

Finally, he excused himself from the table, bid his people good night to their half-hearted cheers, and led his bride up to his room. He made her strip off his clothes, teaching her as she did so how to touch and kiss his flesh. Isolde knelt before him and slid her fingers along his belt, quickly undoing it. She pulled the strap away and untied the laces on his pants.

Sithian was in a state of bliss, already erect when Isolde pulled down his breeches. He taught her all that he knew. He did not sleep at all that night, doing his best to fortify his bloodline as a rare snowstorm raged outside.

Erdwyf turned at the sound of little feet on the stone and smiled as Jaryikin came running. The little elf had grown in the last few months, reaching the maturity of a three-year old human child.

"*E'na!*" she cried, holding out her little arms for her mother.

"What is it, little one?" Erdwyf said as she crouched so that her daughter could reach her.

"*E'na!*" Jaryikin sniffled again, unable to express anything but her want of her mother.

"Are you frightened? Did something happen?"

"*Achien muchen!*"

"Bad people? Where?"

Jaryikin clung to her, obviously frightened. Now there were sounds of more running, the stamping of booted adult feet. Erdwyf straightened, her daughter glued to her chest as Feorien and several guards came running around the corner into her study.

"Queen Erdwyf, Seadueni soldiers are in the courtyard. They are requesting an audience with you immediately," Feorien said worriedly.

He, like all the Blackhavenites who had transferred with Erdwyf, disliked the Seadueni more than the native Narnenians.

Erdwyf sighed, now understanding her daughter's fright. "All right. I will meet them in the throne room."

Feorien rushed off with the guards. Erdwyf set Jaryikin down and made the short walk to the first floor, where the throne room butted up against the back of the castle, the toddler jogging along beside her.

When she had arrived, Nestra, the capital city of Narnen had been utterly decimated. The very walls of the castle had been stained brown with dried blood. It had taken weeks of determined washing to clean it from the cold granite. The work was disturbingly reminiscent of the reclamation of Blackhaven City. Erdwyf had presided over the funeral of the previous royal family, burying them in the graveyard set aside for royalty and high nobility. Her coronation had been a quick affair, with most of the people attending with blank eyes and cold expressions. The only enthused people had been her parents, Lhia and Anuan.

Now, Erdwyf sat more comfortably in the throne though not at ease by any stretch. She had taken drastic measures to turn the devastated kingdom around. It was the smallest province in Nymyños, with the smallest population. Erdwyf now ruled over four thousand, seven hundred, and sixty-two people. Her army consisted of five Blackhaven guards, three old human retainers, and one soldier that had been away on a message delivery when Narnen was razed by the Rahlans. He was eighteen.

Erdwyf had consulted with her parents on the wisest course of action in bringing her homeland out of its ruin. They had suggested carving out an entirely new kingdom. Narnen would remain its name, but even that was under discussion. She had taken down all the standards of Narnen, a yellow and brown quadrant with a black anchor in the yellow squares, and replaced it with a shield form of red, slashed through with black and the white silhouette of a torch in the center.

She had the hideous yellow and brown runners pulled out of the castle and burned, along with the tapestries, other than two, which she had placed in carefully sealed boxes for preservation purposes. The thrones had been taken to the basement of the castle along with the boxes. Everything with the anchor was either demolished, given to the people, or placed in the small room in the basement. In a few weeks, Narnen had become the kingdom of the torch, the kingdom that would remain eternal.

Erdwyf had the crowns of Emar and Atlan taken down to the room in the basement as well, and had commissioned a new one for herself. She would let Ghealan design his own when he arrived. It was a thin band of braided gold and silver with small diamonds and rubies placed alternately along the center. Above her brow, suspended by fine gold and silver wire was a tiny, ornate torch. The flame was embedded with a fire diamond. It was such a rare stone she'd had to pay twenty gold spikes for it, which was worth more than five horses. The crystalline clarity of the diamond was unmatched, but it was the flare of red and orange within the stone that made it so rare and valuable.

It caught the light streaming through the newly cleaned windows now as Erdwyf leaned back in her new throne, carved from a piece of red-veined white marble and cushioned in black suede. Her hands rested on the scrolled armrests as she waited, Jaryikin fidgeting restlessly. Erdwyf gestured to her nurse.

"Would you take Jaryikin to the nursery? I do not want these bastards to see her."

"Of course Queen Erdwyf," the young woman said and held out her hand to the little girl.

Jaryikin obligingly took the hand and tottered off with her nurse, blithely smiling back at her mother. A moment later there was a knock on the door and it opened to admit more than a score of Seadueni soldiers in full armor, missing their weapons. Feorien walked before them and managed to look absolutely wretched.

The twenty-odd elves marched up to the dais and bowed, their armored knees hit the ground with a loud thud. Erdwyf frowned. She never expected submission from Seadueni. As one, they rose and stared at her with their gold, gray, and light green eyes. The closest one stepped forward a little more.

"Queen Erdwyf, my name is Rorse Lach. These are my warriors. We are here to offer you our services as soldiers, if you would have us."

Erdwyf was rigid now, her face unfathomable. "What? You, Seadueni soldiers, are offering services to me, a newly crowned queen, formerly High Advisor to the Throne of Blackhaven? Are you serious?"

"Very. King Stoffnias has allied Seaduens with the human kingdoms of Zaedic and Talenias, and is taking orders from the Rahlan heir. We do not fight for the Rahlans."

"You do realize that Narnen is mostly human, right?"

Rorse hesitated for a moment. His golden eyes flicked to Feorien for a moment before returning to her. "Yes."

"And you still want to be a part of my kingdom? A part of my army?"

"Yes."

"Because Stoffnias allied with Midian and then Sithian?"

"Yes."

Erdwyf stared at the male for a long time as she tried to get her brain to work. Such an event was unprecedented. Finally, she stood and descended the stairs until she stood directly in front of Rorse. He was about an inch shorter than her, but she had always been tall.

"You and your warriors will have to swear fealty to me, to Narnen, and to her people, humans included. You will be charged with protecting the citizens of Narnen, and her allies, including Blackhaven. When King Ghealan arrives, you will swear fealty to him as well. Any objections?"

Rorse looked back at his followers for a moment and then shook his head. "No."

"Then swear to me."

The elf went to his knees and took her proffered hand. He repeated her words and then kissed her knuckles as she did not yet have a ring. The twenty-two other soldiers came forward and swore the same, each kissing her hand before standing and moving off to the side. When they had all sworn, Erdwyf turned to them.

"Welcome. You are now citizens of Narnen. You will have new armor commissioned for you, and your old will be destroyed. Is that clear?"

The elves ran their hands over their well-worn Seaduens armor, and then nodded.

"Do you have a place to stay?"

Rorse shook his head, silent with the weight of his decision.

"Then for the time being, you will have to stay here in the palace as the barracks was demolished in the razing. Feorien, see to it that our new soldiers are given rooms on the second floor, in the west wing. And Feor, there are enough empty rooms in this place to overwhelm a ghost. They can have their own."

The seneschal and advisor bowed, beckoned to the twenty-three elves, and stalked away. Erdwyf collapsed into her throne once they were out of the room, shaking her head in absolute disbelief. She hoped she hadn't just made her first big mistake.

# Chapter 19
## Stoffnias's Mistake

Tlonna, Yayènia, and Aidyn decided to stay for a week to help where they could. For the first three days, they simply fought in the frantic melee, slicing their opponents to ribbons the way only they could. On the fourth, things changed.

The Seaduens Militant finally entered the main battle. They stood tall amongst the humans like bright, deadly beacons. On this day a storm raged like none other but the two sides were in a blood frenzy. Lightning crackled across the bruised sky, sheets of it lighting the underside of the roiling clouds for split-second moments, catching the battle in freeze-frame. Sleet pounded against armor and weapons with merciless abandon while the driving wind whipped it unexpectedly into exposed faces to leave painful welts where it could.

Tlonna wiped a hand across her face yet again to clear her eyes of ice and water. It was dark, though the day was not yet old. Before her color seemed washed away, only the spray of blood was vivid as it flashed across the battlefield. She knew it was a trick of the weather, but the sight was unnerving anyway. A soldier rushed at her, his sword lifted high in the air, his mouth open in a primal scream of bloodlust. Tlonna leaned back as the blade's tip whistled by her face, then crouched and stabbed her own sword straight out.

The howling man impaled himself, unable to stop his headlong rush. His body slid all the way up the blade to slam against the hilt and jar her arm. Blood exploded out his mouth to splatter against her chest and neck. Tlonna jiggled her sword to free it of the corpse, but he stayed on and wiggled horribly with her efforts. She knew getting your weapon caught on something in the middle of a battle was a good way to die.

Her heart began to race as she heard soldiers rushing up behind her, and they did not sound friendly. Gritting her teeth, Tlonna lifted her sword, dead body and all, and swung it about to slash the tip across an elf's face. Her attack took an eye and half his nose. The dead soldier finally flew off the end of her blade and crashed into two others and knocked them down. Suddenly her weapon felt much lighter and Tlonna went after the closing enemy with vigor, her teeth bared in fury. These people were invaders, murderers, rapists. They had no right. *They had no right!*

Aidyn slipped through the milling masses like a shadow, his blades carving a path of bloody violence that filled up with allies as he went. He never felt the sting of an enemy blade, or the blunt shock of heavier weapons. He had left his cloak behind for he knew it would only slow him down in such a press of bodies, so he was simply a slender form flitting through the confusion. Two elves caught sight of him, fire in their golden eyes. They came at the assassin with a wicked vengeance. They flipped like dancers through the air as they did to avoid being slowed by the bulkier humans.

The dark elf waited for them, his scimitars dispatching any fool who thought he was a vulnerable target. When the Seadueni finally reached him they were wild with battle fury. Aidyn ducked low and spun at the same time their longswords came screaming at him. His right scimitar snaked in to score a poke at one of elves' thigh.

He howled and jerked his sword down at Aidyn's exposed shoulder. The assassin rolled and came up between the two. He stabbed out to either side, his arms crossed over his body. A fist sailed toward his face and he dropped down to avoid it and wrenched his scimitars down with him. The elves screamed in agony as their sides were ripped open, the leather straps on their cuirasses sliced apart. Aidyn rolled back again and continued onto his feet. As the elves began to turn, rage contorting their fine features into masks of death, he crossed his arms again, and then with a powerful blow swept his arms out straight to either side to take their heads clean off.

The assassin skipped backward to avoid their falling bodies, and ducked to avoid an oncoming mace. The human wielding it screamed in agony as the dark elf's foot shattered his nose. He hit the ground already dead. Aidyn was headed to the aid of a Blackhaven human being pressed by a Seaduens soldier when a wild, twisted jubilation ripped through his heart, stopped him in his tracks. His green eyes widened as Tlonna's unbridled emotion caromed through him like a fire. It was the oddest sensation he had ever felt. Knowing she was in no danger, the assassin pushed the feeling to the side and continued on to help the poor man.

Tlonna's gaze landed on a most welcome sight. Stoffnias had joined the fray. He was stalking through the fighters like a cat, dispatching humans with great joy, both friend and foe.

"Stoffnias!" she screamed, pointing her bloody, gory sword at him.

The king pivoted at the sound of her voice shouting his name. His face distorted with loathing as he found her standing amongst a ring of dead bodies, many of his soldiers among them.

"Ewôsdírn!" he bellowed and began to shove his way to her. "I am going to rip you apart!"

"Coward! You stupid idiot!" Tlonna shouted back, rising his ire. "You are not even capable of sustaining your own war! You have to ally yourselves with little boys and murdering rapists in order to make yourself feel like a real elf!"

Stoffnias's massive broadsword flew at her, driven by awesome strength and hatred. Tlonna dove to the side and at the same time flicked her own slender longblade out to send the weapon reeling. They pinged together with a ringing clash, both vibrating with the strength of the opposing wielder, sparks flying. Tlonna landed on her side and slid, used the momentum to flip over and get back to her feet. Stoffnias came at her in a blind rage, his braided hair flying out behind him.

The king and queen came together with a hard impact and struggled viciously as thunder overhead bellowed its approval.

"Where is your pretty peasant boy? Too poor to own a sword?" Stoffnias hissed, his teeth crimson with the blood of his enemies as it sprayed in his face.

"Losolin is tenfold the male you are, Lostug, and he would slice you to pieces were he here. But he is off killing all your petty little allies. I will get the pleasure of taking your worthless life," Tlonna growled back as she twisted her arm out of his grasp and brought her knee up into his groin.

The male barely reacted to the blow but narrowed his eyes as he shoved her away. "Bitch. You do not know what a real male is. You have had only mad kings and peasants between your legs."

Tlonna's wrath erupted in an explosion of strength. She tapped her sword against his twice in rapid succession to send it out wide so she had an opening. Stoffnias danced back and quickly reversed his wide-flung broadsword. Tlonna came at him again, furiously parrying his thrusts and jabs. Their swords met crossguard to crossguard and she twisted hers causing both weapons to swing out in a wide arc. Her foot caught him in the sternum and forced him back as he gasped for breath. She leapt forward through the driving wind and sleet, lifted her sword high above her head and aimed for the windless elf. Stoffnias suddenly shifted to bring the heel of his palm straight up. It slammed into her chest so hard it flipped her end over end. Tlonna slammed into the cold, slushy ground and grunted as her armor pressed against her flesh hard enough to bruise. As she tried to get her bearings, a boot smashed into her midriff. The female felt bones pop. Desperately trying to breathe, Tlonna clutched at her stomach, one arm pressed tight to her side.

Stoffnias growled down at her, a hundred years of rejection and humiliation at her hands fueling his brutality. "Oh how I have longed for this day, to see you crawling at my feet where you belong."

Tlonna coughed out blood as she rolled onto her hands and knees. Her triceps undulated beneath her skin as she leaned away from his next kick. As his foot sailed past her shoulder, the queen kicked out at his standing leg and connected hard with the shin. Stoffnias roared as fell, his knee bent back the wrong way. He caught himself just before his head crashed into the ground. He could not do the same for Tlonna's knee. It caught him square in the temple.

The King of Seaduens flopped limply, dead from the edge of her greave that had driven into his brain. She jiggled her leg in an effort to free herself, but Stoffnias's head just nodded at her. Disgusted, she grabbed a fistful of blood-matted hair and yanked. Her greave dislodged with a splatter of gore.

Tlonna rolled onto her feet and lifted her sword to defend herself against any oncoming enemy, but found to her surprise that there was no one around. She stood for a moment to catch her breath, and then bent to grab the dead king. She draped him over her shoulder and jogged back toward camp.

The battle seemed to have died down as the storm gathered in fury. She could barely believe the vehemence of the tempest. Soldiers still battled around her, but most of the invaders seemed to be fighting for a retreat. Tlonna slipped and slid in the gory mud, Stoffnias' armored weight pulling her off balance. Her own warriors shouted at her in glory and shook their various weapons in the dark sky as the lightning flashed around them to give the whole scene a spectral feel.

Finally Tlonna reached the partial wall and slowed, blinking sleet from her eyes. Though it was barely noon, the sky was black as night, which made it difficult to see. Hundreds of her soldiers were headed back to camp and she was caught up in the swarm. The Magin Queen at last reached the command tent, where most everyone was gathered. Ghealan was still out along with Suneelo, but the rest of them were wringing out their soaking hair and clothes by the two braziers.

Faces paled and eyes widened when they saw that she carried someone. Tlonna flopped Stoffnias down on the table and the looks of fear and worry changed to surprised looks of exultation. Yayènia leapt upward as she whooped, her fist punching the air. Losolin grinned at his wife before planting a cold, wet kiss on her lips. Aidyn shook his head as the strange feeling that had stopped him cold clicked into place. A smile brightened his tawny features. Sargotarh and Orthak laughed and danced about with Yayènia, reduced to silliness by their excitement. Thunder rumbled overhead as the tent flap was ripped open and Suneelo and Ghealan strode in to take in the sight.

Suneelo caught Tlonna up in a wild embrace and swung her about like a child as Ghealan went to stand by Yayènia. He was grinning from pointed ear to pointed ear. Finally, when they had all settled down, the High Commander turned to her sister.

"Tell us how it happened?"

Tlonna recounted the battle and left nothing out. Losolin shook his head when she told them about his insults, but didn't seem bothered too much. When she was finished Ghealan grabbed Stoffnias's head and jerked it to the side in order to reveal the gaping hole in his temple. They all examined the wound with relish, Yayènia even stuck her finger in it and wiggled it about to see how deep it was. When she withdrew the finger, it was bloody up to her second knuckle.

"Well done!" she crowed and wiped her finger clean on her pants.

Suneelo rolled his eyes and draped a long arm over his wife's shoulders. "What are you going to do with him?"

Tlonna glanced at her friends. "I just want the head. You can do what you want with the body."

Yayènia, who hated the king more than anyone other Tlonna herself, and perhaps Losolin, yanked out her dagger and gripped it tight.

"Wait!" Tlonna shouted as she jumped forward to stop her sister. "Not on the table."

The High Commander grabbed a fistful of blond hair and dragged the dead king off the table. He landed with a clatter of armor on the hard ground. Yayènia twisted Stoffnias, rolled his body onto his stomach and lifted up his head. It was a gruesome sight. Before anyone else could delay her, the warrior began sawing on his neck, going slow and ragged despite the fact that Stoffnias would not feel a thing. When his headless body finally flopped forward and trickled blood onto the ground, Yayènia lifted the head and held it high, her eyes alight with gleeful madness.

Tlonna held out her hand for the head. When it was handed to her, she stalked outside into the still-raging storm. She found a guard with a spear and asked for his weapon. He handed it over without question, and watched silently as she screwed Stoffnias's head onto the barbed head. Once it was secure, she handed the soldier a silver spike.

"Will that cover your spear?"

The man gaped at her, silver coin held out in his open palm. "My queen, this...I can get a new spear at the weapons hold for free. They are cheap to make. I cannot take this."

"Yes you can, and you will. Thank you," Tlonna said and turned away.

She planted the butt of the spear outside the command tent for the time being, and walked back inside. They had his body completely stripped, and Yayènia was working between his legs.

"What are you doing?" Tlonna cried, sickened by what she thought she saw.

The High Commander finished and twisted her torso, holding up the bloody organ. "I thought Miazie might like to see this."

Tlonna then realized that her sister had been cutting off his member, and not something completely horrible and absurd.

She began to breathe again. "I am sure she will. What will you do with the rest of him?"

Losolin lifted the fire prod from one of the braziers with a grin. "I thought we might send his body back with a little reminder of why you should not mess with Blackhaven."

Tlonna stared at the poker. Unwillingly she recalled the time Losolin had killed Stoffnias's son Iyaner with a similar one at the castle. He had been defending her from the Seadueni prince who believed she belonged to him. She looked up into his oceanic eyes and saw in the depths a lingering lust for revenge. Tlonna realized Losolin hated the Lostugs more than most, perhaps as much as Yayènia, perhaps as much as Tlonna. It was a giant circle of hate.

She nodded and watched as her husband heated the iron poker in the fire and then pressed it to Stoffnias's chest to leave a clear brand of what it was. The sickly sweet smell of burning flesh filled the tent. When Losolin had branded both pectorals, he replaced the fire prod in its rest and stepped back. He seemed...sated.

Ghealan and Suneelo lifted the body and took it out into the storm. They did not return for a long time. The council was having dinner in the front room of Tlonna and Losolin's tent as the command tent was aired out and cleaned when the two returned.

Ghealan dragged a chair over, straddled it, and balanced the plate a servant handed him on the high back. "We took his body to the edge of the battle field and left it there. We waited until they came and retrieved it. At first they did not realize who it was, and then they saw the one testicle, and knew it for Stoffnias. Then they started screaming."

Suneelo grinned as he planted a kiss on Yayènia's cheek. "I have rarely heard such swearing coming from the mouths of elves. They swore vengeance on the House of Ewôsdírn."

"Good. The Lostugs need to be wiped from the face of the earth, the same way we got rid of Athelias and his brat," Tlonna snarled as she stabbed a piece of bannock with savagery.

Every one nodded and a comfortable silence filled the tent.

# Chapter 20

## Seductive Stories

Tlonna, Aidyn, and Yayènia left two days after the fall of Stoffnias. They rode out of the camp before dawn in order to not be seen by the soldiers. Tlonna and Yayènia said their quiet goodbyes to their husbands while Aidyn stood impatiently by, the reins of the three frisky horses in his hands. Soon after, they were riding along the edge of the Purheae Forest, keeping their heads low in the misty morning as the sun rose behind them. As they wound around the tangle of trees Tlonna kept a watch out for any change in the atmosphere. Although Losolin had destroyed the barrier that kept Magins from using their magic within the boundary of Purheae, she believed that there remained a violent force of residual backlash floating about the kingdom.

They rode for one and half days before Tlonna felt it. She gasped in startled pain when the power touched her flesh and tried to recognize it. The other two behind her shifted in their saddles, the shock of discomfort barely registering against their tortured bodies. Aidyn blinked in surprise and looked at Yayènia, who grimaced slightly. They both watched as Tlonna doubled over the horn of her saddle, gagging.

The assassin leapt off Whäd's back and caught his queen before she fell to the ground clutching at her head and dry heaving. Yayènia dismounted and yanked out her sword against a threat she could not see.

"What is it?" Aidyn cried. He grabbed Tlonna's chin and pulled her head back to clear her airway. "What do you need?"

Tlonna's body convulsed with another nauseating heave as she gagged on the thick, tainted magic that choked the air around her. Her head felt as though it was going to explode from the intense pressure and pain now radiating through it. She clutched at Aidyn's hand, nearly breaking his fingers as another seizure wracked through her body.

"Damn!" Yayènia swore and dropped to her knees beside her sister. "She needs clean air! The magic is killing her!"

"What?"

The warrior sucked in a breath, trying to figure out how to explain what she knew to the frightened assassin. "When we were here last Losolin did something to the magical barrier that kept this land safe from intruders with power. It dimmed everything magical, including our traits of sight and hearing. Tlonna died here when Jair overtook her body, but Losolin brought her back by calling forth all the power in the area, including the boundary, and channeled it through his healing power and into Tlonna. He brought her back to life using the very same power meant to keep her away. Now it must be reacting violently to the invasion of her mixed power. I am not sure, but I think she needs clean air," she explained rapidly, barely taking a breath.

"But the border is a day's ride away at the least!" Aidyn shouted as the female in his arms convulsed.

"Breathe into her!" Yayènia screamed back.

"What?"

"Put your damned lips on hers and breathe into her! I cannot do it because I have magic within me that may cause problems!"

Aidyn hesitated a moment longer and then bent over Tlonna and pressed his lips to hers. With his free hand he pinched his fingers against her jaw to pry her mouth open. Blood welled upward to spill over Tlonna's chin. The dark elf gagged as it burst into his mouth. He quickly spat out what he could and dug two fingers into her mouth. Yayènia watched in horrified revulsion as he scooped out the blood that was filling Tlonna's mouth. When it was clear, he locked his lips on hers and expelled a breath into her. Nothing happened.

"Press on her chest when I stop breathing into her," Aidyn said, his lips coated in glistening blood.

Yayènia nodded and leaned forward to press her hands between her sister's breasts. The assassin bent back down and gave Tlonna another breath. As soon as he stopped to take a breath for himself, Yayènia pressed downward. The Magin's eyes snapped open as an agonizing breath rattled from her chest. The dark elf took her expelled air within his body, his insides churning as what felt like burning oil flew into his lungs. Aidyn held her head still and breathed inward repeatedly as Yayènia alternately pressed down to expel the tainted magic.

Several minutes passed as they desperately tried to bring their friend back from the brink of death. Slowly, Tlonna's twitching eased until it quit completely. Her eyes had closed again and she seemed oblivious to the world. Without warning her hand came up to cup the back of Aidyn's head and press his face to hers. The assassin went rigid with shock as Yayènia sat back on her heels, breathing hard from exertion. Tlonna's other hand twisted in Aidyn's hand until her fingers slid between his. Suddenly she was kissing him with a passion that defied logic.

Squirm as he might, the dark elf could not free himself as Tlonna's mouth moved against his. Seconds dragged by as Yayènia watched in baffled fascination. Aidyn's shoulders stood out against his cloak as he tried to detach himself, and Tlonna's eyes began to slide open. They were completely white and staring upward, not at Aidyn, but through him. Then her blue irises began to appear, forming slowly like ink pressed against the back of a cloth. Her mouth froze as her eyes returned to normal, and her hand stopped pressing Aidyn's face against her. The assassin took the opportunity to press his lips together in a tight line lest she start kissing him again. Their eyes met, and Tlonna gaped up at him.

"What?" she whispered, looking utterly confused.

Aidyn pushed himself away and sat back to fall rather ungracefully on his backside. He looked as though he had just been punched in the face with a hammer. Yayènia shook her head, a small smile dancing on her lips as she looked away.

"Welcome back," she said to her sister, and stared at the ground between her knees.

"What?"

Yayènia sighed and looked her queen in the eye. "The magic Losolin destroyed left a residue, which I think you already knew and were looking out for. It caught you as you inhaled a breath, coating the inside of your throat and esophagus with tainted magic that did not like the presence of the magic inside of you. I believe it recognized you, or at least parts of you, as a danger, and tried to eliminate you. We had to get that evil breath out of you and replace it with clean breath."

Tlonna's gaze went to Aidyn, who was wiping the back of his hand across his mouth to clear it of her blood. She said nothing as Yayènia continued to explain.

"I could not do it, because I have magic within me that not only shares a blood bond with you, but is also quite powerful. I feared that it might only cause more of a reaction. You vomited blood into Aidyn's mouth, by the way. You might want to thank him for saving your life after that."

Tlonna watched as the assassin dropped his blood-covered hand into his lap and met her gaze with an emerald stare that set her heart to thumping. "Thank you," she said quietly, disgusted with herself.

Aidyn lifted one toned shoulder in a feeble shrug. "All in the name of duty to the throne, I suppose," he muttered weakly.

An absurd sense of hurt filled Tlonna and she managed a single nod. Yayènia scoffed loudly. "Are you two finished avoiding the fact that you were just about to make it right in front of me?"

"Nia!" Aidyn snapped, his expression one of fury as he spat out another glob of blood that had been sitting in the back of his throat.

"We were not!" Tlonna argued, sitting up and pulling in a deep breath. It felt as though her ribcage was too small, and she winced at the top of the breath. "I...I did not remember who I was."

"Wonderful," Aidyn grumbled, and promptly rolled over to vomit out more blood that was not his.

The females watched the spinal extensors in his back tighten and writhe with the heaves. It was astonishing they could see nearly every muscle through his cloak and shirt. Tlonna finally crawled over to him and grabbed a fistful of his raven hair to keep it out of the way. She combed it backward, felt the silky smooth strands slide between her fingers and against her palm. Aidyn spat out the last globs of her blood and sucked in a few deep breaths.

She had never seen him so revolted with himself and her. Ashamed, Tlonna waited until he got up and then released his hair. She scuttled away from him, not wishing to disgust him further. Aidyn stumbled over to Whäd and yanked his waterskin off his saddle. He tipped the whole thing into his mouth and swallowed great amounts of clear water. When he finished, he dropped the empty canteen and leaned against his horse, his face turned away from Tlonna and Yayènia.

The Magin flopped back to the ground next to her sister. "He cannot even stand to look at me anymore, can he?" she whispered softly, failing to keep the keen of panic from her voice.

Yayènia squinted at her and wrinkled her nose to make a decidedly indignant expression. "You think that is his problem? Disgust? I think it has more to do with male stiffness than anything."

Tlonna blinked at her, unsure of what the warrior meant. Yayènia let out a huff. "Tlonna, he has probably swallowed more blood in his life than both of us contain together. He loves you, desperately, and is going to take every opportunity to savor contact with you. He is an assassin, for bloody sake, not a flaming priest. You probably just made him...happy...enough to take us both."

"You are mad."

"Without question."

"I vomited blood into his mouth."

Yayènia shrugged. "Well, I am sure he did not enjoy that. In fact I watched him gag as it happened, but he spat out what he could and kept going. There was no way a little regurgitated blood was going to keep him from saving your petulant life."

Tlonna scowled at the warrior. "I am not petulant."

"All right, irritable, prickly, whiny, take your bloody pick. He saves your life and spews up the blood you heaved into his mouth, and you think he hates you? What did you want him to do? Swallow it and keep it as a souvenir?"

"No need to be vulgar, Yayènia. You did not see his face when he looked at me. It was like he could have killed me right then and there."

The commander buried her face in her hands, elbows braced against her knees. "You are impossible."

Tlonna's back straightened and she winced again as her chest pulled tight, still burning from the poisoned magic. "All right, say you are right. What then? What do I do? I am married to Losolin, and I love him more than life itself. What do I do if Aidyn is in love with me?"

Yayènia's face came up, her eyes wide and unfathomable. "Love him back. Just because you cannot have a physical relationship with him does not mean you cannot love him. Were it me, I would take every chance I had to be with someone who loved me that much."

"And Losolin?"

Yayènia grinned wickedly. "Two is better than one."

Tlonna gasped and choked at the response. "Would you really? With *both* of them? Suneelo and Aidyn?"

"Yeh," the warrior grunted inarticulately

Tlonna looked away, deeply ashamed and feeling childish. She missed Losolin. Yayènia's voice cut into her self-deprecating thoughts.

"Besides, it was you who was doing the groping. He was trying to get away."

"Aidyn is stronger than I am," Tlonna said, confused.

"Not when it comes to magic. Do you remember anything from the night Jair invaded your body?"

The queen shook her head. "Just when I woke up in Losolin's arms. He was crying, but never told me why. I just know I was terrified beyond reason."

Yayènia took a deep breath. "Well, among other things, you grabbed me by the throat and would not let go. You knocked Suneelo out cold and nearly suffocated me. I could not get out of your grasp. I am physically stronger than you, but I could not move even your little finger from my throat."

"Nia, I did not know, I am sorry."

The warrior shrugged. "You were possessed. When your magic gets away from you, you turn to cold steel. Nothing can budge you. It was much the same. You and I both saw his muscles through his clothing, Tlonna. I doubt there is anyone alive today who is more physically fit or stronger than Aidyn, but he could not get away from you."

Tlonna looked down at her hands. "I am a monster."

"No, you are the Magin Queen. There is a difference."

"I do not see it."

Yayènia lay back, gazing up at the gray sky. "You would not. You are determined to see only the worst of yourself, the faults and fears that you misconstrue into evil and cruelty. You find every physical trait that is different from others and you twist it into a mark of evil."

Tlonna remained silent as the fighter spoke, her voice quiet and a little rough, a bit gravelly from having her throat slit. Aidyn finally returned, looking more composed. He sat down across from the two females and stared at the empty ground between them. Yayènia continued on, almost as though she were talking to herself.

"You refuse to see what everyone tells you because you are afraid that you might actually be the good person we all know you to be. You think that if you are indeed that good creature, then you will not be strong enough to do as you must in the end. You fear that if you are accepted as this guiding post of hope and freedom and you ever make a wrong move you will lose all that you strive for. But you are wrong. You allow yourself to get lost in this mire of self-doubt and self-proclaimed wickedness in order to allow for the mistakes we all make. I have made mistakes. Aidyn has made mistakes. Everyone has made mistakes, Tlonna, but that is not something you accept.

"You believe that everyone around you is perfect, incapable of wrongdoing, when we are just as fallible as you are, and it is not a crime. It is what makes us elves. We are perfect looking, perfect sounding, perfect in every physical way, but our minds are just as flawed as a human's or a dwarf's. We have the same doubts you do, we just realize them to be doubts. We accept that even though we are good people we sometimes have to make decisions that seem cruel or uncaring. We aim to find the answers that give the best outcome for all involved, but when we cannot do so, we take the next best choice, even if that means allowing people to die. You, on the other hand, may take that choice but you berate yourself for not finding a way to reach the ultimate, painless option. You never accept what is acceptable. You criticize yourself for not always reaching perfection."

Tlonna sat there like a disciplined child, her shoulders hunched forward and her expression grim. She started at Aidyn's quiet voice.

"I once told you that we as a people were perfection, and you laughed. Do you remember?"

The elf nodded, unable to look at the assassin. That had been on the night Midian had captured her.

"Why did you laugh?"

She was silent for a bit, thinking through his gentle question. Finally she sighed. "Because I do not believe it. I do not think I ever have. It seems a ridiculous notion with all of our problems. If we were perfect, then we would not be sitting here on the frozen ground discussing my various shortcomings. I would not have vomited blood into your mouth. I would not have even been affected by a thing such as tainted magic. We would never bleed, never get dirty, never sweat, never get headaches or injury, we would never cry or laugh. We would be statues, and would never fail at anything. We fail a lot."

Both Aidyn and Yayènia shared a small smile. The dark elf turned his gaze upon her. This time the look in his eyes was one of such profound understanding it took Tlonna's breath away.

"For five years I have waited for you to say that. I said that we were perfect in an effort to get you to understand that very thing you just said. We would never laugh, never cry, and never fail. We would be empty vessels of perfect proportions. We are people, Tlonna, as susceptible to corruption and failure as any other bipedal creature in this world," Aidyn said passionately, though his voice remained soft and quiet. "You have never understood that, until now. You have always strained to be this perfect creature, this model of untainted idealism, never realizing that doing so would mean to lose all that you are. You would not be capable of love, because love goes hand in hand with struggle and pain. It is something you have to fight for, and a perfect being is not capable of fighting for anything because they already have everything they need. I have wanted you to understand this since you were a child, Tlonna. Even then you were never happy with yourself, constantly striving for something that would destroy you."

Tlonna felt tears of shame running hot down her cheeks, and she looked away from both her companions, feeling inadequate. She wiped her knuckles across her face to remove the tears even though more kept coming. Finally she looked at Aidyn, who was staring at her without expression. His long, toned legs were drawn up with his arms hooked around his knees, his black leather boots nearly touching at the toes.

"How much pain and trial must I make you go through before I am satisfied?" she whispered to him, unable to make her voice any louder.

Aidyn's eyes narrowed dangerously. "What has happened to me happened because I chose to let it happen. I am an assassin, not a soldier. I do not have to fight in any battle, I do not have to do anything but sit in my manor and await a contract from you or Losolin. I choose to stay by your side, to fight in the war, to protect the kings of other lands. It is not by your command, it is who I am. Do not take responsibility for my actions, Tlonna. Only I can do that."

"But you would never have been captured by Sithian, never have fought the Eseirik, and certainly would never have had to fight Rhiannan in the guise of Yayènia."

The commander snorted. "How do you know? These events are happening for a reason, and who is to say that it would not be just someone else causing them? You are a catalyst, yes, but you are probably not the only person able to be it. If you had not survived for some reason someone else would have been chosen to take your place. Not saying that you are replaceable, you are definitely the best suited for it, but one of use would have taken up the torch, probably Losolin. But my point is that you cannot hold yourself wholly responsible for the events that are happening. To do otherwise would be arrogant and foolish in the extreme, and you are neither, at least most of the time."

Tlonna managed a small smile. "You are probably right, but it does not make it any easier. So many people expect me to be...something paranormal. They want me to fix everything, or to destroy everything. No one really wants me around, do they? Other than you lot, and sometimes I am not even sure about that."

Aidyn reached over to pat her knee. "Always, Tlonna. We always want you around. We all love you, and we stick around through the rough times because we believe in the cause you represent and fight for. Otherwise we would sit back and do only what you ordered us to, rather than argue with you or demand that at least one of us be with you on all of your crazy escapades."

The Magin Queen chuckled at his dry humor. "Thank you, Aidyn."

Yayènia's sigh as she got to her feet reminded Tlonna that they were in Purheae for a reason. What reason, she did not know. Aidyn held out his hand to help her up, and soon they were back on the horses and headed steadily toward Eyin's village. Tlonna remained pensive and silent, quite unable to look either of her friends in the eye. Aidyn rode on her left, Yayènia on her right, silent guardians as they traveled across the rough, wild landscape of the savage land.

It took several more hours for them to reach Eyin's home, and it was well past dark when then did. Aidyn rode directly into the village and left Tlonna and Yayènia behind to give Eyin some warning so they did not frighten the people. Several minutes later he reappeared with the young king, Meradyn, and Nebet'thu. The two females dismounted and met the males as they walked up to them.

As they bowed, Tlonna scrutinized the crown on Eyin's head. The horns that spiraled up from his temples glistened dully in the moonlights, and when he lowered his head she saw a bound tuft of hair decorating the back of the iron band.

"Queen Tlonna, High Commander Yayènia, a very great pleasure to see you both again. Welcome to my humble home," Eyin said graciously, sweeping out an arm back toward his village.

Tlonna smiled. "It is good to see you again as well, Eyin. And you, Meradyn."

The young man seemed thrilled to see Yayènia, and he kissed her hand before returning to his feet. "Yes, you too Queen Tlonna. High Commander, I am so happy you are here."

Yayènia gifted her protégé with a beaming grin. "I hope you have been keeping up on your training, Meradyn."

"Oh yes, High Commander. Not a day goes by without me spending at least three hours working myself."

"Excellent."

Tlonna gripped Nebet'thu's shoulder. "How have you been, my friend?"

The plains elf shrugged. "Fair enough, I suppose. I miss home."

"I hope to be able to send you back soon. After we see how things are going on here, I will let you know," the female replied quietly while giving him a small shake of understanding.

The shorter elf nodded his acknowledgement. Aidyn stepped forward. "We need a place to stay for the night, Eyin, and then we will be traveling on into the forest. We may need your help with that, as well."

The human seemed a little overwhelmed. "Ah, well, you can stay with Neb, again. Queen Tlonna and High Commander Yayènia will stay in my yurt. I shall stay with Mer."

"No, we will not put you out. Our tent has served us well this far," Tlonna interjected before anyone could move.

"But...you are a queen."

"And you are a king."

Eyin's expression crumbled with worry. "Please, I must give you the best accommodations available!"

"Eyin, stop it. If it is that big of a deal, we will stay wherever you want us to," Tlonna sighed, not wanting to argue with the boy.

The king let out a breath of relief. "Good. You shall stay in my quarters then. Come into my village."

They followed the shaggy-haired king into the walled village. Yayènia stared in disbelief at the wooden barricade.

"This is your defense structure?"

Eyin looked at her askance. "Yes. Before Nebet'thu came, we had none. For the moment this will have to do until we find the materials to build a stone wall. Do you not approve?"

Yayènia shrugged. "Did it keep out the Seadueni?"

Both Meradyn and Eyin gave her hard stares, which had even Tlonna's back straightening in surprise at their resolve.

"Our village is the only one that had such a structure. Our village is the only one still here," the king replied stiffly, his jaw muscles flexing with his obvious anger.

"Then I approve."

The palpable tension seemed to ease with Yayènia's simple words and they continued on into the center of the village. It was well after dark so everyone was abed, allowing Tlonna a good measure of the place itself. Yurts were lined up in a triple half circle, the center point being a large stone well with a wide rim that, from its worn appearance, was often used as a bench. A few small, well-tended trees dotted the center, and a large garden bereft of all but the hardiest of weeds sat against the wall on their right.

Directly across from the gate was a large ovular building, which Aidyn pointed out as the infirmary. Tlonna lifted an eyebrow at him, pointedly running her eyes down his body as though checking for injury. He responded with half a smile, his white teeth glinting in the moonlights. Eyin lifted a finger and pointed.

"There is where I'll be staying, with Mer, if you need me."

The three looked in the direction of his finger at a larger than average yurt. A black and brown flag sewn with the red stag hung limply in the winter night air just to the side of the door, on which were nailed two spears that crossed in the center. Meradyn looked proud, his shoulders straight and back as Yayènia clapped him on the back. Eyin led the rest of the way through the three rows of yurts to the largest building yet. It too had the flag, but hanging on both sides of the door, and a bit larger. Tlonna eyed the three round buildings that made up the royal suite, as it were. There was an odd light that reflected off the far side of the building, a kind of flickering green and orange that did not seem at all natural.

"What is behind your place?" she asked, frowning.

"The elder council gathers in a sacred house, and also the eternal flame is maintained there."

"Eternal flame?"

Eyin nodded. "A fire of offering to Lord Gagu, god of all humans and plants."

"How do you turn it green and orange?"

For a moment the human looked nervous, as though he were not supposed to be talking about such things, and then he let out a quiet huff. "The elders say it is a magical substance only they can handle, but I snuck into the Temple once, and I saw what they used. To turn it green, they use a copper powder, and to turn it orange they use calcium."

Meradyn looked shocked, not by what his friend had done, but by what he was saying. "My mother always told me it was magic."

"No one could do magic here, until...until King Losolin took down the barrier," Eyin responded, stumbling over the fact that it was in order to save Tlonna's life.

"And what is it for?"

The two young men seemed a bit unnerved by her interest in their esoteric beliefs. "It allows Lord Gagu to see us. If the eternal flame ever goes out, he will be blind to us, and we will no longer be protected by his sheltering hand."

Tlonna eyed Eyin in the darkness, knowing full well he could not see her as well as she saw him. "And do you believe that?"

The king shrugged. "Doesn't really matter if I do, does it? My people do, some of them quite emphatically. I will not destroy their faith just because I know some of their secrets."

Yayènia and Aidyn watched Tlonna's face warm into a proud smile, and they shared a relieved look.

"Good man," the queen said, clapping Eyin on the shoulder. "Now, I am tired. Where can our horses stay?"

Meradyn ducked his head in an unsure bow. "They have already been taken away to the stable. Your things are probably already in place."

Tlonna was a bit surprised by the response, but she did not allow it to show on her face. "Excellent. Then may we retire?"

Both Eyin and Meradyn bowed from the waist, much more graceful than the ones they had given months ago in Blackhaven. Nebet'thu shook his head and motioned to Aidyn.

"If you are to bother me again, I am not going to stay awake for it. You know where to go?"

The assassin nodded. When the three of them were alone Yayènia led the way into Eyin's home and looked about in that scrutinizing manner of hers. Tlonna wondered what she saw, if she saw a potential battlefield, or simply a room full of hides and rough spun fabric. Aidyn did the same thing, though he was much more subtle about it. Tlonna studied the fire in the hearth, which had burned down to a glow. She could see Eyin pacing before it, his muscular arms folded in that stubborn way of his as he worked over some decision his people had presented him with. There was a simple coat tree by the hearth, with a round ball on top similar to the one on her armor stand. While hers held her helmet, she supposed this one held the horned crown.

"What is your plan?" Yayènia asked after a moment of studying.

Tlonna shrugged. "I am not sure. There are two places here that are of interest. One of course is the Tower of Magins."

"*No,*" both Aidyn and Yayènia said the word sharp with emphasis.

"I agree," the queen said, sending them a slant-eyed look. "The other is Tonora's grave."

"Your ancestor?" Aidyn asked, frowning. "I thought she was killed in battle."

"No. She was murdered. It was during the most frenzied time of the war, so the story was spread that she was slain in battle in order to protect her resting place," Tlonna replied, moving over to stare into the hearth. "The truth has been known by few throughout history, the Ewôsdírn line of course, and a few others. Father told me as he lay dying that she was murdered by one who loved her, and hated her because she did not love him. She lies buried somewhere in this forest. Miazie has told me a general location, but she could never pin down exactly where."

Yayènia frowned slightly at her sister's back. "What do you think we will find there?"

"I cannot know. But it seems to me that is a good place to start. Yes?" Tlonna admitted as she turned to face her friends.

Both warriors nodded, and when no one said anything further, Yayènia strode into the room off to the left of the main one. The warrior walked back out, looking a bit shocked.

"The boy has a study! With books!"

"He is a king, Yayènia."

She snorted. "Of what, forty people? I have lieutenants that handle twice that number!"

"He had closer to one hundred and thirty people before the Seadueni showed up," Aidyn countered in defense for the human. "He is twenty-three years old, Yayènia! He is taking command of a land that has been utterly destroyed by past wars."

Tlonna let them argue as she made her way into the right room, which was the bedroom. Eyin's room seemed a blend of the child he was still outgrowing, and the man he was fast becoming. The bed was wide and a bit short, which meant her feet would probably hang off the edge, and was covered in a blanket made from several different furs. She bent down and saw to some amazement that there were finely spun sheets of wool beneath the cover. The walls were covered in hides, a new tapestry that depicted the red stag, a few mounted horns, and to her surprise, a small sketch of Blackhaven Castle.

She felt a presence enter the room and she turned to find Aidyn standing behind her. His tawny hand reached over her shoulder and pulled the drawing off the wall, careful not to tear it. It was well executed, obviously drawn with a fine-pointed stick covered in ash. The image was from the front, the main object being the gigantic stairway that leads from the ground up to the third floor. Even the veins of silver, pearl, and gold were sketched in, though in grayscale the whole thing looked like it was cracked into a several billion pieces.

"Whoever drew it has a fair hand," the assassin remarked quietly. "Which one do you think it was?"

Tlonna took the drawing from him and looked for a signature or mark. She found none, and shrugged. After tacking it back in place, she turned to face Aidyn. She had to lean backward in order to keep her face out of his neck he was so close. He did not move away. A tiny flutter of thrilled panic shivered through Tlonna's body.

"If you are not careful, one of our encounters is going to turn into something troublesome," she murmured as she looked up at him.

The dark elf lifted one winged eyebrow as he studied her face. "Would that be so terrible?" he breathed back, his eyes lidded.

Tlonna put a hand on his chest, fingers spread, and felt his slow heartbeat. "Yes. I am married to, and in love with, Losolin. You are my closest friend, Aidyn, and my protector."

The assassin allowed her to push him back with her hand. His lips curved into a mischievous smile. "As you wish, my queen," he murmured as he picked up her hand and kissed her knuckles. "I shall take my leave."

Tlonna watched him go with her heart in her throat, wishing for a moment that elves accepted polygamy. When that thought fully coalesced in her mind, she violently shook her head to rid herself of it. Disgusted, Tlonna yanked off her boots and stormed about, which caused Yayènia to come running in, katans drawn.

"What is it? What happened?"

"Why does he have to be so, so...smug and beautiful! Why does he have to be so arrogantly flaming perfect? Why does he have to exude that blasted sexuality like a bloody scent?"

"What are you talking about?" Yayènia said as she shoved her blades back into their scabbards.

"Aidyn!" Tlonna nearly screamed, remembering at the last second that the walls of a yurt were not very solid.

"Because that is who he is. Why, did you do something just now?"

The carefully hidden amusement in Yayènia's suspicious question got Tlonna's back up fast. The Magin glowered at her sister. "No. I have more self control than that."

"Ah."

"Why do you have that look?"

Yayènia's expression of knowing smugness slid immediately into her usual stoic blankness. "What look?"

"That look that says you know something and are not sharing."

The warrior hesitated a moment and then shrugged. "Just that when I kissed him, I was barely able to pull myself off of him, and I certainly did not want to."

Tlonna's eyes were wide open and unblinking as she gaped at Yayènia. "When you kissed him? When did you kiss him?"

"Back before we left, when he was in the hospital."

"Why?"

Again the commander shrugged. "I always wanted to know, and it seemed like a good time. He could not get up and chase me away," she lied.

"You have a husband."

"Who knows all about it and finds it rather amusing."

Tlonna swallowed. "What was it like?"

Yayènia's ice blue eyes narrowed. She decided now was not the time to inform her sister that she had lain with Aidyn before, and just did not remember. "You know. You have kissed him as well."

"Yes, but there was a lot of blood between us, and I was not aware of the fact."

The warrior sat down on the edge of the bed and removed her boots, and then her belt before answering. "It was like tasting the sun, hot and sweet and dangerous all at once. There was a moment when I was fully in control of my body, and then suddenly I had very little willpower. I could barely keep myself from ripping off my clothes and riding him. You know that scent he has, that kind of clean, spicy aroma that just about makes your eyes roll up in the back of your head?"

Tlonna nodded, thinking of the clothes she had stashed away that were filled with that very scent. Yayènia swallowed and looked away, obviously embarrassed.

"He tastes like that, only stronger. His lips are impossibly soft, and he is so very skilled with his tongue. So very skilled with everything."

"What stopped you from...what stopped you?"

Yayènia's shoulders slumped. "Suneelo. The thought of betraying him that way rose up in me, and I could not continue. I was worried that even as long as we have been married and as much as we have been though, he would not take lightly to my kissing Aidyn. He was not very happy for a few days, and then he just started laughing about it. Now he teases me mercilessly."

Tlonna sat down next to her sister. "What power does he have that we have such trouble resisting?"

Yayènia shook her head. "I do not know, but I do not think he does it on purpose, or even realizes it. I feel quite bad for Rahna, actually."

"Did you know her?"

"A little, just before she died. They were engaged, you know, and then she left him because she was afraid."

"Of Aidyn?" Tlonna asked, thinking of how much that must have hurt her friend.

Yayènia sighed as she tugged the vambraces off her forearms. "I think that was part of it, but more than that she was afraid he would not come back one time. Only in the last few years has he become the incredible fighter that he is now. He has always been absurdly skilled in fighting and killing, but suddenly he is just...unstoppable. But back then, every now and again he would get hurt pretty bad. It seemed to drain Rahna every time he came back with a little blood on him.

"Then without warning she left him. Their fight echoed through the entire castle, and I was only three doors down from him. I have never seen him act like that, not before, and certainly not after. The life just went out of him."

"Did you ever find out the whole reason of why she left him?" Tlonna asked when Yayènia said nothing further.

"Aidyn never speaks of it, but I am pretty sure it has to do with him being an assassin. She was a gentle creature, absolutely petrified of me. I could never figure out how she could sleep with Aidyn every night, and literally go weak in the knees whenever I was around. Anyhow, she left him, and then there was an attack."

Tlonna frowned as she pulled off her shirt and reached for her nightclothes. Yayènia was untying her breeches and paused to fight with the knot in the laces. When she finally triumphed and pushed her pants down, she started talking again as she too dressed for sleep.

"Hadian Rahlan had just sacked Zeynuwn, though none of us knew it at the time. We figured it was some errant band left over from the War of Monotheism that was trying to wipe out polytheists. Well, the battle somehow poured into the castle itself, and people were running and screaming in panic, searching for some safe place to hide. Aidyn was up on the second floor landing firing off arrows as fast as thought. I was across the landing with Ghealan, fighting desperately with my squad. It was before I was High Commander."

Tlonna's eyebrows rose as she tidied her things and slid into the bed. She had never heard Yayènia talk about her time in the army preceding her current office other than the fight with Ghealan that determined who would become High Commander. No wonder the fight had spilled into the castle. Yayènia would have died before letting that happen. The only reason she had not when Midian had attacked Blackhaven was because there were no soldiers left to fight alongside, and it was stand alone and let Ghealan die from the wounds he had received, or flee and let him live.

Yayènia got into the bed next to her and pulled the blankets up to her chest. "Anyway, I saw Rahna come flying out of a room, the common room just off the landing there."

Tlonna nodded that she knew which room it was when Yayènia looked at her.

"She saw Aidyn and screamed for him. He watched her running for her, but continued to fire off shots, then when she was about a dozen paces away he turned to her, his arms outstretched to take her in, and that is when it happened. An arrow went right through her skull. She had enough momentum to carry her into Aidyn's arms, but she was dead before she got there. His face was so horror-stricken I could barely recognize him, even though I had watched it happen. He picked Rahna up and held her to him as he pulled out his sword and started destroying people. One handed he took down most of the enemy within the castle foyer. I have never seen such rage."

"I cannot imagine such a terrible thing. To have the person you love running toward you for safety and die in such a horrible way just steps away...I could not live with myself," Tlonna said quietly, staring up at the dark leather ceiling.

"Aidyn changed after that. He took no lovers, barely spoke to anyone, including Dietirin, for nearly a year. Even after he began talking again, he remained chaste. Then something happened, and he regained a little bit of his personality back."

"What happened?"

Yayènia froze, realizing that it had been the day after Tlonna's forty-fifth birthday that Aidyn had come back to himself. The night after he had been with her. She scrunched up her face as she quickly tried to come up with an answer.

"I uh...I think he slept with someone."

"Who?"

Damn. "I do not know."

"Well then why do you think he slept with someone?" Tlonna asked as she turned on her side to look at her sister.

Yayènia gave her a pained expression. "He just seemed more relaxed, sated...a little bit happier. You know how males look after they have been bounced. He looked like that."

Tlonna did indeed know, and her mind flashed back to Losolin lying sweaty and exhausted on the cot in their tent, a look of utter satisfaction on his perfect face, his dark blue eyes half-closed and his lips parted as he sucked in air. She flipped onto her back and linked her hands over her belly.

"Does Suneelo's voice get huskier during?" she asked suddenly, thinking of how Losolin's did.

Yayènia choked with shock at such a question. Once she had composed herself, the warrior glared at her sister. "Why? Does Losolin's?"

"Yes."

"Well...yes it does. It gets all scratchy and breathy and sometimes I can hardly understand him, especially when he gets excited about something. One time, afterwards, we got an invitation to a rare book auction. I swear all I heard was wheezing as he shouted at me for half an hour about some book he had been searching for and must be at this auction. It was by the way, and we ended up paying nearly eighty geld for the damn thing."

Tlonna chuckled at Yayènia's sour tone. "What book?"

The warrior flicked a hand in the air. "Something about Serenyi's wars."

"And that does not interest you?"

"No. Why would it?"

Tlonna shrugged against the pillow, which sent up the earthy smell of Eyin. Though it was not a dirty smell, or even unpleasant, it had nothing on the elven males in her life. "Ancient history fascinates me. I love reading about how they fought long ago with different codes of honor and tactics we no longer use. Losolin does too, but he reads any book he can get his hands on."

"I enjoy reading as well, but I like stories that are not real. I like to lose myself in a world that does not require me to make any choices other than which characters I like. Every now and then I will read books on the history of weapons or books on battle, but I find them educating, not so entertaining."

The queen nodded her understanding and lifted a hand to wipe strands of hair from her face. "I wonder if Losolin and Suneelo ever realize how much they are truly alike."

"I do not think so. Look at Aidyn and Aladorn too. Every time they do something similar, they stare at each other in suspicion, all four of them."

"We do not do that," Tlonna muttered stiffly.

"No, we do not," Yayènia replied just as defensively.

"When I met Aladorn, he was so creepy," Tlonna said after a moment of awkward silence. "He called himself Udu."

"That is my horse's name," the commander chuckled.

"I know. It took a long time for Losolin and me to warm up to him. Aladorn actually cut Losolin during an altercation. Then they fought in the courtyard of an inn, and suddenly they were all friendly to each other."

"Aladorn strikes me as a very protective person. He guards himself well from others," Yayènia replied quietly, and then yawned not so quietly.

"I wonder how he and Aidyn realized they were brothers. Seven hundred years is a long time to be separated."

"Maybe they saw each other naked."

Tlonna's snort of laughter escaped her before she could stop it. "What would that prove?" she finally managed.

Yayènia grinned at her sister. "I have seen both Losolin and Suneelo in the buff. They are very similarly sized. I do not know if that is a brotherly trait, or just them, but knowing what Aidyn looks like, and the rumors I have heard about Aladorn, I think they share the same."

Tlonna was gripping her sides as images of the four males marched naked across her imagination. It was not a terrible thing to imagine even as she laughed with the absurdity of Yayènia's suggestion. At last she got her giggles under control and rolled onto her side once more.

"When did you see Losolin naked? And Aidyn for that matter?"

Yayènia's eyes twinkled in the darkness. "I saw your husband stark naked a very long time ago, before you knew each other. I walked in on him getting out of the tub during the short time he lived with Suneelo. He was quite upset with me."

"I can imagine. And Aidyn?"

"Well that was not so fun. Ghealan and I were in Seaduens to take care of a few traitors from Blackhaven when we were set upon by an entire group of the bastards. Aidyn came to our aid, as he had been there tracking an elf who had raped and murdered four women, which was lucky for us because we were a little overwhelmed. We got them all, but Aidyn had been stabbed in the hip and shoulder by an elf named Torsin, one of the ones he killed here a few weeks ago. He was losing so much blood we had to strip him to get to the wounds and stop the bleeding. Even then, when he was laying there unconscious and bleeding to death, I was...quite breathless."

"Indeed?"

Yayènia made an agreeable sound low in her throat. "Indeed."

They lapsed into silence and drifted off to sleep. Tlonna had such wonderful dreams, that when she woke, she had made a rather rash decision.

# Chapter 21
## The Magin Stone

Tlonna and Yayènia met Aidyn, Eyin, Meradyn, and Nebet'thu outside the royal yurt early the next morning. The queen could not help it. Her eyes landed on Aidyn's exquisite face, slithered down his body, and took in all she now knew from her hushed conversation with her sister during the night. She could feel a blush creeping up her face, but she could not look away from his shapely, muscled thighs. Tlonna took in the way his scimitar belt slanted more to the right than the left and the way the split, dagged sides of his *ärdyz* tunic parted just below the telltale bulge in his leather pants, teasing her by hiding what she knew was there. Early morning light winked between his thighs as he shifted his stance, telling all the world that there was not a spare ounce of fat on his legs, or the rest of his body for that matter.

Yayènia subtly nudged her and Tlonna looked up sharply, wondering if seconds had passed, or hours. Aidyn was staring at her with an intense expression, a little baffled, a little pleased, and much more accusatory. His emerald eyes were not blinking as he looked at her, so she turned her gaze away.

"Lord Aidyn said you might need some information from us?" Eyin said, oblivious to the very adult matter that was thickening the air around them.

"Ah...yes. Do you know where Tonora died?"

"Who?"

"Tonora? The elf who fought the Magins in the Tower, the elf who died and became a moon, my ancestor?"

Eyin looked at Meradyn for help, and found none. He bit his lip. "Jorunson would probably know. I will send for him. Why do you need to know?"

Tlonna walked down the short set of steps that led from the yurt to the ground. "I need to visit her grave."

"Why?"

"I just do," the queen muttered.

As Meradyn rushed off to find the literate Purheaen, the small group stood around avoiding each other's gazes. Yayènia and Aidyn were having a staring contest and neither warrior seemed to know why. Tlonna was studying everyone's boots, and studied them all the harder when Nebet'thu pointedly shifted his feet. Finally Meradyn returned with Jorunson, who looked less than pleased to see the elves he had believed himself rid of.

"Yeah?" he demanded, ignoring Eyin's fiery glare.

Tlonna looked the impertinent youth in the eye, having never really liked him. He thought she was a whore. "Do you know where Tonora died, or is buried?"

The young man was silent for a minute as he thought, his hand rubbing against his jaw line. "East of here quite a ways, in the center of the thickest part of the forest. There's not a lot written about her because so few knew of her until much later, but if what I have studied is correct, she's buried deep in the woods. Several miles from the Tower of Magins, I would say."

"Could you point out the general location on a map?" Tlonna asked, still looking Jorunson in the eye.

He lifted one shoulder in an uncaring gesture. "Sure."

"I have maps inside," Eyin said, and then bopped Jorunson on the back of the head. "Stop being a prick."

Jorunson glared at his king with a sullen temper as they filed inside Eyin's home. The king beckoned everyone into the study and bent over a woven basket full of rolled maps. Tlonna was impressed with the collection. He found the one he wanted and spread it out on his desk, a simple affair of four untreated legs supporting a thick, untreated desktop. He handed Jorunson a quill and stepped aside to let his friend work.

"Did you sleep well?" he asked suddenly, mortified that he had forgotten to ask such a thing.

"Very. Your bed is quite comfortable," Tlonna assured him, smiling when she saw Jorunson's body stiffen with confused surprise. "And you?"

Eyin nodded. "Mer and I used to share a yurt before they made me this...thing." His hand swept out to encompass the three-yurt house. "I tried to deny it, told them to use it as the mending house or something, but they would not hear of it." He sounded as though she should be ashamed of him.

Tlonna smiled. "A king should have a special place from where he runs his kingdom. It goes along with that crown on your head."

Eyin's hand lifted to touch one of the horns spiraling up from the iron band. "Still, sometimes it makes me feel a fool."

"It does that to all of us," the queen said gently, touching her own delicate band of silver that sufficed as a crown while she was running about the continent.

"Here," Jorunson said and shoved the rolled map at Tlonna with little grace. "It's all marked for you. Do not get mad at me if it is wrong. I can only tell you what little I have deduced."

"I will not fault you for unintentionally misleading us," Tlonna guaranteed him, making sure he did not miss the inflection she put on 'unintentionally'. "I thank you for your help."

The youth grunted and looked at Eyin, who nodded in a weary sort of way. Jorunson rushed out of the yurt and skipped by Aidyn who was leaning against the doorframe.

"I suppose you will be on your way immediately?" the king asked, his voice disappointed.

"Yes, but we will return when our search is over. Would it be all right for us to leave our horses here? If we are traveling through thick forest I do not want to deal with them being tangled up all the time."

"Sure, sure. Meradyn is teaching some of the younger boys how to take care of the two horses you granted us, and Neb's Leartia, of course."

Tlonna looked back at the plains elf, who was reclining against the wall a few feet away from Aidyn. He nodded his confirmation of the village's competence in dealing with the animals.

"Then we must be off. Thank you for your help, King Eyin."

"You're more than welcome, Queen Tlonna. I hope you find what you are looking for."

"I do too," the Magin said heartily, and led the way out of the yurt.

She hefted her pack and adjusted her weapons around it to make it more comfortable. She saw Aidyn and Yayènia doing the same, though they looked much more lethal than she felt. They set off with well wishes from Eyin, Meradyn, and Nebet'thu.

Tlonna sighed as she, Aidyn, and Yayènia ducked under yet another thick vine. The assassin remained a silent shadow behind her, but the warrior up ahead mumbled and swore as she hacked away at the clogged undergrowth. They had been hiking through Purheae's deep forest for three days now, attempting to follow Jorunson's unsure directions.

"This is ridiculous," Yayènia grumbled as she tugged her katan out of another branch. "We are never going to find her tomb, Tlonna. We should just go back."

"Nonsense. The magical residue is strong here, and getting stronger. She is near," the Magin countered. "Aidyn, what do you feel?"

For a moment the dark elf continued to be silent. Then he huffed in resignation and lifted a finger to rub the scars on his cheek. "I feel a great sadness in the air; murder was done here."

"Then we are very close. Miazie was able to tell me Tonora was buried only a few feet from where she died."

Yayènia shoved her katan back into its sheath and folded her arms beneath her chest. "We should have brought her with us. She is the one who supposedly saw us on this fool errand."

"Miazie is dealing with problems of her own, Nia. She and Sodo are facing problems unprecedented."

The warrior frowned. "What? He is an elf, she is...quarter elf or something like that. What problems?"

Aidyn snorted. "Oh, nothing about Sodo being touched by evil, or Miazie having the genetic memories of two strange elves within her. Their child is going to be different."

"Different how?" Yayènia demanded.

"How am I to know?" the assassin snapped, irritated with the female.

Tlonna snarled in annoyance. "You would think, old as you two are, that you would both know when to keep quiet."

Aidyn grunted and Yayènia snapped her mouth shut with a click.

"*Old* as we are?" the assassin muttered, amusement lacing his voice. "Does not keep you from staring at me, now does it? Get your fill?"

Tlonna spun on her heel and pointed a stiff finger in the dark elf's face. "Just because you happen to be pretty does not make you irresistible," she boldly lied. "Keep your mouth shut or I will slap it off your pretty face."

Aidyn's impish grin caught her off guard, and he leaned forward to plant a kiss on her supposed-to-be-threatening finger, his eyes staying steady on her face. "So glad you think I am pretty. I will have to work on that irresistible part."

"I am married, thank you very much."

"You are quite welcome," the assassin said too brightly and held out his hand in an invitation for her to resume the walk.

Tlonna turned and stomped onward, shoving an amused Yayènia along before her. She was about to tell her sister to stop giggling but stopped instead, going perfectly still.

"We are here."

Aidyn and Yayènia stopped and moved to her side, all teasing mirth gone. Now they were guardians; deadly, focused, ready. They moved a little off to either side, better to watch the surrounding forest as Tlonna took a few more steps forward and gasped when she entered an empty clearing. The Magin closed her eyes and breathed deep, sensing the Weaves. The air shimmered like a heat wave in spite of the chilly winter air. Sparks of light flashed through the clearing. Yayènia stepped backward, gripping the hilt of her longblade.

"What is it?" she whispered as the air began to pulsate slowly.

Tlonna ignored her sister, lifted her hand, and flicked her fingers through the air. The air impacted without sound, knocking the elves to the ground with such force it kept them down for a few seconds. Aidyn recovered first, then Yayènia. They helped Tlonna to her feet and tried to ignore the painful tingling that came from her hands.

Slowly, the three of them looked around at the clearing, utterly surprised. Within the center stood an ancient tomb, its granite surface pocked from weather and age. Moonflower vines had dug into the stone, their tendrils embedded deep into the stone façade.

"How long ago did she die?" asked Yayènia, her mouth dry as she stared at the tomb that had been hidden from them.

"A little more than two thousand years ago. As I said, everyone believed she was killed in battle, only her descendants know the truth."

"And her descendant is you?" the warrior asked when Tlonna fell silent.

"Well, you and me," Tlonna replied, turning to the stunned warrior. "I thought you knew that."

"I knew you were, I guess I never thought that would include me. I still have trouble remembering Selinia and Yinji were not my parents."

Tlonna nodded and took Yayènia by the hand to draw her closer to the tomb. Aidyn stayed back, looking unnerved. As the females approached, the air seemed to thicken until they could no longer move. Panic seized Yayènia but she could not force her hands to her blades, try as she might. Tlonna felt a searching presence and relaxed her muscles, trying to convey her feelings toward her seething sister.

A breath of wind brushed across their faces like cool, tender fingers. A whisper was carried on the air, soft and warm. *"You may pass, my daughters,"* it murmured, and the wall disappeared.

Yayènia's hands shot into the hilts of her katans, uncontrolled, and her knuckles slammed painfully on the edges. She yelped in surprise, her face ashen with fear. "The wind talked, called us its daughters."

Tlonna smiled. "It was Tonora. She felt us, recognized us. Are you ready?"

"No, but I never will be," Nia muttered and stepped to the tomb.

The queen followed her and smiled faintly. Tonora's likeness was carved into the granite, her hands folded restively on her belly. Around her hands in a circle were holes, each accompanied with a name.

Tlonna touched the nearest hole with a reverent finger. *"Sen,"* she moved to the next, *"Shaltisimö,"* and another, *"Blütenar."*

"There are fifteen," Yayènia said quietly.

Tlonna nodded as she untied the blue silk bag at her belt. "The Magin Stones. This is why they came to me. This is why they came to the line of Tonora. This is why Miazie saw us here."

"What will happen?"

"I do not know," Tlonna admitted as she dumped the ordinary looking rocks into her palm.

"Do you think that wise?" Yayènia snapped, grabbing her sister's wrist as she went to place a stone, *Kaltenuss*, into its spot.

The Magin shrugged. "We will find out," she said and dropped the stone into the hole.

It moved sharply as though drawn by a magnet, and then went still. Tlonna quickly placed the stones in their respective spots, each one jerking about for an instant and then going still. When she dropped *Flaridon*, both she and Yayènia took a prudent step backward. There was an odd clicking noise and then different colored light pulsed from each stone to join in the center, directly above Tonora's stone hands to form a cone of colored light. The bar of light flickered between each color and then turned brilliant, pure white. It was so blinding the sisters lifted a hand to shield their eyes.

Then there was another concussion but this one was not silent. The forest trembled with the force of the thunder while birds alighted at the deafening boom. Aidyn was thrown against the base of a tree while Yayènia and Tlonna were laid flat out, their very bones rattled.

"What was that?" the warrior snarled, brushing off the seat of her pants.

Tlonna was silent as she stared at the tomb. The fifteen stones were gone, molded into the granite, turned to gray stone. Above Tonora's hand rotated a new stone, deepest black on the inside, opaque white on the outside. Tlonna gazed at it, drawn and repulsed at the same time.

"What is it?" Yayènia asked, her icy eyes riveted on the stone.

Tlonna shook her head. "I do not know, but it has power, immense power."

"Wonderful, just what we needed. More dangerous magical stuff," the commander scoffed. "Well, take it and we can go."

The queen eyed her. "You take it."

"No, I am not touching that thing!"

Tlonna laughed and lifted her hand, shielding it in a non-invasive Weave. When her fingers wrapped about the stone, it crackled and sparked, but remained passive. Her hand nearly covered the entire thing, a faint light pulsing from between her fingers. She dropped it into the silk bag and tied it to her belt. Yayènia grunted at her and shook her head.

"What is it for?"

Again Tlonna admitted her ignorance. "There is a reason for it, just as there was a reason for the fifteen stones."

"Perhaps it belongs with that thing you always have," Nia said, gesturing to the Staff of Cyree on Tlonna's back.

Tlonna's eyebrows rose as she led Yayènia away from the tomb, back toward an impatient Aidyn. "You may be right. I never thought of that. The staff was made by the Council of Magins, as were the stones. They were both left for me, and they were made to augment magical powers. Maybe they are two parts of one talisman."

They had reached Aidyn and were met by a seething glower. "What in the nine bloody hells was that about?"

"The power of the fifteen Magin Stones has been combined by Tonora's spirit into one stone. Nia thinks it belongs with *Isten shä Talchin*."

Aidyn eyed the staff and the stone Tlonna had shoved in his face with disgust. "More magic?"

Tlonna kissed his scarred cheek. "Always," she chirped and put the stone back.

"What will you call it?" Yayènia asked once they were on their way back to Eyin's village. "Talismans always have names."

The Magin Queen was silent for a while. "The Magin Stone. We do not know what it does, and I do not want to associate Tonora with anything malevolent."

Her companions nodded in agreement. Aidyn let out a soft breath, rubbing the back of his hand across his scars, feeling the lingering memory of her kiss. Yayènia slid him a sly glance, her lips twitching against a smile. He gave a slight shake of his head and bit his own bottom lip. Tlonna continued on ahead, ignoring the silent conversation her friends were having behind her back. The Magin's hand kept returning to the Magin Stone to feel the glorious power that radiated from it.

The assassin crossed his arms over his belly, gripped the hilts of his scimitars, and strolled along comfortably as Yayènia stared at him in judgment. The two warriors kept a watchful eye on the surrounding forest, ever wary as they watched each other. Tlonna knew they were exchanging looks, but found herself not caring. She was one step closer to the end, one more question answered in the riddle of her fate. She knew Yayènia was right. The Stone belonged with the Staff. It was emitting pleasurable warmth from where it sat slanted across her back next to her bow, on top of her pack. It pulsed in harmony with the Stone at her hip. It was all starting to come together.

They were looking for a place to set up camp for the night when the chilling ring of Aidyn's scimitars coming out of their sheaths shattered the silence. Tlonna went into an instinctive crouch as Yayènia's katans followed a heartbeat later. There was a rustle in the canopy of the twisted trees right above them, and the warriors edged closer to their queen.

Tlonna released her hold on her magic and let it fill her until she was awash in the sheer power and waited. The three of them, back to back, waited. There was a low muttering coming from the canopy. With a loud thump, two forms dropped from the height to land directly in front of Aidyn. They were very short creatures with scraggly hair covered in leafs and twigs. Tlonna and Yayènia swung around so that they each flanked the assassin and stared at the two people who came up to their knees.

"State your name." one of them demanded in a whispering voice that was more akin to wind than words.

"I am Tlonna Ewôsdírn, the Everwood. I am the Magin Queen of Blackhaven. This is Aidyn Sestuns, my guardian, and High Commander Yayènia er'Tiena of the Blackhaven Militia. Who are you?"

The creature who had first spoken stepped forward and presented a small bow. "I am Teechus, and this is Beriles."

"An honor," Tlonna said and knelt down to be closer to the creatures' height. "You are Tree Elves, are you not?"

Teechus bowed again. "Yes, High Elf Queen," he said in his whispery voice.

"Have you been following us?"

"Since you entered the forest we have watched you. We are the guardians of these trees. Queen Tonora gave us this duty, and we hold to it with our very lives."

"You lived during her time?" Yayènia asked as she too went to her knees.

Teechus looked at her, lifting his head so that they could see his face. It was a beautiful face, ageless and full of wisdom. His eyes were completely green, with no pupils and no whites. There seemed to be shapes shifting in them, but it could have been the ephemeral twilight reflecting off them. His skin was a pearly white, and the roots of his dark hair were green like moss. Though he and Beriles were small, they exuded a power and wisdom that overwhelmed the tall elves before them. Beriles had yet to look at them, and yet to speak, but Tlonna could see streaks of rusty red in his hair.

"We were here before her, created when the Men destroyed the inner forest that you now stand in. We were the children of Men, once, long ago. But that time is long gone, a near-forgotten legend. We were given a new life, an unending life. Queen Tonora gathered our kind and gave us the same strength and hope she gave her own people. She was the first of her kind, as I was mine."

"What do you mean she was the first of her kind?" Tlonna asked, finding it a little difficult to catch every word in the sighing wind.

"She was an elf like any other except in one regard. She could not heal anything but the most mundane of things, but she could destroy. She was not a Magin as you are, for her powers were more internal. There was no visible representation of what she did. It just happened."

"Tonora is our foremother," Tlonna said, gesturing between her and Yayènia.

Teechus nodded. "Yes. You look like her, but you," he shifted his green gaze to Yayènia, "have her build. You, Everwood, have her mind and her heart, but the Guardian has her body."

"How do you know I am the Guardian?" Yayènia breathed, unhinged by the strangeness of the day.

Beriles finally stepped forward and looked at her with the same ageless face as Teechus, but his eyes were red, as were the roots of his hair. When he spoke it was a harder wind, angrier.

"When Queen Tonora's body was molested and murdered by that foul traitor she lifted her soul above the mortal realm and sent it with her hopes and dreams into the sky. The traitor saw this and was afraid, but he knew his wrongdoing and fell before her mangled body to weep. That extracted soul went into the sky and became a moon, but it served another purpose. It ensured the survival of her essence. When you were born to her line, Yayènia er'Tiena, you had the heart of her, but not the body or power. You were too angry. When you were born, Everwood, her heart had already been taken, but not her body. You received that. Together, you make up Tonora's living spirit."

"Why do you think you cannot die?" Teechus interjected. "Because you are special?"

"I am a Maig," Yayènia said defensively.

"Even a Maig cannot heal a cut throat. Only you!"

The chilly wind in the forest whipped at them with Teechus' declaration. "You cannot die while your sister lives, just as she cannot die while you live!"

"How is that possible?" Tlonna breathed, her eyes riveted on the tree elves.

"You are one being." Beriles said as if that should answer all their questions.

"But...I am three hundred and fifty-four years older than her!" Yayènia protested loudly.

"And you believe that matters? You think three and half centuries means anything to us, who can live forever if we so choose? You think it matters to this prophecy?"

"But, I do not heal. I am not a Maig," Tlonna said, shaking her head.

Teechus stared at her for a bit before speaking again. "Why do you think prophecy appointed you with three Guardians?"

"There is only one mentioned in the prophecy."

"Is there? The Lover shall rule? The Guardian shall fall? The Friend shall perceive?"

"Losolin and Miazie are my other protectors?"

Teechus glanced at Aidyn for a moment but remained silent. The assassin's fingers clenched on his knees as he thought about what Miazie had told him about *that* part of the prophecy. He too remained silent, then Teechus spoke softly.

"Do you not often find yourself torn in two? Does not your heart yearn in two different directions? Do you not wonder at this? Understand that Tonora's being was torn in two by the birth of Yayènia Nefarian Ewôsdírn. Her soul went first, to lend fire to the protector. When you were born, that soul was taken, and so you filled your own. Part of you belongs to *you*, and other to fate, as your heart does. Fighting it will only bring you pain."

Tlonna felt Aidyn shift beside her, and she felt something snap inside of her chest, like a faint click.

Beriles sighed, a rustling of leaves, and shook his head. "Unconditional love is the strongest protection against all emotional attack. Fierce loyalty is the strongest protection against all physical attack. Unbound knowledge is the strongest protection against lies and deceptions. Just because one has the title Guardian does not mean the other two are simply there to be of aid."

"I never thought of it that way."

"Which is why you have been seeking answers you do not need."

"What of the Staff and the Stone then? What can you tell me of them?"

Teechus shifted his little feet on the loamy ground and clasped his hands before him. "Only that you will need them in the end."

"I already know that."

The tree elves exchanged glances. "There are some things you must discover for yourself, Queen Tlonna. We cannot give you all the answers."

"But can you not help me?"

"Have we not already helped you? Opened your blind eyes a little further?" Teechus demanded. "We are not obliged to tell you anything, yet it is for the future of all beings that you fight for. We are not fools. Once all the High, Dark, and Plains Elves are wiped out, the Dark Man will turn for the last of us, the Tree Elves. We have seen this future, and it is bleak."

"Then it is already decided that we will fail?" Yayènia challenged angrily.

"No. This is but one path on the many-forked road that you walk right now. We have seen several futures, not all are bleak, not all are happy," Beriles told her, unruffled by her temper. "We will tell you this. You will need the aid of all good kings in this land if you are to succeed."

"All good kings?" Tlonna muttered, confused. "Who?"

"All good kings, Everwood, all good kings."

"Does that exclude emperors?"

"All good kings."

"What the bloody nine hells does that mean?"

Beriles and Teechus bowed and strode away, disappearing long before they should have, their forms twisting away in coils of wind. Tlonna and her two companions sat on their heels for a long time staring at the same spot in silence. The Magin felt the confidence she had experienced upon finding the Magin Stone fade away.

Downhearted, she slowly got to her feet and helped Yayènia up. Aidyn rose as fluidly as ever, his face void of any expression.

Tlonna inhaled deeply and let it go in a huff. "Well, I need to think about that."

Yayènia snorted as she ripped the pack off her back. "Useless nonsense," she growled as she tore her sleeping roll off the bottom of her bag and tossed it on the leafy ground, having decided that she was done walking for the day.

Aidyn wandered off to find deadfall for a fire, his footsteps nearly silent on the dry ground. Tlonna watched him go, feeling him nestled in her heart like a warm bundle. Yayènia grumbled to herself as she fluffed her bedroll with unnecessary force. Leaving her to her fury, Tlonna stood and followed the assassin, her heart thudding as she decided to act upon her decision.

Aidyn slammed the heel of his boot into the center of a dry log, snapping it half. He bent to pick up the smaller pieces, but pivoted when he heard footsteps behind him. Tlonna stood there, twisting the bottom of her shirt in her hands, looking tormented. The dark elf said nothing, just remained in his crouch as she stared at him.

"You know I love Losolin, right?"

Aidyn narrowed his eyes at her. "Of course."

"I...love him deeply, and I would never want to cause him harm. He stands so strong for me, no matter what I do to him."

The assassin stood and folded his arms, cocking an eyebrow. "Yes, he does."

Tlonna bit her lip and sucked in a shaky breath. "You drive me mad. I lose all manner of control around you. Only with you do I ever think of what it would be like to be with someone other than Losolin. I have dreams like memories, and when I wake all I want is you." Aidyn's heart began to race and his breathing shortened as she moved closer to him. "I do not want anything to be between us," she murmured, sliding her hands down his arms to grip his wrists. Gently, she pulled his arms apart, then tugged his shirt out of his belt.

"Tlonna..." he warned, "I cannot control myself with you. If you go any further, I will not be able to stop. I do not want you to betray Losolin. He is a dear friend and I will not rip the two of you apart."

Her fingers found the trigger on his belt buckle and pressed it. The scimitars clattered to the ground as his belt fell away. "I know," she whispered. "He is my heart and my husband, but if I do not do this, I will regret it for the rest of my life, and it will always come between us. All three of us."

Aidyn did not help her, but he did not stop her as she pressed the other buckle that held his baldric in place against his chest. His sword and bow joined his scimitars on the ground. Tlonna found the laces on his *ärdyz* and swiftly undid them, pushing aside the asymmetrical hem. She slid her hands up his warm torso, gliding over the muscles and scars. Aidyn's chest was moving with his rapid breathing. He kept his hands down at his sides, part of him hoping that she would stop herself, the other part begging that she keep going.

Tlonna pressed her mouth to his throat, which was beating visibly with his fluttering pulse. "No blood, no sorrow," she whispered.

Aidyn felt her grip tighten on his shoulders beneath his gaping shirt, and suddenly she slammed his back against a nearby tree, pressing her body against his. Her mouth was hot and hungry on his, her fingers digging into his hair. He could resist no longer, and wrapped his arms around her, returning her affections with enthusiasm. He lifted her up and reversed their positions, pressing her against the rough bark. Tlonna moaned as he lifted her shirt free of her belt and slid his hands up her smooth back. She could feel the leather straps on his right hand that triggered his hidden blade, but felt a thrill of excitement at the danger.

With a curse, the assassin shoved away and scrabbled at his arm, yanking the contraption off and throwing it to the forest floor with reckless unconcern. He returned to Tlonna, his fingers digging into her hips as she tugged at the laces on his pants.

Their mouths met again, unrestrained and passionate. Aidyn felt his pants loosen, and gripped her backside, lifting her up against the tree. Tlonna wrapped her legs around him, still separated by their britches, but pressed hard against each other. The queen couldn't seem to get a full breath into her lungs and a sort of madness had taken over her. All she knew was the hardness of the assassin's body against hers, the scent of his skin and the shaking desire in his hands. She was desperate for him, hopelessly entrenched in his pull. Tlonna tightened her legs around him and framed his face with her hands, her thumbs against his sharp cheekbones. She kissed him again, sliding her fingers through his silken raven hair. She gripped a handful and pulled his head back so she could press her lips against his throat, her teeth scraping gently against his flesh.

Aidyn felt a moan escape him as he bared his throat for her. His control was in shards, his willpower nothing more than a vague memory. He loved her so desperately. When her hand suddenly dipped low and reached beneath his unlaced trousers, alarm bells went off in his head. Her fingers wrapped around him, and his knees buckled. Her legs dropped from around him and she shifted to hold up her own weight.

With a groan, Aidyn sank to his knees before her. She had released him when he crumpled, but the sensation remained. He buried his face in her lower abdomen and sucked in a ragged breath.

"Aidyn?" Tlonna cried gently, her hands moving to the back of his head.

"I cannot do this," he nearly sobbed, forehead pressed against her belt buckle. "Please do not do this to me."

Tlonna's heart broke at the words. She had never thought to hear Aidyn beg. His fingers dug into her thighs as he pressed her face against her, shuddering. Tlonna slowly lowered herself to the ground and wrapped her arms around him, drawing him close. He lay between her legs, half-undressed, painfully desirous. With a groan he stretched out, fallen leaves rustling as they piled up against his legs.

Exhausted, the assassin crawled up to the base of the tree and held an arm out in invitation. Tlonna rolled against him, face to face. She looked up into his tortured green gaze as she tucked her arms against his chest.

"I thought you would not be able to stop yourself," she whispered.

Aidyn closed his eyes and shifted, driving one leg between hers. "I nearly did not."

"Why did you?"

"Because we cannot be, Tlonna. You are married, and though I know Losolin loves you more than anything in this world, I do not think he would be able to forgive us this."

Tlonna sighed and wormed her way closer to the assassin, pushing against him. "What do I do, Aidyn? I need you so badly."

The assassin drew her mouth up for a final kiss, then rested his chin atop her head. "I do not know," he whispered.

Yayènia sat poking the fire with a stick, feeling torn about what she figured was happening in the trees. It was not a matter of adultery, she knew. Aidyn had been made for the express purpose of being Tlonna's lover, according to the Tree Elves. But, Tlonna had fallen in love with Losolin against all odds. Her sister was being torn in two different directions, one by fate and the other by chance, and she could not fight either.

Suddenly a thought hit her, and Yayènia sat up straighter. Aidyn had been born to this world with the intention of being a lover, to be a consort. With that purpose dashed by chance, his function would have to go somewhere else. Abruptly she knew why no female seemed able to resist the assassin. He was *meant* to be a sensual whirlwind, and without its intended target, those lashes of power reached out and drew in every possible mark, enticing anyone who might become a lover to him.

"Ah gods, Aidyn," she murmured sadly. "The spirits have not been kind to you."

She looked up as a rustle alerted her, and her two companions appeared through the trees. Tlonna held Aidyn's belts and weapons while the assassin carried a bundle of firewood. They both looked distraught. Yayènia noted that her sister's belt and pants looked just as they had when she left, though her shirt was pulled free, but Aidyn's were undone and loose about his hips, and his shirt hung open. His hair was in disarray and his eyes were red. Apparently he had been too upset to put himself back together again.

The assassin dropped the wood by the fire and flopped down next to it, ignoring his half-naked appearance. Yayènia eyed him for a moment then looked to Tlonna, who had leaves in her hair. The commander lifted an eyebrow in question. Her sister shook her head in denial, looking shaky. Yayènia sighed ruefully. Aidyn glanced at her, then seemed to notice his ruffled look. He quickly yanked his pants up higher and tied them, but left his shirt open and simply ran a hand back through his hair twice to smooth it somewhat.

They settled down for the night, speaking very little. They had left the tents behind, as they were too bulky to carry around in such a tight space as the tangled forest, but the trees afforded good cover from the chilly winter. The previous nights they had slept apart, rolled in their blankets around the fire. This time though, they were chilled and nervous, so the three of them huddled together in their blankets to ward off the wintry atmosphere with Aidyn in the middle. The male could hardly move in the middle of the night with both Yayènia and Tlonna pressed against his sides for his warmth. He lay awake, staring up at the dark canopy as firelight danced on the underside of the leaves. Tlonna had surreptitiously wriggled her hand beneath his shirt as she drifted off.

There was no need for a watch as Tlonna had placed a shield around their campsite that would go off like a gong if anything tried to force itself through it. There was a decidedly unpleasant feeling several feet away that warned any wandering creature or person of the danger, but if they were stubborn enough to try, or stupid enough, by the time they reached the barrier the three elves would be ready.

The assassin lay awake anyhow, the mingled scents of Tlonna and Yayènia rising on the air to join above him. Though they smelled different, there was a similar undercoating to their aromas. While Tlonna smelled like freshly harvested alfalfa and wildflowers, Yayènia had the sweet smell of the alfalfa and newly fallen rain. He wondered if only elves had such scents, as he had never been so intoxicated by a human or dwarf. Aidyn turned his face away from Tlonna, whom he very badly wanted kiss again, which unfortunately put him nose to nose with Yayènia, who had her arm draped across his middle in her sleep, inches from where Tlonna's hand lay against his skin.

She looked incredibly peaceful when she was unconscious, he thought. Aidyn took the rare opportunity to study her face. Though similar in shape to Tlonna's, Yayènia had a squarer jaw and higher cheekbones. Their eyes were the same shape, as were their noses and lips, but the warrior's hair was more bronzy gold than Tlonna's, which was the color of turned wheat. The assassin let out a muffled groan when Yayènia's fingers dug into his side in order to draw him closer. Spirits the elf had hard fingers! Tlonna mumbled in her sleep and wiggled her way in closer, somehow rolling under his blanket as well as hers.

Sighing in defeat, Aidyn lifted his arms so both sisters could put their heads on his shoulders, which they both seemed determined to do. Once they were in position, the dark elf dropped his arms onto their curvy sides, mindful of where his hands landed. The night passed very slowly.

# Chapter 22
## A Troubled Relationship

Yayènia woke with a start, momentarily lulled by the sweet smell of ginger and cloves. Then she realized she had her face buried in Aidyn's armpit. Slowly lifting herself away, the warrior gazed down at the assassin who squinted up at her with menace.

"You talk in your sleep."

"I do not."

"Do too. You kept saying I had stolen your boot."

Yayènia flicked his pointed ear. "You did, in my dream at least."

Aidyn snorted, which woke Tlonna. She scrambled away from him so fast she took all the blankets with her, and squashed his arm in the process, which had been draped over her side. Yayènia realized his other arm was under her hip, but he was saying nothing about the pain it must be causing.

"You smell too good," she accused him and lifted her hips up to free his arm.

"My apologies. I will be sure to roll in the stables when we get back to the Stone Hunters' village."

Yayènia swatted at him again, grinning. While Tlonna untangled herself from the blankets, Aidyn sat up and rubbed his arms to get the blood moving in them once more. He curled up and thought quite desperately of his male friends to rid himself of the morning curse. Yayènia lifted an eyebrow at him, obviously unperturbed by such a thing. Tlonna finally succeeded in freeing herself and stood in a rush.

"Sleep well?" Aidyn asked her as he too got on his feet, in control of his body.

"Yes," she replied hastily, too hastily.

"Did you know your sister talks in her sleep?"

"I did. She once accused me of breaking her toe and stealing her cat. I do not think she even owns a cat."

"I did not! And I do not!" Yayènia huffed as she plopped a cooking pot on the fire and filled it with water.

"You did."

"Apparently she always dreams about her friends stealing her belongings. I kept stealing her boot."

"Well how dare you?" Tlonna asked him, planting her fists on her hips.

Aidyn lifted his arms into the air and dropped them with a huff. "I know. I am a mean thief."

Bits of bark flew through the air and hit them both in the temples. Yayènia was glaring at them from the firepit.

"Shall I talk about what you two do in your sleep? Moaning over each other like human teenagers just experiencing their first romp."

Aidyn laughed. "Why not? What is a bit of humiliation between friends?"

The High Commander glowered at him. "Oh, all right Mighty Mast."

The assassin put his hands on his waist and stretched his back, looking unimpressed with her jab. "Nothing to be embarrassed about, now is it love? I have never had any complaints."

Yayènia bit her lip as she caught Tlonna's crimson blush. The queen stamped over to her pack and knelt down to dig through it. She yanked out a clean shirt and shook it at Aidyn.

"Can we please all remember that we are supposed to be adults?" she growled.

The male beamed at her as she ripped off her shirt and tugged on the clean one. As she stomped into her boots Tlonna pointed a finger at Yayènia. "You cannot say such things when we get to Eyin's place, understood? We need to maintain at least a pretense of being old and wise. If he finds out we are just a bunch of jabbering idiots he is not going to be pleased."

"Who are you calling a jabbering idiot?" Yayènia demanded as she shook a finger right back at her sister. "It is about time we discussed Aidyn! I know how close you two came to rolling about in the blankets last night, so do not bother denying it. Since when can we not be honest with each other? I know I would like to discuss the effects of Aidyn's member and the rumored skill he uses it with."

The assassin choked on a biscuit he was gnawing on at the same time Tlonna spluttered out the water she was drinking. "Thank you for that," he finally managed, sounding weak. "How often do you discuss my...me, exactly?"

Yayènia gave him a saucy grin. "Whenever I need a laugh."

Tlonna thumped to the ground, blushing uncontrollably as Aidyn gaped at his friend in stunned disbelief. It was a long time before any of them regained enough composure to start their real breakfast.

A day later they arrived back at the Stone Hunters' village to the disbelieving stare of Jorunson. Eyin stepped out of his large yurt, his horned crown in his hand. "Did you find what you sought?"

"Indeed. I believe that goes on your head."

The young man lifted the crown with a skeptical look. "I find it brings me a great deal of pain and too much ignorance."

Tlonna smiled and touched her traveling crown. "I understand. I thank you and your people for your hospitality and aid," she added so the congregated Purheaens could hear.

"When will you leave?" Eyin asked, hoping the queen did not take the question wrong.

Tlonna smiled at him. "We would beg your patience with us for one more day, and then we shall depart."

The young king held up his hands in a warding gesture. "Please, take all the time you need. I would not rush my friends out of my home."

They all turned when Jorunson walked up to them, his eyes wide. "Did you find it?"

Tlonna lifted the map out of her pack and handed it to him. "Yes. I marked the exact position of it on here for you. Your calculations were very close, within less than a hundred yards. Impressive, Master Jorunson."

The Purheaen shifted his feet and looked down at the ground. "Thank you, Queen Tlonna," he muttered, barely audible.

"You are quite welcome."

Yayènia broke into the awkward silence. "Where is Meradyn?"

Eyin brightened at the change of subject. "In the yard."

"What yard?"

"I will show you."

They followed the human into the village, past the three rows of homes, and into a small barren tract of land. Eyin swept his arm out. "We have been working on it since Lord Aidyn rid us of the Seadueni elves. It is small and not very well equipped, but it's a place we can practice."

Yayènia, Aidyn, and Tlonna gazed out over the two acre plot to where a sweating Meradyn was working through his forms, his lithe body twisting with precision. Yayènia dropped all her things on the ground and walked out to meet the boy. He did not stop working, even when she picked up two practice swords and stepped closer to him. Without hesitation he parried a thrust, and soon the two were involved in a dance of blades, their weapons whipping and cracking in the cold air. Aidyn stood passively by, watching them with a professional eye while Tlonna watched her sister.

Tonora's body.

Then Aidyn stripped off his cloak and pack and jogged to the center of the yard where Yayènia and Meradyn were sparring. He picked up two wasters and joined the fight, an opponent to both of them. Yayènia barely seemed pressed, but Meradyn was panting, and though no word had yet been uttered between the three, they were speaking to each other in the way of warriors.

Tlonna and Eyin watched them for a while in silence, and then the young king turned to her. "How is Prince Haydyn doing?"

The words hit Tlonna like a physical blow hard enough to knock the very wind from her lungs. She clenched her jaw as emotional agony rolled over her in unrelenting waves. Eyin's brow twitched in confusion when she did not reply.

"Are you okay?" he finally asked, putting a steadying hand on her elbow. "Do you need a healer?"

"No, no...Eyin...Haydyn is dead."

The look of disbelieving woe in the young man's eyes broke Tlonna's heart all over again. "How?"

"His sister cut his throat while in the guise of Yayènia. I was under the impression you two did not get along."

Eyin's dark eyes flickered to the ground, to the sparring trio, and then back to her. "We had our differences, but in the end we resolved to set them aside for the betterment of our respective people. I am grieved to know he is gone. He was an honorable person."

"Yes," Tlonna whispered, "he was." His hand on her elbow brought a teary smile to her face. "Thank you Eyin."

"We are in this together, Tlonna, we all are. We shall take our revenge for the loved ones we have lost."

At that moment the elf realized she had never heard the young man mention his parents. He must have noticed her expression for he smiled softly.

"My mother and father ventured out to learn what they could of the world. They never returned. I was eleven. Meradyn's parents as well. They went together."

"And Marc and Jorunson?"

Eyin sighed and folded his muscled arms over his chest. "Jorunson's mother died in childbirth, along with his sister. His father now lives here with him. Marc's parents were of the Deer People, to the north of here."

"Until the Seadueni came."

"Until the Seadueni came," Eyin repeated quietly, a shadow of grief passing over his face. "Luckily Marc was out in the forest collecting things for his experiments when it happened. He was the one who brought us word of the attack."

"And should be given something for his actions," came an angry female voice from behind.

Tlonna and Eyin turned to face a young woman who was glaring at the king with such vehemence the elf had to fight the urge not to slap the girl.

"Marc did his duty to his people, Ressa. If I handed out awards every time someone did something for the community, everyone would have a bloody badge by now!" Eyin growled, his hands shaking at the sky.

The girl, Ressa, did not relent on her scowl. "You turn my brother into a murderer, and you treat my betrothed like a common idiot. You are no king, Eyin Thorn!"

"Ressa!"

Tlonna turned again to find Meradyn running toward them, a look of utter rage on his sweaty face. Yayènia and Aidyn trotted after him, baffled.

"Meradyn, Eyin has yet to award Marc for his bravery."

The young commander scoffed angrily. "Ressa, you are making a fool of yourself before some very important people."

The girl blushed crimson when she finally took in the three elves now standing behind the two young men. Meradyn thrust his hand out, one finger jabbing toward the ground.

"Bow before Magin Queen Tlonna Ewôsdírn of Blackhaven, High Commander Yayènia er'Tiena, and Master Assassin Aidyn Sestuns, Ressa."

The young woman went into a wobbly curtsy and spread out her rough spun skirt. Tlonna acknowledged the attempt with a small smile.

"This is my oldest sister, Ressa Obren. She is betrothed to Marc," Meradyn said stiffly. "She has too big a mouth for her own good."

Ressa's lips pressed together in a thin line of embarrassment and anger, but she remained quiet. Eyin looked annoyed.

Meradyn stomped over to his sister, grabbed her arm, and marched her away, snarling at her under his breath. Tlonna and Yayènia shared a look, wondering if they would have argued like that had they grown up knowing they were siblings. Aidyn snickered quietly.

"I'm sorry," Eyin said, turning back to them. "She has been on my case for several weeks now, saying I am treating Marc unfairly."

Tlonna lifted one shoulder in a shrug. "You will always have those people who think you are not doing what you believe is best for your people, Eyin. Does Marc think he is being treated unjustly?"

"Not that I know of. He's not said anything to me."

"Would he?"

Eyin let out a snort of laughter. "Yeah."

"Then let it ride off your back. Ressa feels as though she is losing her brother to the violent art of warfare, and her betrothed is one of the new king's advisors. She probably feels a little unimportant right now."

"But that's stupid!" Eyin protested, his fingers dragging through his unruly brown hair to get it out of his face. "She's just as important as everyone else, especially now!"

"Why especially now?"

The king blanched. "Well, now that we've lost two-thirds of our people, repopulation is very important to us. She and Marc are set to be married in a few weeks, and...we need her to help bear the next generation."

"True enough," Tlonna agreed quietly. "What of you? You are a king now, you will need a wife, and an heir."

Eyin folded his arms in a way that looked a little too much like hugging himself. "Well, there was a girl at the Academy in Blackhaven. She was from Zeynuwn and her name was Jalel. She...I..."

"Did you sleep with her, Eyin?" Aidyn asked, a bit of amusement lacing his voice.

The young man looked at Yayènia and Tlonna, horror etched in his features. "Ah..."

The assassin dropped his arm around the petrified king's shoulders and guided him away from the females, his head bent closer so he could speak more privately. Yayènia and Tlonna stood side by side, deserted by everyone. They looked at each other, blinking.

"Want to work a little on your form?" Yayènia asked and whacked her queen in the rump with a wooden sword.

Tlonna jumped in surprise and then turned on the warrior. She grabbed the other waster and twisted out of her pack as she retaliated. She swung the wooden blade up to block the whistling attack now coming for her. Her feet moved slower than they should, and Yayènia jabbed her hard in the hip.

"Move!" the commander commanded and pushed her sister back a few steps.

Tlonna cursed as she tried to remember everything Yayènia had taught her about fighting. She could hold her own very well against most opponents, but the warrior was not satisfied with her efforts. Yayènia had her panting with exertion after only a few minutes. As the commander's wooden sword came at her again and again, Tlonna barely got hers in place to block it each time, but block it she did. However, she was too busy defending that she never got close to pressing an attack. Yayènia looked bored as she whipped her waster about and slapped it against Tlonna's hard enough to crack the wood.

"You have let yourself go," the fighter accused, slamming the weapon down again.

Tlonna winced as her arm vibrated, and also because the wood was beginning to splinter. "I have had other things on my mind."

"You should practice at least a half hour every day."

"Aidyn says it is his job, and yours to protect me, not mine."

"Ridiculous. Aidyn's job is to tumble you. You need to know how to defend yourself, and how to take an enemy down as fast as possible. Just because you are a queen does not mean it is okay for you to be a lazy fighter."

Tlonna let out a harsh breath and managed to roll her eyes. Yayènia leered at her and continued to press the attack. A few villagers had gathered to watch, their faces slack with awe. The queen wondered what had drawn their attention until her sister smacked her waster against her own again. The sound was incredibly loud, a reverberating crack more akin to thunder than dueling. This time however, Tlonna's weapon finally gave up and shattered. As the topmost portion of the sword flipped through the air, Yayènia hit her waster against Tlonna's in three rapid moves and then hit it even harder. The weapon splintered into hundreds of little pieces, leaving only a tiny portion sticking up out of Tlonna's fist. Desperately trying to defend herself, the queen threw the chunk of wood at her sister's head. It bounced off her temple, splitting the skin just enough to ooze blood.

Tlonna watched in horror as the blood rage filmed over Yayènia's eyes, a visible blankness that turned this from a regular duel into a deadly fight. The Magin danced backward to avoid the suddenly violent swing of Yayènia's weapon. It whistled scant inches from her midriff, and then reversed with amazing speed and came back around. Tlonna, desperate and a little frightened by Yayènia's ignited ferocity cast about for something to defend herself. She refused to use her power against her sister. Yayènia's lips twisted in a snarl as she stepped forward and at the same time yanked her wooden sword up, nearly catching Tlonna in the chin. The queen launched herself backward, landed on her back and rolled.

She regained her feet a second later only to see a flying black form crash into Yayènia. One moment the female was coming for Tlonna, the next she was gone. Tlonna blinked and then heard a collective gasp from the small crowd. The queen looked to her left and saw Yayènia slam against the wooden wall, Aidyn's arms around her middle. The two warriors tussled for a few seconds and then the assassin's elbow jerked down against Yayènia's shoulder, once, twice, and a final third time. She went limp in his arms, her head thudding onto his shoulder. The dark elf held her still for a moment longer and then stood, the warrior cradled in his arms.

Tlonna panted, pressing her hand flat against her stomach. "What was that about?"

"Her battle fury. It comes upon her unexpectedly, usually when she gets hit, but not always," Aidyn explained, holding Yayènia tight to his chest. "Sometimes when she is challenged she will slip into it as well."

"I thought she was going to bludgeon me to death," the queen gasped, still trying to catch her breath.

The assassin nodded. "She is a deadly fighter."

"What now?"

Aidyn looked at their packs, slumped against each other by the edge of the yard. "If you will grab our things I will take her to Eyin's yurt to rest. She will be sore when she wakes up."

Tlonna agreed and jogged over to their grab their things. Meradyn and Eyin were standing by them, looking unnerved.

"What happened?" the young king asked, his brow knitted in worry.

"Yayènia went into a battle fury," she explained vaguely, not wanting to have to explain to them what Aidyn had told her.

Meradyn nodded. "I saw her do that in Kajgenia when she and Lord Aidyn were dueling. I have never seen such a fight."

"You were there?" Tlonna asked in surprise.

The man shook his head. "I was passing a window in the castle and spotted them through it. I could not look away."

The elf nodded her understanding of his statement and picked up the three packs. "May we use your home again?" she asked Eyin.

"Of course. Should I have a healer come and take a look at her?"

Tlonna shook her head. "No. She is just unconscious. She will be fine."

The two young men nodded and watched her stride away, the packs slung over her shoulder. Aidyn already had Yayènia laid out on the bed and was pulling off her boots when Tlonna entered.

"When will she wake?"

The assassin dropped her left boot next to the right one and twisted, stretching his midriff. "An hour or so. I hit her pretty hard."

"Aidyn..."

"All I saw was you on the ground and her leaping toward you with a raised weapon. I acted."

"Aidyn," Tlonna touched his elbow. "Will you two be all right?"

The assassin inhaled slowly and then looked away, shrugging weakly. After a moment he bent over Yayènia again and undid her belt. He slid it out of the loops and untucked her shirt. When he straightened, the dark elf shook his head.

"We will always be separated by what happened...but we are both too old to hold grudges against each other. If we keep getting into brawls though...I do not know. We have been friends nearly five hundred years, I do not want to lose that."

"I do not know anyone who attacks their friends as much as you two," Tlonna grumped, shaking his arm. "You should probably stop."

"Probably," Aidyn agreed.

Tlonna meant to release his arm, but instead she moved it up to his shoulder. The assassin gave her a half-smile. "Want to try again?" he murmured, turning to face her.

"Desperately."

The assassin grinned wickedly. "You do try my resolve. You know Losolin will kill me if he ever finds out I so much as kissed you, much less anything else."

Tlonna sighed heavily. "He must not find out. I do not like keeping secrets from him, but what you and I have is so uncontrollable."

Aidyn grunted in agreement. "If I make love to you, Tlonna, I will not be able to stop hoping for another chance, and then another."

"You said you would not be able to stop yesterday," she reminded him, tugging him closer.

"We never really started, yesterday. If we go through with this, it will never stop. You consume me, and I will take every chance to get burned, no matter the cost."

"Cannot have that," Tlonna murmured as her mouth closed on his, their fingers linking.

# Chapter 23
## Surprise Guests

Erdwyf watched from the courtyard balcony as the ex-Seadueni elves sparred with each other and the few humans who had trickled in from the countryside to join her paltry army. She was pleased and mildly surprised that the elves had held to their oaths with strict regard, treating the humans with something akin to respect, even friendliness. It had been a little under a month since they had sworn allegiance, and the improvements in her tiny guards' performance were astonishingly profound.

Jaryikin held her hand, silently watching the goings-on down below. Erdwyf knew that her daughter had seen things since coming to Narnen that had deeply troubled her young mind. The room she now slept in had once been Prince Volker's, and also where his body had been found, a knife through his heart. Everything but the washroom items and the massive teak wardrobe carved in an ornate scroll pattern and gilded in silver had been destroyed. His clothing, along with Emar and Atlan's had been given to the people. Now everything else matched the wardrobe, and even the posts on her bed were carved and gilded. Jaryikin's hand suddenly clenched in Erdwyf's, and she looked down.

"What is it?"

"*Lälian*," she murmured, her gray eyes lidded.

Erdwyf had realized her daughter had a strange ability to sense presences coming toward her, even if they were yet miles away, a few days after the Seadueni had come. When she had asked, Feorien had informed her that no one had told Jaryikin about the incoming Seadueni. She wondered where it came from.

"In Hindarün?" she asked, trying to teach the elf-child the common language.

Jaryikin looked up at her. "Elves."

"Love, there are many elves about."

"*Noya*, different elves. Old elves."

"Old elves? What do you mean?"

The girl screwed up her face, not sure how to communicate her thoughts into words. She shrugged one shoulder. "Not like us," she finally muttered.

Erdwyf sighed and turned away from the courtyard. She was halfway to her office when Feorien stopped her. "There is a large ship coming into harbor flying the flag of the corsair Alexander."

The newly crowned queen frowned. "Did we know they were coming in?"

Feorien shook his head. "No, and they look to have been through a hard journey. They are listing pretty hard."

"I will meet them down at the harbor. Would you have my horse saddled?"

The aide bowed and hurried off to do her bidding. Erdwyf turned to her daughter. "Would you like to come?"

Jaryikin nodded.

They collected their winter cloaks and gloves and walked down to the stables where Erdwyf's mare Verity was being saddled. They mounted up, the princess sitting before her mother in the saddle and clutching the horse's mane for support. Erdwyf quickly trotted down to the harbor yard, which was a sad sight when compared to Blackhaven's gigantic port, but brought her many, many memories.

The giant clipper ship *The Silver Crest* was indeed pulling into dock, and did seem to be tilting on the left. The Commodore Alexander stood at the helm and waving his beaten hat in the air at her. Erdwyf waved back and dismounted, noticing as she did that three of the Seadueni elves had ridden up to meet her. They came to flank her, their expressions fierce and unhappy about life. Erdwyf slanted a look at them.

"Commodore Alexander Willis is an old friend," she told them, but they simply nodded and went back to staring forward.

As soon as the ship was in, the gangplank was lowered and the man jogged down, leaving his crew to finish tying in.

"Lady Erdwyf!" he shouted, looking surprised. "I did not expect to see ye here!"

Erdwyf smiled grimly. "My husband Ghealan and I were named the rulers of Narnen a while back when King Emar and Queen Atlan committed suicide, along with their son."

If the man was taken aback by the news, he did not show it. Instead he swept his hat off in a grand bow. "Then I should say Queen Erdwyf, then. And who is this?"

"This is my daughter, Princess Jaryikin. Jary, this is Commodore Alexander. He gave our friends from Blackhaven and me a ride several years ago, when I was pregnant with you."

The elf-child curtseyed and then stared up at the man, his sea-stained appearance apparently fascinating to her. Alexander's face suddenly became grim.

"I am come from a run to Zaedic with a few merchant ships from Blackhaven. When we docked, a woman came on board to speak with me. She wanted to buy passage fer several others, and asked that I take 'em directly to the closest elfin city. She didn't seem to care which one, just as long as it was elfin."

Erdwyf had a troubling feeling she knew who the passengers were but remained silent as Alexander turned to his ship and waved his hand at someone standing next to the railing. The corsair disappeared and a moment later several people were lining up to descend the gangplank. Tall, well formed people.

Jaryikin tugged on her hand. "Old different elves," she said pointedly, a little put off.

Erdwyf shook her head. "I know them."

"I thought ye'd remember 'em," Alexander said, turning back to her. "I had no idea 'twas them 'til they boarded my ship in the dead of night. They remembered us and found out that we pulled in every couple of months. They're fleeing."

"No doubt," Erdwyf muttered as Niander, Syntyche, Seraphia, Lukein, and several other elves walked up to them.

They were Zaedican elves, hundreds of years older than Erdwyf, who was well into her fifth century. They had been frozen in time by a Weave by Hadian Rahlan, Midian's grandfather, and were unfrozen when Midian, who had been maintaining the Weave, was killed the first time by Losolin. They stood now before Erdwyf with a mild look of surprise and recognition on their porcelain faces.

"Niander Saryth," Erdwyf said with a tilt of her head. "I am glad to see your family is well and now safe."

"I am sorry, I recall your face but not your name," the ancient elf said coolly as he brushed back his fine red hair with a slender hand.

"I am Queen Erdwyf er'Tomyvon, this is my daughter Princess Jaryikin."

Niander's face tightened. "I did not know you were a queen."

"Newly acquired title," she said dully and clasped her hands before her. "What can I do for you?"

Niander looked away, his hand about his wife's wrist. "The Rahlan boy-king found out there were elves living on *his* island. Very few of us escaped."

"How many of you were there?" Erdwyf asked, eyeing the nine elves before her.

"Around thirty. Only my family escaped, and only because we knew of Commodore Alexander, and we got lucky."

"Who did you get to help you off the island?"

"There was a girl who had been raped by the king, then he humiliated her by letting her think she could be his bride, and choosing another. She fled to the country and my brother Nasren found her. She agreed to talk to the corsair if we took her with us."

"Then where is she?"

Everyone looked uncomfortable. Alexander pushed his way through the elves. He looked oddly small in the company, though he was a well-built man.

"About halfway through she jumped ship. She was standing by the railing and suddenly she climbed over it and jumped. Axl jumped in after 'er, but she was already gone."

Erdwyf stared at him. "She asked for safe passage, was granted it, and then jumped off when she truly was safe?"

"We were attacked by a Zaedican ship two days later."

"Why?"

Alexander shook his head. "I don't know. They put up quite the fight though, came outta nowhere. Unfortunately Troaz and *Zaedic's Bane* were on a run for Zeynuwn, and Adii and his *Sidyov* were docked in Arseninis. We nearly lost, but then the elves joined in the fight, and the tables turned."

"You waited until they were losing to help them? Why is that?" Erdwyf asked Niander, anger lacing her voice.

The elf's chin came up in defiance. "We were below deck and did not realize there was an attack until we felt the ship shudder. That is when we came out to join the fight."

"It was a fast attack, Erdwyf," Alexander said in defense. "Started and finished within a few minutes."

"Queen Erdwyf," one of the Seadueni guards snarled and stepped forward to shove his sword hard against the corsair's throat.

"Stop!" Erdwyf commanded as Jaryikin shrieked in fright.

The Zaedican elves all stepped back at the same moment the guard moved forward, and very suddenly the situation was very tense. Erdwyf's hand was pressing against the hard abdominal muscles of the edgy elfin guard, which were so tense it felt as though he wore armor under his light tunic. Alexander stood in the middle, less than a foot away from Erdwyf and the only human in sight, a blade scraping his throat. He wasn't cowed.

Erdwyf grabbed the guard's hand and pushed it back, giving him a very telling look. He did not move for another few seconds, and then with a huff yanked back his sword and sheathed it. She was vividly reminded that the elf probably had a very dirty past. Alexander lifted a hand to knuckle away the trickle of blood on his chin and eyed her with a passive regard that deeply bothered her.

"Ye have Seadueni thugs working fer ye?" he asked quietly.

The guards behind her all sucked in a deep breath of insult and rage, but she held up a hand to stall their reaction. "They are sworn Narnenian guards, Commodore, that past is behind them now."

"Well, ye gave corsairs a chance, so I s'pose I can give ex-Seadueni elves a chance," the man said, nodding at the guard.

The elf's jaw muscles flexed as he clenched his teeth, but he nodded in acceptance. Erdwyf silently thanked the gods that the males around her had come to an agreement, if a nervous one. She held out her hand to a wide-eyed and silent Syntyche.

"It is a pleasure to see you again. Please, if you would follow me I will get you settled in the castle."

The Zaedican elves waited until Erdwyf and Jaryikin had mounted before moving forward, flanked by the guards. Alexander signaled something back to his ship and the queen wondered if the other corsairs she knew would sail out immediately for their berth in Blackhaven, or if they would stay and take the time to fix their ship. She hoped they stayed and said so to Alexander. The corsair did not reply.

The large group made their way along the nearly deserted street that ran from the harbor to the city. The castle sat in the middle of it, forcing the road to curve around it in both directions. Erdwyf waited while the guard on top of the wall signaled to open the gate in the granite wall shielding the castle grounds. Then she had to wait while one of her bodyguards jogged inside to check it for safety. When he came back through, Erdwyf clicked Verity along the way and then surrendered her to a liveried stable boy.

She escorted the nervous Zaedican elves inside and showed them to the rooms they could have. Niander and Syntyche dropped their belongings on the floor, made sure their two children were settled in, and then turned to Erdwyf.

"May we speak to you in private?" the male asked, his voice nervous.

"Of course," the queen replied, and handed the fidgeting Jaryikin over to Feorien, who had appeared around a corner.

Alexander followed them to a sitting room without invitation and leaned against the door as the elves took seats. Erdwyf ordered hot beverages to be brought for her guests and then looked back at the Zaedicans.

"What can I do for you?" she asked, keeping her face a mask of serenity though inside she felt a great turmoil.

Syntyche wrapped her fingers in her husband's hand and licked her lips, apparently nervous. Her large eyes widened as she looked at Erdwyf with an obvious plea on her lips.

"We are refugees now, with no place to call home. All of our friends are dead, our home dilapidated despite our efforts to restore it, and hundreds of years taken from us. We remembered the elf you were traveling with, the Everwood, and we decided to call on her for help. We did not expect to find you here in this position, though we are gratefully relieved."

"So what is it you would ask of me?" Erdwyf prompted when the female did not continue.

Niander gave his wife a small smile of comfort and the queen felt a stab of loneliness, missing Ghealan. "Have you found any other elves like us?"

The question surprised her. "Not that I have heard of. I believe the Weave you were under was restricted to Zaedic alone, especially considering that is where the Rahlan's live and rule. We have found that most of our race has been captured, tortured, and mutilated into the creatures known as Darkwights. We are working even now on a way to turn them back to their original state."

"Darkwights. They are those black demons, are they not?" Niander asked, his face slightly flushed.

"Yes."

"We have seen them. I do not recall any of the monsters being around from before we were...stilled, but since we recovered, my brother and I have spotted a few of them out in the wilds of the island. Ghastly things."

"Tortured creatures," Erdwyf argued softly. She did not want to anger the elf. "But now I have a question for you. Do you remember when Hadian Rahlan was alive?"

"Of course."

"Then, do you know any reason as to why he would freeze you in time rather than just kill you? If he was powerful enough to stop and preserve dozens of people, then he was most certainly strong enough to kill you all."

"We have thought of this ourselves, but we have no answer," Syntyche replied, and let out a frustrated breath. "Before, we were a wealthy family, and well-received in the towns about the island. We had fair relations with the other gentry of Zaedic and we believed a decent one with King Hadian. We have also wondered why, if the other kings were aware of the Weave, then why did they wait until now to act?"

Erdwyf frowned, having not come to that question yet in her own mind. She bit her lip, thinking. "Perhaps they did not know what the spell was for. Tlonna...the Everwood, says that there are some Weaves, such as barriers, that are passed down from generation to generation without the Magin's who receive them ever really knowing it. They are maintained by a talisman or other item that holds the threads of the Weave together, and as long as they are fed power by the Magin that they are bonded to, such as a certain bloodline like the Rahlans, then they will continuously hold up their spell. But, if the bonded Magin dies, or for some other reason is unable to be a source of power, then that object will run out of power almost immediately, unless a very large reservoir has been supplied."

All three people in the room stared at her with a slightly blank expression. Erdwyf sat back in her chair, and gladly accepted the steaming mug of peppermint tea a servant held out for her. Syntyche offered the boy a small smile and took two mugs for herself and Niander. Alexander sniffed at the sweet liquid and carefully took a sip. His worn face wrinkled as he tried to figure out whether or not he liked it.

Erdwyf waited for someone to speak, so the silence stretched on for a long time. Finally she set down her mug on the marble table before her and braced her elbows on her knees. "You still have not said what you want from me."

The other elves started, almost looking lost for a moment. Niander finally swallowed and looked her in the eye. "We beg sanctuary."

"Of course. You had it the moment you stepped off *The Silver Crest.*"

"Yes, but we do not know when we will be able to move on. We have no currency, no prospects, and nine people. Commodore Alexander told us that this kingdom was ravaged by war only recently. We do not want to be a burden on an already stretched treasury."

"It is not burden to help those who have suffered from the Rahlans' prickly touch. And the coffers were not as badly touched as many believe. Luckily the former monarchs had a good dose of paranoia and suspicion and hid most of the geld away in several parts of the kingdom. My own parents hold several hundred thousand of it in their protection, and they are not the only ones, plus the hiding spots here in the castle itself."

"So we can stay?" Syntyche asked, relief so thick in her voice it nearly made Erdwyf wince.

"Yes. We will find a way for you to make a new life here. The treasury may not have been utterly destroyed, but we have little geld coming in from trade, less than fifty soldiers, and very little economy. I am sure we can find you and your family members jobs."

"I was a good mason, long ago," Niander replied. "It is how I made my fortune. If you have stone that needs working, I would be glad to help."

Erdwyf smiled. "It just so happens that Narnen is in great need of repair. I shall refer you to the mason's guild tomorrow, if you would like."

Niander nodded his agreement. Syntyche smiled at him before turning her attention to the other female. "I can sew and paint, nothing truly useful I am afraid, but I have a fair hand."

"I am sure we can find you something. What of the others?"

"Nasren is a hunter, and a fighter. I do not know if he is up to the task like your Seadueni guards, but he would be willing to do what needs to be done, I am sure. His wife, Ellia can cook like no other."

The male continued to rattle off the various talents of his companions while Erdwyf nodded and made notes in her head. They would be a useful bunch to have around. When Niander fell silent, a sudden question struck her.

"What of the old woman who was in your house? I do not recall seeing her."

The elves exchanged a glance. "She was our servant. She died almost immediately after the spell wore off. Despite the magic holding us in stasis, her body continued to age. It was not a thing designed for the mortal races. She was only fifteen when we were stilled."

Erdwyf nodded, accepting their explanation. "I am sorry."

Niander waved a hand in the air. "She was human. It was five years ago anyway. At least she did not realize she was dying."

"A relief, if only a small one," Syntyche added softly.

Again Erdwyf nodded, liking the female more and more. "What of your children? They can join my daughter in her studies, though I am sure they are far more advanced than she is, or whatever you want them to do."

"What studies?" Syntyche asked in a motherly way.

"Right now just the basic things, reading, writing, mathematics, and language. She is learning the three Foundation Languages, Parlêthian, Hindarün, and Kierlak."

"You would teach your elven daughter the language of the dwarves?" Niander spluttered, shocked.

"Of course. Our land shares a border with Florwen Hune, land of Dwarves, led by a good friend of mine, King Barukh Odrinsson. Jaryikin will be well versed in all three languages."

"I meant no offense, but it is such a harsh language, hard to form with our elven mouth."

"It has a more difficult phonemic structure to be sure, but I find it an honest tongue. The dwarves are our friends here."

"This seems like such a wonderful, peace-loving land," Syntyche said, her expression one of burden. "I have often dreamed of such a place."

"It is, but unfortunately the Zaedicans, Seadueni, and many Talenians are trying to overrun our morality with brutality. We are in the middle a brutal war for freedom, for peace, and for the eradication of evil."

"Surely you do not believe you will completely erase evil from the face of the world, do you?" Niander asked, his hands on his knees, arms stiff.

"No, for it will always exist but we can destroy those who would gather followers and try to take from others what they covet. We will not stand for such injustices to take place, and so we fight. We shall not condone the atrocious abuse of the Nymyñosian people."

"You say we. Who else is fighting?" the male pressed, eager.

Erdwyf lifted her chin with pride. "King Losolin and Queen Tlonna of Blackhaven of course, King Furntil of Flousen Dua, King Tristan of Kajgenia, King Tyular of Arseninis, King Eyin of Purheae," here Alexander jerked in surprise, "Emperor Tahi-tat of Zeynuwn, and King Barukh of Florwen Hune."

"A list of powerful names," Syntyche murmured. "Yet you still struggle to win?"

"We may have a lot of allies, but that does not mean that they are all able to send forces to the battle front. As of now, only Blackhaven has troops on the front line, but the others are looking at what they can spare from their defenses to send. The enemy has well over fifty thousand soldiers, while that is more than the armies of Blackhaven, Florwen Hune, Flousen Dua, Arseninis, Narnen, and Purheae combined. Tristan of Kajgenia has enough to almost even the odds, but only if he sends out every single soldier under his command, leaving his land vulnerable to Seaduens at his back."

"The odds are not good, then," Niander muttered in a doleful tone.

"Ah," Erdwyf lifted a smug finger, "but you forget who leads the Blackhavenites, and when the others join, she will lead them as well, just as she did at the previous battle to a great victory."

"Who?"

"The High Commander Yayènia er'Tiena," Alexander nearly shouted in his exuberance, finally joining the conversation. "Deadliest fighter in all Nymyños."

"Not quite, but close. At her side is Lord Aidyn Sestuns, Master Assassin of the College of Assassins, who has bested Yayènia twice in equal battle, along with my husband, Ghealan, who has been her partner for three hundred years, her husband Suneelo who is a brilliant warrior, the new Second Commander Aladorn Sestuns who is the equal of Suneelo and Ghealan in battle. You met them all back at your old home."

"I remember them, particularly your husband, my lady, and the female, Yayènia. They were not the friendliest."

Erdwyf chuckled. "No, they are not the friendliest people, but they are fierce and loyal to their cause. You will find no better elves to lead this war than them, any of them."

"Ye say the dark elf can defeat Yayènia?" Alexander asked in disbelief as he took a seat.

"Yes, but their friendship is now stronger for it. You cannot forget that they head the army, all of them, and that makes it nearly undefeatable. They will lose battles, they will suffer heavy losses, but in the end it is their purpose and their passion that will triumph over this plague of evil and darkness. Never forget that."

The three were pushed back by the emotion in Erdwyf's voice, and now they swallowed and felt a rising pride within their respective chests. The corsair stood once more and downed his mug of tea.

"Once me ship is fixed I'll set out once more fer the Sea to block any traffic coming to and from the island. I'll get me boys to check every ship, and if they be transporting fighters, we'll take 'em down."

"Do not put yourself at unnecessary risk, Alexander. You are a good man, and your crew is the best I have ever seen. It would a great loss if those men, and you, were to perish in a battle with the Zaedicans," Erdwyf cautioned him as she put a hand on his shoulder.

The corsair shrugged, grinning. "We have been in this fight fer a long time, it is time it is finished. Never let it be said that Clan Esmoden doesn't hold its own!"

"Never let it be said," Erdwyf repeated, clasping hands with the man. "I will give you whatever you need to fix your ship."

"My thanks," Alexander said, bowed, and departed, leaving Erdwyf with the two other elves.

She turned them and held her arms out to her sides. "Well, all that we can do now is have dinner and get some rest, for tomorrow will be a busy day."

Syntyche and Niander smiled at her as she led the way from the room. Though many things remained a mystery, Erdwyf felt a strange sense of things coming together at last.

# Chapter 29
## The Arrival of Erandur

An ashamed and sore Yayènia was already awake when Tlonna got up.

The queen looked at her sister and lifted an eyebrow. "Are you going to try and kill me again? Because if you are, I would like some warning."

Yayènia's jaw tensed and she looked away. "I am sorry. I...cannot control it sometimes. Did I hurt you?"

Tlonna shook her head. "No, but Aidyn was there faster than a bolt of lightning. He knocked you out before you could do any damage to me or yourself."

"I can tell. It feels like my shoulder is broken."

"Is it? He hit you hard, several times."

The warrior snorted. "He will not stop at anything to protect you, will he? And no, it is not broken. Just feels like it."

"Aidyn felt terrible, Nia. He looked so downtrodden. It wears on him, being my protector, even if he will not admit it. Sometimes I think I am more evil than those he has to kill or take down. I know I am not," she added quickly when Yayènia opened her mouth, "but I do not like the fact that he has to take such a burden on himself for my sake."

"He loves you, as we all do," Yayènia muttered, knowing it was only partially true. "You have to do what you have to do, and we will be there on the flanks to take apart anything that tries to stop you. If I happen to be one of those things, then he will take me down. If he does, then I will take him out, or at least attempt to. Please do not piss him off, Tlonna."

The queen chuckled at the desperate expression on her sister's face. "I will try. Honestly, how do you feel?"

Yayènia grimaced as she stood. "Like hell. Your assassin does not hold back. I think he is stronger now than ever. He keeps getting stronger, but he does not get any bigger or bulkier, which is the way it is supposed to happen. He is still all slender and p...."

"What?" Tlonna asked when the warrior fell silent.

"I think she was going to say petite, which is entirely wrong. I am *not* petite."

The Magin flipped around on the bed to stare at Aidyn, who was leaning against the door with his arms and legs crossed. He looked amused and irritated at the same time.

"I was *going* to say puny. But petite works too, you pipsqueak."

The notion that Aidyn was a pipsqueak was ridiculous in Tlonna's opinion. His shoulders were broad, his body well muscled, and he stood at a solid seven-foot-nine, a full ten inches taller than Yayènia. She snorted at the same time as Aidyn. Yayènia gave him a cheeky grin and rubbed her shoulder.

"You damn near broke it, dark elf," she muttered at him.

"You damn near whacked Tlonna, high elf."

Tlonna shook her head and got to her feet. She pushed Aidyn out of the way of her bag and knelt to drag clean clothes out of it. She dressed while they continued to argue and then grabbed the assassin by the shoulder. He looked down at her with a childishly enthusiastic grin, tiny crinkles at the corners of his eyes. She'd never noticed them before last night, but then there were many discoveries she had made last night, like how his upper lip was slightly shorter than the bottom, and curved upward at the corners, and how his incisors were a little more pointed than most. She pulled at his bottom lip with her thumb and he traced her jaw line with tenderness in his fingers. Yayènia watched them with suspicion.

"Did you two...please tell me it was not in this bed while I was unconscious?"

Aidyn dropped his hand away from Tlonna and grinned at Yayènia. "The less you know the better."

"Tlonna?" Yayènia whimpered, scooting away from Tlonna's side of the bed.

The queen looked up at Aidyn's smoky gaze, still unsure what exactly *had* happened the night before. They had not made love, but had spent the night together, and shared a tenderness she had never expected to find in her assassin. She vaguely remembered snuggling against his near-naked body beneath blankets in the front room before the fireplace, listening to his voice. It was vague because she had wrapped up the memories in her head with a Weave, and done the same to Aidyn, so they would not be driven to experience more.

"You had the bed to yourself, Yayènia," Tlonna finally murmured, still staring into Aidyn's face. "We need to return to Blackhaven. Nebet'thu will be coming with us so that he may return to Asheyl and his life. Are you ready?"

Aidyn nodded. "Any time. Neb has had his things packed since last night."

"Good. I want to be home in less than a week."

"Easy enough. Let me know when you are ready. I will be with Meradyn and his friends until then."

Tlonna nodded and she and Yayènia quickly gathered their things, her sister sending her sideway glances but saying nothing. They rode out just as the sun began its ascent over the canopy of the dense Purheae Forest. Light filtered through the trees just enough to illuminate the ground. They turned and quickly waved to the four figures standing in the entrance to the little village.

Meradyn, Eyin, Jorunson, and Marc watched them go from the gate, waving and trying hard to hold their smiles. Once they were out of sight, Eyin turned to his friends.

"It is time for Purheaens to prove their worth. Mer, you have two months."

As the young commander nodded, Eyin sucked in a deep breath and turned back to his yurt, rubbing his arm that sported the symbolically heavy tattoo.

Tlonna and her three companions pushed their mounts hard to get back to Blackhaven in decent time. Nebet'thu departed their company a few days later to head for home, and they reached the city two days later, exhausted and feeling dirty. Tlonna dismounted wearily, rubbing her legs as she walked toward the door leading from the stable yard to the castle. Yayènia and Aidyn followed her like two lethal shadows, their mere presence a deterrent to foul play, unbothered by endless days in the saddle. Miazie, Sodo, and Aladorn met them in the foyer, regal and formal in their clean clothes.

The queen eyed Miazie's dress with speculation and took in the bump in the woman's middle. The Belau covered it with her hands, smiling serenely.

"I am glad you are home safe," she said as her eyes scanned them.

"I hear you had quite the time acting as regent while I was away," Tlonna said. She pulled off her riding gloves and handing them to a bowing servant, along with her pack. She took out a small box before they hurried off. "Yayènia thought you might like to have this."

Miazie glanced at the suddenly grinning warrior and took the box with wary fingers. She pulled the lid off and shrieked, dropping the box and its contents on the floor. Stoffnias's organ rolled pitifully a few inches before coming to a stop. Yayènia and Aidyn were laughing so hard they were bent over double. Sodo glared at the severed appendage before snapping his gaze up to Tlonna. The queen tried to suppress a smile, but failed.

"What manner of joke is this?" the alchemist asked softly.

"No joke. That is Stoffnias Lostug's penis," Yayènia chortled as she bent down to retrieve the offending member and place it back in the box. "I thought you might like to take care of it."

Miazie swallowed as the female handed her the box once more. "He...he is dead, then?"

"I killed him myself. He can torment you no longer," Tlonna replied solemnly.

A sudden grin bloomed on Sodo's face and he chuckled. "Oh, that does make me happy."

"I thought it might," Yayènia said brightly and gently punched the alchemist in the shoulder.

Miazie secured the lid of the box and held it carefully. "I am going to burn it."

"A fitting way to go," Aidyn remarked.

Aladorn shook his head in resignation, his eyes studying his brother's body, noting the more relaxed way he stood. "Yes, well, we have many things to discuss."

"I am sure, but first I want a bath and clean clothes. Aidyn, Yayènia, you are dismissed for the time being. Go clean yourselves up."

The two warriors saluted in their particular ways and strode off, jostling each other like children. Tlonna lifted an eyebrow at the three before her.

"Well?"

Miazie swallowed. "We can walk and talk at the same time. Tlonna, what did you find?"

The elf grabbed the Magin Stone from her blue silk pouch and handed it to the woman without comment. She gasped, her eyes clouding over with visions and knowledge. Sodo placed a comforting hand on her back while Aladorn moved to the other side of the queen.

"How is he?" the wiat asked, not bothering to elaborate.

"He is nearly fully healed, I believe, in both heart and body. Our bond is back, somehow."

"What happened?"

Tlonna shrugged. "He saw me naked."

Both Sodo and Aladorn stopped in their tracks; Miazie was too deep in the recesses of her scrying mind to notice. "What?" the dark elf wheezed.

"He came out of nowhere, in the forest, and I grabbed my weapon in defense. I had just come out of the Cyree so I only had on a blanket, and it fell off. Suddenly the bond was back in place, taking us both to the ground. It gets stronger each time it is renewed."

"Why would seeing you in the nude bring the bond back?" Sodo asked, but Aladorn's face was gray.

Tlonna shrugged. "Maybe because I was vulnerable. I cannot be sure. Or maybe it was just seeing each other again in full health, and my being naked had nothing to do with it."

Aladorn scoffed at the idea in his head, but remained silent. He knew it was Aidyn's love for Tlonna that had been triggered by seeing her exposed flesh, igniting within him the deepest, most carnal need...to be with Tlonna. The bond was his only way to do such a thing. What a mess.

Tlonna sighed in luxury as she sank into the deep bath, the scents of pomegranate and rose permeating the air and her skin as it swirled in the steam. She let her head fall back against the marble rim of her tub and closed her eyes while she let the filth of travel slough away from her flesh. She breathed in deeply, lifting a heavy arm to the edge of the tub. The female sat for a while longer, unwilling to move, and then finally began to wash. Once she was out and dry, Tlonna settled to the task of overseeing the things that demanded her attention from being gone for a month. After a moment she got up from her chair and moved to the side table by her side of the bed. With a guilty glance at Losolin's pillow, she pulled out the box that contained the clothing with Aidyn's scent and buried her face in it, her lungs expanding with a deep breath. She held the clothing to her face for several seconds and then replaced it in the box. Feeling miserable, adulterous, and lonely, Tlonna lay down on the bed and rolled over to clutch Losolin's pillow. Two males that drove her mad and she couldn't do anything to stop it, or herself. She fantasized about Aidyn, felt there was something deep and rooted in their relationship that neither he nor anyone else was telling her. But she loved Losolin with her entire being. He was her opposite in so many ways, a healer, a gentle soul, albeit with the strength to do what was needed without hesitation. He thrilled her, fulfilled her, and made her feel safe and loved. Aidyn...Aidyn made her feel dangerous and almost wicked.

Tlonna curled up around the pillow and buried her face in it. It had been washed so her husband's own scent was barely there, which made her inextricably sad. She felt foolish and childish, but she didn't care. The world wanted so much from her, and she was in love with two people.

"Why cannot anything be easy? Why can I not have just one thing go right?" she mumbled into the pillow.

With a great sigh, Tlonna flopped onto her back and stared up at the canopy above her bed. She linked her fingers over her belly and allowed herself several minutes of wallowing. Then she got back onto her feet and returned to her desk. The winter celebration of Yule was coming up very soon, and the city was in an uproar. This, like Samhain, would be the first time it was celebrated in over twelve years. Already there were festive candles and Magin lights decorating the city, a gift from the weaker Magins that lived in the city, as all the stronger citizens were at the battle. Celebratory, and sometimes haunting, carols filtered through the air at all hours of the day and night while people seemed cheerier than usual. There was a palpable sense of joy in the air as the city prepared to celebrate.

Tlonna combed her damp hair back with her fingers and thought of calling Carlotta in to take care of it, but decided against it. She let it air dry while she read the reports from Miazie, noting the deep frustration the woman had for the geld problems. The bill the Merchant's Guild had pushed through bothered Tlonna, but she decided not to veto Miazie's strict pass on it. Those problems would be taken care of eventually, when they no longer had enemies at the proverbial gates.

A few hours later, when she was about sick of reports, Tlonna was startled by someone knocking on her door. A liveried messenger strode in when she bade him enter, his back straight and eyes boldly meeting hers. She demanded that of them.

"Queen Tlonna, several people have arrived and request your immediate presence," he stated crisply, bowing.

"Who are they?"

"A Prince Erandur Eldrout, Second Lieutenant Lelfwin, Silver Lara, and three others. They appear to be civilians."

A grin spread quickly across Tlonna's face and she rushed to the door, pausing only to check herself in the mirror as she went by. Her hair was slightly wavy from not being combed straight and was held in place only by her crown. Her plum-colored dress was a working one, split down the middle, and she wore sturdy gray cotton pants beneath.

"Good enough," she murmured and hurried down the winding stairs.

A reviving breeze of crisp, clean air filled the stairway from the openings in the curving wall and lifted her spirits. She hastened to the ground floor where a small group of slender elves and one drained-looking human waited. Lara of the elite *Zephyr Leifen* fighters stepped forward and bowed, obviously exhausted. She was much thinner than when she had left a few months earlier.

"Your Majesty, once again I present to you Prince Erandur Eldrout of Flousen Dua, and High Captain Lelfwin of the Onyx Forest Army. May I also introduce Lord Councilor Vilyneldril, King Furntil's Head Advisor."

Tlonna smiled. "Welcome back, Lara. Go get some rest, and we will debrief you after dinner. You two as well," she said, gesturing to the two male elves flanking the human warrior.

As one, they bowed and hastened off, eager for a warm bath and clean bed. The queen turned to the three elves left standing there, and grinned. "Prince Erandur, it is wonderful to see you again, and you, Lelfwin. I am honored to meet you, Lord Councilor."

"As we are you, Queen Tlonna," Erandur said, returning her genuine smile. "I am however surprised to see you here. We had heard that Blackhaven was on the war path, seeking revenge against those who not so long ago were holding siege against your great city."

"I am just returned from a mission in Purheae, and will be returning to join my people at the banks of the Sethryn as soon as possible. High Commander Yayènia, Lord Aladorn, and Lord Aidyn will be traveling with me," Tlonna replied and gestured for the males to follow her to a more comfortable place. "I regret that my husband, King Losolin, is not here. I know he would have loved to see you again."

Erandur bowed his head in agreement. "I am pleased to hear the High Commander survived the horrible injury she suffered in Alchemian."

Tlonna chuckled, "Survived, and moved far beyond. It is Aidyn who has suffered the most recently."

"What has befallen the great assassin?" Lelfwin asked immediately, concern forming his words.

"He was taken and held captive for many days by Sithian, during which he was viciously tortured. He managed to escape, but suffered grievous wounds in the act and has been recuperating since. He seems to have made a full recovery, but the extent of his injuries was great," the female replied, smiling faintly. "But he is strong and rode with Yayènia and me to Purheae, and fought beside us in our brief time with the army."

"I am sorry to know that, but gladdened to hear that he has recovered," Erandur said gently as he shared a sad look with his lieutenant.

"Is this the dark elf Furntil is so impressed with?" asked Vilyneldril, frowning in confusion.

"*Aiya*, the same. He stands up to the stories, Vily. Just wait until you meet him," Lelfwin said.

"He...has been through a lot in the past few months," Tlonna warned softly. "As have we all." She opened the door to one of the small, informal reception rooms and bade her guests to sit.

Erandur looked at her, straight into her white-pupil eyes and did not flinch. "A friend can accept such changes if he is a true friend."

Tears threatened the queen, but she took a deep breath and nodded. "So I have learned, Erandur, so I have learned. Tell me then, what brings you here at the side of my messengers? What did your father say of my proposal?"

The prince smiled. "I had to bring Vily for a reason. He is my father's chief calligrapher, and he draws up all of our most important documents. I can sign in Father's stead, while Lelfwin here will sign as head of the army."

"King Furntil expresses his deepest regret that he could not come with us, but he fears exposure after so long of being thought dead," Vilyneldril added, his bronze-colored eyebrows lifting as he spoke.

"Understandable," Tlonna replied kindly. "Are you here to sign the Racial alliance and the treaty agreed upon by me, and Kings Barukh, Tristan, Tyular, and Eyin?"

"Indeed I am."

Tlonna blew out a breath of relief, but it was shortened by the hard look Erandur and Lelfwin gave her.

"I have only ever heard of two of them," Erandur said slowly.

Tlonna settled back in her chair and told the Duani elves about Purheae, and about Demetrius's death. When she finished they were all wide-eyed and shaken. The prince was slouched in his seat, long legs spread out before him, his arms limp on the rests of his chair. Lelfwin and Vilyneldril stared blankly at their hands and feet, unsure of what to say.

"Indeed, you did not understate when you said everyone has been through a lot," Erandur noted finally, sighing. "I suppose Father will indeed have to come out at some point now to stand beside these men who so bravely stand beside you. He is anxious to meet you, and all of your companions."

"As we are him. It is not every day you get to meet a hero out of legend," Tlonna chuckled, shaking her head.

"Indeed, it is not," Lelfwin said and his eyes pinned her with meaning. "So, what else has befallen the land while we have been away?"

"Ah," Tlonna grinned. "You should be pleased to hear that Stoffnias Lostug is dead."

"By whose hand?" the prince asked eagerly.

"Mine."

"Excellent! That is indeed great news! So, only two of the brats remain?"

"Yes, Isadorr will become king, and Gothier will move into place as heir-apparent, until Isadorr marries and creates an heir, if such a time will come."

"Well, we are on a roll, are we not? Athelias, Athelan, Midian, and Stoffnias all down within the span of two years. Not too bad for us, is it?" Lelfwin chortled as he rubbed his hands together.

"No, but unfortunately their children all seem to be worse."

"What of Talenias? Who rules it now?" Erandur asked, frowning at his companion.

Tlonna sighed. "At the moment Tristan and Tyular are ruling as joint regents until we can find someone suitable to place on the throne. Lady Erdwyf has been named Queen of Narnen, and Ghealan the king, so they are now out of the question. They signed the treaty when they were named so. The only people I have here that are even plausible options are Miazie Paron, who is technically the queen of Anutch since her father was killed in the siege of Anutch, and her fiancé Sodo."

"Are they willing to take such a position? I remember the alchemist being a bit reluctant to take action."

Tlonna nodded at the prince's words. "He has come around, but I have not spoken to them of such a thing. Right now we have more pressing matters."

"Of course. I will send Lelfwin and Vily back to Duan at dawn tomorrow with word. I will ride with you to the fight."

"Prince Erandur, surely you know that is out of the question," Vilyneldril gasped, nearly coming out of his seat with anxiety.

"Nothing I decide to do is out of the question, Vily. I am the Crown Prince of Flousen Dua, and I shall do as I please. I am sure that I am old enough to make such decisions on my own."

"A mere eight hundred years, my prince, a young elf still."

Tlonna wondered how old the councilor was if he considered eight hundred years young. Then again, King Furntil was well over two thousand years old, so she supposed such a time span really wasn't very impressive in comparison.

"I would greatly appreciate your company, my friend," she interjected before the obviously upset councilor could launch into a tirade, which he plainly wanted to do.

Erandur expertly hid his smile, but Tlonna saw it before he fixed a stony expression on his face. "I am glad. Now, when do we sign this treaty?"

Tlonna stood and led them to the door. "Come, we shall take this to the map room. I shall call High Advisor Miazie in with the documents."

The four elves settled themselves in the large map room and waited while Miazie was summoned. The human rushed into the office and grinned when she saw Erandur and Lelfwin. Vilyneldril gaped at the sight of a human running the affairs of what he considered an elfin kingdom, but they bowed to each other with the formality of advisors.

"This is Lord Councilor Vilyneldril of Flousen Dua, Lord Councilor, this is High Advisor Miazie, Belau."

"A Belau?" the elf gaped, his hand lightly gripping hers.

"Yes sir. An honor to meet you, Lord Councilor."

"Ah, yes, an honor," the councilor muttered as he reclaimed his seat.

Tlonna had the sudden image of an elderly human seeing something he didn't completely trust or understand. She wondered again how old he was. She turned to Miazie.

"Our friends have come to us in order to sign the Great Nymyñosian Alliance and the Nymyñosian Racial Alliance."

"Wonderful. I guess that Prince Erandur will sign for his father?"

The Duani elf nodded, eyeing the tooled leather folder Miazie produced from somewhere. "Yes, and Lelfwin will sign as leader of the army."

"You are here to witness?" the woman asked Vilyneldril.

"*Aiya.*"

"*Sennia*, good," Miazie replied in Parlêthian, a mischievous sparkle in her eyes. "Here is the Racial Alliance," she said and handed over the calligraphic document. It was one of the oldest treaties in Nymyños, laid down by the founders of Zeynuwn, Florwen Hune, and Arseninis. With each passing generation of the human kings it was renewed, so the elves barely read it before signing their names. It was simply an ink and paper representation of what they all believed. When the woman put it away, the mood changed to one of trepidation.

"Well, here it is, The Great Nymyñosian Alliance," Miazie pulled out a large piece of vellum and laid it out on the table.

*"We here signed below do recognize this alliance for the betterment of all the peoples of Nymyños, and her safety. We adhere to the various laws of each individual province of Nymyños, and do hereby agree to uphold each law as lain down by her leaders. When threatened, we shall protect and defend, when ravaged, we shall support and serve, and when corrupted, we shall purge and renew. During times of war and strife, we shall give what aid we can in order to support our neighbors and our people. If any fail to do so, they shall be stripped of title, land, and wealth and exiled to the Liberated Lands to make what life they can. If said offender ever steps within any of the below represented lands, they shall be executed without trial. This alliance to be renewed with each passing generation of Man.*

*Signed this 28th day of Resen, of the Year 547 of the 9th Age*

Queen Tlonna Arune Ewôsdirn er'Grisholm

King Losolin Ullor Grisholm en'Ewôsdirn

High Commander Yayènia er'Tiena

**King Barukh Odrinsson**

**GENERAL GRATIS POESSON**

King Tyular Ambrose

General Tomas Kelton

King Tristan Demetrius Plaukler

**General Richard Bell**

King Eyin Thorn

Commander Meradyn Obren

Queen Erdwyf Lhia er'Tomyvon

King Ghealan Romis Tomyvon

When Miazie finished reading, she handed the document to Erandur, who quickly read it for himself, studying the signatures the longest, and then passed it to Vilyneldril. The councilor read it several times over, frowning with concentration. A thick silence filled the room while they waited. After a bit, he set the parchment down and folded his hands before it.

"I take it the signatures below the royal signatures are the leaders of the armies?"

Tlonna nodded. "Yes."

The elf bowed his head in thought once more and then looked up. "It seems to be well in order. It is quite the entrapment, but I see no foulness in the words. I will agree to it."

Erandur smiled and held his hand out for Miazie's quill. She handed it to him and he quickly scrawled his signature below Ghealan's. He handed it off to Lelfwin, who added his own autograph.

Tlonna leaned back and smiled, greatly relieved. Erandur smiled back at her and ran a hand back through his white-blond hair. Lelfwin gave the quill back to Miazie and slid the parchment over to Tlonna.

"Tahi-tat and General Hatsu are going to have a hard time finding a spot to sign," the elf said, giving her a impish smile.

"That is a good thing, High Captain," Tlonna said.

"I thought you were the High Captain, Prince Erandur," Miazie muttered, half distracted by storing the treaty in her folder.

Erandur shook his head. "Father decided I was needed more solely as the prince. He promoted Lelfwin and gave him command of the army. I still have a say in the goings-on, but Lelfwin is now the head."

"Fascinating," the Belau mumbled and knotted the folder closed. "Did he give you a reason?"

Tlonna frowned at her advisor but did not call her on her questions. The elf prince frowned as well as he folded his hands on the table before him.

"Yes. He said it was time for me to take upon the mantle of leadership not only in a military faction, but in an economical and societal position as well. He said I have had freedom for eight hundred and thirty-nine years and that it is time for me to act as a prince."

"Your father is wise, but he is afraid. He believes his life is coming to a close, and he is readying you for the kingship," Miazie said. "He plans to march at the head of the army in two week's time to augment Blackhaven's ranks. He is bringing with him every last soldier left in Flousen Dua. He is going to throw everything Flousen Dua has at this last war. He is going to be there for the end."

"What are you talking about? How do you know this?" Erandur demanded, coming forward in his seat.

"Vilyneldril already knows this. He has been keeping this from you by order of the king. I have no such orders."

"Miazie, what are you talking about?" Tlonna snapped, shocked and angered by Miazie's behavior.

The Belau looked up and the queen sat back, slightly mollified. The woman's eyes were glazed, she had been taken by a vision without warning, and had no control over herself. Vilyneldril licked his lips as Lelfwin and Erandur turned to him in seething anger. The prince lifted a clenched fist and shook it at the councilor.

"You have betrayed me," he hissed.

"No," Vilyneldril denied, lifting his hands in a submissive gesture, "what she says is true. I was under oath by your father to hold my tongue. He knew you would argue against such an action, so he did not want you to know until the last possible moment."

"Well, he has been foiled. Lel, we need to go. Tlonna, I apologize for this, but I need to get back before my father does something to get himself killed."

"Ride swift my friend," the queen stood to grip the male's hand.

"No!" Miazie reached out to grab their joined hands. "You must not disrupt this path. To do so would spell disaster for all involved."

"When did you become a prophet?" Erandur accused, standing straighter to tower over the human. "You would advise me to stand by and allow my father to put his life in danger?"

"Your father is the most legendary assassin in the entire world, Prince Erandur. He tops even Aidyn, he is no feeble warrior," Miazie nearly shouted.

Lelfwin grabbed the woman's shoulders and pulled her back a little roughly. "Hands off Prince Erandur, Lady Miazie," he warned quietly.

Tlonna turned to Erandur. "She is right, but I understand the desire to protect your father. I killed my own mother in order to do so, though I failed to protect him. I will give you whatever aid you need."

"My thanks. Perhaps..." he glanced at the highly anxious Miazie, "we will stay the night and think on things before we head out. We can make it back to Duan in less than two weeks."

"True enough."

Erandur let out a deep breath and turned to his friend. "Lel, are you ready for this?"

"No, but I will be," the warrior responded dully and let go of Miazie.

"Vily, I will not be beguiled again. You have lost my trust," the prince said, sticking his finger in the councilor's face.

"Prince, I am sorry you feel that way, but I did as your father, my king, demanded. I did what was expected of me."

"My father has not been in touch with the rest of Nymyños for over a thousand years, Lord Councilor, and so his judgment is affected. He is not the warrior he used to be! You have agreed to let him march to his death!"

The councilor stiffened his back and faced his prince. "Your father is a proud, wise king and he did not make this decision lightly. He will stand with the other leaders of Nymyños in this final battle against evil."

Erandur strained against the urge to strike the pompous councilor, but he finally turned away from him and back to Tlonna. "Is there a room for us to stay in while we are here?"

"Of course my friend. I will show you to them myself. Miazie, please go get some rest."

"Tlonna, I..."

"Go."

The Belau sighed and walked from the room, her shoulders slumped in remorse. Tlonna gripped Erandur's arm and gave it a little shake.

"Things will end up all right in the end. If your father does make it to the battle front, know that he will be guarded by the best warriors Nymyños has to offer."

"I know. When do you plan on returning there?"

"I do not know, unfortunately the murder of one of my agents and a sadly depleted treasury demands my attention for the time being. I hope to head out by the end of the month."

"That does not give you much time to deal with such things. Would it be of offense if, when I am returned with my father, I join your husband in the defense of our great union of kingdoms?'

"No, of course not. That would bring much comfort and joy to Losolin and the others, I am sure. Come, I will show you and your companions where you may stay."

Tlonna led the three males to their separate rooms and then went to her office. Aidyn was sitting on the floor by her door, idly playing with one of his numerous knives. When she appeared, the assassin flowed onto his feet with an agility that continued to amaze.

"You look better," she remarked as she took in the dark elf's clean attire and gleaming hair.

"As do you. I hear Erandur has come."

Tlonna tried to ignore his scent when she moved close to him to unlock the door. "He and Lelfwin just signed the treaty."

"That is good. I saw Miazie in passing. She looked upset."

Tlonna led the way into the room and then shut the door behind him. Aidyn leaned his backside against her desk, folding his arms.

"Miazie always looks upset. She is pregnant," Tlonna grunted, desperately wishing Losolin were beside her as she tried to keep her body from reacting to Aidyn's presence.

"True enough. So, when do we return to the battlefield?"

"How many times am I going to be asked that today?" Tlonna exclaimed, throwing her hands in the air. "I do not know. Do you think I enjoy not being there? Do you think I enjoy not knowing whether my husband is alive or dead, whether my people are lying slaughtered on the ground? Well I do not! I do not like it at all! But what can I do? I leave here for a few weeks and my High Advisor murders my agent, and a bill is passed that could actually cripple the kingdom's coffers. I do not know what to do, Aidyn! I do not want to make these choices any longer!"

She did not realize hot tears were splashing down her face, nor did she realize that she was sobbing uncontrollably until Aidyn pulled her close and put his arms about her. She buried her face in his chest and wept, digging her fingers into shoulders.

"It will all be okay, Tlonna. It has to. Life does not stop, even if we fail in something. You cannot let it all get to you. You will get old that way."

"What?" Tlonna sniffled, unwilling to move from his comforting embrace.

Aidyn's chest rumbled with a chuckle. "Stop worrying and let things come as they will. Deal with each problem singularly and try to think of solutions, not the problems. You have a lot of people to share the load with, so share it."

"I love you Aidyn. I really do. You are the best friend I could ever ask for."

"I love you too, Tlonna," the assassin murmured and rested his chin on top of her head. "So, share the load. What can I help with?"

"Well, for one you could tell me what you were doing waiting outside my door," the queen responded and reluctantly pulled away.

Aidyn stopped her from leaving his embrace all the way and looked down at her. "Ah, well that is easy. I wanted to tell you that there was a message waiting for me in my room. Something has happened at the College and I am urgently requested there."

Tlonna let out a resigned breath. "When will you leave?"

Aidyn lifted one raven-black eyebrow at her. "I was actually going to ask if you, Yayènia, and Aladorn might come with me, and if we might simply make it a detour on our way to the Sethryn."

"But...the College is supposed to be top-secret, is it not?"

The assassin shrugged. "Yayènia already knows where it is, Dietirin knew, so you should know as ruling monarch, and Aladorn is my brother. I am the Master Assassin, and can do as I please with the College, anyway."

"Do you get urgent summons often?"

Aidyn's face tightened slightly. "Only once, when Master Driszn died and I became the Master. Not in over seven hundred years have I received another."

"Then we shall go."

"I am glad. Now, what else?'

Tlonna shrugged. "Well, there is this Merchant's Guild bill that Miazie passed, albeit with strict reformations on it. It bothers me for some reason. Then there is this unsettling note from Erdwyf. She says that a squad of Seadueni elves have sworn fealty to her and become her guards. She says that they disagreed with the way Stoffnias was running things, and wanted out. Now they are in full support of us, Blackhavenites, their sworn enemy for one hundred and fifty years."

Aidyn frowned and let her go so he could read the letter himself, of which she had reached around him to grab. "Well that is unexpected, but what is bad about it? Seaduens elves may be a bucket full of trash but when they make an oath they keep it just as any elf does."

"I know, but why now? There is no way they could know that Stoffnias was dead when they swore, will that affect their decision? Will they regret their choice to abandon the Lostug regime when they find out Isadorr is now king?"

Aidyn grabbed her face and forced her to look at him. Tlonna could feel the iron strength in his slender fingers, and she recalled his old nickname. She smiled naughtily, catching him off guard.

"Yes, Fingers?"

His emerald glare set her heart to racing, and she reached up to tug on his fingers, which were pressing into her cheek. He moved so fast she could not stop him from twining her fingers with his, trapping them. "One problem at a time. You have no control over what is happening over there in Narnen, so push it from your mind."

"Okay," Tlonna breathed, unable to look away.

Aidyn smiled, revealing a glimpse of his pearly white teeth, and kissed her chastely. "Relax, Tlonna," he said and released her face and fingers to rub her arms. "You need to calm down."

"I am trying. I really am."

"I know. Now sit."

Tlonna sat, looking up at him with wide eyes. "What?"

Aidyn lifted himself onto her desk and looked over her head. "Isadorr being king of Seaduens is going to cause problems. Of all of them, I would prefer Gothier to sit on the throne, but that is probably not going to happen. Isadorr is much more cautious than any of his predecessors, and I am sure he will be even more so now. The only good thing is that Isadorr hates humans more than the rest. He may simply abandon the fight and head for home."

"Do you think so?"

The assassin shrugged. "Impossible to know, but it is a possibility. As for the Merchant's Guild pushing their weight around, let them do it. If it causes a riot, we will put it down. The geld issues," he sighed, "those will never go away. All we can do is hope that this war ends soon, and we can focus on the economy. Until then, hand those responsibilities over to Daphne, and forget about them."

"You should be in my seat," Tlonna muttered. She glared at his knee, unable to meet his gaze.

"I would just kill everyone who irritated me. There would be very few Blackhavenites populating the kingdom."

The queen snorted. "That is almost exactly what Yayènia said when I offered her the throne." She reached up and placed her hands against his thighs.

"We are very similar in that," the assassin said, smiling faintly.

"Yes, I suppose you are."

Visible beneath the taut leather were the two raised scars in the shape of a T. She traced it with a finger. "You make me want to do bad things," she whispered.

Aidyn's lips quirked, but he stayed on her desk. "I want to let you do them."

Tlonna growled at him. "You are impossible," she said as she stood up between his knees. "But I really need my friend right now."

The assassin held his arms out, and she stepped into them, finding comfort in his simple embrace.

# Chapter 25

## Breaking Apart

Vilyneldril and Lelfwin departed the next day, leaving Erandur behind. The prince watched them go with shadowed eyes, his hands clasped tightly behind his back. Tlonna and Aidyn stood on either side of him to lend their moral support. His decision to stay behind weighed heavily on the prince, but he had decided it to be the best course of action. The trio watched them until the two were out of sight, and then turned back to the castle with pensive hearts.

Time moved slowly by as Tlonna got the kingdom back under her control and began to sort through the mess of papers on her desk. Aidyn disappeared often, worrying and confusing everyone, though he appeared to be quite well. Only Tlonna knew he was in the indoor training room housed in the inner courtyard, putting himself through rigorous training routines to get his body back into full working condition. Miazie was beginning to waddle and Sodo walked around with a stupefied expression on his face. Erandur and Aladorn sparred in the courtyard, and even Yayènia kept herself busy and somehow serene. It was an odd, in-between time.

A week or so after Lelfwin and Vilyneldril's departure, Tlonna was in her office reading a report from the castle kitchens and wondering why she was reading it. She nearly leapt out of her seat when her door banged open to slam against the wall and rebound. It stopped with a loud smack as it hit Yayènia's open palm.

"What is it?"

The warrior was seething. "Rioting in the streets. I do not know what is going on, but people are getting trampled, Tlonna, dying in the streets of Blackhaven!"

Tlonna shot out of her chair and grabbed her sister's arm, the sharp edges of her vambrace digging into her palm. "Who started it? What is it about? Where is it centered?"

"I do not know. Miazie was on her way up here, but I beat her. Aidyn and Aladorn are already outside trying to calm things down."

The queen cursed. She knew how those two would calm things down. She did not need more deaths on the hands of her council. "Where was Miazie when you saw her?"

"Headed up the stairs. Sodo had just rushed outside to help the brothers."

Tlonna nodded and the two ran down the corridor and met up with the human halfway down the staircase.

"Tlonna! The Merchant's Guild!"

"What?" the queen squeaked in surprise.

Miazie gulped in air and clutched at her belly. "The riot was caused by the Merchant's Guild. Count Iranyo started it, telling the nobility that it was at the behest of the elves and dwarves and other faery creatures that the strict regulation on their tax benefit was placed."

"This is about geld?" Yayènia gaped, gripping Miazie's shoulder.

"Greed can drive people to great lengths. Tlonna, it's my fault. I passed the bill that cut their request in half. I did not think this would happen."

Tlonna cut her hand through the air in a dismissive gesture. "How could you? I let it pass as well. Now, tell me about Iranyo while we walk."

The Belau nodded and turned with the elves. "He has been a forerunner in racist movements for years. He is the Master of the Merchant's Guild, which gives him a lot of power, particularly over the middle class people. He can raise and lower prices of the goods the Guild provides for the craftspeople according to whim."

"Why have I not heard of this? I would not have allowed that, ever!" Tlonna demanded as she nearly dragged the human down the stairs.

Miazie shook her head. "That is the main reason for the existence of the guilds and colleges. Just like you have little say over what Aidyn does with his assassins, you have little say over the Merchant's Guild's price-setting. You are allowed to set a limit on tax, but within that limit they can fluctuate prices without ever telling you. It was a law set down by Damian in order to protect the working people from corrupt nobility. At the time it was a sensible law, being that the population was less than half it is now, and the community was much closer knit. But in today's society, it is unreasonable."

"Then why has it not been revoked?" Tlonna asked, thinking hard as her advisor spoke.

"Because there hasn't really been a reason to bring it into the light. Most complaints that deal with taxes and prices are brought to petition and are taken care of that way. Never before has there been an uprising on this scale, at least not here. They are quite common in the human kingdoms, but not here."

"So what does Iranyo have to do with this one?" the queen inquired as she swung around a newel post onto the ground floor.

Miazie swallowed and gasped, winded by the elves' fast pace. "He started it by standing in the a city square and hollering about how it is the corruption and greed of the faery creatures that drives the prices up, that with their long lives they amass great quantities of geld, but are stingy with it. He says that elves and dwarves hold out against the humans, wanting better quality items without revealing how wealthy they are. This causes the warehouses and suppliers to have to import finer materials, which costs more, therein driving up the bottom line price for consumers."

"But that is nonsense. We are no wealthier than humans are," Yayènia snapped, her hand grabbing hold of Miazie's other arm, and shook her.

The human's toes were off the ground now and she hovered between the two elves like a child. "It's not nonsense, not really. I mean the hoarding is, of course, but not the idea. That is how prices get driven up."

"Wait a moment, you said Count Iranyo? The bastard who tried to start a lynch mob against all non-humans all those years back, before the initial siege?" Yayènia growled.

"The very same. He's a dangerous man, and now he has just proven his corruption," Miazie looked ashamed for a moment, "he was one of Martin Crotes' informants."

"Would the murder of that man have anything to do with this, do you think?" Tlonna asked dangerously, setting her down so that her shoulder was lifted high by Yayènia, but she now stood on her own feet.

"Perhaps," Miazie mumbled, looking away. "I have reason to believe Iranyo was in on a plot to kill you."

"How delightful," Tlonna said, sarcasm heavy in her voice. "Was?"

"The plot was abandoned when Martin died, according to one of his sneaks I pulled in."

"Well there is some good news," Yayènia spat and let go of Miazie's arm with a shove. "I think we should kill him."

"Not a bad idea, but not by you," Tlonna said, her finger pointed at Yayènia. "Come on, we need to get this thing under control. Miazie, you stay here."

"But-"

"No, you are vulnerable. Stay here and be safe. That is an order," Tlonna said and moved her finger to the woman.

The Belau bowed her head in acquiescence. "As my queen commands," she murmured and walked slowly back up the stairs.

Tlonna sighed and pulled Yayènia's longblade out of its sheath. The warrior jerked in alarm, and then lifted an eyebrow as Tlonna rested the blade against her shoulder.

"You do not have any weapons on you?"

"Apparently such things are not befitting to a queen," Tlonna said. "So, what do you know about stopping a riot?"

Yayènia shrugged unconcernedly. "People are easily frightened."

The Magin Queen smiled slowly. "No collateral damage, High Commander."

"*Eann munnasae alt*," the warrior said loftily, an acerbic phrase meaning 'by your command'.

Together, the two females strode out of the castle into the city, where they found the city in a complete uproar. People ran amok in mobs, throwing flaming torches into the hastily boarded up shops and attacking wealthy-appearing bystanders. One such group came at Yayènia and Tlonna, realizing at the last second who it was they were about to attack.

"Queen Tlonna!" a youth shrieked as he skidded to a halt. He dropped his torch in the street.

Tlonna stuck her hand out over the burning brand. A trickle of white light expanded out of her index finger and extinguished the flame. Yayènia stepped forward and whipped out her twin katans in a motion so swift it made people wonder if the blades had been in her hands all along. She crossed them at the youth's gulping neck.

"I would suggest you boys run along and hide before you get caught up in things far too deadly," she hissed in a menacing tone, bending down a little to press the blades against his flesh.

"Yes, High Commander er"Tiena, Queen Tlonna, we will."

"Good. Go."

The group fled, bumping into each other in their terror. The sisters turned down the street, hurrying toward the city center, encountering more and more mobs at each turn. They sent them all running in absolute dread. By the time they reached the hub of the riot, Tlonna was at the end of her tolerance. In the only paved area of Blackhaven city stood a twisted, hollow tower that existed only to make the eye wander. A sturdy railing twisted up its entire length, affording brave souls a stunning view of the city, but that was it. There was no entrance inside, and therefore was a subject of theories and stories all on its own. It was to this architectural eccentricity that Tlonna now headed.

Yayènia grabbed a gawking teenage dwarf and heaved him from the beginning of the stairs to send him bouncing across the cobblestone. Tlonna gave her a warning glare as she began to ascend the winding steps. Once they reached the top, the queen took a moment to look at the scene far below, at the teeming mass of people swarming the square. Guards moved through the crowd, trying to install some order. They were failing miserably.

She also spotted a moving bubble, and saw Aidyn in the center of it, walking unhindered through crowd, Aladorn and Sodo just steps behind him. The people who parted for them, or for the assassin alone more correctly, seemed to lose all fire and stand quietly. Even this remarkable feat was not enough to stop the chanting, screaming, heaving mass of people. Tlonna took a deep breath and handed the longsword back to Yayènia with thanks. She'd had to use it a few times to knock people down.

Again she sucked in a breath and held it as she lifted her hand in the air, palm facing the afternoon sky. A violent concussion rent the air, eliciting different screams from the seething crowd. The bubble of space around Aidyn, Aladorn, and Sodo stopped moving as they halted. When they saw what had caused the interruption, the males began moving again, this time toward the tower. Yayènia cursed and bent low against the railing, not liking the rattling sensation in her bones from standing too close to Tlonna's Weaving. Again the air impacted with a sound like angry thunder. When that sound faded, five crackling bars of light shot up from Tlonna's outstretched fingers, coming together in a cone shape far above them. Each bar was a different color, sparks of white dancing about them. The magic disappeared into the clouds, and then came rushing back, but as it touched the place where the five pillars separated, it spread out in a solid dome.

Yayènia gave up on steadying herself and released the railing to clutch at her head, clenching her jaw against the painful rumbling in her body. Tlonna stood rigidly, her face hard as she held the dome up to encompass the entire city.

"This is your queen," she began, and her voice reverberated throughout the entire dome, amplified a thousand times over. "I am disappointed in my people. You have fallen victim to a nefarious lie meant to elicit racism and hatred. I believed better of my people. I believed them above the petty issue of race, but I was wrong. You are slaves to an old, broken ideal. You bow to the dubious passion of wicked people like slavish miscreants. This is a kingdom of conscience, a kingdom of intelligence and acceptance. Do not make a mockery of my kingdom. If you believe yourself mistreated then by all means come and speak with me about it, I am here to help you, not to beat you into submission with strength, geld, or words. I ask you only to consider the consequences of your actions, to look at the people standing next to you, look at the elves, dwarves, humans, sprytes, dryads, and half-breeds among you, and seek in them the cruel intention you are so intent upon punishing."

When Tlonna paused, a low murmur rose from the crowd along with a slight shifting as people looked at each other in shame. The Magin Queen was not finished, however.

"Each of you chose to live here, whether you moved or were born, you have chosen to stay. Why? Because this is a land of freedom, a land where we defend our rights to live as we choose. It is in our motto! 'While we stand, we shall guard!' We defend our right to live as individuals with the freedom of speech, of religion, of culture, and of choice. You have the right to protest the way things are, but when you take that right and turn it into violence, you take that right from others! You are a hypocrite! I will not stand to have such injustice in my kingdom! If you find this unfair, you have the right to leave! I bid you take that right and rid us of your prejudice!

"People have died here tonight, because of your actions! You have all taken part in murder! You may think yourself innocent because you were simply doing as everyone else was, but that makes you ignorant, not innocent! It is the person who stands alone to defend what they believe is right that is a hero, not the person who follows another because they get caught up in the passion of violence."

Yayènia turned her head as Aidyn stepped up beside her and placed his booted feet on either side of her. She did not know how he could stand the agony of standing next to Tlonna with all that power vibrating around her, but she felt protected, and leaned against his thighs. He reached one arm down and touched her shoulder in comfort. Aladorn and Sodo stood far below at the base of the tower, and blocked the way up the stairs.

"Now, I bid you either go home and think on the things you have done this terrible day, or leave this kingdom forever. Make your choice now while others can be witness to your bravery or your cowardice."

Tlonna waited a few seconds longer and then lowered her hand. The crackling dome swirled inward and then imploded high above them, shaking the very foundations of the tower. The Magin let out a heavy breath and stumbled back to lean against the twisted face of the tower. Aidyn's thighs flexed against Yayènia's back as he leaned over to bring Tlonna into his free arm. The commander slowly stood and rolled her shoulders to rid them of their tightness. Her sister's voice had been so loud in her head!

When Yayènia turned, she watched Tlonna collapse into Aidyn and her head thunk onto his shoulder. He did not know she was watching as he inhaled deeply against her hair, his emerald eyes half closing.

"Aidyn."

The assassin looked at her with a cold expression. "We will wait until the crowd is gone before going down."

"Of course," Yayènia responded quietly as he held his love against his body.

They stood and waited for a long time. Many of the people below lingered, staring up at the trio, trying to get a glimpse of what was going on, but only elves could see clearly that far, and they were mostly all holed up in their homes. Finally, when the last few stragglers shuffled away from the square, Aidyn gently hoisted Tlonna into his arms and carried her down the winding stairs, Yayènia on his heels. Aladorn and Sodo turned when they approached, concern etched on their faces.

"Is she okay?" the alchemist asked as he eyed Tlonna.

"She used a lot of power to do that," Aidyn mumbled. "She is simply asleep."

"I will call a carriage," Sodo said and rushed off.

The four waited in silence until the tainted elf reappeared, leading a covered carriage. Aidyn carefully carried Tlonna into a seat and held her close. Yayènia and Aladorn shared the other bench. Sodo climbed up next to the driver.

"That will be the gossip for a long time to come," the wiat remarked quietly, not looking at anyone.

"Do you think anyone will leave?" Yayènia asked him. She knew he was more in touch with people than her or Aidyn.

The dark elf lifted a shoulder in a shrug. "Hard to say. She may have insulted quite a few people, but those are the kind we do not want here. Some will leave the city, I suppose, but not the kingdom. They know what they have here."

"I heard someone say the Merchant's Guild was behind it," Aidyn said. "If this was about geld issues..." the assassin broke off, unable to come up with anything to explain his disgust.

"It was. Count Iranyo was behind it," Yayènia told them, shaking her head. "Only he would think of putting a racial spin on a geld problem."

"I hate that man," Aidyn muttered, glancing at Tlonna's sleeping face.

"Who is he?" Aladorn asked, frowning.

While Yayènia explained to the wiat who the man was, she watched his brother watch her sister. It was unsettling the way the assassin's face went soft when he simply looked at Tlonna. The ride back to the castle was rather quick as there were few people left in the streets to hinder their passage. Aidyn carried Tlonna all the way to her bed, and then took up a vigil at her bedside. Yayènia shook her head as she left, ushering Sodo, Miazie, and Aladorn out of the royal bedroom. She looked back once to see Aidyn bury his face in hands.

Tlonna came to her senses with a start. She sat straight up in bed and gasped. Aidyn stiffened in his chair and then relaxed when he saw no threat. They looked at each other in silence. Finally the queen swung her legs to the floor and smiled.

"My hero, as always," she joked softly and shook her head.

The assassin snorted, leaned back and stretched his spine. "If you would stop needing heroes I would much appreciate it."

"Then you would be out of a job."

The dark elf chuckled as he stood. "How do you feel?"

"Do you not know?" Tlonna asked, pressing her hand to her chest, directly over her heart.

Aidyn studied her for a moment before answering. "I feel many things, so I must ask what it is you are feeling strongest right now. You used a lot of power."

"Did it work?"

"Aye. Your people are sufficiently cowed."

Tlonna sighed. "I feel sad, like everything is breaking apart. How can we hope to win if the people we are trying to protect are railing against us?"

"There will always be malcontents, Lonna, always. You cannot let them get to you."

The queen rolled her head in an attempt to soothe her aching muscles. She realized he was the only one who called her Lonna. Everyone else called her Loni, or her actual name. She wondered why. "There were so many people in that square, so many willing to give in to gratuitous violence on the mere word of some greedy noble."

"Why do you think those soldiers are fighting right now?" Aidyn asked, tilting his head to give her a lecturing look. "On your word, they marched to battle. On your word they are willing to lay down their lives to protect their country. On your word. Most of those soldiers have not seen any of the Rahlans, never been at the receiving end of their evil, but they will fight against them because you say they are evil."

Tlonna was fighting back tears, and losing. "Am I that terrible? Am I a dictating tyrant who sends her people to slaughter just because I have been slighted?"

The assassin joined her on the bed to put a comforting arm about her shoulders.

"No, what I am saying is that words have power. But you said the same at the Cyree, about Brandon Stynbek. Some use that power for wickedness, some for good and there will always be people susceptible to both. It is for the ruler, the queen, to seek out those who use that manipulative ability for cruel actions. Iranyo is such a person, a nefarious, greedy man who hates to see anyone succeed more than him. You are a queen, a leader of her people, and words are going to be your best friend at times."

"You are my best friend," Tlonna muttered, her head resting on Aidyn's strong shoulder.

"As you are mine, but my power rests only in my ability to use a blade."

"No," Tlonna sniffled, "you have a greater strength. You bring me comfort and advice. Security and peace. Love."

The assassin had to control his breathing so he wouldn't be caught up in her scent, in her touch, in the very sound of her voice. "I always thought I was a pest. Your father always called me a thorn in his side."

Tlonna chuckled and sat up and took a deep, steadying breath. "You can be, but a pretty one."

"Always with the pretty. I am male, I am not pretty."

"You are," the queen chided gently. "Too pretty."

Aidyn rolled his eyes and stood once more. "As you wish, my beautiful queen."

Tlonna hesitated and then stood, steeling herself for what she was about to ask. "Aidyn."

The assassin turned to her and noticed her stiff posture. His face went from friend to killer in an instant, and she felt a shiver go up her spine. Never before had she asked him to do the very base of his job, as she was about to do.

"Aidyn, my dear friend," she began again, her heart thumping as his eyes narrowed suspiciously. "I need him...taken care of."

Aidyn's eyes brightened knowingly and he grinned slowly. "Long have I waited for this day. How do you want me to handle the situation?"

Tlonna winced and put a restraining hand on his forearm. He looked amused.

"I need it to be quick, and immediate. Let there be no doubt as to who did it, but with no proof. There must not be any proof that I ordered the termination."

The assassin shrugged, nonchalant. "Easily done. I can do it this very night, if need be."

"No, tomorrow morning."

"Morning?"

The queen nodded. "Talk to Miazie, see if she knows anything about the man's personal life. She may have some information that would be valuable to you. I need you to search his house as well."

The prospect of assassinating Iranyo had his blood pumping heatedly. "What should I be looking for?" Aidyn asked, his mind already planning the execution of the racist old human.

"Letters, symbols that might tie him to our enemies, anything you find suspicious. I give you full lead on this, do whatever is necessary to take care of him."

"Who will take his place?"

Tlonna tapped a finger against her chin as she thought. "I will ask the young Viscount Markus, currently overseeing the village of Hastert. His brother can take up his position as Viscount."

Aidyn nodded. "Then it shall be done as you wish, Your Majesty. By the Honor of Assassins I accept your contract and shall fulfill it to the best of my ability, and only my death shall prevent success."

Tlonna took his proffered hand and kissed his tawny knuckles as was the formal way of sealing a contract. The air seemed to thicken around them and Aidyn went to his knees. He looked up with a solemn expression. "Between a Magin and an Assassin," he whispered and without another word the dark elf walked away, *ärdyz* cloak flowing out behind him. She watched him go in amazement.

# Chapter 26
## Two Broken Bodies

Aidyn found Miazie in her office and walked in without knocking. She glared at him.

"What can I do for you?" she asked snappishly, not appreciating the dark elf's perfect features when she felt so sweaty and fat.

The assassin lowered himself into a chair with that damned fluid grace that came so naturally to him and rested an ankle on a knee. Son of a goat. "What can you tell me about Iranyo's daily routine?"

The Belau gaped at him. "Why?"

"Are you going to question the orders of the Royal Assassin, High Advisor?"

Miazie blanched and looked down. Only Tlonna and Losolin outranked the Royal Assassin, as he was level with the High Commander. "No, Lord Aidyn."

"Then what do you know?"

She got up from her chair and walked over to a cabinet. After unlocking it, the pregnant woman rifled through the folders within until pulling one out and moving back to her desk. "This is all that I have on him," she said and opened the file. "He is seventy-five, the second wealthiest count in Blackhaven, has been married twice, his first wife died from a fever thirty-some years ago. Oh, this is interesting. He has a mistress named Phoebe who arrives at the manor house every weekday morning precisely at ten, once the Countess has gone for her daily excursions about the city."

"You know all that? That is convenient."

Miazie gave him a long-suffering look. "Aidyn, I have inherited all of Erdwyf's files, which over the course of three hundred years she has compiled through the clever use of spies and other agents. You would not believe the amount of information that elf gathered during her tenure. There is even a file on you."

Aidyn scowled. "Give it to me."

"I think not."

"I do. Give me the file, Miazie."

"It is classified information."

"I highly doubt that any information you might have read about me is unknown to me. Give me the file, or suffer the consequences."

"Are you threatening me, Royal Assassin?"

"I am, High Advisor, and not idly. My very existence depends on my personal details remaining secret."

Miazie sat back in her chair, inwardly petrified, outwardly confidant. "Your personal life has long been in the public view, Aidyn. Your romancing of the various ladies of the nation has taken care of that."

The dark elf resisted the urge to hit the woman through the balcony door. "Are you jealous I did not sleep with you, Miazie?"

The Belau's mouth dropped open and she managed a look of indignation. "No! Hitting me won't do you any good! But you are a lecher and I know what you did to Tlonna!"

"You know nothing, woman."

"Oh? I know every little sordid detail, *assassin*. I see it every now and then, sometimes it wakes me up in the middle of the night and I have to spend the next few *hours* in the bathroom sweating and panting on the floor, praying to the gods Sodo doesn't realize why I look the way I do when it happens. I know what you look like, how you move, how you *feel*. You may not have physically made love to me, but I know what it's like anyway. You took Tlonna's virginity and you have coveted her ever since. *You* are the jealous one, not me."

"Then tell her and see if she believes me a lecher! Tell her and find out if she thinks my love is a curse!" Aidyn shouted, his fingers digging into his side to keep from killing the human.

Miazie blushed as she realized what she had said, and what he had just admitted. "I'm...I'm sorry, Aidyn, but I...I don't quite feel myself these days. I did not realize you felt...that way."

The dark elf had drawn blood on his waist. His breath was coming in hot, fast huffs. "As I said, you know nothing. But you should know that nearly all the rumors of my licentious activities with the ladies of this kingdom are fabrications. I have been with one woman in the past two years, and that was at Tristan's coronation. I have no desire to be with anyone other than she whom I love, and I cannot be with her so I do not lay with anyone. Put that in your damn file. Thank you for the information. And stay out of my head!"

"Aidyn..." the Belau began, but he was already gone.

Aidyn walked into his room and threw open the doors of his wardrobe, the wood creaking in protest as it rebounded. Trying to calm his fury and focus on the job at hand, the assassin pulled out a large chest with several different locks on it. After inserting the keys in the correct order and placing his fingers in all the appropriate spots, the locker lid popped open and inside sat his implements. There were torture tools and grappling hooks, several varieties of rope, chains, even a few masks.

The elf took a deep breath and closed his eyes, picturing the manor house in his mind, turning the image this way and that to decipher his mode of entry. When he had settled that issue, Aidyn pulled out a small rucksack and placed a light grappling hook and rope inside, followed by a small bottle of a powerfully odorous anesthetic and a rag. That was all he packed, and then he sat restlessly for the remainder of the night, his excitement building as he pushed his fury away and thought about the kill. When the morning came he was out the door, gone before the morning mist had completely dissolved.

Aidyn flitted through the street like a wraith, barely disturbing the swirling mist as he passed. Several minutes later he was standing in the shadows of a large birch willow a few yards away from the manor house of Count Iranyo. A fifteen foot wall separated him from his target, but the dark elf took out his hook and rope and readied it for his climb up. He waited patiently as the sun rose, heard the city come to life, and then he heard Countess Marith depart in a flurry of barking lapdogs and shouting henchmen.

Aidyn was up and over the wall in seconds. He pulled the rope after him so no one would find it. Then he was slipping through the back door, soaking rag of chloroform in his hand. The first man he came across turned as the assassin purposefully scraped his boot along the floor and then he was down, knocked unconscious by the powerful odor. Two more servants suffered the same before the dark elf reached the upper floor where Iranyo was getting ready for his rendezvous with the imminent Phoebe.

"I have waited a long time for this," Aidyn said quietly, which caused the man to start in fear.

"Lord Aidyn! What are you doing here?" the nobleman asked, but the answer was already in his frightened eyes.

"You have angered the wrong people, Iranyo, and it is now time to pay for your crimes. May your corrupt, racist soul burn in the ever-flames of the nine hells," the assassin intoned and in a quicksilver move slammed into the man.

Iranyo landed on his back on the bed with Aidyn atop him, his tension spike buried deep in the man's lung. The Count was already dead when the elf retracted the weapon and climbed off the bed. Knowing the wound was identifiable by its unique appearance, the dark elf pulled out his dagger and inserted it carefully into the inch-wide hole. With a violent jerk, he yanked the blade upward to create a wicked laceration that went through bone and muscle all the way to the man's armpit, eviscerating the evidence of his one-of-a-kind blade.

Quickly, Aidyn cleaned his gear and then went through a systemized search of the house, knowing his time was running short. He found a few letters and one enameled pin with the Zaedic crest on it. Then he jogged to the cellar, deciding at the last minute to check it for propaganda. When he opened the door and light from the kitchen illuminated the large room, the elf nearly howled in rage.

A female dark elf hung listlessly from her arms, her legs half bent as she did not have the strength to stand. She was naked and her body was covered in welts, bruises, and cuts. Aidyn's breath caught and he found himself unable to move. She was a true dark elf, her skin dark gray, her hair an indecipherable light color, and Aladorn's stories of their long dead brother Aolan came rushing back. Finally he gathered his wits and rushed forward to the female.

"Can you hear me?" he asked quietly as he lifted her chin with his finger. "Do not be afraid."

Her eyes fluttered but she did not speak or make any other movement. Swearing under his breath, Aidyn quickly picked the locks on the shackles about her wrists and caught her as she collapsed against him. Gently, the assassin set her down and removed his cloak. Once she was tightly wrapped in the black garment, he expertly tied her to him, alarmed at her feathery weight, and rushed from the cellar.

The first man he had taken down was beginning to stir and lay directly in Aidyn's path to freedom. Cursing again, he kicked the man in the face before he could open his eyes enough to identify him and fled the house, the tortured female clutched to his chest. He tossed his hook up the wall and hoisted himself over, careful not to jostle the victim. Seconds later he was resting his back against the wall on the other side, his heart beating unusually hard.

The female in his arms stirred slightly, her eyes cracking open for a moment, and Aidyn caught the startling color of amber. For a moment he stared down at her, entranced, and then once again his wits came rushing back. Making sure he had everything, the assassin made his careful way back to the castle, staying within the deep shadows of the forest, away from the people. It took him nearly an hour to make it back, having to wait several times for the path to clear.

When he did, he slipped inside the kitchen door, not wanting to attract attention. The cooks rushed him, noting his stressed features.

"What is it, Lord Aidyn?" the head chef asked, his eyes riveted on the large bundle in the dark elf's arms.

"I need to get to the infirmary without being seen. I need to use your passages," the assassin replied quickly, holding the female tighter to him, protective.

"As you will, sir. Follow me," one of the servants said and led the male into a narrow passage.

The servant ways lined the entire castle and opened up in different rooms where there were large gatherings or important meetings. They allowed the servers and the maids to get about without being hassled or getting in the way of the milling castle inhabitants. Now Aidyn rushed through them on the heels of a confused but determined cook, and in half the time it would normally take, they were standing in the infirmary prep room, where food and medicines were readied for the patients. Aidyn thanked the cook and burst into the hospital, shouting for a healer.

Braden, the young man who had nursed the dark elf back to health after his ordeal with Sithian nearly jumped out of his shoes when the assassin appeared out of the supposedly sealed room.

"Lord Aidyn!" the healer gasped, his hand pressed to his racing heart. "How did you do that?"

"Servant ways, Braden, I need a private room."

"Of course," the young man said without hesitation and led the way into a small sealed off resting chamber.

There, Aidyn laid the female on the bed and removed his cloak, hissing at the sight of her ravaged body in the full light of the infirmary. Braden stared down in disbelief and shock. Aidyn then frowned as well; her hair was not white or gray like most ash-tones, but silver. Even her eyebrows had a hint of the color to them.

"Wha..."

"She is a true dark elf, the full blooded elves of my ethnicity. I found her in a cellar, chained by her wrists," Aidyn explained quickly and gestured to her swollen and bruised hands, ignoring his surprise at the color of her hair.

Braden nodded and bent to her and ran his fingers over several of the wounds to check their severity. After a long time, he straightened and rolled his shoulders. "She will heal without too much scarring, but there will be some. I'm mostly worried about the ah...injuries to her inner thighs and nether regions. She was raped, repeatedly, and brutally...not always with a phallus."

Aidyn squeezed his eyes shut in revulsion and pity. He suddenly wished he had drawn out Iranyo's death. "I need to get Tlonna. And Braden, you must not tell anyone, not even your fellow healers. Not yet."

"As you wish, Lord Aidyn. May I borrow your cloak for a while longer? Our blankets are all down in the wash or in use."

The assassin wordlessly handed over his rare garment and hastened from the room. He found Tlonna standing outside the entrance to one of the small reception rooms, a local baroness at her side. Aidyn walked up to them and smiled inwardly when the woman abruptly ended her rapid-fire monologue and stared at him. Tlonna's eyes looked weary when she met his gaze.

"My Lord Aidyn," the Baroness Nadine intoned and curtseyed. "I am grateful to know of your full recovery. My husband, Baron Nathaniel Dawson, is a great admirer of yours." She put a single finger on his elbow and looked up at him through her lashes. "We would be greatly honored if you would celebrate Yule with us. We are having a little, *private* fête at our manor in the Peerage District on the eve."

"The honor is mine, Madam, but I must decline. My duties demand that I be with Queen Tlonna at all public functions."

The woman's gaze turned to her ruler and she very nearly pouted. "Certainly you do not demand that of him, Your Majesty? Can he not have but one night off?"

Tlonna suppressed the urge to hit the baroness. "I would love to, but unfortunately in times of war the edict is quite strict on such matters. Lord Aidyn's oaths bind him to protocol as much as mine do. Please accept my apology, Baroness Dawson."

"Of course, Queen Tlonna, if you will excuse me. Lord Aidyn," she said stiffly and stalked off, her back rigid.

"Ambitious young thing," Tlonna muttered.

"She is a twit like all the rest. What did she want of you?"

The Magin sighed and idly brushed a stray bit of fuzz off her assassin's shoulder. "She wanted to know when the castle would host the season's festivities. I told her it would be on the night of Yule, as usual. She did not like that and told me that she and her husband were holding their own on the eve if that was indeed the case."

Aidyn shook his head. "Well, we have more pressing matters. Iranyo is dead, but I found a female dark elf in his cellar, beaten and raped, nearly comatose. She is in the infirmary."

"Iranyo was keeping an elven pleasure slave?"

The assassin nodded. "She does not look well."

Tlonna pinched the bridge of her nose and squeezed her eyes shut. "Lead on, then."

They hurried to the hospital wing and were greeted by a frantic, frightened Braden.

"She is awake," was all he said.

The assassin rushed by him and into the little room despite the protests of both his queen and the healer. The female looked up at him with nearly glowing amber eyes, fear and undeniable murder roaring in their depths.

"*Leae feaen dü?*" she demanded in Parlêthian, her voice thick with agony.

Aidyn stared, unable to respond. She had thrown his cloak to the floor and stood unashamed before him. Blood caked her body like a second skin, new and old scars crisscrossing her flesh in more places than even the assassin had.

"I am Aidyn Sestuns, Assassin for the Throne of Blackhaven," he answered in kind. "You are safe here," he added in Hindarün.

"*Lãn moyrkeľ?*"

"Yes, I am an assassin. What is your name?"

"Lavandyra."

"Lavandyra, would you please lay back down, or at least sit? You have suffered grievous injuries and I do not want you to compound them."

The female was about to comply when she suddenly went rigid, the murder back in her eyes. Aidyn turned around to find Braden and Tlonna standing in the doorway, completely stunned.

"We are friends, Lavandyra. We are here to help you. This is Tlonna Ewôsdírn-er'Grisholm, Queen of Blackhaven, and Healer Braden."

"Miss Lavandyra, please lie back so I can examine you. You are losing a lot of blood still, and I am very worried," Braden said calmly.

When Lavandyra did not reply, he moved closer to her and slowly reached out, his hand steady. Then she moved. Her hand snapped up to Braden's throat and slammed him against the wall, her other hand pinning his arm by the wrist.

She loosed a string of Parlêthian curses and threats, but Aidyn found himself paralyzed. He kept envisioning his brother Aolan, and her purplish gray skin transfixed him.

Tlonna swore and firmly wrapped her fingers about Lavandyra's. She pulled the dark gray hand away from the healer's throat. Braden watched her calmly despite the lack of air. When the female finally backed off, she slumped dejectedly, her dark shoulders rolling inward.

"I apologize," she said in a foreign accent, turning about to include Aidyn in her words.

The assassin jerked his eyes upward as she turned, fearing her reaction, but she only frowned a little. "You are the first of our kind I have seen in many years, Lord Assassin. Do you know how beautiful you are?"

Aidyn swallowed, for once at a loss for words. "I am not..."

"You are. Every aspect of you is desirable, even your scent. You are truly exquisite in every detail, though you are thin."

The dark elf managed to blush in spite of his tawny skin. He never paid much attention to his own appearance before, and always argued with Tlonna and Yayènia when they said such things, but he could not muster the mental faculty to contradict Lavandyra.

Tlonna found herself nodding in agreement with the strange female until she noticed Aidyn's dumbstruck expression. Lavandyra seemed unaware now that she was completely naked as she walked the few steps to the stricken male, combing back her thick silver hair with her fingers as she did so.

"I wish to know more of you," she murmured as she moved her hands to Aidyn's face and ran a thumb over the triangular scars. "Where did you get these marks of evil?"

Aidyn cleared his throat and backed away. "You should heal, and then we will talk, I promise. But first...heal."

Lavandyra nodded once and sat on the bed, looking to Braden. He spent the next hour examining her injuries more thoroughly; asking her questions of which she only answered a few. Tlonna and Aidyn stayed out of the way and tried to discuss the items the assassin had found in Iranyo's house and the reason for keeping Lavandyra.

"What I do not understand is why," Tlonna muttered softly. "If he hated elves so much, why keep one as a pleasure slave?"

Aidyn looked at her from the corner of his eyes. "For the same reason Midian kept you. Power."

The Magin fell silent with his statement. She reached out and gripped his hand after a moment, gave him a small smile. "You think she is beautiful?"

The assassin returned her gaze. "You are beautiful to me, only you. She is a pureblood dark elf, a nearly extinct race of elf. Legend says that they came from a place far south of here, called Anlinylath. It is said that Anlinylath was so beautiful that any who set eyes on it could never leave again. The people who inhabited Anlinylath were elves just like any other, but they began to turn against their god, and so he punished them by burning their flesh with rays of light that reflected off the diamond-white beaches. They prayed for mercy and he acquiesced, granted them their beauty, but forced them to keep their darkened skin as a reminder. In truth, being as far south as it is, Anlinylath was most likely just really hot and humid, so they adapted over time and their flesh darkened as a defense, but that is the Legend of Anlinylath."

"I thought the dark elf trait was a genetic mutation," Tlonna asked, perplexed by the story.

Aidyn shrugged. "It is in a way. The original dark elf was my ancestor Ikari, brother to Akitor, my...great grandfather. The ship she was on disappeared during the voyage to Nymyños and my family is of the opinion that her ship landed on Anlinylath. The dark elves that may have migrated from Anlinylath after hearing word of the Serenyi high elves reappearing on a giant mass of land up north would have been integrated into society. Just like any genetic code, the dark skin, the white or gray hair, the 'sunrise' eye colors would all have been diluted by high elf traits, only to reappear in rare cases. The brother that I never knew, Aolan, was an even rarer case, a dark elf with pure traits, called an Ash Tone. Lavandyra may be one of those, or she may be a direct descendent of an Anlinylathian."

Tlonna looked over to where the female lay quiescent while Braden worked on her. "I have never heard of this. No one has ever found Anlinylath?"

"No. Several explorers have tried, but no one has ever gotten past the Fãrthyn Expanse. After that, the tide pull from all the moons just destroys ships. As for never hearing about, there are only a few books, and most of them were destroyed during the persecution of dark elves back around when I was born. Aladorn has a copy of the legend that he recovered from a ruined library in Zeynuwn long before you were born. Other than that, people do not like to talk about it. Dark elves are still regarded as different, strange. We are the twisted mutants of high elves, a genetic anomaly no one understands."

Tlonna shook her head. "We are an advanced society that is nine thousand years old and yet we still cannot accept something different from ourselves. It is disgusting and disappointing."

Aidyn shrugged again. "It is the nature of people, Tlonna. Blackhaven was founded on principles of equality, freedom, and diversity. The rest of Nymyños was not. The Liberated Lands exist because there were humans who wanted nothing to do with rest of the races that inhabit the continent, so they went into self-imposed exile to get away from the inadvertent economical and societal relationship with non-humans. Seaduens built up a border protection that separated them from the rest of the world. Zeynuwn barricaded the passes through the Bijoz Mountains and watch every single person who travels in or out of the kingdom. Most of the Twelve Kingdoms make it difficult to be of a race foreign to the dominant one, and so it has been since the founding of Nymyños itself."

Tlonna was about to reply but was cut short by Lavandyra screaming. Braden cursed and went into a flurry of action, calling for help. More healers rushed into the room and bent over the female. Aidyn went pale and he stood.

"We should leave them to their work. I am going to go help Aladorn finish up Martin Crotes' death duties."

"Why is he doing that?" Tlonna asked as she followed the assassin out of the room.

"Because Miazie cannot, being the killer, and you were gone."

The queen frowned. "What is left to do?"

"Well," Aidyn rubbed the back of his neck, "the family has been notified, the funeral has been taken care of, I think he is just finishing up the distribution of Crotes' assets. Unfortunately, the brothels he ran were also convenient meeting places for the group who were planning your *assassination*." He said the word with such disgust Tlonna made a face at him.

"It is insulting that such morons thought themselves assassins."

"I am glad you are so concerned for my safety," Tlonna snorted.

The dark elf dismissively waved his hand. "There was never any threat, Lonna. Those idiots would never have made it beyond the doors of the castle, or wherever you happened to be."

"Was Martin in on it, then?"

"No. He would never dirty his hands in such a way, but that is not to say he would try to stop it. He was always a man who looked to the winning side. Why he thought those people were the winners, I have no idea, but with both Crotes and Iranyo dead, whatever plans the rest of them might have had are surely finished."

"Do you know who else was conspiring against me?"

Aidyn lifted one shoulder and massaged it for a moment. "Not for sure, but Al and I have our theories. Unfortunately, when Miazie killed Crotes and reeled in one of his spies they all went to ground. The brothels shut down, the prostitutes fled, and the buildings were put to flame."

Tlonna gaped at him. "This does not sound like my city, Aidyn."

The assassin stopped and turned to face her. They were now standing on the landing between the second and third floor stairs. "Lonna, think for minute. Blackhaven Kingdom has a population of just under forty thousand, and the city itself has a little more than half of that inside the walls. You have an assassin as your personal protector, and we are at war. This is the way our society works."

The queen dropped her gaze and nodded. "You are right, as usual, but I guess now it just seems more...visible. The people who did not agree with me before always seemed to either be upfront about it or blatantly try to kill me, or they would just lurk in the shadows and complain. Now it is like all the barriers are down and anyone can try and take me out."

Aidyn rubbed her arm and gave her a bright grin. "Well, you do not have to worry about that, right? That is why you have me."

Tlonna nodded. After a minute she scowled at him. "Why do you call me Lonna? No one else does."

The assassin's grin faded. "That is how you introduced yourself to me, and it just sort of stuck. If I recall correctly, Dietirin brought you into my room when you were just two years old and told you to introduce yourself. I had already seen you of course, but that was the first time we were formally introduced. You pointed at yourself and said 'Lonna' and then you pointed at me and said 'Ayden'."

"I called you Ayden?"

"Everyone does when they first meet me. After that you clung to my leg for an hour while Dietirin and I spoke about...something. I cannot remember."

"You let me?" Tlonna chortled as they began walking again.

"Yes. What was I going to do? Tell the princess of the realm to go away? I think not."

"You have no problem with it now."

"Well," Aidyn smirked while he tugged on a lock of her hair, "you are not going to run off and cry in a corner until one of the servants finds you."

"You never know, I might."

They shared a chuckle and Tlonna realized they were now standing in the deserted hallway a few feet away from the entrance to the inner courtyard. She looked up at Aidyn and felt her heart stutter. With a deep breath she pushed him up against the wall and then buried her face in his shoulder, her arms tucked against his chest. The assassin went rigid.

"Aidyn, please just hold me for a minute while I lose control," she whispered into his neck, tears already sliding down her face. "I feel so weak, so...lost."

The dark elf softened his body and wrapped his arms around her. "As long as you need me to, Tlonna."

"Do you think Lavandyra will live?" she mumbled in an attempt to regain her senses.

Aidyn hesitated and then sighed. "No. Maybe if Losolin were here, but she is in terrible shape."

"I am sorry."

"I am too, but there is nothing we can do about it."

Tlonna nodded and relaxed against him, drawing in his warmth. It was a peaceful moment and she could not find it within herself to feel guilty. Aidyn was her friend if nothing else, and she needed comfort. One of his arms moved from around her shoulders to her lower back and pulled her closer, his eyes closing. For a moment, the world felt right to him, and then he heard a gasp and stuttering feet on the floor. Aidyn reluctantly opened his eyes and glared at the servant who had stumbled upon them.

"I...I'm sorry Lord Aidyn...Queen Tlonna. I..."

"It is all right, girl. We are having a moment of friendly support," the assassin said quietly, but Tlonna heard the constrained frustration and rage in his voice.

"Oh. I see, forgive me. I'm sorry."

Aidyn gently disengaged from Tlonna as the servant began to back away and then he moved so quickly the queen blinked in surprise. The dark elf grabbed the girl by the shoulder and backed her up against the wall.

"Breathe a word of this in any foul light, and your life is forfeit. Start a false rumor, and I will kill you. Do you understand?"

The servant's skirts dampened and she began to cry. Finally she managed a nod. Aidyn released her and she fled the corridor. Tlonna gaped at Aidyn in shock.

"Was that necessary?" she demanded once she could speak again.

The assassin looked at her with blazing eyes. "Yes. Unless you want the entire city to be gossiping about how the queen is having a lusty affair with the royal assassin while her husband the king is away at war."

"Well, we sort of are..." Tlonna's voice faded as she accepted Aidyn's words. "Never mind."

He shook his head and walked away. Tlonna watched him go with a heavy heart, confused and conflicted.

# Chapter 27

## Lavandyra

Aidyn was in the indoor training room of the castle, a large vaulted chamber off the southeast end of the rear courtyard. Shirtless and shoeless, the elf was deep inside a training exercise in an attempt to get his emotions under control. His body gleamed in the sunny winter light streaming through the windows, his muscles gliding and bunching with each motion as he flowed through the formations. He held no weapon, instead the last two fingers of each hand bent inward while the other two and his thumbs stood straight out. His breathing was deep and even, his eyes closed. The assassin moved slowly, forcing his limbs to maintain a steady, enduring pattern that stretched the muscles and kept them limber.

So deep was his concentration that he did not hear her enter, nor did he realize she was watching him with lidded eyes. Only when he halted his routine to retrieve the heavy weights he strapped to his arms and legs to increase strength did Aidyn see her.

"You are allowed out of the infirmary?"

Lavandyra nodded once. "The human knows I know I am going to die. He allowed me this freedom before the end," she added in her lilt.

"I suppose you want that talk, now?" Aidyn asked, not at all surprised by her easy acceptance of her pending death. He felt the same way.

"If it would not be of hindrance to you, yes."

Aidyn moved away from the weights and bent to his things. Pulling on his shirt, he turned to the female. "What would you ask of me?"

"Where did you come from? Who were your parents? How long have you been accepted into the high elf community? How did you become accepted? How did you come to attain such powerful friends?"

The assassin could only shake his head at the questions.

"What?"

"You act as though it is something I did. It was not. I was born in Arseninis City to Bailan and Alena Sestuns, who were high elves.

Except for the first few weeks of my life I have always been a member of the 'high elf community' as you call it. There are laws here in Blackhaven that protect us from such racism."

"You cannot be protected from thoughts," Lavandyra snarled.

Aidyn lifted one shoulder in a think-what-you-will shrug. "It is your job to protect yourself from the thoughts of others, or be strong enough to take them without being provoked. As for how I came to be friends with the most powerful leaders, it all has to do with my profession."

"Being an assassin brought you into the fold of a monarchy?" the ash-tone scoffed and folded her ebony arms.

"I received the job of Royal Assassin at the age of nineteen, and have held it ever since. In that capacity I have run missives, helped forge and uphold treaties, taken down kings and tyrants, and in the end, yes, I count myself lucky to name many kings and queens among my closest friends."

Lavandyra uncrossed her arms and moved close to the assassin, paying no attention to personal barriers. She pressed her hand against Aidyn's throat in as threatening a gesture as one can do.

"What would you do with me now?" she hissed, narrowing her amber eyes.

The male did not flinch or swallow. Instead he gazed down into those eyes. "I would do nothing with you now. It is your life to live as you will. Do with it as you please. No one here will stop you unless you try to bring harm to anyone who does not deserve it."

Lavandyra's hand pressed harder against his throat, squeezing off his air supply. She guided him back against the wall, and then pressed her hips against his. "Would you have me as your lover? Would you demand sex of me?"

Aidyn did not stir beneath her movements, which seemed to surprise the female dark elf. "As I said, your life is yours to live. I will not, and cannot, demand anything of you. Only you can decide what to do."

"Do you not want me?" she whispered, her black lips near his.

"I belong to another," the assassin stated.

The ash-tone stepped away from him and stared hard. "I have never met anyone like you. You are a surprising killer, Aidyn Sestuns."

"So I have been told. What of you? How did you end up in Iranyo's basement?"

Lavandyra licked her lips and turned away. "I was born in Pyúrhe thirty-one hundred years ago, when there were many of us. During the War of the One God, nearly all of us were murdered by humans frightened by our dark appearance. I, along with nearly a dozen others, escaped into the ocean. We sailed north, far north until we came to an island."

"Pyúrhe? Zaedic?"

"Pyúrhe was the first name of Purheae. The humans could not pronounce it, so they mashed into a terrible sound. I do not know what Zaedic is, but our island was small and full of trees. We made a life there, a peaceful life, but then humans came. They burned it down around us. They were rough humans, wanting only to bury themselves in the females, and to bury their swords into the males. They slaughtered nearly all of us, but they kept a few of us alive as slaves. I was one such. I escaped a few decades ago, stole one of their boats and sailed south as fast as possible. I landed in Seaduens, where I was taken captive by high elves. When Blackhaven rose from the ashes of oblivion, I was sold to Iranyo as an offering. My body for information."

"Who sold you, do you know?" Aidyn asked.

Lavandyra pinned him with an amber glare. "High elves."

"Yes, but do you know their names?"

"No. All I know is their size and skill."

The assassin eyed her without pity for he knew it would probably just offend her. "I am sorry for your misfortune," he blandly said after a moment. "Many of us have suffered because of racism and greed."

Lavandyra lifted a silver eyebrow. "Your marks?" she assumed.

"Aye. Two scars among a hundred others. These were given to me by a Maginic weapon wielded by hybrid assassins. The first but not last time I have come close to death for this war."

"You would seek pity?"

"No more than you, lady."

Lavandyra was about to reply when the door opened behind her and in strode Aladorn, who stopped and nearly fell over at the sight of her.

"Aolan," he wheezed, his eyes staring beseechingly his brother, who understood his pain.

"Lavandyra, this is my brother Aladorn."

The female stared at the newcomer in astonishment, her lips parted. "Two of you?"

"Yes, two of us. You are not alone here," Aidyn replied walking over to his stricken sibling, and steadied him.

"I see that. But I will be dead soon and again there will only be two of you."

"If you believe so, then yes."

Lavandyra continued to stare at Aladorn with a look that defied logic. The wiat finally got himself under control and met her gaze with a verdant one of his own.

"How do you do?"

"I am dying. Internal bleeding that cannot be stopped."

Aladorn blinked, unsure of what he should say. Finally, he moved his gaze from her eyes to take in all of her. "Your hair is silver."

"Yes, very astute. A leftover trait from those of us who are gone."

The two brothers waited for an explanation while the female studied them both. "You are wider than Aidyn Sestuns," she said bluntly to Aladorn.

"He is a skinny one," the elder brother said slowly.

"I like your body. Your brother is much more beautiful, but you have a more masculine waist. We would fit well together."

Both males went rigid with the comment, one in wonder, the other in embarrassment. Aladorn lifted his hand to scratch the tip of his nose.

"Ah..."

"My mother came from Anlinylath. I heard you telling the high elf in the hospital about it," her gaze moved to Aidyn. "It is no legend. It is there but like Serenyi it fell to disaster. You are correct in the knowledge that Ikari Sestuns and her husband Korgoran were the beginning of us. Ikari had a son with another elf, a High Elf named Sören before they all fled Serenyi, but the boy was with his father on the ships and it is assumed they made it here. Few survived the Exodus, and less survived the voyage here. The Serenyi high elves had already built Shisandr. They feared the Anlinylathians when we arrived, for Sören, Akitor, and the others had departed for other lands and no one recognized us, so our people moved north and found the wild trees of Pyúrhe. There, only doom came to us. I am the last survivor," Lavandyra stated as though unaware that her audience was completely off balance by her manner.

"Ah..." Aladorn grunted again.

"How old are you?" Aidyn finally asked her.

Lavandyra looked at him curiously. "I already told you. I am three thousand, one hundred and forty-six years old. You?"

The brothers exchanged stunned glances. "I am seven hundred and eighty-nine. Aladorn is eight hundred eighty-two."

"Children yet. And your high elf queen?"

Aidyn narrowed his gaze at her. "Why?"

"She has old eyes."

"One hundred and forty-seven."

Lavandyra's face went slack with surprise. "Is that all? An infant runs your kingdom!"

"She may be young in years, but she has seen a full lifetime of experiences, do not doubt that. No one is better suited than Tlonna Ewôsdírn," Aladorn stated calmly.

Aidyn shook his head. "Well, what are you going to do now?"

Lavandyra frowned. "I do not yet know. I have rarely gone more than two days without having someone inside of me, and not at all in the last two years. What should I do in the hours remaining to me?"

The brothers shared another look. "What did you do on your island?" Aidyn queried.

The ash-tone thought for a second, as though trying to remember. "I was a painter, I think."

"Do as you wish, Lavandyra, as I said, it is your life," the assassin told her as he moved back to his things. He strapped on his scimitar belt and his longsword baldric. As he tugged on his tension sheath, he heard Aladorn's sharp intake of breath.

Aidyn spun to find Lavandyra very close to his brother, her fingers running over his features like a blind person trying to learn a face. The female seemed to have no concept of personal barriers.

"Yes, I find you quite attractive, not pretty like your brother, more masculine. I like your thickness."

Aladorn sent Aidyn a pleading look, but the younger sibling ignored him. He was too busy muffling his laughter at the idea of anyone thinking his brother thick. The wiat was as slender as any elf, perhaps a little more muscular than most, except Ghealan and

Suneelo, but still very trim. He was, however, getting a little irritated at females calling him pretty. Her next words brought him fast out of his mirth, though.

"I shall take you as my mate, I think. For much of my life I have been the plaything of males. In death I shall take a male I choose," Lavandyra stated calmly and departed, leaving behind a disturbed, stunned Aladorn and a disgusted Aidyn.

"Is everyone around here bent on getting their romp on?" Aidyn snapped as he got to his feet. He felt like being irrational.

"You want to sleep with that? Go right ahead, *bruun*," Aladorn nearly shouted. "She is flaming crazy!"

"I never said I wanted to lay with her, but it would sure be nice if someone would think I am bloody well *pretty* enough to want!"

"You are jealous? Of that? Nine hells, Aidyn, you cannot be serious?"

The assassin stopped short and pulled in his emotion. He wasn't jealous, not at all, but he had not been with anyone for a very long time and it was starting to gnaw at him. The recent closeness with Tlonna was nice, but it also sharpened the cutting edge of his love for her.

"I am sorry. I guess I am just...a little lonely."

Aladorn gave him a small smile. "You have been spending quite a lot of time with Tlonna, lately."

Aidyn gave him a warning look. "That is not up for discussion. She and I are working through our problem."

"Problem?"

"I do not wish to discuss it. Suffice it to say, I am quite on my own."

Aladorn gave him a knowing look. "I know how you feel, I do."

"Yes, well, it does not look like you are going to have that problem for a while, Al. She has made her decision. Will you agree to it?"

The wiat hesitated. "No. I will not make love to someone just because that is what they are used to doing. As alluring as she is on the outside, I cannot do such a thing, especially to a dying female. Not to mention the fact that she is completely out of her mind."

"You hesitated."

"It has been a long time for me too, little brother. Since Miazie, actually."

"Did you need something from me? Why did you come down?" Aidyn asked after a moment's silence.

His brother shifted back to purpose with a start. "Erandur and Sodo wanted to talk to us."

"What about?" the assassin asked as he stomped into his boots.

"Something about the chemical used to induce the fires when we routed the army. The alchemist was itching to tell us something, and I think Erandur just wants something to do."

"I do not blame him. Lead on, thickness."

"Do not start with me, pretty one."

Aidyn smirked at his brother's broad shoulders as he followed him out of the training room.

# Chapter 28

## Unusual Training

Aidyn left the meeting with Sodo and Erandur feeling a little off-balance. It had proved to be pointless and boring for him. The only thing the alchemist had of interest was the separated chemicals of the Nytrynhimmel and naphitha. The rest of it was a mindless conversation about females that Aidyn did not care to enter into. Aladorn had been right. Erandur was simply bored. The assassin was musing on the prince when Yayènia popped out of room and gestured to him. Frowning slightly, the assassin moved to her side and gave her a suspicious look that made her roll her eyes.

"I have been thinking for a long, long time about my recent past," the warrior began in a low voice. "And I believe you are the only one who could take such a task upon yourself and not lose who you are."

Aidyn frowned again. "Take what task upon myself? What are you talking about?"

Yayènia took a deep breath. "I have noticed something about my ability to heal. I have received much more grievous wounds recently than ever before, and my...regeneration process, if you can call it that, has sped up, but it is not fast enough. I want to be able to heal myself immediately, no matter how bad the injury."

"What do you need me for? I have no magical powers," the dark elf inquired, curious and wary of her intentions.

Here the warrior hesitated as she squinted up at him as though unsure how to proceed. Finally she sighed, resigned. "I get faster the more I get hurt. I need you to work with me, I need you to hurt me."

Already Aidyn was shaking his head. "I think not, Nia. I cannot do that to you. You are my friend, I would never intentionally harm you!"

"Please Aidyn! I need to get faster! The pain is not an issue for me, as you well know. I need the injury in order to heal it. Please?" Yayènia cried, clutching at his forearms in perhaps the most helpless manner he had ever seen her in.

"Why not ask someone else? Your husband, perhaps?" the assassin asked, desperate to get away from the idea.

Yayènia scoffed. "Like Suneelo would ever agree to this. I need you, a kindred soul who can take the atrocious inflictions upon yourself without too much psychological damage. You are the only person who can help with this."

"What kind of injuries are we talking about," he demanded, hating himself for even considering her request.

The look of relief that crossed her face left him a little stunned, but then she shrugged. "At first just little cuts and glancing blows. By the end, I want to be able to fix a broken bone in seconds."

Aidyn gaped at her. "You want me to break your bones?" he nearly shouted, but remembered at the last second to keep his voice quiet.

"Not for a while, but yes, eventually. How else will I learn?" the commander shot back, giving him a look of utter disbelief. "Why are you suddenly so weak-hearted? You are the same elf that drove a scimitar through my belly, are you not?"

"Not *your* belly!" Aidyn retorted, but with little heat.

Yayènia eyed him for a second, and then lifted her chin. "Be at the compound tonight at seven. I have a free hour between drills."

Aidyn shook his head in disbelief, but she was already beyond him and did not see, or care.

The assassin took a deep, steadying breath and entered the military indoor training hall where stacks of wasters, stuffed targets, strength tools, and dozens of other such equipment lined the walls. The center was a bare floor painted with rings and targets, made of oak wood slats. Yayènia stood in the center with her back to him, wearing none of her armor, which made her seem terribly small and vulnerable. When she turned, Aidyn noticed that her hands were busy tying a looped knot into a piece of thick rope.

"What is that for?" he asked when he approached her. He took off his cloak and tossed it to the side.

"To bind my hands," the warrior replied softly, finishing the knot. "I do not want to lash at you if I go into battle fury."

Aidyn shook his head and stepped very close, his hand closing over hers and the rope. "I will not tie you up, Yayènia."

"But if I-"

"You will not," he whispered, tugged the rope from her hands, and tossed it aside. "You will not."

The high elf took a steadying breath and nodded, stepping away from the dark one. "All I need you to do is cut me in several different places, as fast as you can. I would do this part myself, but I find my hand trembling too much. I have not the strength to do it."

"So you expect me to?" Aidyn asked as he unbuckled his scimitars and removed his longsword.

"No, but I hope you will. I am frightened, Aidyn," Yayènia replied and rushed him, coming to stand very close once more. "Ever since Alchemian I have been terrified of my own mortality. And then Rhiannan so easily overcame me, albeit with my own strength, but it was shameful to me and painful for others, most especially you. Please, I beg of you, find the strength."

Aidyn stared down at the top of her head, which was buried in his chest, her small, fragile-looking hands clutching fistfuls of his shirt, pressing her entire body against his. He felt her shudder and realized with a start that she was crying. Unnerved, the assassin gently put his arms about her shoulders and held her for a moment, just like he'd held her sister only a few hours ago, until she stepped away and looked up at him, still gripping his shirt.

The male smiled gently and brought his hands to her face, thumbs pressing against the tears that were so unfamiliar to them both. He then bent and kissed her forehead.

"I do not want you to be scared, Nia. I will find the strength for you. I promise," he said after a moment and she pulled fully away.

"How will you do it?" she asked, already turned away from him.

Aidyn pulled his throwing knives out of their sheaths and held them between his fingers. "I will throw them, and hit you along the sides of your arms, legs, and stomach. I will stop when you say, or when I run out of blades."

Yayènia nodded and turned back to face him, her eyes fierce with determination. "Do it."

Steadying his thudding heart, the assassin lined up his aim and let fly, one, two, three, until the final blade had flown from his fingers, a dozen all total. Yayènia took each slice stoically, barely flinching. When the twelfth knife clattered to the floor behind her, she rolled her shoulders and looked down at herself. Ruby lines stained her along the edge, two on each of her arms, three on each leg, and one on either side of her torso. She lifted her shirt and her body contorted with such concentration that Aidyn could see every abdominal muscle distend against her ivory skin. Slowly, the lines against her ribs disappeared to leave only red smudges that she wiped away, leaving no trace of the wound. The same had happened all along her arms and legs.

The assassin retrieved his daggers, and the hour passed slowly for both of them. At one point a dagger came in a little harder against Yayènia's shoulder and her eyes hazed over in manic fury. Aidyn tensed, ready for a battle, but the female sucked in a hard breath and shook her head, and when she looked up at him her eyes were clear once more.

"Are you all right?" the assassin asked, two daggers in his hands. He would not throw them if she was unstable.

"Yes. Continue," she said, her body shifting.

By the end, Yayènia was covered in a sheen of perspiration and Aidyn was sick to his stomach, full of self-loathing.

"The last cut disappeared almost instantly, did you see?" the High Commander asked as he retrieved his belongings.

Aidyn nodded silently and straightened, his cloak settling about his strong shoulders. He looked down at her with his emerald gaze and swallowed.

"I am sorry I have to ask this of you, my friend," Yayènia said quietly as she came to stand before him. "But I believe it necessary."

"Whatever you believe, I am not immune to seeing you in pain, especially when I am the cause, no matter how honorable my intentions."

"I know, but I hope you will continue to help me in this."

Yayènia reached up, ran her fingers through Aidyn's sable hair, and then dropped them to his shoulder. "You really are too...breathtaking...for your own good, or anyone else's for that matter."

The male snorted quietly as he took her hand in his and kissed the deceptively delicate knuckles. "So I have been told," he replied. "You should change before your Silvers show up and try to kill me."

Yayènia looked down at her blood- and sweat-soaked clothing and nodded. "Then I shall say goodbye for now, Aidyn. Will you come back tomorrow?"

"So soon?" the assassin said as he turned to leave.

"The faster we go, the faster it will end," Yayènia replied, already stripping off her soiled tunic.

"Then tomorrow it is," Aidyn replied, looking back for an instant to see her bare back, crisscrossed with as many scars as his own.

Tlonna was sequestered in her office, reading reports from the battlefront, wishing she could be there, when there was a knock at her door.

"Enter," she called, both grateful and annoyed at the interruption.

"Tlonna, I'm sorry to bother you, but this needs your attention," Miazie said as she entered, her expression alarmed.

The queen looked at her advisor with a frown, her eyes shadowed by weariness. "What is it?"

"There is...someone to see you."

"Who?" the elf prompted when the Belau said nothing further.

"Gothier Lostug."

Tlonna's mouth dropped open in disbelief, and she slumped back in her chair. "What does he want? Is Isadorr with him?"

"No, he came alone, and is waiting rather impatiently in the garret room, with Yayènia."

Tlonna swore and shot up from her desk, fearing that the Prince of Seaduens was already dead. The elf pushed by Miazie and sprinted down the hallway, across the narrow bridge that spanned the walkway four stories below, and to the other side of the castle. Within less than a minute she had crossed the entire breadth of the castle and was striding through the heavy door to the vaulted tower room. To the Magin's vast relief, and shame, Yayènia was lounging easily in a chair, her shapely legs stretched out before her, crossed at the ankle. One hand was resting on the huge round table, the slender fingers tapping a constant rhythm, while the other was wrapped loosely about the hilt of her longblade. Gothier was pacing back and forth, his hands worrying at each other, his thin face pale white and nervous.

"Prince Gothier," Tlonna said to gain their attention.

When the Seaduens prince turned to her, he suddenly seemed to lose whatever nerve he had left. His legs trembled and his eyes fluttered weakly.

"Perhaps you should sit down," the queen said and took her own advice.

Yayènia remained as she was, watching her hated foe with deceptively sleepy eyes. When Tlonna took a seat next to her, the warrior's lips turned up slightly, her hand tightening on her blade's hilt. Gothier fumbled into a chair and sat staring at the two females, his hazel eyes unblinking and wide.

"I take it you came here for a reason?" Tlonna asked pointedly, confused and slightly troubled by the elf's behavior.

"Ah...yes, actually. Thank you for seeing me on such short notice."

"I could hardly keep the Prince of Seaduens waiting," the queen replied blandly.

Gothier wheezed faintly, his eyes bugging. "That is...ah, part of the problem. See, Your Grace," he began.

Yayènia twitched, unaccustomed to politeness from any Seadueni. Tlonna too was dumbfounded.

"Isadorr and I were going through the birth records of our family, as is custom when a new king is crowned, when we came across something...troublesome."

"Which was?"

"Enyis Lostug was not my mother."

Yayènia's head snapped up, obviously finding something in the statement alarming and possibly dangerous, her hand slipped off the table to grip a dagger. Tlonna sent her sister a look and then stared at Gothier.

"I am sorry, but I am not sure what that has to do with me, or anyone here in Blackhaven. Did your brother exile you for not having the same mother as he? Certainly Stoffnias was your father...?"

"Yes, he was, and no, Isadorr did not exile me, though he desperately wanted to. Constancias Ewôsdírn was my mother."

Complete silence greeted the male's words as Tlonna gaped at him, and Yayènia thunked her head down on the table, which elicited a nervous tick in her sister's cheek. "What?"

"I am your brother," Gothier stated quietly and dropped his gaze.

"Constancias could not have borne two children without anyone noticing!" Tlonna roared suddenly, leaping out of her chair.

Yayènia's head came back up and she glared at the male. "Do you know what you are saying? Is this some sort of scheme to get the throne of Blackhaven? Are you completely insane? You do know that your father is dead because of us?"

Gothier's look of disgust seemed more common to his features than the shame that soon replaced it. The prince produced a single sheaf of parchment from his pocket. "This is the record page."

Tlonna yanked it out of his hand and read it, her stomach twisting. She tossed it at her sister. "Where in the nine hells is Miazie?" she asked, and then stormed out of the room looking for the Belau.

The woman was in the hallway outside, pacing nervously. When the queen appeared, she spun about and gawked at the furious elf. "What is it?"

"Get in there and tell me whether that useless male is telling the truth!" Tlonna bellowed.

Miazie jumped nearly a foot in the air in fright and then hurried into the room, her eyes wide. "What happened?"

Yayènia shoved the parchment at the woman, her face set in a hopeless plea. "Is this genuine?" she whined.

The Belau took the paper and read it, her eyebrows climbing her forehead as she did. Tlonna had moved back inside and slammed the door shut behind her, trapping the four of them inside the garret room. She scryed it, and sighed.

"What answer do you want to hear?" she asked uselessly, already knowing.

Yayènia and Tlonna scowled at her, the looks so identical Miazie nearly laughed. Nearly. "I'm sorry."

Slowly, the two females turned to stare at Gothier, their brother.


"What is it with this place? Family members popping up all over the bloody country!" Tlonna grumped once she had told everyone the news.

Aladorn, Aidyn, and Sodo all sat staring blankly at the queen, their mouths open in incredulity. Aladorn and Sodo were studying their hands, not wanting to meet Tlonna's angry eyes. Considering that Sodo was the only one in the room who did not have any blood ties, no one could argue the point.

"Where is Yayènia?" Aidyn finally asked, noticing the absence of the warrior.

Tlonna shrugged. "She stormed away and I have not seen her since. I should probably check on Gothier, make sure he is still breathing."

"I will do it, you should probably stay away from him for a while," the assassin remarked, got to his feet, and departed the room in a swift, blurry movement.

Once alone, he jogged up the stairs to the fourth floor and found the room in which Gothier had been detained. The prince looked up in surprise and fear as the assassin poked his head into the room. With a legendary glare, Aidyn checked the elf for injury and then slammed the door behind him. Moments later he was standing outside Yayènia and Suneelo's suite, knocking on the door.

The warrior yanked it open and then stopped short when she saw Aidyn lounging against the jamb. "Aidyn, what do you want?"

"To talk, let me in," the assassin said and suited action to words as he pushed by the surprised female.

Yayènia shook her head as she locked the door behind them. "Only you can get away with that sort of thing," she grumbled as the male flopped into a chair.

"And why is that?"

"Because you are the only person who can best me in a fight," she replied flippantly and sat across from him. "What do you want to talk about?"

"Gothier."

The High Commander's face contorted with disgust and rage but she quickly calmed herself. "That useless brat. And Constancias! I knew she was a whore!"

Aidyn smiled faintly as Yayènia got to her feet and began pacing. He realized then that she did not wear her knee-length boots and so her legs from the knee down were uncovered. He studied her feet, which he had never seen bare before. They were small, almost disproportionately small, and she walked on the balls of them, her heels rarely touching the ground. Shapely calves with rock hard muscles glided beneath pale skin as she paced, hypnotizing him.

"... during the months she was gone I knew something was amiss, the stupid cow. But I never honestly believed that she had been unfaithful to Dietirin. Such a thought was so horrible to consider. I am sure now, that Dietirin knew. He must have. He never said anything to you?"

Aidyn shook his head. "No, he never mentioned anything about Constancias to me. When he was not with her she did not exist. Although..." the assassin frowned as something the king had once said to him came to the fore of his memory. "He once told me his heart was shattered by the inability to love. I thought it such an odd thing to say at the time, but now...he must have known."

Yayènia gave him a startled look and sat back down, crossed her legs and began bouncing the top one. "He knew I was his daughter? And Gothier his son?"

"I am starting to believe so."

"Why would he never say it?" she queried, hurt.

The dark elf shook his head again. "Dietirin knew the ways of people, and their hearts, better than anyone alive. He knew what would break them, and what would lift them up. Think about how you would have felt if he had come up to you one day and said, 'Yayènia, I am your father, and Constancias is your mother. You are the rightful heir to the Wind Throne'. Had he acknowledged you, you would have been forced to give up most everything you love in order to fulfill your duty. And with your house motto, it is not something you could ignore."

"*Zuskadi naht xellt*," Yayènia intoned, "Duty above all. I suppose you are right, as usual. You are getting to be as annoying as Miazie in that realm."

"It happens," Aidyn replied, shrugging. "So, what do we do about your brother?"

The female looked at him sharply, noting the too-calm way his fingers rested on the arm of the chair, the relaxed way he lounged. "You want to kill him."

"It is what we do, you and I. He is a problem that can be eliminated. I just looked in on him and he is absolutely petrified. He will be easy to destroy."

Yayènia's lips curled into a half smile. "I have taken two of his brothers out, Losolin another... it would indeed be fitting," she murmured. "But alas, no. Tlonna would never allow it."

"We do not need Tlonna's permission. I am the royal assassin, you are the highest authority of military force. Who is going to stop us?"

The High Commander studied the assassin for a long time, their eyes identically cool and glittering in the firelight. "Yes. Who indeed?"

Aidyn grinned and stood, flexing his wrist to release the tension blade. Yayènia grinned back and followed him out of the room, excitement building in her chest. Together they moved down the hallway, soundless, two figures of strength and lethality, their muscles tense with anticipation. Aidyn slowly opened Gothier's door and pushed it all the way open so that it revealed him and Yayènia to the frightened elf.

He gulped and stood up from his chair, wringing his hands and shivering, looking nothing like the proud Lostug he had once acted as. "What do you want?"

Yayènia drew a curved knife as Aidyn held up his wrist spike and shut the door behind them. Gothier began to hyperventilate.

"You create problems that we do not need," the assassin crooned as he moved beside him to look over the prince's shoulder at Yayènia, who smiled.

With a lightning fast move he kicked Gothier in the back of the knees and shoved him downward. He lifted his arm to drive the spike into his right shoulder as Yayènia did the same on his left, but just as they began to move the door blew open and the two elves were thrown to the wall. Gothier collapsed on the floor, his hands over his head as he sobbed in terror. The door shut again and Yayènia and Aidyn dropped to the ground, crouched in a feral stance of defense. Tlonna stood before them, her shoulders thrown back, light pulsing from both hands.

"You have an unfortunate habit of trying to kill my family members, Aidyn," she commented dryly, her eyes on the hysterical Gothier.

"And you have an unfortunate habit of getting in my way," the assassin replied. He released the spike and straightened.

Across the room Yayènia did the same, fury writ on her face. "He is my family member too, Tlonna, and I want him dead. He will cause us no end of trouble."

"Do you know that?"

The warrior sniffed and looked away, disregarding both her siblings. "He is Constancias's son, not Dietirin's. No good can come from that."

"You did, as did I."

"Dietirin's blood runs through our veins. Stoffnias's runs through his."

"So now we judge based on whose blood we come from?" Tlonna asked calmly, the light fading from her hands. "You are becoming bitter in your old age, Nia."

"*Aiya*, and much less patient with meddling fools," the female warned, annoyed. "How did you know we were here?"

Aidyn looked curious now as well, rather than indignant. The queen smiled. "You both were supposedly alone, as was Gothier. I know you better than that."

Yayènia and Aidyn shared a look, quite resentful. "It looks as though you live for another day, Lostug," the assassin growled and strode from the room. When he pushed Tlonna out of the way, his hands were gentler than she expected them to be.

"You will be safe here as long as you cause no harm to others," the queen promised her new relation.

"Why?" the prince asked as he got to his feet, shame lining his once-proud face. "You two are the reason three of my family members are dead."

"They threatened our lives, or the lives of our loved ones. We had no choice but to take theirs," Tlonna replied quietly as she studied the prince.

"They were cruel people," Gothier stated, closing his eyes. "I am not like them."

"Then why do you care that we killed them?" Yayènia snapped.

"They were still of my blood, the father that raised me, the brothers I played with and learned from. What would I be if I were ambivalent toward their lives?"

"If you learned from them then how are you so different? I remember your actions when last you were here, boy," the female demanded, her ire rising once more.

"I did not used to be different, but I began to feel wrong about our actions, and slowly I realized that our way of life was not the just way, and I needed a change. Isadorr and I grew apart daily, until we realized we could not stand each other. Then we came across the record, and I decided to leave. It was the only course of action I could think of, knowing it very well could be the end of me."

"A very astute observation," Yayènia snarled sarcastically, "Stay away from me, Gothier. I do not need another brother."

"Nia," Tlonna began, but the High Commander was already gone, striding down the hallway back toward her room. Turning back to Gothier she shook her head. "Stay out of their way, Gothier, I may not be fast enough next time."

"Why do you care?" the prince suddenly demanded. He strode toward her, his cowardice forgotten.

Tlonna lifted an eyebrow at him. "Unlike you and your family I do not take pleasure in murder. However, if you even look at me wrong I will not hesitate to rip your beating heart from your chest."

Gothier's bravado faltered, and he held his arms out to the side in a hopeless gesture. "What am I going to do? I am not who I thought I was, and I have nowhere else to go. I am an elf with no home; my enemy's castle is now my only sanctuary. I knew that here, even if I could not prove my claim of blood I would be given a slim chance of acceptance. Anywhere else in Nymyños I would be killed on sight."

"Even though Seaduens and Blackhaven have been at odds since my birth, you ran here in the slight hope that you would be treated fairly? Makes your family's vendetta sound a little foolish, does it not?" Tlonna asked while she moved slightly closer to her half-brother.

Gothier looked away, licking his lips. "I hope to make amends for my part in that, you must believe me. I know the likelihood of any Blackhavenite trusting me, but I ask you to allow me the chance to try."

"You are here, are you not? And still in one piece."

The prince nodded, the muscles in his jaw flexing. "True enough."

Tlonna made to leave again, but stopped and turned back. "Gothier, what does your brother plan to do with the soldiers at Sethryn Lake? Will he continue on with his father's foolish choice to side with Sithian?"

"I am not sure. When Father's body was brought back into camp," the male hesitated, glanced at her with a measured look, "Isadorr was furious. He blamed you, of course, and Sithian, and the traitorous Talenians. We left soon afterward to bring Father home and lay him to rest. It was then that the coronation took place, and the record was found of my birth. Once my true lineage was discovered, Isadorr stopped confiding in me. He hates Sithian, he hates all the humans, but he hates you more. He had not yet made any decision when I fled, at least none he told anyone about."

"And what of your mother? She obviously knew you were not hers, but did Isadorr see her silence as treachery or loyalty to your father?"

Gothier blanched. "He...he stripped her naked before the city, tied her to a pole, and left her there. I tried to free her, but the guards would not let me pass, and they took me down when I fought them. Isadorr labeled her a traitor and a whore."

"It was your father and our mother who were the adulterers," Tlonna commented, but the prince seemed not to hear.

"The next morning, she was dead. She had been beaten, raped, and humiliated in the last hours of her life. I watched Isadorr take her down, made sure she was buried next to Father, and then I fled. He never knew I watched. He cried over her body though it was his fault."

"The people did that to their queen?" Tlonna asked, horrified.

Gothier looked at her sharply. "As you said, my people, my family, take pleasure in murder."

"I am sorry, I truly am." The queen hesitated, questioning herself before she even voiced her thought. "Would you like to see your birth-mother's grave?"

The male stared at her. "You buried her?"

"Of course."

"In Seaduens we burn traitors."

"Yet your brother buried your mother, who he had labeled a traitor."

"I see your point," Gothier muttered, and grabbed his cloak. "I...yes, I would like to see it."

Tlonna took a deep breath and remembered the angry oath she had made to never visit Constancias's grave. With a contingent of guards, she led Gothier to the cemetery, and pointed him toward the marker.

"She lies there."

The prince hesitated, and then moved off alone to stand at the foot of the simple grave. What thoughts went through his head, Tlonna did not know, nor care to. She stood silently in her ring of guards, who stood just as quietly, their cloaks flapping in the stiff winter breeze. Yule was in two days, and snow was piled thickly against the headstones and trees that dotted the place of the dead. Finally Gothier turned to her.

"You will not come closer?" he asked quietly, his voice carried on the wind.

Tlonna shook her head. "I made a promise to myself that I will not break. Constancias murdered my father, and for that I will not stand before her grave."

The prince nodded his acceptance and walked over to stand beside her, causing the guards to shift slightly, prepared for anything the Seaduens prince might do. Together they walked back to the castle, pensive and unsure. Finally, when they were standing back at Gothier's room, she lifted a hand toward him.

"If you prove yourself to be of changed heart and mind, then I will welcome you into the family of Ewôsdírn. Until then, you must be careful around here. My people, most of whom are rather passionate, are understandably unfavorable toward Seadueni."

"I will," Gothier said with conviction. "Please," he said suddenly, lurching forward, "you must go to Seaduens. I know it will be dangerous, but you must go there."

"Why?"

"While many people have lost their way, there are many more who are trapped there. Please, Queen Tlonna, you must go there."

"That would be like walking blindfolded into a viper's nest, Prince Gothier."

"But...the people..."

"Have chosen to live in Seaduens. I just had to illustrate that choice to my own people and re-enlighten them to the fact that they have the opportunity to leave or stay. Do not the citizens of Seaduens have that same choice?"

Gothier paused before answering. "Where would they go? They are Seadueni, Queen Tlonna, and therefore not well-received anywhere."

"And what would you have me do if I went? If I survived?"

The prince shrugged. "Tell them they have a place to go."

"They do not have a place to go," Tlonna said harshly. "If I allowed even a hundred Seaduens elves into my city, with my pledge that they would be safe, I would be hard pressed to keep it. And who knows if they would be peaceful citizens? If they come here of their own free will and ask for sanctuary, they will be given it, but I will not put my own people at risk, especially the humans and dwarves, for the sake of them."

"You will not even go? You will not even take a few days to see?" Gothier accused, shaking his head. "I thought you were of higher morals than the rest of us."

"My morals have nothing to do with this, Gothier. I simply do not trust the morals of Seaduens at large."

"At least give them a chance."

Tlonna sniffed quietly and left the room, baffled by the oddities of life.

# Chapter 29
## Yule

Tlonna and the others stood in surprise as Losolin and Suneelo rode through the gates the next day, looking neither hurried nor worried. Yayènia and Tlonna rushed down the stairs to embrace their husbands, who swung them about in affection while others looked on with expressions of great tolerance. When Losolin put Tlonna back on the ground, she pushed him out to arm's length.

"What are you doing here? Has something happened?" she asked breathlessly as she stared up at her husband in joy.

"No, nothing has happened. Truly, nothing has happened. There has been silence on the front nearly since you left. In fact, Isadorr pulled back all his troops and they have not been seen since. We know not if they have returned to Seaduens or if they are just waiting on the sidelines, but without the elves filling their ranks, the Zaedicans seem less inclined to attack."

"Yes, well, there is more to that story," Tlonna warned him, and explained Gothier's appearance. "But what are you and Suneelo doing home?"

Losolin kissed her forehead and began walking toward the castle, his arm about her shoulders. "Well, Yule is tomorrow, and with things so quiet, Ghealan told us to return here for a few days. He said he would send word if he had need of us. He wrote to Erdwyf, and she said that Narnen was too broken to celebrate just yet, so there will only be a small fête, too small for him to feel any guilt for missing it. That and," here the king paused, his face a mix of disbelief and wonder, "King Furntil Eldrout arrived with his host of Duani warriors the day before we left. Tlonna, he stood before me! Furntil Eldrout!"

Tlonna waved a servant away, who seemed intent on being of use, and squeezed Losolin's waist. "I was wondering. Erandur is here, and I am so glad you are here. I have missed you so much."

"What of Purheae? Did you find anything useful?"

"Yes," Tlonna assured him, and told the story.

Losolin looked at the stone she held out to him with a frown. "I did not like those Magin stones, and I do not particularly like this. I remember the night they tried to trap you in the past."

"I remember it too, Losolin, but this at least it is another step in the right direction."

"Toward what end, though?"

Tlonna shrugged and looked back in time to watch Yayènia and Suneelo enter the castle holding hands. Aidyn and Aladorn walked in behind them, annoyed. The reason appeared in the form of Lavandyra. The ash-tone had taken to wearing a simple white dress of cotton, hemmed in gold. It set off her dark complexion quite nicely, but Tlonna knew the stranger had some sort of design on either or both of the Sestuns brothers, and she was not immensely pleased about it. It was truly a marvel the female was even still alive. Braden had told Tlonna just yesterday that he didn't expect her to live for more than a few days now.

Erandur, Sodo, and Miazie all came down to greet them with exuberance, Suneelo and Losolin grinning at the Duani elf with genuine liking. Losolin told the prince of his father's appearance at the frontline, along with High Captain Lelfwin. Erandur nodded solemnly, resigned to his father's decision.

Once all the greetings were finished and the mood calmed down, Tlonna looked about the faces surrounding her and felt peace in the knowledge that these beautiful, strong, loyal people were all fighting alongside her. Her hand warm in Losolin's, she shared a private smile with Yayènia.

The group all stared at each other for a few seconds of silence and then the questions began, becoming a very loud tumult of nonsense. Only when Tlonna suggested moving to the dining hall for refreshments and a more orderly conversation did it quiet.

Yule in Blackhaven City was a relatively calm, joyous affair. Gifts were given out by family and friends, great feasts were laid on groaning tables crammed with relatives, and carols both haunting and jovial were sung on every street the entire day long, and well into the night. The castle hosted a ball for the entire population, and couples appeared in their most expensive finery to parade themselves before the court.

Tlonna was bedecked in a sparkling white gown of velvet, blue and silver ribbons fluttering about the gathered elbows and hem. Losolin wore a simple outfit of light gray, his snug cotton pants lightly embroidered along the seams in white snowflakes. Apparently Mattie the couturier had been well prepared for the slim chance that the king would be home for Yule. Yayènia and Suneelo stood next to the royal couple, also in festive, warm garments. The High Commander had on a dark blue overdress and white leather breeches, and her twin katans, which somehow matched because of their braided white and blue hilts. Suneelo was in a startling red coat with the same color pants, gold thread dancing down the seams and sides of the sleeves in a swirling design.

On Tlonna and Losolin's other side stood Aidyn, in black as usual, and Aladorn, who surprisingly enough had Lavandyra on his arm. The wiat was in green satin and black leather, his billowy emerald shirt the same color as Aidyn's eyes.

Miazie and Sodo stood next to Yayènia, looking prime in their holiday garments, the Belau's navy blue and purple dress let out to allow for her rapidly swelling belly. The alchemist stood tall next to his fiancée, his own green and gray outfit offsetting her dark. Even Erandur was dressed in a rich suit of black and green, the colors of Flousen Dua, and he blended in with the rest of the noble crowd.

As the wealthy people of Blackhaven came forward to bow or curtsey before them, Tlonna and Losolin smiled and returned their festive small talk. The queen was highly annoyed when Baron Nathaniel Dawson and his irritating wife appeared before them.

"Baron and Baroness Dawson. I thought you were holding your own celebrations," Tlonna said stiffly, though she attempted to sound decent.

"Oh, Your Grace, we would never miss a palace function. We held our party last night, like I said we would," the baroness tittered. "King Losolin, I am so glad you are home from the battle. We always worry so much for you, and for Lord Aidyn of course. Such dangerous males you are."

Tlonna felt her eyes narrow and stopped herself from openly glowering at the woman. Losolin looked bewildered and Aidyn was simply bored. The baron cleared his throat and turned to face the assassin.

"My wife and I are very eager for your company at one of our delightful feasts. I'm sure your stories would greatly entertain our guests."

"Or make them vomit," Yayènia muttered as she shifted her stance and glared at the couple. "Besides, everyone knows of your sordid little orgies, Dawson. No one here is interested. Go away."

Tlonna's mouth dropped open and Losolin choked on the wine of which he'd just taken a sip. The noble couple blanched.

"Queen Tlonna, will you allow the soldier to speak to us in such a way?" Nadine gasped, her hand pressed against her chest in an offended manner.

"If you speak of High Commander er'Tiena, yes. I am certainly not going to reprimand her. Are you?"

The woman went sheet white and curtseyed. "Thank you for your time, Majesties."

They rushed off, but the baron looked back over his shoulder and gave Aidyn a little smile. The assassin shuddered in revulsion. Tlonna shook her head and stood, her hand lifted in the air for silence.

"Tonight is a time of reflection, joy, and appreciation. It is the turning of the year, as it is a turning of fortune for the world. People of Blackhaven, put aside your worries and your fears and smile with hope at a new world. As we say goodbye to this dark season of winter, we look forward to victory and peace. The good spirit, the Lord of Light is with us now, and he shines down upon us with favor and with promises of victory. Tonight, we toast all the wild spirits, the good, the bad, and we rejoice in the love we have for each other and our kingdom. May you all be blessed on this day, and live out the new year with love in your hearts," Tlonna said, and then lifted a crystal goblet of holly wine in a toast to her people.

The High Hall, which was decorated with pine trees and glowing Magin lights was soon filled with music and laughter, the clink of glasses and the swishing of skirts. As the council moved to join the dance, Aidyn and Erandur moved to sit next to each other, watching with slight envy as their friends danced in delight. The assassin turned to the prince after a while and clinked the edge of his goblet against the other's.

"To bachelorhood," he intoned.

Erandur smiled softly. "Aye. To that."

"So, there is no princess of Flousen Dua?"

"No, there is not. Perhaps at one time there might have been, but I scared her off. She has since married a councilor's son, and has a thirty-year-old son. What of you?"

Aidyn shook his head. "My fiancée Rahna was killed in a battle with Hadian Rahlan, an arrow, right through her head." The dark elf tapped a finger against his temple to illustrate his point. "Never sought another."

"Would you?"

The assassin lifted an eyebrow at the prince. "Would you?" he countered.

Erandur's slow smile was full of self-deprecation. "No, no I would not. But I see your brother has found a creature of unusual complexion."

"Ah yes, *Lavandyra*," Aidyn muttered, unintentionally saying her name with sarcasm. "She is an ash-tone, probably the only one left in the world. He apparently has no willpower around her. Not two days ago he was fleeing her presence. She has only days left to live anyway."

"Really? Are you envious?" Erandur asked, intrigued.

Aidyn shook his head. "She was held as a pleasure slave first by human raiders, then by the Lostugs, and finally by a count here in the city. I killed him and found her in his cellar. And no. She is absolutely mental. Beautiful yes, but crazy."

"Are not they all?" the prince chuckled, gesturing to Yayènia who was twirling about in Suneelo's arms.

The assassin had to concede the point. Not long after the end of their conversation a blushing young water nymph stuttered out a request to dance with Prince Erandur, to which he graciously accepted and left Aidyn alone on the small dais. The dark elf leaned back in his chair, resigned to watching everyone else. He noticed a group of females staring his way from the refreshment table, but as soon as his gaze landed on them, they went crimson and giggled helplessly. He sighed.

Tlonna closed her eyes and pressed her cheek to Losolin's neck, breathing in his scent of harvest and sighed in contentment. Their bodies moved together in perfect harmony across the ballroom floor though they were oblivious to the jealous and appreciative stares. The Magin Queen smiled into her husband's throat, the feel of his slow pulse against her lips reassuring. Losolin's chest rumbled with a moan, so Tlonna pulled back her seduction and grinned up at him.

"We cannot leave yet, Loni," he warned her, his dark eyes dancing with lust.

"Too bad," she murmured and spun with his turn.

Losolin rolled his eyes, smiling all the while, and brought her back into his arms. Together, they waltzed along with the falling and rising melodies of the orchestra, lost in their love.

Aidyn looked up when Gothier flopped into a chair next to him, dressed in casual white and green clothes, and looking slightly rumpled. The assassin glowered at him, but said nothing.

"I thought for sure you would be inside a lady already," the prince stated boldly, not looking at the dark elf.

"You thought wrong."

"You do not even have a partner?"

Aidyn was growing weary of the constant assumptions that he was accompanied by females at all hours of the day. "I do not need one, like some people," he shot back.

Gothier lifted his hands in a gesture of surrender. "I was just making an observation, assassin. No need to get defensive."

He was about to say something more when he became very rigid, his entire body coming forward in his chair. Aidyn watched him, his hands crossing to grab hold of his scimitar hilts.

"Who is that? I have seen her before," Gothier said and pointed at Aladorn and Lavandyra.

The assassin's eyes narrowed dangerously. "Where?"

The prince turned to the dark elf. "In the bedroom of my brother, I am positive. She was his pet for quite some time. He called her Lavender. How is she here?"

"Your brother sold her to a count here in Blackhaven in trade for inside information. I rescued her when I assassinated the bastard two weeks ago."

Gothier leaned away from Aidyn in transparent fear. His hazel eyes shifted to the dark elf's hands, which were still wrapped around his hilts. "I mean no threat, Aidyn."

"You *are* no threat, Gothier," the assassin retorted honestly.

The prince nodded his agreement. "True enough, I suppose."

Aidyn shook his head in disgust and looked away, his gaze landing on a pretty brown-haired elf sipping a glass of cider. When she noticed his gaze, the female dropped the glass, sending hot droplets of golden liquid spraying across the floor. A host of servants rushed to clean it up before anyone slipped, but the elf did not notice. She had the fled the hall in terror.

"Well done," was Gothier's haughty remark.

"Watch it, or you will end up with your head inside one of the cider barrels," the assassin threatened him, one deadly eyebrow lifted.

The two slowly looked away from one another, and in complete silence they watched the festivities meander to a late end.

# Chapter 30
## Secrets Unveiled, Bonds Tested

Winter dragged by without too much activity. While Tlonna's close-knit group of companions rode continuously back and forth between the frontline and the kingdom, nothing much seemed to happen, other than finally meeting the legendary assassin Furntil. He had slain the tyrant Brandon Stynbek to free the elves and dwarves who had fallen into his brutal clutches. The king cut an imposing figure, tall and broad-shouldered, his silver hair falling free to his shoulders.

Furntil's pale blue eyes were aged with the wisdom of centuries lived, and he spoke in a quiet voice that nonetheless commanded attention. Aidyn nearly fell over when he met the First Assassin, his usually perfect composure shattered. For his part, the great king seemed as equally star-struck by the dark elf, and even bowed his head over Aidyn's hand in greeting.

Erandur smirked in the background, knowing how impressed with Aidyn his father was. Perhaps even envious of the assassin's reputation. Furntil did not speak much, however, and seemed content just to sit quietly at the table while decisions were made, deferring most of the time to his warrior son.

The invading force, while huge and taking an economically devastating toll on the Liberated Lands, seemed content to sit and wait out the winter while the defenders used the time to fortify their position, and their safety route back through Kismath.

By the time spring began to appear, the wall had been completed and the soldiers on both sides were ready and willing to spill blood. Tlonna sat with her council in the map room as they tried to decide the best way to move. Yayènia refused to stay behind any longer, explaining that Aidyn was more than enough protection for the queen. Tlonna reluctantly agreed. Plans were made for the High Commander, her husband, and Erandur to depart for good the following morning. Tlonna, Losolin, Aladorn, and Aidyn would follow in one week's time, enough to settle the last remaining issues with the Merchant's Guild, and Gothier's presence.

Though the prince had been nothing but quiescent, no one yet trusted him, and he was growing bored. Tlonna finally succumbed and went to speak with him, as he had been requesting for days.

"What do you wish of me?" she demanded of the male.

The prince stared at her for a long time. "I am your brother by blood," he finally said. "I am a prince of Seaduens, and of Blackhaven, as hard as that is for both of us to accept. I have been as quiet and as malleable as one can be for the duration of my stay here, and yet nothing has changed."

"What did you expect? You are given a very loose leash, and though I admit that I hold the end of that leash, I neither tug on it, nor tighten it. You have not been mistreated, but for that first day. Do you deny this?"

"No, but I am not used to being ignored by people I am above in status," Gothier spat, coming to the head of his issue.

"There is your first mistake, Gothier," Tlonna warned. "You are not above anyone in status. You are no better than a scullery maid, nor am I, for that matter. We are all people, equal from birth. It is how you grow from the day you are born that decides your so-called status, and that is the very foundation of Blackhaven. Some of us may have been given more opportunity than others, but that does not deter us from making bad decisions, or good ones, whichever the case. We are all equal, man, woman, elf, dwarf, spryte, nymph, half-blood, and so on. You would do well to remember that. Tyranny at any level leads only to failure. Those who set themselves above others without true cause have only a greater distance to fall when the oppressed rise up. Until you stop looking down your nose at everyone, including me, you are not going find yourself accepted, much less liked. Get off your high horse and down on the ground with everyone else."

"You sound like one of those bleeding monotheists," Gothier accused, disgusted.

"No, I do not agree that everyone is only as good as the lowest creature, not at all. It is our choices and our determination that make us who we are, and where we end up on the ladder that is society. The lowest peasant can become king; the wealthiest king can become worm food, all because of the choices we make. Do not make the wrong choice."

Gothier could not argue against her logic, or her passion, so he backed down. "Will you at least put me in the records?"

"Why?" Tlonna demanded.

"Because as of right now, I have no home, and no family, as Isadorr has surely stricken me from the annals of Seaduens, and you have yet to accept me into yours. I am an elf without a land, a prince without a kingdom."

"You realize you will never sit upon the throne of Blackhaven, correct?" Tlonna said, her voice breathless with urgency.

"I would be a fool to expect such a thing, of course."

"Good. I will write you in, but do not expect a throne. You are my brother, but you are the son of Constancias, not Dietirin. You have no blood ties to the Ewôsdírn line, and only an Ewôsdírn can claim the Wind Throne."

"I understand this, I simply want to be acknowledged."

"Very well, as I said, I will write you in," Tlonna replied, and left the prince's company.

The next morning the deadly triad of warriors rode out of the city gates toward Sethryn Lake, and the frontline, while those left behind waved in farewell.

Sithian stirred his index finger in the swirling, foggy liquid within the wide basin, his sapphire eyes hooded and glittering. Slowly, three separate faces loomed in the scrying pool, and he grinned down at them. With a deep breath, Sithian lifted his hand and pressed it against the other, palms, thumbs, and pinkies together, the rest of his fingers spread outward to create a blossom effect. From his fingertips lifted slowly undulating threads of Spirit, Earth, and Air, which he Wove gently into three separate braids.

He lowered his hands and sent the Weaves into the three faces, watching as their eyes widened in shock and confusion, their mouths opening in agony.

"Hello," he crooned.

Hundreds of miles away Tlonna and Losolin clutched at their heads and went to their knees, fighting against the sudden intrusion of their minds. Across the palace, Aidyn too gripped his head, sitting rigid in his chair. The knife he'd been sharpening flew across the room as he convulsed in an effort to free himself from the mind grip. Despite all of their efforts, their three minds were snagged and dragged into a foggy gray room furnished with a table and chairs. Their bodies were there already, sitting listlessly in three of the chairs, one on each side of the square table. Seconds later they were staring at each other in confusion and trepidation, unable to move their bodies, but able to turn their heads.

"What is this?" Aidyn demanded, his gaze on Tlonna.

The queen shook her head, frowning. "I do not know. I have never heard of such a mind trap, not one with a physical manifestation of the mind's corporeal form."

"I am so flattered to hear that, Mother! What a compliment, to hear from the Magin Queen herself that I can do something she cannot," Sithian laughed as he materialized inside the room, standing behind the one remaining chair. "I have waited a long time for this, so long to be able to have you all here, at my every whim."

"If we are at your every whim, we would already be dead, boy," Losolin snarled and gave the Magin a vicious glare.

Sithian's smug look deflated a bit and his knuckles turned white on the back of the chair. "We are going to have a little chat," he finally said, and sat.

"About?" Tlonna asked cordially, giving her evil offspring an overly interested look.

The Zaedican King sneered at her, but his dark eyes shifted to study Aidyn with a deeply knowing air. The assassin glared back at him, his chin rising in stubborn defiance. He wasn't about to display the nugget of fear in his chest.

"I have been studying, a lot, on prophecy, history, and downright fascinating scry journals," the boy said finally.

"Scry journals?" Tlonna asked, still feigning interest.

"Mm," Sithian nodded, his eyes riveted on the dark elf. "Things the Rahlans have scryed over the years and written down. I thought to share some of them with you. Thought you might enjoy them. Are you prepared?"

Suddenly Aidyn's breath became short as he stared at Sithian, already knowing what at least one of the topics would be. His emerald eyes flickered to Losolin, who was watching him in concern, and then dropped his gaze to the table. Sithian chuckled cruelly and then waved his hands over the table so that a scroll materialized before him. He flicked his fingers up and the scroll opened, spreading upward so that an image was portrayed before the three elves.

"The first of two, see. I shall show you the important one last. This one is a vision from Hadian before even my grandfather was born, before your sister murdered Ethan. It is simply for entertainment purposes."

Yayènia, Ghealan, and Suneelo stood side by side, all looking much younger and less careworn than the present day. They were each in full armor, but it was different from that which they now wore, covering more of their bodies, and much less decorated. Even the plumes on their helmets were shorter, and did not have tails.

The younger Yayènia lifted a hand and pointed to something outside the vision. "There are about fifty of them down there, and a handful of priests."

"What were Constancias's orders again?" Suneelo asked, his sword to resting against his shoulder.

Yayènia shifted. "She said to kill them all."

"And do we follow them?" Ghealan asked.

The female shrugged indifferently. "Why not? She may be a hag, but at least we have justification to kill them."

"Orders do not equal justification, High Commander," Suneelo said, and those in the room realized then that this had to have taken place right after Yayènia's ascension to the post, only a few years after her and Suneelo's wedding.

"They do when I want to kill them," the female replied and yanked out her own sword, a wickedly curved shortsword with nasty barbs for tearing into flesh near the crossguard on the back of the blade.

With the statement, the three elves let out a wild whoop and rushed down the hill they had been standing on into a startled group of humans. Without mercy the trio cut down the defenseless people, whose only returning actions were to fall to their knees and lift their hands in surrender. Hands that were quickly sliced off by whistling swords that were then stabbed into the unprotected chests of the victims. In moments the slaughter was over, but the vision seemed to shift to Yayènia, who stood with a weeping, screaming man kneeling at her feet.

"Why would you do this? We are peaceful people! Why?" he cried, trying to comfort his bleeding wrists, where his hands should have been.

The young High Commander licked her lips with a disturbing expression of malice and enjoyment. "You are Monotheists, yes?"

"Yes, but we are peaceful people!"

"You are the children of murderers."

"Blood does not claim perception!" the man keened, obviously near the end of his life from blood loss.

"Still, you die this night," Yayènia chuckled and shook her head. "I do not like Monotheists. You offend me with your dogmatic lies, your preaching, and the way you try to shove your religion on others, try to make them abandon theirs for yours. So, you die tonight."

"Please!" the man cried, but Yayènia's blade silenced him, violently tearing through his heart. She bent down and looked him in the eye as she twisted the blade to finish the kill.

"I love my job," she whispered when Suneelo and Ghealan came to stand beside her.

"Aye," the other two agreed, and slid grins over the female's head.

The vision faded, leaving the room deadly silent. Sithian smiled at the horrified looks on his captives' faces and leaned back in his chair.

"I just thought to show you just how truly sick and twisted your friends really are. But this next one, oh this next one is truly a gem. The reason I brought you here, actually. You say your bonds of friendship are unbreakable, that the strength of conviction and mutual respect are enough to get you through any obstacle. Let's just see how true, or false, those words are."

Again he brought out a scroll and opened it so that it filled the entire room, darkening until the image was all they could see. The first few moments were of Aidyn, minus the black scars on his cheek, standing outside a door they all knew very well, the door to the Heir Apparent suite, the Tower of Moons.

Suddenly the door opened and Tlonna stood there, younger and much more innocent looking, her pupils black and her eyes filled with joy and lust. Words were spoken, though they were silent to the watchers. Tlonna's face ranged from slightly curious to shocked, then eager. She let Aidyn into the room, and the vision moved with them.

The young Tlonna wore only a thin robe over a nightgown, and she laughed as Aidyn said something.

Slowly he approached her, and her mirth faded to nervous expectation. Aidyn reached out and brushed her hair away from her shoulder. Then they were embracing, fingers scraping through hair, peeling off clothing, breath coming hot and fast as their lips met, hands sliding into intimate places. A few torturous minutes later Aidyn and Tlonna were on the bed, the former moving his mouth down her jaw and throat, his hand dragging across one breast to grip her slender waist. It seemed to the three watching, unable to close their eyes or turn away from the image that filled the room, that the passionate scene went on for hours.

As the younger Tlonna arched her back and gripped Aidyn's shoulders as pleasure rolled through her, her white legs wrapped around the assassin's waist, the older one was crying, tears running down her humiliated face. The scryed Aidyn nipped Tlonna's shoulder as his own body shuddered in response, then moved his mouth to hers, covering it in a passionate kiss that was all too familiar, and the present one nearly gagged in shame, his gaze turned away from Losolin.

The elven king's breath was coming fast and hard, rage boiling inside him as he seethed at the image of his wife and the assassin lying together, sweaty and sated. Behind the image, Sithian giggled in vindictive joy as he looked between the three expressions of shame, humiliation, and fury. The image now showed Tlonna lying still beneath Aidyn, her face one of pure contentment. They spoke again, Aidyn shook his head and Tlonna's face crumpled. Then she said something and Aidyn framed her face with his hands, kissing her gently. As the image began to fade, Tlonna was reaching for the assassin once more, passion rising in her eyes.

Again, a horrible silence filled the misty room until Sithian stood and grinned, winked at Aidyn's furious expression. "Way to go, assassin. Got the first nibble of a delicious pastry."

"That is your own mother you are talking about," the dark elf snarled in a voice thick with wrath and other emotions too strong to control.

Sithian shrugged. "And I was indeed quite ill after seeing the image, I can honestly say. Disgusting, in my opinion, but you, oh you long for her yet, love her yet. When you're with others, you see her face, say her name in your mind while you're saying theirs to them. I know of kisses shared, embraces in covert hallways. Maids always talk. Remember," he said, turning to Losolin, "it was I who brought the truth to you, not any of your friends, several of whom I am positive know about this. Enjoy."

With a loud whooshing sound, Sithian, the room, and the furniture all disappeared and the three elves found themselves back in their respective places in Blackhaven. Aidyn recovered first, shot up out of his chair and grabbed up his weapons. He strapped them on and whipped his cloak about his shoulders. He grabbed a large purse of geld and prepared to run.

Across the way, Tlonna stared at Losolin for a split second before the king launched himself to his feet with a roar. He burst through the doors of their apartment, sped down the spiraling stairs, and sprinted onto the fourth floor of the castle. The elf exploded into Aidyn's room and flung himself at the assassin, who was tying a rope about the railing of his balcony.

Both elves went flying over the railing as Tlonna screamed for them both in frustration and terror. The freshly knotted rope went taught seconds later and she heard a frightened scream echo through the night air. Sobbing, the queen gripped the quivering rope and went down it as well, mindless of the stinging burn from the friction. Below her, Aidyn and Losolin were struggling against each other in a violent fight, fists flying and feet moving in fast, perfect form.

Losolin had a hank of Aidyn's hair in his fist and he was repeatedly slamming his knee into the dark elf's groin. The assassin was still grappling with Losolin despite the obvious agony he was in, and had even gained the upper hand, enough to free himself. Tlonna hit the ground several feet away and sprinted to their side, nearly retching from the agony that blossomed in her heart from the bond.

With a tremendous heave, she shoved them apart but Losolin reached around in a lightning fast move, slammed his fist into Aidyn's mouth, and snapped his head back. The assassin reeled backward, his hands reaching for something to catch. He caught Tlonna. They landed hard with the female on top, Aidyn's legs bent on either side of her waist. For a second they stared at each other, passions at war. Then reality came rushing back to them in the form of Losolin ripping Tlonna up and away from the assassin.

"Losolin!" she screamed as she tried to get a hold on her enraged husband.

"Bloody lecher!" the king bellowed and slammed his boot into Aidyn's midriff. "Thrice damned traitor!"

"It was a hundred years ago!" the assassin wheezed while he tried to crawl away. "Before we even knew you!"

The words had no effect on Losolin, but they knocked into Tlonna hard. She staggered backward, clutching at her chest. Before she had known Losolin, she had been with Aidyn. Suddenly it all made sense, their relationship, the way she always felt around him, the way his mere presence made her happier, the nearly uncontrollable desire he caused in her. Though, despite the knowledge of the fact, she did not remember it. She found herself wanting that memory more than any other.

The dark elf was back on his feet, hardly fighting back. Instead, he was trying to explain things to the deaf king while continuing to defend himself. Then Losolin swung hard at his face and Aidyn ducked, spun around, and slammed the high elf into the wall of the castle, twisting his arm behind his back.

"Stop, or I will break your shoulder," he snarled as Losolin struggled in vain against his hold. "You need to listen to me. It was a hundred years ago, and I did it at the behest of Dietirin. It was her birthday, and we feared she would soon be married off to one of the Lostugs. I, *we*, wanted her to know what true love felt like, wanted her to know real passion and lovemaking. When she met you, I was the farthest thing from her mind. She loves you, Losolin, she married *you*, not me."

"You sound a little disappointed," the king snapped, his face pressed against the cold obsidian blocks.

Aidyn hesitated for a moment as he wondered whether he should finally set out the truth or keep it hidden a while longer. He sighed in resignation. "I love her still, yes, but I would never come between the two of you. Ever. You must realize that, after everything we have gone through these past years. What has happened between us recently has been two friends giving comfort and support."

Losolin struggled for a few more seconds and then his shoulders slumped. He closed his eyes and nodded. "I know."

Aidyn gently released his arm and stepped away, walking carefully for the sensitivity in his groin. Tlonna stepped up to him and watched as Losolin turned to face them. He shook his head and took a deep breath.

"This is a cruel life," he muttered, staring between them.

Tlonna huffed. "Are you telling me you were never with anyone before we met? And no one in the eight years we were lost to each other? Losolin, you were conscious for them, I was not. What did you do?"

The answer was plain on his face, a deep-rooted shame that turned his cheeks red. "But none of them are here; none of them are our friends."

Aidyn let out a deep breath and folded his arms, which were cut and bruised in several places. "I was going to leave, and I will still do so if it is your wish. You know the truth now; I am at your mercy."

"Hardly," Losolin retorted. He sported several superficial wounds even though he'd been the aggressor. "But I do not wish you to leave."

Tlonna nodded in agreement and then looked up sharply. "I heard someone scream when you went over the railing."

Aidyn winced. "Lady Morgana was standing in the yard when we came down, and she ran away."

"Then we will have some serious explaining to do tomorrow," Tlonna replied dully, and sighed yet again. "And we cannot tell them the truth."

"Then let us think on it tonight, and agree on it in the morning," Aidyn said quietly, his gaze turned away.

Tlonna sat on the edge of her bed, her mind whirling as emotions and memories washed through her, though she still did not remember the night with Aidyn. Losolin sat on the other side, also silent. It had been silent in the room for a very long time.

"Do you love him?" the king finally asked, his husky voice quiet after so long of disuse.

"Yes," Tlonna had to admit, "I love him very much. But not the way I love you. Nothing could ever compare to my love for you."

"What happened while you were in Purheae?"

Tlonna did not respond for some time, thinking through her answer. "We came very close, Losolin, very close. He pulls at something within me that I cannot control. I decided that with him, I would fall to some temptations, but I would not cross that line. I kissed him, several times, and I cannot regret it. He tries so hard to restrain himself, but I think I pull at him too. I love you Losolin, and I love him. I know how that sounds, and I know you probably hate me for it, but I cannot deny it. You are my heart, and he is my soul. I cannot live without either of you," her voice broke and she fell quiet.

The bed bounced slightly as Losolin crawled over to her. His legs unfolded on either side of her, and she leaned back against his chest.

"I always felt there was something deeper between us," Tlonna whispered, lacing her fingers through his, her palms against his knuckles. "Perhaps that is why our bond, the oath, is so strong, because of our love."

"Then why can I not have the same?" Losolin asked and rested his chin against her shoulder.

"Because the oath is between an assassin and a Magin, a queen no less. Father told me Aidyn had once had the same oath with him, until he released Aidyn to be my guardian. I have longed to have the bond with you, Losolin, to know if you are well, what you are feeling, but it cannot be."

"Will you keep it with him?"

"Would you have me remove it? You cannot deny he is the greatest protector I could ever have."

Losolin was quiet for a time, holding his wife close. "No," he sighed at last, "I wish you had told me how you feel. I know he would never betray us in such a way. I just wish he had told us."

"Yayènia knows, so I am sure Suneelo does, and if it is a memory I do not have, Miazie knows as well, and therefore Sodo," Tlonna told him and turned her head to look at him from the corner of her eye.

"No wonder the two of them have been so at odds lately," Losolin remarked, thinking of the tension between the assassin and the human. "Miazie has little control over what comes out of her mouth, sometimes. I am sure she has used it as blackmail against Aidyn."

"Do you believe that?" Tlonna gasped, also thinking of the strained relationship.

"Aye, I do. I am sure the two have been irritated at each other long enough for such a threat to come forth."

"She is a surprising creature," Tlonna agreed.

Losolin did not respond for a while, his mind on something far more disturbing. Finally he could hold it in no longer. "Tlonna, do you remember what you told me Jair said?"

"Yes, why?"

"Remember who loved you first and longest for in the end it will be he who is your saving grace," Losolin murmured quietly, his heart breaking even as he said the words. "Aidyn is the Lover named in the prophecy, not me."

"Oh, Losolin! It cannot be so!" Tlonna cried. She twisted in his embrace to wrap her arms about him and hugged his waist. "I love you so much it hurts! Why is this happening?"

The king buried his face in her shoulder, breathing in her sweet, glorious smell, his eyes squeezed shut against the tears that threatened him. "No matter what, I will always love you," he breathed into her ear.

They clung desperately together, both unwilling to move as their hearts broke and reformed many times over.

Aidyn sat outside, his back against the castle wall as he stared blankly into the courtyard. He felt listless and empty, his chest heavy with Tlonna's mixed emotions of grief and understanding. He did not know how long he had been sitting when Aladorn appeared beside him with a look of concern on his dark features.

"What has happened?" the wiat asked his brother and sat on the bench next to him.

"Sithian somehow managed to capture my mind, along with Tlonna and Losolin's, and he showed us two images. The first was of Yayènia, Ghealan, and Suneelo mercilessly slaughtering a group of unarmed monotheists."

"Why would he show you that?"

Aidyn shrugged. "Another attempt to weaken our bonds. The other was of Tlonna and me, the night we were together."

"Ah, *bruun*," Aladorn breathed, understanding what that simple sentence meant. "What is going to happen?"

"They said they do not want me to leave," the assassin told him, shaking his head in wonder. "I know I would want the male who took my wife's virginity to get as far away from me and her as possible."

"They love each other, you cannot deny that, and that gives them strength to endure many hardships. I doubt Losolin would want you to leave. He may be hurt, insulted, feel betrayed, even worried that Tlonna might desire you, but when he comes to his senses, which it seems as though he already has, a little, he will realize that you are nothing but a devoted friend to both of them."

"A devoted friend who is still in love with her," Aidyn reminded him.

"And would you betray them by acting on those feelings?"

"I already have," the younger dark elf replied. "In Purheae."

Aladorn's eyebrows climbed his forehead. "Well...does he know *that*?"

Aidyn sighed. "Yes. He knows now."

"So you and Tlonna were together...in Purheae...and he did not kill you."

"We did not copulate, Aladorn, we just...slept together. Kissed a few times."

"And they realize that, I am sure. So many times you have had the option to take Tlonna to oblivion and back, but you have not. You have restrained yourself with admirable strength."

Aidyn shook his head. "Sometimes it is all I can do to not cry out that I love her and see what happens. There have been times when I have been tempted to simply walk up to her, kiss her, and then run away."

"Well, do not do that," Aladorn chuckled, though so little was humorous at the moment.

The assassin snorted quietly. "No, that would not be a wise thing to do, though it hardly matters now."

"You will find, little brother, that some friendships can withstand even the most egregious of wounds."

"So wise in your old age."

"Yes well, give it time and you too shall be this old."

"And you will be older yet."

"So it must be, but remember this, and I tell my son this all the time; no matter how old and wise you get, I will always be older and wiser."

Aidyn, despite his depressed mood, could not help laughing.

# Chapter 31

## Alchemist and Assassin

A rumor began the next day that Aidyn was teaching the king the art of assassination, and all the subsequent fighting skills. The nobles who passed Losolin in the corridors of the castle tittered and battered their lashes at him, believing that the dark elf must also be teaching the king everything else he was legendary for. Losolin bore it all as he did everything else, with silent resignation. He and Tlonna had not slept at all. Instead they had sat against the headboard of their bed and discussed all the options and decisions they had left to make. Aidyn was not seen for most of the day, but the Magin sought him out in his apartment, where he stumbled upon the most unusual scene.

Losolin knocked on the door and then entered without waiting, and found Aidyn sitting in one of his chairs and strumming quietly on a six-stringed instrument akin to the lute. The assassin looked up at the king and stopped playing, his nimble fingers moving to rest on the wooden neck and bulge of the guitar.

"Well, you are going to discover all my secrets, huh?" Aidyn muttered as he set the instrument aside.

Losolin lifted an eyebrow. "I think people might find this one to be the more shocking of the two, to be honest."

The dark elf gave him look somewhere between disbelief and consent. "You are probably right. Did you know that I have not lain with ninety percent or more of the females who claim I have?"

"I am not sure I am the one to tell, Aidyn, considering."

Again the older male had to concede. "Well, are you here to rip me to pieces?"

Losolin gave him half a smile. "I certainly thought about it, but in all honesty I believe you would survive, and I would wind up in the infirmary."

Aidyn chuckled. "Ah, the curse of being me, I suppose."

The king moved a stack of papers that looked to be letters from the only other chair to the floor while the dark elf watched him in silence. "I am here," Losolin began as he sat, "because Tlonna is too afraid to look at you right now."

"Afraid?"

"That is what she told me. Can you not feel it through the bond?"

Aidyn rubbed the heel of his hand against his chest. "She feels so much that I usually cannot pick out one emotion from all the rest unless she is in a fit. Right now I feel hurt, shame, fury, love, fear, but mostly confusion."

"I need to tell you something, and it is not something I want to tell you," Losolin muttered and looked down at his hands.

The assassin did not respond, just waited as his friend tried to find the words. Finally the king bit his bottom lip and looked at him.

"Tlonna was told by Jair, before she absorbed him, to 'remember he who loved her first and longest, for he would be her saving grace'. We...we thought he meant me, but obviously it is about you. It also means that you are the Lover named in the prophecy."

Aidyn did not look surprised. Losolin's eyes narrowed. "That does not shock you," he stated more than asked.

The assassin sucked in a breath, held it, and then let it out with a groan. "No. The time has come for complete honesty, I suppose. Miazie told me she had figured that out a couple years ago, back when she realized Sithian was the true evil, not Midian. She only just told me before I went to find Tlonna and Yayènia at the Cyree."

"Is that why you went?"

"No. The reason I went is that she said she saw me and the girls in Purheae Forest, and I had to go to Purheae to get rid of the Seadueni thugs squatting outside Eyin's village anyway."

Losolin leaned back in the chair and covered his face with his hands. "So all this time," he began, his voice muffled, "you have known that I am just a hiccup in her fate, a misstep of destiny."

"You are not, and quit being a fool. If Tlonna loves you, then that is how it should be. Just because I loved her first does not mean I am right for her. People who love me have a nasty habit of dying anyway."

"What do you mean? Are you talking about Rahna?"

Aidyn tilted his head slightly when Losolin looked at him. "Her, and another named Elva. She was my first...everything. An enemy of mine killed her in order to get to me. Needless to say he did not live long afterward, but still."

"I did not know."

"The two who did are now dead."

"Dietirin and Demetrius."

"Yes. More examples right there. But what I do not understand, and what Miazie could or would not tell me, is how I even fit into the prophecy. I do not rule anything, but you do. You are a peasant become king, the ultimate rise in station."

Losolin shook his head. "It all has to happen in sequence in order for it to be valid. The Guardian has fallen, that was Yayènia. She had to fall because otherwise Tlonna could not have found the rage to rip him apart like she did, which was the only way to kill him. We talked about it last night. Midian was never the true darkness, the real foe. It is Sithian, wrought of the two strongest bloodlines in Nymyños, perhaps the world. His soul is twisted and his mind enthralled by ideals dark enough to destroy everything. He is very strong and determined to succeed."

Aidyn blinked at him. "So?" he said after a minute. "What does that have to do with you?"

"I became the king before Yayènia fell, so that cannot be what the prophecy was speaking about. Whatever it is will probably happen soon, Tlonna thinks, because she says she can feel the very air tensing for some great cataclysm."

"And you believe her?"

Losolin gave him an incredulous look. "I have found it a bad idea to not believe the things she says. Aidyn, she has more power in her right arm than half the Magins of Nymyños combined, and she is very rapidly learning how to control it, refine it, even undo it. She sees magic in separate elements now and can pick it part until it simply falls away. She reads Veries Gurgen's journal every night, along with the other Magins' Journals, *The History of Magic and Its Uses*, and any other book on magic she can find. Even Dietirin wrote down some of his experiments with the magic, and she has gone through his notes several times."

"All right," Aidyn lifted his hands in a gesture of surrender. "I know she is very strong, but she has not been using her power for very long after all, only a few years. Dietirin told me he spent over three decades as a novice under his father's tutelage, and that was just the magic, not any of the duties of kingship. Thirty years, Losolin, not long in our lifetimes, but thirty years as a *novice*?"

"I know, but this is Tlonna we are talking about. I trust her judgment in this."

Aidyn sighed in defeat. "I suppose...I suppose it would be foolish not to."

"Aye, it would be."

The assassin fell silent once more as he tried to absorb, to accept, what the king was telling him. Finally he rubbed his fingers against his forehead and sighed. "So...what does that mean? I do not rule anything, nor do I have the inclination to do so."

Losolin eyed him darkly. "Tlonna believes it to be the College of Assassins that you rule."

"Ah ha!" Aidyn shouted and jabbed his finger at the king. "I have been Master Assassin for seven hundred years! You two were not even born yet! Your own logic proves you wrong!"

The high elf shook his head. "No. The assassins do not swear allegiance to you, do they? They swear it to the college."

"And that will never change."

"Will you be quiet?" Losolin snapped, his eyes glaring at the dangerous male across from him. "Trust me, I argued with Tlonna about this for hours last night, but she is convinced, and every argument you are coming up with I already have, and she discounted them."

"Well then get her over here, and have her explain it to me!" Aidyn demanded, throwing his arms into the air. "Or else I will find her!"

Losolin stood as the assassin did, suddenly very aware that his friend was walking very close to the killing edge. Aidyn shoved by him and yanked his door open with such ferocity it rebounded against the wall hard enough to knock a few books of the shelf next to it. The king huffed in aggravation and followed the dark elf out.

Aidyn stormed across the castle, his fists clenched and his entire body rigid with helpless fury. He violently pushed protesting guards out of his way when he reached the door that led to the winding stairs inside the Tower of the Winds. One of Tlonna's private guards, Alij, tried to bar his way with a tall spear, but the assassin grabbed hold of the weapon and jerked down, at the same time slamming his knee into the man's groin. Alij doubled over in grunting agony, and Aidyn stepped over him onto the threshold of Tlonna's door. Behind him, he heard Losolin running up the stairs.

Aidyn leaned back and kicked the door in, heedless of the hundreds of tiny pieces of wood that splintered into the air as the handle went flying. Inside, he heard a startled gasp. He picked up Alij's spear and walked inside with it, and then slammed the destroyed door in Losolin's furious face. Aidyn jammed the spear crosswise against the door, effectively barring passage from the outside.

He turned slowly to find Tlonna standing above him, staring down in utter shock and absolute terror. Such a look he prayed he would never see on her face again.

"Tlonna."

"Aidyn..." she breathed, her hand convulsively going to her heart. "What do you want?"

"An explanation."

"For?"

The assassin ignored the pounding coming from the other side of the door as he walked up the steps to stand very close to his queen. He continued walking which forced her to back up with him. When he finally reached the wall, he placed his hands on either side of her face and glared down at her.

"Now you know how I feel about you, Tlonna. Now you know how I have felt for a century. But still you cannot find the courage to face me, to tell me that you believe me to be the one named in that gods-forsaken prophecy that has utterly devastated our lives. How is it that you send Losolin, he who must be hurting the most right now, to talk to me when even you cannot?"

Tlonna swallowed, the heady scent of the seething assassin and her own fear doing a fair job of making her mind fuzzy. She sucked in a breath and let it out as a shivering sigh. "Do you remember that night I came to talk to you, the day you tried to kill Sithian?"

Aidyn nodded, unable to speak.

"I fell asleep in your arms, but I woke up alone. I remember waking up in your bed, breathing in your scent and finding a stray hair on your pillow. At that moment, I realized I loved you. It tore my heart into a billion little pieces because I love Losolin as well, but they are *such* different loves. With him I find safety, peace, compassion, and a simmering desire that never seems to fade. You...you make my knees weak with desire. I want to bury myself in you and never come out. Aidyn, you set me on fire."

The assassin shook, his entire body and his heart straining against his mind. He nearly lost control when she placed her open hand on his chest, over his beating heart.

"That is why I did not come to you to tell you. Even now I want to tear your clothes off and take you into nirvana. Knowing that you feel the same about me makes it that much harder."

"Because you are married."

"And I love Losolin with my entire being," Tlonna confirmed, her hand dropped to his sword belt.

This time it was Aidyn who swallowed as the devilish monster within him reared up and purred as her knuckles brushed his abdomen. "Tlonna," he sobbed, his head hanging as she tugged him closer.

The queen lifted her arms and hugged the assassin close, burying her face in his neck. "Oh, gods, how are we going to get through all this?" she keened, her back hard against the obsidian wall, Aidyn's body hard against hers.

"Somehow," he murmured in her ear. "Somehow."

Finally he pulled away from her, every cell in his body screaming at him in mutiny as he did so. He looked away from her red-rimmed eyes. "So. What about the College do you think is going to change to make me a ruler?"

Tlonna took a moment to gather herself and then shook her head. "I cannot know. I just know that something will. You must understand, Aidyn, how I perceive things. When I look at you, sometimes I see images and auras. Most of the time I do not because I have learned to control it, but every now and again they are so powerful I cannot help but see them. Right now, I see a dismembered hand holding an orb above your right shoulder. It is a symbol of power, authority."

"Why did you not tell me?"

"I only saw it once we were free from Sithian's mind cage," the female murmured, folding inward as the emerald gaze of the assassin bore into her. "That is why I knew something had changed, something horrible is going to happen."

Aidyn let out a slow breath and studied his queen. "I do not want this, Tlonna. I do not care about the Darkwights or whatever they may be. I care about you, and I do not want to see you suffer anymore."

She shrugged, resigned. "Caring about me, worrying about me, it means nothing anymore. Our situation is not going to change because we are emotionally attached to one another."

"So cynical. I remember when you used to find a way to laugh at everything, no matter how bad things became. You were always so full of life and cheer, and all around good charisma," Aidyn stated and sat on the edge of the royal bed.

Again Tlonna shrugged and joined him. "I guess I grew up. After so long of being miserable why even put forth an act of happiness?"

The assassin slumped. "It breaks my heart to hear you talk so, Tlonna. Surely you find happiness some days?"

The incessant pounding on the door from Losolin finally stopped, which left the room filled with an almost empty quiet. Tlonna looked down at her folded hands and shook her head. "There are moments, yes. But they are overshadowed by such pain. I have lost my son, my father, many of my best friends, soon to lose another when Ghealan leaves, and my other son murdered my daughter. It is so hard to find the strength to even smile."

Aidyn refrained from taking her into his arms, knowing his self-restraint was tenuous at best. Instead he nudged her with his shoulder. "I will have to learn some jokes then, to make you laugh."

Tlonna chuckled wetly. "I do love you, you know. I even kept the clothes I was wearing when I fell asleep with you, I could not wash them. They are in that cupboard," she pointed at her night table.

The silence that followed was palpable, and painful. Aidyn let his head fall back and stared up at the dark canopy of the bed. The bed he wanted to sleep in every night with the beautiful creature sitting next to him. His chest expanded as he sucked in a deep breath, his eyes closing against the emotional torture that he had not been trained to endure. Tlonna watched him in concern, unsure of how to deal with the heartrending display of agony.

Finally he looked at her, his exquisite face a mask of determination. "Ah, Lonna," he murmured, his gaze flicking over her face as though trying to memorize it. "If I had not been a cowardly fool a century ago..."

Tlonna smiled sadly and grabbed his hands in a hard grip. "We would not have the friendship we have now."

Losolin turned as the stairs beneath him rumbled with the heavy footfalls of a running human. He lowered his bloody knuckles and turned to the panicked guard. He frowned as he tried to place the man. The guard bowed, huffing as he tried to gasp his message out.

"Take your time, man," Losolin said and patted the guard on his shoulder.

"Sire...sire something happened. The seneschal, she's gone."

Both Tlonna and Aidyn jumped when Losolin burst through the door, shattering the blocking spear as though it were kindling. The bang after so long of quiet startled them both, but nothing more so than the way the king looked when he reached them. Losolin looked like a madman, his right fist bloody and torn, covered in writhing green power, anger etched onto his normally composed face. He surveyed the scene with dark, angry eyes.

"You are treading dangerous waters, assassin," he muttered softly.

"And you are creating those waters," Aidyn returned, eyeing the furious king with wariness.

"Losolin," Tlonna said, an edge to her voice. It was not an edge of anger, but of worry. "What is it?"

"Narda is missing," Losolin replied, furious. "Her office has been searched and there is no trace of her."

The queen seemed to snap into focus. "What? Who saw her last? Where was she? Who told you?"

Losolin shook his head. "I know nothing other than that. A guard came running. He had been sent to her office from Daphne's with a coffer of geld, and found her office decimated."

Aidyn stood and situated his sword belt more squarely on his slender hips. "I will head into the city and find a trail."

"Good, we will search her office and see if anything important is missing," Tlonna agreed, standing as well.

"Does she know anything vital?" Aidyn questioned as he headed toward the door.

Tlonna sighed. "She knows the castle inside and out, she knows all the personnel, she is at most of our meetings, and she is in the City Council. She knows enough to be extremely useful as a captive."

"I will get Aladorn and find out what we can."

"No, your brother is too public now. Take someone else," the Magin said as she grabbed her husband's tense arm and pulled him through the door.

Losolin stopped her and held a hand out to Aidyn. "Before we go anywhere we need to get something straight."

"Losolin, now is not the time," Tlonna said stiffly.

"It is now, or not at all. You," he pointed at Aidyn. "She is *my* wife. Mine. You love her, and she loves you, but she also loves me and I love her."

Tlonna scowled at the statement, but let her husband speak. Losolin's grip on her hand trembled and he let loose a ragged breath. "You be there for her when I cannot, you hear me? You protect her with your life, you hold her when she is afraid or lonely. You do whatever is necessary to keep her safe and happy, when I cannot. However, if I catch you in *my* bed, I will tear you apart. No, I catch you in *any* bed, I get to tear you apart. That is the line I am drawing. No further than Purheae. Understand?"

Both Aidyn and Tlonna stared at him. Losolin scowled at them both. "I know what I came between, I get it, but nothing more than what happened in Purheae. I cannot...I cannot share that part of my marriage."

Tlonna put her hand on her husband's shoulder. "You do not have to do this, Losolin."

The king took her chin in hand and stared down at her with nothing but love in his gaze. "Yes I do. I know I cannot command you to do anything, but I would like to think our marriage means something. I love you, and I would see you happy. If that means allowing you to cuddle up with Fingers when I am gone, then so be it. Just do not make love with him, please."

"Losolin," she breathed, tears threatening.

"We have fought and railed against every bit of our fate, and I am tired of it. We three, we shall bend a little, and allow this to be what it is. Aidyn?"

The assassin watched the couple with agony in his heart. "I would not come between you, willingly."

"I know that," the king said simply. "Do you agree to this?"

The two stared at each other for a long time, and then the dark elf nodded once. Losolin's mouth thinned, but he kissed Tlonna before heading out. She followed him, looking over her shoulder.

Aidyn watched her go, his mind whirling. Finally he sighed deeply, the excitement of the day completely flipped on its head, and turned to search out Sodo.

"You want me to go with you?" the alchemist asked in surprise when the dark elf found him lounging in Miazie's office.

The Belau stared at Aidyn as well, suspicious. "Will it be dangerous?" she asked coolly, fiddling with a quill, not about to forget that he was probably still furious with her.

The assassin snorted. "Of course it will, Miazie. Everything involving kidnapping and subterfuge is dangerous, especially when I am brought into the picture. So, will you go with me?"

Sodo blinked at him with his mismatched eyes. "What for? How will I help?"

Aidyn huffed in annoyance. "I do not know. Two people are more threatening than one."

"You do a rather good job at threatening alone," Miazie laughed cynically. "You want Sodo to go so you don't get bored. You and Aladorn are the ones who usually do this kind of thing, but your brother is now in a position of public power, so he cannot be used for such things anymore, am I correct?"

The dark elf sent her an emerald glare full of frosty irritation. "What Aladorn does with his time is up to him. Will you go? I do not have the time to stand here and convince your lover that I will not get you into a fight," he snapped the last at Sodo.

"I do not see why not. Let me grab my cloak and I will join you," the alchemist said, shrugging.

When Miazie opened her mouth to say something further, Aidyn pointed a finger at her. "His life is not yours to command. This is a mission of information gathering and very little else. Now stop being a craven human and allow your mate to live life as he should."

Sodo began to turn back at the last comment but the assassin shoved him roughly out of the office. He turned back to give the stunned Belau one more withering glare. Once the alchemist had retrieved his cloak the two elves set out into the city. They headed northeast into the rougher part of the market district. The sun broke through the tree-lined streets to bathe the citizens in a warm light, offering a nice reprieve from the chilly spring wind that seemed a constant companion in the early months. Sodo and Aidyn quickly found a seedy tavern and walked inside, the latter hiding his well-known face in his cowl.

He also slumped his shoulders and roughened his gait, which masked his supreme grace and agility. Sodo glanced at him once, surprised. He started to pull up his own cowl but Aidyn's barely discernible shake of his head stopped him. The alchemist's features, though odd, were not known outside the Academy and castle. Next to the shuffling assassin, he felt for once the more attractive, and he smirked slightly. Aidyn's brown hand lifted and pointed to a far table and the two moved to it, sliding into their chairs with ease.

"I have never heard you so much," Sodo murmured in amusement.

Aidyn's green eyes grinned at him from within the deep hood. "It takes a talent to be loud and ungainly. I learned it from my years at the College of Assassins, among humans of great stealth. They never realized I was mocking them."

"Were you the only elf in the College?" the high elf asked, intrigued by the dark one that so befuddled the general population.

"Aye. For a long time. At least, the only elf that survived the Three Terms. Most die in the second term, the torture is too much for their kindly souls. Once I took over as Master however, more elves seemed to find the coldness that is necessary. Even though we do not kill out of hand or without reason, it takes a cruelty to exterminate a life without any personal connection behind it."

"I am not a fighter, but I have always been attracted to the life of the warrior. Now, knowing you and Yayènia and Suneelo, really everyone, it seems even more glorious," Sodo replied quietly, unsure as to why he felt so comfortable with the deadly killer.

Aidyn's barely-visible cheek lifted slightly as he made a face of bafflement. "I have been told that many times, and I tell you now I do not understand it. We are this way because we did not have any other option. Nia and I...we were practically forced into the life of killing because without it our lives would have been worthless and easily forgotten, brutalized and abused as we were. The same with Suneelo and Ghealan. Suneelo had more choice than the rest of us, but he still felt the need to earn his place in society, rather than just inherit it from his forefathers. Ghealan was orphaned as a child and left to die, but he fought his way through life and became one of the world's greatest fighters. It is not a life I would recommend to anyone who had a choice."

"Is it so bad? I mean, when I fought at Alchemian I took lives but only because they tried to take mine first. I do not have any doubts or regrets about it. Miazie tells me that everyone in the 'family' carries with them deep shames and hidden wounds, but I do not understand it. Everyone is so noble, so honorable, and I cannot comprehend why you and the others would be ashamed of what you have done. You fight for your beliefs and moral integrity. How is that wrong?"

Aidyn leaned back in his chair, his arms stretched on the table before him, hands fidgeting with an iron candle holder. "Every one of us has taken an innocent life, whether by accident or purpose. I have probably taken the most, but have the least regret about it. It takes a great deal of willpower and special resolve to take a life that has done you no personal wrong. Many of the others, Tlonna probably most of all, have not found the necessary darkness to be able to do so and not break a little on the inside. We are beleaguered souls, Yayènia, Ghealan, and I, and it is because of that that we are the warriors we are. And it is good that it is so. Tlonna and Losolin would be terrible leaders if they did not have the kindness and genuine moral decency they do." *Except when a certain Magin finds out you slept with his wife a century ago,* Aidyn added silently.

Sodo was silent, never having heard the dark elf say such a lengthy personal monologue. After a moment, he looked up as a server walked up to their table, disinterested in the hunched, cloaked figure but eyeing Sodo with great interest. He sneered, repulsed by her obvious lust.

"Something you want?" she asked, her eyebrow lifting at the shadowy Aidyn.

"Mead," the assassin said in a gruff voice and flicked a copper spike at her. "Two mugs."

Sodo once again was stunned by the *humanness* of Aidyn, but he masked it well. He looked at the woman with a blank expression that made her blanch at his tainted eye. When she was gone, the elves smirked at each other, enjoying their charade.

"So why did you really ask me to come?" the alchemist finally queried, curious.

Aidyn shrugged. "Miazie was right, Aladorn is too public now. And you are a good conversationalist. And we have a connection now, a physical similarity that makes it easier for me to be around you than several others."

Sodo watched Aidyn's hand reach into his cowl briefly to touch the black scars on his cheek, and the alchemist realized that they had indeed both been touched by evil. He looked down as he ran a hand through his black-streaked pale hair and shook his head.

"I never thought of that," he murmured. "I do feel relaxed around you, which seems like a stupid, incredibly naïve thing."

Aidyn's teeth glinted in the shadows as he smiled. "I only kill when you are not looking at me. Though sometimes you just look so bored I feel as though I should attack you just to bring you from your melancholy."

"Please do not do that," Sodo laughed, shaking his head. "I would probably humiliate myself beyond reprieve. But you are astute, my friend. There are days where it all seems the same. I love teaching, and I would not give it up, but sometimes I just want to throw the books in the air and run away."

"What stops you?"

The alchemist paused, thinking. "Miazie," he finally said, locking gazes with the assassin. "She may be less than an elf, but she has a passion to her that makes up for it. I do love her."

Aidyn continued to watch the pale elf from within the shadows of his cowl, noting the way his companion's eyes grew soft when he spoke of the woman. Their drinks arrived and neither elf looked up at the server. Sodo took a drink from his mug and shuddered.

"Vile," he muttered, but continued to drink it. He figured Aidyn had ordered it for a reason.

The assassin lifted his vessel and downed half the liquid in one gulp. He hid his disgust well, but Sodo, who had been watching, saw his teeth glimmer as he grimaced. After a moment of quiet, the alchemist dared to ask the thing he had dreaded since knowing the dark elf.

"Miazie told me she once lay with Aladorn, back in Arseninis. Did she...did you... ever? She never gives me a straight answer."

Aidyn was silent for a few seconds, his eyes on his drink, which made Sodo very nervous. Then he sighed and dropped his hands to the table. "No, I never did. She kissed me once, when we went to retrieve the recruited army from the Seadueni, but that was it. Something always stopped her, and I believe it was her love for you."

"You say something stopped her, what stopped you?"

Again the killer was quiet, pensive. "I love another, and so carnal passion with anyone else always seems superfluous to me. I do not live a celibate life, I do not always refuse coitus when it is offered but I will never make the advance. I suppose that would be the answer. I do not seek it."

Sodo was dumbstruck by the admission. Even he had heard the rumors about Aidyn's virility and had always thought the male was a bit of a skirt chaser. Apparently the dark elf was used to the misconception, for he sniffed amusedly at Sodo's expression.

"Thought I was a lecher, did you?"

Ashamed, the alchemist shrugged one shoulder. "A little. But the stories...you know."

"I do indeed," Aidyn chuckled, honestly amused. "When people do not recognize me, like now for instance, I have been privileged enough to hear about my own 'libidinous expertise'. It is always rather interesting to hear how the stories grow and warp."

Sodo laughed along with his companion, rather gleeful at the thought that Miazie had never lain with him. Then suddenly Aidyn went silent, his body becoming rigid even though he stayed in his relaxed position. The alchemist studied his face for a second and then slid his gaze over the rest of the tavern, searching out what had caused the change. He saw the man as he sat down at a table in the middle of the room, his back toward the counter, facing them. A minute later another man got up and inconspicuously moved over to sit across from the other. Their hands met under the table to exchange a small bag of something.

Aidyn nudged Sodo with his boot and glanced pointedly at the mug in front of him. Obediently, the elf took a swallow of the foul drink, careful to be casual. He kept his peripheral on the two men and noticed that the assassin across from him was now sitting up, leaning on the table with his forearms, shoulder blades sticking up as he kept his head low.

"Go to the bar and order another two mugs. When you pass the table, try to get a look at the nearest man's left hand, between forefinger and thumb," Aidyn murmured quietly, passing him another copper.

Wordlessly, Sodo took the spike and strode to the bar, his expression indifferent. His heart skipped a beat when he spotted the strange tattoo on the man's hand as he picked up a bottle of spirits. He ordered two more meads and then returned to their table, slid a mug over to Aidyn.

"The mark looks like three colored circles and a yellow star. Right here," he pinched the web of flesh between his thumb and forefinger. "It looks faded and old."

The assassin hissed angrily, startling his companion. "Midian's sign. The bastard is a Zaedican."

"Do we have our target?" Sodo asked in a nearly inaudible voice.

"Aye. This is the one tavern that caters to people like that anymore. It is a hive for treason and sedition, well-known to those of us in the more shadowy professions. I knew if we were to find the perpetrator it would be here. Come, finish your drink and we shall leave."

Sodo obediently drank the rest of his mead and soon they stood from their table and departed, weaving through the now crowded tables with ease. Aidyn still affected his rough, shambling gait, walking before Sodo like a middle-aged human. Once they were outside, the assassin dropped the disguise and in spite of himself, the alchemist gasped as Aidyn's movements became so refined they were almost blurry, his footfalls so silent he had to look to believe the elf was walking beside him.

"Here," the dark elf said quietly and stopped before a section of street several yards away from the tavern door, hedged by a thick bush and two elm trees. A scrolled stone bench sat low to the ground.

Sodo followed his companion into the little area and sat beside him on the bench. They waited for nearly an hour, speaking only occasionally as some thought crossed their minds. They had reached a point in their relationship that allowed them to be comfortable in silence, though the alchemist noticed his companion seemed by far more relaxed than he had ever seen him. Aidyn sat with his elbows on his knees, his face in his cupped hands, and his eyes half closed as he pondered the thoughts that always plagued him. At one point something the dark elf had said spurred Sodo into speaking.

"You said that inn was known to be a place of disloyalty?"

"*Aiya.*"

"Why not do something about it?"

Aidyn scratched his chin. "If we took it out, the people who use it as their place of discretion would find another, someplace we do not know about. This way, as long as we are careful we can watch them without their knowledge. The innkeeper is one of ours, a spy that Erdwyf hired a long time ago. He has been running the place and keeping us informed for many, many years."

"An elf?"

"Half-elf, which is perfect. Humans think he is on their side, elves think the same. Truth is he is as racially indiscriminate as one can get. Does not give a damn about either race."

Sodo chuckled softly and fell silent once more. After another moment he could not help himself from asking. "Why were you and Losolin really fighting last night?"

Aidyn stiffened and then shook his head as he realized the alchemist probably already knew about him and Tlonna through Miazie. "He found out I was the one who took Tlonna's virginity and am the Lover in the prophecy."

Sodo was quiet for a moment and then nodded. "Miazie had said something like that to me a while back, after she spent the entire night in the bathroom on the floor, wrapped in a blanket." He fell silent and then looked sharply at the assassin. "She retains that memory, then. That is why she looked so odd. She..."

"Yes. She has that memory, and when it happens to revisit her, she experiences...well...me, because it is Tlonna's memory, not mine."

"So technically, she has been with you."

Aidyn shook his head. "No. Not emotionally, and certainly not physically."

"In alchemy there is this philosophy that if there is a memory or a thought, then there is reality, sort of a duality of mind and matter, heavens and earth, body and soul. What happens in here," Sodo touched Aidyn's temple, "or here," he moved his finger to the assassin's chest, "happens out here." He spread his arms out to indicate the world. "Or at least that is how I always interpreted it."

"Not the smartest way to interpret it at the moment, Sodo. Miazie is yours. Besides, I have already fought one husband over their wife for something I did over a hundred years ago; I do not want to fight another."

"Miazie and I are not married, yet."

"No, but you might as well be. She carries your child, yes?"

"Yes, but..."

"You love her, you are the father of her child, you respect her and care for her, after that marriage is simply a formality."

The alchemist fell silent with the statement and then looked at the dark elf. "Thank you."

Aidyn's jaw flexed and he looked away. "Truth is what you believe in your heart. Never let another's actions dictate your values."

Sodo nodded, and silence once again descended between them.

Finally the man who had paid the Zaedican appeared in the tavern door and the assassin slid off the bench into a crouch. His hand released the steel spike from the tension sheath with a faint click. Sodo followed his motion, trying to be as silent. When the man moved down the street in the opposite direction, Aidyn strode swiftly from their cover, silent as shadow, deadly as poison, Sodo following.

When they were less than two yards from the man, Aidyn gestured to the alchemist to stop moving, and then launched himself onto the human. He did not have time to shout as the elf landed on him, at the same time driving the spike into his spine. In a matter of seconds it was over. Aidyn dragged the paralyzed human into the alley between two shops. Sodo followed him, on the lookout for witnesses. By the time he reached Aidyn, the elf had the man propped against the wall and was squatting before him.

"What is your name?" the assassin demanded, coldly ignoring the man's quiet pleas.

"Morvan."

"What are you doing here?"

"I'll never-"

The man's denial was cut short by his own scream of agony, muffled by Aidyn's forearm, which he had shoved into the human's mouth. Sodo was confused by the scream until he saw that Aidyn had his wrist blade buried deep into his victim's knee, just below the kneecap. When the assassin asked the question again, the man quickly complied.

"I was paid to pay another for services to the Throne of Zaedic. The man at the tavern was supposed to capture an official from the castle and get answers about the layout of the castle, and who slept where."

"Why?" Aidyn demanded and twisted the blade slightly.

When the man stopped screaming, once again muffled by Aidyn's left forearm, he had to gasp out his answer.

"I was not told details, other than that the kidnapper was supposed to find out some information about a certain elf staying at the castle."

"Gothier," the dark elf murmured, glancing up at Sodo. "Where is the dryad?"

"Dead, somewhere in the city. Probably in one of the gardens. He wasn't supposed to kill-"

Once again the man's words were cut off, but this time Aidyn drove his dagger through his throat hard enough to slice it clean through. He ignored the crimson spray that coated his face. Sodo was sick, but not from the murder. He had liked Narda, and so had everyone else. Aidyn withdrew his wrist blade and carefully cleaned it before releasing it back into its sheath.

"It looks like you are going with me to find poor Narda," Aidyn said when he finished and led the way out of the alley.

Sodo frowned. "What does Seaduens have to do with all of this?" he asked, trailing the remarkable dark elf.

The assassin shook his head. "It could be a number of things, but most likely Sithian, along with the help of Isadorr, plan on killing Gothier here in Blackhaven, within the castle itself. That would allow Isadorr to call Tlonna a murderer, and launch a citizen-accepted war against us. Retribution, it would be called, and with that sort of frenzy behind it, we would be hard pressed to stop it."

"But we are already at war with them, and have been since they tried to take the city," the alchemist replied, confused.

"No, we have been at war with the Lostugs and their bastardized version of culture since Yayènia killed Herrich, the eldest of the sons of Stoffnias. It has always been under the table, a simmering mutual hatred held at bay by Constancias, the only thing she ever did for this kingdom, though it was her fault it started at all. Now that they have openly declared an alliance with Zaedic and the rebels of Talenias, they can afford to move the offensive," the dark elf explained, shaking his head again. "Neither of our kingdoms will rest until the other is obliterated."

Sodo merely nodded his understanding, his hands buried in his pockets. Though he usually wore his caste robes, the alchemist allowed himself the freedom of fashion whenever he was not in public attendance or teaching. He even had a long knife attached to his belt, a gift from Ghealan before he had departed for the battlefront. He stopped when Aidyn caught the arm of a passing dwarf, his beard more gray than red.

"Have you seen Seneschal Narda recently? A dryad, about this tall," the dark elf held his hand up to his shoulder.

"Nay, Lord Aidyn, but I'da ask around near da tower."

"My thanks," the elf said and released the dwarf.

"The tower?" Sodo inquired, frowning. "What tower?"

Aidyn let out an amused snort. "It is the viewing tower in the middle of the markets. Built by a rather delusional dwarf, it stands about one hundred feet above the roofs and has become quite the tourist spot. It is where Tlonna addressed the city when they were rioting."

The two males quickly traversed the quiet streets and found themselves standing at the base of the tower minutes later. Sodo stared up at it in humor and a little awe, shaking his head. He'd not really noticed the oddness of it on the day of the riot. People stood all along its length, some only ten feet off the ground, others leaning over the highest point, shouting and laughing in bravado, obvious terror in their actions.

Aidyn swore an oath of resignation and began shoving people out of the way, an amused Sodo behind him. The tower goers muttered in angry offense until they noticed the face, weapons, or clothes of the assassin. They became very quiet once they realized who he was.

Aidyn and Sodo both grabbed a young human couple as they tried to flee in fright. The dark elf easily pinned the terrified boy against the tower wall and gave him the legendary emerald glare.

"How long have you been up here?"

"About ten minutes, sir. Please, we ain't done nothing."

"Shut up," the assassin muttered, scowling absently.

Sodo, who held the girl, shook his head in frustration. "No one here will have been here long enough to have seen her. What now?"

"Seen who?" the girl asked as she stared up at the handsome elf that held her. She batted her eyes.

Sodo glanced down at her once and then looked back at Aidyn. The assassin sighed and released the boy, who was glaring at the girl in a jealous fit.

"Has anyone spotted a dryad in these parts, accompanied by a large human?" he asked the general crowd.

Murmurs broke out with the dark elf's words, but a commotion down on the square below caught his attention, as well as many others'. A man, the same Zaedican Morvan had spoken with at the tavern, broke out into a sprint across the busy plaza. Swearing enthusiastically, Aidyn yanked his bow off his back and knocked an arrow, following the man's movements as he sighted down the shaft of the arrow. Sodo shoved the now very curious and thrilled crowd back, forcing them all back a step through sheer desperation as the assassin waited for the people in the square to give him a clear shot.

There was a sudden lull in movement and Aidyn released the arrow, dropped his bow and tossed Sodo the end of a rope which he had about his person at all times, the other end of which he had wrapped about his hand.

"Are you nuts?" the alchemist shouted, but Aidyn did not hear him, for he had already vaulted over the railing.

Sodo cursed as the assassin sailed out over the square, one of the few places within the city that was paved with cobblestone. He wrapped the end of rope around his hand, up onto his elbow, and then grabbed more of it with his other hand, braced against the railing. Seconds later the line snapped taught as the length was used, swinging Aidyn down in a lurch. Sodo grunted as he was yanked against the railing, the twisted iron digging into his hip, but he kept his back straight, straining against the force of Aidyn's flying weight. Though the assassin was light, as were all elves, he carried a lot of equipment, and had more muscle than most, so he packed quite a punch when pretending to be a pendulum.

Aidyn felt his arm wrench as the line jerked taught, but he kept sight of his goal, the struggling man trying to escape. Struggling because he had Aidyn's arrow buried deep in his calf. He grimaced as he slammed into the side of the tower, which scared the people on the railing next to him, and kicked out, all the while hoping Sodo would not let go of the rope.

The assassin coiled his body as he neared the end of his range, and let go of his end. He somersaulted through the air, landing with a thud on the stone plaza, his thigh twingeing where Sithian had stabbed him. He sprang upward whilst drawing his right scimitar as he did so.

When he landed again he was directly behind the limping man, and he spun in his crouch, swept his blade out, and hamstrung the killer.

The man screamed in agony as his leg collapsed under him, which forced him to fall on the arrow protruding from his other leg. After Aidyn stood and sheathed his blade, he spun about in surprise as cheering applause erupted in the square. Unsettled by the positive reaction to the violent attack, the assassin looked back to the tower in time to see Sodo land on the ground next to the rope, rubbing his hands against his hips at the burning sensation. He wiggled the rope and someone standing at the railing graciously untied it and sent it sailing toward the elf.

"Impressive display of acrobatics," the alchemist commented dryly as he handed the coiled rope to the assassin.

"I could not let our friend get away," Aidyn said and shrugged. "He knows where Narda is."

The grim purpose of their task settled on Sodo once more and he glowered down at the screaming man. "Can you shut him up?"

Aidyn knelt by the man's head and grabbed it by the chin, viciously twisting his face up so that he could look at him. "What did you do with the dryad?"

"Deed! I feckin keeled 'er!"

Both elves started at the foreign brogue, recognizing it from the strange little green orb Losolin had once used to record an accent similar to the Cleick who had possessed the Death Pendant.

"Where is her body?" Aidyn demanded coldly.

"A weerhowz!"

"Weerhowz?" Sodo asked, baffled.

"Warehouse," Aidyn supplied. "Which makes our job easier. There are only three warehouses in the city. What was stored in the warehouse?"

"Feebric end dees. Aah! Ye keelled me!"

"Not yet," Aidyn snorted, and then obliged the man by breaking his neck. He looked up at Sodo and grinned wryly. "There is only one warehouse that keeps fabric and dyes, it is about four streets away. Coincidentally enough it was under the control of one Count Iranyo Tod. I will stay here if you will go get some guards and bring them here, please."

Sodo hastened away from the scene, amazed by Aidyn's calm. Minutes later he returned with three guards in tow, who then took custody of the body of the murderer. Aidyn wiped his hands and beckoned to his friend. Together, they rushed to the warehouse and found the manager.

"Let us in," Aidyn demanded.

"I'm sorry sir, but only those with an official pass can go inside the warehouse. Surely you understa-"

He was cut short by Aidyn's longsword pressing against his neck. "Is this pass enough? Let us in."

Seconds later he and Sodo were striding through the dark warehouse, scanning the abundant shadows for a sign of the missing seneschal. Aidyn patted about his body for a light source, and found none. Suddenly a flame appeared inches away and he spun in surprise to find a smirking Sodo holding up a tiny vial. A wick stuck out of the top, burning with an intensity many times its size.

"Impressive," the assassin said honestly.

"You have your acrobatics, I have my chemicals," the alchemist said nonchalantly, turning about in a circle to illuminate the warehouse.

Aidyn pointed into a dark corner and moved toward it, pulling Sodo along behind him. Narda's beaten body came into view as the two males approached, her grayish brown skin stained with crusty blood, her thick hair matted to the floor with the same scarlet liquid. Her eyes were swollen shut and her nose splattered over her face. The assassin gently pressed his slender fingers to her throat and gasped in hope.

"She lives yet," he breathed. "She lives."

Sodo backed quickly away as Aidyn carefully gathered the dryad into his arms to cradle her against his chest. They ran back to the castle as fast as possible, not daring to stop and check on Narda as they did so. They burst into the infirmary, surprising several healers and a few patients with their loud arrival.

"Braden!" Aidyn shouted as he laid Narda down on a free bed. "Braden!"

The young healer appeared down the hall and rushed to the assassin's side. "How many more are you going to bring me?" he asked, his eyes worried.

"She is severely injured. Can you help her?"

The human checked the dryad over for several minutes, continuously taking vitals. After a while he moved back and sighed.

"She is too far gone. I'm afraid even King Losolin would not be able to save her."

"Why not?"

"With every race other than elf-kind, and the heartiest of dwarves, such injuries are fatal, no matter what kind of treatment they are given. If King Losolin used his magic on her now, the small amount of energy it would take from her would kill her as surely as doing nothing. All we can do for her now is make her as comfortable as possible."

"How long?" the assassin demanded, frustrated that he could not save her.

"Due to the severity of her wounds, I am surprised she yet lingers. Within the hour, if not immediately," Braden said in a quiet voice, the desperation in the eyes of the two elves mirroring his own. "I am sorry, I liked her too."

"Get Tlonna, Losolin, Daphne...get everyone down here. She should be surrounded by her friends," Aidyn said to the healer, who immediately sent someone to find the entire council.

Daphne was the first to arrive. The treasurer rushed to her friend's side and went to her knees, tears streaming from her eyes. "Narda...I'm so sorry. I should have been there for you."

As everyone filtered in, from Yayènia to Edwin the Steward of the Wall, Narda opened her gray eyes. She looked at everyone surrounding her bed, nearly a score of people. With a tiny nod at Aidyn and Sodo, she breathed her last, a faint smile on her lips.

# Chapter 32

## Another Assassin

The next day, after Narda's well-attended funeral, a report came of stirring activity in the enemy camp at Sethryn Lake. With much worry and sorrow, Losolin and Aladorn departed quickly, the need to be at the front drawing them away from their respite. Tlonna and Aidyn watched them go with heavy hearts, wishing they had more time to settle matters. The king gave Aidyn a stern warning glare as he left.

With a small shake of her head, the queen led the way back to the castle, Aidyn following closely. Once they were nearing the library, Tlonna turned to the assassin. He was standing very close.

"Narda was murdered for a reason. We need to find out why."

Aidyn scraped his fingers back through his hair and sighed. "The two men I spoke with were definitely not from here, and they said they had been bidden to find out the layout of the castle and the schedule of a certain elf. Did Losolin ever tell you what I told him back in Kajgenia? About what the Eseirik said?"

"Nothing specific, no."

"He said our people had only one kingdom left; that we are in a dire situation. I told Losolin that I believed there might be trouble in Seaduens."

Tlonna frowned slightly, Gothier's desperate request of her echoing in her mind. She said nothing, so Aidyn continued on talking.

"My thoughts are that they kidnapped and tortured Narda for information about Gothier's position in the castle. Where is he allowed to go, at what times, where does he take his meals, does he eat alone? Does he have his own sleeping chambers, and so on. I think Sithian, or Isadorr, or perhaps the both of them are planning on having Gothier murdered."

"Then they would blame it on me, and have a validated reason for waging a desperate, bloody war," Tlonna finished for him, her voice horror-stricken.

"Yes."

"Will it never stop?" the Magin muttered.

"No."

"Thank you for that."

Aidyn snorted. They were near Aidyn's room when someone shouted from behind them. They turned and watched in confusion as Locton, Aladorn's son ran up to them.

"Uncle Aidyn, *help me!*"

Tlonna watched in astonishment as the young elf went to his knees in front of his uncle and clutched his boot tops. Locton began shivering and then hugged his arms around Aidyn's knees.

"What the...*Locton,* what are you doing?" Aidyn gasped as he tried to back away from his nephew's clutch.

Tlonna looked up from the odd spectacle in time to see Lavandyra slip from Aladorn's room, a sheet wrapped around her body. "Hold it!" the queen commanded loudly, causing the dark elf to halt in her tracks.

Aidyn's eyes bugged as he stared down at Locton. "Are you sleeping with Lavandyra?"

"No! She...she is barking mad! I was in Father's room checking on his things as I always do when he is away, and she came in and attacked me! Uncle, she tried to force me!"

Tlonna crooked a finger at Lavandyra and the other female sulked over to them, her bare feet peeking out from the sheet with every step.

"What were you thinking?" Aidyn snapped before Tlonna could speak. He bent and hoisted his nephew to his feet. "Aladorn was falling for you and the moment he is gone you try to seduce his son?"

Lavandyra fixed him with a murderous glare but said nothing.

"Lavandyra, explain yourself," Tlonna demanded coldly though her eyes were on Locton's shaken expression as he clung to his dangerous uncle.

"I am free, dying, and I can do as I please, you said so yourself," Lavandyra said to Aidyn.

"That does not mean you can seduce my brother *and* my nephew!" the assassin nearly screamed.

"Aidyn," Tlonna said quietly and laid her hand on his shoulder. "Take Locton and wait for me in the library. Now."

Lavandyra watched the males leave with glittering amber eyes. When Tlonna shifted her own gaze to the ash-tone, she lifted her chin in defiance.

"Are you going to punish me now?"

"I should," Tlonna snapped, "but that is not my place. Now listen. You leave Aidyn alone, and you leave Locton alone. Here in Blackhaven when you choose to seduce someone, you remain loyal to them!"

"Do you?"

Tlonna narrowed her eyes. "Yes."

"I have seen the way you act around Aidyn Sestuns, though. Your face goes soft and you stand closer to him than anyone other than your husband. I do not understand."

The queen squeezed her eyes shut and let out a soft groan. "Aidyn and I are very close, yes, but Losolin and I are married. Lavandyra, you must understand that the relationships here in the castle, among the city council, are very special. We are all family, and we will each defend each other to the death. That way we are stronger. Many times our enemies have tried to break us apart by revealing dark secrets and unwanted truths, but in the end we have just grown closer. We all love each other as a family does, unconditionally and irrevocably. Were I you, I would tread carefully for you are in danger of treading on one of my brothers' hearts."

"You speak of Aladorn?"

"Yes. Why are you with him if you mean to simply turn into someone else's arms the moment he is gone?"

Lavandyra blinked at her. "I am a pleasure slave. It is what I do."

"You *were* a pleasure slave. No longer."

"Aladorn will not lie with me, though he does not push me away. He seems only to want to make me happy in my last days. But he left, so I am alone. I wanted him badly, he is attractive and obviously limber. I imagine Aidyn Sestuns would be like bedding a wild animal, dangerous and thrilling. I do not want to lose a limb, so I choose instead to turn to the young Sestuns, this Locton. I believe he would be more agreeable than his father, less sure, and therefore willing to learn. I wanted only to give him the gift of experience."

"Did you now," Tlonna muttered softly. "Lavandyra, this is a royal order. You are to return to your quarters and remain there until I or High Advisor Miazie gives you leave to move about the castle once more. At that time, you are to remain away from Aidyn and Locton Sestuns indefinitely. Am I clear?"

"As you command," Lavandyra murmured and curtseyed gracefully with her sheet. Without another word, she turned and walked back toward her room.

Sighing, Tlonna found Aidyn and Locton in the middle of a quiet argument in the library.

"I said no!" the assassin hissed as Tlonna entered and turned to look at her with wild eyes. "Well?"

The queen slumped into a chair. "She said she wanted to give Locton the gift of experience."

"What? She believes me a virgin?" the young male said. Young in terms of elves, the wiat's son was in his mid-seventies.

"I doubt it, but she imagines you to be much more eager than your uncle," Tlonna grumbled, not mentioning the ash-tone's description of his father's sexual allure.

Locton went scarlet anyway while Aidyn slammed his forehead onto the table. "I am *sick* of everyone talking about me and my wildly exaggerated libido!"

"I get it, Aidyn. You are a crotchety old elf with no carnal pleasures whatsoever. Give over," Tlonna snapped.

The assassin shut his mouth with an audible click. Locton shook his head. "Uncle Aidyn says I should not tell my father about this."

"I agree with him. Aladorn does not need his world shaken at this time. I have ordered Lavandyra to stay away from the both of you, but as a precaution, I believe you should spend as little time in the castle as possible, Locton. Aidyn..." Tlonna shrugged.

"She comes near me I will break her licentious little neck," the assassin growled angrily.

Locton sent his uncle a wide-eyed stare. The Magin sighed wearily. "Go on, the both of you. I have work to do."

When the males left, Tlonna sat alone in the great library, surrounded by the stories of so many others, wishing hers was guaranteed a happy ending for someone. Anyone.

Later in the day, Tlonna found Lavandyra's quarters and knocked. She did not want to walk in on the dark elf without reason. After a moment she knocked again, but received no answer.

"Lavandyra?"

Tlonna frowned at the door and grabbed the knob, anger rising in her chest at the thought of the female disobeying her direct order. With a grunt, she broke the handle and wiggled the lock free. The queen pushed the door open and stepped inside the dimly lit room. She found Lavandyra curled up on the bed, her eyes glassy and staring sightlessly at the wall. Tlonna's heart sank and she sat on the edge of the bed.

"Poor creature," she whispered and drew the coverlet over the female's head. "I am so sorry. May you at last find peace in Summerland."

She departed Lavandyra's deathbed and found Miazie in her office. The woman looked up at her with red-rimmed eyes.

"Tlonna, I'm sorry I didn't tell you about Aidyn. I should have, but I couldn't betray him in such a way."

Tlonna held her hand up for silence and shook her head. "It was not your place to tell me. It was not Sithian's either, but so be it. It is done, and we must move on. I need you to take care of something for me. The dark elf Aidyn rescued, Lavandyra, has died. She is in her quarters, on the bed."

"Hers was a sad story," Miazie said softly, "that could not be rewritten by any of us. I will take care of everything, but where do you want her to be buried?"

"In the castle cemetery. I think here she may have found at least a small bit of solace."

"Of course. I'll get on it. Tlonna, I...I have missed you."

The elf smiled faintly and moved around the advisor's desk to hug her gently. "And I you. I promise, when this is all over, we shall spend more time together."

Miazie smiled back, though she knew the words for a kindness with little truth. "Aye."

The short memorial was a small ceremony in one of the side courtyards of the castle a few days later, and Tlonna felt the need to attend, as no one else did. She and a priest, along with Locton who was there only for his father were the only ones present. She stood silently on the side, her mind wandering. It was a pleasant day, warm, with a slight breeze to take the edge off the newly invigorated sun. Tlonna thanked the gods that winter and its incessant snow was finally gone. Soon she would have to get up and cast a blessing over the coffin.

Aidyn leaned against the railing on his balcony and watched the ceremony below him. He could just barely hear the words being spoken. A sudden calm washed over the assassin as he gazed down at the happenings, the feeling he always got before he killed. It startled him, for he had no reason to assassinate anyone, so he frowned. His instincts were what he relied on to survive, and he was loath to ignore them now, but it seemed ridiculous to interrupt such a run of the mill funeral because of his gut. Folding his arms, Aidyn shifted his position and watched as Tlonna mounted the dais, her golden hair catching the sunlight.

"I do not like this," someone said from the doorway of his balcony, and he turned to see Miazie.

"Aye. It does not sit well with me, either."

As the woman joined him at the railing, they both looked down at the tiny funeral and, with identical thoughts, considered ruining it. Aidyn was watching Tlonna when a flicker of shadow caught his attention and he looked up just in time to see the edge of a boot disappear around one of the thin bell towers. Cursing, the assassin shoved Miazie and nodded in the direction of the shift, forgetting for the moment that he was irritated with the human, and that she was not one of his more physical friends or in any shape to be pushed around. The High Advisor frowned at him as she rubbed her sore shoulder.

"What?"

"Did you see that? Stay here," Aidyn said and sprinted through his bedroom, down the hall and out onto one of the other bridges, trying to find the best possible route.

He saw a gray-cloaked form standing in the shadow of the bell tower and slid to a stop, halting Miazie with a single motion, as she had disobeyed him and followed him out. Again, he gestured in the direction of the stranger, and she nodded, having seen him at last. She watched the assassin eye the distance between the bridges, grabbed his shoulder, and shook her head.

"You will never make it," she hissed when he brushed her off.

The male smiled slowly, cocked his head in denial. "You have never been with me during an assassination. Now is your chance."

"What?"

"Now you get to see me in my element, Miazie. Trust me."

The woman started to reply but Aidyn crouched, his hands reached between his legs to grip the obsidian bridge, his knees up near his ears. Suddenly he was in the air, lithe body stretched out, arms straight out to the side. Miazie stopped herself from shouting out in fear for her friend, but then the assassin rolled in midair and landed with barely a scuffle on the far bridge, once again crouched on the edge. She swallowed in disbelief as Aidyn stood, though he was still bent over in order to remain undetected by the doomed infiltrator. She saw his shoulder twitch slightly, and knew that he had released the deadly iron blade out of the tension-sheath on his inner forearm.

Aidyn moved along the bridge, his eyes trained on the gray back of the stranger, his fingers braced carefully on the knife attached to his wrist. Seconds later he was upon the individual, one arm tight across his throat, the other pressing the wicked blade hard into the kidney.

"Who are you?" the dark elf whispered, his mouth near the other's ear.

"Aidyn Sestuns."

Aidyn snorted in disbelief. "Wrong. I am Aidyn Sestuns. One more try?"

The captured assassin struggled vainly against the elfin one, his hands prying uselessly at the tawny arm across his throat. "Jidair."

A wave of betrayal shot through the dark elf. "No."

"Yes, Master, it is I."

"But...why?"

Jidair let out a huff. "Who am I to refuse my king?"

"You are the Master of the Seaduens College! You always have a choice! Or do you believe assassinating the one person who can put an end to this ridiculous war is a noble idea?"

"Who says I am here to assassinate anyone? Master Aidyn, are you telling me that every time you are given an assignment it is to murder someone, or do you sometimes do the difficult tasks that no emissary could ever do?"

"If that were true, why sneak into the city, into the castle itself and climb onto a bell tower overlooking a ceremony that the relatively unguarded ruler is attending?"

Jidair huffed again, his air still restricted by Aidyn's arm. "Who says my target is the Everwood?"

"What?"

"Forgive me, Master Aidyn," the Seaduens assassin breathed and lunged forward.

Aidyn was dragged forward as the other took a flying leap off the tower. They hung suspended for the merest second, and then began to freefall, plummeting toward the ground. Behind and off to the side Aidyn heard Miazie scream in horror, but his mind was already working. He tucked his smaller body against the back of the suicide assassin and slammed the blade into Jidair's body until his knuckles pressed up against the bloody cloth.

Jidair howled in pain as he snapped his arms and legs out, folds of cloth billowed out to catch the two in midair and swept them upward, though only for a moment. Aidyn yanked his blade out as they began to fall again, though at a slower rate. Seconds later, only feet from the ground, the elf launched himself upward, curled into a ball and rolled backward. As soon as he began to descend, he leaned forward. Aidyn hit the ground hard but rolling, and he used the momentum to get back onto his feet. Locton and the priest had already leapt to the side, having both watched the terrifying descent and seen the desperate look in the stranger's eyes.

Aidyn spotted the other assassin running full tilt toward the dais, his wing-like cloak discarded on the ground nearby, blood staining a large portion of it. Sprinting after him, the dark elf felt the distinct edge of pain up and down his legs and back, but ignored it as he followed Jidair. The traitorous assassin was on the dais, headed straight for a cold-faced Tlonna, but he was unarmed.

Roaring out in pain and adrenaline, Aidyn dropped into a crouch and sprang through the air, wrist blade out and winking in the sun, already crimson with blood.

Tlonna watched in fascination as the stranger pivoted away from her at the sound of Aidyn's cry. Her assassin was already in the air, his legs tucked under him as though he were crouching, his right arm cocked back at the elbow, the left straight out, fingers splayed. For a moment, it seemed as though time had slowed, that the dark elf was hardly moving at all. Then, with a loud crash Aidyn landed on Jidair, his feet on either side of the assassin's shoulders, his right fist pressed to his throat, the left palming the stranger's face.

The killer thrashed about for a moment and then went very still. Slowly, the dark elf stood, withdrawing the deadly blade as he did so, and Tlonna saw what had killed her would-be assailant. With the tensing of his hand, Aidyn sent the bloody blade back into its sheath, and he looked at Tlonna. There was blood soaking his shirt, but he ignored it.

"Never thought I would fly," he muttered with a shake of his head.

"Where did you come from?" Tlonna asked, utterly confused.

Aidyn didn't answer, for suddenly he stumbled to the side as though struck, his face going pale. The queen lunged forward and caught him as he fell, his eyes fluttering weakly.

"Aidyn?"

The assassin's breath caught and he clutched his side, tore at his shirt. When he finally got it free of his belt, Tlonna's heart stopped. Just above his hip was a deep puncture that tore down in a laceration down the side of his thigh, though it appeared nothing was truly damaged. The dark elf let his head fall back and he groaned as someone rushed up to the dais.

"Dear gods! No!" Miazie shouted as she arrived at the scene. "Aidyn!"

Tlonna shook her head and pressed her hand to the wound in an effort to stop the bleeding. The assassin looked up at her with hazy eyes. "Tlonna," he breathed, fumbling for her hand. "Here we are yet again."

"Indeed, now shush," she replied as the male's head rolled listlessly onto her bicep, his chest moving with deep, rapid breaths.

Miazie dropped to her knees beside them. "Is he...?"

"No, unconscious. Is there a healer on the way?" Tlonna replied as she cradled her friend.

"Yes. Where is Losolin when you need him?" Miazie sighed, brushing the sable hair out of Aidyn's face.

The queen shook her head. "I wish he had not gone to the battle. He is needed here. If Aidyn dies because of that decision, I will not make it."

"He will not die. He's been through too much to die from this," the advisor said calmly as Aidyn's breathing became normal even though no healing had yet been done on him.

When she noticed once more the priest and Locton still staring in horror at the dais, she raised a hand to the nearest guard and he nodded. The priest went silently, but Locton shook the guard off.

"He is my uncle, and I am staying."

The guard looked to Tlonna, who nodded. After a minute or two, they were alone but for the dead body of Jidair, Locton, and the guard. Tlonna could not move from Aidyn's side as her hands were pressed to the bloody laceration, but Miazie crawled over to the other assassin's body and dragged it closer. When she flicked the hood off, they stared in confusion at the foreign features.

"Who do you think he was?" Tlonna asked finally. She drew Aidyn's body closer to her so that his forehead rested against her neck.

"He's an elf, but other than that I have no idea. Perhaps Aidyn knows but we will have to wait on that. No insignia, no colors, jewelry, nothing. An assassin of some skill though, that is for sure."

"Why?"

Miazie related the story of the stranger's and Aidyn's descent, still amazed at the dark assassin's agility. "I have never seen anyone move about in the air like that. Ah, look," she said after flipping open Jidair's hand to reveal a slender dirk, stained crimson with Aidyn's blood. "He must have gotten it up in time to stab Aidyn before he died."

Tlonna nodded and looked up at the sound of running feet. She spotted a healer sprinting toward them and sighed in relief. When the man reached them, he hissed in shock.

"Lord Aidyn again?"

Both females looked up in surprise, then recognized the healer Braden. The young man was becoming well-respected through all his work on the assassin and Lavandyra.

"Aye, please, help him," Tlonna replied as she scooted to the side to allow the man room to work.

They sat on the dais for a long time while the healer labored, and slowly the sun sank into the horizon. When darkness had enveloped the courtyard, the healer sat back, awash in the orange glow of torchlight. "I can move him now, up to the infirmary or his room, whichever. There's not a whole lot left for me to do, he just needs to rest and let it heal."

"Bring him to my room and I will make sure he does not move," Tlonna replied while she got to her feet.

"As you wish," the healer said and motioned for the guard and Locton to help him move Aidyn onto a stretcher.

Several minutes later, they were reversing the process in Tlonna's room, depositing the assassin on her bed. Locton had returned to his room, gray in the face. The queen ordered the guards to set an extra watch on the door and shut it behind her.

"Why do you want him here?" Miazie asked as Tlonna began untying Aidyn's boots.

"If he woke up in his room, or the infirmary, he would not comply, and would probably not heal correctly, like last time. This way I can control him."

"And you get to see him in the flesh," the advisor added as Tlonna pulled off the assassin's boots and started undoing his belt.

Tlonna scowled. "I already have, though you know that. Though truly, who would deny themselves the pleasure? I always wonder why he is such a good assassin when assassins are supposed to be visually forgettable."

"Aye," Miazie agreed as she took the scimitar belt from her friend, "but when you are as good as Aidyn, it does not matter what you look like. And as for knowing about you and Aidyn...believe me the memory doesn't bring me any pleasure. It made me ill the first time."

"Why?"

"I'm not an elf, and experiencing that through your mind was almost painful. It was like when I was forced by Stoffnias and Isadorr. I'm not built to endure that sort of...endurance."

"I am sorry."

Miazie shrugged. "Not your doing."

Quickly they removed the rest of Aidyn's clothing until he wore only bandages. Tlonna stared at him in nearly overwhelming desire. Miazie glanced at him once and then folded her arms. She'd experienced enough of Aidyn already. She cleared her throat in order to gain Tlonna's attention.

"Which is Losolin's?" she asked when Tlonna spun away, running a hand over her face as she tried to pull her mind's eye away from Aidyn's body.

"The left. There should be a pair of cotton pants somewhere inside," she said, her eyes pinned to the floor.

After a moment of rummaging, Miazie emerged triumphant with a pair of loose, white cotton trousers. They quickly got them onto the fallen assassin and stepped away in relief, no longer thick-tongued with desire.

"Where will you sleep?" the advisor asked and looked around the large room.

Tlonna shrugged. "The bed is big enough for eight. I only take up one edge of it, Aidyn can have the rest."

Miazie face split into a wide grin. "Just because he is unconscious does not mean he won't wake up to the right administrations..."

The queen shoved her, also grinning, relieved to be joking about the situation. "True, but I love Losolin and the one thing he denied us was fornication. I would hate to be disappointed with him after being with Aidyn."

"Oh? And why would you be disappointed?" the woman asked coyly, grinning.

Tlonna snorted. "Do not pretend ignorance on that."

"Honestly Tlonna, were it not for Sodo I would still be whimpering on the washroom floor. But he holds nothing for me now."

"Truly?" the queen asked in surprise and risked a glance at the sleeping dark elf.

Miazie shrugged. "Sodo...he is the very sun in the sky to me. How could I not be satisfied with that? Aidyn's physical attributes do nothing for me. Not anymore."

"I wish I could say the same. What do I do, Miazie? How do we get beyond this?"

The human smiled slowly. "Take him. Take him and move on. I would."

The Magin shoved her pregnant, chortling friend out of her apartment and quietly readied for bed. As she slid beneath the covers, Aidyn stirred slightly, but otherwise remained asleep. The queen scooted over to his side, brushed the now flung-about hair back from his face, and pulled the covers up to his shoulders.

"I owe you so much, Aidyn," she whispered, gazing at him with sleepy eyes. "I only hope that I can one day repay you."

When he rolled his face away from her, Tlonna snuggled against his arm and fell into a light doze.

Aidyn woke sometime late in the night and suppressed a groan of pain as he gingerly sat up and attempted to figure out where he was. When he looked over and saw Tlonna sleeping a few inches away, he slid back down and dropped his hands over his face, wondering why in the nine hells he was in her bed. That was the one thing Losolin had forbidden. When he realized that his clothing and affects were piled neatly across the room and he was wearing some sort of loose pants that were slightly too big, the assassin's heart nearly seized in panic.

When he pushed back the covers and swung one leg over the edge of the bed, Tlonna woke with a start and shot upward, pointing at him with a very stiff finger. "Do not even think about it. You are not to move for a *week*."

"What?" Aidyn gasped, still unsure what all this was about.

"Get back in bed," Tlonna growled, dropped her hand, and crawled over to him. "If I have to tie you down, I will."

"What is going on? Why am I in your bed, in Losolin's clothes? Did you undress me?" the assassin wheezed as the queen carefully pulled him back, pushed him down, and casually checked his bandages. She lifted the stretchy band of his pants, ignoring his surprised yelp, to check the neat row of stitches along his hipbone.

"You are here so I can keep an eye on you, and you are in Losolin's pants because it was the loosest thing we could find."

"We?"

"Miazie and I."

"You both? Why?" Aidyn asked, slightly embarrassed and more than a little disturbed.

Tlonna sat back, her arms folded. "Because you are our friend, and you saved my life, yet again. Besides," she shrugged, "what do you have to be worried about? Miazie was not impressed."

"Fantastic," the assassin muttered, his fingers laced together behind his head in spite of the painful tugging on his abdomen. "And what of you?"

The Magin eyed him in the dark, unable to suppress her desire, and she licked her lips unconsciously. When Aidyn's eyes widened, she blushed, thankful for the shadows. "I had expected to be able to resist more than a day," she managed after an awkward moment and lay back down, curling against him.

The assassin snorted. "Are you sure you can control yourself then?" he teased, looking over at her.

"No," came the unexpected and dangerous reply.

Aidyn sucked in a breath as her warm hand suddenly danced up his chest and pulled his chin over. Her mouth was there, ready. Aidyn tucked his arm around her and drew her closer, rolling onto his side for better leverage. Ignoring the laceration in his hip, the assassin pinned her against the mattress and delved into the taste of his queen. When they finally broke apart, Tlonna gasped in a breath and shivered.

"Ah, gods," she murmured, licking her lips. "I will never get used to that."

"What?"

Tlonna let out a shaky breath. "You are like kissing fire. Sweet fire. I want to burn in it." She looked up at him, leaning above her, almost nose to nose. "Get some rest, Aidyn, you will need it."

Aidyn was still staring at her long after she fell asleep.

# Chapter 33
## Warning Signs

The next day went by quickly with the guards examining Jidair's body for clues and reports from the battlefront trickling in. It seemed things were as steady as could be considering. Miazie complained as she waddled about, but smiled when Tlonna pressed her hand against the woman's belly and felt the child within kick. They were taking the time to dine together.

"I am so happy for you, my friend," the elf said softly.

Miazie cradled herself and smiled serenely. "One day, Losolin will give you a child, and you will know this feeling. Of course, you will not get sick, or have to run to the washroom every twenty minutes, or get stretch marks..."

The queen gave her friend a gentle hug. "You are still beautiful, Miazie. Always will be."

Evening came and Tlonna retired to her chambers, forgetting for a moment that she had a prisoner. Aidyn glowered at her from the bed, the blankets pushed down to his feet and his arms crossed. There were books strewn about the pillows, and a pile of knives down on the floor. They looked freshly sharpened and oiled. His green gaze followed her as she walked over to her vanity and removed her crown, then kicked off her shoes and undid the pins from her hair. He said nothing. Tlonna strolled over to the bed and turned her back to him.

"Laces?" she asked.

The assassin grunted but she felt his fingers tugging at the delicate strings a moment later. When the dark red dress loosened about her body, Tlonna stepped away and pulled it off, sighing as the elaborately embroidered silver chemise and petticoat joined it on the floor. Behind her, Aidyn sighed. She turned, clad in only a thin shift and undergarments. The assassin was looking down at his hands, which were fiddling with a book between his thighs.

With an arched eyebrow, Tlonna pointedly grabbed the shift and lifted it over her head. Aidyn squeezed his eyes shut. "It is only fair, assassin," she said coolly. "I have seen you naked on multiple occasions, and suffered for it."

"Suffered?"

Tlonna drew on a light robe and walked over to him, tying the belt. "*Aiya*, suffered. Been frustrated, distracted, and helpless to alleviate my own desire. Suffered."

Aidyn opened his eyes as she joined him on the bed. She pushed aside a pile of books and inspected his stitches, ignoring his long-suffering sigh. When she replaced the hem of his pants, Tlonna smiled. "Healing well, I see."

The assassin glared at her. "Hard not to when all I do is sit here. As much as I enjoy your bed, I would enjoy it much more if I were not by myself."

Tlonna laughed and brushed the stubborn strands of hair out of his eyes. They returned the moment her hand left. She touched his face, running her fingers over the angles and curves, gingerly brushed the tip of one over the triangular scars. He winced.

"Do they hurt?" she asked softly as he removed the book he'd been fiddling with.

"Sometimes. Sithian said he could control me through them, cause me pain," Aidyn shrugged. "Since having them, I can sense the darker intentions of people."

Tlonna made a sound in her throat, leaning forward. She gently pressed her lips to the scars, then his jaw, and then the corner of his mouth. "He will not touch you again."

Aidyn wrapped his arms around her and dragged her across his body so she was on his right side, away from the wound and the scars. She moaned as his grip moved to her waist, the robe bunching up beneath his hands. He shoved it aside and placed his hands against her bare skin, warm and soft. "No further than Purheae," he murmured as he bent down to nuzzle her throat.

Tlonna nodded mindlessly as his hands pressed her against the soft mattress and he straddled her, running his mouth over her mouth and neck. Her fingers dug into his back. After some time, Aidyn pulled away from her and lay down against her side, their legs entangled. The queen had her eyes closed and her mouth parted slightly. She gulped and looked at him.

"It is very difficult to stop there," she said huskily.

The assassin snorted. "Yes."

They lapsed into silence for a time, then Tlonna sought his hand. "Had...had things been different, the way they should have been...would you have married me?"

Aidyn started, his muscles tensing, but he relaxed a breath later. "Yes."

"You would have given up being an assassin and taken the crown and throne?"

The dark elf nodded. "Anything. I would have given up anything. I still would. Tlonna I love you with my entire being, every part of me. Had things followed as they should have, I would have been yours from the first moment you reached adulthood. There is nothing in this world that I care about more than you and your happiness."

"Oh, Aidyn," Tlonna whispered, leaning into him. "I love you."

He smiled faintly in the dark and held her close, his chin on top of her head as she fell asleep.

Tlonna stepped from the stairs onto the fourth floor of the castle the next morning and found herself face to face with her brother. "Gothier."

The prince looked away, as though in shame, and shuffled his feet. "I just saw the assassin."

"Aidyn? How? He is in my room."

"No, no...Jidair. Tlonna, I know him."

"What?"

Her voice must have come out much more forceful and acerbic than she intended, for the male winced and swallowed. "He is from Seaduens, one of Isadorr's assassins, the best."

"What is your brother doing sending an assassin after me? Certainly he knows that is one of the absolute worst mistakes he could make."

Gothier's eyes narrowed, but in a more thoughtful expression rather than anger. "I am not sure he was after anyone. Jidair was also a College Assassin, close to Aidyn's caliber, and I doubt anyone came closer."

Tlonna studied the male with interest. "Then why was he here? If he was of the College, that explains how he managed to get onto the bell tower in the first place. And if he is an assassin, why would he even be here, stab Aidyn of all people, and try to kill me if he was not after anyone?"

Gothier shrugged. "I cannot be sure, but Isadorr knew I was here, he knew where to find me."

Tlonna was silent for a moment, thinking. Finally she cocked her hip and folded her arms to give Gothier a speculative look. "You think your brother is trying to send you a message? A threat? Does this have to do with Narda's death?"

"The dryad? Most likely. As for a threat, I do not think so. He may be embittered toward me, but I do not think he wants me dead. Your guards would not let me inspect the body, but I would like to."

"Why?"

The prince hesitated, as though worried about how to tell her. "There may be a message on him."

Tlonna shook her head. "We searched Jidair thoroughly, Gothier. There was no letter, no insignia, no jewelry. We found nothing."

The male squinted and shifted again. "That is why I would like to inspect him. I knew Jidair, and I know my brother. Please, let me see him."

The queen sighed. "Very well, follow me."

Gothier seemed to relax as he fell into step beside his half-sister. Tlonna eyed him from her peripheral.

"What do you think you will find? Or hope to find?" she asked after a while.

"I do not know. As I said Seaduens is not in the shape you believe it to be in. I truly do not know what to expect. Perhaps I am wrong and Jidair was sent here to kill you or Aidyn, perhaps both. As I said, I do not know. But I do know that Isadorr is not foolhardy or stupid."

They continued on in silence until they reached the morgue. Tlonna held her hand up to stall the guards' protestations when Gothier followed her in.

"Jidair is from Seaduens, and he knew Prince Gothier. You are excused."

"But, Queen Tlonna, we cannot allow you to be in here alone with..." the guard began, his eyes shifting to the Seaduens prince.

"Prince Gothier is both my brother and your prince. I am perfectly safe with him, you may be assured."

The guard and his two companions bowed and took the dismissal as it was and shut the door behind them. Tlonna looked at Gothier to find him staring at her with an expression of utter surprise.

"What?"

"I never thought I would hear you defend me in such a way. The cursed and hated Everwood Queen, defending me? The Prince of Seaduens?"

Tlonna chuckled quietly. "Things are all based on perspective, Gothier. We were grave enemies, and now we are siblings. Now, what do you see?"

The male moved to the side of the table on which lay Jidair's body. He bent down and lifted the assassin's hand. He studied the fingers, the wrist, and then moved to inspect the other one. Tlonna waited in silence as she watched him. The elf searched the feet, the elbows, the neck, and even the hips of the high elf assassin. Gothier let out a deep breath and straightened with a dismal expression.

"Well?" Tlonna asked.

Gothier nodded. "There is a message, certainly, and not at all what I would have thought my brother would send. See this?" he lifted Jidair's left hand.

Tlonna bent down to look at the tips of the elf's fingers, and found tiny tattoos on the forefinger and the ring finger. "A sun and a torch?"

Again Gothier nodded. "Symbols. Here, on his neck, is a sword. And on his right hip there is a dead tree."

Tlonna waited for an explanation. The prince huffed out a breath, his cheeks rounding with the force.

"The torch and sun on Jidair's fingertips indicate allies, but the fact that they are on his left hand mean they are unstable allies. The torch is Narnen, and the sun is Talenias. The sword here, is Zaedic, and because it is on the neck it means it is a threat, that Zaedic has its sword at the neck of Seaduens. This tree, on his hip, is a symbol for Blackhaven in Seaduens."

Tlonna lifted an eyebrow at him. "A dead tree for your hated enemy?"

Gothier gave her a small smile. "Yes, but what is more disturbing is that it is on his right hip."

"Why?" Tlonna asked, amazed at the complexity of the symbolism on Jidair's body.

"Had it been on his left, it would have meant that Isadorr was warning me of Blackhaven's intentions, but because it is on the right, it is telling me *to* warn Blackhaven."

The Magin was now completely confounded. "So, what is the whole message?"

Gothier bit his lip before speaking. "Isadorr is telling me to warn Blackhaven, to warn you, that Seaduens is in trouble, at the mercy of Zaedic, and that Narnen and Talenias are in the same situation, or will be soon. Soon, when Zaedic has seized control of Seaduens, it will turn everything it has toward Blackhaven."

"You can tell all that from four little tattoos on the body of a dead assassin?" Tlonna asked incredulously.

Gothier nodded. "Messages like this have been used for centuries in Seaduens. They are discreet, and impossible to break if you do not know the language. To most people they look like simple tattoos, nothing special about them."

"And so your brother inked up the greatest Seadueni assassin and sent him to his death to send a message of what, warning and a plea for help? Why not let him live, and tell us in person?"

"You forget that Isadorr hates you, and probably figured Jidair would be a good attempt at taking *someone* out, and he could be reasonably sure I would see the body and receive the message."

"Ah."

"You asked me if I believed Jidair's presence had something to do with the dryad's death, I say yes. My guess is that she was kidnapped with the intention of finding out what limitations I had here in the castle, and if there were any sort of events taking place soon."

"Narda could not have known about the funeral because Lavandyra was still alive when she died, but she knew that the dark elf was about to die and the likelihood that she would be buried here, and she knew about you and your position," Tlonna said. "Aidyn suspected much the same thing. So, one mystery solved, but there is another. Her kidnapper was from Zaedic, paid through someone else, to capture her and find out information about you. What is Sithian's stock in this? Is your brother double dealing?"

Gothier shrugged. "Could be. If Sithian thinks Isadorr is going to try and kill me, he is going to jump on that wagon. If I die here, outcast or not, Isadorr would rally all of Seaduens against you. He may have tried to do such a thing, or at least make Sithian think he was, in order to fuel the people's hatred of Blackhaven."

"There is by far too much deceit going on around here," Tlonna grumbled. "You say your brother could be trying to send you a message in good faith, or trying to kill you to feed the war frenzy. Which is more likely? I know which I would figure."

"*Aiya*," Gothier nodded at her, "but I know which one is more likely. Isadorr may be cold-hearted and cruel, but he is my brother. He is not completely bereft of goodness, either. He was sending me a message, I would stake my life on it."

"I think you already have," Tlonna stated wryly.

"True enough. But there is also this. Isadorr would have received word that you had Count Iranyo assassinated, so he would be reasonably sure that someone would have found out about Lavandyra. She was his pet for a long time, so she must know something. Else why was she here? Why attach herself to Aladorn the Wiat so quickly when Aidyn, by far the more sought after brother, is just as available?"

"Aidyn said she found Aladorn's body more to her liking. He said she said he was too thin," Tlonna pointed out.

Gothier shook his head. "Aladorn has just been made Second Commander, yes?"

The queen nodded.

"Who better to attach a leech to than one of the highest military officers in the most powerful kingdom? Pillow talk, Tlonna, is one of war's best friends."

"Aladorn would never...he knows how to be discreet."

Gothier gave her a pitying look. "My queen...my sister...do you retain all your mental facilities during sex?"

Tlonna shook her head. "But I do not shout out all my secrets either. Aladorn has led a life of discretion, a life of hiding. He would never betray us, even in such an innocent way. And he never slept with her."

"Would you stake your kingdom on it?"

The words sent a shivering chill down Tlonna's spine as she looked at Gothier. "I have to go to Seaduens."

"Yes, milady, I am afraid you do."

"How can I be sure I am not heading into a trap?"

Gothier spread his hands. "On my word? I suppose you cannot be."

"Wonderful. I shall make plans. You are coming with me."

"Why? I cannot return there!"

Tlonna lifted an eyebrow at him. "Do you think I would leave you here alone, with my city? Oh no, Prince Gothier, you are coming with me."

He gave her a pained expression, but knew he had no choice.

When Tlonna told Aidyn, Miazie, and Sodo about her decision, her friends simply sighed in resignation and nodded.

"I am going with you. I am not so injured I cannot ride," Aidyn stated.

"Of course you are, but I doubt that will stop you. Miazie, Sodo...try not to kill anyone this time. Daphne is helping the new seneschal settle into her duties, and I have put a stop on all incoming bills, so you will not have to deal with that, at least. We are leaving immediately. Tomorrow morning. We will be taking a roundabout route to the College of Assassins with Aidyn's agreement," Tlonna stopped to look at her assassin. He nodded in assent. "And then we will head for the frontline. We will gather those that we can, and then head directly for Seaduens. I plan on making a stop in Kajgenia on our way in, and Florwen Hune and Narnen on our way back. Any questions?"

"Do you think it wise to take Gothier with you?" Sodo asked as he leaned forward.

"More wise than leaving him here. Anything else?"

When no one said anything further, Tlonna stood. "Then I shall prepare, and see you all tomorrow, early."

# Chapter 34

## On the Road Again

Tlonna, Aidyn, and Gothier rode out at dawn, their horses' hooves throwing up sodden chunks of earth, still wet from the previous night's rain. The sun rose to their left, slowly illuminating their path through the forest. By midday Aidyn took the lead and led them southward, veering onto a tiny, barely discernible track through the trees. A few hours later he stopped and turned in the saddle to eye Gothier with deep suspicion.

"You may not come any further."

"What?" the prince yelped.

"This is my order. If you want to survive in the next few seconds, you will obey it. You are not to move beyond this spot."

"But I-"

Aidyn cut him short with a whistle and out of the trees dropped a darkly clad figure. When the person straightened, he revealed himself to be a slender, plain-looking human swathed in *ärdyz* silk. Two hilts lifted above his shoulders, and a brace of daggers rimmed his waist, attached to his baldric.

"Master Aidyn," the assassin bowed low, his voice a reverent rumble.

"Enzo, keep watch on Prince Gothier. If he moves from here, kill him. Am I understood?"

"By the Honor of Assassins, I shall do as you command, Master." Enzo moved forward and grabbed hold of Gothier's bridle.

The prince looked alarmed, but he let go of the reins without a fight. Tlonna looked to Aidyn, who beckoned her onward. She looked back at Gothier with a shrug. He stared after her, doleful. It took the two elves another hour to reach the College of Assassins. Tlonna gaped at the stately old manor, the trees edging right up to the wall. Aidyn led her to the stables and dismounted. The dark elf stared about in confusion at the dozen or so horses already there. Baffled, they left Whäd and Takîreaes munching happily on grain and dried apples.

The assassin and the queen walked into the house and were immediately set upon by three novices. They stared up at their leader with nearly mindless devotion, sparing their queen a few quick bows and nods.

"Master Aidyn! You have returned to us so quickly! We had feared our message would not reach you!" one of them exclaimed, bowing again.

"What is going on? Why are there so many horses in the stables?" Aidyn demanded, unnerved. "Where is Moiran?"

"I am here, Aidyn. You three! Bow before your sovereign queen! Idiots!" the present master of the house said from atop the stairs.

The three novices immediately went into deep, respectful bows before Tlonna as they stammered their apologies. Tlonna moved closer to Aidyn and clutched his hand. His fingers were warm in hers.

"They are so young," she murmured as they dispersed to attend to their duties.

"I was seventeen when I joined," the dark elf told her. "It is easier to start them young. Otherwise they fight, and often break."

Tlonna nodded and they mounted the stairs, closing on Moiran. He watched them with hooded eyes.

"Master Aidyn," the man said and bowed to him. "Queen Tlonna."

"Moiran, what is going on?" Aidyn demanded immediately.

The man looked uncomfortable. "Please, let us speak in private."

The two elves followed the assassin into his office, which Aidyn told Tlonna had once been his study and observatory. Moiran sat down behind his desk with a heavy thud. Once they were seated, he pinned them with a heavy stare.

"After the battle at Alchemian, the Shitan-Kulata found themselves desperate and leaderless. Their general had been slain, the man who had replaced him died in the battle, and over two-thirds of their numbers were obliterated. Two of our brothers," Moiran looked away from Aidyn's suddenly disbelieving stare, "succumbed to the guild's pleas. They obtained oaths of obedience and secrecy from the bastards, and led them here. Aidyn, you have sixty-three new recruits sitting in the basement of your College."

Tlonna sat on Aidyn's old, creaky bed and watched him pace. It was disconcerting being in his room, seeing things from his previous life. She had been watching him for over an hour now, and felt a twinge of guilt for Gothier. She hoped he wasn't dead. Finally Aidyn let out a groan and flopped onto the bed next to her. He lay back, his booted feet still on the floor.

"What do I do, Tlonna? How can I allow the flaming *Shitan-Kulata* into my College? Gods, what do I do?"

The queen patted his thigh. "You gave them hope, a promise of honor and glory, at Alchemian. They came when you called, *you*, their greatest competition. What does that say about them? And about you?"

Aidyn muttered something darkly and sat up. "It says I am a fool, and they are desperate."

Tlonna gave him a small laugh. "I do not see that you have a choice, Aidyn. I told you something would happen."

"Yes but why? I do not want to rule anybody!"

"Oh, come. It is not so bad."

The dark elf glowered at her for a moment and then stood. "All right. Come on," he held out his hand to her.

"Where are we going?" Tlonna asked as she took it.

"To the basement."

The queen and the assassin hurried to the kitchen, and then walked down the narrow stairwell into the large basement. Crowded into the space were scores of navy blue-clad men who all stood as one when they entered. Aidyn squeezed Tlonna's hand briefly and then released it.

"I am Master Assassin Aidyn Sestuns, Master of the College of Assassins and Lord of this manor. Who is your leader?"

One man stepped forward and sketched a hasty bow. "I am Aran Connor of the Shitan-Kulata. I was a lieutenant under the command of General Damon Suutson, and then of General Haiwe Tsin. Captain Hirshono, his brother, also perished in the battle at Alchemian. I am the highest ranking officer left."

"What do you want?" Aidyn snapped and folded his arms, not at all cowed by the large human before him.

Aran too folded his arms. Tlonna refrained from shaking her head in wry amusement. *Males.*

"We used to number over two hundred, now we are sixty-three. All of our leaders are dead, everywhere we go we are jeered at, taunted, despised. We have seen the way people respect you, even love you. You stand hand-in-hand with your queen. We want that as well. We understand that the mistrust and general dislike between our two sects is not going to be erased in a few short months, perhaps not even years, but we are good fighters, good assassins, and we tire of leading soulless lives. When we were led here by two of your men, they forced us to swear oaths in your name, and in the name of your Honor of Assassins to obey and to maintain the secret of this location. We stand by those oaths. We are at your mercy, Master Aidyn."

Tlonna watched her friend's gaze take in the weary, almost desperate faces of the men before him. She watched his shoulders slump and he turned to her.

"This is it, is it not?"

"It is," she confirmed quietly and took his hand. "Aidyn...for what it is worth, I am sorry."

The dark elf nodded and tightened his grip. "I am too," he said softly. When he turned back to the gathered assassins, his face was a mask of resignation. "Here are the conditions of your acceptance into the College of Assassins. You will have to undergo the training we have all had. Be prepared, several of you will die. You will take the Three Oaths that will bind you irrevocably to the Honor of Assassins at the end of your training, and..." here Aidyn's voice faltered and he sucked in a steadying breath, "you will swear obeisance to me, immediately."

As one, the gathered men fell to their knees and bowed their heads to the floor. Aran touched his fingers to Aidyn's boots. "We swear to abide by your word, to follow every order and to live our lives in the hope of pleasing you. As we are Men, we do swear to you, Aidyn Sestuns."

They stood in a rush and waited in silence for their new master to command them. The elf's hand trembled in Tlonna's, and he pointed to the stairs behind him. "You are to report immediately to Master Moiran for training."

The assassins filed quickly past the two elves and up the stairs. When they were alone, Aidyn sank to the floor and buried his face in his hands. Tlonna went with him, concerned.

"Are you all right?" she asked him and brushed his sable hair back.

Aidyn shook his head. "No."

"Is there aught I can do?"

"I should have denied them. Then what? The prophecy would not be fulfilled and you would survive. Tlonna, what did I just do?"

"You did what you had to. I might survive anyway. Just because you might not have said the words, they would have sworn allegiance to you anyway, in their minds and hearts. So far we have not really understood the prophecy, even though we thought we did. Have a little faith."

"In what?"

"Yourself, me...all of us. We are not so helpless, after all."

"No, but we still seem to be losing a lot."

Tlonna chuckled humorlessly. "Well, at least we are still around to complain about it. Now come, if we stay down here much longer people will begin to speculate."

"They do that already."

Again Tlonna laughed darkly and kissed him. "For good reason."

They strode back into the kitchen to find a fiery-haired chef shouting at no one in particular. Aidyn immediately went to the side of the flustered dwarf and put a hand on his shoulder.

"Master Aidyn!" the dwarf bellowed so loud it made Tlonna jump. "Seventy-eight people in residence! Seventy-eight! Where are these people supposed to sleep? How am I supposed to feed them all? Seventy-eight! There haven't been that many assassins in the Blackhaven College ever! Perhaps in the all the Colleges in Nymyños, but certainly not in one!"

The dark elf chuckled faintly and undid the purse on his belt. He handed it over to the dwarf. "I know, Ruben. I will take care of it. For now, this should help."

"But...Master Aidyn how will you eat if you have no geld?" the dwarf asked, his eyes wide in his ruddy face.

"This," Aidyn held a hand out to Tlonna, "is Queen Tlonna, Ruben. She will pay my way."

"I will?"

"You will," the assassin told her blandly. He turned back to the chef. "Divide that between yourself and Talor to take care of the newcomers."

"By your command, Master Aidyn. Will you stay for dinner, then?"

"Alas, I cannot. But..." the elf held up a hand to forestall the protestations about to burst forth from the dwarf, "we will take some to go."

"Oh, oh!" the chef bounced and began shoving various vittles into a monstrous bag. He rattled out what each was as he shoved it into the rucksack, completely baffling the elves. A few minutes later Aidyn hoisted the bulging bag over his shoulder and led Tlonna out of the kitchen. Moiran met them just outside the manor.

"You are leaving?" the assassin asked without preamble.

"We were merely making a stop, Moiran. We cannot stay," Aidyn said. "You know how to train new recruits. These men are just that. I have extracted oaths that bind them completely. Are you worried?"

"By the spirits, yes! I cannot do this Aidyn!"

"Yes, you can. I will have additional funds sent to you as soon as possible. I gave Ruben a substantial sum to split between him and Talor. The novices' personal needs are already being seen to. The rest is up to you. Train them well."

Moiran huffed out a breath and nodded. "As you command, Aidyn, like always. Queen Tlonna, it was an honor to meet you at last."

"The same, Master Moiran."

With a shake of his head, Aidyn led Tlonna to the overcrowded stables and away from the College of Assassins. When they were some distance away the queen halted Takîreaes and waited for Aidyn to do so as well.

"What is it?" the dark elf asked, his hand halfway to his longblade hilt.

Tlonna studied him in silence for a long while, which caused him to shift uncomfortably in his saddle. Finally, she looked away. "Aidyn, I know the strain I have put you under. I just want you to know that, whatever happens, I will always love you, though I should not. There are few people in this world that would so unceasingly stand by a person such as myself. You are truly an incredible person. I understand if you ever wish to leave."

The assassin lifted an eyebrow at her. With a click of his tongue, he set Whäd to moving again, his head shaking.

They reached Gothier a while later and found him sitting against a tree trunk, his horse hobbled off to the side. The assassin Enzo was leaning against a tree across the track, idly cleaning a dagger. When the two elves came into view, Enzo snapped to attention, the blade sheathed with a quicksilver move that had Tlonna unnerved.

"Get up," Aidyn told Gothier, who obeyed slowly.

"Where have you two been all day?" the prince asked as he wiped debris from his pants.

"Swearing in the remnants of the Shitan-Kulata to the College of Assassins. Come on, we can reach Sha Bridge by nightfall."

Tlonna sighed softly as she shifted in her saddle. Enzo bowed low to Aidyn as the dark elf turned Whäd around in the direction of Obsidian Way.

"Well done, Enzo. Ah...give this to Moiran when you return to the manor," Aidyn said and handed a sealed letter to the other assassin. "I know he would not accept it from my hand."

"As you command, Master Aidyn. Travel swiftly."

"Courage to you, Enzo."

The three elves rode carefully through the forest until they emerged onto Obsidian Way. Then they let the horses have their heads and gallop as long as they cared to. It took the rest of the day to reach Sha Bridge, and when Aidyn slowed to dismount, Tlonna stopped him.

"Do you need to rest?" she asked her companions, who both shook their heads. "Then I say let us ride on as long as we can. I want to be with my husband and my soldiers as soon as possible."

"I agree," Aidyn said and led Whäd into a ground-eating trot over the bridge.

They traveled well into the night and stopped just after midnight to set up a swift camp. Aidyn made a light dinner while Tlonna and Gothier set up the tents, all in silence. Once they were seated and eating, the queen turned to her assassin.

"What did you give Enzo?"

The dark elf was silent for a time, debating whether or not to tell her. Finally he shrugged a shoulder and looked into the fire. "It was instructions to be followed upon my death. I named a new Master of the College, and for all the remaining geld left in my coffers after my death duties to be given to him. I meant to give it to Moiran, but he was rattled enough as it was."

"Do you believe this war so hopeless?" Tlonna asked quietly.

Aidyn shrugged again and looked at her. "It is always good to be prepared. Driszn had named me several years before his death. We are assassins, and, excepting a few, our life spans are typically rather short."

"Who did you name? Moiran?"

The dark elf snorted. "Hardly. Moiran is well beyond his prime, and is more used to sitting behind a desk than fighting anymore. No, I would have named Jidair, but being as how I killed him...I named a Duani elf called Thanat. He was trained by Furntil himself, according to his records."

"You can name someone from another province?" Tlonna asked in astonishment.

Aidyn slanted her a look. "I thought you knew."

"Knew what?"

"I am Master Assassin of the College of Assassins. The *entire* College of Assassins, which includes the Blackhaven College, Seaduens, Flousen Dua, Arseninis, and Narnen. Each College has a Master: Moiran, Thanat, Senkuh, Ove, and until recently, Jidair. Two of them are elves, and Senkuh is the only woman."

"And you preside over them all? I have never heard you mention any of these people," Tlonna said, thunderstruck.

Aidyn shrugged with glance at the interested Gothier. "It is not something I like to talk about. I get missives from each Master at the end of every month, along with my cut of their earnings, which is usually only a few dozen geld, and that is the extent of our communication. The only time I ever visit them is if a Master dies and I have to name a new one."

"Did you know it was Jidair when you attacked him?" Gothier asked, speaking for the first time in many hours.

"Yes. He knew it was I, too, before he dragged me off the bell tower. He betrayed me, and the College. I do not know why. All his correspondence was fairly satisfactory."

"I am sorry," Tlonna said gently and linked fingers with him.

"Betrayal always stings, but there is one in every faction," the assassin said mildly.

"A cynical view, dark elf," Gothier muttered.

Aidyn pinned him with a stare. "Yet you sit here, a prince of Seaduens, sitting with the assassin and the queen of Blackhaven."

"Point well made," Gothier chuckled darkly.

"Did you know Nydis, then?" Tlonna queried suddenly.

"Who?" Aidyn asked with a frown.

"Nydis Karnahan, the elf you ran down in Blackhaven when we flushed out that group of infiltrators that Arganor had let into the city."

"Ah, no, I did not. He may have been a College assassin, I do not know all of them, but I doubt it. He was too easily downed."

"You shot him in the knee," Tlonna muttered.

"You think we were not shot during our training? Tlonna, arrow wounds are among the least of our training."

"I knew him," Gothier said into the sudden, strained silence. "He was my father's favorite assassin. I know he was not of the College. He was a free-lance killer until Father brought him off the street and set him up in the castle itself."

"You sound bitter," Aidyn remarked dryly.

Gothier shrugged. "He treated the murderer like another son."

"Well then, it should please you that we cut off his head," the dark elf told the prince.

Gothier stared at him in utter silence.

The trio made the battlefront two days later and made their way directly to the command tent. Inside were Yayènia, Losolin, Erandur, and Furntil Eldrout. Tlonna, Aidyn, and Gothier marched inside without announcing themselves and caught the four by surprise. Aidyn automatically went to his knees before Furntil, his head bowed in reverence.

"Stand, my son," the ancient elf murmured in his deep voice and placed one slender, pale hand on the other's shoulder.

"My Lord Furntil," Aidyn said breathlessly when he stood, still amazed that his idol stood before him, though this was not the first time they'd met.

"Master Aidyn. I heard of your daring actions to defend both a seneschal and your queen. Truly, I am in awe."

Tlonna gently pushed the slack-jawed assassin out of the way and smiled at her fellow monarch. "King Furntil, a joy it is to meet you at last."

"Ah, the Everwood Queen, my humblest respects," the first assassin said, bowing from his waist, his left hand sweeping gracefully across his chest.

"Y-you are...Furntil Eldrout?" Gothier stammered, his face bloodless.

"At your service, young one. Whom do I have the pleasure of meeting?"

"Pleasure is a dubious word, my lord. This is Gothier Lostug," Yayènia butted in before anyone else could speak.

"Ahh..." Furntil breathed, a faint smile on his narrow face. "Yes, I had heard one of Malihk's descendants had joined our cause."

"Malihk?" Losolin asked, frowning.

"My grandfather," Gothier supplied and eyed Furntil with unease. "He died in the middle of the Sixth Age."

"Yes, I remember. Slain by Amram himself in a bloody battle for the forest of Pyúrhe," Furntil mused, rubbing his chin as he looked back upon history even the eldest in the tent, other than him, had not been alive to see.

"Our families have been killing each other for over three millennia," Yayènia growled at Gothier. "And it should stay that way."

"Oh, child, calm your fiery heart. Bloodshed is never the only answer."

The High Commander sucked in a deep breath and visibly calmed herself. "Still, my lord, his family is a nuisance."

"He is of your family, Yayènia, and I do not consider you a nuisance," Furntil blithely replied with a smile at her wide-eyed look.

Erandur finally spoke up and shook his head at his father. "It is called Purheae, now, Father. Remember, none of us were around before the late Seventh Age."

"I do not forget, Eran, but I am old and I prefer the ancient names. They bring me peace."

The Duani prince shook his head again and reclaimed his seat. Losolin moved past Furntil and took Tlonna in his arms. "How are you? Have you come to stay?"

The Magin embraced her husband, who eyed the younger assassin over her head, and then pulled away. "No. I have another favor to ask of you, but I would rather wait until everyone is here. Please, tell me what has transpired."

Yayènia slumped into her chair and sighed heavily. "Since Isadorr pulled his troops back into Seaduens the humans have been less inclined to mount full-scale attacks on us, but still they are persistent. General Orlando drives them hard. It is as though he gone mad, Tlonna. He heads the charge each time, retreats last, and comes back the next day howling like a man already damned."

"What of Sithian?"

"No sign of him," Losolin muttered as he turned back to the table. "We have nearly obliterated their Magin ranks, and without his presence the remaining ones are not quite as willing to throw their lives away."

They continued to discuss the goings-on of the battle for quite some time before any of the others returned from their duties on the battlefield. Ghealan and Suneelo were the first to enter, swiftly followed by Aladorn, who gripped his brother's shoulder in a loving way. Once all the greetings were done with, Tlonna gestured for everyone to take a seat. They did so with some reluctance, knowing their queen and friend too well to be assured by her calm demeanor.

"As I am sure you all suspect, I am not staying. In fact, I hope to be on my way tomorrow. I am to Seaduens. Now, before you all leap down my throat, let me explain. There was an assassination attempt on me a few days ago, which was thwarted by Aidyn. The assassin's name was Jidair, who happened to be the Master of the Seaduens College, and also Isadorr's royal assassin. Gothier here does not believe the attempt was the true purpose of Jidair's presence in Blackhaven. He was tattooed with symbols that gave the message to warn me that Seaduens is at the mercy of Zaedic, and that Narnen and Talenias are in the same situation, or are soon to be. Once Zaedic has seized control of Seaduens it will turn everything it has toward Blackhaven."

"And we are to believe this?" Ghealan asked blandly, his light green gaze on Gothier with a suspicious glare.

Tlonna ignored the question. "In Kajgenia, Aidyn questioned the Eseirik who murdered Demetrius, and was told that the elven race was down to one kingdom. It is reasonable they did not realize the extent of Flousen Dua's survival, as we all did not, and no other place is more inhabited than Seaduens and Blackhaven. Due to several similar signs of Seaduens' duress, I feel the necessity to go there myself and discover the truth. I plan on traveling through Kajgenia to get

Tristan's knowledge of the place, and of Talenias's situation. Then, once in Seaduens I want to go directly to Amaden to speak with Isadorr. On our return I will pass through Florwen Hune to speak with Barukh, and Narnen to see Erdwyf. I do not plan on being gone for more than two or three weeks.

"I would ask that Yayènia, Suneelo, and Aladorn accompany me, along with Losolin and Aidyn. I realize that once again I ask too much, but truly, I fear the trip to Seaduens and I want my protectors around me," Tlonna explained, not having to feign her unease at traveling to the violent kingdom. "Ghealan, I would love to have you along as well-"

The large elf stopped her with a lifted hand. "Do not think on it, Tlonna. I meant to see this battle through, and I shall. Leaving would only make it harder to return, especially if you are to see Erdwyf. I am not sure I am strong enough for another farewell."

"Thank you," the queen said, nearly choking on her appreciation.

Yayènia sighed and smacked her hand onto her husband's shoulder. "I do not like the idea of leaving my troops again, but I dislike the idea of you traveling through Seaduens even more. We go."

"I too shall go with you. Someone has to protect my reckless little brother, eh?" Aladorn chuckled and shook Aidyn.

Furntil leaned forward. "Tlonna, do not take too much upon your slender shoulders. This is not just your battle. This is a battle for all our freedom, for justice, and coexistence. Truly, I feel as though I started this war when I crept into King Brandon's room and slew him, and I am glad to be here for the end. Please, go with the assurance that your efforts will be upheld by me, and my people as well as yours."

Tlonna had to swallow before nodding her gratitude, unable to speak. The others fell to planning the basic defenses during their absence, and she sat back, feeling hollow inside. Aidyn reached over and squeezed her hand in a gentle reassurance. She managed a small smile of appreciation.

The next day found the seven elves riding out of the camp with no fanfare just before dawn. They took the Corridor of Astinus for a short while and then swung east into the rolling hills of the central Liberated Lands. A day later they rode into the calm Forest of Ullor, passing very near to the place Tlonna had woken several years ago with no knowledge of who she was. They made good time and reached Kajgenia a mere three days after leaving the camp, and Derid a day after swinging around Kajgen Lake and turning onto King's Road, the most heavily used road in all of Nymyños. They rode into the capital city at dusk and immediately were granted entrance to the castle. Tristan met them in the foyer wearing his new crown with a little more confidence than last they had seen him.

He embraced all of the warmly, but for Gothier, who he openly glared at. "What brings you to Kajgenia? Certainly not more ill news," the young king said, his gray eyes wide with worry.

"No, not news, really. We are simply passing through on our way to Seaduens. Please, I know it is late, but may we speak with you?" Tlonna asked as she adjusted his black and teal coat in a motherly way.

"Of course, follow me."

Soon, the seven elves and one human were ensconced in a plush sitting room, where they were promptly served ciders, teas, and all manner of hors d'oeuvres. Tlonna sat back in an overstuffed chair and began her tale of Jidair, the Eseirik's message, at which Tristan scowled dangerously at Gothier, and finished with her desire to go to Seaduens.

"I see," was all he said for a while.

When the silence grew uncomfortable, Tristan leaned forward, his elbows braced on his knees. Tlonna and all her companions could not help but see his late father in the pose. When he spoke it was with a grave tone that belied his two decades of life.

"Both Tyular and I have been ruling as co-regents of Talenias, but even so we are losing our control over there. We are aware that a good many Talenians are swelling the ranks of Sithian's horde, and that nearly all of them are fanatics devoted to Athelias or Athelan. The people left are frightened, desperate, and terribly unorganized. Nothing we do seems to help. We have sent our own soldiers in to try and restore order, but they are cursed at by confused fathers and denounced by frightened mothers. Only last week Tyular actually went himself and spoke to the Talenians. They listened and blessed him for delivering them from the Embinas but they demand a new ruler, a single ruler, not two kings from other provinces. We do not know what to do."

"What of the Cleicks? Has their presence been a bolster to the fright?" Losolin asked.

Tristan shook his head. "They have actually mostly disappeared. Tyular and I suspect they are fighting your troops. It would make more sense for them to be there than anywhere else."

"I saw some of them during a few skirmishes," Yayènia confirmed. "Nasty buggers the lot of them."

Tristan nodded. "Aye, as for Seaduens, I do not know much. The sightings among the border have certainly lessened, that's for sure. There hasn't been an attack in weeks, and it used to be that there were Seadueni gangs molesting Kajgenians and Arseninisians every other day."

Everyone looked at Gothier, who blanched. "I offer no excuse for my people's actions."

"Good, because there are none," Yayènia spat at him.

"If you honestly believe that speaking with Isadorr will accomplish anything, then I say it's worth a try, but I have found that one cannot hold to hope. Perhaps if you do solve anything I will be able to pull my troops away from the border and send them to aid you," Tristan said, and then sent Gothier a suspicious glance. "Unless of course this is all an elaborate plan in order to get me to do exactly that. It would leave Kajgenia naked to attack from behind."

Gothier shook his head. "As far as I know, Isadorr wants nothing to do with Kajgenia, or any other province than Seaduens."

"How comforting," the king replied monotonously.

"I do not deceive you, King Tristan. Truly, I do not."

"Yes, well, unfortunately I do not believe you."

Aidyn smiled at his friend with pride. Tlonna shook her head in sadness at the bleakness of the young man's voice. Tristan gently slapped his hands to the arms of his chair and stood.

"We shall see what this venture gains you. Can I assist you in any other way?"

Tlonna and her entourage stood. "Yes, you can rest, Tristan. I can see the weariness in your eyes, even if you do not acknowledge it. We will depart in the morning and send word of our success or failure, whichever it may be."

The king nodded wordlessly, and after sharing a brief embrace with Aidyn, left them in the hands of his servants.

# Chapter 35
## Seaduens

The seven elves rode their horses over the wide stone bridge that spanned the Ivory River, which separated Seaduens from the rest of Nymyños, a day and a half later. Two towers flanked the bridge with archers lined up between the tall crenellations with drawn bows. Only Gothier's presence saved them from being showered with arrows the moment they stepped off the bridge. An officer came down to meet them with a furious glower on his angled face.

"Prince Gothier, you lead our enemies to the heart of our kingdom?" he demanded loudly and grabbed the elf's reins.

"Remove your hand, Captain, or else lose it," Gothier replied coldly, his hand going to the sword at his belt.

The soldier did as he was told, but did not move from their path. "What is your purpose here then?"

"Am I not allowed to move about freely of my own kingdom? Get out of the way."

"Your brother, King Isadorr has executed your mother for treason, and named you a deserter. This is no longer your kingdom."

Behind her, Tlonna heard Yayènia ardently swear. Suddenly she was surrounded by Suneelo, Aladorn, Losolin, and Aidyn, all holding up a shield or arm to block her from incoming arrows as Yayènia rode to the front of the group.

"You treat your prince as though he were nothing? You are scum! Get out of the way or die for your trouble!" she shouted as she drew a katan and shoved it in the elf's face with little subtlety.

Gothier noticed that the warrior had placed herself directly beside him, which meant that the archers could not shoot her without risking the possibility of hitting him. He mentally chuckled at it. The captain swallowed as Yayènia's sword nicked his throat hard enough to draw a pinprick of blood. With a slight bow, he moved aside to let them pass.

Once they were safely out of range of the bows, Gothier looked at her. "Well done."

"Shut it," she snapped and rode back to her position behind Tlonna.

Near nightfall, the group saw a faint glow rising from the ground nearly a mile from their position. Tlonna rode up to Gothier and pointed at it.

"It is the memorial to the elves that fell during the War of Monotheism. They are all buried there. At least, all who were able to be recovered."

"May we go see it?" she asked, curious.

"It is a public sight, though there are some restrictions to gain access. First, you must be an elf."

"No problem there," Tlonna replied, looking back at her companions who stared at her with little to no expression.

"Second, you have to be barefoot."

"Why?"

Gothier shrugged. "The priests who attend it say that only through the touch of the naked flesh can you experience the true horror of the war. I have walked it a few times, and all I ever felt were stones digging into my soles."

"Well, we shall see if any of us feel anything different," Tlonna told him and urged Takîreaes onward toward the site.

Not long after, the seven were dismounting before a gigantic ring of upright stones, the entrance marked by three stones that formed a large doorway. A white-robed priest came to greet them and bowed low.

"Welcome to Nosferâth, please remove your footwear and weapons. This place is sacred, and has already seen too much blood."

As they complied, the priest gathered the items and placed them neatly in a cubby. He seemed nearly traumatized by the amount of weapons each of them carried, but said nothing about it. His fingers shook horribly when Aidyn finally managed to remove every dagger, knife, and hidden blade about his person and had to hand them to the priest with both hands. Yayènia stifled a giggle. When they made certain their affects were securely under lock and key, they followed the still-trembling priest through the archway and into the ring of stones. Tlonna gasped when she realized each behemoth was carved with a list of names. Thousands of names.

The priest stopped them just inside the doorway and licked his lips. "The War of Monotheism, also called the War of the One God, was one of the bloodiest conflicts in history, including that of Serenyi. Over a million total died, Elf, Man, and Dwarf. Each race gave their all to protect that which they loved most, their freedom. The war was started by a council of Men who claimed to have been visited by Gagu, Lord of Plant-life and humans. They wrote strict decrees of what they claimed Gagu had told them, and brutally enforced them. They were not kind decrees. They demanded sacrifice of offspring, the burning of so-called heretics, pagans, and heathens, and the total submission of all, to these few Men.

"They incited a fiery rage in the hearts of thousands, who blindly followed their words in the hope of finding the answer to life, and death. These poor mislead souls were viciously manipulated by the Gaguín, those Men who claimed to have been god-touched. For over a millennium the war raged across the face of Nymyños, obliterating ancient kingdoms, places of worship, and wiping out entire cultures. In each of their turn at rule, every monarch did their best to defend their homeland from the ravages of these deluded people who killed in the name of their god. Finally, when all seemed lost, the armies of Nymyños rallied together, and with the aid of the Monotheists who truly loved their god, and knew the actions of their fellows to be wrong, turned back the tide of murdering savages.

"In that final battle, glorious and bloody, nearly half of all the casualties of the war fell. Over thirty thousand elves died, seventeen thousand dwarves, and four hundred and fifty thousand humans fell on that single day and night. In the end, when the dead had been counted and the living looked about in disbelief at their survival, no one could truly remember why such a terrible thing had happened, and at such a cost. It had been so long that none quite knew who the Gaguín were, or why the enemy had screamed 'in the name of God!' as they died. In the decades that followed, Monotheists would be found hiding in secluded places around Nymyños, and would be swiftly eliminated. Today those that remain are quite lucky, though the descendents of those who turned to fight their own in a last desperate act to redeem their religion are accepted throughout many of the kingdoms."

The priest walked over to a carven stone and placed an open hand upon it, bowing his head. "It was a tragedy that could have been avoided had one faction simply accepted the difference of the others. It is a tragedy that we are still fighting this war, though we put a different name to the values. Walk among the stones now, and *remember.*"

Humbled and saddened, the seven elves moved about the monument in complete silence, the two couples holding hands with their spouse while the others wandered in forlorn silence. Tlonna felt a faint warmth emanating from the stones that could not have been residue from the day, as it seemed to pulse beneath her feet. She clutched Losolin's hand and opened her mind to the spirits that whispered. Jair was strangely subdued, his presence more akin to someone looking over her shoulder than an angry sentience inside of her. The spirits hummed a lament, softly filling her mind with all they felt. Tears ran swiftly down her face as she walked with Losolin.

Aidyn stood before a stone and scanned the list of names, each of them burning into his memory. He knew he would never forget them. And then he saw it. Swallowing, he beckoned to his brother who was reading the stone next to him.

"What?" Aladorn whispered.

"Look," Aidyn said, pointing to a name near the top of the list.

*Aisund Sestuns.*

"He was Father's father," Aladorn told him.

"I never knew."

"Aye, he was slain not long after Aolan's birth. Father fought in the War too, did you know? So did I."

"You did?"

Aladorn nodded shortly. "When I enlisted in the Warriors of the Shadow, we fought for about a year in western Nymyños. It was before Ghealan joined. After that, the fighting went into a sort of simmer and we felt we were no longer needed. Apparently we were wrong."

Aidyn shook his head, still staring at his grandfather's name, carved into a stone in Seaduens. "I remember hearing of the final battle, but I was young and rich and did not really care. I was a fool."

"As you said, you were young. I was nearly three hundred by then, and had experienced the bloodlust of war. I was in Arseninis at that time, a lieutenant in the army. Why I was not sent out to fight, I will never know. I was grateful at the time. I recall the endless screaming of mourners, the tolling of bells announcing the thousands lost from Arseninis alone. It was terrible," Aladorn breathed and lifted a finger to run it over his grandfather's name.

The brothers fell silent then as they stared at the name Aisund Sestuns.

After a long while, the seven turned to the priest, ready to leave. The elf bowed to them again.

"I know who you are, all of you," he said softly. "Warriors, assassin, rulers the lot of you. Prince Gothier, I hope you know what you are doing. This kingdom has no more need of bloodshed. If you hope to bring peace to your people by leading Blackhaven's heart to your brother, then I commend you for your courage, and know that my hopes ride with you."

"Thank you," the deposed prince murmured.

"Go now, with the memory of those fallen, and the hope of those still alive," the priest intoned, and unlocked their items.

A day later, when the seven felt sufficiently distant from the gravesite to talk, Suneelo rolled his shoulders and looked at his brother. "When you were here with the White Hands, did you feel a thickness upon the air?"

Everyone looked at the captain, relieved that someone had finally mentioned the discomfiting feeling. Losolin nodded with a glance at Gothier who looked confused.

"*Aiya*, it is strongest in Amaden. It comes from unhappiness."

Yayènia sent him a scornful look. "Unhappiness?"

"Yes. The elves here, many unbeknownst to themselves, are miserable. What little earth magic our race retains anymore is tainted, unable to truly purify the earth as it does in Blackhaven because it is dimmed by misery."

"It certainly feels unhappy," Aidyn muttered, shifting uncomfortably. "It makes me want to kill someone, which makes me feel guilty after seeing the memorial. I do not like feeling guilty."

"You always want to kill someone," Tlonna remarked dryly, which elicited soft chuckles from everyone else, even Gothier.

The assassin smirked and glanced at his brother who grinned back. "I just do it for the geld."

Again everyone laughed and the air around them seemed to brighten. Gothier's look of confusion melted into wonder.

"I never realized it before, but after spending so much time in Blackhaven, I do feel it! Is it truly brought on by unhappiness?"

Losolin nodded. "I remember not liking it the first time I was here, and even then, when I did not know who I was, what I was missing," he reached for Tlonna's hand, "it saddened me. I looked it up in the library a few years ago. There is a book that details the sort of earth magic we used to have, and the outcome of it. Blackhaven, and I would assume Flousen Dua, have a pure atmosphere to them because the elves within strive to be peaceful and caring. The book said that only through the absolute despair of a large number of elves could the natural purifications of the air be polluted, and that it had happened in Purheae during the Council War."

"Fascinating," Suneelo commented, edging closer to his brother. "Did it explain why we have lost so much of our ability?"

Losolin dove into the explanation, talking about the transitioning of the world from a majority of elf and dwarf to human, the advancement of technology, and so on while the others in the group looked on with resigned amusement. Tlonna released Losolin's hand and urged Takîreaes next to Yayènia, who was staring off into the distance. She had been withdrawn since the memorial, and her sister thought she knew why.

"Nia, may I ask you something?"

"Of course."

Tlonna took a moment to collect her thoughts and then said quietly, "Did Losolin tell you about the mind-trap?"

"Yes."

"And did he tell you what we were shown?"

"Somewhat. He said there had been an image of Ghealan, Suneelo, and I from long ago, and another of you and Aidyn on your night together."

Tlonna involuntarily glanced at Aidyn who rode a few feet to her left. He must have felt her eyes on him for he met her stare with a curious one of his own. She quickly turned back to Yayènia.

"The first one was of...it was you, Lan and Suneelo butchering a camp of Monotheists on Constancias's order."

Yayènia's jaw tightened, but other than that she did not react to the admission. "Yes, that happened. It was less than a year after my ascension to the post of High Commander."

"What precipitated it?" Tlonna ventured nervously.

She expected an explosion of anger, but instead she got the Ice Face. "A group of them had been terrorizing a small village, that which eventually became Hastert. We were sent out to eliminate them. There happened to be two groups in the area, one was malignant, the other benign. We had no information other than that there was a group of Monotheists in the area. We eliminated the wrong one."

"Yayènia..." Tlonna said softly and reached for her sister's hand.

"It was a long time ago," the warrior said shortly and rode off a bit to be by herself.

The queen slumped in her saddle, miserable. A warm hand touched hers and she looked up into Losolin's concerned face. For some reason she had expected Aidyn's, but the assassin was still off to her side, stoically looking forward. Tlonna gripped her husband's hand and sniffed. She told him what Yayènia had said, and when she fell silent, Losolin nodded.

"I know. I asked Suneelo. He said it is the only thing he has done since joining the Blackhaven Militia that has caused him nightmares and a steady stream of guilt."

"What a horrible thing to have on your conscience," the female whispered.

"But they weather it like everything else, by accepting the fact that nearly everything they have done has been in the service of goodness."

Tlonna nodded silently, and drew strength from Losolin's hand in hers.

Amaden was the capital of Seaduens, situated half in the White Forest, half in the rugged terrain of the Silarnim Highlands. The city sat in a bowl, ringed on one side by sheer cliffs and the thick, tangled White Forest on the other. All along the natural wall were towers, upon which stood deadly archers accompanied by snapping green and gold pennants sporting the White River of Seaduens. When they neared the two towers that flanked the road into the city, Tlonna looked to Gothier, who nodded.

Behind them, Yayènia and Aladorn unrolled the Tree of Blackhaven and the Ewôsdírn Sun and Star and set the butts of the standards in their stirrups. Aidyn and Suneelo rode forward to flank Tlonna and Losolin, acting as shields. Gothier took the lead and urged his horse into an easy trot.

They moved around the towers, which sat up against a foreboding cliff face, the road hewn right through it. Rounding the natural wall, Tlonna received her first view of the oldest surviving elven kingdom. The road stretched on to eventually cross a small river and wind up another cliff, atop which sat Seaduens Castle. From afar it glimmered white in the sunlight, looking more like a dense cloud than a building. On either side of the road was the city. On the western side, to her left, were sprawling open-air houses, markets, and other buildings, spaced widely apart on the grassy plain sheltered by the monstrous jutting earth that surrounded it. On the right-hand side crept the forest, sheltering smaller homesteads and businesses, though they too were spread out. Considering its geographical placement, Tlonna understood why the city had never been under siege.

Few people wandered the street, elves all, their faces more narrow and feline than the Blackhavenites'. Their light-colored eyes watched them pass with a curiosity bordering on oppressed anger. Tlonna was suddenly very glad she had insisted on bringing her companions. Gothier rode in front of her, his back rigid and his head held high in defiance of his brother's decree of desertion. Once they were beyond the bridge that crossed over the narrow river, the homes became very large and ornately carved. Nearly all of them were made from block-cut white marble, though the striations differed greatly from house to house.

Gothier did not falter as he led the way up the narrowing road. The seven began the ascent up the hill, staying in the center of the road as it twisted and turned up the face of the unforgiving rock. When they at last stood upon the top, just inside the towers flanking the entrance, Gothier's shoulders lost some of their stiffness. He turned to them.

"After we are rid of the horses, we will find my brother. He is sure to be in his solarium on such a fine day."

Tlonna nodded and followed him to the castle steps, where they dismounted and handed their horses over to liveried hostlers. Gothier took a deep, steadying breath and walked inside his ancestral home. Immediately he and his six companions were blocked by guards.

"You are not granted access, not with these people, Prince Gothier," one of the guards growled, his spear shoved forward in a threatening gesture.

"Then you will have to go and bring my brother here."

The fear on the guard's face told them all what that meant. Gothier smiled humorlessly.

"So, risk the wrath of your king by fetching him from his duties, or allow us to go ourselves to find him, leaving you without too much risk for it."

The guard glanced at his companion, and then moved aside with a huff. "On your head be it, then, Prince."

"Indeed," Gothier muttered and beckoned to the six to follow.

Gothier shoved the blocking guard out of the way and opened the door to the castle's solarium without announcing himself. They found Isadorr inside the sunlit room as expected, enjoying the company of two females who did not appear to be native Seadueni. He lay slouched in a large chair, his long legs stretched out before him. He languidly rolled his head over to his brother. His eyes widened marginally when he took in the six elves in the doorway. With a hand, Isadorr gently pushed the female between his legs away and retied his breeches. When he stood, Tlonna saw that the mantle of kingship rested heavily on his shoulders, despite his indolence.

"Gothier, you are full of surprises," the king said softly. "Do you plan to depose me?"

"I met Jidair in Blackhaven," was the prince's reply.

"Did you? How fortunate."

"Yes. He is dead."

Isadorr's amber eyes flicked to Tlonna, and then Aidyn. "I am not surprised. Leave us," he said to the females, who knelt behind and in front of the chair.

They obliged silently and scampered out of the room in a flutter of silks.

The king waved vaguely at the chairs around the solarium and then reclaimed his seat. Tlonna, Losolin, and Gothier sat, the four others remained standing to take up positions behind the king and queen, their arms folded and their feet planted. Isadorr eyed them mildly.

"I would think that my life is the one in jeopardy at the moment," he told them.

"Never trust a Seadueni," Yayènia hissed at him.

"Same to you," the king replied. "So, what now?"

Tlonna glanced at Gothier. "I understand you have withdrawn your troops from the battle?"

"Yes. I do not fight alongside men in order to advance their plans."

"Is not their goal also yours? To eradicate Blackhaven once and for all?" Losolin demanded, much less diplomatic than his wife.

Isadorr shook his head slightly, his eyes closing for a brief moment. "That was my father's goal, yes. Mine is less...vindictive."

"What is it, then?" Gothier asked, his voice thick with confusion. "You claim not to want total annihilation of Blackhaven, yet you sent your best assassin after its leader?"

Isadorr smiled. "I never said my dislike of Blackhaven was gone. I sent Jidair with the expectation that he would die, but I needed someone who I could count on to at least infiltrate the castle itself."

"Why?" Tlonna said shortly. "Why not just send a letter?"

"Would you have trusted it? By inking an encoded message on the body of my very best assassin I guaranteed that my dear brother would be the only who could decipher it. If you came, then I would know that you have at least an inkling of the honor and integrity everyone claims you do, and also that Gothier has at least managed not to make a complete ass of himself. Also, by having only one person in your entire bloody kingdom able to read the message, I guaranteed that it could not be read by someone it was not intended for."

Gothier shifted in his seat. "Isadorr, you hired a man to kidnap the seneschal of the castle, a dryad called Narda. She was brutally murdered, and the man who did it was from Zaedic. What is Sithian's stock in this?"

"I had heard about that, yes. She was not supposed to die. I have no quarrel with dryads. I told Sithian that I intended to have you assassinated, so I needed to find out your daily routines. I convinced him that with your death inside the walls of Blackhaven, I could incite a rage in all my people and they would willingly throw themselves into the war. Your son may be a ruthless tyrant, but he is not very smart," Isadorr said to Tlonna.

"He is only a child."

"And a murdering brute."

"On that we agree," Yayènia muttered.

Isadorr appraised her a moment before continuing. "Sithian agreed to pay the fee for hiring a kidnapper readily enough, and after that it was a simple exercise in patience. When I had heard that the dryad had been murdered and the kidnapper publicly executed," he pinned his gaze on Aidyn, "I feared all was lost. But then I received a missive detailing the goings-on of the castle, Gothier's routine, and all out-of-ordinary guests. It was simple enough from there. Jidair was to penetrate the castle, locate Tlonna, and make a big enough ruckus that he was sure to be at least captured. At that point I held it on faith that Gothier would find out about it and insist on seeing him. Hence the message was relayed and this meeting a possibility."

"Why? What do you want from me?" Tlonna asked, dumbfounded.

Isadorr's eyes flashed in the sunlight and she caught the first glimpse of true fear in his gaze. "Midian Rahlan had a hold over my father, what it was, I cannot know. What I do know is that when he died and your thrice-damned son took over his rule, there was an occupational presence already here."

"I saw no army," Losolin interrupted.

"You would not, for it is not an army of men. Darkwights have taken over the forest and have been feeding on my people for years."

"Feeding on them, more like turning them. Darkwights are all elves, Isadorr. Tortured and twisted, their soul ripped from them in the process. And they convert elves rapidly. The entire foundation of this war is because of that simple fact. We are trying to find a way to free them," Tlonna told him quietly.

The king looked ill. "Be that as it may, Seaduens is choking. While we were in battle, Sithian had thousands of Darkwights here, unbeknownst to me or anyone else, and slaughtered the civilians. There are less than two hundred people, apart from the army, left in Amaden."

"That is why you need our help," Tlonna said, horrorstruck. "You have to get your people out of here. I will write to Tristan, see if he would be willing to harbor them until they can make it safely to Blackhaven."

"You honestly believe Demetrius's son would willingly allow Seadueni into his kingdom?" Isadorr scoffed.

"No more than I was, not ten minutes ago," Tlonna replied coldly. "What else can you do? If they stay here they will be either butchered or turned into Darkwights. If they flee, at least they have a chance at survival."

Isadorr fell silent as he studied the faces before him with little expression. His gaze lingered the longest on his brother's, who stared back at him with resolve. "What say you, then? You have the blood of both our lines in your veins."

Gothier folded his hands in his lap and bit his lip. "All I know is that despite even *my* treatment of Blackhaven's people, when I fled there in naïve hope, I was not mistreated. There were a few rough times, but generally I was welcomed as a...mistrusted...guest. Our father's hatred of them was personal, not political or even justified. He was slighted and so he made them an enemy. Isadorr, I believe that only there do we have a chance."

The six Blackhavenites stared at Gothier. Aidyn and Yayènia shared a smirk over Tlonna's head, which Isadorr caught.

"I take it you two are responsible for the rough times?" he asked, a small bit of humor in his voice.

"It is our job," Aidyn replied blandly.

"Well then, what now? When I sent for you I did not know what I hoped to accomplish, I just knew that you had to see for yourself that Seaduens is not the enemy you believe it be, or even the enemy it was when my father was alive."

Losolin snorted. "We are responsible for half your family's death. How are you not our enemy?"

Isadorr glared at him. "I never said we were friends, Grisholm, just that we are not the enemies you think we are."

"You raped my good friend, your brother tried to rape me," Tlonna cut in angrily. "Your father attacked my city, my people, and allied himself with my greatest enemy. Believe me, Isadorr, there is no chance of friendship between us."

"I have raped no one," the king defended, furious.

Aladorn scoffed. "You and your father raped Miazie Paron back when you held our army hostage in Purheae. Do you think we have forgotten," he waved at his brother, "that you did so, while keeping us bound?"

"That was not rape. She agreed to it."

"To save our lives!" Aidyn shouted, nearly drawing steel. "You held her against her will for nearly twenty hours! She is human for spirit's sake and you treated her like a whore for longer than even the most libidinous elf can go!"

"You would know!" Isadorr yelled back.

Swords came out so fast and in unison it left the air ringing. The four standing elves had drawn steel, each with a weapon in both hands. It was a startling sight, and Isadorr went pale. Gothier looked ill and sank down in his chair, which was directly in front of Suneelo, a dangerous place indeed.

Tlonna sighed wearily and put a hand on top of both Aidyn and Yayènia's swords and pushed them down. "What you did to Miazie was deplorable and cruel, and I cannot forgive you for that, but your people should not suffer for your actions."

"Then you will allow them succor?"

"I will, but first you and I need to talk, alone."

"Tlonna..." everyone behind her said, their weapons still drawn.

"I can very well handle King Isadorr," she told them dryly as she leaned back in her chair and removed her hands from the two blades on either side of her.

Losolin shook his head. "As king, I demand my right to hear what he has to say."

"I will give you that," Tlonna replied and reached over Yayènia's two swords to grip his hand.

"As your guardian I demand my right to stay!"

"Denied Yayènia. All of you. Isadorr?"

The Seadueni stood and opened the door. "Lead these four, and my brother, to the private courtyard. They are not to be harassed."

"Yes King Isadorr," one of the guards said from beyond the door, and the king stepped aside to allow the five room to exit, though they did so with great reluctance.

Once alone, Isadorr dropped some of his arrogance. "What do you want?" he asked the other two monarchs as he flopped back into his chair.

"What do you know of the attack on Demetrius? Why did Stoffnias include himself in that fiasco?" Tlonna asked, leaning forward to brace her elbows on her knees.

Isadorr shook his head. "Not much. I know that it was planned by Athelias. He had some grievance against the old man and enlisted

Sithian's aid, probably in hopes of leeching onto your son as he did Midian. My father disliked Demetrius with a great passion, mostly because of Kajgenia's indelible ties to Blackhaven. My guess is that is why he added Seaduens' mark to the attack. He was never against hiring mercenaries to carry out the dirtier deeds he had done."

Losolin frowned. "The Eseirik were no mercenary band. For one, the leader of each group had a pewter disc burned into their hip that sported rudimentary symbols for Seaduens, Talenias, and Zaedic."

Tlonna dug the medallion from her belt pouch and handed it to the male. He took it with a scowl and studied it a bit before handing it back.

"All I can tell you is that I know little of these Eseirik, and if there are any in Seaduens, I do not know of them."

"There are none. Aidyn killed every last one of them when Demetri died," Tlonna told him.

"Did he now? I may not like him, but I have always been in high regard of his talents," Isadorr stated quietly. "Anyway, as I said I know nothing of Father's involvement with these people. How a pewter emblem with the Ivory River on it ever made it into the flesh of an assassin, I cannot know."

"You seem to not know a lot," Tlonna commented dryly.

"Yes, well I had not expected to become king quite so early," he snapped, his look telling her that he knew exactly who had killed his father. "This is what I do know. Athelias, Midian, and Stoffnias all had ties to each other, admittedly Midian was usually the leader because of his power. Athelias was always a pawn, like a lap dog constantly trying to make itself loved by its masters. Father and Midian worked together with an uneasy alliance, their hatred of each other's respective race always making things tense between them. The only thing they truly agreed upon was a desire to annihilate Blackhaven. However, even their goals in that were different. Father simply wanted it gone or in his power, either would have made him happy. Midian wanted you, for the reasons you obviously know."

"He needed the strength of my blood and race added to his, to make invincible heirs," Tlonna said quietly.

"Precisely, and he got just that."

"But why did he not do that when he first had me? I mean, he took my memories from me and left me for dead after parading an image of my fleshless body in front of the gates of Blackhaven. Why wait eight years?" Tlonna questioned, frustrated by her lack of knowledge and the seemingly erratic plots of her enemies.

At this Isadorr smiled faintly. "That I do know. When Midian managed to capture the two of you, he did not know about the power of combining your two bloodlines. He simply needed to get you out of the way. He did not kill you then because he knew about the prophecy, but did not understand it. Any fool knows that messing around with prophecy before having at least a simple understanding of it is disastrous. He refrained from killing you because he was afraid of the implications. That is also why he did not kill you even after you had given him three heirs. For your life to end before the time dictated by the prophecy would be a cataclysmic mistake."

"Before the time..." Tlonna muttered and shook her head. "Your father certainly did not seem to give a damn about that. He tried to kill me on the battlefield."

Isadorr shifted in his seat. "Father never cared about the prophecy. He just hated you."

"How very pleasant."

"Well, what do you expect?"

"Not a lot. Now, what is your opinion about Talenias?"

"Tlonna?" Losolin asked, his voice full of warning.

Isadorr looked confused for a moment. "Why does my opinion matter? It is a human province, therefore no concern of mine."

"That is not true. You are part of this continent, and whoever becomes the ruler will be on equal plane with you. You will have to deal with them as King of Seaduens."

"The flaming place can fall into the ocean for all I care. Tyular and Tristan seem to have it all planned out."

"They are being resisted."

"What do you want me to do? It is an odd kingdom that worships the sun. The entire southern half is inhospitably cold and rocky, and the rest is infested with humans and vagabonds. As I said, I do not care what happens to it."

Tlonna gave him an indecipherable look. "Miazie Paron and her fiancé Sodo are being considered for the throne."

Isadorr's eyes widened at that. "That could be uncomfortable."

"Yes, unless you advocated her for the throne along with everyone else. I do not know if she would even agree, but it is worth asking."

"It is unprecedented, the rulers of other kingdoms planting a new and untried ruler on the throne they helped to overthrow, with no plans of regency. Honestly, you and the other three eastern kings are the oddest bunch of rulers around. Why are you all so pleased with your present situation?"

"If you are talking about our respective kingdoms, it is because our people are happy, our lands are healthy, our ties of friendship and mutual trust stronger than ever, and our borders are big enough to support many times the population that already inhabits them. What do we have to be displeased with, other than the fact that other rulers are intent upon destroying our freedom?"

Isadorr remained quiet, unable to counter her statement. Tlonna leaned back in her chair and folded her hands upon her lap. "In your message, you also inferred that Narnen and Talenias are in some sort of trouble?"

"Ah...yes. As you may know, some of my soldiers deserted the war effort and swore themselves into the service of your friend Erdwyf, the Queen of Narnen. I understand their reasons, and I have decided not to burn their names with desertion. I do not want to see them die."

"Why would they die? Narnen has no more troops left to fight," Losolin muttered, shaking his head.

"Precisely. From the last correspondence I had from Sithian, he alluded to another attack on Narnen, this time burning it to the ground. He also plans on taking over Talenias. He will sail around Nymyños in order to reach it without conflict, and then march from there to join his troops facing off with yours. He also intends to, at the same time, land what is left of his forces in Narnen and obliterate it. There will be no mercy granted."

"How does he have the troops to do this? Where in all the nine hells does he get his soldiers from?" Losolin demanded angrily, frustrated.

Isadorr chuckled humorlessly. "From the north. There are, according to him, hundreds of islands up north of Zaedic, populated with hundreds upon thousands of Men. None of them speak the same language or have the same culture. It is quite amazing, actually."

"How have none of us ever known of these islands?" Tlonna wondered, blown away by the revelation.

Isadorr stood and walked to one of the glass walls, light streaming in to bathe him in soft golden light. "Who would dare sail that far north? With the wild tides we have to contend with, sailing along the coast is nearly all we can do. Travel between Nymyños and Zaedic is rendered calm by High Reef and Norman's Reef, but beyond that, it becomes a frenzied ocean. Sithian claims that the only reason his family knows about the islands is that a few castaways washed up on Zaedic, claiming to be from a small group of them called the Scattered Isles. After that the Rahlans invested in building wide-bottom ships that could handle the rough waters, and charted them out. They stopped their exploration when they came to a giant land covered completely in ice and snow.

"Sithian says that his grandfather Aderiaen figured that was far enough, and bade his cartographers come home. Then Midian began scouting the islands, forcing the people to bow to his rule. Ever since then Zaedic has filled its ranks with islanders not native to Zaedic. Now, however, Sithian has depleted all his sources and will use the last of them to overtake Narnen and Talenias."

"He told you all of this?" Tlonna said, doubtful.

Isadorr pinned her with a bland stare. "Your son likes to brag."

"You have that in common," Losolin muttered darkly. "What I want to know is what did your father have to do with the kidnapping of myself and all the male inner-council members of Blackhaven?"

The prince turned back to the window-wall and clasped his hands behind his back. "That was a foolhardy risk Athelias orchestrated. Sithian, I know, did not care for it, but he figured that if anyone managed to take one of you out of this world then so much the better. Father thought it a great laugh, especially when the Eseirik never even made it out of Blackhaven Kingdom, and the fact that it was four females who stopped them. Of course, no one even remotely intelligent would mean to suggest that the four females who did stop them were incapable in anyway, but still...it was a fantastic distraction for a time. A short time. Basically, Athelias wanted the Eseirik to nab the six of you, because Sithian had warned us that his sister had sent a woman there to accuse the other one...Haydyn—"

Tlonna squeezed her eyes shut against the agony that name brought forth. Isadorr didn't notice.

"— of rape. Athelias believed doing such a thing would throw the head of the kingdom into anarchy, therefore making it much more acceptable that the woman's accusations were valid. It turned out to be a great catastrophe, as of course you did not indict your son with the bogus charges, and the woman managed to kill herself before anything else could come of it. The abduction was foiled, and Athelias was at the mercy of Sithian for a time and received the beating he should have been given long ago. I saw him a few days after. Poor bastard could barely open his eyes. That is why he broke so easily at Tristan's coronation. He had already been severely punished for the deed, and to think that someone else might take credit for any part of it, no matter how disconnected, simply snapped his mind."

"What do you mean? How do you know all this? Was it not your father, Sithian, and Athelias who orchestrated Demetrius's murder?" Tlonna asked as she stood and moved next to the king. His amber eyes slanted over to her.

"Sithian and Athelias, yes. Father and Demetrius were used to each other. Neither liked the other one to be sure, and Demetrius often threatened Father with invasion if he did not stop or at least try to control the border attacks, but all in all they understood each other. Young Tristan, on the other hand, is much more prone to violent vengeance than his wise sire. He has upped the amount of men he has at each entrance between our two lands, and even though nearly all of my people are here in the city or fled into the Assassin's Forest, he keeps them there. Did you not see them when you crossed over?"

"We saw them, but were distracted by your guards pointing arrows in our faces," Tlonna replied wryly.

Isadorr shrugged. "They did not shoot you, did they?"

"Obviously not," Losolin grumbled. "But still you have not explained what Demetri's murder and our abduction had in common, other than the Eseirik."

"Is it not obvious?" Isadorr asked, his eyes wide as he turned to regard the other king. "They were both Athelias's ideas. He above all hated Demetrius. Oh, how he hated him. I daresay he hated Demetrius more than my father hated the two of you. Sithian just went along with them. I think he enjoyed watching Athelias try, fail, and beg for mercy. Actually, Father was rather ticked when he heard about the old man's death, particularly when he learned that your Aidyn was right there."

"Why would Aidyn's presence cause more anger in Stoffnias?" Tlonna asked, scowling at the sunlit courtyard.

"When your assassin is involved, things tend to get a bit sticky for us. He is a master at his art, may very well be *the* best ever to walk this earth. Aidyn harbors a simmering hatred of just about everything not involving you or Blackhaven, and probably hates some of that too. Would you want him as your enemy?"

"Certainly not, but I do not particularly want anyone as my enemy. I just seem to collect them," Tlonna muttered dryly.

Isadorr gave her a knowing look and nodded, lifting one shoulder as he did. "Just so. Father concluded, as you have proven to me today, that he would be a suspect in the involvement of Demetrius's death. Knowing Aidyn was there with him pretty much means that the assassin is going to want revenge, and will most likely get it. That is why Father was not happy about the old man's death, and Aidyn's involvement. He did not want to die a painful death at the end of one finely placed scimitar. Or perhaps simply a fist. I have seen what the dark elf's punches can do to a person's face," the Seadueni shuddered delicately.

Losolin slapped the arms of his chair and stood, stretched his back. "So, what have we concluded? Your father is innocent in Demetrius's death, he laughed when I was kidnapped, you know nothing of the status of his relationship with Midian, and you do not care about Talenias?"

"Losolin," Tlonna murmured and shook her head at her husband. "Isadorr has told us quite a bit, answered many of our seemingly endless riddles. I am appreciative."

"I believe this to be unprecedented, Tlonna."

The Magin looked at the king with a questioning look. Isadorr gave a small chuckled. "The King of Seaduens and the Queen of Blackhaven working together for a common goal."

"Not so," Losolin snorted. "Constancias and Stoffnias got along just fine. Better than fine, apparently."

"Fine, a common goal that more than they alone shared," Isadorr amended with a faint smile. "Though I am loath to call you my friend, I shall not consider you an enemy, whatever you may think. You can worry no longer about Seaduens coming to your gates in force."

"I will not, then. If you have parchment, I will write to Tristan and ask him to harbor your people until such a time as they can make it to Blackhaven. Though I do not believe his answer will be favorable to you, no matter what it is," Tlonna returned, a profound sense of relief washing over her.

"As long as my people are safe, I will be pleased," the king said and handed her a sheaf of vellum on which to write her message. After a moment he shifted enough that Tlonna looked up at him. "I have only my suspicions, no proof, but...watch Gothier. My trust in him is as solid as ice on a summer's day. He is less violent, and less brave than the rest of my family, but he is ambitious. He will align himself with the most obvious winner."

"You believe him to be misleading us?" Losolin asked as Tlonna continued to write.

Isadorr shrugged. "As I said, I have only my suspicions. I appreciate you not killing him the moment he arrived on your doorstep, but he is holding something back."

"He has been nothing but compliant this whole time, even grateful, obviously terrified that we might turn on him at any moment," Tlonna murmured as she finished the letter.

She had Losolin sign it and then sealed it with her personal signet. As she handed it to the guard Isadorr had called in to take it, Tlonna turned to the glass walls and started. The sun was nearly to the horizon and darkness was falling fast.

"A snake does not always announce its presence before striking, Everwood," Isadorr replied softly.

Tlonna lifted an eyebrow at him. "Indeed. May we stay the night?" she asked, half-disbelieving the fact that she was asking Isadorr Lostug, King of Seaduens, if she and her entourage could sleep beneath his roof.

"As you wish. I do not think your companions will be happy about it, though."

"That is why I am queen, and they are not."

"True enough."

They found the five elves sitting idly in a small, walled courtyard. Aidyn was stretched out on a bench, his legs on either side so that his feet were planted on the ground, thigh muscles straining against the leather of his pants. Aladorn leaned against Aidyn's right shin, half faded out and dozing. Yayènia and Suneelo were playing some sort of game involving their belt knives, a square made of notched twigs, and three pieces of copper geld. Yayènia dropped the geld into the square and they both slammed their knives down, eyes closed. Tlonna hiccupped in surprise, but both the sharp blades landed inside the square, Suneelo's directly between two of the coins, and Yayènia's a scant inch away. She groaned and her husband laughed, gathered up the geld.

Gothier watched them from another bench, his back hunched over and his hands laced loosely between his knees. They all looked up when the three elves entered the courtyard, flowing to their feet so swiftly it almost appeared as if they had been standing all along. Suneelo shoved the coins into his wife's pocket as he sheathed his knife.

"Well?" the High Commander demanded, her arms folded, the stance slightly ruined when Suneelo's gauntlet caught on her shirt and tugged a part of it out of her pants as he pulled his hand out of her pocket.

Tlonna shook her head. "Not tonight, please. We will be staying here for the night, and then continuing on to Florwen Hune. I do not want to be away from the troops any longer than necessary."

"We want explanations, Tlonna," Aladorn said as he moved to stand beside his brother.

"And you shall have them, but for now I must think on what Isadorr has told Losolin and me. Suffice it to say that I have sent a letter to Tristan asking him to harbor the refugees until they can come to Blackhaven."

"He will deny them, as he should," Aidyn said stiffly.

Tlonna shrugged. "Perhaps I will free the Darkwights before they have need to go to Blackhaven. We cannot know. As it is, I am weary, so I am going to bed. Have a good evening."

She took Losolin's hand and followed Isadorr out of the courtyard, trailed by her companions. When she at last lay in the soft, gold-blanketed bed, Tlonna sighed and curled up next to Losolin. He lifted an arm so that she could rest her head on his shoulder, and she inhaled his aroma.

"I do so love you, Losolin, against all odds," she murmured, already half-asleep.

"Mmhmm..." he managed to grunt before sleep took him as well.

Aidyn waited until the sun was long departed and then slid from his bed, still fully dressed. Across from him slept Aladorn, his brother's features turned away from him to face the moonlights streaming through the window. Smiling faintly, the assassin crept from the room and hurried out of the castle, unnoticed by all the guards. He sped down the road and into the city proper, silent as a shadow. He reached the bridge and stopped to study the guards placed at either side. With a silent curse, Aidyn ducked under the bridge and smiled. Iron rings were spaced evenly along the underside of the arch in order for repair boats to be tied at each interval. Making sure all his items were securely attached to him, the dark elf grabbed hold of the first ring and swung his body out over the cold water of the Ivory River tributary. His free hand connected with the next ring, and he made his way along the bridge. When he reached the other side, Aidyn clambered onto the bank and moved along the edge in order to get away from the alert guards.

A few minutes later he was striding along a grassy path in the forested part of the city, on the lookout for demons. It did not take long for them to find him. The assassin stopped moving when he heard the first faint rustle of cloth, his hands hovering over his blades. Three Darkwights stepped out from behind the trees and cackled wickedly, thinking they had just found easy prey.

"Come on, then," Aidyn whispered, turning as the demons approached.

One lunged, its clawed hands outstretched and the dark elf threw his body backward, pulling out his longsword at the same time. The blade slammed into the Darkwight's head so hard it split it in two and cleaved it all the way down to the jaw. Aidyn spun, threw his blade out in order to dislodge the dead demon from it, and kicked out, his boot heel connecting hard with the next creature's sternum. The demon howled and stumbled backward, gasping for breath as the third one came in, now determined to recruit this deadly fighter into the ranks.

The dark elf ducked low and reversed his sword, now freed from the Darkwight's head, and slashed it across the belly of the demon, shredding clothes and skin alike. Aidyn skipped backward as the second creature came back into the fight, slashing and clawing with abandon. Pressed on two sides, the assassin dove into a roll and came back to his feet, spun around and pulled out his right scimitar. The shorter blade parried blows, severing twisted fingers as it did so, while he kept his longsword in a dance with the third demon. They were skilled fighters, strong and quick, but Aidyn was stronger, and quicker. He crossed his swords in front of him, trapping a demon hand between them, and scissored them, spraying blood everywhere. At the same time he kicked out to the side and smashed in the nose of the other Darkwight. Both creatures fell back howling, clutching at shattered bones. The assassin did not give them time to recover. He leapt into the air and spun, both blades swept out to the side. When he landed, the demons fell to either side, their necks severed and spouting blood. Aidyn stayed where he was to catch his breath. Then he turned, cleaned off his swords, and returned them to their respective homes. Without another thought, he continued on his journey, moving swiftly and smoothly through the trees.

Several minutes after his encounter with the three Darkwights, he slowed. Before him, surrounded by a low stone wall sat the Seaduens College of Assassins. It was a simple building, made of rough-cut black granite and timber. Aidyn did not hesitate as he walked to the front door and inside. He had not taken a step further inside when two blades came whistling through air, one from behind and the other from the front. Aidyn sidestepped and lifted his arms, vambraces out. The daggers slammed into the metal armor and rebounded away to clatter against the floor.

"I would not do that again, were I you," he said coolly as he dropped his arms and turned back inside.

"Master Aidyn!" one of the throwers shouted, the one from inside the college. "Please forgive us!"

"I will if you bring Trainer Eltïar and Punisher Kidvig to me."

"Of course," the assassin said and hurried off.

Aidyn studied the rather surprising college as he waited. He had only been there once before, just after he had ascended to Master of the College of Assassins, and then he had been quite taken aback. The furnishings had more the feeling of a lodge than an elfish home, or even an assassin's home. The inside walls were the same as the outside, the exposed timbers delicately carved or hung with tapestries. Giant chairs sat before an even larger hearth, an old, weathered table between. Hallways split off from either side of the main room, and a short set of stairs took up the middle. Aidyn did not have to wait long before the assassin returned with Eltüar and Kidvig. The three elves descended the stairs with their eyes pinned to their leader.

"Master Aidyn," Eltüar said in unison with Kidvig, bowing. "What brings you here?"

"Jidair is dead. You are in need of a new College Master."

"Jidair? But...how?" Kidvig asked, his sea-green eyes wide with confusion.

"He tried to kill Queen Tlonna, so I killed him. You need not know more than that. I only have a few hours so I need to meet all your assassins in residence immediately."

"Of course. Griffith, rouse your brothers."

The assassin rushed off once more while the three elves studied each other. Finally Eltüar lifted his arm to point down the left hallway. "That way is the dining hall. It is the biggest room here."

"Then we will meet in there," Aidyn said and moved off. He hated this part of his job.

Soon enough, all the present Seaduens assassins were gathered in the hall, blinking and yawning at their legendary, deadly leader. There were seven of them, not including Eltüar and Kidvig. Aidyn stood and folded his arms.

"Your Master Jidair has fallen in the line of duty. I am here to name a new Master of the College of Seaduens. Whomever I name will be placed by oath to receive correspondence from King Isadorr, along with my orders, and any requests you attain from your various informants and cohorts. This person will be accorded all rights to execute or punish any assassin who is a threat to the College and its brothers. They will also have the right to induct any new assassins. Each of these rights is also a responsibility that I will hold you to under the strictest of hands." He continued to lay down the many responsibilities of the Master of the College before the slowly widening eyes of his people. When he finished, Aidyn took a deep breath and pointed at Eltüar and Kidvig. "I will need to see Jidair's office."

"Yes, of course. It is this way," Eltüar said and beckoned for the dark elf to follow him.

The field assassins watched them go in silence, and then began muttering to each other in excitement. It was not often any of the Colleges received a visit from the legendary master.

Alone with Eltïar, Aidyn sat in Jidair's office and sighed. "Typically, the College Master leaves a will of some sorts. I will need about an hour alone to go through his files."

"Jidair kept all his papers in there," Eltïar pointed at a carved box on the corner of the desk. "Aidyn, who are you thinking?"

The dark elf looked at the Trainer, his emerald eyes reflecting the pulsing lamplight. The black scars on his cheek seemed to absorb the light, and Eltïar swallowed in sudden fear.

"I will...uh...leave you to it, then," he said and hastened from the room, shutting the door behind him.

Aidyn grunted and opened the box, riffling through the little stack of parchment Jidair had set aside for such a time. It was always hard, but every assassin in the College accepted the fact that their death was more than likely to come early rather than later. The dark elf appeared to be the exception. Aidyn leaned back in the chair and let out a heavy breath, his hands holding the parchment naming Jidair's suggested replacement. Eltïar. Aidyn was not surprised; the Trainer was much like Jidair; strong, independent, stubborn, wicked fast, and deadly with his favorite weapon, a lightweight but dense hammer with a sharp claw on the back for tearing apart his enemies.

After reviewing all the Seaduens assassins' files, their triumphs and downfalls, Aidyn was in agreement with Jidair. Kidvig was too impatient, too quick to anger, a common trait in the Punishers. He shook his head at the memory of Gadrin. Griffith was too ambitious, and too inexperienced. There were others, Kytmar and Sorison, Rheme and Blais, but they all were too young or too bold, too inexperienced or too violent. It was a problem Aidyn simply sighed away with all of his young assassins, they joined for a reason, and it was his and the College Masters' task to temper their want for vengeance and retribution with ideals of justice and honor. After nearly an hour of study and review, Aidyn stood and grabbed Jidair's box. He left the study and went back down to the dining hall where everyone was still gathered, some gnawing on bread and cheese.

They silenced when he entered. The dark elf carefully and purposefully set the box on the table and took his time aligning it with the edge. He then backed away and folded his arms. He pinned each high elf before him with his famous glare.

"Jidair had his predecessor in line, and I agree with him. Eltïar, come here."

The elf swallowed and went to stand next to the dark elf. Aidyn grabbed his hand in a death grip and placed the ancient leather ball in his hand, opposite the one scored when one is sworn into the College the first time. Then he tensed his hand and released the tension spike. The assassins gathered in the hall gasped as the weapon shot out of nowhere. Eltiar licked his lips as Aidyn spoke again the Three Oaths of Nobility, Loyalty, and Bravery. Each time Eltiar swore, the Master Assassin slid his blade across the College Master's hand, mirroring the old scars. When blood flowed freely over the ball, Aidyn lifted it and held it so that all could see it.

"Behold, the Stain of Blood upon the Orb. Behold Master Eltiar of the Seaduens College of Assassins."

Everyone present other than Aidyn bowed low to Eltiar, who looked pale. When they stood straight once more, the dark elf replaced the leather ball in the box and handed the whole thing to Eltiar. Then he clapped him on the shoulder and gave him a mischievous grin.

"Good luck, Eltiar. I think Griffith should be your Trainer."

"A good choice, Master. Griffith, report to my study at once."

"Yes Master Eltiar," the younger elf said, his voice unsteady. "Well? What now?"

Aidyn frowned. "Things continue on. I must get back to the castle however, my company leaves in a few hours. I will expect your first correspondence at the beginning of next month. I have letters for each of the other Colleges that I need you to send out immediately. I am asking that every assassin who is in agreement ride to the battlefront of Blackhaven and fill their ranks with warriors of unshakable courage and honor. As it is our creed, I cannot command you, but I implore you. However, if any of you come, we will stand together under my banner, and that of the College. If the College of Assassins is in attendance, the clawed orb will fly with the rest of the great houses."

"You can be sure Seaduens College will stand beside you, Master Aidyn. I believe Griffith and Rheme fought with you at Alchemian. We all realize what this war is about."

"Good. Then I shall see you on the battlefield."

"Indeed. It has been an honor, Master Aidyn."

"Yes. Take care of them, Eltiar."

"I will."

Aidyn smiled faintly and left, hurrying back to the castle. No demons attacked him this time, and he swung beneath the bridge without any incidents. An hour after leaving the College he was moving through the halls of the castle. He slid into bed and immediately fell asleep, only to be awakened three hours later.

# Chapter 36
## Retracing His Steps

The group left Amaden after bidding a tense farewell to Isadorr who watched them leave with hooded eyes. Gothier hesitated on the threshold, looking back at his brother as though hoping he would rescind his decree of desertion, but Isadorr simply looked away, his face turned away almost as though he were ashamed of his decision. Tlonna and Losolin knew better.

The queen watched Gothier, her expression carefully neutral. Isadorr's warning repeated itself in her head and she couldn't help but doubt his integrity. In spite of her misgiving, she reached over and rubbed the back of his arm in an attempt to convey support. His eyes widened as he felt her contact. Gothier swallowed and awkwardly patted her hand. Yayènia saw the motion and lifted an eyebrow until it came close to climbing off her forehead.

Tlonna gave her a deadpan look and flicked Takîreaes's reins just enough to send him into a trot. She moved up next to Aladorn, who sent her a dazzling smile of welcome to his position.

"You seem cheery this morning," she remarked as they began the trek down the cliff on which Castle Seaduens sat.

"Any day I get to leave my enemy's home is a good one."

Tlonna laughed and shook her head. "Ah, this reminds me of simpler times."

"Like what?" the wiat asked, a carefree smile still on his face.

"Oh," the female sighed, "you and Losolin arguing futilely in the back courtyard of a whorehouse. You and Losolin arguing futilely in a dark camp. You and I discussing Nymyñosian history while Miazie argued with you about facts and theories."

"It seems all your memories of me include an argument," Aladorn chuckled, feigning insult.

Tlonna grinned at him. "It is what you do best, my friend."

"Indeed."

A comfortable silence followed until the queen remembered Lavandyra's actions just before she had left. "Aladorn...does your son have a lover?"

"Locton? Not a steady one, no. Several fly-by-night ones, though. The boy is too blasted pretty for his own good. Why?"

Tlonna ignored the question and looked away. "Does he...want one?"

The wiat snorted a laugh. "Why? Do you have girl lined up for him? Believe me, I would love to see him settle with someone, if even for a year or two. But alas, he is young and reckless and does not give a bloody damn about what his father thinks."

"That is how they show their love," the queen muttered thinking, painfully, of Haydyn. Her lost star. She suddenly wondered why he did not become a moon, for he had died violently, as was the requisite. Or Rhiannan, for that matter.

Aladorn chuckled, oblivious to her inner agony. "That is true. Ah well, if you find a girl, introduce them, please."

"I shall," Tlonna murmured and dropped back to ride beside Losolin, who was speaking quietly with Aidyn. The assassin's expression was wary.

They both looked up when Takîreaes nudged his way between Whäd and Neñyos and gave her another set of dazzling smiles. She wondered why all the males in her life had to be so beautiful, and careless of the fact. Though they said nothing to her, she, Aidyn, and Losolin rode in companionable silence, somehow having come to a silent understanding about their triangle.

Once out of Amaden and around the protective, hilly barrier, Gothier took the lead and led them northwest, headed for Florwen Hune. The land gradually calmed and flattened out, making their travel easier by the mile. They camped a few miles east of the bridge connecting the two kingdoms, and started out early the next morning, reaching the bridge soon after the sun had completely crested the horizon.

The seven crossed the stone arch over the Ivory River as it rumbled and spat out leaping fish. As a whole they sucked in a breath once they crossed the barrier between the two lands. While Seaduens suffered with a disease of sorrow, the air still held much of the same purity as Blackhaven and Flousen Dua. Florwen Hune's atmosphere was much different. Losolin, and those who had traveled through the kingdom years ago had hardly noticed, so driven by their quest as they had been. Now they took note, and glanced at each other in surprise. The Dwarven province seemed as clean as any elven one, but it held a thicker, earthier quality rather than the airy, rejuvenating feel of the latter. It brought to mind that of permanent and undying strength, an aroma of thick soil and ancient stone.

"Still better than a human land," Suneelo chirped to make his companions chuckle.

They rode for several hours through the flat, unchanging meadows of Florwen Hune, often punctuated with carved stone pillars. Some were short and stubby, others tall and spindly, and more somewhere in between. Each was masterfully done, though some seemed to sport too-careful carvings or ungentle chisel marks. Tlonna, her curiosity overwhelming her, finally rode Takîreaes over to one such pillar and dismounted. She tilted her head to study the images. They went from blocky and malformed to elegant and inspiring. She frowned at it.

Suneelo dismounted next to her while the others waited off on the road and watched them. "These are the pillars dwarf children learn their trade upon," he said, gesturing to the lower etchings. "They start very early and with each passing year they come and add something to their pillar."

"So each pillar belongs to a single dwarf?"

"Or family, depending on wealth or status. This one appears to be a single dwarf's."

"How do you know?"

Suneelo smiled at her, his indigo eyes sparkling. "I read."

Tlonna giggled and playfully nudged him. He laughed and remounted. "Their culture is not that different from ours, really. They are caretakers of the land, masters at their craft, and lovers of all things pure and natural. The only difference, other than our physiology of course, is that we enjoy the surface, they enjoy the underside."

"You truly are a beautiful person, Suneelo," the queen said, smiling at him. "Your heart is as kind as any I have ever come across."

The warrior blushed faintly at the praise. "I simply enjoy learning."

"I am glad."

They rode back to their group, most of whom were shaking their heads in amused resignation. Losolin simply looked empty. Tlonna eyed him, worried. Ever since they had crossed into Florwen Hune he had become shuttered. He gave her a blank look and urged Neñyos into a steady trot.

It was some hours more when a figure appeared in the distance, running swiftly toward them. They halted and pulled out their banners. Yayènia let out a resigned sigh as Anadin the dwarf-elf came marching up, his long blond beard swaying with every heavy step. The entourage watched him come in silence as the only sound came from the banners flapping in the strong wind. Tlonna sat tall, her back rigid and her hands still in her lap, Takîreaes's reins looped loosely through her fingers. Next to her, Aidyn sat just as stonily, the hilts of his scimitars jutting out from his hips, forced that way by Whäd's ribs. As the large half-breed reached them, he bowed from the waist, both hands gripping the wide leather belt at his waist.

"Welcome to Florwen Hune, Majesties. I give you the blessings and warm welcomes of King Barukh Odrinsson. May the stone beneath your feet be smooth and warm," Anadin said in his throaty voice, his words inflected as though he were being especially careful to be formal.

"Merry meet, Master Anadin," Tlonna returned with a bow of her head. "I am glad to finally visit your noble kingdom."

The dwarf-elf beamed. "An' glad we are to have ye," he said in his regular manner. "If it please ye, I'll take ye and yers to King Barukh."

"It would indeed please me," Tlonna replied, smiling back.

Behind her and off to the side she heard Yayènia huff loudly and pointedly check her longblade in its scabbard. Anadin heard and saw her, and laughed.

"A repeat of our first encounter, elfling?"

Yayènia remained silent, but her glower was all the reply that was needed. Suneelo grinned and reached across the small gap between their horses and rubbed her shoulder. "Take it easy, love. No need to fight our friend."

"But it would be such a pleasure," the warrior mumbled, with a sullen look as the group moved off after Anadin.

Aidyn snorted and rolled his eyes, which elicited another glower. He patted Whäd's splotched neck as he gave his friend a cheeky grin.

Losolin was silent as his mind returned to his previous trip through Florwen Hune with much of the same company as now. The memories haunted him, tugged at his resolve and sent him whirling through pains he was only now beginning to appreciate.

Tlonna noticed her husband's ragged breathing and tense grip. "What is it?" she whispered to him, reaching to touch his arm.

The king returned her gaze with one full of old misery. "The last time I rode through this place with these same people, you were lost to me. I was lost. Every moment was a splintered and deepening agony, every breath a mockery. I did not sleep, or eat, or see. I thought only of the pain of losing you forever, of never feeling your touch or hearing your voice. You were taken from me, and I did not know if I had the strength to get you back. Now I find myself willing to share you, because I know that I am not supposed to be with you."

"Oh, Losolin," Tlonna breathed and squeezed his hand hard enough to stretch the back of her leather riding gloves. "That time is over, our lives restored to us. Let go of your lingering pain and see the future before us. We have a fight to win, and we will win, and when it is over our life together will be bright and glorious. You are my husband, and anything I do with Aidyn is different from what we have, somehow less, though not lesser. Release your nightmares. Remember, long ago, I said I would guard you from them, and I meant it."

"I do remember that," Losolin replied as he pulled her hand up to his lips and kissed the leather-clad knuckles.

Neñyos and Takîreaes snorted at each other, by now used to their riders wanting to be so close. The elves ignored them. Aidyn glanced at Tlonna, saw her preoccupation, and dropped back to ride beside his brother. Aladorn gave him a warning glance.

"What?"

The wiat snorted quietly. "You do not seem to even want to try to make an effort anymore."

"To do what?"

"Be simply a friend."

Aidyn rolled his eyes. "Giving them privacy is not an act of cowardice, *bruun*. It is considerate."

"Whatever helps you get through the day," the wiat answered back shortly.

The assassin lifted an eyebrow at his sibling's irritability. "Do you miss Lavandyra?"

The older brother let out a short breath, frustrated for no particular reason. "No...not really."

"You know she is dead, right?" Aidyn blurted without tact.

Aladorn nodded once. "Yes. I received a letter from Locton about it. And Tlonna mentioned it as well."

"What did Locton have to say?"

"Just that she had been found dead in her quarters, obviously from the wounds she received. It was a miracle she survived at all, really. Her willpower must have been beyond normal capacity."

"It was. It often was with true dark elves, according to the records I have been able to find."

Aladorn shook his head. "She was very sad, you know. Her life was void of affection of any kind, she did not know love or kindness, or even true happiness. She could not remember her life before being a pleasure slave."

"Sadness that she masked with arrogance and debauchery," Aidyn snarled.

"I did not encourage that," the wiat murmured softly, "nor did I steal her from you."

"No, you did not," Aidyn replied, his voice suddenly cold. "Had I wanted her I would have taken her. You know that. I am trained to be seductive, to lure, to seduce without mercy. I can frighten with sex or terror. I can weaken personal boundaries with a single touch, even a look if necessary, I can slide a blade into a lung without my victim noticing because their mind is so overwhelmed by lust they cannot process thought. Male, female, I can destroy their morals until they are on their knees begging me for release of any kind. I am the reason people fear and crave the night, the reason flesh shivers when silk whispers in dark winds. I am the reason people are afraid of their own desires."

"Dramatic arrogance does not become you, little brother," Aladorn muttered.

Aidyn gave him a scandalized look. "It is me, Aladorn. An assassin without confidence and self-assurance is a dead assassin."

"You sound bitter."

"You sound worried."

Aladorn eyed his brother's hands, which rested on his thighs; the reins hooked around one finger. "I am worried, like always. At times you sound as though you are ready to commit *Haithen* at any moment. Like now, for instance. And at others you seem determined to wipe out all unattached life that surrounds you. Can you not find any joy in your life? None at all?"

The assassin's emerald eyes slid across his brother's face to land on Yayènia who rode on Aladorn's other side, appearing to be lost in thought, but he knew she was listening. "I get my happiness from the joy of others, and in a few stolen moments. People such as me rarely come across that on our own."

"What do you mean people like you? Assassins?"

Aidyn squinted one eye at him in an expression of disgusted frustration. "In a way. Masters of warfare, dealers in the 'dark arts' of life. Yayènia and I, for instance, Ghealan and Erandur. We live secular lives full of moments that could be our last, why waste what time we have dwelling on the things we do not have? It is a wasted practice."

Aladorn said nothing as his brother sneered at the back of Whäd's spotted neck.

"Think about how much more pain is brought on us by the frustration and anger that is caused by the acts of frustration and anger in the first place. Why rail against something that you cannot win against? Why get depressed about something that you have brought on yourself? There is no point to it. If I had wanted Lavandyra, I would have taken her without a pause. I was attracted to what she represented, but I did not like her. She irritated me. I found her personality licentious and offensive, and her brusqueness rubbed me the wrong way. Whatever you chose to see in her was your prerogative and I do not care either way."

The wiat stared at the back of his horse's head, unsure of what to say. "Lavandyra...I wanted to help her, Aidyn. I wanted her to know happiness before she died. I do not think I succeeded, but I did try. I could not lay with her though. It seemed...cruel. To use her that way seemed like a betrayal."

"What did Locton think?"

The dark elf smiled faintly. "He said he was glad I was finally giving up being a bachelor. He also said we need to find you a nice pair of legs."

Aidyn snorted, amused by his nephew. "Tell him to find himself a pair."

Aladorn groaned. "My son has more lovers than you and I combined. Trust me; he does not need any more pairs of legs. He needs a good slap to the head. Tlonna and I discussed this just yesterday."

"I did not know Locton was such a philanthropist," the assassin laughed quietly, enjoying his brother's obvious frustration with his son.

"More a lecher. You know what he says to get their attention?"

When Aidyn shook his head, Aladorn let out a long-suffering sigh. "He tells them he is your nephew and, if they are nice enough, he may introduce them to you."

The assassin let out a real laugh that startled his companions. "Does he now? Apparently none of them have been nice enough because he has never introduced anyone to me."

"Apparently not," the wiat conceded, glaring at his brother. "Apparently not."

The entourage traveled swiftly across the landscape, eager as they were to return to the battle. Every evening Yayènia, Suneelo, Aidyn, and Aladorn would spar, their contest a deadly dance of grace and violence. There were no rules, no set team, just a simple matter of staying in the fight. At times all three would gang up on Aidyn, try to defeat him, but he would slip by their defenses and step inside the smallest opening to claim a victory. Then they would spin and gang up on Yayènia, who moved so fast they could not catch her, and her parries would send them into vulnerable positions they could not recover from quickly enough. Anadin would watch them with a strange mix of greedy awe and contempt in his eyes while Tlonna and Losolin simply watched. Gothier sat hunched beside his half-sister, his eyes riveted on the campfire as though trying to find answers within the flames.

Every now and then, the king and queen would join in the exercise, which would elicit startled expressions from Gothier and Anadin. The six elves spun through the mock battles, a lethal dance of spiraling footwork and arcing blades, ducking and leaping over jabs and swipes. It kept them from becoming overtly frustrated by their absence from the real fight, forced their minds to stay sharp and focused on the task at hand. Even Losolin, who was still having a hard time with the journey, found himself more able to relax afterward.

One evening, after their exercise was done, Yayènia and Aidyn disappeared into the shadows, as they had done every so often since the start of the trek. Suneelo watched after them with more worry than suspicion, but the others could see it lurking in his eyes. When they returned, Yayènia appeared bone-weary and aching, while the assassin simply looked empty. Once they were all settled in for the night, Tlonna rolled out of Losolin's arms and crawled over to where her sister lay.

"Nia," she whispered and gently pushed the warrior's shoulder.

Yayènia came out of her sleep with a gasp, her eyes zoomed around the area before settling on Tlonna. "What?"

"Come."

The two females walked away from the camp and stopped when Tlonna found a suitable stone pillar to lean against. "How did you get Aidyn to agree?" she asked without preamble.

Yayènia scowled at her. "Agree to what?"

"To do whatever it is he is doing in order to help you perfect your healing abilities?"

"How do you know that is what we are doing?"

Tlonna lifted an eyebrow. "There is only one thing that can put that dead look on Aidyn's face, and that is having to hurt someone he cares about in some way. The only time you look completely exhausted is when you have to heal yourself from more than simple bruises and cuts. Deductive reasoning, Yayènia."

The commander turned and walked a few steps away. "I asked him to help me. To hurt me so I could learn how to heal. He...it hurts him more than it does me, but he knows that I am afraid of being crippled by injury, even for a moment. My cowardice forces him to take the strain upon his soul, to bear the burden of my weakness."

"It is not cowardice to be afraid of pain," Tlonna began, but her sister shook her head.

"I am High Commander er'Tiena, the most famous military leader in Nymyños. I am not afraid of pain, nor am I afraid of death, I know it will come, and most likely I will not see it when it does. What I am afraid of is being unable to fight up to that moment, of being vulnerable and weak. What Aidyn does for me is get me to that point of helplessness, and then I work to bring myself back."

"But how? What does he do?"

Yayènia turned back around to face her queen. "At first he cut me, threw knives and such to slice my skin. Now...tonight he shattered my entire leg. He had to gag me so I would not scream loud enough to alert you and the rest. It is the first time we have done anything so drastic, but I feel that time is becoming short. I can heal even a shattered bone in mere seconds now, Tlonna. As long as I can keep hold of my faculties for a few seconds, I can heal anything."

"At what cost?"

Yayènia sighed with a shrug. "I knew that if anyone could handle it, Aidyn could. He keeps together better than even I expected. He does not panic or cry when I fail, he just holds me until I regain control and can heal. He just...does what I ask and then goes off for a bit. I do not know what he does during that time, but when he comes back, he seems perfectly fine."

"*El shä Rók*," Tlonna muttered. "I have seen the scabs on his arms."

"I figured."

"You two will break each other," the Magin snapped angrily. "I do not know why you both seem so intent upon pushing yourselves to the brink of madness and over. One day you will not return."

Yayènia snorted. "That day has come and gone, Tlonna. If you think there is a way we could possibly be one hundred percent sane anymore, you are just as mad as us. Someone has to be in order to do our jobs the way we do, and come out victorious every time. If anyone could do it, everyone would. We are the warriors who stand solid in the face of overwhelming odds," she jabbed a finger into her own chest, "we are the soldiers who are on guard every day, who expect death to come around every corner, and know how to stop it when it does. What sane person could do that?"

Tlonna shook her head. "That is not what I meant. I understand that what you do takes great sacrifice, but why must you test Aidyn so much, and why he you?"

"Because it allows us to share our burden with each other. Pity does not become us, neither does gentle affection. We need violence to anchor our minds, for that is all we have known. Only the past few decades have shown us true gentleness, and we are not accustomed to it yet."

It was the next day when Anadin turned them north; away from the path those who had been there before had taken. By late afternoon, the land had turned rather wild and they left behind the flat expanses of pillar-dotted grass. Here the stonework was much more elaborate, some newer, some much older. There were simple obelisks and ornate statues, arches and basins to catch the rain, there were sculptures and shrines, every piece masterfully worked with hammer and chisel. The elves noticed they were going up a slight incline as the day progressed while Anadin strode along in front, completely unconcerned about his companions.

Tlonna noted the lack of real trees with mild interest, but said nothing. Instead, the land was now covered not only in stonework but high-standing shrubbery and small, twisted trees with tough sticky needles that clung to the warped branches. The top of the trees reached to a maximum height of six feet. The branches curled inward and outward, never standing straight, and looked like something out of a child's storybook.

By nightfall, the entourage had reached the base of a medium sized plateau with a narrow defile cut through the center. Anadin turned to his charges.

"Dushvata lies beyond, and the Hall of Mahaya, where sits King Barukh. We wait here tonight, and tomorrow I'll bring ye to the capital of all dwarves. Ye might want ta set yer tents tonight."

"Why?" Losolin asked as he studied the small area they stood in.

It was a rather surprising spot, surrounded all around by tall bushes, some tall enough to block out the sky. A few yards to their left began the narrow passage, and to the right a little waterfall that splashed into a pool the size of a bathing tub. A trickle of water rushed away and bubbled cheerfully as it did so. Unsettling mist furled out of the defile like reaching fingers, only to be blown away once it touched the open space.

"Because when the sun sets on the other side of the plateau, the wind rushes through the pass. It chills the air and can get strong enough to steal yer blankets. Picket yer beasts near the fall, so they don't get frightened by the keen of the wind."

Tlonna and her companions did as the half-breed suggested. Once the camp was set and a fire was going in the center, Anadin took a deep breath. "This'll be the first time an elf sets foot within Dushvata, much less Mahaya, in more'n two centuries. Be prepared for some dissent."

"But we have no quarrel with the dwarves. The elf-dwarf relation has been strained at times, but not in the past thousand years," Losolin replied with a frown.

"Not ye Blackhaven elves, no, but we border Seaduens," Anadin replied quietly. "They're not so friendly." His gaze pinned Gothier with a deadly threat.

Tlonna shook her head. "We just came from there, my friend. Though the Lostug family has been cruel and unjust, many of the people were less than slaves, even the upper class. They were overrun by Midian Rahlan's hordes, several thousand turned into Darkwights, and many more slain. What is left of the population is rather desperate. They were under the violent thumb of the Rahlan's, forced to do their bidding or watch their family die or become demons. There were more graves than people."

"That may be true, but I saw many of 'em in my day as a border guard. They smiled as they did their deeds. Smiled as they raped, smiled as they murdered. Give 'em any excuse you want, they still smiled."

Gothier hung his head. Everyone remained silent as Anadin's quiet, growling words hung in the air. Later that night, as Tlonna lay against Losolin's back in their tent, she felt a slight tug on her blankets. Sitting up, a little groggy, she saw Aidyn crouching in the entrance of the tent, his hand held out to her. Quietly, she gathered her cloak and crawled outside. It was rather cold, and the wind was as fierce as Anadin had said it would be. Tlonna followed the shadowy form of Aidyn away from the camp, wondering at his intentions. When they were several minutes away, the assassin turned and grabbed her by the wrists.

Startled, Tlonna leaned back away from him, but he simply held her wrists and stared at her in the dark. Finally he let go and sighed. "I need your help."

"With what?" Tlonna asked, concerned.

For an answer, the assassin lifted his shirt and showed her the stitches that tracked along his hip. "I cannot see half of them, I need help removing them."

"Of course. Lay down."

Aidyn obliged and Tlonna knelt beside him. She Wove and a small globe of light danced above her shoulder. She tucked the assassin's nightshirt up around his ribcage, then used tiny slices of power to sever through the thread of those visible against his hip. She carefully used her fingers to pull the cut stitches away, piling them to the side. Her fingers brushed over his lower abdomen as she tugged his pants down enough to reveal the rest of the stitches. She quickly removed them, then bent over to press her lips to the new scar he had earned for her.

His fingers tangled in her hair as her mouth brushed over his hipbone. "You are going to get yourself in trouble," he murmured softly.

Tlonna grinned and slowly walked her fingers up from the low line of his pants to his chin. "You are the one who brought me out here in the dark," she reminded him.

Aidyn sat up and brushed his fingers over her cheek. "He is not away," the assassin said quietly.

Tlonna conceded. "No, he is not. Come, my dark one."

They walked back to camp, hand in hand. Aidyn kissed her knuckles as he stopped in front of his tent, which was right next to hers and Losolin's. He ducked inside, and Tlonna returned to hers. Losolin rolled over and held his arm to her. She doffed her cloak and gratefully climbed back in the blankets.

"What was that about?" he asked softly.

"Aidyn needed his stitches taken out," she told him as she pushed up against his warmth.

The king grunted. "How many this time?"

"Almost twenty."

"Spirits. Is he all right?"

Tlonna smiled against his shoulder. Only he would be concerned about the male who openly carried on an affectionate relationship with his wife. "Yes, I believe so. Thank you."

Losolin grunted again. "Just so long as you come back to me," he murmured into her hair.

"Always."

Morning came too swiftly, and the group, weary from their stresses and long travels, quickly washed in the trickling water while Anadin made breakfast. Though he was half elf, his dwarven genes seemed much more prominent, for he did not feel the necessity to wash every day when possible, or comb out his thick hair. Only his smooth, unblemished skin and height belied his mixed heritage. Before the sun had fully crested the horizon, the seven elves and their grumpy guide went into the pass. They immediately felt the pressing, looming closeness of the lichen-spotted walls that seemed to curl up and over them due to the sheer narrow height. Water dripped from unseen places to splash with quiet conversation to the rubble-strewn ground. An oppressive quietness dominated the narrow defile; the only sound that of the water and the clacking of disturbed pebbles.

Tlonna shared an uneasy look with Losolin just before entering, knowing it was the last time she would see his face for a few hours or so, as the path was barely wide enough for one horse, much less two. The wind drifted into their faces, warm and moist with the droplets it picked up from the wall. It was incredibly calm when compared to the howling maelstrom that it had been during the dark hours, and the elves appreciated the fact. The mist however, lingered. It swirled about their horses' hooves, distorted the ground and made them uneasy.

"Do not look up," came Anadin's voice once they had entered and were a few minutes away from the threshold. "The sight has been known to disorient, frighten, and disturb many people."

Against their will, all seven elves looked up when he said the warning. Tlonna's stomach lurched. The top of the crack seemed miles away, an impossibly thin ribbon of brightening light that glowed at the very top. The walls seemed to grow larger as she stared, seemed to come in closer, squeeze her. Gasping quietly, the elf dropped her gaze to Anadin's back, and tried to settle her lurching insides. Behind her she could hear the others having much the same reaction.

"No small wonder why Dushvata has never been conquered," Yayènia said after a moment or two of silence. "One warrior could defeat an entire army here. Line archers up along the top of the canyon, and not a single invader would be able to escape."

"It is true no enemy has set foot within Dushvata," Anadin replied, his voice carried back with an echo through the pass. "The north side of the city lies within the base of the plateau, against a sheer rock wall of a thousand of feet. Ye'll see."

"And how do you get trade in and out? Certainly caravans do not come through this passage?" Losolin asked, curious as always.

"There are tunnels spread throughout Florwen Hune, laid and founded with stone carved over two thousand years. They open up in various locations, and many are equipped ta deal with merchant caravans and the such."

"Do these tunnels not negate this pass as far as security, then?"

The half-breed's hair moved as he shook his head. "The caravans are met at predetermined locations, then blindfolded and led into the tunnels. Once a mile inside, they're permitted to take off the blindfolds."

"And what of the dwarves who build, maintain, and guide these people? I know of the strong loyalty of your people, but recently even my kingdom was nearly undone by treason. How is this dealt with here?" Tlonna asked, hoping the male did not take her question as a threat, or worse.

He surprised her by chuckling softly. "Their tongues have been cut from their mouths to prevent 'em from speaking, and they have only their three center fingers, no thumb or pinky, to prevent 'em from writing directions."

"I am surprised Barukh would allow this butchery to take place, even if it does insure total safety," the queen murmured.

"King Barukh didn't start the tradition, his great granddad Dreash did, back durin' the Devil War."

"Devil War?" Tlonna asked, confused.

Anadin's shoulders shrugged. "I think ya'll call it the War of Monotheism or some such."

"Ah, that we do, Anadin," the queen replied softly with a nod even though the half-breed had his back to her.

The conversation dwindled into silence as the day warmed to an unpleasant humid tepidity. Beads of sweat glistened on Anadin, though the elves remained cool to the touch. Yayènia and Suneelo tugged at their armor and wished they could remove it. Aidyn unhooked his cloak and let it drape across Whäd's rump, then tugged at the laces on his tunic so that it gaped open. The pass twisted and turned for miles, switchbacks sometimes turning them in completely the wrong direction, only to turn sharply back once more. Tlonna was glad they were going to visit a friendly nation rather than a hostile one, for surely they were like herded animals within the defile. At times it was so narrow she had to squeeze her legs tight against Takîreaes to avoid scraping them on the rock. She would have dismounted were there room to do so without making a huge fuss.

It took them hours to traverse the corridor. After a while Tlonna realized they were going up a slight incline, the air getting cooler and dryer as they moved. Finally, when the sun was to their backs, off to the left, Anadin turned them down yet another corridor, but this one seemed much larger, and it rose slightly steeper than any of the others. The queen let out a relieved breath when she saw that the crack above was widening, getting closer.

Minutes later, they came up out of the defile, and grassy plains spread out before them. They were high up on top of the plateau, the pass twisting off into the evening shadows, that looked like nothing more than a narrow fissure. Tlonna felt Takîreaes take a deep breath beneath her and patted his strong neck.

"Welcome to Dushvata!" Anadin said loudly, his arms spread out wide.

"This is it?" Aidyn asked as he frowned at the flat expanse. It was interrupted only by a hillock and two accompanying fluted pillars that held up a scrolled post. From the post hung the standard of Florwen Hune, a heavy tapestry with brown on the left, gray on the right, and a black pickaxe in the center. Its black tassels flapped feebly in the slight breeze.

For a moment Anadin looked confused, and then he grinned. "Ye stand atop it, elfie! That is the entrance to Dushvata."

He pointed one thick finger at the pillar-flanked hillock. When the elves stared at him, silent, the half-breed stomped toward the mound and beckoned them after. When they stood before the mound, Anadin lifted a massive hammer and swung it at the grass, which made a surprisingly loud, hollow *bong*.

The seven elves jumped back in surprise, and then instinctively gripped weapons when the hillock began to open. A crack appeared in the center that widened as two halves were pushed outward to open up at a sharp angle. Anadin grinned at them as the doors fell back with a loud thud. Two dwarves holding heavy poles, which were attached to thick iron rings on the inside of the door so it could be pushed open, stared at them in shock.

Tlonna was completely dumbfounded. Before her was a well-lit marble entryway carved from white-veined tan marble and wide steps that descended downward. The doors that now lay open were encased not only stone and iron, but had a small circle of bronze in the center of each, bowed outward so that the deep chime could echo for a long time through the halls.

"As I said, welcome ta Dushvata," Anadin said, his voice brimming with pride. "Yer beasts will have to come inside as well, I suppose. Come on, we need ta get the doors shut."

Looking at each other, the seven elves followed the giant half-breed down the marble stairs, past the grinning guards, and into the dwarven city of Dushvata.

Gilded torches lit the entire stairwell and corridor like daylight. As they descended however, the ceiling, which had started out a few feet above their head, grew farther away until it became encased in shadow. What they could yet see was vaulted and carved with various symbols and designs. Tlonna gripped Losolin's hand in one hand and Takîreaes's reins in the other, as she tried to remain calm in the pressing underground. Once the stairs ended, the corridor leveled out and brown carpets hemmed in black and silver trim lined the center. Here, vast fluted columns rose up to support the now invisible ceiling, though here and there a shaft of light cascaded down to add natural illumination, allowed by well-hidden, iron-covered grates laid into the top of the plateau.

About halfway down the corridor, intersections began to appear, and dwarves teemed through them. Tlonna stared about her, her face lit up in amazement. The dwarves, dressed from fine velvets to uncured leathers, stared back as they rushed by. Dwarf children skipped along, mostly dragged by their parents so fast their feet rarely touched the ground. Anadin stood like a beacon amongst the tough people, their heads rarely coming past his elbow, but many called out to him in good nature.

"This way, elfies," he growled as he waved at his fellows.

The dwarves paused to let the seven elves pass and eyed their horses in bafflement. Everywhere there was the cry of "Elves! They be elves!"

Tlonna looked back at her friends to see Yayènia and Suneelo looking decidedly uncomfortable, even holding hands in the foreign place. Aidyn and Aladorn strode along much like usual, the former's eyes flicking back and forth, always watchful, and the latter staring straight ahead, his jaw tense. Gothier looked ill. Yayènia gave her a tight smile.

"This is incredible," the queen whispered to Losolin, who nodded.

"I think our castle was built by the same dwarves who built this place. The stonework is much the same style."

Tlonna felt the reins in her hand tug sharply and looked back, frowning at her stallion. Takîreaes had his head up in a very proud stance, but his ears flicked back and forth as two dwarf children stood under him, gaping in awe. The elf queen let out a laugh and caught the attention of the children, one a boy, the other a girl. They stared at her in utter terror.

"Would you like a ride?" she asked in the hope they understood Haithen, the common language.

They continued to stare at her until Losolin moved beside her and stroked Neñyos's nose. "Where are your parents?"

The others had stopped behind them and were watching them with resigned looks, while Anadin watched nervously from up front. The boy shrugged.

"Down in da mine, probly," he said, his eyes pinned to the ground.

"Perdy," said the girl and reached up to touch Tlonna's thigh.

The Magin Queen smiled and caught the little girl's hand. "Would you like to ride Takîreaes?"

She nodded, and the elf gently picked her up and settled her in the blue leather saddle. The child squealed in fright and glee, thumping her stubby legs against Takîreaes's sides. He ignored her. Losolin swept the boy up and placed him on Neñyos. He grabbed at the reins and stared at the elf with wide hazel eyes. Tlonna and Losolin clicked to their animal friends and began walking again, smiling at Anadin, who looked as though he had been punched in the head.

The seven followed him once more as the two children whooped with joy at riding horses as they wiggled about in the saddles and thumped their feet against their ribs. Several minutes later Anadin stopped before a set of huge, brass-bound oak doors carved with a giant pickaxe slanted across the two.

"Within lies Mahaya. Yer horses'll have to stay out here. There're some stables off that way, which haven't been used in my lifetime, but I'll get someone to take 'em there," he said and turned to a liveried guard who stood stiffly next to the doors, a tall axe in his hand.

The guard nodded and stomped forward, holding his hand out. "I'll take the beasts, then. Off with ya," he added, shooing the children, who could not get down.

Yayènia and Aidyn, who were standing closest looked at each other, and with great sighs, picked the children up and set them down. The girl sucked on a lock of coarse black hair as she stared up at the assassin. She picked at his leather pant leg, trying to find something to grab. She settled on grabbing his leg, her face level his lower thigh.

"What?"

"Yer perdy too," she said, blushing.

"How nice. Go on," he replied and stepped back.

The girl gripped his leg tighter and moved with him.

"Morka," the boy snapped. "Morka he don't want yeh. Let 'im go."

Everyone stared at Aidyn and the girl as she continued to grip his knee. Suddenly she was hugging his leg, her little hands wrapped around his thigh, her face pressed into the side of his knee. The assassin's face went bloodless and he stood ramrod still, his hands clenched at his sides.

"I don't *wanna* let 'im go. 'E's so perdy. I ain't never gonna see anyone this perdy again!" Morka cried and clutched Aidyn's leg in a death grip.

"Aidyn," Tlonna began but stopped as she tried to control the laughter that was bubbling in her throat.

He stopped her with a glare, and then bent down to pry the girl's fingers off his leg. She let him and then gazed up at him in complete awe. "Morka?"

She nodded enthusiastically, her lip pinched between her square teeth. Aidyn sighed, resigned. He held out his hand to her, and she gripped it, her tiny appendage looking frail in his large hand, and pale against his tawny skin. He had to bend over quite a bit to allow her to stand on her own feet, but did so with only a grimace. Suddenly the boy had his other hand, beaming with disbelief.

"I'm Draken."

Aidyn gave them a sickly smile, but did not say anything back. Hunched over, with two dwarf-children clinging to his hands, he followed a giggling Tlonna into Mahaya after Anadin, who shook his head. Behind him, he heard the others chortling quietly.

# Chapter 37

## Dwarven Grandeur

Mahaya, Hall of all Dwarves in Nymyños, was a magnificent feat of architecture. Settled inside the backside of a giant plateau, its height was far beyond even an elf's need for space. The entire floor was paved in white-veined tan marble, each massive tile edged with scrolling. Giant pillars three times the width of those holding up the great Stair of Blackhaven rose from the ground into the inky darkness above. As with the city itself, shafts of light were cut into the ground above to offer those who walked within it a teasing view of the vaulted, ribbed, ornately carved ceiling. The sunlight landed on the floor to illuminate carved statues depicting heroic dwarves, honored dwarves, philosophers, great engineers, legends of royalty, and warriors of renown. Tlonna and her six companions gaped in utter awe.

Off to both sides of the massive hall were what appeared to be buildings carved out of the side of the plateau itself. A few dwarves peered out of arched openings, each of them finely dressed.

"Those are the houses of the nobility," Anadin told them with a gesture to either side. "King Barukh waits through there," he pointed at a grandly decorated archway directly in front of them.

Tlonna studied the entrance, a stairway the only thing visible beyond it. "Are you not coming with us?" she asked the giant half-blood.

He shook his head. "No, nor are they," he pointed at the children who clutched Aidyn's hands. "Beyond is fit only for royals and their noble companions."

Morka and Draken released the assassin's hands with reluctance when Anadin said something to them in Kierlak, the language of the dwarves. They scurried off, leaving behind a very relieved dark elf. Anadin bowed and departed as well. Tlonna took a deep breath and looked to her friends, including Gothier in her gaze.

"Let us see what Barukh has to say," she said and headed for the doorway.

Beyond the archway was a short, wide stair that flattened out into a large landing. Two openings sat on either side, and another set of stairs continued on. They mounted the stairs, and passed two more landings before coming to a halt before a single door carved with the pickaxe and bound in silver. Two guards stood before it, and they stared in undisguised incredulity at the seven strangers.

"Who are ye?" one of them asked once he had gained control of his mouth.

Tlonna dipped her head. "I am Magin Queen Tlonna Ewôsdírn of Blackhaven, this is my husband, King Losolin, and they are High Commander Yayènia er'Tiena, Captain of the Guard Suneelo Tiena, Second Commander Aladorn Sestuns, Lord Assassin Aidyn Sestuns, and...Prince Gothier Ewôsdírn. We seek admittance to King Barukh to speak with him as friends."

"My...your highnesses, my lords and lady..." the dwarf stammered, gaping at his companion in shock.

"Please, enter, and be welcome in the Hall of Mahaya," the other said, slightly more composed.

"Thank you," Tlonna said and passed through the now open door.

Beyond was a smaller hall of black and tan marble accentuated by silver torch sconces and draperies. A few yards in front of them was a raised dais upon which sat Barukh Odrinsson, King of the Dwarves. He was slumped in his magnificent throne of black marble and brown leather, another dwarf knelt before him with his head bowed. When the door opened and the seven elves entered the hall, Barukh looked up and his creased face went slack with astonishment. He shot to his feet, surprising the guards, attendants, and the dwarf before him.

"My friends!" he cried and opened his arms wide as he descending the steps of his dais.

"Barukh," Tlonna called in greeting and went to him.

There were murmurs of wonder and confusion among the dwarves assembled, and they increased when Tlonna wrapped the dwarf in a tight hug, having to bend only a slight bit to accommodate the taller than average dwarf. She had not expected to be so overwhelmed by his wise face, or his friendly greeting, having only met him once for a short time. But the king embraced her back just as tightly, giving her a final squeeze before he backed away. Once everyone had greeted the king in warmth and joy, Tlonna brought forth Gothier.

"Barukh, some things have come up."

"So I see," he rumbled, his eyes hard on the male. "Prince Gothier. I never thought I would see you here, in present company."

"Nor I, good king, nor I."

Barukh seemed taken aback by the humble greeting, and he turned his gaze to Tlonna. She spread her hands in supplication.

"I am sorry to descend upon you like this, with no forewarning of our coming. I am deeply apologetic to be such an interruption."

"Never so!" the dwarf bellowed. "A friend is never an interruption! I imagine you have quite the story for me, and I will be glad to hear it, but first, I must attend to this final matter before me. Please, make yourselves comfortable. Please, please!"

Tlonna and the six others were guided by servants to plush benches against the wall and they sat while Barukh climbed back to his throne. The supplicant lifted his head and the king gestured for him to continue. What his story was, the elves did not know, but finally Barukh lifted a hand and leaned forward.

"Prendle, I have asked you many times before now to think about your actions, and you promised me you would. Now, you are here once more, and your tale has not changed except in its gravity. I have no choice but to sentence you to a year's exile. When and if you return, you shall start once more at the bottom of the ladder. Perhaps, with acceptable behavior, you can lift yourself once more to your present status. Fail to redeem yourself and you will be outcast for the balance of your life. This is my order. Do you understand?"

"But Barukh! I am your cousin!"

"You are a thief and an abuser! One year, Prendle!"

The dwarf howled in dismay as guards came forward to drag him out of the hall while Barukh buried his face in his hands. After a moment he gathered himself and walked over once more to speak with the elves.

"I am sorry you had to see that," he told them solemnly.

Losolin gave him an understanding smile. "It is the duty of rulers, no matter how hard it may be."

"Aye, that it is," the older king agreed. "So," he clapped his hands together. "What brings you here?"

Tlonna lifted her hands in a weary gesture. "We have just come from Seaduens. Recent discoveries there have revealed that Gothier is in fact the son of Constancias and Stoffnias, therefore my brother. He came to Blackhaven to seek aid." She told him the story of Jidair and the subsequent journey to Seaduens.

At the end of the tale the dwarf king was stroking his beard in thought. "So Isadorr pulled all his soldiers back as soon as his father was dead, hm?"

"Yes," Tlonna confirmed with a glance at Gothier.

"My father was always hasty when it came to Blackhaven. He always felt insulted by it, and therefore was inclined to do anything in order to defeat it. He was blinded by hate. Herrich, Jaichrin, and Iyaner followed the same path, each having been denied Tlonna's hand, and therefore Blackhaven's throne. Isadorr and I never had such ambitions. Neither of us wanted to marry you," the prince looked at his sister.

She snorted a laugh. "I am certainly glad about that. Barukh, I need your help."

The dwarf nodded solemnly. "It has been a long day. Please, join me for dinner and we will talk in the morning. I am afraid I cannot give you any focused answers tonight."

"I understand," Tlonna said as she stood and stretched. Her six companions followed her example, standing head, shoulders, and more over the denizens around them.

They followed Barukh back through the corridor, down two of the sets of stairs and into a grand eating hall. Surrounded by massive brown marble pillars, the tan floor glimmered in the torchlight. The seven elves and the dwarf king sat at a long table, clustered at one end. As they were served Barukh questioned them each on various topics, concerned typically with their individual aspects of the war. By the end, everyone was exhausted. The king was highly intelligent and his queries were often hard to answer in full, even for elves.

Worn and weary, Tlonna and Losolin bid goodnight to the others before entering the room Barukh had given them. It was a less spacious suite than what Blackhaven boasted, but richly adorned. The marble floor was covered in plush brown rugs, and the carved bedposts were hung with chocolaty curtains. They stowed their packs in the corner and flopped onto the bed, too exhausted for anything else.

Tlonna rolled into Losolin and buried her face in his strong shoulder. "Why am I so tired?" she asked, her voice muffled by his body.

Losolin groaned in agreement. "I think the stress of Seaduens was more than any of us cared to admit. And now we are here, and none of us really know why, except for you."

"I am going to ask Barukh to fight with us. I am going to ask him to give everything he has. I want this war done with Losolin, I want it all finished."

"We all do, but I think we are too afraid of what that might mean."

Tlonna folded her body against him, not daring to look into her husband's eyes. "I am sick of being afraid."

Losolin's big hands pressed against her back to lend his strength and support in the silence that filled the room.

# Chapter 38
## One Good King

Barukh met them in his hall the next morning, resplendent in his country's colors of gray and brown. Tlonna and Losolin entered first, followed by Yayènia, Suneelo, Aidyn, Aladorn, and finally Gothier. There, the Queen of Blackhaven laid her request before the King of Florwen Hune. By the end, her friends looked upon the dwarf with hopeful, disillusioned eyes, and he looked back at them with great sorrow for their suffering.

"My friends," he said as he spread his arms and stood upon the step that allowed him to be eye-to-eye with the elves. "My courageous, determined friends. When I saw you walk into Mahaya yesterday, I knew you to be here for reasons that weigh heavily on all of us. I know the amount of sacrifice each of you has given, the pain endured, and the fears yet to be realized. Believe you me, I have no desire to see this war continue, or for the antagonists to win it. That said, I will call to Anadin, who will collect all the available troops Florwen Hune has to offer, and they will march behind you. I will march beside you."

Tears threatened Tlonna as she felt a shift of weight on her shoulders. "Barukh, what a relief. I know this to be a hard decision; I myself have faced it too many times already. I, and all of Blackhaven, am in your debt."

"No. We are nations of peace, Tlonna, and when that peace is threatened it is our duty to protect it, no matter who the threat is aimed at. Think no more on it."

"Barukh," Losolin murmured as Tlonna was nearly overcome. "Our deepest thanks, then."

"Aye, lad. When do you depart?"

Losolin gripped Tlonna's shoulder in an effort to steady her. "We must be on our way as soon as possible. We cannot afford to be away from our soldiers much longer."

"I understand. I will have Anadin get the army together immediately."

"We are headed for Narnen to speak with Erdwyf. Have you had any correspondence from her?" the elven king asked as his wife turned to grip Yayènia's offered arm.

Barukh studied the trembling Tlonna with concern, but he turned back to Losolin a moment later. "No, I haven't, at least not recently. She is desperately busy putting back together a decimated kingdom. Last I heard she had taken in some Seadueni deserters."

"That is the last we heard as well."

"Losolin...perhaps you should stay another day, catch some rest," Barukh said and grabbed the elf's wrist as he began to turn away.

"I would love nothing more, but we have not the time."

"Haste is often more slowing than gradualness, lad."

Losolin swallowed as he looked at his depleted wife. "I know, Barukh, I know."

The dwarf released his wrist and let him go, watching the elves depart with regret. Anadin met them once more outside the doors of Mahaya, and escorted them to the giant stairwell that led them to the top of the plateau. Their horses were brought, and the doors opened. As they emerged into the daylight, the seven blinked in dazed surprise after the dim halls of the dwarven kingdom. Anadin made sure the doors were securely shut and then turned to them.

"I'm ta muster our force, but I'll lead ye to the proper exit. From there ye'll be on yer own."

"Our thanks, Anadin," Tlonna muttered as she mounted Takîreaes, sighing as she settled into the saddle.

Aidyn shared a look with Losolin, one raven eyebrow lifted in worry. The group followed the dwarf-elf in the opposite direction they had come in, looking back at the lonely pillars flanking the hillock as they did. A short time later they stood at the entrance to a steep, dark tunnel entrance.

"We have to go in there?" Yayènia asked, unease in her voice.

"Ah, don't ye worry yer pretty head off, High Commander. It opens up a bit o' the way down. Ye just have to get beyond the cliff face. Once there ye'll be on the side o' the plateau and there'll be a trail leadin' down. Only way down."

"Why can we not go out the way we came in?" Aladorn asked as he tried to settle his nerves, which were on edge from the unpleasant thought of such a small tunnel.

Anadin snorted loudly. "That's the way in. Not out."

"It is fine, thank you Anadin," Tlonna said to cut off more protestations from her friends.

"I'll be seein' ye," the half-breed said and strode off, blond hair blowing in the fierce wind.

Taking a deep breath, Tlonna dismounted and led a balking Takîreaes into the tunnel after securing the stirrups on top of the saddle. It was tight, the walls scraped the horse's sides every so often. Behind her she could hear the others following, muttering their displeasure. The light at the entrance eventually faded to nothing and they were surrounded in complete darkness, unable to see anything. Every breath was amplified by the closeness of the walls and the absolute absence of sight. The only smell was of musty dampness and it wafted around them like an oily presence. Claustrophobia set in quickly for the elves, who reveled in the freedom of the open earth. Tlonna tried to illuminate the way, but the ball of light only made it more obvious that they were in a very tight space. Yayènia asked her to get rid of it after only a few moments.

Gothier felt it first, his chest rising and falling with each rapid breath, his shoulders heaved as they came faster and faster. Behind him he could hear Yayènia muttering to herself, the words too low for him to hear. Then her words cut off and she sniffed. Ahead was Aladorn who was completely faded out, though no one could tell for the darkness. Behind the stiff-shouldered Tlonna walked Losolin who had his lips parted to suck breath in order to calm his racing heart. Suneelo closed his eyes, though it made no difference, and held his horse's reins in a death grip. Aidyn held himself together the longest, stoically ignoring the darkness and the closeness of the walls. Then he swallowed and licked his lips, forced himself to stay calm.

Slowly they moved along, their feet shuffling against the rocky ground so that they didn't stumble and fall. Though the tunnel lasted less than a quarter-mile, it felt as if it went on and on for hours. Suddenly they turned a corner and sunlight hit them full in the face. Tlonna cried out and threw an arm up to shield her face as tears streamed from her dilated eyes.

The others reacted the same as they crowded at the mouth of the tunnel. Directly below them was a sheer drop of several hundred feet. Off to the left was a narrow trail that twisted and turned its way along the face of the cliff, barely wide enough for the horses. Turning back to her companions, Tlonna looked them all in the eye.

"We must be careful not to slip," she told them.

They nodded, their eyes so full of experience, wisdom, and grief tightened with nerves and unease. She began the descent, tugging Takîreaes along the slender path. It was a harrowing journey, one that took several hours. At different points of the day, each horse slipped, bellowed out in surprised fear until their person was able to calm it. Even brave Udu and Takîreaes were trembling by the time they reached the floor of the valley.

Once they were all safely on level ground, Aidyn tenderly stroked Whäd's lathered neck. "Swords, murderers, an entire flaming army I would rather face than that ever again. Why would they have such a ridiculous way in and out of the place? I understand the desire to be well protected, but that is just suicide!" he grumbled to the nods of his companions.

"At least it is over," Tlonna said heartily, though she too was weak-kneed. "Come on, we have farther to travel yet this day."

With heavy sighs the group mounted their weary horses and continued on the way. They traveled swiftly across the flat land of western Florwen Hune and soon enough they were approaching the bridge at Longman's Forge. Now Suneelo took the lead as they crossed the bridge into Narnen. The captain leaned over Smithy's broad neck and laughed as the stallion tossed his head and seemed to dance as his person gave him his head. The other elves grinned at each other, followed Suneelo's lead, and allowed their stressed horses to let loose and stretch their muscles.

They passed by Rhaeetigan Manor without stopping, unwilling to delay any longer. They camped for a few hours several miles beyond the house and rolled out of their blankets before the sun had fully crested the horizon. Suneelo led them unerringly to Nestra and into the capital city itself. Tlonna looked about in saddened understanding at the nearly abandoned city. The Blackhavenites shared looks of disturbed remembrance at the broken homes, the desolate streets, the echoing alleys. They were halfway through the city when several armed and armored soldiers thundered toward them from the castle.

"Halt in the name of Erdwyf, Queen of Narnen! Who goes there?" one of them called in a distinctly Seadueni accent.

Gothier started, his shoulders pulled back in surprise. Aidyn slanted a look at him, unsubtly tapping his fingers against his scimitar hilt.

"I am Queen Tlonna Ewôsdírn of Blackhaven. My companions and I are traveling to see Erdwyf."

"On what business?" the soldier demanded as he danced his mount sideways to block their path.

"It is none of your concern, the business between two friendly monarchs. Move out of the way," Tlonna said sternly, her back tall in the saddle.

"It is my duty to monitor all traffic in and out of Nestra. I will not foreswe-"

"Oh, stuff it Lach," Gothier interrupted and moved up next to Tlonna. "Take us to the queen now."

"Prince Gothier!" the soldier exclaimed, his eyes popping wide. "Of...of course."

He turned his horse in the street and gestured his squad back to the castle, and took the lead of the seven others. Tlonna shook her head at Gothier and chuckled. He laughed with her.

# Chapter 39
### Erdwyf's Promise

Erdwyf looked down from the ladder she stood upon when Jaryikin came running around the corner, her nurse fast behind her. "Hand me that one," she said, pointing to a white and black swath of cloth.

"Please my lady, allow me to do this!" the servant said as he handed his queen the long drape.

She laughed and carefully hung the material over the arching doorway. "I am perfectly capable of doing this. Besides, you cannot reach the top of the door, Jordy."

The human shook his head and looked down when Jaryikin tugged on his pant leg. "Jordy...Rorse is coming."

"Jaryikin, Rorse should not be out. Where did he go?"

The princess blinked up at him. "He is bringing in elves from outside. High elves, and even dark elves!"

"Dark elves?"

"Aidyn and Aladorn!" Erdwyf cried as she descended the ladder in one graceful jump. She swept up her daughter and lifted her skirts to run.

She ran down the halls, out of the castle and leapt down the steps in twos and threes. When she saw Rorse Lach heading the septet onto the castle grounds, she let out a cry of joy and waited impatiently for them to reach her. Tlonna and Yayènia barely let their horses slow before dismounting and running to their friend. The three females embraced, laughing.

"Oh! Tlonna, Yayènia! How good it is to see you!" Erdwyf cheered as she kissed her friends on their foreheads.

Losolin, Suneelo, Aladorn, and Aidyn dismounted to greet their friend as well, unable to contain their grins. Gothier hung back and ignored Rorse's questioning looks. When everyone had quieted, Erdwyf swallowed, her eyes desperately searching the group.

"Ghealan could not come, Erdwyf. He said that to do so would only make it harder to leave again," Tlonna said softly.

"He is well, then?"

"Very, but he misses you," Yayènia supplied and gave Erdwyf an understanding smile. "He is consumed by your absence."

The queen of Narnen sucked in a shaky breath and nodded. Turning to her suddenly very frightened daughter, she held out her hand. "Jaryikin, do you remember any of them?"

The young elf stared at the fierce elves with wide gray eyes. "Commander Yayena. Queen Tlonna. King Loslin. Lord Ayden. Lord Aldorn. Captain Sneelo."

"Close enough," Aidyn chuckled and folded his arms across his chest. "How are you, Princess Jaryikin?"

"Good, Lord Ayden."

"Aidyn, love, *Ai*dyn," Erdwyf laughed.

Jaryikin blushed crimson and hid behind her mother's skirts. "So, what brings you all here?"

Tlonna stepped to the side to reveal Gothier. Erdwyf's eyebrows disappeared into her hairline.

"Queen Erdwyf."

"Prince Gothier. What a surprise," she replied in monotone.

"Indeed," Yayènia said. "He is our brother, Erdwyf," she pointed between Tlonna and herself. "Constancias was a flaming whore."

Erdwyf nearly swallowed her tongue. "*What?*"

"Gothier is the son of Constancias and Stoffnias. He fled Seaduens to escape the judgment of his brother, Isadorr. He is one of us."

"Is he now," Erdwyf said dryly, her statement not a question at all.

"Yes." Tlonna said boldly. "May we come inside?"

Erdwyf blanched. "Of course! Oh, forgive me! Please come in. Rorse, take care of their horses, will you?"

"As you will my lady," the elf said with a bow.

They traipsed inside, looking around at the blank walls of the castle. Only bare tables and iron-wrought sconces broke the solid gray of the granite. The foyer was bare of all decoration except for red and white ribbons tied to the carved newel posts on the staircase. Erdwyf led them into a left corridor and little by little, the desolation eased as the few castle workers made their slow progress.

"It has been difficult," the queen said to them as she noticed their wandering gazes. "Everything was ruined, burned or stained with things I do not care to know. It took weeks to wash the grime from the walls. Luckily for me the coffers were not hit too bad, so we have been able to order new tapestries, runners, and furniture, but little of it has arrived. I am considering changing the name as well. At first I thought it would only anger the people, but as I have spoken with them, they do not want to remember the Narnen that was."

"What would you call it?" Tlonna asked, surprised her friend would take such drastic measures to wipe clean the kingdom's slate.

Erdwyf shrugged. "I want Ghealan's input on it, of course, and the peoples', but my idea is Nouraeva. *Nourven* means strength in ancient Hindarün, and I think that would be a comfort to the people."

"I like it. Similar enough to Narnen to remind them of who they are, but different enough to give them a new start. If you decide to do so, know I will back you," Tlonna said and put an understanding hand on the other queen's shoulder. "But I must tell you it is a relief not to be the only queen in Nymyños anymore."

"Well, I just hope I am not one that stands out in history for being miserable," Erdwyf chuckled as she held open the door to a room off the small corridor into which she had led them.

It too was sparsely decorated, but there were chairs and a table, along with a carved marble fireplace. "This used to be Atlan's study. I am thinking of making it mine."

The seven crowded in the doorway, and when Erdwyf laughed at them, they filed in to take their seats. Tlonna sighed as she sank into the wing-backed chair. "How are the others settling in? Feorien and the others?"

Erdwyf shook her head. "Well enough. We all miss Blackhaven, but we have been so busy here that we have hardly had the time to dwell on it. Feorien has been a godsend, surprisingly enough. He is loyal to me and is willing to do any task. His wife, Sharntun, has been a soothing presence to me as well, with her harp. Jaryikin loves her, yes?"

The princess looked up at her mother and nodded, her gray eyes staring at each of the newcomers with the boldness of youth. Erdwyf refrained from asking her friends why they were there, though the question seemed ready to burst from her lips unbidden. Losolin leaned forward and held out his hand to Jaryikin. Like all children, she was drawn to him. She gripped his big hand in both of hers and then hoisted herself into his lap.

"Did you get the letter I sent to you a while back?" he asked as the child leaned against him.

Erdwyf nodded. "I did. I have little objection to it, for I know that it will be a grand protection for west Nymyños. What I fear is the others' reaction to it. The eastern kings, barring a select few," she glanced at Gothier, "are good people, but cutting off half the continent will set them on their toes."

"I informed them as well, and have spoken to Barukh, Tristan, and Isadorr about it. They all cautiously agreed it is the best choice right now. We will tear it down in the future," Losolin explained. "I know Tyular will not be against it, and that leaves only you and Tahitat."

"Well as I said, I understand the need for it and so I will not oppose it."

Talk continued for many hours, during which Jaryikin had her mother call for her nurse and left the boring adults to their chatter. Erdwyf simply laughed when they told her of Miazie's actions since receiving her office. Then she winked at Aidyn.

"You *should* see the file I had on you. Makes for an interesting read."

The assassin smirked at her. "I will get it, do not worry."

Erdwyf paused to take a drink of tea that had been brought in by a servant and then her eyes went wide with excitement. "I forgot to tell you! Do you remember the elves we encountered on Zaedic? Well, they are here! Apparently Sithian discovered them and had them hunted down. All the others were slain, but Niander and his family was able to escape because as fortune would have it, Alexander was in port and they were able to make it on board in time."

"The entire family is here?" Yayènia gasped, remembering the tense encounter all those years ago.

"Everyone! Syntyche, Nasrin, all of them. They have been successfully integrated into society, such as it is. Syntyche is actually the one in charge of the castle interior. I am thinking of making her my seneschal."

When everyone's back went stiff, Erdwyf's expression froze. "What is it?"

Tlonna took a deep breath. "Erd...Narda is...she was murdered. I am sorry. I know you were friends."

The queen's eyes saddened and she looked down. "She is but one among hundreds we have lost in this blood-thirsty war."

Yayènia nodded. "Know that she spent her last moments among friends. Aidyn found her and brought her back to the castle in time. We were all there."

"I am glad. It eases my heart to hear that."

She was about to say something more when a knock sounded on the door. Feorien entered and smiled at the elves gathered in the room.

"Merry meet, Feor," Tlonna said, rising.

"You as well, Queen Tlonna. It is good to see you again, all of you. Erdwyf, Niander is here with the reports you requested from him."

"Of course. Will you bring him in?"

Feorien nodded and disappeared for a short time before returning with the Zaedican elf in tow. When he entered the room, he stopped in his tracks, staring at the elves before him. Losolin broke the uneasy silence.

"An honor it is to see you again, Niander."

"Uh, yes. Losolin, right?"

"Indeed, and this is my wife, Queen Tlonna."

"Hello, Niander," Yayènia said and extended her gauntleted hand.

The Zaedican tilted his head to the side. "The warrior. I certainly remember you, High Commander."

Yayènia dropped her hand and smirked. "Good."

As everyone else reintroduced themselves, Niander nodded to them, a little befuddled. "I do not know what Queen Erdwyf has told you, but know that had she not been here and given us the refuge she has, we would have gone to the Everwood City. It was our acquaintanceship that got my family and me out of Zaedic before were slaughtered, so I have you, and of course Queen Erdwyf, to thank."

"You helped me out once, I am glad the favor was returned, even though I was not the one to do so," Tlonna said. "And I am relieved your entire family made it out. Not many can say that."

"No, I am afraid not. None of the others survived, so we count our blessing and look forward to building a new life here, in the city of new beginnings."

"Good," Losolin replied and clapped the other elf on the shoulder. "It is always best to look to the future rather than dwell on the past."

"Indeed. I shall leave you to your discussion, but it is good to see you all again. May peace find you on each road."

"You as well," everyone said as Niander turned to leave.

Once they were alone again, Tlonna set her glass of tea down with a decisive clink. "May Losolin and I speak with you alone, Erd?"

The room became still and quiet while Erdwyf studied her friends. "Of course," she said softly. "I am afraid the guest rooms are all rather spare at the moment, so you will all just have to deal."

Yayènia snorted. "Oh no, whatever shall we do? Nine hells, Erd, it is just us. The only one you have to worry about pitching a fit is dandy Prince Gothier."

The male opened his mouth to protest but everyone was laughing too hard to hear. Suneelo led the way out of the room and soon enough the three elves were alone. Erdwyf crossed her legs as her smile faded.

"Whenever you two get those looks, bad things tend to happen. What is it now?"

When Tlonna looked away, Losolin sighed and leaned forward. "We need you to promise us something, but first tell us about your Seadueni guards."

"What about them? They deserted because they did not believe Stoffnias was doing the right thing by teaming up with Sithian. When they found out he was dead, every one of them decided to stay on. They have been true to their oaths and have performed admirably. I think some of them have even begun to form friendships with the humans."

"We have learned that the elves of Seaduens are not what we thought," Tlonna muttered.

Erdwyf gave her a meaningful look. "I have noticed. Yayènia has taken it hard."

"How do you mean? She seems fine. A little frustrated but so am I," Tlonna replied with a frown.

"You would not know, I suppose," the other queen said with a heavy sigh. "She has always been more than adept at masking her feelings. For all the terrible things that have happened to her, I expect it is necessary lest she lose her mind completely. However, when you have known her as long as I have you get to know the signs. When Ghealan brought me home to Blackhaven, it was the first time he had been there since leaving Nia. Do you recall the sword she had with her in Purheae, the one with the elephunt?"

"Ghealan gave it to her before he left," Losolin said.

Erdwyf nodded. "I asked him about it. Apparently the Warriors had been called to a dangerous mission, one that they fully expected to lose. He did not think he was going to survive. But he did, and the Warriors came here to Narnen to regroup and prepare for their next assignment. That is how Lan and I met. I was here in Nestra on a shopping trip with some friends and we were being hassled on the street. Lan was walking by and put a stop to that quick enough. Well, details aside, I was smitten immediately and I guess he was intrigued enough to abandon his comrades when they rode out.

"It is surprising now, because when I think back on it I actually can remember Aladorn, though when we first encountered him back when you were tracking Midian, Losolin, he appeared to be just another stranger. To be fair, he was quite a bit different three hundred years ago, more volatile, in your face." Erdwyf chuckled. "He was built more like Aidyn then too, a bit more slender and agile. Funny how much alike they really are."

"Aladorn is a connection to us all, it seems. Aidyn's brother, our first contact, Ghealan's ex-comrade, now partners yet again," Tlonna mused with a faint smile. "They still do not get along very well."

"Nor will they ever, I do not think. Too much history," Erdwyf pondered. "But I meant to tell you about Yayènia. Ghealan asked me to marry him, and so I did. When we arrived in Blackhaven, Nia had found out somehow that the Warriors were returning. She had slipped out of Raith's grasp and was waiting at the gate, holding that sword. I looked over when Ghealan nearly fainted from blood loss. Her face..." the queen shook her head and looked away. "I have never seen such a transformation. One moment she was smiling, her face lit up and her eyes bright with joyous tears, the next...nothing. No expression, just emptiness.

"I thought for a moment that she would kill me, but she just walked away. Over the next few months, every time we encountered each other she had that expression. Slowly it went into a softer stage, and seemed to evaporate when she met Suneelo, but every now and then it reappears. Say Gothier's name, it is there."

"I call it her Ice Face," Tlonna said. "I never paid much attention to her with Gothier, I guess. It was such a shock to me as well."

"Indeed," Losolin grunted, shaking his head. "I wonder if that is why Constancias was so bitter towards you. You were her third child but the only one she could acknowledge."

"She could have acknowledged Nia. It was only her prejudice that stopped her," Tlonna growled. "Gothier was a different matter, he was, is, a product of her treachery."

"The revelation of Yayènia's true parentage was a shock to her, as it was all of us. She hides her pain of betrayal just as she does everything else. You can always tell though, if not through her than with Suneelo. She sits very still, clenches her jaw every so often, and her eyes become a little hooded. He gets tenser, shorter. He is the only one she is ever truly honest with."

"So what do you want us to do? She has not said anything. The first day she and Aidyn tried to kill him, but since then there have been no problems."

"Tried? That term is not often used with those two."

Tlonna sat back and folded her hands. "I stopped them."

Erdwyf chuckled softly. "That would do it. But no, Yayènia is hurting, bad. And of course she has not said anything, nor will she. She will talk to Suneelo, but no one else. As with all of us, our trust is not easily given, and kept only by those we love. She and Neel have been through hell together, just as you two have been. Had you seen them back when Midian was occupying Blackhaven, you would understand the depth of devotion they have to each other. Yayènia ran and fought on legs that were literally only held together by ligaments to rescue him. He forced her to escape nearly at the expense of his own life. Just like you two, they have placed their own safety and sanity on the line for each other. I would say Gothier's life hangs by a thread, and Yayènia holds that thread."

Tlonna shook her head. "Two months ago, I would agree, but Nia has changed a lot recently. She and I spent some time alone a couple weeks back, and I saw a side to her that I had never seen before. It was enlightening. She is an incredibly kind person who does not put up with nonsense or intolerance. Her life has forced her to make some difficult choices, but they have also made her very strong and loyal. I do not think she would harm Gothier unless he tried to hurt one of us, or her," Tlonna replied gently.

"She put herself in the line of fire to protect him in Seaduens," Losolin commented when Erdwyf looked skeptical.

"Perhaps, but I have watched her slice the neck of an innocent man just to keep him from being used as a tool by Aderiaen. She is unpredictable at best and unafraid of personal consequences. Watch her, Tlonna, I implore you."

"You sound as though you do not trust her, perhaps even fear her," Losolin accused, scowling.

Erdwyf leaned back. "Only a fool does not fear her at least a little. As for trusting her...I would place my life in her hands any day, but have you never been at the end of her battle lust?"

Tlonna shrugged as she vividly remembered the way her sister's eyes had clouded over and had nearly bludgeoned her to death in Purheae. "She does what is necessary to get the job done, no matter what it is. If the cost of such skill comes at the price of momentary lapses in sanity, then so be it. We can handle her. Erd, I have never heard you speak such doubts against Yayènia."

"They are not doubts, just warnings. I have known her for three centuries, and half of that time was spent in near abject terror of her. Only in the last one hundred and fifty years have we become the friends we are. The rift caused by Ghealan's supposed betrayal was really only healed a few years ago, when we came through Narnen in our search for you. She is a true friend and an invaluable companion, but I would not put the life of a known enemy in her hands if I did not want him to die."

"Gothier is not a known enemy. He is an ally and a member of our family. Yayènia will not harm him," Losolin countered stiffly. "As hard as that is to believe, it is the truth. These days our lives are full of hard choices, and harder deeds. We cannot afford to doubt each other."

"I forget sometimes how young the two of you are," Erdwyf sighed wearily. "Give it some time and your high-horse ideals will not seem so gallant. Betimes you have to accept the flaws in yourself, and those around you. Take me for example. I am petrified of making the wrong choice, so I wait until I no longer have the luxury of time, and end up making hasty decisions that could be detrimental to my people."

"We all do that, Erdwyf, it is part of being a ruler, no matter how experienced, but it is how you handle those decisions, and their resulting consequences, that is what true leadership is about. Give it some time and you will grow accustomed to it. As for being young, I think we have experienced enough in our lives to be considered sufficiently careworn," Tlonna remarked dryly with a shake of her head. "Do not let that crown on your head blind you to real life, and its hopes. Do not let it turn you bitter. You have a kingdom to protect, and a people to support. That is actually what we must speak with you about."

"Indeed, we need you to promise us that no matter what happens, unless your land is directly threatened, you will not ride to war. Promise us that no Narnenian or Nouraevan as such, will go to war," Losolin said gently, his oceanic eyes steady on the female.

"I will not stand idly by!" Erdwyf nearly shouted, her back rigid. "How can you ask me such a thing?"

"You have no military, Erd, other than your guard. What good would it do to throw away those few lives on a battle where numbers count for little? If Nouraeva is to become a new kingdom of Nymyños it needs a population. Spare your people, they have already suffered enough," Tlonna said soothingly. "Besides, if we all perish the land will need a strong figure to lead them into the next era. Eyin Thorn is too inexperienced, Tristan as well. They will follow you, but only if you survive. Give yourself a chance. Think of Jaryikin."

"It seems that is all I do, think of Jaryikin. You have placed me in a rough spot, Tlonna. How can I agree to such a thing when every moral fiber of my body screams for me to throw myself into the battle? At the same token, every rational fiber demands I stay and protect my people from complete annihilation. What do I choose? Allow my friends and family to die, or let my people die?"

"There is no certainty that we will die, but if you lead your people to war, they will," Tlonna said quietly. "Promise us."

Silence reigned for a long time while Erdwyf stared blankly into space, her eyes troubled. Finally she wilted. "I promise."

Tlonna and Losolin gave each other small, relieved smiles before standing. "Thank you, Erdwyf," the queen breathed. "I am thankful you do. Otherwise, things were going to get nasty."

"How do you mean?"

Losolin folded his arms. "We would have sent troops in to blockade all exits into Nestra. You would have been completely isolated until the end of the war."

"You would do that?" Erdwyf gasped as she stood.

"Absolutely. We were not about to let you commit suicide."

"You two have gotten tougher since I left. I am sorry."

Tlonna shrugged. "Makes us harder to wound. Goodnight Erdwyf, I hope you can forgive us one day."

"Come back alive, and I will throw myself at your feet," the queen replied, hugging her friend. "Just...come back alive."

"I will do my best," the Magin promised.

# Chapter 40
## Nouraeva

The group left Narnen the next morning, uneasy from being gone from the battle after so long. Erdwyf watched them go with a heavy heart, her eyes sad. She feared she would never see some of them alive again.

"If anyone can survive the coming trials, it will be them," Feorien said from behind her. "We must focus on the task before us. We have a new kingdom to forge, or rather, you do. Erdwyf, are you sure you want to change the name?"

The queen turned to eye her advisor. For so long she had despised him as Constancias's lapdog, but he had proven himself an intelligent advisor. "Yes. Narnen has had too much bloodshed in its past. I intended to make this land flourish again, and to do so I must begin anew, and I have decided I can no longer wait for Ghealan to arrive. It has to be done now, else I will lose all courage and this darkness will linger. Call the people to the city center at noon, and we shall make Narnen a bad memory."

"As you wish, Erdwyf."

At midday Erdwyf gathered Jaryikin into her arms and rode to the city center. A small stone dais sat in the middle of a cobblestone square, used year-round as a gathering place for caravans, fairs, and celebrations. The remnants of the population were already there, staring about in confusion as the guards gently blocked off the dais. Erdwyf lifted her hand to acknowledge the cheers that were directed her way, and though they were sincere they were weary. The people were tired.

The queen dismounted and walked with Jaryikin onto the dais. She studied her people in silence for a few moments before speaking. "My friends, I share your pain. Narnen is my birthplace, where I blossomed into a young adult, and where I met my husband, your king. I have returned here after many years in Blackhaven at the behest of the late King Emar and Queen Atlan to take up the throne. Since my arrival I have striven to lift Narnen out of the ashes of destruction, but I have thus far failed. While it is true that markets are beginning to open up, and lives are being reclaimed, we still bow under the weight of a brutal invasion. I have spoken with many of you about what can be done, and there seems to be one recurring theme. Remake Narnen. But one cannot simply remake a kingdom.

"I have tried. I have sanctioned a new standard, I have forged anew the crown, I have even remade the throne in attempts to ease the terrible burden that sits on all our shoulders. After the recent visit of the monarchs of Blackhaven, I have come to a decision, and I pray you do not loathe me for it. I have come before you to say that I have decided to do away completely with Narnen. It shall fade into history and we will be new. I have chosen a new name for our great land, one that shares in both human and elfin history, but stands for all the races of Nymyños. Nouraeva. It means strength, and that is what we need. Are you with me? Shall we all be called, from this day forth, Nouraevans? Shall we be reborn with the strength of our bloody past and the hope of brightening future?"

A great cry went up from the haggard people, one of pure elation and joy. Erdwyf was taken aback. She had expected resistance, to be called a usurper and a tyrant. Instead they lifted their arms and faces to the sky and cheered. Once the cheering had quieted some, Erdwyf held up her hand.

"So be it, then. I shall send to all the rulers of Nymyños and tell them that Nouraeva stands on the ashes of Narnen, that this is a kingdom reborn!"

Again a cry went up and this time it did not stop. Erdwyf looked to Rorse Lach and Feorien who stood side by side behind her, and grinned. They beamed back, witnesses to history.

Tlonna shook her head as her early morning conversation with Erdwyf went through her mind yet again. *Nouraeva.* A new land. Losolin shared her bemusement. She understood it, of course, but to change the entire face of a kingdom seemed risky.

"Perhaps we should change the name of Blackhaven to Moonland," Losolin said as if reading her thoughts.

"Moonland?"

"Well if all the bloodline monarchs become moons when they die..."

"You are terrible."

The king laughed. "Yet you married me nonetheless."

"Indeed. Hindsight, my love, hindsight. But...do you believe Erdwyf has made the right choice?"

"We cannot know. Time will tell, of course and that is something none of us have at the moment."

"Your comprehension of the apparent is inspiring, Losolin," Suneelo teased as he came up behind them.

"Jealousy does not become you, old one."

"Oh! Age jokes. How appropriate."

Tlonna laughed as the two brothers began trading insults like children, jostling each other in the saddle. Aidyn and Aladorn twisted to see what was going on behind them, their eyes narrowing as Yayènia gave them a look of expectation.

"Unlike those two," Aladorn began, but was cut short when Aidyn shoved him hard in the shoulder. The wiat disappeared he was so shocked.

By the time he had righted himself, Aidyn was several yards away, looking forward in complete innocence. Tlonna and Yayènia were laughing too hard to sit up as Losolin and Suneelo tussled, and the always-calm Aladorn blustered at his assassin brother.

It took two solid days for them to reach the camp of the Blackhaven Militia once more. All hilarity had been wiped from them by the time the sight of the battle came into view. Smoke from burial pyres blackened the sky on both sides while carrion birds circled between, searching for any missed corpse.

"How recent?" Tlonna voiced to her companions.

Yayènia sighed. "Less than a day. Looks as though both sides took massive casualties. What caused such a melee to break out?"

"Only one way to find out," Aidyn said and spurred Whäd toward the camp defenses, which were still several miles away.

When they reached the command tent they found everything in chaos. Healers and servants rushed to and fro, their faces white and red with fear and exertion. Tlonna nearly flew off Takîreaes in order to get into the tent as fast as possible.

"What has happened?" she shouted in the tumult, hoping someone heard her.

"Lord Erandur took a hit to the shoulder, my queen. He's lost a lot of blood," someone shouted back.

"Losolin!" Tlonna bellowed, inadvertently quieting the tent when everyone stopped to notice her.

"Tlonna!" Ghealan cried from one side of the tent, looking pale and exhausted. "Thank the gods you are here."

Losolin shoved inside and by Tlonna, not bothering to ask questions. He disappeared into one of the smaller rooms held aside for injured officers and a new hush filled the tent as a green glow came through the canvas walls.

"What happened Lan?" Yayènia asked as she appeared next to her sister.

The large elf shook his head. "The general, Orlando, has lost his wits. Just after dawn he came roaring over the hill like always, but this time he did not stop when they started to lose. He threw everything he has at us, including what appeared to be the last of the Magins in camp. Admittedly we were a little taken off guard by the ferocity of the attack. Never before has he just crashed into us. This time there was no battle plan, no discernible tactic. It was like a giant tavern brawl.

"Erandur was trying to move his men off to flank when a Darkwight came out of nowhere. Stabbed him in the shoulder, all the way through. He kept fighting until the end, but he exerted himself so much that I fear he may lose his arm, if not his life."

"How long ago was he hurt?" Tlonna asked, craning her neck to see around Ghealan's broad shoulders.

The commander shrugged. "At least an hour or so, perhaps longer. Incredible endurance, that one."

"I assume you are talking about my son, Ghealan?" Furntil Eldrout said quietly as he moved up beside the big elf.

"Indeed. Only two other people in this world can fight with such severe wounds, and they stand in front of you."

Yayènia and Aidyn shared a look when Furntil nodded at them. "Your arrival was fortuitous, my friends. Losolin says he may be able to save Eran's arm enough that he will be able to use it again."

"If anyone can save it, it will be Losolin," Tlonna assured him. "Any idea what brought on such a ferocious attack?"

Both males shook their heads. Yayènia grunted. "Whatever it was, I am sure we will not like the answer. How many did we lose?"

"Over a thousand dead, nearly as many wounded. It was a hard hit," Ghealan said, scrubbing his hand over his face. "We have been fighting every day for hours, sometimes at night. No one is getting any rest."

"We need to finish this soon," Tlonna snapped, frustrated. "And we need to know why Orlando forced such a battle."

"I think we may have our answer," Furntil said and nodded to a pale man who had just entered the tent, wearing the garb of a scout.

"Uh...Major Bergeson, my lords and ladies. High Commander. I saw the young king, uh, Sithian. He's back, and he doesn't look too happy."

"Brat never does," Suneelo muttered. "But I would wager my life that he is the reason Orlando did what he did. Did he have anyone with him? Did you see him arrive?"

The major nodded. "Aye sir. He had a whole bunch of people with him, looked like civilians the way they were dressed, and all types, too. Men, women, skinny, fat, certainly not soldiers. There were a couple of them demons too, the 'wights."

"He brought in more Magins. How many would you say?" Tlonna queried with a scowl.

Bergeson licked his lips. "I'd say around fifty, only a dozen or so of them were demons."

"Fantastic," Yayènia said, sarcasm thick in her voice. "Anything else, Major?"

"No ma'am."

"Return to your post once you have refreshed your supplies. Dismissed."

Once the man was gone, Tlonna turned to the warriors before her. They all looked at her with cautious eyes, wondering what she would do when the inevitable encounter with her son happened.

"I will do my part. I need you all to be focused on the battle, not me. Yayènia, your army is hurting, but you can pull them back together. I know it. Suneelo, do the same with your guards, this is not where they ever expected to be, but they are here now. Keep them standing strong. Aladorn, Ghealan, get over your past, it was three hundred years ago. You are commanders, act like it."

The two males shared a sidelong look, their arms folded across their chests. Tlonna pinned them each with a warning glare. She turned to Aidyn and pressed her hand to his face, her thumbs skimming over his cheekbones.

"I am going to need you to be strong for me. Stronger than you have ever been, my friend. Can you do that?"

The assassin took her hand in his and kissed her knuckles. "Whatever you need, I will do it."

"Good. Furntil, let us go see how Erandur is fairing," Tlonna took the ancient king's arm and led him back into the small room where Losolin still stood over the prince.

"Eran?" Furntil said softly as he peered around Losolin to look at his son.

"Father. I am all right," came Erandur's weary voice.

"He will have to sit out for a few days, but he should regain the full use of his arm," Losolin said, his hands still pulsing with green light. "He did a lot of damage to the muscles and tendons inside his shoulder, but I was able to reconnect them all. Now I am knitting the skin back together. Unfortunately I was not here soon enough to stop the scarring, but at least he will not have any lasting effects."

"Good, good," Furntil said, patting his son's calf. "How do you feel?"

Erandur shrugged his good shoulder, smiling faintly as Tlonna edged around his father to stand on the other side of the bed. "I think this is the worst injury I have ever had, but it was not so bad. I was too mad, too desperate to think about the pain. I just kept swinging my sword and screaming at the top of my lungs. I do not think I even realized I was hurt until Ghealan hauled me onto his horse and galloped back here."

"I have noticed that," Losolin chuckled. "The worse you are hurt, the less you realize it until later. Then it is like a kick in the teeth."

The prince nodded and chuckled slightly. "Indeed. I am glad you arrived when you did. If I had to look at another panicking healer's face, I think I might have cut my arm off myself just to spare them the fright."

Tlonna smiled. "They do that. On hindsight, we should have had Aidyn's healer come down, Healer Braden."

Losolin nodded. "He is good, one of the best I think. Perhaps we should send for him."

"Speaking of sending to Blackhaven, the engineers wanted to speak with you when you returned," Erandur told them, brightening a bit. "They had an idea."

Tlonna found Yayènia, rather than wait for Losolin to finish with Erandur, and together they found the engineers. The two men had been set up at the back end of the camp, which gave them more room to work. Wood shavings and discarded objects littered the ground around their shared tent, workhorses and tools placed haphazardly to make a workshop. Lukan Morholn stood behind an odd contraption as he made tiny cuts along an arm of wood when they arrived.

"Master Lukan, merry meet," Tlonna said as she stepped onto the pile of sawdust.

"Heyo," the engineer sung, either oblivious to who she was, or uncaring.

"Is your partner around?" she asked with a smile as the man continued to work.

"Yup. Matt! Get out here!"

The other engineer popped out of the tent with a confused frown on his face. "What, Lukan?"

"The queen's here to see ya, and so's the commander."

"So he is just irreverent," Yayènia whispered to her sister, chuckling.

"I prefer that to the incessant and false bowing I get from most people," Tlonna told her, also grinning. "Ah, Master Matthias. Pleased to see you again."

"Aye. I must say my lady, it is almost luxurious to work in your war camp. I can actually get things done! When I worked for that tyrant Sithian, he was in my face all the time about working faster and harder. I never slept! Begging your pardon, of course."

"Why? I am glad you enjoy your job."

"Well, he's your son, isn't he? That's what we were told," Matthias said, paling.

"Unfortunately, yes. But I know he his cruel, you do not need to fear a reprisal from such a statement. I would however appreciate it if you kept the gossip to a minimum."

"Of course, Queen Tlonna. But I surmise you are here because of my idea?"

"Prince Erandur told me you wanted to see me, so I am here. What idea?"

The engineer turned to throw his arm out towards the object Lukan was chiseling on. "I know you said you did not want a war machine, but from what I have seen of the battles, you need one. Desperately. This is a smaller version of the mangonel that Sithian used to attack your wall. We can make a score of them, and use them to throw items into the air."

"Why would we do that?" Yayènia asked as she moved in to inspect the thing.

Matthias moved with her, gestured for Tlonna to follow. "What would happen if sand or grit was thrown into the air at high velocity toward an advancing line?"

"It would get into their eyes, noses, mouths, they would not be able to see very well," Yayènia said, her voice changing from confused to enlightened with every word. "We could wait until the air had cleared and hit them hard before they had a chance to recover. It would be a slaughter."

"Exactly. If we make twenty of them and launch barrels of sand at the bastards, it would be enough to fill the air for several minutes."

Tlonna gripped Yayènia's arm. "Nia...Kismath. Flying icicles."

"What about them?"

"Glass, old blades, twisted iron. Imagine that flying through the air."

"It would tear apart the ranks like nothing else. It would not just blind them, it would decimate them."

"Something that heavy though," Matthias began, stroking his chin, "we would need larger catapults."

"Not necessarily," Tlonna walked off a little, deep in thought. "If we can just get the stuff up into the air, I can hold it still until the time is right, and then I can use a Weave to push it into the ranks at speeds faster than even the sand would hit. It would be like a million flying daggers. I just cannot lift it all."

"That would work," Matthias said, nodding. "We can have them made in two weeks."

"It needs to be sooner. If I sent you some people, would that help?"

The engineer looked to his partner. Lukan nodded. "We could use them to do the basic steps. Depending on how many you send us, we can have them made in a few days."

"Excellent. I will find some people immediately. Good work, gentlemen," Tlonna said, shook Matthias's hand, and then Lukan's.

She and Yayènia returned to the main camp and went different directions, the commander to find the officers of her army, and the queen to write letters. The first went to Braden, and the second to Miazie. The latter requested all unused glass objects, spare iron, blades, and any sort of sharp object to be transported to the camp immediately. Then she found Ghealan.

The commander was speaking with a few of his soldiers when the queen walked up to him. The soldiers bowed away and left the two alone.

"How are Erdwyf and Jaryikin?" he asked, having not had the chance to do so earlier.

"They are well. Erdwyf misses you greatly, Lan. I am sorry you must stay here."

"I must do nothing. It is my choice to finish this out. Narnen can wait."

"That is what I want to talk to you about. Narnen no longer exists. Erdwyf has changed the name to Nouraeva to give the land an entirely new start. I do not know what the peoples' reaction was to it, for we left before the announcement, but that sort of change is immense. It will take time for Nouraeva to be a kingdom worth its salt. I know she wanted to wait for you, but something must have made her decide to push it ahead. Perhaps it was our visit that spurred her decision, I cannot know. But as king, you should know that your kingdom is no longer called Narnen."

Ghealan shrugged. "Erdwyf has always done what she thought was right, no matter the cost. I did not think this would be any different. Whatever changes she makes will be for the betterment of the land, of that I have no doubt. Perhaps Emar and Atlan knew that when they decided to make her queen. She has the courage to do what they were always afraid to do. She will stand tall and proud against any enemy, just like you. If anyone can remake a kingdom, it is Erdwyf. I am just part of the package."

"No, you are not. You are one of the best warriors to live, a paragon of honor, and an incredible person. Never consider yourself part of a package. You are Ghealan Tomyvon, King of Nouraeva!" Tlonna said and shook him gently.

"Thank you, but I am not feeling much like anything right now. Over a thousand deaths, possibly several hundred more. It is hard to not hate yourself over something like that."

Tlonna swallowed. "I know. But it is not our fault those people died, Lan. It is Midian's, and Sithian's, and Aderiaen's before them. We cannot allow ourselves to bend under the pain they have brought to this land. The forces of fate have led us to this point, and all we can do now is make sure we win. If we do not, someone down the line will have to rise up and start this all over again. It is our job to end it, here. Now."

Ghealan smiled faintly and crushed her into a breath-stealing hug, something he had never done before. "We will triumph!" he roared loud enough to make Tlonna wince.

All around cries went up, ululations of determination and bloodlust. Ghealan released her and she grinned at the soldiers surrounding them as they shook their fists and weapons in the air. It was an uplifting sight.

# Chapter 41
## The Erroneous General

When the next attack came, they were ready. Tlonna and Losolin stood side by side, weapons in hand and their various protectors all around them. Yayènia walked up a moment later, her back straight and the plume on her helmet standing tall. She turned to her soldiers and they looked up at her with the eyes of veterans.

"Today is a day for revenge!" she screamed, lifting her longblade high in the air. "Make them pay with blood!"

The Blackhaven Militia and its Duani allies burst into savage cries and near-animal howls. It was an unnerving sight, and Tlonna felt a shiver go up her spine. Then the enemy came pouring over the rise and they crashed together with a crimson spray. Tlonna bared her teeth and slashed her sword across the face of a screaming Zaedican. Bits of bone and steel from his helmet splattered across Losolin's face, which caused him to stumble in surprise. Tlonna leapt over to his side as a man came in swinging a morning star. She blasted him backward, a hole torn right through his chest.

Losolin straightened and looked at her, wiping gore from his face. "Thank you for that."

Tlonna shrugged. "Duck, next time."

"Mmm," was all the king said as he rejoined the battle.

Tlonna laughed and followed suit.

Ghealan spun about to block a wicked mace as it hurtled toward his back, his warrior's sense on high alert. He caught the weapon on his forearm, grimacing at the dull pain, and shoved his sword into the wielder's belly. As the man fell, another form took his place that moved with the surety of a fighter.

"Ghealan Tomyvon, I know you," the bulky human said coolly as he swung his broadsword like a pendulum.

"Should I know you?" the elf replied, wiping his face with the back of his wrist, recognizing the massive human immediately.

"You will soon enough, never fear," the man said and poked his sword out in a testing manner.

Ghealan deflected it easily but did not retaliate. Again the man jabbed outward, this time a little faster, a little harder, and again the elf swept it away but did not respond.

"Fight me!" the man demanded, eyes dark with anger.

"I will know your name before I do," Ghealan replied lightly.

"Orlando, General of the Zaedican Force," he snapped, irritated with the nonchalant elf.

"Pleasure," he replied and then snapped his sword forward and swept it down a split second later, surprising the big man with his quickness.

Orlando brought his giant blade up and crossed his body with it, parrying the quicksilver elfin blade just in time. Then he swung it outward in a vicious swipe, which forced Ghealan to dance back a step and then another on the return swing. The elf pivoted and ducked low, bringing his weapon up and at an angle, aimed for Orlando's belly. The human jerked his hand down in an effort to block the deadly blade, his sword out too far, and hissed as a line of blood appeared on his forearm.

"First blood, impressive," he said flippantly, ignoring the pain.

Ghealan did not reply as he was already moving. He ran forward a few steps and then leapt straight up, his arms held high, both hands on the hilt of his blade. Orlando lifted his sword to try to skewer the elf, but the commander had other plans.

Rather than strike with his longsword, Ghealan snapped his leg hard into his adversary's face. Orlando flew backward, blood sprayed from his shattered nose and split lip. The elf landed lightly and was already running, meaning to finish off the cocky human when Orlando put up his sword in a pitiful expression of fear. Ghealan snarled and brought his weapon around a blur, aiming at the man's gut, but Orlando scrambled away and disappeared in the milling fighters.

The commander blinked in surprise and disgust. "Flaming coward," he muttered and turned back into the fight.

Orlando walked into the tent and met Sithian's seething gaze. "Well?"

"I cannot fight them on even ground. They're too strong, too fast. I need an edge," the general replied as he picked up a rag and held it to his broken face.

Sithian watched him for a moment and then turned to his desk. "I will find a Weave, but perhaps you should train more. You were not out there long."

Orlando's lips thinned in anger but he wisely stayed silent. The King of Zaedic twisted slightly to give his general a wry smile. "Which of them did you fight?"

"Ghealan Tomyvon."

"Ah...his wife was just crowned Queen of Narnen, was she not, and he King? What is he doing here still, fighting for a cause that is no longer his? Is it a weakness we can use?"

The massive general shook his head in doubt. "He headed the Blackhaven Militia for nearly two hundred years, such loyalties are not easily broken, I would assume. And he and Yayènia er'Tiena were once lovers."

Sithian's brow rose at the last fact, but he said nothing, his mind elsewhere. When the young man continued to be silent, Orlando ducked from the tent and went to his own, seeking rest, wishing once more that Learia was still alive, or that his king was dead.

The next day began as usual, a few hours rest and another wailing attack. The previous battle had been won with little loss, for the attacking enemy had retreated soon after their general fled the field with a broken nose. It would have been a pleasant day if not for the war, the temperature one more fit to sit in the shade of a favorite tree than swing a sword. The sun beat down on the land while heavy thunderheads amassed on the very far horizon. The Blackhavenites once again stopped the charge and began to reverse it. Soon enough the battle was a full-on frenzy yet again.

Yayènia sprinted across the battlefield, leaping over bodies, both prostrate and standing; her vision focused on the massive man creating havoc with his giant broadsword, his face bright red and swollen from the broken nose Ghealan had given him. She flipped over a pair of struggling soldiers, sliding her blade across the throat of the Zaedican that sprayed hot blood over the face of the surprised Blackhavenite man. She hit the ground running, her mouth open in a primal scream of rage and hatred. Orlando turned to her and smiled a cruel grin of eagerness.

The warrior ducked under his whistling sword and jabbed at his knees, spun around to slice across his hamstrings. She blinked in surprise when he did not scream in agony and fall to the ground. Yayènia landed on her shoulder and rolled, came back up to her feet in an instant. Orlando was there, his massive sword cleaving down at her head. She danced back to dodge the barbed edge and snarled, her eyes flashing dangerously.

"Come on pretty elfling," he taunted as he flexed his fingers. "I've been waiting for you."

Yayènia remained silent, not one to engage in conversation with her enemy. She moved like lightning and sliced her blade deep into his side. She jerked back as his arm came toward her, enraged that he was unharmed. The warrior skipped out of range once more and stood staring at him.

"What? Problem?" Orlando hissed and bared his teeth in what she supposed was a smile.

The elf sneered back at him, examining his body for a hint. A soldier bumped into her back and she pivoted in time to take his head off while one of her own tumbled into her. "Get out of here!" she screamed at him and shoved him away.

The human looked more terrified by her shouting at him than the bloody battle raging around him. He gladly dove back into the fray and Yayènia turned back just in time to leap out of the way of Orlando's attack. She rolled and lost her helmet in the action. With Orlando hot on her heels, the commander got back to her feet and swung at him in fury, but her blade passed through him like smoke. She turned and ran, tossing daggers back at him as she did. The man walked through them as though they were not real, not even bothering to deflect them.

Yayènia swore, and then swore louder when his hand grabbed the back of her head. She lurched forward, ripping away from his fingers, which caused her braid to come loose in his fist. He laughed and tugged backward sharply. Yayènia's feet came out from under her and she felt her rump hit the ground hard. The wind was driven from her lungs in a sharp breath but she strained forward in an attempt to get away from the inhuman human. There was an unexpected jerk against the back her head and suddenly her hair was falling all about her face, barely reaching her collarbone. The bastard had sliced her braid off, but she was free from his grasp.

Yayènia snarled in defiance and frustration as she shot forward, caught her rolling body on the palms of her hands and lifted upward into the air. Standing on her hands, she kicked upward, and the heels of her boots slammed into Orlando's chin.

They connected solidly and shoved him back. Her mind already steps ahead of her body, Yayènia dropped onto her back and kept rolling until she was on her feet once more. Spitting out the strands of hair that had gotten into her mouth, the warrior tossed her sword up in the air and caught it by the blade itself, careless of the razor sharp edge digging into her flesh.

"*Dûmvadyn!*" she screamed as the battle rage slammed into her full force. Orlando reeled back in surprise and horror as the elf wrapped both hands about the blade and swung it at him. Her fingers already slippery with blood, the weapon caught more momentum than either fighter expected, and the hilt cracked across the Zaedican's face with such force that it crushed his jaw, shattered teeth and bone. Howling in agony, he stumbled back again, wildly lashing out with his sword and caught Yayènia in the hip and threw her to the side.

The elf spun and kicked her leg out, slammed it hard into the small of his back. Orlando stumbled and dropped his sword to cradle his pulverized jaw. Yayènia readjusted her grip on the slippery blade and leapt, landing on the disoriented Orlando with both feet. Bellowing mindless gibberish Yayènia bludgeoned him, completely unaware that one of her fingers was missing, and another about to be. With a final, disgusting splat Orlando's face caved in, brain and bone exploded upward to cake Yayènia's crazed visage in a thick, visceral mask. Stepping away from the mauled corpse, the elf dropped her sword and looked at her hands for the first time, shaking with the pain.

Her left forefinger was gone, missing from the bottom knuckle, and her right thumb was nearly severed. Quarter inch and deeper cuts laced the rest of her fingers and her palms, the tendons and phalanges visible in many areas. Gritting her teeth, the Maig quickly healed her decimated hands, thanking Aidyn for his help in that though her missing finger was gone for good. Flexing her remaining fingers, her thumb in particular, Yayènia was relieved to find that they worked, if a little stiff. Turning about, she picked up her crimson sword, carefully wiped her blood off the silvery blade, and sheathed it.

She crouched to gain some time to recover her wits before dancing back into battle. Lowering her face, Yayènia saw the uneven edges of her hair catch on her cuirass and then fall free to hang in wavy tangles to her chest. She ran a gauntleted hand back against her scalp and felt every strand that caught and pulled on the iron studs. Her hair ended a few inches below her shoulders at the back, several feet shorter than it had been for nearly three hundred years.

The commander crawled over to where the coiled length of her hair lay splattered in mud and gore. She picked it up and twined it about her belt, not about to leave a prize for an ambitious foe. Yayènia went back to Orlando's body and yanked at the leather ties on his pants. Once she had a good length free, she severed it and used the leather to tie back her hair. Yayènia wiped away a hot tear that fought its way onto her cheek and shook her head at the ridiculous thing.

"Nonsense," she muttered and turned, shoving her helmet back onto her head. All around people struggled, heedless that the two commanders of the opposing armies were mere feet away, one an unrecognizable mess, the other nearly as altered.

Yayènia finally got to her feet and stretched her sore muscles. She began to walk back toward the melee but turned back, thinking better of it. Bending down, she grabbed Orlando's splattered face and twisted it. Pulling out a knife, she tested it against his exposed throat. The flesh resisted. Smiling grimly, the elf sawed through his neck and severed his head. Tying it to her belt, she searched his body for any other recognizable items. She found a ring with the Rahlan symbol on it, the three connected circles with the yellow four-point star in the center. She pocketed that. Sighing as she stood once more, Yayènia tested her grip on her sword and found it manageable.

Wishing she could trust her mangled left hand to hold onto one of her katans, the High Commander launched herself back into the fight. She hacked and slashed away, howling mindlessly as blood sprayed against her face from a slit carotid artery. At one point she felt someone's shoulder push into hers and she looked back, startled. Shoulder to shoulder stood her family in a ring; Tlonna to her left, Aladorn on her right. Beside the queen it went Ghealan to Losolin with Aidyn between the king and Aladorn. Somehow they had managed to meet up in the middle of the battle, their shared hearts bringing them side-by-side for a moment. None of them had any time to notice the head tied to her belt or the lack of braid, for not a moment had passed before they were all springing out in different directions once more, weapons swinging.

Tlonna looked up when someone gasped in a mournful way, her heart thudding unexpectedly. She saw Yayènia enter the tent, her helmet looking slightly off. The warrior threw a lumpy object onto the table and made a beeline for Suneelo, who looked stunned and pale. Yayènia sniffed, *sniffed!* and pulled off her helmet. Everyone gasped. Her hair fell far too short, and she seemed to be missing a finger. As everyone converged on the female, Tlonna went to the table where strings of clotted blood had whipped across the papers and maps strewn about from the horrible item leaning on its side. She pushed it around with a finger, her nose wrinkling when the face came into view.

Orlando's mandible, nose, and cheekbones were completely caved in, his forehead completely covered in dried blood. Tlonna felt her gorge rise and wondered what exactly had happened between the man and Yayènia.

"He had a Weave about him that made him invincible to a blade, but not to blunt force. He was not expecting the hilt of my sword to break his face," the warrior said as she came to stand next to her sister. "But the bastard cut off my braid."

Yayènia handed Tlonna the heavy length of hair. "Nia, I am sorry."

The warrior shrugged, her face oddly more feminine with her hair in disarray about it. "It will grow back eventually."

"Your finger will not."

Again she shrugged. "Better a finger than my life."

"True," Tlonna agreed and offered the commander a small smile. "Well, you certainly dealt them quite the blow today."

"Aye. Here is this, too," she handed the queen the ring. "Can you, uh...can you make it even?"

Tlonna eyed her sister's hair. "I imagine so. Aidyn, give me your sharpest dagger."

The assassin surrendered his weapon and watched in fascination as Tlonna went about evening up Yayènia's ragged hair. When she finished, the commander's hair was just long enough to brush her collarbone.

"There you go," Tlonna said, handing Aidyn back the dagger, who took it with a look of befuddled amusement. "Much better."

Yayènia muttered something in the way of thanks and moved off to stand near her husband, who drew her close with one arm. Aidyn cocked his head when Tlonna turned to him.

"She looks different."

"Of course she does. She just lost about four feet of hair and a finger. How about we shave off all of your hair and see how you look?"

"I suppose it would be much less hassle."

"Oh forget it," Tlonna snorted, "you would still be pretty."

Aidyn shook his head and laughed. "I cannot get away from that, can I? How many times do I have to tell you, I am *not* pretty!"

"Lies do not suit you, Fingers," Losolin said as he happened to walk by, his hand held out for Tlonna.

"Ah, *leif,*" the assassin swore and folded his arms.

# Chapter 42
## Under the Clawed Orb

Tlonna and Aidyn sat atop their mounts on the fortified foothills of the Kismath Mountains. The wall was nearly complete, and the rigged traps winding their way through the narrow pass in the mountains were finished, ready for use at a moment's notice. Tlonna knew that course of action was not one that anyone wanted to accept or even think of, despite the losses they had already suffered and would still suffer.

Below them the Jaquisa River rumbled along, oblivious to the turmoil happening all around it. The sun was a glowing orange sliver on the far horizon when Aidyn shifted in the saddle, his focus deepening.

"What is it?" Tlonna asked quietly, turning her gaze in the direction the assassin was staring. A tiny dot on the grasslands below them caught her attention and she frowned, her hand slowly moving toward her bow.

"No." Aidyn said, though he did not look back at her. "I cannot believe it."

"What?" the Magin stressed, deeply curious.

"Eltïar did it. I cannot believe he did it."

"Who? Did what? Aidyn!"

Finally the dark elf turned to her. "When we were in Seaduens I took care of the succession within the College there, because of Jidair's death. I sent out letters from there asking for the assassins' aid in the war. Eltïar, the elf I lifted to Master, said he would come. It appears as though he brought nearly all the assassins in the entire College, not just Seaduens, but all of them. This is incredible. It has never happened before. Ever." His excitement was palpable, and he leaned forward to grab Tlonna's face, pressing a kiss to her mouth in jubilation.

When he released her, looking a little punch drunk, Tlonna carefully moved Takîreaes closer to the edge of the pass and peered downward in wonder and no little fear. She could see them now, over fifty mounted figures racing over the landscape, their clothing all the same inky black, eye-tricking *ärdyz*. One of them held a standard, a black flag with the strange emblem Aidyn had on all his buckles and weapons.

"I thought you said that was your own symbol."

"It is, but about a century ago the College asked if they could make it the standard. I agreed. No one else is allowed to wear it, but it hangs in all the colleges. They must have had a banner made," Aidyn told her, sounding a little off. "We need to get down there."

"Why are they coming from that direction? How did they get beyond Sithian's camp?" Tlonna asked as the dark elf began to descend from the pass.

"They are College Assassins, Lonna. They could get by *our* defenses in broad daylight and not be noticed. Sithian's mercenaries would not have a chance."

The queen shook her head but allowed the assassin to lead her down to level ground. Once there he took off, Whäd's mane and tail flying out behind her. Takîreaes snorted and moved into a gallop to match the mare. They flew past the sentries, not bothering to explain, and a few minutes later were on an intercept course with the assassins. When they met, the collegiate warriors quickly surrounded the pair, their horses stamping and snorting in the early morning dark.

"Master Aidyn! Good morning," someone said as they pushed to the front of the throng.

"Eltüar," Aidyn replied with a smile. "Who have you brought with you?"

"Masters Moiran, Thanat, Senkuh, and Ove, of course, and their respective colleges."

"All of you?" Aidyn asked, obviously dumbfounded.

Tlonna kept her gaze moving, for every time she met the eyes of an assassin she felt a shiver race up her spine. These people were the deadliest in all the land, and it did not matter that their leader was her closest friend, and partial lover, she was still a little edgy. The Magin stiffened when four others materialized out of the crowd, each one diverse but similar in body language. They were ready to kill, and damn near ready to die. The only woman was a hard-faced little thing. She glanced at Tlonna with unreadable brown eyes and immediately dismissed the queen as unimportant and focused on her leader. Moiran, Tlonna recognized, and he dipped his head to her. The other two were as foreign as the rest of them, one an elf, the other a man, both hardened by a life of shadows. Thanat, the elf, Tlonna appraised a little longer, remembering what Aidyn had told her about him. Reportedly trained by Furntil himself to be an assassin. Ove was nearly forgettable, discounting the amount of weapons he wore of course.

Aidyn reached over and grabbed her hand, which elicited raised eyebrows and cheeky smirks from the fifty or so assassins around them. Tlonna lifted her chin in defiance of their suppositions.

"This is Tlonna Ewôsdírn, Magin Queen of Blackhaven."

The smiles melted away with his words and several heads bowed. Many did not. Senkuh openly glared at her. Tlonna wondered if she was jealous of her proximity to Aidyn.

The dark elf once again addressed the crowd. "I thank you all for your commitment to the freedom of Nymyños. The fact that you are here tells me that you understand your oaths more than most would. I would suggest you all camp in the same area, rather than petrify the regular soldiers with your presence. This is an army of diversity and skill, and all together you make a frightening sight. They will know you for what you are. While you are here you must obey every order I give you, or in lieu of myself, the High Commander Yayènia er'Tiena or any of her officers. Tlonna and King Losolin as well. This is war, not a simple assignation. If you have objections, leave."

Tlonna waited for them all to turn around and ride away, but not one of them even touched their reins. Aidyn looked at her and smiled faintly.

"We should let Nia and the others know, and find a place for them to set up camp."

"Agreed," Tlonna said softly, still unnerved from being surrounded by the assassins.

Aidyn chuckled and turned Whäd around. The assassins opened up their ring to allow them out of the center, and then fell in behind them as they rode back to camp. By now the sentries were on their toes and wondering what was going on. Tlonna had them stand down as the assassins filed within the defenses to the petrified gazes of the guards and anyone else within visual range. Once everyone was inside the defenses, Aidyn had them wait while someone went to fetch whatever officers could be found.

Yayènia, Suneelo, and Sargotarh were the first to appear, all of them looking unperturbed by the group. Yayènia stood before them, her arms folded and her face unreadable. Most of the assassins stared back, unsure who this formidable, armored female was.

"How many?" Yayènia asked.

"Fifty-six," Aidyn told her with a shake of his head. "I thought maybe ten would come at most, not all the field assassins and House Masters. Never before has this happened."

"Their leader called, and they came. Now you know how I feel all the time," Tlonna said, gripping his shoulder. "Now what do we do with them?"

"You heard me tell them to stay together, to make a camp as a company and not single assassins. This is a new world for them. My actions at your and Dietirin's side has always been a topic of confusion for most of them. I told them to obey our commands, so they will, but their social interaction will be quite the experiment."

"Perhaps you should introduce Furntil and Erandur to them, play a little on their motivation," Yayènia said, still staring at the silent group of assassins.

"I will, though Thanat and his College already know them, so not a really big thing for them."

Tlonna shrugged. "Perhaps seeing their king and prince here will make them want to prove themselves more."

"Well, we are talking about College assassins here," Yayènia interjected, "the best of the best. I do not think we have anything to worry about."

"Indeed," Aidyn snorted and dropped his hands onto his scimitar hilts. "This battle is over now. Those bastards have no hope of victory. My boys who were at Alchemian numbered only a few. Imagine how great an advantage this will be!"

"Are those who were at Alchemian here as well?" Yayènia asked.

"All but one. Masya died a few months later, she was ambushed outside of Talenias."

"I am sorry," Tlonna said.

Aidyn shrugged. "Part of being an assassin. Very few elves make it beyond fifty years, twenty of that being just training. Humans normally less than thirty-five. Some live out their lives in retirement, but not many. I somehow broke that rule."

"Somehow," Yayènia snorted. "Like you do not know."

"Well, I try not to flaunt it, unlike some."

"There is nothing wrong with flaunting, my dear," the warrior said, patting his cheek. "Now, introduce me."

Aidyn shook his head but he turned to the assassins and held his arm out to Yayènia. "This is High Commander Yayènia er'Tiena. She is in charge of this battle, and even I typically do what she says because she knows what she is doing, and does it well. You have all heard of her, I am sure. That reputation was not earned with ease. Behind her is Captain of the Guard Suneelo Tiena, third in command, and Yayènia's husband. I would advise you not to piss him off. He sleeps with her. And this is Captain of Cavalry Sargotarh. He once disemboweled a Shitan-Kulata assassin with a chair. I trained him."

Tlonna stared at the captain with wide eyes, his deceivingly young face hard as cold iron. His eyes shifted to her for a moment and a tiny smile lifted the corner of his lips. The queen shook her head in amazement and turned when she heard the others approaching. Losolin, Aladorn, Ghealan, and Erandur, his arm in a sling, slowed to a stop when they realized who the group was.

Aidyn moved his arm out to point at them. As he introduced them, including each of their most acclaimed or vicious achievements, the assassins' looks of boredom changed to something more akin to disbelieving uncertainty. Thanat nodded to Erandur, an expression of disapproval crossing his face when he saw the sling on his prince.

When Aidyn finished, he turned back to Yayènia. "Where can they set up camp?"

The commander chewed on her lip, thinking of a spot big enough. "There is a place between the main camp and the *Zephyr Leifen*. It is going to be one hell of a spot though, assassins and the Silvers right next to each other. Talk about a deadly situation for anyone who happens to meander in there."

"Sounds like a good place, then," the dark elf said and relayed the command to the assassins.

They moved off, the only sound that of the jingle of harnesses and saddles. The five House Masters remained however, their arms folded and standing perfectly still before the group of leaders. Aidyn eyed them for a moment before looking to Tlonna.

"We should probably introduce them to the rest of the family," he said quietly, his green eyes searching hers for any sign of wariness. He found none.

"Aidyn, they are yours. I trust you so I trust them. Have no fear," she said and pressed her palm to his cheek.

"Follow us, then," Yayènia said to the five assassins, who looked a little put off by her casualness.

Tlonna dropped her hand from Aidyn's face, but it inadvertently skimmed down his arm and over his knuckles. While neither of them paid it much heed, Senkuh's eyes went wide with rage. The queen noticed as the woman's hand jerked toward her belt knife and then away.

"Aidyn," she began, her trust suddenly a little shaky. "How well do you know Senkuh?"

The assassin shrugged as he moved off to follow Yayènia and the others. Losolin fell into step beside him as Tlonna hurried to catch up. "She is good, one of the best human assassins I have ever known. She can be pretty violent, and has been known to lose control of her temper when she is really riled. Why?"

"Because I am pretty sure she is in love with you, and stupid with it."

"What?" Aidyn yelped. "Are you mad? She is not in love with me, I guarantee it."

"She is," someone said from behind them and they turned to find Thanat walking a few steps away. "When she saw you two together, she threatened to 'kill the bitch that was clouding her Master's judgment and hording his bed.' She nearly did just now when you two were standing so close to each other. Master, I do not want to overstep my bounds, but I would watch her, were I you."

Aidyn's expression was one of complete shock. "But...she never...why?"

Tlonna let out a gusty sigh. "Thanat, correct?"

The elf nodded with a small smile that brightened his angled face.

"Aidyn does not believe he is beautiful, nor does he seem to care. It does not matter how many times a female falls over in a dead faint when he walks by; he just assumes it is someone else. I do not know what to do about it. Ideas?"

The assassin swallowed back a laugh. "Well, Queen Tlonna, you could always tie him up in a roomful of females and see what happens."

"That would be rape, Thanat," Aidyn muttered.

"You would enjoy it, Master," the other assassin retorted with a grin. "Anyway, you definitely need to watch your back, Queen Tlonna. Senkuh does not like you."

"A lot of people do not like me, Thanat. Unfortunately it comes with the territory of being the prophesied destroyer of evil. Believe me, I can handle myself."

"I would never doubt it from the Everwood. Now if you will excuse me, I must find out why my prince has his arm in a sling," Thanat said, squeezed between the two, and hurried off to fall into step beside Erandur.

Aidyn glanced back to see Senkuh's smoldering glare turn into careful mask of nothing when she caught his eye. The three other masters all gave him a pitying look and shook their heads. Moiran appeared to be trying not to laugh.

"Ah... spirits," he muttered as he turned back around.

Losolin and Tlonna gave each other amused looks and linked hands as they walked. The king gave his wife a curious look, then glanced pointedly at Aidyn's hand. She frowned back at him. He lifted their intertwined fingers and lifted his eyebrows. "If we are going to do this, we may as well do it right," he murmured gently.

Tlonna gazed at him for a moment as they walked along, then slowly reached out and took Aidyn's hand. The assassin's fingers automatically slipped between hers, but then tried to twist away when he realized what she had done. Tlonna tightened her grip, and the dark elf looked sheepishly at Losolin, who shrugged. "Maybe you should give her some of your soap," the king mused and then bit his lip to stop from grinning as the three of them walked along, each holding onto Tlonna.

"What? Why the hell would I do that?" Aidyn snapped, and then his face turned to understanding.

"Sayoir!"

"Indeed, Sayoir."

"I do not think Senkuh would appreciate the gesture. I would most likely get it thrown back in my face, along with a fist. What am I going to do?"

"Keep her from slicing me to ribbons would be a good idea," Tlonna said, unconsciously swinging her arms, and Losolin's, and Aidyn's.

# Chapter 43
## A Warrior of Some Skill

Yayènia shook her head as she passed the assassins' camp on the way to the *Zephyr Leifen* camp. It seemed like a patch of darkness amongst the lighter silvers and blues of the militia, the eye-tricking *ärdyz* material wafted softly in the breeze, which made her feel slightly unbalanced. She hurried by when some of the deadly gazes of the assassins fell on her; not out of fear, but common sense.

"High Commander, we were wondering if you would come by today," one of the Silvers said as he inclined his head when she stepped into the ring of tents.

"Of course. I wanted to speak with all of you about the assassins."

"Are they really here on the command of Lord Aidyn?" Laren said as he came up to her, his short stature allowed her the chance to look down at someone for once.

"Close enough. He requested their presence and every single one of them came. He is in command of them, but has also told them to follow the regular chain of command of the militia. I do not foresee any problems with them, just be on your guard. With them here, our chances of success triple, if not more. With the combined strengths of *Zephyr Leifen* and the assassins, we will be unstoppable, but only if our factions work together. You all know how to fight as one, now you must adapt to allow the assassins the freedom to fight as they do. You have seen how Aidyn fights, yes?"

There were appreciative nods from every single warrior before her. Yayènia folded her arms and looked each of them in the eye. "Though none of them are quite up to par with him, they are all incredible fighters, nearly unparalleled. Pain has no meaning to them, and they will fight to the death in every situation. Just as you are the elite of the fighting forces of the twelve kingdoms, they are the elite of the freeform fighters of Nymyños. Treat them with the same respect you are given by others, and it will be returned to you. If I hear of an incident, be sure that Lord Aidyn and I will be down to rectify the situation. Is that clear?"

"Aye, High Commander!" came the ringing reply as her special squad snapped into their military bow. She frowned when Yaedin, her informal second within the Silvers, narrowed his eyes and moved his gaze to beyond her shoulder.

Yayènia turned and felt her back stiffen. Behind her stood nearly all the assassins, silent and watching, their hands braced on nearly every sort of weapon imaginable. Some had straps all across their body holding several, and others had one or two. One assassin even had some sort of metal band on both his knuckles; his lower face was covered with an *ärdyz* bandana and his hood up to shadow everything but the gleam of his eyes.

"High Commander er'Tiena?" one of them said, and the warrior vaguely recognized the elf as one of the Masters Aidyn had introduced.

"Master Thanat?" she risked as she turned fully to face him.

"Aye. We heard your words. They are wise and generous. Know they will be heeded by us as well."

"Good. Aidyn is one of my oldest friends; I would hate to have him disappointed in those who follow in his steps."

Thanat smiled faintly, his silvery-blue eyes crinkling slightly at the edges with the movement. It was not a sign of age, but of the angled nature of his face. Yayènia half turned back to the Silvers, who were as tense as harp strings. Yaedin and Laren had taken a few steps forward to flank her. She sent them sidelong glances, a smile on her lips.

"Hear that, boys and girls? The assassins will heed my warning. I expect you to as well."

Again the Silvers performed their aggressive bow, their knees snapped halfway to the ground, hands crossed to grip whatever weapons they had on either side of their waists or shoulders, and it was done with purpose. Glancing over, Yayènia watched some of the assassins' eyes widen slightly. She couldn't help her smile this time. With a clap to Yaedin's shoulder, she marched off, doing her best to appear unbothered by the presence of so many deadly warriors.

Yaedin watched his commander stride away, admiring her sense of pride and unshakable confidence, then turned his gaze on Thanat. "I am Lieutenant Yaedin Mahys of *Zephyr Leifen*," he said and held his hand out to the darkly clad Duani.

"Merry meet, Lieutenant Yaedin. I am Thanat Skare, Master Assassin of Flousen Dua College. An honor it is to meet you."

"And for me as well," Yaedin said as his hand was unintentionally crushed by the assassin. "Lord Aidyn is an elf of great honor and skill. I have known him for nearly a century now, and there is no one I admire more."

"Yes, he is…extraordinary. Your High Commander, she is sister to the queen? To Everwood?"

Yaedin frowned. "Yes. Why?"

Thanat shook his head. "Something my king once told me, about that lineage. I am sure it is simply hearsay, however. I shall leave you to your duties. Blessed be, Lieutenant."

"Aye…blessed be," Yaedin muttered as the assassins melted back into their camp.

More days of battle passed and the conjoined forces of Nymyños quickly adjusted to their new, dangerous comrades. It was a week after the assassins had arrived that Tlonna sent out the word that all Darkwights were to be offered sanctuary, but any who declined should be killed. Though many of her soldiers and councilors disagreed, they all acquiesced to her order.

Aidyn grunted in pain as the Darkwight knocked him to the ground with a powerful blow. The assassin tried to roll out of the way but the demon hissed in denial and cleaved his sword downward, only to have it stopped by Aidyn's crossed scimitars, inches from the elf's face.

"I know what you are!" the dark elf gasped in an attempt to follow Tlonna's decree.

"You know nothing," the Darkwight snarled in a guttural voice, his accent that of Zaedic.

"I do," Aidyn panted, straining against the immense strength of the demon. "You are an elf, or…you were. All of you were. Queen Tlonna can change you back; take away the pain of your soul. Let us help you."

The demon's eyes widened slightly, but then narrowed once more and its distorted face crumpled into a hateful sneer. "No one can help me."

Aidyn grunted again as the Darkwight enhanced his efforts in getting his sword through the elf's skull. "Have it your way!"

Squirming a little, the assassin got his knee up into the demon's chest and jerked it forward. His knee slammed into the pommel of his assailant's sword, knocking the weapon out of the surprised demon's hands. The Darkwight fell forward, his neck slid between Aidyn's crossed scimitars and the blades' keen edges sheered right through the flesh and bone to sever head from body. The elf grimaced as blood splattered over his face, but he pushed the body of the demon away and got to his feet.

A few yards away stood Yayènia, her armor sprinkled with crimson, her face half covered in soot and grime. Two Darkwights lay dead at her feet, though she ignored them, instead focused on something else. Aidyn looked around for a moment before realizing it was him she was staring at.

"What?"

The High Commander shook her head as though coming out of a trance. "You have exploded."

"I certainly hope not. What are you talking about?" Aidyn said, concerned. The female was staring at him as though they had never met.

"For the last three hundred years I have watched you fight, seen you spar, even fought you myself, and been the victor. But now, you have bested me twice, quite thoroughly, and now you fight with skill that amazes even me. I do not know what has happened to you, but you are invincible, it seems."

"Yayènia, the last time I *bested* you, it was not you, but Rhiannan in your body. She had all of your talent, but none of your heart, which sets you apart from everyone else. You fight with a purpose. I fight to kill," the assassin mumbled, slightly embarrassed by her words.

The warrior smiled up at him, her teeth bright against the grime on her face. "Well...whatever it is, it is certainly working. You just took out one of the older Darkwights, the stronger ones Midian created."

Aidyn turned to examine the headless body of the Darkwight he had just slain. Shrugging, he eyed the snarling head. "I gave him the chance to join with us, and change back into what he used to be. He refused."

Yayènia shrugged, indifferent. "His choice. Come, we must find our queen and make sure she is alive."

"She is," Aidyn said automatically and unconsciously rubbed the heel of his hand across his heart.

The female eyed him suspiciously. She sheathed her katans as they began walking, the area around them clear of fighting for the moment. "What does that bond tell you? You two seem to be incredibly close lately, even more so than normal. Oh...Aidyn, you cannot be...Losolin will kill you! *I* will kill you!"

The assassin's mouth fell open. "Well, you can try, at least, but no, Tlonna and I are not sharing the sheets. I would never do that to Losolin, nor would she. If I tell you, you must swear to me you will keep our secret."

Yayènia looked at him, her lips slightly parted in surprise. "All right...I swear."

"Tlonna and I are bound by oath to each other, and not just any oath, but the oath between assassin and queen, Magin and elf. It is a connection between us, and I cannot willingly part her company for more than a few days before I must return. If I do not, I die. It tells me what she is feeling, a vague direction of where she is, and if she is hurt or tired or whatever. Losolin knows about it, and he...gave us...permission."

"So that is what it is. How long have you had it? Permission for what? How did you get her to agree to such a thing?"

"Well, she did it accidentally in Kajgenia years ago, and when she released me so I could go after the Eseirik, it left us both rather empty. When I returned, I asked her if she would reaffirm it, and she did. It brings us both a great measure of comfort and security."

"What happened when she was captured by Midian? You were separated for months. What if one of you dies?"

Aidyn shrugged. "If one of us is taken by force, the bond tears in order to protect the other half from whatever hell the other one is going through, at least that is the way I understand it. I was able to more fully tear it when Sithian had me but not completely remove it, which is why it returned to us at the Cleshnoe so unexpectedly."

Yayènia slanted a look at him. "Yeah, Tlonna would not tell me what it was about. I knew you had some sort of link, and I knew you were bound to her by oath, but I thought it was just like my oath of service and loyalty, not an actual magical bond. What permission did Losolin give you?"

The dark elf frowned slightly. "I had it with Dietirin as well, but it was not as potent. There is something more between Lonna and me that makes it stronger, most likely our...affection for one another. I can feel her, Nia. Her emotions, her pain, her strength. She has to be feeling them particularly strong, but I can still feel them. It helps me protect her," Aidyn explained, pointedly ignoring her other questions.

"And if one of you dies?" Yayènia asked again, this time in a darker tone.

Aidyn stopped and looked at her. "It would do one of two things. The other would die shortly after, or they would be released."

"You do not know?"

"Tlonna and I have talked about it, but we have decided that we would rather not know."

"Then how did you mask it when you were with Sithian? She said she could no longer feel you, and then when you saw each other at the Cyree it took you both to your knees, or nearly so. I do not understand."

Aidyn shrugged, tensing as another wave of Zaedicans came into view. Behind and off to the side, the main army turned toward the new threat and moved back into formation and thousands of arrows screamed through the air to drop as many enemies.

"I do not know. Perhaps it was simply willpower. I could not allow her to know what I was experiencing for fear that she might come to me again and risk damage to herself, or feel the pain I was in. Whatever it was, it blocked it for a good long time. When I saw her, so vulnerable, so frightened, it must have shattered that block."

Yayènia scowled at him. "She was not frightened when she came out of the pond."

"She was. I could see it in her eyes. Something she saw down there terrified her, though she will never tell us, I am sure. It is part of who she is, I think, to take such burdens upon herself and keep them from us."

"Well, whatever it is, I suppose I am glad for it. There is no better protector for her. What permission, Aidyn?"

Aidyn grinned and then ducked low as the wave of enemy soldiers hit them. He tossed a bellowing soldier over his back and slammed his tension blade into the belly of the next.

Yayènia jerked her shoulder and head out of the path of a flying spear, barely dodging it. At the last second, she snapped her hand up and caught the end of the pole and twisted, whipped the spear about her body and jerked it up into her armpit so that the point stuck up above her head, her forearm against the lower part of the haft. The demon that had thrown it sneered at her, completely unimpressed.

Yayènia strode forward, sheathing her longblade and cocking her head. "You waste this beautiful weapon by your lack of skill, demon," she said as she tapped her forefinger against the haft.

"You wasste my time, elf," the demon replied, his sibilant voice uncaring.

Yayènia shrugged, and with the same motion flipped the spear around her back and brought it out in front of her, the tip quivering slightly as she held it in check. The demon danced backward, no novice to skilled battle, and brought his forearms up to block the now whipping spear. The elf launched herself in the air, her legs rotated over the end of the haft so that she landed with her back to the Darkwight. Her instincts on full alert, she touched ground less than a foot away from a charging soldier and slammed her open palm into his chest and knocked him to the ground, where he was then trampled. She moved about the end of the spear and drew her longblade, slicing away at the enemies that had noticed her distraction.

Behind her, the demon did a desperate dance at the end of the spear as Yayènia kept it in constant motion so he was not able to slip away. Finally the area cleared and the elf put her blade away once more, slid under the spear and turned about. She yanked the weapon back and forth, her body in tandem with the velocity of the spear.

At the other end of it the Darkwight could only keep his arms before his face to knock away the lurching spearhead before it took off his face. Yayènia spun again, and slapped the middle of the haft across her shoulder blades to give it the momentum she needed, and then slammed the heel of her palm against the spinning weapon.

The pole shattered a split second later as the head lodged itself between the demon's eyes and nose, cloven through half his face. Yayènia let go of the remaining part of the haft while she was still spinning, and it whistled away to impale another Darkwight in the eye, killing it immediately.

The elf blew out a breath and walked over to stand before the dead demon, the spearhead and a few inches of its pole sticking out of his face. "I told you," she muttered and walked away, longblade in hand once more.

A few yards off Aidyn appeared to be toying with three humans who were trying to stab him. He twisted and spun between their blades, barely even using his own weapons to parry. Yayènia blinked when a shadow appeared behind one of the men and a red line gushed from his neck. Aidyn let out a rolling belly laugh and, in a quicksilver motion, sliced the throats of the other two. When all three humans dropped, the female saw one of the College assassins standing on the other side.

"Ruin my fun, Enzo," Aidyn chuckled and slapped the young elf on the shoulder.

The other assassin grinned. "Looked as though you were getting tired, Master Aidyn. You *are* getting up there in age."

"Ah, the insolence of youth, eh Nia?"

"Aye," she muttered, baffled at the odd relationships Aidyn sometimes revealed. "Have you seen any of the others recently?" the warrior asked suddenly, turning to survey the battlefield. "Where is Suneelo?"

Aidyn looked out over his friend's head. "Last I saw him, he was charging like a demon toward a surge of reinforcements."

Yayènia looked sharply up at the assassin and forced her heart to start beating again. "I did not see him go. Do you...do you see him at all?"

Aidyn peered again around the battlefield, his eyes shaded with one of his scimitars. Finally, he sighed. "No. I am sure he is fine, Nia. He is a warrior, and this is a war."

"I know. But he is also my husband."

"This area seems to be cleared for the moment. Go find him. I will return to Tlonna's side."

"I will. Protect her Aidyn, for the love of the gods, do not let her do anything reckless."

The dark elf grunted. "It is my job, Yayènia. Get going."

She nodded to him as she called Udu over and rode off, searching for her husband.

Suneelo spun about in surprise as the earth itself seemed to revolt against the battle. It erupted as magic-wielders fought with abandon; the Nymyñosian Magins roared their defiance as they leapt wildly through the battling soldiers. Suneelo ducked as another explosion rocketed through the air and threw debris and body parts everywhere. He swore as he threw himself to the ground as the earth beneath his feet rolled angrily, cracking and splitting like a piecrust, rumbling with discord. He looked about for a sign of his wife and friends but saw none of them, only the shaken soldiers of both armies. A Magin loomed out of the ensuing dusty air, purple light flickering about his hands, and for a moment, the captain believed his life at an end. Then the man looked down and sloppily saluted, casually stepped over the prostrate elf and continued on his way. Suneelo glared after him until he saw the Magin throw himself at another, presumably the one who had caused the first explosion.

Suneelo climbed to his feet and looked around, wincing at the absolute devastation wreaked by Maginic warfare. All about him soldiers, both friendly and not, lay very still; a few moaned in agony as they breathed their last. The captain shook himself and jogged onward to find his companions. Then suddenly there were soldiers all around him, sprinting away in panic. Most did not even notice his presence, and those few that did only looked back and waved him to follow. Frowning, Suneelo turned and saw three figures chasing the fleeing soldiers. There were only a few more Blackhavenite fighters straggling behind, most of them wounded severely. The elf braced to face this new challenge.

The three Magins did not even stop running. They simply lifted their hands and Wove. Suneelo tightened his grip on his sword and dove at them, his teeth bared in a feral grimace. The first one lost his hands and then his head, but it was too late for the others. They tossed their hands upward in unison and the world obeyed. Balls of roiling white fire erupted from the ground, which tore great holes in the earth and threw Suneelo up in the air like a rag doll. He twisted and cursed as he lost his grip on his sword. He landed hard and groaned in pain but there was no reprieve. The Magins had already finished their next Weave and let it loose. Suneelo rolled to avoid most of the whipping rocks and weapons that had been picked up from the ground by the magical maelstrom, but still a knife sliced across his cheek and a rock smashed into his knee, pulverizing it.

Suneelo cried out as he continued to roll desperately in an attempt to avoid getting torn apart by shrapnel. He yanked out his boot dagger and swiped the back of his arm across his face to clear his vision. He watched as one of the Magins turned his head, looking away, and the other began to move toward him. With a quick prayer to the spirits, the captain let fly his dagger and grimaced at the awkward throw. He didn't see the dagger land, but the Magin stopped and twisted a little before falling to the ground. Before he could get out another weapon, the enemy let loose a retaliation that tossed Suneelo another few yards, spattering clumps of dirt against his armor.

When the debris settled, the elf stopped rolling and lay panting, his arms tucked beneath his chest as he closed his eyes against the agony radiating from his decimated knee. The Magin appeared at his side and glared down at him, his fingers twitching.

"Not again!" Suneelo growled and grabbed the man's leg. He placed one hand on the knee and the other on his calf.

The Magin stumbled backward in surprise and then fell as Suneelo rolled over onto him, jerking his knee under him. The elf kept one hand on the man's leg as he continued to roll, pulling on tendons and muscles without mercy. His free arm he lifted and repeatedly brought his elbow down onto the Magin's face, howling all the while. When the man stopped squirming, Suneelo dropped the leg and collapsed onto his side, his chest rising with short, rapid breaths.

After a while he lifted his head and looked around, waiting for the sight of dusty boots. When he saw none, Suneelo summoned his remaining strength and pushed himself up with trembling arms. Slowly he got onto his good knee and managed to slide it up enough to stand. He took one hobbling step and fell with a groan of agony. He lay for a long time, his breath shallow as he tried to control the pain, and then he heard the sound of a heavy, running man. Once more certain he was about to die, the captain rolled onto his back and blinked the blood out of his eyes so he could see the sky.

"Captain!" came a horrified cry and Suneelo lifted his head to stare at the man running toward him.

"Nathan, what-?" he began, and then saw what had his man so frightened. In the too-near distance a line of advancing cavalry loomed, weaving in and out of the dead bodies littering the ground. "Run!"

"Captain Suneelo, I will not leave you!" he cried and scrambled to a halt by Suneelo's head. He held out a dirty, bandaged hand. "Come on, I'll carry you."

The elf shook his head. "No, I am too injured. Go on and warn the others. That is an order."

"Come on, I'll not be the one to tell the High Commander I left her husband on the battlefield to die," the exhausted human said as he gripped Suneelo's trembling forearm and hoisted him up, ignoring the older male's cry of anguish.

"Thank the gods you're an elf, sir," Nathan grunted as he turned and began to jog, his commanding officer slung around his shoulders.

"Thank my parents for that, Nathan," Suneelo muttered, the back of the guard's head digging into his midriff.

"I shall."

Behind them the advancing cavalry appeared to have spotted them, for cries arose and the sound of galloping hooves thundered through the air.

"Damn!" Nathan cursed and began to run, the air scraping in and out of his lungs as he desperately sprinted over the fallen bodies of fellow soldiers.

"Drop me and get yourself to safety!" Suneelo yelled, struggling.

"I will drop you when I die, sir. Now with all due respect, stop wiggling!"

Suneelo obliged. He didn't want to exhaust his man further. He scanned the empty horizon for sight of friendly forces. Where in all the nine bloody hells had they disappeared to? He heard a whistling behind him and craned his neck to look. He jerked his body, which caused Nathan to fall just in time to avoid a crossbow bolt getting buried in his spine. The two males rolled over the unpleasant ground; the elf wincing every time his knee connected, the human jangling as his weapons were all twisted about his body.

"Well sir," Nathan said after a moment, his voice weak and ironic, "I never thought I'd have the honor of dying at your side."

"Who said anything about dying? Come on, help me up," Suneelo said as he searched the dead Darkwight he'd landed on. When he triumphantly held aloft the long scimitar, Nathan grinned.

The human got to his feet and helped the elf up. Suneelo braced his back against the guardsman's, and linked his left arm through Nathan's baldric. The cavalry was nearly upon them now, and the two turned so that they both had their sides to them. The equestrians hollered and whooped, their weapons swinging above their heads. Suneelo and Nathan ducked at the last moment and took out the horses' legs. The riders screamed as their mounts slammed into the ground and took out several behind them.

Again Suneelo slashed at the legs and necks of the horses nearest him, jerking Nathan around to avoid getting skewered. The human had his sword and long dagger out, fending off the cavalry soldier who hacked at him with a claymore. Suneelo spun again and stabbed the soldier in the kidney, howling as he torqued his knee. He could feel Nathan's ragged breath against his back and knew the human would not last much longer.

"Hold on Nathan, just a little longer!" Suneelo shouted as he ducked under the swinging blade of a horseman and poked at the horse, which caused it to rear up and dump its rider onto the ground.

Yayènia sucked in a breath when she saw the ring of riders circling two figures, one of whom she instinctively knew was her husband. "Hold on Suneelo, just a little longer," she whispered and moved Udu into a gallop over the unsteady battlefield.

Most of the troops had been called home as the enemy had fled, but pockets of angry fighting still continued, and she knew she was needed elsewhere, but Yayènia rushed to her husband's side. Duty be damned for once, she would not let him die.

She slammed Udu's massive bulk into the outer rank of cavalry and leapt off his back as the Zaedicans turned to see what had caused the commotion. She flew through the air with a wild cry, her katans flashing in the sun. Blood sprayed as she landed on the back of a soldier and jerked her swords out to either side. The men fell, gurgling as their throats bled out. Yayènia slammed her helmeted forehead into the back of the man she sat behind and knocked him senseless. She saw Suneelo fall, barely supported by an equally exhausted looking man and her heart began to race.

Desperate, she dropped one of her katans and began yanking throwing blades out, tossing them as quickly and accurately as she could. While she turned her head to find another target, agony exploded in her right arm. A soldier let go of her shattered elbow and smacked his fist into her cheek, thinking her done for. With a grimace, she jerked her shoulder around, swung the fractured arm and called upon her innate healing power. The bones reunited in seconds, her hand twisted back into its proper position as the soldier's eyes went wide.

"Bad idea!" she screamed and hit him as hard as she could with her healed arm, which drove the studs on her gauntlet through his jaw.

Only a few riders remained and they struggled to get to her and the center of the ring where Suneelo and Nathan lay. The horses stomped and reared, tried to escape from the entangled ring. Yayènia stood on the saddle and then quickly ran over the backs of the horses toward the remaining soldiers. With a howl, she leapt off the last horse and took down two of them as she fell. The warrior kicked one in the face and stabbed the other, twisting to avoid the cutlass aimed at her side from a third man. She ducked under his horse's belly and yanked him out of the saddle before she slashed her sword across his throat. As the remaining two approached, Yayènia grabbed a fallen morningstar and threw it at one. He flew off his horse as the chain wrapped around his throat and the spiked head of the weapon slammed into his back. The other rider turned and fled.

Yayènia made her way through the panicked horses to the center. Suneelo lay curled into a ball, blood crusted the side of his face and soaked his entire left leg. The man who had fallen on top of him stared at her with blank eyes, a sword buried in his chest.

"Neelo? Oh gods, Neel!" she cried as she pushed the dead guard off her husband and rolled him over.

Suneelo cracked his eyes open and groaned, barely conscious. Desperate, she shooed the horses away after pausing to untangle a few. Udu stood a few yards away, his legs spread and his head low.

"Come here," she said with a gesture to the stallion.

Yayènia draped Suneelo over her saddle and then picked up the guard, not willing to leave him among the dozens of Zaedican dead. She spotted her left katan and sheathed it as she took up as many of her daggers as she could find. Once finished, she grabbed Udu's reins and ran back toward camp, her heart thundering the entire time.

# Chapter 44

## The Chiming of Glass

Tlonna smiled faintly at Yayènia as she ducked out of the mending tent. "He is awake and complaining, so he is doing fine," the warrior said.

"I am glad to hear it. When I saw you running up with someone slung over your shoulders and another over Udu I feared the worst. Still, poor Nathan. He was so young."

"A lot of them are. Suneelo said that he refused to leave his side. He said he owes Nathan his life, and wants the boy to be recognized."

"Fair enough. I will write him down on the list of accommodations. How are you doing?" Tlonna replied as she eyed her sister with distrust.

Yayènia shrugged. "I am as I always am. Fine. Another wave is coming. I can feel it. We will get no respite."

"Right you are, Nia. They are coming now," Ghealan said as he walked up to them, covered in gore. "Two companies straight on, another four from the flanks."

"Another six thousand, after the massacre we just saw. How many more do they have?" Tlonna nearly wheezed, shaking her head. "This cannot go on much longer."

"We can always retreat back into the pass. That was the original plan, was it not?" the commander said, frustrated.

"Aye, but I like it less and less. We have a good position here, and we have held strong. Every time they come against us they break apart, the only problem is it seems they have countless numbers to throw away. So I am going to initiate the plan Yayènia and I thought up."

Yayènia frowned. "Which one?"

Tlonna smirked faintly. "The wagons of glass and debris arrived today."

"Ahh..."

"As soon as Suneelo is fit to fight, we shall begin."

"Why wait for Suneelo?" Ghealan asked, confused.

"Because I want us to lead a devastating charge after the glass is finished, and tear through them like fire in a dry field. I will need every leader possible with me."

"Braden said once Losolin can get to him Suneelo will be perfectly able to get up and fight," Yayènia told the queen.

"Losolin should be here any moment. He was headed back to one of the other mending tents to heal some of the more seriously wounded," Tlonna said, looking around for her husband. "Have you seen Aidyn?"

"He is in camp with his assassins. I saw them fighting today, one big black weapon cleaving through the ranks. It was incredible," Ghealan commented and shook his head. "It was like they were harvesting wheat, people just fell all around them, all manner of weapons flashing through the sky. Single ranks too, just a wedge that went right through. I have never seen anything like it."

"Aidyn and I were together for a bit and he was just toying with three of the Zaedicans when one of his assassins came up and slit one of their throats. I did not even see him approach. Aidyn just laughed. The assassin could not have been more than twenty, Enzo, I think." Yayènia muttered as she slapped her gauntlets against her palm.

Tlonna chuckled. "I met him, he is a cute lad. I am glad they are on our side. Ah look, there is Losolin."

The king walked up to them, leading Neñyos. He looked exhausted but he smiled. "Glad to see you three," he said and kissed Tlonna, then grabbed Yayènia around the neck and kissed her temple.

"Losolin, Suneelo was hurt today. Braden is in with him, but he needs you," Yayènia told him, reliving for a moment the terror she had felt when she'd seen him curled up on the ground, covered in blood.

The Magin nodded, his face falling. "Take me to him."

Yayènia led her brother-in-law into the tent and to her husband's side. Suneelo lay sleeping, his pant-leg cut open to reveal his pulverized knee. Healer Braden looked up as the king entered.

"King Losolin, good to see you."

"When did you get here?"

"About three hours ago. Hell of a first day," he said, shaking his head. "His kneecap is shattered, and the tibia is fractured."

Losolin nodded and laid his hands on his brother's calf and thigh. As his green magic pulsed out of his hands, Suneelo twitched, his face tightening. Yayènia moved to his side and placed a hand on his shoulder. The blood from his head had been cleaned off to reveal several deep lacerations on his temple and around his left eye. As Losolin's magic coursed through him, the skin began to knit back together.

"He is scarring," she said softly as she watched small welts of flesh form around his eye.

Braden sighed. "I did not immediately stitch them closed because I knew King Losolin would be able to do better, with less scarring. They are not too bad."

Yayènia nodded. "No, they are not."

The scars were a dark red now, four slashes that crisscrossed around his eye, and one that went through his eyebrow, skipped over his eye, and ended just below it.

Losolin let out a deep breath and stumbled back, his eyes closing for a moment as fatigue threatened to undo him. Suneelo groaned and opened his own eyes, glancing about as he gained his bearings. He squinted his left eye, grimacing.

"Losolin?"

"Aye brother," the king murmured and leaned against the cot. "How do you feel?"

"Not spectacular, but I will survive."

"Give yourself a few minutes before trying to move," Braden commanded as the warrior began to shift. "Otherwise you will probably undo all my work, and King Losolin's."

"All right. Nia, thank you."

Yayènia took his hand and kissed his knuckles. "Never would I stand idly by while you fought. Never."

"I know, my heart. You are my savior."

"As sweet as this is," Ghealan began as he walked into the tent, "there is another wave coming."

Losolin pressed his hand to stomach in an attempt to fend off an attack of nausea. "How long?"

"Half hour if we are lucky."

Suneelo looked at Braden, who sighed and moved away from the bed. The captain swung his legs over the edge and stood, stumbled a little but quickly regained his balance. Yayènia hurried to his side and put a steadying hand on his shoulder. "I wonder if you should sit this one out," she murmured.

"Hardly," he snorted and gave her a sidelong look. "Honestly Yayènia, you have become more and more protective in the last few weeks."

The High Commander flushed as the four males present pinned her with their stares. Tlonna let out a gusty sigh. "If we worry, you get offended, if we do not worry, you get offended. So we worry and you can bloody well deal with it. Come on, we have six thousand more Zaedicans to kill before sundown."

"Let's give 'em somethin' to cry about!" Suneelo yelled in the human dialect, laughing.

The others laughed along with him. They were all weary and sick of war, sore and injured and any excuse to laugh was taken. They were nearing the entrance to the tent when it was ripped aside and Sargotarh entered, followed by Aidyn. The high elf was covered head to toe in blood, his eyes a shocking blue against the red.

"There was a surprise attack from the south. Thank the spirits the assassins were over there doing drills; otherwise we would have been overtaken."

Aidyn looked furious, his jaw clenched. "Even so five of them died. Five! We need to make them pay."

Tlonna moved to him, pressing her hands against his torso and chest. "Are you hurt? Sargotarh, is that your blood?"

"No, at least not most of it. Maybe some. I do not know. We stopped them but not for long. There is another several thousand marching from the main encampment, and then another fifteen hundred or so that we blocked off."

Aidyn gently removed Tlonna's hands from his body, pushed by Sargotarh, nodded at Braden, and grabbed Yayènia. "We need to go, now."

"Wait...just wait," Tlonna said, her hand out to stall him. "Ghealan, get all the Magins in camp to meet me at the front line. Braden, check Sargotarh, the rest of you, come with me."

The queen hurried out of the tent and toward the engineers' camp. The two men were standing next to one of the wagons full of glass. They turned when the elves approached, bowing their heads.

"The mangonels are ready, Queen Tlonna. And the glass arrived a few hours ago. When do you want us to get it to the front?" Matthias asked.

"Now. Right now," Tlonna said. "We need it immediately. We are here to carry the mangonels."

"Your majesty, they may be small but they are heavy," the engineer said, but cut off more protestations when Yayènia lifted two and walked off with them without a word.

"We can handle it, I promise," Tlonna said as she picked up two more. "Get those wagons down to the front."

As the elves walked off with the tiny machines of war, the engineers directed their helpers to hook the wagons up to the draft horses and get them moving. Tlonna adjusted her grip on the miniature mangonels and jogged with the rest of her friends to the front line. She had each of them positioned fifty yards apart and then turned when Ghealan called her, followed by a large group of people. She frowned at the turnout, surprised by the number.

"Are you all here as Magins or soldiers?" she asked, her voice ringing in the evening stillness.

They looked uncomfortable beneath her gaze, but they seemed to turn slightly to a middle-aged human among them. He swallowed his anxiety and stepped forward. "We are here in both capacities, your majesty. We are here as healers, fighters, whatever is needed."

"Good, good," Tlonna murmured, "but how do you feel about being merciless killers?"

The man swallowed again, unsettled by such a question. "We...we will do what is necessary to preserve our lives and the lives of our fellows."

Tlonna smiled at him, one void of humor. "Good answer. I have a plan that will stop the enemy in its very tracks." She turned to indicate the mangonels behind her. "These have been constructed in order to throw glass up into the air and into advancing ranks. However, what we are going to do will be much more devastating."

She picked up a piece of glass she had taken from the wagons and held it in front of her face. She took her hand away from the glass, but it stayed up in the air, rotating slowly before her. With a splintering crack, it shattered into several pieces, each jagged in form, the evening sun glimmering off the uneven edges.

Tlonna's eyes moved from the rotating shards to the gathered Magins. "We have wagons of glass and iron headed our way right now. Each shard will be cut just as unevenly as these, and hung in the air as the army approaches. You are all going to link with me and I will break them into even smaller pieces, and we shall hang it in the air. Once the enemy is close enough, we will send it flying toward them."

"But won't they see it, my lady?" a rotund woman asked, nervous.

The Magin Queen again smiled maliciously. "Indeed, but it will be too late. It will destroy them."

"But their Magins will put up a wall, and it will be a useless attempt," a brave soul countered, hidden somewhere in the crowd.

Tlonna shook her head. "No, not from this. Only I and their king can put up a shield Weave strong enough to block non-magical items for an entire army, and you can bet Sithian will not be shielding them."

Silence filled the air, disturbed only by the faint clinking of the floating glass as it occasionally glanced off the edge of other pieces. Finally Tlonna pinned the Magins with an iron glare.

"I need all of you to help disperse and hold the glass in the air."

"We will do it," the man said, again speaking for the whole group.

"Good. Everyone, load the debris into the barrels and then come back here. You will all need to link hands. Losolin, I will need you next to me."

"Always, Tlonna."

"Yayènia, Ghealan, make sure our people are behind us. If they are out front...just make sure they are behind the line."

Yayènia saluted and began signaling her officers as Aidyn, Suneelo, and Ghealan mounted their horses and rode off in separate directions to make sure their contingents were where they needed to be. Tlonna watched as Lukan fitted the barrel into the mangonel in front of her, the clanking of glass and iron filling the air.

"If it works it'll be quite the sight, majesty."

"Do you doubt it will?"

The engineer shrugged. "Either way, it'll be an experiment I don't want to miss."

"You may not want to stick around, Lukan. This will be a massacre," Tlonna told him and then took a deep breath as the rumbling sound of a large moving group of people reached her ears.

"Aye, and a justified one. All right, you're good to go. Good luck," the man said and rushed off to the next one.

Moments later the engineers and their helpers were clearing the area, headed back to the defenses where they could watch. Yayènia and Aladorn rode up, dismounting smoothly. They hurried to her side.

"We have the archers positioned down in the first trench where they will be able to get off several volleys before the bastards are out of range, depending on how close you let them get," Aladorn told Tlonna, making sure his sword was loose in its sheath. "Aidyn has his assassins waiting with the Silvers in the center, down there," he gestured at the small slope they stood on where the black and silver group patiently stood.

"A dangerous group, that," Tlonna muttered with a glance at Yayènia.

"Lan and Neel have their flanks ready to go as soon as you give the all-clear. Erandur, Orthak, and Sargotarh are split into phalanxes behind the archers. They will follow the flanks."

"Good. Here they come. Losolin!"

The king was running toward her as the other Magins fell into one line on either side of the queen. He reached her and they clasped hands, gesturing their two friends back. The advancing army was a dull rumble on the other side of the battlefield, rushing towards the flimsy-looking line of unarmed civilians. Tlonna closed her eyes and opened herself to the spirits, to Jair, to the power that coursed through her. She felt Losolin's hand jolt in hers as she tapped into him, and the other Magin on the left of her do the same. Slowly she pulled deeper into them, moving onto the next one as soon as they were fully linked with her. A few sagged but stayed upright, determination etched on their faces.

"Now," she said, and kicked the lever on the mangonel before her.

All down the line, others did the same. With a deafening crash, the barrels of glass and iron were thrown up into the air, careering wildly about. As soon as it began to fall, Tlonna let loose a portion of the power she held in check. An eerie silence filled the air as the debris was stopped in midflight, and then, with a sound like crackling thunder, every piece shattered into many more as Tlonna let go of the next Weave.

As the pieces stopped breaking and began to rotate slowly, Yayènia swallowed and nudged Aladorn. "Do you hear it?"

The wiat nodded, staring at Tlonna as she stood illuminated by her own power, and that of fifty others, many of whom were on their knees in a stupor. A quiet, almost peaceful chiming filled the air as millions of pieces of glass and iron tapped against each other every so often as they rotated slowly in suspension.

"It is incredible," he whispered, shaking his head. "If it works, she may take out a full quarter of the damn attack."

"It will work," Yayènia told him and sucked in a breath as the army poured over the rise of the battlefield like a black shadow. "It will."

Tlonna felt the magic scouring through her body, felt the individuality of each as it went through her. She could feel the exhaustion and terror of many of those she was linked with, but that did not stop her from pulling more and more. Only Losolin remained steady, his hand solid in hers. She could feel his weariness as well, but also the steely determination to stay with her. It gave her strength.

The army became a single entity to her, one massive wave of evil. The sweet tinkling from the rotating glass was louder to her than the rumble and roar of the enemy. Jair moaned in ecstasy as the power washed through her while the spirits sang in harmony with the magic. Tlonna's eyes turned completely white.

"Tlonna?" Losolin asked as the men got closer and closer.

"Now..." she whispered and let loose the final Weave.

Losolin fought off his fatigue with sheer stubbornness and held tight to Tlonna's hand. He watched her irises change to pearly white to match her pupils and knew something tremendous was about to happen. There was a sound like a loud chime as the floating debris seemed to snap to attention and became still in the air.

Tlonna's fingers tightened in his and her face lowered toward the ground, her shoulders going back. The first line of soldiers was barely fifty yards away when she let out a grunt. The glass and iron shot forward as if it had been released from a slingshot, quickly gaining speed as it flew through the air. The dying sun glanced off the edges of each twisted piece and threw prisms of color across the bloodstained ground. The first line was slammed to the ground by the devastating attack, squirming and screaming as their flesh was ripped open, veins severed and organs punctured. The translucent weapon kept going, unabated by the first hit. It razored through the next several lines before it began to falter.

Losolin again looked to Tlonna and cursed when he saw the sweat rolling down her face. "Come on!" he yelled to the Magins standing with him. "Anything you have left, give it to her!"

He felt a pulse of magic go through him and knew that it was all they had. Tlonna began to sag, color returned to her eyes in pale blotches. The wave of glass and iron finally fell, though it had sliced through well over a third of the advancing lines. Tlonna's knees gave out from beneath her and Losolin caught her up just in time. He screamed at the Magins to run as he turned back toward the waiting army.

"Go! Yayènia! Now!" he bellowed even as he sprinted across the uneven ground. He heard the command go up, followed by the responding roar from his army. Riders approached and swept up the exhausted Magins, dragging them bodily onto horses before wheeling about and speeding off, sent by Aladorn.

The assassins and the Silvers rose up around Losolin as he ran into the small depression. The king stumbled and would have gone down had a black-clad assassin not grabbed his arm.

"Steady there," he said in deep rumbling voice, "you're protected now."

Losolin gulped in a breath and looked around to find himself completely surrounded by Aidyn's brethren and Yayènia's elite. "Thanks. How close are they?"

The assassin who held him up looked to a silver-cloaked warrior. "Yaedin, how much longer?"

As he spoke several thousand arrows screamed over head, followed almost immediately by another, and then another as the three ranks of archers let loose their volleys. The Silver turned and slightly bowed his head to Losolin.

"Another thirty seconds before we go. Do you need Hanrin to escort you and the queen back to camp, King Losolin?"

Losolin looked to the assassin, Hanrin, and shook his head. "No. Good luck. I know of no group who is better equipped to take these bastards out. I almost pity them."

The assassins and Silvers all chuckled and then Yaedin whistled sharply. "Form up!"

Losolin hurried out of the way as the warriors shifted expertly into a loose triple wedge formation, which gave each fighter room enough to swing their blades. Tlonna mumbled against his shoulder and he looked down at her, checking to see if she was awake. She was not, but the perspiration was drying up. Yaedin looked at the tall figure to his right whom Losolin vaguely recognized as the Master of the Seaduens College, and nodded. When the nod was returned, the warriors burst from their cover and rose up against the nearing Zaedicans like avenging angels, the silver cloaks and nauseating *ärdyz* clothing distorting the eye.

Losolin watched for a moment more and then turned and ran back toward the camp. Yayènia met him halfway with their horses and dragged Tlonna up onto Takîreaes with a glower.

"That was one flaming show of power. I did not realize she would keep it going for so long. Took out well over two thousand of them in seconds. I saw you stumbling back and just knew it was over. Bloody nine hells, Losolin, is she okay?"

"Yes, just asleep. You would not believe the amount of power she just channeled through her body."

"I would actually, I saw it. Get back to camp, this battle is not over yet, but your part is done."

Losolin nodded. "See you tonight, Nia."

The warrior nodded as she slammed her helmet onto her head. "As usual."

It was a quick fight as all the separate companies of the Blackhaven and Flousen Dua armies poured out from every angle, led by the *Zephyr Leifen* and the assassins. Yayènia almost felt sorry for the soldiers that fell so easily to her blade, almost. They died screaming, clutching at hemorrhaging wounds and shattered bones. It was a slaughter, and the warrior knew it. But she also knew that the next day there would be just as many, for the army seemed to have no end of recruits, and only the size of the battlefield stopped the enemy from simply overrunning them.

Yayènia looked up as she pulled her blade from yet another victim and saw Sargotarh slash the throat of a snarling Darkwight. Then she saw the Magins creeping up behind him.

"Sargotarh!" she screamed, "move!"

The elf instinctively threw himself to the ground and rolled as she grabbed a dagger from a corpse and let it fly. The enemy Magins saw her move and Wove together to form a shield that was able to deflect her attack. Yayènia sprinted over to Sargotarh, used his back as a springboard, and, katans whistling in the air, took a standing leap toward the two men. Too late. Yellow magic flashed and she was knocked sideways, slamming bodily into her soldiers, blood squirting from her mouth and nose as she landed hard. She rolled onto her front and lifted herself up, grimacing as the arm she'd broken and healed twinged with the motion. Her lungs burned but she stood anyway and shook her head to remove the lingering fuzziness from being tossed about like a doll. The Magins ran at her, Weaves glowing bright on their hands. They were trained War Magins, wrought by Sithian to be devastating and suicidal on the battlefield.

Yayènia caught a glimpse of the soldiers around her, humans, defending her, an elf, as the Magins descended upon them. She danced back a step to avoid a lash of power and cursed as the men formed a protective ring. She got a glimpse of the soldier who appeared to be in charge of the group and swore.

"Aselios, fall back! Fall back! Get your men out of here!" she shouted at the small Knight of Aman from Arseninis, a true veteran of the war. "I can deal with them, just get away!"

"High Commander, it has been an honor," he said and turned slightly to look at her. Yayènia was behind him, just inches away, reaching for his shoulder. Suddenly he exploded outward, sword raised in defiance.

"BLACKHAVEN!" he roared, and then continued onward, uttering a wordless howl. He took one of the Magins out by sheer velocity, slamming into him so hard the Magin's throat was torn open by his gauntlet. It was the yellow wielding Magin, the one that had thrown Yayènia. The other one lashed out, blue magic enfolded Aselios like a cloak. Yayènia cried out as the man writhed in mid-air, agony in his every movement. There was a flash of silver, the Magin twitched, and the blue Weave faded. Aselios dropped like a wet rag, his sword buried deep in the Magin's throat, a perfect throw.

Yayènia burst out of the ring toward him, landing on her knees by his side. He was already dead, his face composed in the peace of death. Grabbing his hands, she wept bitterly, for all those who had died, and for all those who had yet to die. She was tired of the fight. For the first time in her life, she was tired of the fight.

"High Commander, we must go, there's no one left to fight," someone said quietly, sorrow deep in his voice.

"No."

"Please High Commander, we can't stay out here alone."

Yayènia shuddered with a sob. "The Courage of Men. There is nothing stronger than the courage of men," she whispered, and folded Aselios's hands over his chest. "All my long years, I have been wrong. So wrong. Forgive me, my brother," the Maig whispered to the dead man, and stood to let the unknown soldier lead her away.

Losolin jerked his sword down, tearing it out of the belly of a screaming Darkwight, its mangled hands clawing at him as it died. The king spun away and sliced his blade upward, cleaving a crimson line through the face of a tattooed human. Losolin stepped away as the body fell. Just as he turned something exploded to the left of him, making him wince. His ears rang with a high-pitched keen and he blinked, disoriented. Instinct forced his body to the side and just as he vacated the spot another explosion went off, this time tossing him and a few others, friend and foe, to the ground. Losolin pushed himself up, ignoring his deafened ears and watery vision. He tightened his grip on his sword and balled up his left hand into a fist. He blinked a few times to clear his vision. A blurry gray-robed figure stood a few yards away, something orange and flickering in his hands. Losolin swore and sprinted toward the form. Just as he lifted his sword to strike, his vision cleared and the elf saw the face of a frightened human, framed by a deep gray hood.

Losolin hesitated as the light brown eyes widened even further. The man's chin trembled and his face crumpled into terror-stricken weeping. "Please, please don't kill me. I'm just following orders."

"We all are," Losolin growled, grabbing the man by his collar. "We saved your people, your camp. What are you doing?"

The alchemist dropped the lit brand he had been using to light his bombs so he could reach up and grab onto Losolin's hand. "S-some of us were hired by General Orlando. We weren't given a choice."

"You had a choice. You are coming with me," the elf snarled and began dragging him bodily through the fighting. A half dozen soldiers broke off their duels and formed a circle about their king, creating a guard.

They fought their way back to camp and there Losolin dismissed the soldiers. The alchemist was shaking violently by the time the king tossed him bodily into the command tent. Suneelo and Orthak were inside, quietly discussing tactics over the maps spread on the table. They both looked up as the human landed hard on the ground before them. Suneelo's eyes narrowed in what his brother recognized as a sign of dangerous temper. The captain crouched before the man and flicked his hood back.

"What is this?" Suneelo asked quietly, glancing up at Losolin.

"Alchemists. Seems Sodo was correct in his belief that they betrayed us."

The man scrambled onto his knees. "No, no we didn't betray you. We were *hired*. We are neutral, see? You took Alchemist Sodo, General Orlando hired some of us...we don't take sides."

"Sodo is not here, throwing *nytrynhimmel* grenades at us," Losolin said softly, riding the killing edge. "He is home, with his pregnant wife."

"That trollop Miazie?"

Suneelo's fist slammed into the man's stomach, doubling him over. He held himself up on trembling arms and spat out blood. He coughed and gagged, shuddering. Suneelo's indigo eyes were lidded, his face void of emotion as he gripped the man by his hair and slowly pulled his head back, exposing his throat. "How many of you are here?"

"F-forty came. Seven are dead."

Orthak stumped over and glared down into the man's eyes. "Who allowed ye to be hired?"

"It is not a matter of allowance," the man gasped, his head wrenched back. "High Alchemist Kryll was simply following our creed. We are hirable by anyone who has the funds."

"When we left, Ardenay was High Alchemist," Losolin said sharply.

The alchemist's eyes rolled over toward the king. "She died. Something went wrong with one of her experiments, and she was killed."

"Sodo must not know," Suneelo said to his brother.

"High Alchemist Kryll forbade any contact with the traitor Sodo."

"What is your name?" Orthak muttered.

"Darmian. Darmian Gray."

Losolin shared a look with Suneelo. According to Miazie's accounts of Alchemian, Darmian had been the lover of the spryte, Kryll. "Kill him. We have what we needed."

Darmian shrieked and writhed in Suneelo's grip as the elf dragged him out of the tent by his hair. The shrieks cut off abruptly, and a moment later Suneelo reappeared, sheathing a dagger. He looked at Orthak. "Send a letter to Miazie and Sodo, inform them of this. I will find Nia and tell her." The dwarf nodded and set about his task. Suneelo gripped Losolin's shoulder for a brief moment before both of them returned to the battle.

Yayènia yelled at her troops to fall back and regroup behind her. The land heaved and rumbled as dark Magins advanced, their steps purposeful and their hands outstretched. The allied forces did as she bid, scrambling away from the wielders. As the last few stragglers passed her, Yayènia turned and spotted Aladorn sprinting toward her, his blade out and gleaming dully with bright red blood. Just as the dark elf reached her, the earth erupted and they stumbled into each other. Aladorn wrapped his free hand about her arm and began tugging her back toward the retreating troops. She went willingly, using him to balance. The ground trembled beneath their feet and explosions harried them on both sides, sending them reeling and twisting about each other, fighting to keep their feet.

Yayènia lost her grip on Aladorn's shoulder as she was tossed upward. She managed to wrap her hand in the dark elf's black shirt as she came back down, now on the other side of him. His arm came around her shoulders and they stumbled forward, trying to outpace the war Magins.

"*Leif*," the commander grunted as they flinched away from yet another detonation only inches away from Aladorn's foot.

Then suddenly they were both in the air, spinning wildly as they tried to control their fall. Yayènia landed hard on her back, her helmet bouncing away. She wheezed as the air was knocked from her lungs, then grimaced as Aladorn landed on top of her. His body covered all of her, his black hair spread across her face. He smelled like Aidyn, though a bit muskier. Suddenly Aladorn's body tightened above her and he curled inward, pressing her legs together between his, wrapping his arms around her waist and shoulders. His chin came down against her neck. Yayènia gasped and let her head fall back against the churned ground. She rested her face against his, cheek to cheek. He smelled so *good,* blocking out the dirt and blood.

Opening her eyes, Yayènia started. Color was leeched from the world, faded and nearly gone, but everything was sharper, more defined. Tensing, the High Commander thought they were done for as a Magin approached; his face seemed carved from stone, set above the high collar of a stiff dark coat that fell to his knees. She tightened her body against Aladorn's as the black boots crunched by her head, then continued onward without pausing. Suddenly she realized he was somehow projecting his ability onto her, making them invisible.

She peered through the strands of dark hair that was spilled over her face, lifting her head so she could look over his shoulder. Aladorn stiffened as she cursed and dropped her head back down, burying her face in his hair, hoping it would help him keep her shielded.

"Three more," she whispered into his ear.

The wiat nodded once and tightened his arms and legs around her. Yayènia's hands were pinned to her sides, level with his hips. She wriggled her fingers beneath his belt to keep them from shaking, the backs of her fingers against the warm, soft skin of his lower abdomen and the sharp ridges of his hipbone. She could feel his muscles, tense and solid as iron as he pressed down over her. Several minutes passed, ticking away slowly as they lay there on the battlefield, holding tight to each other in a much more intimate way than they ever foresaw themselves being. Finally Aladorn's face lifted and his dark green, nearly black eyes scanned the horizon. He grunted and lifted up onto his hands and knees, straddling Yayènia. Her hands were still tucked into his trousers as he did so. She plucked them free as she rolled onto her stomach, still between his arms and legs. The four Magins were receding, arrogant in their power.

Aladorn stood and helped her up, silent. He gave her an unreadable look as he tucked his shirt back in. Yayènia eyed him in a new light. He did look a mighty lot like his brother. She found her helmet and slid it back over her head. Together, they went after the Magins, now with the element of surprise. Aladorn took the closest one out with a garrote, slipping up behind him, invisible. Yayènia watched as a line of blood appeared out of nowhere on the man's neck, dropping him. Aladorn flickered back into sight as the second Magin turned, pale blue light crackling about his body. Yayènia dodged a bolt of blue fire and swept her leg under his feet. As the Magin fell with a curse, she stabbed her dagger down into his chest, ripping it out in a spray of blood.

The last two humans turned, the powerful one in the dark coat glowering in surprise as he spotted the two elves. Aladorn twisted as the closer Magin shot a net of dark green wires out of his fingers. A knife gleamed just before it buried itself in the man's throat. The dark net disappeared just before it reached Aladorn. The wiat ran to retrieve his knife as Yayènia sprang onto her hands, then flipped back to her feet, avoiding the shots of gray magic the last Magin hurled at her. His feet were spread, hands splayed toward the elves. Aladorn leapt in front of Yayènia and went to his knees. The female launched off his back and drove a katan straight down. The Magin collapsed as Yayènia landed, her sword buried in the top of his head. All around them, the land stilled as Weaves died along with their creator.

Breathing hard, the High Commander yanked her blade out in a spray of bone and brain. Aladorn strolled over to her, casual as can be, and used his thumb to wipe away a bit of blood from her cheek. She wrinkled her nose at him. Together, they walked back to their retreating troops. As they neared the rear line, Suneelo trotted up on his horse. He eyed their dirty, splattered appearance with a critical eye.

"Magins," Yayènia told her husband as he dismounted, looking behind them. "Four of them. I think the fight is over for the day."

Suneelo nodded, his eyes scanned the emptying battlefield. "That is good. Losolin was attacked by an alchemist earlier. Forty of them were hired out to Orlando by Kryll, a spryte who took over when Ardenay died."

Aladorn growled and Suneelo nodded. "Apparently Orlando's death does not affect their contract. The one Losolin captured was Darmian."

Both elves narrowed their eyes, recalling Miazie's recollections. Yayènia sighed heavily and scratched at her nose. She no longer wore gauntlets because they didn't fit right with her missing and mangled fingers. She ordered Suneelo back to camp, and continued to walk back with Aladorn, discussing the next steps.

# Chapter 45
## The Friend Perceives

The days became hotter as summer moved into full swing and the war continued to drag on. Tlonna kept a constant correspondence with Miazie, who still sat as regent in Blackhaven, Sodo by her side. The human confessed herself fat with child and uncomfortably sweaty at most times, which made Tlonna laugh. The kingdom appeared to have moved into a period of steady economy, and the Belau reported that though it was still dangerously low, the treasury was seeing its first increases since the occupation by Midian. She also wrote that the spies sent out by Martin Crotes, and whom she had taken into confidence since his untimely death, had returned and reported a massive military movement among all the allied kingdoms.

This news troubled the queen and she showed Losolin the letter when he ducked inside their tent after meeting with Orthak and Sargotarh to discuss options.

"What do you think?" Tlonna asked when her husband set the letter down.

Losolin shrugged. "They are either headed our way as reinforcements, or are simply preparing for our eventual defeat, guarding their borders. It is not illogical for them to do so."

"Tristan, Tyular, and Barukh would not leave us to die," Tlonna argued quietly, shaking her head. "They are good men, good kings."

"No doubt, Loni, but everything is possible."

"I know. What did you decide upon with Orthak and Sar?"

The king flopped into a chair and kicked off his boots. "We are wasting time here. Every attack we think will cripple them just sets them back a little. We got, what, a week's reprieve with the glass? We have the traps set up in the mountains, but you and Nia are right about not moving back. Here we have a solid defense, they have never broken through. Still, we are accomplishing nothing. This needs to end. Now."

"I need to lure Sithian out. He has not been seen for weeks. I know he is in camp, but he never comes out to the fight. That will end this," Tlonna said and rolled her head back to stare at the canvas ceiling of their tent.

"I would rather fight this war until my bones turn to dust than have you do that, Tlonna."

"There truly is no guarantee that I will die, Losolin. We have been so wrong about the prophecy all along, perhaps we are wrong about this too," she lied, recalling the images drawn on the cave walls beneath the Cyree.

Losolin snorted. "As if the real interpretation of the prophecy is any great thing anyway."

"Oh, love," Tlonna breathed, turning her head to look at him, "do you doubt my love because of a few ancient words? Or because Aidyn was crafted to be my lover?"

"Never, I just...I feel thwarted."

She couldn't help it. Tlonna laughed, giggling hysterically at Losolin's words. "That is utterly ridiculous!" she managed to wheeze.

Losolin chuckled at her. "I know. But the thought of that pretty assassin running his hands over you just sets my teeth on edge, no matter what I promised."

"Aye, I know. You could always join in," she said saucily. "Anyway, it never goes any further than kisses. You, my love, get all of me."

He looked up at her with an incredulous laugh. "I am willing to give that assassin more of you than any husband should ever be, and I will admit that you both seem happier, lighter, and that makes me happy. However, not to save the world would I jump in the middle of *that*."

Tlonna laughed and bent down to kiss him. Losolin grunted and stood, preparing to take her into his arms when Ghealan strode into their tent. The commander took off his helmet and wiped the heel of his hand across his forehead.

"There are uh...riders coming. A lot of them, from the west," he mumbled.

Tlonna got to her feet and pressed her hands to the big elf's face. "Get some rest, Lan. You are going to run yourself into the ground."

He shook his head. "I have not the time, Tlonna."

"Nonsense. You will do us no good if you fall asleep in the middle of a fight. I temporarily relieve you of duty until morning. Go to your tent and rest. Now," Tlonna said firmly but gently.

Ghealan gave her a sulky glare but did as she commanded, his shoulders slumped with exhaustion. Tlonna and Losolin hurried out toward the west end of camp. They passed the *Zephyr Leifen* section and the assassins', their eyebrows raised at the mingling going on between the two.

"Tlonna! Hold on!" came a cry from the area and Aidyn materialized from the crowd. "Where are you two headed?"

"Lan said there were several riders coming from the west. We were going to meet them," she told her friend, linking arms with him and her husband.

"The west? Nebet'thu?"

Losolin looked surprised at the idea. "I did not even think of him. Perhaps."

The assassin shrugged one shoulder. "I cannot think who else it might be."

The trio moved beyond the formal camp lines and into the sentry lines, grabbing torches from the guards standing watch. They hurried out to the final ring of sentries and were met by a face from their past. The human Tyre smiled as he bowed.

"I did not know you were here, Tyre!" Tlonna cried as she hugged him.

The man laughed as he patted her back. "I would never stand aside, Tlonna. I was in it from the start, and I intend to be there for the end. I take it you are here because of the army?"

"Army?" the three elves said in unison, their eyes going wide.

Tyre nodded. "Yeah, we spotted them about twenty minutes ago, coming out of Purheae Forest, it seems."

"How many?" Aidyn asked, moving out behind the range of the torch.

"Thousands. *Thousands*," Tyre said, his voice dull. "Is it possible we were flanked?"

Tlonna let out the breath she had been holding and shook her head. "I do not know. How long until they are within visual range from here?"

"Another hour, perhaps a bit more. They are moving very slowly."

"All right. I want all second rank officers and up here in twenty minutes, full armor, and two standard-bearers, tell Ghealan I apologize. Aidyn, will you meet us back here with one of your assassins?"

"Of course," the dark elf said and hurried off, disappearing into the night.

Tlonna and Losolin left Tyre to gather their own gear and horses. Fifteen minutes later they were sitting atop Takîreaes and Neñyos in full armor watching as everyone rode up. Yayènia, Suneelo, Aladorn, Sargotarh, Orthak, Erandur, and Ghealan sat in a line more daunting than anything Tlonna had ever seen before. Aidyn and his chosen second Thanat were a little off to the side, two inky-black figures melding into the night. Behind all of them were the Second Rank Captains Tyre, Erich, Bryce, and Aselios's replacement, Joshua, along with the two standard-bearers. Tlonna eyed them all with pride, her battle-hardened friends and colleagues.

"I have you all here now because of the possible threat heading our way. If it is yet another enemy, or more of the same, we will meet them and let them know we will not stand idle. They will see the steel that leads this army. If, by some miracle of the gods, they are friends, then we will meet them with honor. It is time," the Magin Queen said and turned her stallion westward.

They rode quickly and within a half hour the approaching behemoth came into view. Tlonna reined Takîreaes in and peered through the dark, trying to see the fluttering banners. None of her entourage carried a torch, so she took the Staff of Cyree off her back and planted it in the ground, leaving a Weave upon it so that it glowed like a beacon. A cry arose from the advancing army and several riders dispatched from the body. The standard-bearers with Tlonna rode up to flank the Staff while everyone else moved into a single arcing line, drawing bows and notching arrows.

She looked down the line to see the set determination of fourteen warriors, friends, family, and trusted companions all. Their arms were steady, their gazes unwavering, their arrows each aimed at the heart of a rider. She was glad she was on the fletching side of the missiles.

"Should we give them something to think about?" Yayènia muttered, glancing at Aidyn and Suneelo, who were on either side of her.

"Put your arrows right before their horses' hooves," Losolin said when Tlonna nodded.

With barely a second passing between the first arrow let loose, which was Aidyn's, and the last, Bryce's, the arrows flew almost in a straight line. They landed just feet away from the advancing horses, which stopped the beasts and made them rear and buck. The riders cried out but did not draw weapons. They got their mounts under control and as they rode by, grabbed the arrows up out of the ground.

"What in the name of...?" Aladorn muttered as the figures got closer.

"Dear gods, can it be?" Suneelo said, moving his horse forward a bit as he stared outward.

"Not a nice thing to do to friends!" one of the riders called and Tlonna nearly burst into tears.

Tristan, Eyin, Meradyn, Tyular, Barukh, Nebet'thu, Shin-Hatsu, and Isadorr halted their mounts before the others. It was Tyular who had spoken, his voice full of mirth as he waved an arrow at them.

"We ride for months around south and western Nymyños gathering troops and you welcome us with arrows? Honestly."

Tlonna sucked in a shaky breath and pulled her helmet off, still fighting back tears. "You are here, all of you! You all came?"

"Well, we like to think of ourselves as good kings and generals, Tlonna," Barukh said in his gravelly voice.

"All good kings..." Yayènia said, sharing a look with Aidyn and Tlonna.

"Isadorr?" Losolin questioned, shocked.

The Seaduens king bowed his head. "When King Tristan sent me back his letter saying he was willing to give my people sanctuary, I came to the realization that though we are separated by borders and races, we are all Nymyñosians, we are all of one true nation. I will not be the selfish coward my father was. I will stand and fight with my neighbors."

"I am glad to hear you say that, your...*our,* brother will be pleased. Eyin...what are you doing here?"

"You told me once that I must make my decisions and act upon them, and that will be what history will remember of me. I want to be a good king, Queen Tlonna, and how could I be viewed as such if I sat back and let the entire continent go to war without offering what aid I can? You gave me every opportunity to make my people into something more than tribal barbarians. We are here to begin repaying that generosity," the young king said, his strong chin raised in pride.

"We did not do that for repayment," Losolin said, shaking his head.

"This is another reason we are here. You showed us kindness without any real promise of return. This is a new world, King Losolin, and we will be a part of it."

"It is their choice to be here. Allow them to keep their honor," Tyular said, giving the young Purheaen a small smile.

Tlonna shook her head, not in denial but in disbelief. "I cannot believe you are all here, with your armies. Shin-Hatsu, I did not think to see you again."

The Zeynuwnian general shrugged. "I told you I would ride beside you whenever needed, unless explicitly barred by Emperor Tahi-tat. When Kings Tristan, Barukh, and Tyular came riding into Kyiji with word of war and encroaching evil, he gave me the command to march with them."

"Your Hindarün has improved," Yayènia remarked dryly.

"Your life has been restored," Shin replied in kind. "Seems we are both capable of miracles."

Everyone chuckled until Barukh rode forward and eyed the gathered people before him. "Had we been enemies, what were you planning to do? Everyone person I see has signs of high rank upon them. You could have decapitated your entire army by coming here."

"If you knew what we had been up against these last few months, you would understand our reasons for drastic measures. Had you been an enemy, we would have taken down as many as possible and then retreated back to camp, all the while sounding the alarm," Yayènia told him. "We want this to be done."

"Understandable," the dwarf king said, nodding.

"Gothier is not among you?" Isadorr asked as his eyes flashed through the ranks.

Everyone frowned. "I have not seen Gothier for a few days, actually," Aidyn said, scowling.

"He has not been found among the dead," Yayènia added, her face darkening.

"I am sure we have just missed him in the mayhem," Tlonna muttered, not wanting to think about such things at the moment. "Come, bring your much-appreciated soldiers into camp."

Tyular studied her for a moment before grabbing a horn that lay at his hip and blowing three long blasts on it. A faint cry went up from someone in the ranks, and the army began marching forward. With a signal, Yayènia sent the bannermen into motion and the rest followed.

The first battles that the vast army of Nymyños fought together were creations of grace and brutality, devastating the enemy as they never had before. The massive Nymyñosian Army worked together like a well-oiled hinge, separate parts melding together under a single purpose. A week later, Yayènia forced Tlonna to stand on a rock and address the thousands of soldiers who followed her. The Magin Queen had commanded her Magins to stand down, sensing their exhaustion, and worrying about what might happen to them when she finally unleashed her power, and so only warriors stood before her now. The queen looked down at the group of friends and family that had been by her side for so long and felt their love wash through her.

"My friends, we are not here because we have committed some sin against our aggressors, or because we have we done evil that demands us sacrifice our lives in retribution. All we have done is live in freedom and peace, in community and love. These wretches that day after day throw themselves at us in a desperate surge of violence have come here out of jealousy and illogical hatred. So we have defended, we have pushed them back hard every time, and we are yet standing!"

Tlonna threw her arm out to point behind her, where the enemy sat hidden from view. "Those are evil people! They are blind in their hatred and vicious in their ignorance. Today, we end this. Today, we drive them into their graves and whatever sacrifices we make here today will be for freedom, for glory, for justice, but most of all for love itself. Love of our families, our homes, and our land. So I say let them come!"

She turned around to face the horizon and threw her arms out wide. "Come to us and we will triumph! *Yeste eshoun akod, klamen günna vont traeta!*" she screamed in both Hindarün and Parlêthian, causing a great roar to erupt from the massive army.

Yayènia helped her down with tears in her eyes, her heart beating slow and hard beneath her armor. "This is it," she said to the queen.

"Yes. This is it," Tlonna replied, looking each of her companions in the eye, and drew from their ferocity, their resolve, and their support. "I hope to see you all at the end. Blessed be."

Miazie was listening to a dry report from the raw materials warehouse manager. The man droned on, listing the exact revenue of each product and checking it against the crown's treasury. She stifled a yawn when he paused to take a breath, his knobby finger keeping his place on the chart. Then he disappeared.

Startled, the Belau nearly fell out of her chair, but it would not have mattered, for her mind was no longer in her office, or even in Blackhaven. She was staring at a beautiful elf identical to Tlonna who was kneeling at the side of a dying child in the middle of a forest village. Miazie watched as Tonora stood and turned to face Astinus the Seer. The scene unfolded as he told her about the prophecy. Stunned and upset, the Belau wheeled through time. She saw Tonora fall in love with Aeron and give birth to the infant Jair, the subsequent murder by Jesper. She witnessed firsthand Jair's destruction of the Tower of Magins and the Council. It was a long and bloody vision, filled with more horror and despair than any other of which she had been prey.

Miazie gasped as the vision faded. She was on the floor, curled into the fetal position and gasping hopelessly. Her fingers were digging into her scalp, hard enough to draw blood. The warehouse manager was gone, replaced by Sodo and a few guards. Miazie recoiled from her fiancé's touch, feeling too vulnerable for even that simple connection. Her eyes burned with tears both mournful and furious. The Belau felt sick, violated and desperate.

"Miazie..." Sodo breathed, sitting on his heels a few inches away, not daring to touch her again. "My love what is it?"

"Blood, so much blood. Why is there always so much blood?"

"Where? Are you hurt?"

Miazie cackled softly. "My mind."

The alchemist shooed the guards away and knelt by the woman. "Miazie...tell me. What happened?"

Slowly, brokenly, she told him, her eyes staring blankly at his knee. When she finished, Miazie clutched at her swollen belly.

"I must destroy it."

Panic seized Sodo and he grabbed Miazie by the shoulders, ignoring her frantic attempts to get away from him.

"I am not right! I am shattering into a billion pieces Sodo! Please! I cannot force this life onto a child!"

Sodo shook his head and pinned her arms above her head so she couldn't claw at her belly. "Miazie, stop it! Calm yourself! Listen to me, hear my voice. What you saw was in the past. There is nothing you can do. Our child will be healthy and whole. You are safe."

He began to sing in Parlêthian, soothing her as he once had years ago when she'd been burned by Nytrynhimmel. Her violent thrashing slowed until she lay still on the floor, breathing heavily, tears running down her face. Sodo started to ease up when she let out a terrible scream. His heart tried to gallop into his throat as the woman he loved twisted and contorted into a grotesque position, her fingers scrabbling at the air.

Her beautiful green eyes opened wide and the pupils expanded until they took up nearly her whole eye, a sliver of white barely visible on the edges. Fear threatened to undo Sodo as he watched, helpless. Then she screamed again, this time for what seemed like an eternity. On the other side of the door he could hear the frantic questions of nobles, servants, and council members.

Sodo still had his grip on her wrists when a dark, inky vapor started rolling from Miazie's mouth and nose. He swore, bewildered and terrified. There was a loud detonation and he was thrown backward to slam against the wall. The alchemist slid down to the floor, dazed. Through his watery vision he saw Miazie flop listlessly, her limbs flaccid, her chest barely moving. The mysterious vapor was gone.

Shaking his head to clear his vision, Sodo crawled to her side and lifted her head and shoulders into his lap. "Miazie?"

The woman's forehead crinkled and she moaned. Slowly her eyes opened, staring up at the elf. "Sodo?"

"What in all the nine hells was that?"

"What? Why am I on the floor?"

Sodo scowled. "You had a vision of sorts, about Tonora's death and the destruction of the Tower of Magins. Then you started convulsing, and this odd black fog came pouring from your mouth and nose. It exploded, I think. At least it knocked me into the wall."

"I remember the vision." she frowned, looking lost. "Sodo...I feel different."

"I would imagine. What is going on, Miazie?"

The woman sat up with a groan. "I...do not know." Her eyes went blank, into her trance-like state, but she resurfaced almost immediately and gripped his wrists. "Sodo, it's gone! I cannot find the answers!"

"What do you mean?"

Miazie took several deep breaths and tried going back into her mind again. When she failed over and over, she looked up at her lover. "I am no longer a Belau."

"How is that possible?"

She shrugged, weak. "I do not know. Sodo, I'm frightened."

The alchemist nodded. "As am I. Come, you need to rest, and I think so do I." He picked her up and opened the door.

Dozens of people were standing just outside, worried. Sodo ignored them as he pushed through the crowd. Without a word he carried her to their apartment, laid her on the bed, and watched her sleep for hours, anxious.

# Chapter 46
## Prophecy's Final Price

It began as any other fight, a clashing of flesh, steel, and bitter anger. There was no mercy given on either side. Soldiers, mercenaries, heroes and assassins met on a field of bloodshed that was at last equal in terms of numbers. As each fighter met a new foe, they hardened themselves against the possibility that their story might be at an end.

Eyin howled as he led his men into battle, barely keeping his seat on the galloping horse. Behind him, Meradyn bellowed just as loudly, though he had one arm raised, his sword poised to strike. The Purheaen men who had ridden with them shouted and whooped, some of them whipping slings and clubs around as they slammed into the fight. Only a few seconds in, Eyin's horse was cut down, which sent him flying over its head. He landed hard and rolled, groaning in pain. He climbed to his feet and looked around, surprised he was still alive. All around him was fighting, bloodletting, and screaming.

A soldier rushed the young king, his scraggly teeth bared in a feral snarl. Eyin lurched backward, Yayènia's drills scrambling up in his head. For a moment he thought himself done for, and then the idea of his fledgling people falling back into their reclusive poverty drove him forward. His arms mindlessly went out in front him and he yelled. The soldier swung at him but the young man ducked under it and came up very near to the Zaedican. With a growl he slammed his hands into the soldier's face, digging his thumbs into the man's eye sockets. With a scream the solider flailed, let go of his sword as he writhed to the ground, Eyin's thumbs digging ever deeper until they popped like a cyst, staining his hands.

When the soldier finally stopped twitching, Eyin stood and shook the gore from his hands, his stomach lurching. Gasping in a breath, he pulled out his sword and looked around for Meradyn, praying to Gagu that he and his friend would survive the day.

Meradyn shifted in his saddle, his hand loose on the pommel as sweat made his grip unsure. He hit the line of enemies and felt his horse shudder, but Commander kept pushing forward while men and demons scattered before the cavalry charge like mice from a cat. All around him heroes from legend whooped and hollered as they plunged into the Zaedican force. Slightly ahead of him, High Commander Yayènia held her blades out to either side, slicing through the foes as her massive warhorse bit and kicked his way through the throng. A dwarf captain laid about with a mace, the spiked ball the size of Meradyn's head. Just on the edge of sight he could see King Losolin urging his leggy gelding forward as bodies flew away from him, crumpling from sword and magic alike.

These thoughts took a heartbeat, and then Meradyn was focusing on the people before him. He jabbed his sword downward, sliding through a man's defenses and stabbing him in the chest. As the body slid off his blade, Meradyn felt fingers grab his opposite leg. With a curse, he had Commander turn, slamming his broad hindquarters into the pressing mass. A Darkwight had hold of his ankle, claws digging into his skin through the thick wool of his pants and leather of his boot. With a groan, Meradyn sliced downward, but the demon yanked him out of the saddle.

The young man hit the ground and rolled. He winced as Commander was cut down and the enemies on his other side stabbed the horse repeatedly. Meradyn regained his feet and turned to face the Darkwight. The demon laughed at him, a coarse, wet chuckle. Somewhere in his thoughts flickered the knowledge that this blackened creature had once been an elf, now turned to the dark side. A curved and notched sword darted out, but Meradyn knocked it aside with his own. The demon's orangey-red eyes narrowed and the blade slithered out again, this time switching directions mid-swing. Meradyn barely avoided it and spun, going low for an attempt at the creature's legs. The Darkwight kicked his sword, jarring his arm. With a curse, Meradyn adjusted his grip and stumbled over a corpse. He didn't look down to see if it was friend or foe, for he was set upon by two Zaedicans he had fallen between. Meradyn slashed out, slicing one man open from shoulder to hip, and then twisted, jabbing his sword into the lower gut of the other. Both fell and Meradyn scrambled back to his feet as the demon advanced.

They dueled for a moment, both testing, and then the Darkwight launched forward and his blade scratched Meradyn's arm, barely deep enough to split skin. Tiny beads of blood rose to the surface, but did not fall. Gasping, Meradyn touched the cut with his sword hand. It burned to the touch. The demon held up his sword and twisted it in the sunlight. A clear liquid gleamed in multi-hued waves along the edge of the weapon. Poison. With a howl, Meradyn went after the demon. The Darkwight stumbled back from the sudden attack. Reckless, the young human battered away at his foe, cutting through his defenses with sheer force. Screaming a guttural, animalistic bellow, Meradyn leapt into the air and shoved his sword down, kicking out his leg to add momentum. The blade buried itself in the Darkwight's chest, and the creature fell, sword still protruding from its body. Meradyn landed and his legs gave out. His knees hit the bloodied earth and he moaned. He touched the score on his arm. It burned with hellfire and was already blackened and swollen. When his fingers brushed it, the cut split open and greenish-gray fluid gushed out to run down his arm.

Nauseated, Meradyn struggled to his feet and picked up a discarded weapon, a cutlass some dead fool had dropped. Through blurry, darkening vision he spotted a woman standing in a bubble, alone. She was quite pretty, rather skinny in a ragged black dress that whipped with a torrent of wind, though no breeze stirred Meradyn's hair. With a snarl, he stumbled toward her. She saw his approach and gray light expanded out from her body. Her eyes widened when Meradyn simply walked into it, already numb from the poison. He did not feel his skin begin to peel away in flakes. With his last remaining strength, the Commander of the Purheaen force raised his blade high in the air and brought it down on the shocked Magin. The sword cleaved through her neck and lodged against her collarbone. She dropped, gray light all around snapping back, freeing struggling soldiers from its acid grip. Meradyn smiled faintly as friendly soldiers turned to see him fall. There was the blue cloak of Blackhaven, teal of Kajgenia, brown of Florwen Hune, dark green of the Duani elves, green and gold of Seaduens, green and red of Zeynuwn, and the yellow of Arseninis. These colors filled his vision, creating a sight of unity, and then his world darkened forever.

Aidyn slid his scimitar out of the belly of a surprised looking Zaedican, spilling his entrails on the ground. He still looked surprised as he hit the ground, and the assassin stepped over him. The dark elf lunged low and hamstrung a Darkwight an Arseninisian man was fighting. The man didn't hesitate, but stabbed his broadsword down into the demon's throat as it fell. He nodded to Aidyn in thanks, and the assassin lifted two fingers from his scimitar hilt in acknowledgement, already moving on. The lines of cavalry had broken, and the fighting had descended into mayhem once again. Arrows flew overhead, punching into the lines that had yet to mix. It was a beautiful day, really. Aidyn spotted an *ärdyz* cloaked figure a few yards away, then noted the bronze line across the assassin's knuckles. Aonis, one of the few half-elves Aidyn knew that had been raised happily by both parents. He had become an assassin after his human father passed from old age and his elven mother fell into depression. He killed for money.

Aonis dispatched the Darkwight he had been fighting, tearing through its face with a bronze-fisted punch. The half-elf joined Aidyn and the two assassins walked through the battle, dispatching foemen every other step. Aonis wore a black veil across his face, concealing all but his eyes. He said it was because he didn't want his victims to see the same face his mother saw. Aidyn didn't care why he wore the damn thing; the half-breed was a bloody good assassin.

Suddenly Aonis lurched to the side, brushing against Aidyn. The dark elf steadied him, looking about for the cause. A ball of leaves spun by, spinning faster than any wind could ever make them go. The two assassins watched in astonishment as the leaves barreled into the back of a Zaedican and began slicing him to ribbons. Aidyn let go of Aonis as a tiny creature stepped into view, barely reaching his knees. Moss green hair and bright green eyes in a face that was too familiar.

"Teechus?"

The Tree Elf bowed his head. "How fares the Lover?"

Aidyn shrugged uncomfortably as Aonis gave him an odd look, eyes crinkling above the veil. "Alive yet. Did you bring your people to aid us?"

Teechus nodded once. "All mature enough have joined the battle. Has Everwood accepted you?"

Aidyn knelt down, ignoring Aonis's curse. "She has, somewhat, though she holds to her marriage vows with Losolin."

The ancient creature gave him a faint smile. "Good. All must experience love and passion before the end. Love her, Aidyn of House Sestuns, and all will be well."

"I will, always," the assassin said. "Listen, there are rogue alchemists among the enemy. Can your people target them?"

Teechus closed his large eyes for a moment and then breathed out. He nodded. "It shall be done. Fare thee well, Lover of Everwood."

"You as well," Aidyn murmured as Teechus trundled off, his ball of leaves wreaking havoc among the dark forces.

Aonis tugged at his veil when Aidyn stood. "What the nine hells was that?"

"Tree Elf."

"No, about you and the queen?"

Aidyn smiled mysteriously. "That is a long story, my friend, and we have no time for it now."

Aonis shrugged, and they waded back into the fight.

Aladorn wiped his forearm across his face, which left behind a smear of blood that did not belong to him. The day was heating up, and the kicked up dust in the air stuck unpleasantly to every bit of exposed flesh. He jerked to the side just in time to avoid a swinging axe and slammed his fist down on the hand attached to it, forcing the owner to drop the weapon. The soldier looked up just in time to see Aladorn's knee smack into his face hard enough to shatter bone. The man reeled backward as the wiat punched his other fist into the side of his head. The soldier was barely aware of the knife Aladorn slammed into the base of his skull, which dropped him to the ground.

He took one step forward to progress into the battle and found himself surrounded. They sneered at him from every side, believing him overwhelmed. Aladorn ducked low and spun, kicking in kneecaps and avoiding blades. He came up quickly and slammed his sword across the belly of another, spinning and dodging. Around him fireballs exploded against the ground, gifts of the traitorous alchemists. Aladorn eliminated them all, leaving a ring of corpses around him. He pivoted one last time to search for more but something smashed into the back of his head hard enough to make him stumble. The wiat faded from view but it was too late. The man who had clubbed him acted as a target for the spear thrower. The missile thudded into his chest hard enough to throw him backward. Aladorn gasped in agony, clutching at the wooden shaft as blood leaked from his chest. He had returned to view the moment the spear touched him, and now he lay weak and vulnerable against the pile of bodies, his vision clouding as he sought out a familiar face. Instead, he saw a roiling, twisting ball of green flame hurtling toward him. Aladorn closed his eyes and waited for the end.

Losolin watched helplessly as Aladorn stumbled forward, disappeared, and then reappeared with a spear though his chest. The king cried out in dismay, struggling futilely toward his fallen friend. Enemies blocked his path with every step, and though they fell before him like grain to a scythe, more and more blocked his way. Cursing, Losolin prepared the Weave anyway, fighting with one hand as he sought to reach the dark elf. It was hopeless. Aladorn slumped weakly, his fingers slipping from the spear. With an enraged howl Losolin threw his hand out in a desperate and useless movement, straining. Consequently, he was stunned when the Weave slid from his hand like water, sailed through air, and engulfed Aladorn, which caused him to jerk weirdly.

For a moment, the king stood motionless, hoping though doubtful. His heart did a double-take when Aladorn stood slowly, the spear falling away. The wiat's hands explored his chest, searching for the wound but found none. The two males shared a look, full of profound relief and gratitude. But they only had a moment before the battle once again demanded their attention.

Ghealan plowed his way through the enemy horde, barely pausing between victims. He no longer cared about the possible preservation of any Darkwight he came across. He just killed them. The fight had gone on too long, his wife and child had been away from him for over a year, and he was finished. He wouldn't leave the battlefield until the enemy was defeated, or he was.

He bashed in the face of one screaming Zaedican, yanked the man's weapon out of his hands, and stabbed it into the belly of another. Ghealan stalked on, moving in a straight line, leading his company in deeper. A few feet away from him Tyular and Barukh guarded his flanks, cutting down any fool who tried to come in from the sides. The large elf came up against a man nearly as tall as he, and twice as wide.

Ghealan swung low, took out the soldier's legs and then slammed his elbow into the man's nose as he fell, which shattered the cheekbone and torqued the neck. The Zaedican's sword hilt whacked into Ghealan's throat but he barely noticed, for he had just spotted Yayènia.

The Magin lifted his arms and prepared to attack. Yayènia yanked on Udu's reins and jerked the warhorse's head around. She wasn't fast enough. The blast of magic hit the ground just behind Udu's hooves and sent them both flying. Yayènia flipped over the stallion's head as he let out a terrified squeal. A second bolt of power hit her in the back. The elf was blasted across a stretch of battlefield, blood whipping from her body in crimson strings. She landed hard in the gory dirt, just yards away from Ghealan's feet. Cascades of earth and debris landed on top of her. Ghealan shouted out in horror as the Magin loomed out of the dust to stand right at Yayènia's feet. The High Commander had not moved and the dirt around her was tinted red from the spray of blood.

Ghealan snarled in fury and began to move, but the Magin lifted his hands again at the same time the mound of earth heaved upward. Yayènia roared as she lifted herself up onto her hands, dirt pouring off her body. Teeth bared in a primal grimace, the warrior rose to one knee. The Magin's face froze in terror. Yayènia slowly lurched to her feet, lips curled in pain. As she stood, her hand scraped along the bloody mud, caking her fingers. For a mere second, her eyes connected with Ghealan's.

The blood-rage madness that he knew lurked in the back of the commander's mind was visible, taking control. She snarled, he shuddered. With a tremendous groan, Yayènia reached over her shoulder with one hand and drew a katan. Ghealan watched in horrified fascination as Yayènia pulled back her arm, spun, and shoved the curved blade into the Magin's belly. With the High Commander's back to him, Ghealan saw the fist-sized hole blasted through her shoulder. Slowly the warrior pulled her sword out of the Magin's gut and kicked him hard in the chest. He flew backward to land in the hole he had created with his magic, dead. Yayènia turned, bloodied blade dripping onto her gauntleted fist. With a pained grunt, she arched her back, the hand covered in sludge dragging across her face in an agonized, unconscious motion to leave a dark stain across her eyes like some macabre mask.

She straightened with a violent tremor, popped her neck, and strode over to Ghealan. He had to fight hard to contain the shiver that wanted to run through him again. Blood ran down Yayènia's face from the slanted streak across her eyes and nose. Green eyes met ice blue. Insanity raged behind the High Commander's gaze, though her expression was calm. Ghealan could not stop the third shiver.

Yayènia's eyes slid away from his to where Udu was getting to his feet. Slowly she bent and picked up her helmet, which had been thrown several feet away.

"Almost got me, that one," she said coldly, spat out a glob of blood, and began walking toward Udu.

"Almost?" Ghealan breathed as he followed her. "He did get you. You just healed it before you died of blood loss!"

"See? I am harder to kill than death itself," Yayènia said and showed her teeth in a gruesome parody of a grin.

Ghealan shook his head, about to respond, when he looked up and saw enemy soldiers advancing. Yayènia followed his gaze and cursed. With a groan she grabbed his hand and yanked him along, calling Udu. The horse snorted and trotted after them.

"Nia," Ghealan croaked, his bruised larynx coming on full force. "Nia just go. I will make it on my own."

"Quiet," she snapped, turning when Udu reached them. She mounted and pulled her partner up behind.

Ghealan studied the charred hole in her armor as she urged the warhorse into a canter. The flesh was whole, albeit red in the exposed area. He gently brushed his fingers over the area, making her shiver slightly, remembering their past.

"Lan..."

"Would that I had your gift, Nia."

"It is a curse to be unable to die. I would give it up in a moment, if I could."

Ghealan rested his head against her back for a moment, his eyes closed. "I am sorry, so sorry I brought you into this life. Were it not for me you could have lived in peace. I wish I had left you alone the first night we met."

"The damage had already been done, Lan. This is who and what I am, what I was meant to be. Regret nothing."

"I have caused you so much pain, and I can do nothing to rectify that mistake. Just know that I am sorry."

Yayènia snorted as she guided Udu through the bodies that littered the ground. The battle had moved back toward the defenses, pushing hard on the Nymyñosians. They arrived behind friendly lines and found Tlonna and Losolin. The king and queen had apparently just met up, for they were embracing. Tlonna started wiping at Losolin's face as they dismounted. Yayènia patted her brother-in-law on the shoulder and he turned to her with a grin, a ghastly sight for half the king's face was covered in blood, though none of it appeared to be his.

Tlonna sucked in a deep breath. "Nia."

There were shadows under the warrior's filth-painted, raging eyes, and Tlonna knew that her sister had not slept in days, barely even stopped to rest. Her body seemed hale and functioning, but the Magin Queen knew the kind of toll Yayènia could withstand without faltering.

"Tlonna. How are you?"

"Fair enough. We have not had the chance to count casualties though. How many more do you think are left?"

"Thousands, I am sure. There was another wave coming."

The queen sighed heavily. "Any sign of Sithian?"

Yayènia shook her head. "Not yet. But I have seen some actual soldiers in Zaedic armor so I believe we are getting close. He tends to keep them nearby."

Tlonna nodded her understanding. "I will find him."

She turned to Losolin who had his hand flat on Ghealan's chest. The green light pulsed and the commander took a deep breath.

"We need to find Aladorn and Barukh. I want their companies to lead a charge directly through the front lines. Everyone else I want coming in through the flanks. Yayènia, arrange it. Ghealan, come with me."

The queen set off to the sound of a horn blasting three sets of four staccato notes, signaling all upper officers to assemble. Ghealan strode along beside her, worried.

"What are you planning, Tlonna?"

She sighed. "I cannot allow any more people to die when I can stop it."

"At the cost of your own life."

Tlonna shrugged. "One for a million, Lan. There is no just way for me to continue living when my death would save them."

The warrior shook his head. "I still say there is another way. There has to be."

"Perhaps, but we have run out of time to find it."

"Why do you want me, then?"

"Because your interest is more about finishing the fight and getting home to your family. I know where your loyalties lie."

"They lie with you, Tlonna, as always."

She smiled and gripped his arm. "I know, but your heart and soul is in Narn...Nouraeva. That is where you need to be."

Ghealan looked away. "You are right, as always. My only consolation is that I know Erdwyf and Jaryikin are safe. That brings me peace in this hell."

"I am glad. I need your help."

Ghealan glanced around, studying Tlonna and Losolin's tent. "With what?" he asked, suspicious.

"I need you to help me get my armor off."

"Why?"

Tlonna sighed. "Maneuverability."

The male huffed out a breath, but he began undoing the clasps. "Losolin will kill me, not to mention Aidyn and Yayènia."

"I ordered you to do it, as the Magin Queen."

"That will make no difference and you know it."

Tlonna sighed again. "I know, Ghealan, have a little faith in me, please. If everyone already thinks I am doomed to die in this, then I already have."

Ghealan shook his head as he pulled her cuirass off. He knelt and began removing her greaves, his fingers deftly undoing the straps on her thighs and lower legs. Tlonna slid her vambraces off and unlaced her blood- and dirt-stained tunic. When Ghealan stood, he moved back a few feet as she stripped it off.

"Are you going to tell anyone?"

"To what point? They would only try to stop me. I will do what needs to be done, Ghealan, as we all do."

"I know, so do they, but it makes it no less difficult. You are loved by so many people, Tlonna, surely you understand how hard it is for us to accept your determination in this."

"I do. But I cannot do nothing when I have the power and responsibility to do everything."

Ghealan nodded slowly. "Well, promise me you will do all you can to come back to us."

Tlonna stretched up on tiptoe and kissed his cheek. "I promise. Ghealan, thank you for all you have done for me. I cannot..." her breath hitched as she gazed into his stormy green eyes. "I love you."

"I love you too, Loni. I will see you at the end, and all will be good."

She sniffed and hugged him, stubborn tears making her vision blur. Ghealan held her tightly and then he was gone, leaving her to prepare.

Tlonna turned and found the items she knew she needed. The Staff of Cyree, the Magin Stone, the Ivory Sword and the Death Pendant. The queen quickly redressed in fresh clothing, put on sturdy boots, and strapped on the sword. She swung the thin black cloak Andramaky had given her over her shoulders. The pendant rested heavily against her chest, too cool. Tlonna drew the Magin Stone from the blue silk bag and positioned it between the prongs of the Staff. For a moment, nothing happened and then the Stone began to shine and then snapped into place. Tlonna let out a breath as the Staff glowed more pure than it ever had.

The queen stepped from the tent and hurried off, feeling vulnerable without her armor. She ducked through the rows of tents and wagons and made for the struggling line of soldiers. Over the din she heard Erandur shouting commands. Though his arm was still injured, the prince refused to sit back and let others do the fighting. Tlonna smiled to herself as she thought about Aidyn's face when he had recognized Erandur.

It worried her that she had not seen the assassin for several hours, not since the start of the battle. But she knew that if Aidyn were dead, she would know. Tlonna melded into the battle, using only magic to destroy her enemies. They flew away from her, screaming as their life was yanked out of them.

Tlonna walked nearly unhindered through the melee, enemies being flung away over the heads of her allies. She ducked and pivoted beneath blows, time and sound of less importance to her than ever. Before too long they were running away, dropping their weapons and begging for mercy. She moved faster and faster until she was sprinting across the field, headed generally eastward. When she arrived at the edge of the battle, Tlonna realized she was completely alone in hostile territory. Without pausing, the elf leaned back and hollered her son's name at the top of her lungs. A few minutes passed and the young man appeared through the haze of dust, the dying sun cast his shadow long and thin beside him.

"Mother," he said without any of his normal arrogance and surety.

"Sithian, in the end, has it been worth it?" Tlonna asked, moving forward a step.

"I brought over seventy thousand people, I have less than ten left. You tell me."

Tlonna shook her head. "You never pretended to care about your people. Why start now? What value are they to you other than arrow fodder?"

Sithian jabbed a finger into his chest. "They are like me, outcast and despised. They are pureblood humans! They are the future of this world!"

"You are half-elf, Sithian! What makes you think they will accept you as lord and master after you drilled them to hate anyone with another race's blood in their veins?"

"I am a god to them. I am their savior!" Sithian roared, his hands lifted in the air.

"You are their pawn."

The mad king howled in fury and his body erupted in blue flames. "I will destroy everything you are, Tlonna!"

The Magin Queen stepped back and opened herself to the magic. Jair sighed in contentment, apparently sensing the end was near. Tlonna stepped back again, not in fear but in preparation. She felt her hands curl into loose fists, wreathed in colorfully flecked white power. The two stared at each other in silence, waiting for the next move. Sithian's patience ran out first and he jerked his hands up. Tlonna didn't move as the whips of magic slashed at her, crackled against her wall. Sithian sneered, Wove again. His mother remained still, simply took his attacks without weakening. Finally he stopped, furious.

"Fight back damn you!"

Tlonna gazed back, calm. "You know what will happen if I do. We will both die."

"Then end it. For the gods' sake, Mother, end it all!" Sithian's voice went shrill in the end, his eyes wide.

The words shocked her. They seemed sincere. "Why?"

He laughed bitterly. "What does this life have to offer? I am a god lost amid peasants."

Tlonna shook her head. "You are child, and a foolish one at that."

Sithian scoffed and then cocked his head. "How is dear Aidyn?"

The anger those words caused filled Tlonna with fire. She snarled and moved her body into a crouch, prepared to do battle. "He is a thousand and more times the male you are. Your petty attempt to control him did nothing. What was the point, Sithian? Why all the useless, ramshackle attempts at creating chaos? The kidnapping, the Eseirik, killing Rhiannan and using her to imitate Yayènia and attack Aidyn? You must have known they would fail."

Sithian shook his head. "It is true they were weak attempts, not very well planned and to be honest I was barely involved in most of them. I used the ineffectual plots of others to further my own singular plan, and also to keep your eyes from Zaedic itself."

Tlonna nodded, hoping to keep her son talking while she subtly moved closer. "Yes, Isadorr told me you were quite indulgent toward Athelias, Stoffnias, and even Orlando, your general."

"Orlando was a traitor who deserved all that bitch Yayènia gave him and more. Athelias and Stoffnias were fools blinded by their jealousy and hatred of you. Midian exploited that, and I continued to do so. As for Isadorr...well let me just say his heart does not carry the taint of the Lostugs, unlike your mutual brother."

Tlonna's heart began to beat faster. "Gothier is yours, of course. That is why no one has seen him for days."

"Was. He fulfilled his purpose, acting as a double agent for Isadorr and me. He was to pretend anger and hurt that his brother had outcast him for being the son of an Ewôsdírn whore, and before he fled to you, he set the seed of uncertainty in his brother's mind, which prompted him to send the tattooed assassin. It lured you and all your troublesome gang into Seaduens, allowing me to set the next stage in my plan."

Tlonna frowned. Nothing truly significant had happened since then, at least that she knew of. Her son chuckled madly.

"By the way, all your traps in the Kismath Mountains are gone, your soldiers destroyed. I couldn't get my army through the narrow pass without risking everything, otherwise you already would have been destroyed," he admitted. "But it would have been a nice surprise had you finally decided to retreat. However, we both know there will be no retreat, not from this battle. And if you did, you would not return to the same kingdom you so foolishly left behind."

"What are you talking about?" Tlonna demanded, a shiver running up her spine.

"Miazie Paron Ughtren!" Sithian gleefully shouted. "She was created just as I was! Darren Ughtren allowed Midian to take his wife, plant his seed, and manipulate it for his needs. A child was born, a girl with the power to see beyond the present moment, able to see both the past and the present. A Belau but more. She was born to be a tool, and so she has been. The visions she sees are controlled, Midian played them out so you would follow precisely where he led."

Tlonna felt sick. "No."

"When Darren tired of having your worthless, lifeless body in a cell, he had his men drop you off in a forest and give you the painful antidote to your induced coma. And what do you do but wander right back into his kingdom! You caused your own downfall! You took Miazie from her controlled environment and set her loose on the world. For a while you blinded Midian. He couldn't find her in order to control her, and in that time she told you who you were and became your friend. It was only in Kajgenia that she came visible to Midian once more."

"The pendant," Tlonna whispered, and clutched at it.

Sithian nodded. "All the while your little friend has been feeding you information that pulled you our direction. She tried to fight it when you were in Purheae, when she became aware that something was not right in her mind and ended up telling you too much, but she is relatively weak in that regard. She is an unreliable means, but a necessary risk."

"You mean she does not know she is being used?"

"A tool that knows it's a tool is rarely useful."

Tlonna's sense of betrayal lessened and she looked quizzically at her son. "You are telling me an awful lot of secrets."

"One or both of us is going to die soon, and it won't really matter," he said, shrugging.

Tlonna silently agreed. She was closer now, only yards away. "I am surprised Midian told you this. I was unaware he trusted you so."

Sithian snorted. "Who else could he trust? You corrupted Haydyn, destroyed Rhiannan, and converted Kelus. I was his only refuge, his only family. Why wouldn't he? After all, I was his heir."

"And look at all you have done. Brought more war to the mainland, caused the deaths of thousands, and the agony of many more."

"I am continuing the legacy begun by my grandfather Aderiaen. I am finishing their dream."

"No matter how you play it Sithian, you are a tyrant. A vicious murderer who needlessly kills even his own people to further his barbarous plans."

Sithian dismissed the accusation with a flick of his hand. "In the end, what does it matter? Death comes to each of us, and I tire of this endless talking. What was your plan? Distract me with words while your heroes come to kill me?"

Tlonna sighed, resigned. "You know very well that is not going to happen. This is between you and me, as it was always meant to be."

"Really? You have not spoken to Miazie recently?" He sounded surprised.

"No."

"Well perhaps you should, before you die."

"It does not matter, Sithian. If she has Seen something or not, this moment is here and I am not leaving this battlefield until you or I am dead."

"Very well, if you care not to know what she has perceived then it is of no consequence to me," Sithian said, pulling his arms back, hands fisted.

This time Tlonna reacted. She sprinted to the side and threw her hands out. The ground trembled as it tore open and knocked Sithian to his back. She didn't hesitate before turning toward him and calling on the sky. Lightning snapped down from the cloudless, late evening sky. It struck the king as he crawled from the hole he'd landed in, but he lifted his hand at the last second. The electricity ricocheted off his palm, shot out in all different directions, and shocked fighting soldiers. Tlonna swore and in seconds had another Weave at her fingertips crackling loudly as she let loose on her son.

Sithian cried out as the magic hit him square in the face and launched him skyward. He spun uncontrolled through the air before slamming to a halt, suspended. There was a concussive blast as he threw his arms out and shoved Tlonna back a few steps. The king lifted his arms again, and this time stones, boulders, and debris followed. They pelted Tlonna hard enough to knock her down as they bit into flesh and shredded her clothing. She hissed in pain as a jagged piece of stone sliced into her cheek.

She lay still for a moment to give herself time to gather her courage to do what was necessary. Sithian was no match for her, but she would need his added strength to do the final task of her life. She checked the Staff and the Stone, the pendant and the sword. With a shaky breath, Tlonna got to her feet and met her son's sapphire gaze. He was standing less than ten feet away, blood trickling down his arm and temple. For a moment her heart faltered. He was her son, despite everything, he was her only child left.

"Please Sithian, please do not make me do this. You know I will destroy you. Please."

He shook his head. "I will never stop. I will fight against everything you stand for. I will hunt your friends, raze your cities, and enslave your people. If you want it to stop, you must forsake your soul and kill your own son. Bow to evil, Tlonna."

His words were said in a voice so calm and quiet they sounded almost sane. Sithian's eyes were steady on her face, rimmed by lashes so like his father's. He simply stared at her. Tlonna was the one who looked away, tears rimmed her eyes but she did not let them fall.

"Such a beautiful shell," she breathed and pressed her hand to his cheek. "Why did you turn from me?"

Sithian's eyes became lidded and dead. "You offered rules, ethics, and responsibility. Father offered freedom, and unbridled power. He gave me women and geld, control over others."

"Those were all simple payments for a life of damnation and you cannot tell me you feel no responsibility for the lives lost here. Because of you."

He shoved her hand away. "It does not matter now."

Tlonna closed her eyes for a brief moment. When she opened them to look at her son one more time, they were with the eyes of a queen, the Magin Queen. Sithian took a step back, started to turn away. Tlonna pulled free the Ivory Sword and with a howl of despair and self-loathing, she rammed it into his chest, directly into his heart. Sithian's eyes opened wide and he gasped, wheezing in a desperate breath. He hadn't expected her to attack him in such a mundane way. His face contorted in helpless agony.

As she looked into her dying son's eyes, into the depths of hatred, corruption, and tyranny, Tlonna understood. Without the greatest sacrifice, evil would prevail and life would end.

*All* life would end.

In that single moment of complete and utter understanding, Tlonna heard the spirits' whispers. She heard Miazie reciting the worst prophecy Astinus had ever seen. She heard the Cyree's cryptic words, coupled with the cave drawings. She heard them all, and finally, she perceived them.

Tlonna pulled every ounce of strength, energy, and power she had left. The light around her darkened as the brightness of her magic consumed it. Wind howled, lifted her hair and whipped at her clothes. Sithian, still clinging to life, shook his head once, twice, as he stared at his mother.

The entirety of magic coalesced into a single dense ball around Tlonna's hand and then travelled over the hilt and into Sithian. He screamed in agony as his power was shredded within him. In the last second of his life, he let out a faint sigh, his lips twitching up in a smile. The magic travelled back over the sword, touched Tlonna's hand and crawled over her arm and into her body. The Ivory Sword shuddered and then shot out of Sithian's body on its own accord, jerked out of her hand. It spun away, slicing across her ribs as it went, and then shattered, landing in bits all over the ground.

Sithian crumpled to the ground, lifeless, his face calm and peaceful. Tlonna looked down at him, expressionless. Blood poured from the gash in her side, completely soaking her shirt and pants. She didn't notice. Dark blue magic writhed around the injury and then sank inside her body.

The elf twitched, took a step back, twitched again.

Hundreds of yards away Yayènia looked up and watched Tlonna's body jerk violently. The warrior squinted in confusion. Her sister was on the edge of the battle, nowhere near the enemy soldiers, facing the sunset. She saw Aidyn turn, ignoring whoever he was fighting, his expression one of unadulterated fear. Without hesitation,

Yayènia burst into a full-out sprint. She had not taken five steps when silent thunder shook the earth. The warrior was shaken to her knees. Everyone around her was on the ground as well, confused. Yayènia looked up, but her gaze was stolen by a face only feet away, staring blindly. She reached out, fingers trembling, to close Sargotarh's bright blue eyes. Around him lay over a score of Zaedicans and Darkwights, slashed and lacerated in sweeping lines, the mark of the captain. Face frozen with fury and grief, Yayènia wrenched her gaze up, steeling herself. Tlonna still stood but her face was tilted up. A massive aural shield of pulsating blue and white light was slowly expanding from her body.

Suddenly the shield imploded as a pillar-sized beam of power burst out of Tlonna. Sound was ripped from the world. Dirt and debris flew everywhere. Yayènia shot forward, cloak billowing in the wind as she ran, leaping over fallen bodies, ducking under flying spears and arrows. She drew both swords in desperation. A wall of power and air slammed into her. Through the dust she saw Tlonna fall to her knees. Another wall hit her, and another, one after the other. Fighting against it, Yayènia caught a glimpse of Losolin, Ghealan, Suneelo, and all the others doing the same. She looked at Tlonna, her heart hammering.

Aidyn watched Tlonna stagger backward as his heart tried to explode. Crying out in dismay, the assassin turned away from the demon he was battling and sprinted toward her, his scimitars flashing through the milling fighters. From the corner of his eye he saw Yayènia dashing toward Tlonna as well, her cropped hair flying out behind her, loosened from its tie. A concussion knocked everyone down but Aidyn bent into it, howling into the sudden silence. All around him stunned soldiers were trying to get back to their feet, struggling against each other even on the ground.

The assassin kept moving, his feet barely touching the ground as he leapt and flipped over confused soldiers. Tlonna's arms flung outward as a blinding bar of light shot up from her body. Aidyn slapped a fighter in the face with the back of his hand, paying no attention to whether he was friend or foe. Again a rolling wave of power knocked the entire battlefield to the ground and this time he was unable to avoid it. He slammed headfirst into the churned ground, a little stunned. He rolled onto his feet with a groan and saw Tlonna fall to her knees, clutching her chest. Aidyn let out a desperate noise that rolled unbidden from his throat and he raced over the last several yards to her side. Yayènia was just now getting back to her feet, too far away. She watched in stunned panic as Aidyn soared into a pillar of light, a blotch of darkness against the blinding bright. It looked as if he began to unravel. She broke once more into a desperate run.

Tlonna was encased in an intense heat, but it did not burn her flesh away as it should. It went through her, scouring her soul instead. Before her, Sithian's crumpled body lay at her feet, his reign of terror at an end. Everything seemed to slow for her, as though having finally reached the end, the world wanted to savor every last second of her life. Then there was the pain. It was expected but she could not have predicted the staggering amount of it. She was unable to scream it was so great. It was the same pain she had briefly touched when linked with Aidyn during his captivity.

A war was being waged inside her body, a vicious brawl that tore at her soul with reckless abandon. Then the visions came. They struck Tlonna with fear and rage, utterly devastating all she held dear. Murder, rape, torture, all manner of gratuitous violence assaulted her mind. She whimpered as hot tears rolled down her face. She managed to shake her head.

"That is not all there is in this world!" she screamed as loud as she could. "There is goodness and love. There is heroism, selfless acts. You cannot have it all!"

Tlonna did not know whom she addressed, and didn't really care. Within her, Jair clutched at the warring magics and wrestled with them, adding his own madness to the melee. Every time an image battered her mind, Tlonna replaced it with one of her own.

A man raping a woman. Sodo laughing as he swung Miazie around in a dance.

A bloody, endless war. Blackhaven's Samhain festival.

Two males bludgeoning each other in a brawl, blood on their knuckles. Losolin and Suneelo wrestling, laughing as they tripped each other up.

On and on it went, each terrible image of senseless brutality replaced by the laughing, teasing, loving group Tlonna called her family. When the visions tried to turn even those against her and replace the anonymous faces of the vicious deeds with the warriors she knew and loved, the Magin Queen nearly lost the battle.

Ghealan kicking in the face of a howling soldier, blood spraying beneath the heel of his boot.

Suneelo cutting the throat of a defenseless Monotheist, his face a merciless snarl.

Aidyn slamming his tension blade into the body of a screaming dwarf over and over again, his emerald green eyes wide above a vicious grin.

Losolin shattering the arm of a man with his shield, grimacing as blood splattered across his face.

Then there came one that she could not recall seeing in her life, but knew it had happened nonetheless. It was Yayènia. She was on her knees at the edge of a silent battlefield, bodies piled around in careless heaps, abandoned by the living. She was weeping, heartbroken. Behind her appeared Suneelo, drenched in blood and sweat. He dropped his sword and knelt next to his wife. They embraced, crying over the bloodshed that they had led. Led, but not incited. A conversation with Yayènia came to her then, washing away the rest of the horrifying images.

"*We must always fight back, never fight?*"Tlonna had asked.

"*Always and never,*" Yayènia had responded.

"Always and never!" Tlonna screamed to the sky above, though all she could see was the blazing bar of light.

The visions faded away, leaving her with a soul cleansed, a heart mended. She lost strength in her legs and fell to her knees. She wrapped her hand about the Staff of Cyree and propped it up in the dirt so she could allow the Weave to filter through it. A bursting, overwhelming sense of power began to rise up from her belly and she began to shake. It was time. Finally, it was time. Then something dark enveloped her.

"Tlonna!" Aidyn breathed and wrapped his arms around her.

"Aidyn," she replied, her voice barely audible. "What are you doing here? You cannot be next to me."

"I will always be next to you, Tlonna. Always."

"No, you have to leave. Get away from me," Tlonna whispered desperately, her hand moved up to weakly push against his chest.

"I will not. I need to get you to Losolin so he can heal you," Aidyn argued gently, picking up her hand and kissing the knuckles.

"There would be no point. You must get out of here."

"Yayènia is coming."

Panic flared in Tlonna's eyes and she shook her head. "No, you must stop her. Aidyn please!"

The assassin began to respond but Tlonna's body convulsed and her mouth and eyes opened wide as her head threw back against his arm. Aidyn clutched her tightly, unable to do anything but watch. Her fingers dug into his thigh.

Tears rolled unbidden down his face as she went rigid. "Aidyn, please! Go!" she hissed between her clenched teeth.

"No, I will not leave you!"

Tlonna stared up at him in desperation, trying to will him to leave as she felt her power build inside, an uncontrollable strength roiling to the surface, pulled by Jair's angry presence and the ever-whispering spirits. They were determined to fulfill the prophecy, collateral damage be damned.

"*Please*, Aidyn!"

Aidyn shook his head and looked away from her desperate eyes to watch Yayènia's determined struggle toward them. Tlonna's hand moved from his leg up to his face, where it cupped his chin, her thumb rubbed against his cheekbone.

"I am sorry," she cried, tears splashing down her face. "I am so sorry!"

Aidyn pressed his own hand against Tlonna's, holding it to his face.

"Tlonna...Tlonna do not leave me! Fight it! Please fight it!" Aidyn shouted through the light that seared through him, unwilling to let go of her even though the pain was excruciating.

Their linked hands, pressed against his face, trembled. The dark elf's tears dripped onto her face.

"I love you," he cried as her eyes began to close.

Aidyn bent over her and pressed his lips to hers in a moment of weakness, staring down at her face. Out of her eyes, her mouth, her nostrils, out of every pore came light, pure blinding light. Her face, her beautiful, perfectly formed face bathed in light was the last thing he saw. Her eyes stared up at him, bright with tears and emotion that was too profound to define. The light, a thick bar of power, went through him, and into the sky.

Yayènia stared through her tears at the horrific, unbelievable scene before her. Tlonna's body lay slumped in Aidyn's arms, his head slack to his chest. For a moment, all was still and then she saw movement off to the side, behind Tlonna. Sithian moved, his knees came up and he slowly climbed back to his feet.

"Gods, no!" she screamed as what was left of her world came crumbling down. The words echoed in a sudden silence.

The boy's face appeared blank and soulless, but his eyes opened and stared at Yayènia. "You think one sacrifice will be enough? You believe you have won? You cannot win against raw power! You cannot defeat a god!"

Yayènia glanced at Tlonna, Aidyn, and the scene around her. Everyone was still moving, but so slowly. She could count the debris flying through the air. Her heart hammered and she gripped her sword hilts with a snarl.

"You are not a god, Sithian. You are dead. I saw you die."

"You watched my father die too and you saw how well that worked out for you. I am more than he was. I do not need a trinket to keep me alive. I am the darkest dark, the almighty; I am the one god of all Men! I am more than was prophesied, I will not die!"

The warrior tensed when Sithian dragged a foot forward. She scowled. "Your body is dead. You cannot survive without a body, magic or not. I will destroy you."

The king's body lurched forward and the earth beneath Yayènia ripped open. She tossed her swords to the side and grabbed hold of the edge. Beneath her yawned a chasm of several thousand feet. Unbearably hot steam billowed up toward her and she gasped for air. Sithian's dead, possessed form appeared in front of her and his mouth opened in a parody of a grin.

"You're going to die, Commander. I'm going to kill you, and then Tlonna will be able to die the way she's supposed to."

Yayènia grimaced as the earth beneath her fingers crumbled and she had to reposition her grip. Her feet sought purchase on the edge as she listened to his threats. Sithian swayed slightly and she tensed again for whatever was going to come next. Pain lanced up from the back of her calves and she screamed. Yayènia risked a glance down and saw the three-inch thick thorns that had come out of the earth and impaled her flesh. She was pinned to the edge of the chasm. Blood poured down her legs to pool in her boots and soaked the dirt she was clinging to.

"You are...already dead. I will not...be killed by...a corpse!" she panted.

Sithian laughed horribly and slouched down to look her directly in the eye. "Say goodbye, Commander," he whispered and the chasm began to close.

With a howl, Yayènia grabbed him by the collar and dragged him over her head. Sithian's body flipped over into the rift with a startled cry. His hands scrabbled at her, yanking her head back as he seized her hair and a fistful of her shirt. Yayènia let go of the chasm's edge with one hand and pulled a knife free from her belt. With a jerk, she shoved the blade back into Sithian's body. The boy slid down, his fingers burning lines through her shirt and leaving scorch marks on her cuirass. Yayènia howled and elbowed him in the face, then reached around and pulled her knife out of his side. With a grunt, she shoved it back into him, punching through to his lung.

Sithian screamed as he lost his grip on his aunt and fell backward into the abyss. A searing flash of steam and fire hissed up at Yayènia moments later and she pressed her body to the crumbling precipice. The rift was closing rapidly and her legs were almost completely numb from blood loss. With a gasp the warrior jerked herself upward and kicked backward at the same time. The giant thorns tore free of her flesh and she sobbed in agony. With her vision failing and her head swimming, Yayènia scrabbled up onto solid ground just as the chasm slammed shut. The right toe of her boot was caught and she had to dig it free.

As soon as the dust settled, the world resumed its natural pace and she heard the screams of battle surrounding her. She turned once more toward Tlonna and Aidyn but was knocked back by another concussion that flattened her to the ground. Weak and suffering from severe wounds, Yayènia rolled onto her stomach and willed her body to heal. It took only moments, but seemed an eternity as waves of power rumbled over her. Finally she managed to get back onto her feet and bent into the force.

Losolin and Yayènia exploded forward when the last pounding concussion faded. They were stopped by an impenetrable wall of pulsing power mere feet from Tlonna, who was knee to knee with Aidyn, bent backward in his arms, the Staff of Cyree a beacon of blazing light clutched in her left hand. The dark assassin's body seemed somehow less substantial than it should be. Losolin clawed at the barrier until his fingers were crimson with blood. He kicked and slammed his fist into it, but it stayed, uncaring. Suddenly Suneelo and Aladorn were there, staring in mute horror at the scene before them. Yayènia pressed her open palms to the wall and cried. No one understood.

Tlonna shuddered as something was ripped from her soul. With it went Jair, and all the spirits, all the twisted, leftover Magins. Their magic departed her body with a sense of unrestrained glee.

*Yes,* they whispered as they left her body.

The Everwood, the Magin Queen, opened her eyes one last time to see Aidyn's beautiful, stricken, love-filled emerald gaze staring down at her. She watched as, so slow she could see reflections in it, a tear dropped from his sooty lashes and fell toward her face. It splashed on her cheek. Then light enveloped them, and it was over.

# Chapter 47

## The End of Everything

None of the group surrounding the wall of light noticed the rolling waves of power that expanded over the battlefield and on anymore. They were too stricken by the sight before them, but had they noticed it would have been a sight they would never forget. Once again, the soldiers of both armies were knocked to the ground but this time there was no getting up. The power simply ran them over, pressed them into the ground so that they couldn't move. Each ripple was a different color, every base color of the magic there was. It started as black and each one lightened until it was pure white, brighter than even the sun.

Darkwights screamed as their very flesh was flayed from their bodies, peeling away in flaking rolls. Beneath was the pale, whole skin of the elven race as they were reborn to the world. Oily, clumped hair fell away to be replaced by shimmering waves of blond, auburn, black, and brunette. Their eyes became white where once they had been black, and they sighed as the constant pain of the demon race was wiped away.

Every Magin in the vicinity was stripped of their power as the waves coinciding with their particular color rolled over them and added their magic to its strength. Wounds were healed as the green ripple rolled over the field and beyond.

Across Nymyños people were thrown to the ground as pulsating waves of color rolled over them, preceded by an ominous rumble. They regained their feet slowly, exchanging confused and frightened glances with their friends and family.

Walking hand in hand, Miazie and Sodo strolled down the corridor leading to the throne room for the last business of the day. It was a calm evening, warm and peaceful, the music of birds filling the air with a sweet innocence that the inhabitants of Blackhaven did not take for granted. Neither did the couple, for they had only just recovered from the shock of losing Miazie's ability. As they neared the end of the corridor, approaching the door that led into the throne room, a low rumbling met their ears. The couple stopped, frowned at each other as the sound became louder and louder. Then came the screams. Suddenly Miazie's arm was wrenched backward as Sodo was thrown to the ground by some invisible force. She screamed in fright as the rumbling became a wave of rolling light and crackling magic. Sodo skidded along the floor to hit the wall, stopping with a jolt. He curled into a ball, his hands clenching into fists and pressed against his temples.

"Sodo!" Miazie cried, going to her knees beside him.

So sudden it left a deafening ring in her ears, the rumbling stopped, and the light continued on its rolling way. Sodo let out a gasp and his legs slid to the ground and he slumped, exhausted, against the wall.

"Sodo?" Miazie asked, her voice trembling with fear for her beloved.

The alchemist's brow tightened for a moment and then he looked at her, his lips parted in disbelief and shock. His eyes were the same. The sable that had streaked his pale hair was gone. The taint was gone from him. That which the Darkwights had forced upon him all those years ago had been undone.

"Tlonna," he whispered, reaching out to grip Miazie's hand.

Tears splashed down her face, for she knew what that meant. The Magin Queen had succeeded in freeing the Slaves of Death from their tortured prison, and in doing so had sacrificed herself. Miazie began to shake in both profound relief and sorrow. She had started Tlonna on that long and dark path, and she had given her the knowledge to fulfill the prophecy. She had told her how to die.

"Miazie..." Sodo breathed, gazing upon her with eyes that were white and green as they had not been for nearly a decade.

"She...she did it."

"I know. Come to me."

The woman crawled to the elf and curled up beside him, his arm heavy and warm against her back. She buried her face in his lap and lost herself in the agony of what that must mean.

Losolin fell forward when the wall disappeared and scrambled toward his wife. She was leaning backward still, Aidyn's arms around her waist. A trickle of blood ran from the corner of her mouth and her eyes stared blankly at the dark sky. The sun had set. He grabbed her arm and shook it, shouted her name again and again. Tears blinded him as he gathered her up in his arms, howling madly. Oblivion overcame him and he lost all sense of the world.

Aladorn grabbed Aidyn's shoulder and pulled him back, meaning to ask what had happened. The assassin's head rolled onto his chest and he flopped lifelessly onto the ground. The black scars on his cheek were gone, but his emerald eyes stared up at his brother, empty and unblinking. Aladorn shook him, confused. The assassin's clothes were shredded, his skin smeared with blood. When he realized Aidyn's chest wasn't moving, Aladorn began to scream.

Yayènia's body went numb and she collapsed, sobbing uncontrollably at the sight of Tlonna and Aidyn's lifeless bodies. Her stomach heaved and she vomited. Her heart felt as if it were trying to beat itself out of her chest. She keened as she crawled to Tlonna's left side, mindlessly shoved away the charred remains of the Staff of Cyree and the Magin Stone. The warrior pressed her face into Tlonna's shoulders and wept hopelessly, clutching at her sister's shirt.

Suneelo couldn't feel anything. His mind was blank as he stared down at the scene. It was as if every nightmare he had ever had was come to life. His every fear realized. For a moment more he stood there and then he collapsed to the ground, tears rolling from his eyes as he curled in against himself.

Ghealan shook violently, his entire body in pain from the grief. He had allowed this to happen. He could have tied her up and none of this would have happened. He could have gotten the family together and they could have stopped her. They could have stopped her.

Eyin clutched Tyular's arm, staring in complete horror at the deaths before him. Not Tlonna. Not Aidyn. For all the gods' sake, not them. The older king felt sick as he wept at the sight.

Erandur, Tristan, Barukh, and Isadorr stood together in silence, unable to comprehend the outcome of the battle. For the young human king, Aidyn's death was a blow as painful as his father's had been. The great assassin had been his best friend for nearly all his life. Now he was gone too.

The moons had not risen. The blackest night of the year came on the day everything ended.

# Chapter 48

## Choices

For several days after, nothing happened. The two enemy armies ceased their fighting, for the ruling monarchs of both had been slain. The Zaedican army no longer had the advantage of the Magins and so they quickly departed, sailing back toward their island home. The Nymyñosian army stayed. They lit giant pyres for the thousands of dead. The body of Furntil Eldrout had been found beneath a mound of nearly a score of Zaedicans, a deadly fighter to the end.

Those left alive in the war council could barely move so strong was their grief. Of all the lives lost, there were five that shook them to the core. Losolin could not even speak. He simply sat and stared, tears rolling down his face. Yayènia screamed and rampaged, shouting that as long as she was still living Tlonna could not die. Aladorn turned inward, unable to function. Erandur wept for his father, but he had known it was coming. He was the first to depart with his remaining soldiers to take his father's body home and prepare to take the crown himself. Eyin sat by Meradyn's body and sobbed, hating himself.

Suneelo slowly walked through the battlefield, the wind tugging at his ragged silver cloak and the mangled blue and black crest on his helmet. Around him were the twisted bodies of the dead: human, elf, dwarf, the occasional faery creature, and the Darkwights. Tlonna's magic had scoured clean the skin of the living, but the dead had remained twisted and blackened. Suneelo pointed to two of the bodies, an elf and a spryte that had died back to back. Behind him, a squad of soldiers pulled up a cart and gently lifted the bodies up. They left the enemy dead where they lay. As Suneelo crouched to check the armor of a human, to see which side he had fought on, something silver caught his eye.

Standing, the elf strode over to a pile of Darkwights and scowled downward. A worn pole stuck out from the center of the pile, ending a foot above the bodies in a splintered break. Beneath a demon fluttered a scrap of silvery cloth, that which had caught his attention. With his foot, Suneelo shoved the top demons off to reveal a Blackhaven banner and its bearer. He carefully extracted the ragged flag and pulled it free of the shattered staff. As more soldiers surrounded him, pulling the victorious dead from beneath the enemy, Suneelo bundled the bloody, destroyed flag against his chest and looked around. Fires burned in a long line along the field, large pyres for the dead that couldn't be brought home.

Slowly, Suneelo walked over to the nearest pyre and looked into the flames. Four bodies, their races unidentifiable, burned within. With a sigh, the elf unbundled the flag of Blackhaven and flung it into the fire. It billowed out against the flames, the Tree stretching in an instant before the fire flared white and consumed the fibers. Suneelo saluted with his left fist against his chest, opposite his heart, his right hand clenched at his side. The wind gusted, tugging again at his cloak and crest, but he ignored it. The fire ate the borders of the flag in a flash of white fire, then died back down to red-orange, licking at the bodies. Suneelo dropped his fist and looked around, surprised to see a dozen or so Blackhaven soldiers and allies standing around the pyre, saluting as proper to their nationality. It brought tears to his eyes, as so much did these days, but he blinked and tightened his lips. The time for grief was not now.

Finally Tristan, Tyular, Barukh, and Isadorr left, their shoulders lowered with sadness. The battle was won, the threat of the Darkwights and the Rahlans lifted, and a new hope for Nymyños was on the horizon, but the sacrifice needed seemed too much. Brothers lost, friends, and the greatest queen any of them had ever known.

The order was given by Ghealan to the army to begin preparations to return home. He ordered the temporary wall torn down, and he dismissed the engineers Matthias and Lukan from employ. Then he looked northward, to his wife. He found Suneelo in his and Yayènia's tent, packing.

"I am going to Narn...Nouraeva. My part in this is done. I will bring Erdwyf back for the...for Tlonna and Aidyn."

Suneelo nodded. "Go in peace, Lan. It has been an honor. I will see you in a week or so, then."

Ghealan nodded and said his goodbyes to everyone he could find. Losolin blinked at him and said nothing. Yayènia nodded, unable to speak. She pulled him into an embrace and wept into his shoulder. Aladorn sighed, his eyes swollen and red from tears.

"Ghealan...I am...forgive me for my judgment of you. You are an incredible leader and you were right to leave the Warriors."

"Speak nothing of it, Aladorn. Lead them well in my place, I know of no one better to replace me. May the gods be with you."

The wiat managed a half smile and he gripped hands with the large commander. "And with you. Give my regards to your family."

"I will." Ghealan said and then he left, riding north toward Nouraeva and away from the pain of grief.

The Blackhaven Militia arrived home a week later, battered, stricken, but victorious. Miazie and Sodo met the family at the gate of the castle and there were weeping hugs passed all around. The wagon with Tlonna and Aidyn's bodies was brought up, shrouded in hundreds of cloaks from the soldiers. It had started with Tyre, who had draped his cloak over the wagon as it passed him, and from then on every soldier who could reach it threw their cloak over it. It had been a moving scene.

When Miazie saw Aidyn's body next to Tlonna's, she let out a grief-stricken scream and collapsed on the ground, weeping hopelessly. Sodo gently gathered her up in his arms and carried her back with the rest of the group. There was little to say as the queen and the assassin were lovingly carried into the chamber used to prepare the bodies of the royal family and high-ranking nobles.

When they were alone, Yayènia looked at Losolin and shook her head. "I do not understand. The tree elf said Tlonna could not die as long as I was still alive, and the same for me. She should not have died."

Losolin took a deep shuddering breath and spoke the first words since Tlonna had died. "But she did."

There was only darkness for what seemed to be eternity. Tlonna, a formless creature floating in the endless oblivion, waited. A minute speck of light moved toward her, growing as it approached. Slowly, it formed into a female shape, tall and willowy.

"Your life ended sooner than it should have, my child."

Tlonna would have blinked had she eyes to do so. "I know you. You are Tonora."

The graceful, agonizingly beautiful female smiled slightly. "Yes."

"What is this place? Is there no plane of heaven as we are told? Is there only this emptiness after death?"

Tonora's smile faded. "You are dead, Tlonna, and you gave up your life to preserve virtue. You martyred yourself to resurrect our kind and to bring peace to Nymyños. Those who died in the battle, those millions who have died throughout the ages moved on to either the plane of heaven or the valley of the hells. There are some, however, who die before they are meant to. Neither the plane nor the valleys are ready to accept you, Tlonna."

"So I wait here for eternity? Why are you here?"

"I came back to this oblivion for you. To offer you a choice."

Suddenly Tlonna had a form, her body. She frowned. "What choice?"

Tonora's hands lifted and in them, she held two pendants, one black and one white. "You know these, yes?"

Tlonna nodded.

"Before I explain the choice before you, I must give you another explanation. This is the one you have been searching for all these years. You were never meant to be the Destroyer of Evil, Tlonna. That was my fate, but, like you, I was murdered long before my time. I was unable to fulfill the prophecy, and so it landed on you. I know the Tree Elves, Teechus and Beriles, told you of the connection between you and your sister, Yayènia Nefarian er'Tiena. You should know that she yet lives. They also told you that the Lover would be your saving grace. You are aware that Aidyn Sestuns was the Lover."

"Aidyn came for me..." Tlonna whispered, a sickening sorrow in her heart.

"Yes. He loved you more than anything else in the world. You turned destiny on its head when you fell in love with Losolin Ullor Grisholm instead. You and Aidyn were the ones chosen in my stead, and in my Lover's. His name was Aeryn. Aeryn and Tonora, Aidyn and Tlonna. You see the connection?"

Tlonna nodded, overwhelmed. After a moment she said, "He loved others, though, before me. I was not his only love."

"The two before you would never have fulfilled him, and in fact it was manifestly impossible for there to be any true love for him, other than you. The first, Elva, was murdered by descendents of Tayrn Verla, who thought they were obeying prophecy, but were in fact guided by the hands of the gods. The second, Rahna, was taken at a moment of weakness. The arrow that struck her was meant for another, but the gods guided it in an impossible path, so that she would be removed. Thus, Aidyn was kept free from other hearts. He was meant for you, and you were to be his only wife. Ever."

Horrified, Tlonna felt tears burning in her eyes. "Then why make him live so long before me? And why, when Losolin came along, did you not remove him as well?"

"We were not sure when you would come along, such things are unknowable even for us. However, we knew that Aidyn must be given the time to become perfect. We gave him his unmatched beauty, his ability to learn and retain, and his ambition. It would take many years for him to learn all that he could, and master it. More than seven and a half centuries' worth of practice saw to this. His skill in battle and in bed was honed to perfection, above any others. We did not know what would attract you to him outside of his appearance, so we gifted him the ability to learn music, writing, dancing, painting, even sewing. All these things he could do, and did better than most. His taste for reading was vast, his thirst for knowledge unquenchable. Codes and riddles unraveled before him like loose knot work. He was made to be flawless, and so he was. There was nothing at which he could fail. It was not allowed. Any time he faltered, he was pushed onward."

"But I fell in love with Losolin."

Tonora's fathomless blue eyes softened. "Yes. Yet you loved Aidyn as well. In this, it was not his failure. Losolin Ullor Grisholm was a chink in the plan. His removal was attempted, but each time you interfered, until his life was grudgingly accepted, and attention was turned on you. Your attraction toward Aidyn was manipulated, and his toward you, until it became unbearable. The intent was to make you abandon Losolin for your intended partner. Plainly, this only partially worked. You and Aidyn found yourselves unable to resist each other, yet your love for Losolin was true and strong, and could not be fouled. His love for you was such that even when it shattered his heart, he gave you leave to love an assassin, and did not hate you for it."

Here the spirit paused, hesitated. "There was to be a child. You were supposed to bear the seed of Aidyn Sestuns. The child would have had your power and spirit, *my* spirit, and his perfection, the strength of a family that has survived since Amades and Ullor walked the earth, the Sestuns blood is stronger than any other. He would have been the greatest of us all, a king strong enough to survive the next chapter of Nymyños, of Himmle."

Tlonna felt a painful sense of loss...a child with Aidyn. Tonora nodded.

"Aidyn died in your place. He loved you so much that when the magic to free the Darkwights from their slavery needed a sense of love and righteousness, he overwhelmed it. He cured not only the Darkwight blight, but also any injury ever given by a weapon wielding the same form of taint. His love, his honor, combined with yours, erased the smear of true evil from the face of the world, not just . Nymyños."

"The drawings in the cave, there was a dark figure in the flames, replacing me. It was Aidyn all along."

Tonora nodded. "Yes. Neither Astinus nor anyone after him realized it was the assassin's destiny to die for you. All that was ever seen was the darkness. An assassin, a dark elf, so many things construed as evil when in fact in him they were simply a part of his honor and integrity."

"What of Miazie? Sithian said that she was a traitor. What did she perceive that she did not get the chance to tell me?"

"The woman Miazie Paron Ughtren was never a traitor. She loved you. She believed that what she was telling you would help you, and in the end it did. You were talented and willful enough that you managed to turn even the direst of situations into a victory. She saw only what I just told you, that it was not you in fact who was originally destined for this. It was the last of the prophecy. It was at that moment that her ability as a Belau left her. To know what would happen after that would have destroyed her."

"You mean my death?"

"No. What comes next."

"Which is?"

Tonora again held out the pendants. "The Resurrection Pendant was tossed upon the grave of Midian Aderiaen Rahlan by Sithian Midian Rahlan, a place where spirits and gods have lease. We retrieved it from there. The Death Pendant was around your neck when you came to us. They are your choice. One will send you back to the living, unchanged, to continue your life. The other will allow you to come with me, to Summerland. Be warned however. If you choose to return, the bond with your sister will be broken. If she dies, she dies. If you die, you die. You will not have the power you once had. The addition of Magin Jair," Tonora smiled and Tlonna realized that at last she had her son back, "and the other Magins and the spirits will no longer be with you. You will be strong, but not invincible."

Tears cascaded down Tlonna's face. "There is so much pain in life," she said quietly, thinking of living in a world where Aidyn no longer walked, where a child with their mingled blood would have grown.

Tonora nodded. "In heaven there is no pain, no grief. You will be forever content and sooner or later your loved ones will join you. The draw you felt from Aidyn will be gone. Your love for him will remain, but not the unstoppable desire."

"What happens if I choose life? Will I be permitted to Summerland when I pass?"

"As long as you stay true and virtuous, yes."

"This is not an easy choice."

"It should not be, but you must make it," Tonora said and held out the pendants.

Tlonna stared at the white pendant, glistening with life, with love and happiness. Her gaze moved to the black, shining with death, with pain and grief. She frowned. They both represented elements of each choice.

"Which one is which?"

Tonora gazed at her descendant. "Do you not know?"

After a moment, Tlonna nodded. Reaching out she said, "I am done," and grasped the Death Pendant.

In a flash before all went white and blind, Tonora reached out and placed her hand over Tlonna's womb, and searing warmth spread outward through her body. Then came peace.

# Chapter 48
## The Conclusion of the Aftermath

Tlonna's funeral attracted thousands from all over the nation. Each ruler from the kingdoms came, including Isadorr, King of Seaduens. Her white marble coffin sat on the dais within the throne room, replacing the thrones themselves. Losolin, Yayènia, Suneelo, and Aladorn stood behind it as Miazie struggled her way through the eulogy. It was long, but filled with the stunning achievements of Tlonna's relatively short life.

"She was only one hundred and forty-eight, an incredibly young elf with the experiences of a much older ruler. She lost nearly everything and still kept going. She was a friend to everyone, a person who would listen to your problems even when she herself had such worries and sorrows we can only imagine," Miazie choked on her words and had to take a few deep breaths to steady herself. "Tlonna Ewôsdírn was the queen we all loved, a monarch that will be remembered for all of eternity, not only for her sacrifices and her triumphs against evil, but for her heart and soul. She loved with a passion that defied reason. She detested racism and judgmental biases. Her heart beat for the sake of everyone else. She loved an assassin, a warrior, a peasant, even a human. She had friends among dwarves, elves, humans, and all the faery folk. She..."

Miazie stopped midsentence, frowning, tears still glittering on her cheeks. She met Losolin's gaze and he stared back with the same confused look. There was a low rumble coming from inside the coffin. Yayènia slowly drew her longsword and stepped back, looking around. The rumble grew until it filled the entire throne room. People began to shout. The marble began to crack and split apart, light spilling from each tiny crevice. The five upon the dais felt a vibration coming from inside and their hearts filled with disbelieving hope.

The coffin exploded outward but instead of crashing to the floor and smashing into the congregation, the pieces stayed suspended in the light, each ray to each chunk, no matter how small. A blinding white form stepped out of the remains of the pale blue silk and the hall filled with screams.

"I am Tlonna Ewôsdírn, Magin Queen, come back to you now," Tlonna's voice said, echoing with power, reverberating off the obsidian walls.

The slabs of marble floated over to land in a neat pile inside the remains of the coffin and the light faded. Tlonna stood before them, clad in the black dress with the silver tree of Blackhaven upon it. Her hair was pure white but her eyes had returned to their normal state of blue with black pupils. If possible, she appeared more beautiful than ever before. Losolin's knees hit the floor.

"I have died, but my place in heaven was taken by a soul greater than mine. I was shielded by a love that knew no bounds, a faith that knew no limits, and an honor that could take any doubt. I am here now because of Aidyn Sestuns, who gave his life in place of mine. Give your thanks to him."

The gathered crowd lifted their voices and their arms in praise, weeping in boundless joy as their beloved queen stood before them, radiant and alive. The kings of the nations, Erdwyf and Ghealan included, bowed before her with tear-filled eyes, laughing even as they cried. Suddenly she was accosted from behind and the reborn queen turned to find Yayènia and Miazie clutching her. Losolin remained where he was, kneeling by her coffin, sobbing unashamedly. Suneelo and Aladorn stared at her with streaming eyes, smiling.

Tlonna gently extracted herself from her sister and Miazie and went to her husband's side. She took his face in her hands, wiped away the tears, and kissed him fervently before the entire hall. His shaking hands reached up to grip her head, running his fingers through the silky white lengths.

"Losolin," she cried, breathing in his scent. It had always calmed her.

"Tlonna, oh gods, Tlonna. How? How?"

The queen pulled away so she could look him in the eye, and wiped the fresh tears away. "Aidyn. We owe it all to Aidyn."

"That damnable assassin," Losolin laughed, and then hugged his wife close.

After a long time she pulled away and turned to Aladorn, who was looking at her with a mix of sorrow and joy. Tlonna put a hand on his shoulder and then hugged him.

"Al...I am so sorry. He would not leave me. I tried to get him to, but he refused. He is at peace now. Nothing more can hurt him. *I* cannot hurt him anymore."

The wiat nodded, blinking away more tears. "He loved you, and he died for you. It is what he would have wanted, it was an honorable, beautiful death. He will live on in us."

Tlonna nodded and hugged him again. "Yes. Yes he will."

Yayènia looked about to explode when Tlonna opened her arms and her sister rushed into them. "Ah, spirits Tlonna, you damn near destroyed me. I knew it. I knew you could not be dead. I was still alive. I was still alive!"

Tlonna laughed as she stroked the back of Yayènia's head, feeling where her hair ended just below her shoulders. It was completely loose, not a single braid. "He said you were coming, Nia. Aidyn said you were fighting to get to me. You were there when it mattered, as always. Thank you."

Yayènia nodded into her sister's shoulder, hot tears spilling from her eyes. "When next I see him, I am going to kick his pretty little butt for getting there before me."

The queen laughed again and opened her arms so Suneelo could hug her too, squashing Yayènia between them. The male kissed his fingertips and pressed it to her mouth.

"Glad to have you back, little sister," he said.

When she finally turned to Miazie, the woman could not look her in the eyes.

"Miazie...I have all my memories back. Every one of them."

"Tlonna, I am sorry. I swear to you I did not know I was being controlled. I don't know what to say."

The elf smiled and shook her head. "You need not say anything. You are and always have been my friend. Feel no regret."

Miazie cried out and rushed to her friend, mindful of her swollen belly. "Oh, thank the gods you're back! I missed you so."

Tlonna hugged her carefully, worried that the woman might give birth at any moment. Then she was surrounded. Erdwyf and Ghealan, Tristan, Tyular, Eyin, Erandur, Lelfwin, Tahi-tat and Shin-hatsu, Barukh and even Isadorr. They all hugged her, their faces full of wonder and awe. Isadorr was the last and he hesitated before the queen simply wrapped him up in her arms and nearly lifted him off the ground. His eyes widened and he gasped. When she set him down he straightened his tunic with an air of dignity that made everyone else laugh and he blushed.

"Tlonna...I know what my brother did. I did not know of his treachery, I promise you. I found his body the same day you...on the last day. Know that Seaduens stands behind the rest of Nymyños. I will sign your alliance."

"Thank you Isadorr. This day begins a new era for Nymyños," she lifted her voice so all could hear. "We must all stand together as one nation, separated by land but bonded by blood and by heart and mind. We are alive today because of the sacrifices of many others. We shall not let their deaths be in vain!"

There was a great cry as her words were received and praised. Tlonna turned and held her hand out for Losolin. He took it and held it tight, his face still pale with emotion. The queen took a deep breath and led her family from the throne room, and away from the shattered remains of her coffin. Once ensconced in the library, she told them what had transpired during the battle with Sithian, her and Aidyn's death, and Tonora's explanation.

"So you and I are no longer linked," she said to Yayènia, who nodded in understanding. "The Staff of Cyree and the Magin Stone were created for the sole purpose of channeling the magic through the earth and into me, and therefore into the physical world so that I could erase the taint of the Darkwights."

Sodo lifted his hand and ran it back through his pale blond hair. "It was a powerful blow, Tlonna. Knocked me into a wall. I cannot even imagine the force of it right next to you."

Tlonna smiled. "It was rather painful for me too."

Erdwyf frowned. "I heard that every single Magin in the vicinity was stripped of their power completely. That is, every single one except for Losolin."

The king nodded. "It is true. I retain my powers."

Tlonna smiled again. "It is because of the same reason you and I cannot touch each other with our magic without causing extreme pain. It comes from the same source. It was simply washing over you, blind to you really, because it was the same magic. That is why there would have been a radius around us that was not touched by the waves. I would assume that around that area it just appeared as light, rather than the colors that the rings were."

Tristan nodded. "It was, but there was a wind like no other. I could barely keep my feet."

The queen shrugged. "I have no explanation for that except that there was a lot of power in that area. Also..." her hand lifted to her throat where the Death Pendant had once hung. "The two pendants were destroyed when I chose life. For an instant I saw power coming out of Tonora's hands, and then she was holding nothing. It is the last thing I saw before I woke up in that damn coffin."

"And the Ivory Sword was found in thousands of pieces, and blackened as well," Suneelo told her. "We gathered the shards and placed them in the treasury."

"That is fine. It can stay there for all I care. What of Sithian?" the words hurt to say, but she had to know.

Everyone looked uncomfortable. Finally it was Yayènia who spoke. "I saw his body right before you unleashed the magic, but afterward, he came back, or his body did. He nearly killed me, but I tossed him into a chasm he had created to swallow me. Where it happened there is just this...barren patch of earth. Where you and Aidyn were, there is a veritable flower garden. None of us understood it."

"The Graves of Good and Evil," Miazie murmured quietly and shared a look with Tlonna.

The queen agreed. "Was anything done for them?"

Yayènia nodded. "We used some of the parts of the wall to build a fence around the area, and the engineer Matthias put up a stone plaque telling the story of what happened."

"Good. And...Aidyn?"

When everyone fell silent once more, Tlonna could feel the sorrow in the room. It was Aladorn who spoke at last.

"We buried him yesterday. Nearly as many showed up for him as for you. The entire College of Assassins was there too. He is next to Dietirin, I hope that is all right."

Tlonna wiped her tears away. "It is more than all right. It is where he belongs. I want...I want a statue of him put up in the city. And another on the castle grounds. He will not be forgotten."

Everyone nodded, and the conversation moved on to slightly lighter subjects regarding Zaedic and its apparent downfall. Erdwyf had discovered that Sithian had found a new wife, but had failed to get her with child. The Rahlan line was officially ended and the island kingdom was severely under populated as nearly all the men had been unwillingly drafted into the war. It would no longer be a problem.

# Chapter 49

## Epilogue

Tlonna shook as she turned the well-worn handle on Aidyn's door. It swung open with a light push and she stood on the threshold for a few moments, gathering the courage she needed to enter. The foyer was dark, the curtains drawn against the light. The queen stepped inside and shut the door behind her, shivering though she was not cold. The room smelled like him. It was a mockery. Tlonna walked slowly across the small foyer, dragged her fingers over the worn black suede of Aidyn's favorite chair as she passed it. When she reached the windows, she pulled the curtains to the side and illuminated the entire room. She gasped, for a moment she thought she saw Aidyn standing next to his chair, but he was not. He was gone. Forever. Light sprayed across the obsidian floor, caught the deep crimsons and sables of the many rugs and seemed to burn in her gaze. Against the wall leaned a bow with a frayed grip and dented cap, waiting for its owner to return and mend it. Everything seemed to be waiting for the great assassin's return, sitting in stasis as though nothing was wrong with the world.

Tlonna spotted a bookshelf and walked over to it, having never noticed it before. She ran her fingers over the titles, tilting her head to read. *Furntil Eldrout, First Assassin* and *The Fables of Mattimus* seemed oft-read, their bindings loose and frayed. Others like *Ages of War, A History of the 7ᵗʰ and 8ᵗʰ* and *Understanding Serenyi* appeared to have been read once and never again. Tlonna shook her head, suddenly thinking of questions she wanted to ask her friend. Why did he have a book of children's virtue stories and why was it worn so much? Had he wanted children? Again the thought of Tonora's touch warmed her.

The female blinked rapidly to stop herself from crying as she turned away from the shelf. There were other oddities in the room she had never noticed before, a small carving of a vixen stood proudly next to a model ship, and on one windowsill was a multicolored glass ball that threw splashes of color across the room. A little overwhelmed, Tlonna hurried into the bedroom and stopped, swallowing back her grief. Aidyn's bed was made, the black duvet brushed clean by the maids. The wardrobe sat polished and gleaming against the wall, the little painting of Rahna in its position above it. Tlonna opened the wardrobe and frowned. Among all the black silk, *ärdyz*, and leather was a tunic of dazzling white. Puzzled, she pulled it out and studied it. The hems and collar were embroidered in a gold knot pattern, the material a fine silk. She had never seen it before, and wondered why in the world Aidyn would have a white shirt. There was a small tag attached to the sleeve from the seamstress.

*Aidyn Sestuns, Wedding Tunic, 27 Laynyan, 9362.*

The shirt was for his marriage to Rahna, which had never happened. Tlonna swallowed in sadness as she replaced the tunic and then noticed the latch in the bottom of the wardrobe. After a bit of pulling and pushing, the hidden compartment revealed itself and Tlonna gasped. She picked up the heavy trunk and placed it on the floor. She studied the shattered lock and then pushed on the worn brass fittings positioned on either side of the trunk. The lid popped open. Inside were Aidyn's tools of the trade. Shiny, little knives, perfectly balanced for throwing; ropes and hooks; an ornately decorated hatchet; several bottles of liquid, some foul and some intoxicating; and a myriad other things. Tlonna winced when she accidentally pricked her finger on a stiletto dagger. The damn thing was sharp!

When she got to the bottom of the trunk, the elf's throat constricted when she saw an old, faded piece of parchment shoved against a wall, wrinkled and missing a corner. Gingerly picking it up and deciphering the ink faded to brown but still holding the flowing, precise script of the assassin, Tlonna read the most personal words of Aidyn Sestuns.

*Rahna,*

*My love, I wish you would return to me, at least to the castle. It is not safe for you to be alone; it is not safe for anyone to be alone at this time. Please, I beg of you, honor this one wish. I understand if you no longer desire my company, but is not your life more important than your disappointment in me? Dietirin has issued a blanket security on the castle. Anyone coming or going must be checked by guards before going anywhere. This will ensure your safety, for no one will get beyond the guards. You have my word, my heart, that if you would do this one thing, I will stay as far away from you as you wish. I know you are in pain, and I realize it is my fault that it is so, but know that everything I do is to protect you. I love you.*

*Always,*
*Aidyn*

Across the bottom of the letter in a different, lighter hand were scrawled four harsh words that tore into Tlonna.

*Do not contact me*

Rahna had denied Aidyn's plea for her safety. There was a record of the blanket security that Dietirin had passed, and it was during the battle between Blackhaven and Hadian Rahlan's forces. It was in that battle Rahna had died whilst running toward the male who loved her. Tlonna wondered if Rahna's move had been one of true, desperate love or unbridled fear. People tended to flock to Aidyn's side whenever there was imminent danger, she was no exception. Tlonna suddenly hated Rahna with every cell in her body. The damn fool had taken Aidyn's love for granted, thrown it away as soon as things got a little messy, and then counted on that same love to save her wretched life. The bitch had denied him!

*So did you,* crowed a little voice in her head.

Tlonna refolded the letter and placed it back in the trunk, and carefully put everything back. Then she pulled out one of Aidyn's *ärdyz* tunics and carried it to the bed. She curled up on the duvet and clutched the shirt to her, trembling. Her fingers danced idly over the slippery material. One caught on a raised bump along the side of the shirt. Frowning, Tlonna lifted her head to inspect the anomaly. It was a stitch.

Without warning a memory of Aidyn slammed into her head. It was when he had saved her from the Seadueni assassin Jadir. She remembered standing in her room with Miazie as they tried not to look at him. On his left side, just above where his hipbone protruded against his skin was a scar, about seven inches long and slightly raised. She had kissed it, trailed her fingers over it, over all his scars, and had tried to take them away.

Tlonna's body convulsed as a sob was wrenched from her throat. He must have been wearing this tunic when he'd been hit there. She brought the stitching up to her lips and kissed it, crying softly. Then all at once, it was too much. She buried her face in the shirt and turned into the pillow, and screamed. She screamed and wailed in anguish, her fingers rigidly digging into the side of her head.

A year later, Tlonna stood next to Losolin in front of a black-draped lump of stone, a hand upon her rounded belly. She had not seen the statue since she had commissioned it and had approved of the carver's sketches. Today was the unveiling. Within her womb grew a child of Losolin's seed, mingled with that essence of Aidyn given her by Tonora. The child would be of all three. They were standing in a central square of the city, facing toward the gate. Newly launched was the free academy Haydyn had dreamed of, its doors opening onto the square. By her side stood Yayènia and Suneelo, who were glowing with the fresh knowledge that they too were to have a child. Miazie, holding her half-blood son Aydin, stood with Sodo's arm wrapped around his wife; Aladorn and his son Locton stood on the other side of Losolin. Ghealan and Erdwyf were in Nouraeva, still trying to bring the decimated kingdom out of the ashes of the war. Only Tristan had been able to make it for the unveiling, as the other kings of the east were busy counseling the new king of Talenias, Haldred Ughtren, Miazie's older brother who had been found taking refuge in Zeynuwn. Eyin, newly married to the Zeynuwnian girl Jalel, was busy forging his own new kingdom.

The carver, a dwarf from Florwen Hune, stepped up and looked at Tlonna for confirmation. She nodded. The black cloth was whipped off the statue and it took her breath away. Aidyn was depicted perfectly, even down to the set of his mouth. His right arm was pulled back, holding his scimitar, while the left was straight down, the tension blade extended. His cloak billowed in the wind, held against his back by his bow and longsword, bits of his hair lifted in strands with the same breeze. He looked eastward, toward the rising sun, to forever guard the entrance to Blackhaven. His armor was portrayed exactly as it had been in real life, the red and black symbol carved out of corresponding marble, while the rest was in pearlescent white. His twin statue was in the courtyard of the castle, though it was much smaller.

Tlonna stared at it for a long time, gazing at the stone face of the one she had been made for. Finally, she turned to Losolin, the one she had thwarted fate in order to love. He smiled and held out his hand. He understood.

Together, the quiet group turned back toward the castle as the sun rose to its full height. The land of Nymyños brightened with it because of the sacrifice made by one great assassin. As the sunlight hit his stone visage, the shadows on Aidyn's face lifted into a mischievous smirk, so familiar to those who had known and loved him.

This concludes the story of Tlonna Ewôsdírn and those who sacrificed so much to better the lives of all those who lived in Nymyños, and those who continue to live there.

# Parlêthian Grammar and Vocabulary List

Grammar

The use of double and triple vowels is very prominent in the elfish language of Parlêthian. In each set, they always make the same sound regardless of their position in a word or sentence, as follows:
- (Aa)-air
- (Ae)- ay
- (Ai)- eye
- (Ao)- ayo
- (Au)- aw
- (Ea)- ee
- (Eae)- eh
- (Eoa)- eeoh
- (Ia)- eeya
- (Ìa)- aya
- (Iae)- eya
- (Ie)- ee
- (Ou)- ow
- (Ue)- ueh
- (Uu)-oo
- (Yè)- yee
- (Yi)- yih

✷ The use of double consonants is rare, but again make the same sound regardless of their position in a word or sentence, as follows:
- (Dd)- dth as in wi*dth*
- (Nn)- long n sound, as in ho*nn*ey
- (Rr)- rolled across tongue.

Suffixes are universal but for some words that are simply random throughout the language. There are no prefixes.
- a. Anc or nce-add 'to (*nori* – deliver becomes *norito*- deliverance) If the word ends in TO, repeat 'to
- b. Er- add 's(*aru* – brave becomes *arus*- braver) If the word ends in S, the sound is simply lengthened with another S.
- c. Est- add 'si (*aru* – brave becomes *arusi*- bravest) If the word ends in S, only add the I.
- d. Ed- add 'sa (*aru*- brave becomes *arusa*- braved) If the word ends in S, only add the A.

e. En- add 'su (*kuch-* dark becomes *kuchsu-* darken) If the word ends in S, only add the U.

f. Ing- add 'en (*aru* - brave becomes *aruen* – braving) If the word ends in E, only add the N.

g. Ist- add 'ta (*myrra-* illusion becomes *myrrata-* illusionist) If the word ends in T, still add the TA

h. Ness-add 'il (*kuch-* dark becomes *kuckil-* darkness)

i. Y-add 'lin (*arus* – braver becomes *aruslin-* bravery)

Ownership is achieved by placing an A at the end of words. If it already ends in an A, then there is nothing added.

j. Losolin's book –Losolina dultren

k. Tlonna's book- Tlonna dultren

Plurality is often achieved by placing an E at the end of words and is pronounced as "eh". If it already ends in an E, then there is nothing added. There are few words in Parlêthian that have different plurality markers, but they must be simply known.

l. Chair- isant becomes Chairs- isante

m. Sword- kantle remains Swords- kantle

Also often used are accent marks. They are as follows:

o The caret ^ mark is used on vowels. They are always preceded by a consonant, and used to harden that consonant.

- Examples:
  - Ewôsdírn – Ee- VOS- dEErn
  - Takîreaes - Tuh- KEER- ehs
  - Parlêthian - Par- LEE- thee- an

o The grave (`) is used infrequently, typically in names. It is used to **stress** the long sound of the vowel on which it is placed

- Example:
  - Yayènia pronounced Yah- YEE- nee- uh
  - Lälìan pronounced Leh-lih-awn

o The acute( ´) is used infrequently, typically surnames. It is used to **indicate** the long sound of the vowel on which it is placed.

- Examples:
  - Ewôsdírn - Ee- VOS- dEErn
  - Rók - R- OH- k

- The umlaut ( ¨ )is used on vowels to change the pronunciation from that of the traditional vowel sound to the more cultured sounds as follows:
  - Ä- eh
  - Ë- ye
  - Ï- yi
  - Ö- er
  - Ü- oo
  - Ÿ- ai
- The breve (˘) is used on vowels to change the pronunciation from long to short.
  - Examples
    - Ă- ay
    - Ĕ- ee
    - Ĭ- eye
    - Ŏ- oh
    - Ŭ-yoo
- The tilde ( ˜ ) is also used on vowels to indicate a change in pronunciation, typically from the nasalization to the circumflex, or to the soft rather than the hard sound. It is also used on the consonant N to lengthen the stress of the letter which is achieved by pressing the tongue to the roof of the mouth and speaking from the bottom of the mouth.
  - Examples:
    - Lãn- Lawn
    - Neñyos- Ne*nn*- yose
    - Nymyños- Nim- ih- *nn*ohs
- Also used, though very infrequently is the separating apostrophe. This appears in few words and names and is used to add a pause within, which is achieved by cutting the air off with the tongue and then continuing the word.
  - Examples:
    - Nebet'thu- Neb- eT- Thoo
    - A'da- Ah- Dah

✱ Pronunciation
- The letter C is found only in the form of CH and SC. The form SC makes a slightly harder sound than SH. Ch make a soft sound, produced by making an o with the lips, pressing the back of the tongue against the roof of the mouth, and expelling air forward to produce a sound similar to '*whe*'

- o The letters D and T are pronounced strongly, as is the form TH, which is said by placing the tongue between the teeth and pushing air out quickly to make it a hard sound.
- o The letter J is pronounced softly with a hissing sound made by placing the tongue at the roof of the mouth and breathing outward.
- o The letter Q, unlike in English (Hindarün), is not always followed by U, and is pronounced slightly softer than K.
- o The letter R is most often rolled softly off the tongue unless it is found after (ar) or other long vowel sounds, in which case it is a soft sound like (er).

✳ Married Names
- o When a female elf marries a male elf, she takes his name, with the addition of er'(name) in order to denote that she is married. If a male elf marries a female elf of royal lineage, he takes her name as an addition with en'(name), and the female adds his as well.
  - ▪ Examples:
    - • Suneelo Tiena
    - • Yayènia er'Tiena
    - • Tlonna Ewôsdírn er'Grisholm
    - • Losolin Grisholm en'Ewôsdírn
- o A child of a royal line with a maternal bloodline to the throne will take the combined name with the connective el'(name). His wife will take full name and er'addition, but their child will carry only the name of the father.
  - ▪ Example:
    - • Tonoran Ewôsdírn el'Grisholm
    - • Ferana er'Ewôsdírn el'Grisholm

✳ The difference between Elfish and Elven
- o Elven is an adjective used when speaking of, or meaning, the living race, including attributes such as strength, will, and physical appearance.
  - ▪ Examples:
    - • Elven Race
    - • Elven might
    - • Elven ears
- o Elfish is used when speaking of, or meaning, the language, cities, and material items.
  - ▪ Examples:

- Elfish sword
- Elfish city
- Elfish dialect

＊ Use
  o The elfish language is meant to be spoken in an unbroken manner so that it flows together without break or pause between words except for when taking a breath, which should be done between sentences.
  o The words should be spoken passionately and precisely, with clear pronunciation particularly on all accented letters.
  o In Parlêthian, there is no such thing as a contraction and Hindarün (English) words are rarely used in such a form, and typically in slang or mockery.

The following is by no means an exhaustive list of words, but includes the most oft used words by the people of Nymyños, their Serenyin ancestors, and their descendants. Included is both an English (Hindarün) to Parlêthian and a Parlêthian to English translation. A full dictionary is in the works.

A-

A- Lãn
Able- Lorr
About- Brã
Above- Ajudi
Abyss- Orvã
Accept- Youl
Act- Mimai
Add- Qiit
After- Mynda
Again- Qela
Against- Itaen
Age- Edoh
Agenda- Slír
Ago- Sikkeae
Ahead- Owaen
Air- Essimö
Alas- Erda
Alive- Asen
All- Xellt
Allegiance- Fueldereae
Allow- Nuz
Alone- Gorae
Also- Oh
Always- Fírev
Am- Sïm
Among- Ubóth
An- Lãn
Ancestor- Mauna
And- Nó
Animal- Kulai
Another- Buche
Answer- Jaxea
Any- Jempt
Apart- Rhi
Appear- Han
April- Kayab
Archer- Elantian
Are- Feaen
Area- Térn
Arisen- Yelt
Army- Sanf
Arrow- Neñyos
As- Pe
Ask- Huedd
Assassin- Moyrkel
Asunder- Ayanu
At- Teo
August- Kankin
Away- Bolecke

B-

Back- Tauon
Bad- Achien
Badger- Isidil
Bane- Oad

Bark- Chi
Base- Widne
Bastard- Dûmvadyn
Battle- Inös
Beautiful- Estoun
Beauty- Estadd
Because- Shälda
Be- Eaf
Bed- Riah
Bee- Blaet
Been- Abya
Before- Elba
Began- Uol
Begin- Uo
Beginner- Uos
Beginning- Uoen
Behind- Neben
Being- Sumyan
Belief- Le
Beliefs- Lesh
Believe- Let
Believed- Letsa
Believer- Lets
Believing- Leten
Bells- Melnon
Bent- Ifer
Best- Ealla
Betray- Dak'na
Betrayal- Dak'hana
Betrayed- Dak'nasa
Betrayer- Dak'nas
Betraying Dak'naen
Betrays- Dak'nat
Betroth- Iy
Betrothal- Iyd
Betrothed- Iysa
Betrothing- Iyen
Better- Eally
Between- Edlam
Beyond- Nebt
Big- Gröm
Bird- Flieger
Birth- Kes
Bit- En
Black- Kairho
Blade- Thafn
Blademaster- Thafnlyna
Blaze- Kata
Bled- Blot
Bleed- Blöt
Bleeder- Blots
Bleeding- Blöten
Blessed- Mlek
Blood- Blöd
Bloodied- Blö
Bloody- Blöda
Blue- Skai
Boat- Reffer

Bodies- Quen
Body- Quene
Bond- Olt
Bone- Wróth
Book- Dultren
Books- Dultret
Boot- Olea
Boots- Oleas
Bored- Tam
Boring- Tamen
Born- Flett
Borrow- Pwoe
Both- Wedd
Bow- Köl
Boy- Flaydon
Boys- Flaydot
Box- Qued
Branch- Fili
Brave- Aru
Braved- Aru
Braver- Arus
Bravery- Arulin
Braves- Arue
Bravest- Arusi
Breakfast- Hetr
Break- Hri
Breaking- Hrien
Breathed- Lausa
Breathe- Lauf
Breather- Laus
Breathing –Lauen
Breath- Lau
Breeches- Oloons
Brilliant- Legathe
Bring- Chounsi
Broke- Hru
Brother- Bruun
Brought- Choul
Build-Zasnuil
Burn- Bãn
Busy- Heth
But- Ubr
Bye, Buy, By- Eann

C-

Call- Awin
Called- Awinsa
Caller- Awins
Calling- Awinen
Came- Sün
Can- Jerwlyn
Cancel- Setuil
Cape- Ridda
Care- Thallaa
Carry- Rret'a
Carve- Chued'a
Castle- Flüken

Cause- Älda
Cemetery- Klaguerd
Center- Maullo
Certain- Chouda
Chair- Isant
Chairs- Isante
Changed- Ruletensa
Changer- Ruletens
Change- Ruleten
Changing- Ruletenen
Check- Twe
Child- Jen
Children- Jened
Choice- Fraken
Choose- Fralop
Chosen- Frason
Cipher- Klyph
City- Geth
Class- Heaema
Clean- Shou
Cleanse- Shouf
Clear- Krystes
Cloak- Altenias
Close- Giadef
Cloud- Gleepth
Cloudy- Gleepthi
Coast- Delz
Code- Siira
'Coinage'- Oma
Cold- Bĕtira
Color- Wíramer
Comb- Brästl
Comes- Yeste
Come- Yest
Coming- Yeste
Command- Alt
Commanded- Altsa
Commander- Konyia
Commanding- Alten
Commands- Alts
Comma- Stuet
Common- Pĕtiir
Complain- Maiter
Complete- Duul
Contain- Vrial
Correct- Parra
Cough- Ech
Count- Trefui
Country- Duned
Course- Dülle
Could- Naelos
Cover- Kiyua
Crash-Gwen
Creed- Leh
Creek- Krel
Cross- Ängä
Crumble- Braech
Cry- Luteaer

Cursed- Teysa
Curse- Tey
Curves- Quais
Cut- Afroi
Cyree- Talchin

D-

Dad- Dâd
Damn- Leif
Damnation- Leiflil
Damnedest- Leifsasi
Damned- Leifsa
Damning- Leifen
Dance- Raine
Dancer- Raines
Dancing- Rainen
Darkening- Kuchsuen
Darken- Kuchsu
Darkest- Kuchsi
Dark- Kuch
Darkness- Kuchil
Daughter- Klyshet
Dawn- Illian
Day- Loon
Days- Loone
Death- Syp
Debt- Rók
Debts- Róko
December- Lamat
Decide- Elöda
Dedicated- Saykl
Dedication- Sayklis
Deep- Uha
Defeat- Ushna
Defend- Alpro
Deliver- Nori
Demon- Svonwy
Deserve- Nya
Deserved- Nyasa
Deserves- Nyas
Deserving- Nyaen
Destroyed- Nasen
Destroyer- Nass
Destroying- Nasen
Destroy- Nas
Determined- Sunosa
Determine- Suno
Develop- Wegni
Devil- Sævulen
Did- Dond
Died- Gonsa
Die- Gon
Dies- Gons
Differ- Didua
Dinner- Gethan
Direct- Niir
Disgrace- Shamer

Does- Eonn
Dog- Zeyla
Doing- Vlen
Done- Finat
Do- Nyn
Doomed- Uduan
Doom- Udu
Door- Pŏtal
Doubts- Zerchte
Doubt- Zercht
Down- Buen
Draw- Yiln
Drink- Trasnel
Dry- Frey
Droned- Lemmësa
Drone- Lemmë
During- Throin
Dusted- Sheethsa
Dust- Sheeth
Duties- Zuskadin
Duty- Zuskadi

E-

Each- Haldedd
Early- Latak
Earth- Zarouchen
Ease- Hausil
East- Owne
Easy- Hausten
Eat- Szesa
Elf- Lälian
Else- Bearn
Elves- Läliane
Ending- Zerten
End- Zert
English- Hindarün
Enough- Nodolu
Eternity- Seryean
Even- Na
Ever- Einen
Every- Einel
Evil- Brütel
Example- Pyltak
Excellent- Aargen
Exclamation- Gausten
Exile- Quesio
Explain- Oncherath
Extra- Veyn
Eye- Zso
Eyes- Zsoe

F-

Faces- Yethers
Face- Yether
Fact- Indiil
Fail- Ruben

Fair- Erdwyn
Fall- Booka
Fallen- Bookak
Family- Rae'da
Far- Jarka
Farm- Olsun
Fashion- Styk
Fast- Vas
Fate- Whäd
Father- A'da
Fear- Ika
Feather- Plumès
February- Shuak
Feel- Seno
Feet- Lardoun
Fell- Buou
Fence- Alden
Few- Lir
Field- Dell
Fiend- Olua
Fifth- Fêna
Fight- Rula
Figure- Endarea
Fill- Nid
Finally- Winka
Final- Wink
Find- Yolom
Fine- Ende
Finish- Se
Finished- Sesa
Fire- Xuten
First- Krant
Fish- Skel
Fit- Tiln
Fix- Feld
Flame- Luma
Flee- Leth
Fleer- Leths
Flesh- Koruli
Flower- Insot
Fly- Hinarï
Foe- Muura
Fold- Bri
Fog- Thedreth
Follow- Orner
Food- Sembas
Foolish- Kulten
Fool- Kulta
Fools- Kultae
Foot- Greiol
Force- Fedd
Forest- Buwai
Forever- Laushden
Forget- Lada
Forgotten- Läda
For- Ka
Form- Tref
Fortune- Fli

Fortunate- Flil
Found- Aklm
Forth- Iwen
Fourth- Skola
Fox- Bâbãye
Free- Libré
Friday- Uloon
Friend- Dü
Friendship- Dukata
From- Äoslan
Front- Uster
Frost- Ýlt
Frozen- Ýltid
Full- Lewn
Fury- Aaldoor

G-

Game- Damé
Garden- Yardos
Gave- Seage
Getting- Uleaen
Get- Ulea
Gift- Wella
Girl- Chärdon
Give- Sage
Gives- Sages
Giving- Sagen
Glad- Zaysa
Glee- Vich
Glory- Hallis
Go- Venae
Goal- Nol
Going- Sayd
Gold- Gläs
Gone- Queeta
Good- Sennia
God- Gwemh
Got- Glusheb
Gossamer- Galamial
Govern- Erdia
Grade- Alk
Great- Sied
Green- Emdri
Grey- Siva
Grief- Hespaa
Ground- Himwró
Group- Uhj
Grow- Waev
Guardian- Neelo
Guard- Nee

H-

Had- Jela
Hair- Len
Half- Umble
Hall- Hölle

Hand- Souv
Hands- Souve
Happen- Ikly
Happily- Liedes
Happy- Lied
Harbor- Vwen
Hard- Duneda
Harm- Torseth
Has- Stuna
Have- Yercht
Haven- Tuss
Head- Kjos
Heal- Gris
Heard- Zered
Hearing- Zeres
Heart- Uka
Hear- Zere
Heat- Stealik
Heed- Wer
Hell- Vuuka
Hello- Karinium
Help- Adi
He- Pola
Here- Boun
Her- Sääb
Hers- Sääbe
Hidden- Qredsu
Hide- Qred
Hiding- Qreden
High- Zo
Him- Sään
His- Sääne
Hole- Dyr
Hold- Bai
Hollow- Thiaeth
Home- Duned
Honey- Syak
Honor- Stoyet
Hoped- Synsu
Hope- Syn
Horse- Miea
Hot- Meaelta
Hour- Sae
House- Neyn
However- Udwa
How- Sïnd
Human- Akaid
Humans- Aikaid
Hunt- Nerty
Hurt- Fleab
Hurts- Fleabe

I-

I- Inkan
Idea- Wâdeh
If- Halo
Illusion- Myrra

Impossible- Nyneideae
Innocent- Andre
In- Serbe
Inch- Kwell
Inside- Feda
Inspirational- Risnla
Inspired- Risa
Inspire- Ris
Inspiring- Risen
Instrument- Wehtun
Interest- Nrein
Into- Talis
Invade- Malte
Invincible- Inviktu
Irreverence- Noyaistruktto
Irritable- Myachna
Irritated- Myach
Irritate- Mya
Iron- Fairv
Is- Puscheb
Island- Xeema
It- Shaiben
Its- Shaeben

J-

Jade- Noyv
January- Xul
Jape- Kupa
Jasper- Alda
Joke- Pheak
Joy- Lil
Joyous- Lilit
Judge- Las
Judgment- Laskil
Juggler- Ien
Jugglers- Iene
July- Tala
Jump- Piat
June- Mol
Just- Dochea
Justice- Xeyna

K-

Keep- Sardun
Kick- Notio
Kill- Slaughta
Kills- Slaughtas
Killed- Slaughtsa
Kind- Neaus
King- Eld
Kingdom- Eldion
Knew- Paed
Know- Peaf
Known- Pear
Knowledge- Hemios

L-

Lady- Eria
Lake- Elumña
Language- Lingui
Land- Jord
Large- Qrer
Last- Finst
Late- Joot
Laugh- Narth
Laughing- Narthen
Lay- Tael
Lead- Reage
Leaf- Laen
Learn- Riima
Least- Smek
Leave- Gehr
Left- Nift
Leg- Arra
Legs- Arrae
Legend- Varia
Legendary- Variania
Less- Mer
Let- Noyena
Letter- Yestoma
Lie- Froh
Lies- Freoh
Life- Sen
Lift- Nist
Lighted- Leaen
Lighten- Leasu
Lighter- Leas
Lightest- Leasi
Light- Lea
Lightning- Leatran
Like- Arbe
Likely- Arben
Likes- Arbee
Lily- Ileñias
Limb- Diav
Line- Joa
List- Jian
Listen- Saif
Listening- Saifen
Little- Ittin
Lived- Bayno
Live- Bay
Lives- Baye
Lock- Dobrin
Longing- Haba
Long- Keiden
Look- Hochan
Lord- Erion
Lose- Meaklim
Loss- Meaken
Lost- Meakes
Lot- Yeeh
Loved- Yayenasa

Loveliest- Yayeni
Lovely- Yayen
Lover- Yayenas
Love- Yayena
Loving- Yayenaen
Low- Ghi
Loyal- Lãrmo
Lunch- Fouo

M-

Made- Mentay
Magic- Förunderverk
Maiden- Leatsu
Maidens- Leatsue
Maid- Leat
Main- Lîsna
Make- Ton
Male- Tañd
Man- Kaid
Many- Souden
Map- Kartyl
March (Month) - Muan
March (Verb) - Shlock
Mark- Zêmbyl
Mask- Vilda
Mass- Zeym
Master- Lyna
May (Auxiliary) - Fo
May (Month) - Maen
Maybe- Tauron
Me- Kayn
Mean- Krum
Measure- Jevuu
Meet- Jenu
Memory- Emyar
Men- Kaide
Mercy- Kalise
Metal- Barluk
Might- Llek
Mile- Aalew
Mind- Lumaa
Mine- Särabeae
Mine (Noun) - Matsu
Minute- Ruunin
Misfit- Rayla
Miss- Sintaradö
Mist- Leala
Moment- Minn
Moments- Minne
Monday- Yaloon
Moon- Lälimyina
More- Krosa
Morning- Illion
Most- Iist
Mother- E'na
Motion- Pölya
Mountain- Tuln

Move- Polyp
Moves- Polypa
Much- Vena
Music- Wetron
Must- Glüpen
My- Säära
Myself- Sârtyn

N-

Nails- Vekae
Nail- Veka
Name- Shpa
Near- Bo'la
Needed- Lädönsa
Need- Lädön
Never- Kinë
Next- Sloshea
Nice- Svean
Night- Noie
Nights- Noien
Noble- Darem
Noise- Hëtrecht
No- Noya
North- Kaden
Nose- Slel
Note- Mletch
Not- Flounen
Notice- Zii
Nothing- Behkt
Noun- Sûn
November- Ealieaes
Now- Melas
Number- Nrekin
Numeral- Nreklis

O-

Oak- Kethna
Oath- El
Object- Zîth
Ocean- Vekla
October- Resen
Off- Shtan
Of- Shä
Often- Whim
Oh- Ih
Old- Al
One- Fou
Once- Zonn
On- Mün
Open- Kree
Or- Ib
Order- Elten
Organize- Wônt
Our- Munna
Out- Zunaa
Over- Flok

Owe- Maelda
Own- Jdere
P-

Pages- Yanae
Page- Yana
Pale- Elen
Parchment- Radsun
Pass- Tu
Passage- Tuuk
Passion- Yen
Path- Kuer
Pattern- Ilianria
Pay- Gohnut
Peace- Yi
Peer- Lainli
People- Muchen
Perhaps- Imluu
Period- Nashtan
Person- Mach
Picked- Leuftsa
Pick- Leuft
Picture- Udre
Piece- Iw
Place- Oyer
Plain- Truy
Plan- Deviko
Plane- Grress
Plant- Alamiah
Play- Haphen
Point- Lexla
Port- Sedika
Pose- Friem
Possible- Eideae
Pound- Staabe
Power- Deaet'he
Preserved- Nasior
Press- Mallif
Pressure- Mallifitha
Prison- Druuj'ta
Problem- Prreh
Produce- Iwagi
Product- Iwaga
Promise- Vila
Prophecy- Sharn
Prophetess- Sharntoun
Prophet- Sharntoul
Pull- Wrent
Pure- Talenia
Purify- Taleni
Purifier (Noun) - Tal'enis
Put- Eth

Q-

Queasy- Andil
Queen- Ela
Query- Inter

Question- Interoa
Questions- Interoae
Quick- Vas
Quickened-Vasusa
Quicksilver- Leatran
Quiet- Shyn
Quite- Da
Quit- Sanq

R-

Race- Tubä
Rain- Ulsen
Ran- Qual
Reach-Nold
Read- Flon
Reads- Flone
Ready- Enegadeae
Real- Kïmleth
Rear-Bathel
Rebuild- Kruen
Record- Dubliir
Red- Orltan
Reign- Zek
Rejoice-Gath
Rejoicing- Gathen
Remain- Suddi
Remember- Soyem
Remembered- Soyems
Remembering- Soyemsu
Remind- Dian
Reply- Ait
Rest- Ük
Return- Sa
Returned- So
Revere- Istrukt
Rid- Aald
Ride- Lauk
Right- Flous
Righteous- Flousen
Righteousness- Flousil
Rite- Serel
River- Ólva
Road- Korrido
Rock- Weir
Room- Inaem
Round- Kusra
Rounded- Kusrasa
Rubble- Slad
Rule- Phyr
Run- Qualpe
Running- Qualpesu

S-

Sad- Vwan
Sadly-Vwani
Sadness-Vwanil

Safe-Hovan
Said-Jona
Sail-Xanen
Same- Reez
Sanctum- Qar'tali
Sand- Dule
Saturday- Raloon
Saw- Plet
Says- Zuanas
Say-Zuana
School- Preriim
Science- Förunderverk
Sea- Fäyla
Seas-Fäylie
Second- Vente
Secret- Misarea
Seen- Ocheanas
See-Ochean
Seethe- Fyö
Seek- Oduun
Seem- Vizil
Seep- Ling
Self- Eaegè
Sell- Hók
Send- Wedavii
Sentence- Uerd
September-Laynyan
Serious-Idian
Servant-Leath
Serve- Thèvea
Set- Werij
Sever- Praet
Several- Dosduna
Shape- Fjorlat
Shade-Dua
Shadows-Xetiane
Shadow-Xetian
Shall-Vont
She-Oya
Shield- Rahn
Shine-Tauroun
Shining-Taurounen
Shore- Gravä
Shoulder-Hoift
Shoulders-Hoifte
Should-Peka
Show-Teza
Sigh-Log
Sighs-Loge
Silent-Rekie
Silver-Zephyr
Sing- Ehli
Singer-Ehlis
Sister-Flari
Sit-Elenea
Sitting-Eleneaen
Sir (Knight) – Syr
Sixth-Srêna

Sky-Poth
Slave- Sævulen
Slay-Möden
Slays-Mödene
Sleep-Fealos
Smallum- Tollapia Senn
Smell-Jerpen
Smoke- Lyz
Snow- Thyn
So-Est
Soft-Touve
Solitude- Elysia
Some-Ollean
Son- Ed'a
Song- Ehla
Sorrow- Sinyain
Sorry- Klysm
Soul- Mur
Sound- Vausa
South- Bruul
Space- Darf
Speak- Eyaba
Spear- Mie
Spend- Kea
Spirit- Daesis
Staff- Isten
Stand- Stadya
Star- Bällä
Start- Fineal
State- Datistva
Still- Vothe
Stone- Dwon'na
Storm- Mae
Story- Tallis
Streak- Afle
Street- Way
Strength- Styeladd
Stride- Ulo
Strong- Styela
Stubborn- Mou'ü
Sun- Tagh
Sunday- Talonn
Supposed- Klümen
Sword- Kantle
Swordmaster- Kantlelyna
Swordsman- Kantlekaid

T-

Take- Rraf
Taken-Rrafsu
Tale- Sön
Tall-Boutan
Task- Mehl
Teacher-Larkum
Tears-Yire
Tear-Yir
Teasing-Zaden

Tell-Quet
Than- De
Thank-Gifte
That-Hyan
Their-Iwi
The-Klamen
Them-Keyna
Then-Rodu
There-Konuae
These-Tate
They-Suto
Thing-Son
Think-Nystand
Third-Trêna
This-Taietan
Those-Taiet
Though-Kayet
Thought-Nystra
Thousand- Dakana
Three- Enya
Thrive- Pospit
Thrives- Pospitet
Through- Ekoch
Thunder- Kumuu
Thursday- Kalonn
Thus- Chuke
Time- Ülen
Tire- Weersa
Tired- Weer
Today- Eran
To-Eshoun
Together- Rakna
Tomorrow- Oleas
Too-Eshounün
Tool- Erkae
Touch- Nyach
Town-Dûr
Track- Werkes
Tree- Heta
Triumph- Traeta
Trouble- Hetera
True- Geaef
Truth- Geaes
Tuesday- Paloon
Tunic- Elton
Twisted- Ruic
Two-Ve

U-

Unbreakable- Noyahrik
Under- Mati
Underneath- Matisa
Understand- Föstuil
Unfortunate- Noyaflil
Unhappy- Noyalied
Unheard- Eftar
Unit- Ehj

Unless- Noyamer
Until- Fost
Up- Zaheun
Upon- Fiaer
Urge- Pes
Urgency- Kells
Urgent- Kell
Us- Akod
Use- Waellt
Usual- Ormel

V-

Vague- Meldd
Valley- Kerrsay
Value- Qal
Verily- Fakt
Very- Öulen
Vice- Nis
Victor- Shindar
Victory- Shindaroun
Violence- Bregi
Violent- Brega
Viscera- Gelid
Visceral- Gelit
Viscous- Viski
Voice- Holm
Void- Abys
Vowel- Khal

W-

Wait- Korna
Wake- Nan
Walk- Besat
Want- Kea
War- Echt
Warm- Steaem
Warrior- Takireaes
Warriors- Takireaese
Wary- Koun
Was- Intan
Watch- Mych
Watching - Mychen
Water- Himmel
Wave-Haill
Ways- Vweke
Way-Vwek
We- Günna
Weak- Nujt
Weapon- Nygrahda
Weapons- Nygrahdae
Weaponsmaster-
Nygrahdalyna
Wear- Xalt
Weary- Ëll
Weather- Rugde
Wednesday- Narloon

Week- Jülp
Weight- Sopwe
Well- Finy
Went- Zaha
Were- Qimp
West-Vel
What- Quea
Wheel- Torin
When- Kresna
Where- Lault
Whether- Rulte
While- Kresno
Whispers- Rigis
White- Pül
Who- Leae
Whole- Kepta
Whore- Ärda
Why- Quleten
Wild- Nurmenga
Will- Bene
Will (Constitution) -
Daelon
Win- Bulae
Wind- Keaem
Winless- Bulanoy
Winter- Sardö
Wish- Ealone
With- Quena
Within- Nida
Wonder- Dän
Wood- Eralië
Word- Setk
Words- Setke
Work- Lobar
World- Tolkean
Worry- Feaer
Would- Meano
Wretch- Käll'da
Write- El
Writer- Els
Writing- Elen
Written- Elis
Wrong- Yurg
Wrote- Elit

X-
Xenophobe- Kowa

Y-
Yeah- Ai
Year- Uhr
Yearn- Lell
Years- Uhre
Yes- Aiya
Yesterday- Omeateas
Yet- Ustan
You- Valõn
Young- Jeun

Your- Munnasae
Yours- Munnasaed
Youth- Jeul

Z-
Zeal- Fel
Zealot- Feldd
Zealotry- Felddi
Zealous- Feldde
Zest- Spik

One- Fou
Two- Ve
Three- Enya
Four- Skol
Five- Fên
Six- Srên
Seven- Viin
Eight- Eln
Nine- Nis
Ten- Zor
Eleven- Nar
Twelve- Ven
Thirteen- Ene
Fourteen- Skole
Fifteen- Fêne
Sixteen- Srêne
Seventeen- Viine
Eighteen- Elne
Nineteen- Nise
Twenty- Veo
Twenty-Five- Veofên
Thirty- Enyao
Forty- Skolo
Fifty- Fêno
Sixty- Srêno
Seventy- Viino
Eighty- Elno
Ninety- Niso
One Hundred- Foudan
One Hundred And Five-
Foudanfên
One Thousand- Zerdan
One Hundred Thousand-
Zerzordan

- I love you- *Inkan yayen valõn*
- (Motto of Blackhaven)-While we stand, we shall defend- *Kresno*

*günna stadya, günna*
*vont nee*
- (Elfish Proverb)-
  While we love,
  nothing can defeat
  us- *Kresno günna*
  *yayena, behkt*
  *jerwlyn ushna akod*
- 'Good morning'-
  *Yndrysl*
- Blessed Be- *Mlek eaf*
- Duty above all-
  *Zuskadi naht xellt*
- Blood traitor or
  bastard- *Dûmvardyn*

# Hindarün to
# Parlêthian

## A -

A'da-Father
Aaldoor-Fury
Aald-Rid
Aalew-Mile
Aargen-Excellent
Abya-Been
Abys-Void
Achien-Bad
Adi-Help
Afle-Streak
Afroi-Cut
Aikaid-Humans
Ait-Reply
Aiya-Yes
Ai-Yeah
Ajudi-Above
Akaid-Human
Aklm-Found
Akod-Us
Alamiah-Plant
Älda-Cause
Alda-Jasper
Alden-Fence
Alk-Grade
Al-Old
Alpro-Defend
Alt-Command
Alten-Commanding
Altenias-Cloak
Altsa-Commanded
Alts-Commands
Andil-Queasy
Andre-Innocent
Ängä-Cross
Äoslan-From
Arbee-Likes
Arbe-Like
Arben-Likely
Ärda-Whore
Arrae-Legs
Arra-Leg
Aru-Brave
Aru-Braved
Arue-Braves
Arulin-Bravery
Arus-Braver
Arusi-Bravest
Asen-Alive
Awin-Call
Awinen-Calling
Awinsa-Called

Awins-Caller
Ayanu-Asunder

## B-

Bäbäye- Fox
Bai-Hold
Bällä-Star
Bän-Burn
Barluk-Metal
Bathel-Rear
Baye-Lives
Bay-Live
Bayno-Lived
Bearn-Else
Behkt-Nothing
Bene-Will
Besat-Walk
Bĕtira-Cold
Blaet-Bee
Blö-Bloodied
Blöda-Bloody
Blöd-Blood
Blot-Bled
Blöt-Bleed
Blöten-Bleeding
Blots-Bleeder
Bo'la-Near
Bolecke-Away
Booka-Fall
Bookak-Fallen
Boun-Here
Boutan-Tall
Brä-About
Braech-Crumble
Brästl-Comb
Brega-Violent
Bregi-Violence
Bri-Fold
Brütel-Evil
Bruul-South
Bruun-Brother
Buche-Another
Buen-Down
Bulae-Win
Bulanoy-Winless
Buou-Fell
Buwai-Forest

## C

Chärdon-Girl
Chi-Bark
Chouda-Certain
Choul-Brought
Chounsi-Bring
Chued'a-Carve
Chuke-Thus

## D

Dâd-Dad
Daelon-Will(Constitution)
Daesis-Spirit
Dak'hana-Betrayal
Dak'na-Betray
Dak'naen-Betraying
Dak'nasa-Betrayed
Dak'nas-Betrayer
Dak'nat-Betrays
Dakana-Thousand
Damé-Game
Dän-Wonder
Da-Quite
Darem-Noble
Darf-Space
Datistva-State
De-Than
Deaet'he-Power
Dell-Field
Delz-Coast
Deviko-Plan
Dian-Remind
Diav-Limb
Didua-Differ
Dobrin-Lock
Dochea-Just
Dond-Did
Dosduna-Several
Druuj'ta-Prison
Dua-Shade
Dubliir-Record
Dü-Friend
Dukata-Friendship
Dule-Sand
Dülle-Course
Dultren-Book
Dultret-Books
Dûmvadyn-Bastard
Duned-Country
Duneda-Hard
Duned-Home
Dûr-Town
Duul-Complete
Dwon'na-Stone
Dyr- Hole

## E-

E'na-Mother
Eaegè-Self
Eaf-Be
Ealieaes-November
Ealla-Best
Eally-Better
Ealone-Wish

Eann-Bye,Buy,By
Ech-Cough
Echt-War
Ed'a-Son
Edlam-Between
Edoh-Age
Eftar-Unheard
Ehj-Unit
Ehla-Song
Ehli-Sing
Ehlis-Singer
Eideae-Possible
Einel-Every
Einen-Ever
Ekoch-Through
Elantian-Archer
Ela-Queen
Elba-Before
Eldion-Kingdom
Eld-King
Eleneaen-Sitting
Elenea-Sit
Elen-Pale
Elen-Writing
Elis-Written
Elit-Wrote
Ëll-Weary
Elne-Eighteen
Eln-Eight
Elno-Eighty
El-Oath
Elöda-Decide
Els-Writer
Elten-Order
Elton-Tunic
Elumña-Lake
El-Write
Elysia-Solitude
Emdri-Green
Emyar-Memory
En-Bit
Endarea-Figure
Ende-Fine
Enegadeae-Ready
Ene-Thirteen
Enyao-Thirty
Enya-Three
Enya-Three
Eonn-Does
Eralië-Wood
Eran-Today
Erda-Alas
Erdia-Govern
Erdwyn-Fair
Eria-Lady
Erion-Lord
Erkae-Tool
Eshoun-To

Eshounün-Too
Essimö-Air
Estadd-Beauty
Estoun-Beautiful
Est-So
Eth-Put
Eyaba-Speak

F-

Fairv-Iron
Fakt-Verily
Fäyla-Sea
Fäylie-Seas
Feaen-Are
Feaer-Worry
Fealos-Sleep
Feda-Inside
Fedd-Force
Feld-Fix
Feldde-Zealous
Felddi-Zealotry
Feldd-Zealot
Fel-Zeal
Fêna-Fifth
Fêne-Fifteen
Fên-Five
Fêno-Fifty
Fiaer-Upon
Fili-Branch
Finat-Done
Fineal-Start
Finst-Last
Finy-Well
Fírev-Always
Fjorlat-Shape
Flari-Sister
Flaydon-Boy
Flaydot-Boys
Fleabe-Hurts
Fleab-Hurt
Flett-Born
Flieger-Bird
Fli-Fortune
Flil-Fortunate
Flok-Over
Flone-Reads
Flon-Read
Flounen-Not
Flousen-Righteous
Flousil-Righteousness
Flous-Right
Flüken-Castle
Fo-May(Auxiliary)
Förunderverk-Magic
Förunderverk-Science
Fost-Until
Föstuil-Understand

Foudanfên-
Onehundredandfive
Foudan-Onehundred
Fouo-Lunch
Fou-One
Fou-One
Fraken-Choice
Fralop-Choose
Frason-Chosen
Freoh-Lies
Frey-Dry
Friem-Pose
Froh-Lie
Fueldereae-Allegiance
Fyö-Seethe

G-

Galamial-Gossamer
Gathen-Rejoicing
Gath-Rejoice
Gausten-Exclamation
Geaef-True
Geaes-Truth
Gehr-Leave
Gelid-Viscera
Gelit-Visceral
Gethan-Dinner
Geth-City
Ghi-Low
Giadef-Close
Gifte-Thank
Gläs-Gold
Gleepth-Cloud
Gleepthi-Cloudy
Glüpen-Must
Glusheb-Got
Gohnut-Pay
Gon-Die
Gonsa-Died
Gons-Dies
Gorae-Alone
Gravä-Shore
Greiol-Foot
Gris-Heal
Gröm-Big
Grress-Plane
Günna-We
Gwemh-God
Gwen-Crash

H-

Haba-Longing
Haill-Wave
Haldedd-Each
Hallis-Glory
Halo-If

Han-Appear
Haphen-Play
Hausil-Ease
Hausten-Easy
Heaema-Class
Hemios-Knowledge
Hespaa-Grief
Heta-Tree
Hetera-Trouble
Hetr-Breakfast
Hëtrecht-Noise
Hety-Busy
Himmel-Water
Himwró-Ground
Hinarï-Fly
Hindarün-English
Hochan-Look
Hoifte-Shoulders
Hoift-Shoulder
Hók-Sell
Hölle-Hall
Holm-Voice
Hovan-Safe
Hri-Break
Hrien-Breaking
Hru-Broke
Huedd-Ask
Hyan-That

I-

Ib-Or
Idian-Serious
Iene-Jugglers
Ien-Juggler
Ifer-Bent
Ih-Oh
Iist-Most
Ika-Fear
Ikly-Happen
Ileñias-Lily
Ilianria-Pattern
Illian-Dawn
Illion-Morning
Imluu-Perhaps
Inaem-Room
Indiil-Fact
Inkan-I
Inös-Battle
Insot-Flower
Intan-Was
Interoae-Questions
Interoa-Question
Inter-Query
Inviktu-Invincible
Isant-Chair
Isante-Chairs
Isidil- Badger

Isten-Staff
Istrukt-Revere
Itaen-Against
Ittin-Little
Iwaga-Product
Iwagi-Produce
Iwen-Forth
Iwi-Their
Iw-Piece
Iy-Betroth
Iyd-Betrothal
Iyen-Betrothing
Iysa-Betrothed

J-

Jarka-Far
Jaxea-Answer
Jdere-Own
Jela-Had
Jempt-Any
Jen-Child
Jened-Children
Jenu-Meet
Jerpen-Smell
Jerwlyn-Can
Jeul-Youth
Jeun-Young
Jevuu-Measure
Jian-List
Joa-Line
Jona-Said
Joot-Late
Jord-Land
Jülp-Week

K-

Kaden-North
Ka-For
Kaid-Man
Kaide-Men
Kairho-Black
Kalise-Mercy
Käll'da-Wretch
Kalonn-Thursday
Kankin-August
Kantlekaid-Swordsman
Kantlelyna-Swordmaster
Kantle-Sword
Karinium-Hello
Kartyl-Map
Kata-Blaze
Kayab-April
Kayet-Though
Kayn-Me
Keaem-Wind
Kea-Spend

Kea-Want
Keiden-Long
Kells-Urgency
Kell-Urgent
Kepta-Whole
Kerrsay-Valley
Kes-Birth
Kethna-Oak
Keyna-Them
Khal-Vowel
Kïmleth-Real
Kinë-Never
Kiyua-Cover
Kjos-Head
Klaguerd-Cemetery
Klamen-The
Klümen-Supposed
Klyph-Cipher
Klyshet-Daughter
Klysm-Sorry
Köl-Bow
Konuae-There
Konyia-Commander
Korna-Wait
Korrido-Road
Koruli-Flesh
Koun-Wary
Kowa-Xenophobe
Krant-First
Kree-Open
Krel-Creek
Kresna-When
Kresno-While
Krosa-More
Kruen-Rebuild
Krum-Mean
Krystes-Clear
Kuch-Dark
Kuchil-Darkness
Kuchsi-Darkest
Kuchsu-Darken
Kuchsuen-Darkening
Kuer-Path
Kulai-Animal
Kultae-Fools
Kulta-Fool
Kulten-Foolish
Kumuu-Thunder
Kupa-Jape
Kusra-Round
Kusrasa-Rounded
Kwell-Inch

L-

Lada-Forget
Läda-Forgotten
Lädön-Need

Lädönsa-Needed
Laen-Leaf
Lainli-Peer
Läliane-Elves
Lälian-Elf
Lälimyina-Moon
Lamat-December
Län-An
Län-A
Lardoun-Feet
Larkum-Teacher
Lärmo-Loyal
Las-Judge
Laskil-Judgment
Latak-Early
Lau-Breath
Lauen-Breathing
Lauf-Breathe
Lauk-Ride
Lault-Where
Lausa-Breathed
Laus-Breather
Laushden-Forever
Laynyan-September
Leaen-Lighted
Leae-Who
Leala-Mist
Lea-Light
Leasi-Lightest
Leas-Lighter
Leasu-Lighten
Leath-Servant
Leat-Maid
Leatran-Lightning
Leatran-Quicksilver
Leatsue-Maidens
Leatsu-Maiden
Le-Belief
Legathe-Brilliant
Leh-Creed
Leif-Damn
Leifen-Damning
Leiflil-Damnation
Leifsa-Damned
Leifsasi-Damnedest
Lell-Yearn
Lemmë-Drone
Lemmësa-Droned
Len-Hair
Lesh-Beliefs
Let-Believe
Leten-Believing
Leth-Flee
Leths-Fleer
Letsa-Believed
Lets-Believer
Leuft-Pick
Leuftsa-Picked

Lewn-Full
Lexla-Point
Libré-Free
Liedes-Happily
Lied-Happy
Lilit-Joyous
Lil-Joy
Ling-Seep
Lingui-Language
Lir-Few
Lîsna-Main
Llek-Might
Lobar-Work
Loge-Sighs
Log-Sigh
Loon-Day
Loone-Days
Lorr-Able
Lumaa-Mind
Luma-Flame
Luteaer-Cry
Lyna-Master
Lyz-Smoke


M-

Mach-Person
Maelda-Owe
Maen-May(Month)
Mae-Storm
Maiter-Complain
Mallif-Press
Mallifitha-Pressure
Malte-Invade
Matisa-Underneath
Mati-Under
Matsu-Mine(Noun)
Maullo-Center
Mauna-Ancestor
Meaelta-Hot
Meaken-Loss
Meakes-Lost
Meaklim-Lose
Meano-Would
Mehl-Task
Melas-Now
Meldd-Vague
Melnon-Bells
Mentay-Made
Mer-Less
Miea-Horse
Mie-Spear
Mimai-Act
Minne-Moments
Minn-Moment
Misarea-Secret
Mlek-Blessed
Mletch-Note

Mödene-Slays
Möden-Slay
Mol-June
Mou'ü-Stubborn
Moyrkel-Assassin
Muan-March(Month)
Muchen-People
Munna-Our
Munnasaed-Yours
Munnasae-Your
Mün-On
Mur-Soul
Muura-Foe
Myach-Irritated
Myachna-Irritable
Mya-Irritate
Mychen-Watching
Mych-Watch
Mynda-After
Myrra-Illusion


N-

Naelos-Could
Na-Even
Nan-Wake
Nar-Eleven
Narloon-Wednesday
Narth-Laugh
Narthen-Laughing
Nas-Destroy
Nasen-Destroyed
Nasen-Destroying
Nashtan-Period
Nasior-Preserved
Nass-Destroyer
Neaus-Kind
Neben-Behind
Nebt-Beyond
Nee-Guard
Neelo-Guardian
Neñyos-Arrow
Nerty-Hunt
Neyn-House
Nida-Within
Nid-Fill
Nift-Left
Niir-Direct
Nise-Nineteen
Nis-Nine
Niso-Ninety
Nist-Lift
Nis-Vice
Nó-And
Nodolu-Enough
Noie-Night
Noien-Nights
Nold-Reach

Nol-Goal
Nori-Deliver
Notio-Kick
Noyaflil-Unfortunate
Noyahrik-Unbreakable
Noyaistruktto-Irreverence
Noyalied-Unhappy
Noyamer-Unless
Noya-No
Noyena-Let
Noyv-Jade
Nrein-Interest
Nrekin-Number
Nreklis-Numeral
Nujt-Weak
Nurmenga-Wild
Nuz-Allow
Nyach-Touch
Nya-Deserve
Nyaen-Deserving
Nyasa-Deserved
Nyas-Deserves
Nygrahdae-Weapons
Nygrahdalyna-Weaponsmaster
Nygrahda-Weapon
Nyn-Do
Nyneideae-Impossible
Nystand-Think
Nystra-Thought

O-

Oad-Bane
Ocheanas-Seen
Ochean-See
Oduun-Seek
Oh-Also
Olea-Boot
Oleas-Boots
Oleas-Tomorrow
Ollean-Some
Oloons-Breeches
Olsun-Farm
Olt-Bond
Olua-Fiend
Ólva-River
Oma-'Coinage'
Omeateas-Yesterday
Oncherath-Explain
Orltan-Red
Ormel-Usual
Orner-Follow
Orvă-Abyss
Öulen-Very
Owaen-Ahead
Owne-East
Oya-She

Oyer-Place
P-

Paed-Knew
Paloon-Tuesday
Parra-Correct
Peaf-Know
Pear-Known
Pe-As
Peka-Should
Pes-Urge
Pĕtiir-Common
Pheak-Joke
Phyr-Rule
Piat-Jump
Plet-Saw
Plumès-Feather
Pola-He
Pŏlya-Motion
Polypa-Moves
Polyp-Move
Pospitet-Thrives
Pospit-Thrive
Pŏtal-Door
Poth-Sky
Praet-Sever
Preriim-School
Prreh-Problem
Pŭl-White
Puscheb-Is
Pwoe-Borrow
Pyltak-Example

Q-

Qal-Value
Qar'tali-Sanctum
Qela-Again
Qiit-Add
Qimp-Were
Qreden-Hiding
Qred-Hide
Qredsu-Hidden
Qrer-Large
Quais-Curves
Qualpe-Run
Qualpesu-Running
Qual-Ran
Quea-What
Qued-Box
Queeta-Gone
Quena-With
Quen-Bodies
Quene-Body
Quesio-Exile
Quet-Tell
Quleten-Why

R-

Radsun-Parchment
Rae'da-Family
Rahn-Shield
Raine-Dance
Rainen-Dancing
Raines-Dancer
Rakna-Together
Raloon-Saturday
Rayla-Misfit
Reage-Lead
Reez-Same
Reffer-Boat
Rekie-Silent
Resen-October
Rhi-Apart
Riah-Bed
Ridda-Cape
Rigis-Whispers
Riima-Learn
Risa-Inspired
Risen-Inspiring
Ris-Inspire
Risnla-Inspirational
Rodu-Then
Rók-Debt
Róko-Debts
Rraf-Take
Rrafsu-Taken
Rret'a-Carry
Ruben-Fail
Rugde-Weather
Ruic-Twisted
Rula-Fight
Ruleten-Change
Ruletenen-Changing
Ruletensa-Changed
Ruletens-Changer
Rulte-Whether
Ruunin-Minute

S-

Sääbe-Hers
Sääb-Her
Sääne-His
Sään-Him
Säära-My
Sae-Hour
Sævulen-Slave
Sævulen-Devil
Sage-Give
Sagen-Giving
Sages-Gives
Saif-Listen
Saifen-Listening

Sanf-Army
Sanq-Quit
Särabeae-Mine
Sardö-Winter
Sardun-Keep
Sa-Return
Sârtyn-Myself
Sayd-Going
Saykl-Dedicated
Sayklis-Dedication
Se-Finish
Seage-Gave
Sedika-Port
Sembas-Food
Sen-Life
Sennia-Good
Seno-Feel
Serbe-In
Serel-Rite
Seryean-Eternity
Sesa-Finished
Setke-Words
Setk-Word
Setuil-Cancel
Shaeben-Its
Shaiben-It
Shälda-Because
Shamer-Disgrace
Shä-Of
Sharn-Prophecy
Sharntoul-Prophet
Sharntoun-Prophetess
Sheeth-Dust
Sheethsa-Dusted
Shindaroun-Victory
Shindar-Victor
Shlock-March(Verb)
Shou-Clean
Shouf-Cleanse
Shpa-Name
Shtan-Off
Shuak-February
Shyn-Quiet
Sied-Great
Siira-Code
Sikkeae-Ago
Sïm-Am
Sïnd-How
Sintaradö-Miss
Sinyain-Sorrow
Siva-Grey
Skai-Blue
Skel-Fish
Skola-Fourth
Skole-Fourteen
Skol-Four
Skolo-Forty
Slad-Rubble

Slaughta-Kill
Slaughtas-Kills
Slaughtsa-Killed
Slel-Nose
Slír-Agenda
Sloshea-Next
Smek-Least
Sön-Tale
Son-Thing
Sopwe-Weight
So-Returned
Souden-Many
Souve-Hands
Souv-Hand
Soyem-Remember
Soyems-Remembered
Soyemsu-Remembering
Spik-Zest
Srêna-Sixth
Srêne-Sixteen
Srêno-Sixty
Srên-Six
Staabe-Pound
Stadya-Stand
Steaem-Warm
Stealik-Heat
Stoyet-Honor
Stuet-Comma
Stuna-Has
Styeladd-Strength
Styela-Strong
Styk-Fashion
Suddi-Remain
Sumyan-Being
Sün-Came
Sûn-Noun
Suno-Determine
Sunosa-Determined
Suto-They
Svean-Nice
Svonwy-Demon
Syak-Honey
Syn-Hope
Synsu-Hoped
Syp-Death
Syr-Sir(Knight)
Szesa-Eat


T-

Tael-Lay
Tagh-Sun
Taietan-This
Taiet-Those
Takireaese-Warriors
Takireaes-Warrior
Tal'enis-Purifier(Noun)
Tala-July

Talchin-Cyree
Talenia-Pure
Taleni-Purify
Talis-Into
Tallis-Story
Talonn-Sunday
Tam-Bored
Tamen-Boring
Tañd-Male
Tate-These
Tauon-Back
Tauron-Maybe
Taurounen-Shining
Tauroun-Shine
Teo-At
Térn-Area
Tey-Curse
Teysa-Cursed
Teza-Show
Thafn-Blade
Thafnlyna-Blademaster
Thallaa-Care
Thedreth-Fog
Thèvea-Serve
Thïaeth-Hollow
Throin-During
Thyn-Snow
Tiln-Fit
Tolkean-World
Tollapiasenn-Smallum
Ton-Make
Torin-Wheel
Torseth-Harm
Touve-Soft
Traeta-Triumph
Trasnel-Drink
Tref-Form
Trefui-Count
Trêna-Third
Truy-Plain
Tu-Pass
Tubä-Race
Tuln-Mountain
Tuss-Haven
Tuuk-Passage
Twe-Check

U-

Ubóth-Among
Ubr-But
Udre-Picture
Uduan-Doomed
Udu-Doom
Udwa-However
Uerd-Sentence
Uha-Deep
Uhj-Group

Uhre-Years
Uhr-Year
Uka-Heart
Ük-Rest
Uleaen-Getting
Ulea-Get
Ülen-Time
Uloon-Friday
Ulo-Stride
Ulsen-Rain
Umble-Half
Uo-Begin
Uoen-Beginning
Uol-Began
Uos-Beginner
Ushna-Defeat
Ustan-Yet
Uster-Front

V-

Valðn-You
Varia-Legend
Variania-Legendary
Vas-Fast
Vas-Quick
Vasusa-Quickened
Vausa-Sound
Vekae-Nails
Veka-Nail
Vekla-Ocean
Vel-West
Venae-Go
Vena-Much
Vente-Second
Ven-Twelve
Veofèn-Twenty
Veo-Twenty
Ve-Two
Ve-Two
Veyn-Extra
Vich-Glee
Viine-Seventeen
Viino-Seventy
Viin-Seven
Vila-Promise
Vilda-Mask
Viski-Viscous
Vizil-Seem
Vlen-Doing
Vont-Shall
Vothe-Still
Vrial-Contain
Vuuka-Hell
Vwanil-Sadness
Vwani-Sadly

Vwan-Sad
Vweke-Ways
Vwek-Way
Vwen-Harbor

W-

Wâdeh-Idea
Waellt-Use
Waev-Grow
Way-Street
Wedavii-Send
Wedd-Both
Weersa-Tire
Weer-Tired
Wegni-Develop
Wehtun-Instrument
Weir-Rock
Wella-Gift
Wer-Heed
Werij-Set
Werkes-Track
Wetron-Music
Whäd-Fate
Whim-Often
Widne-Base
Winka-Finally
Wink-Final
Wíramer-Color
Wônt-Organize
Wrent-Pull
Wróth-Bone

X-

Xalt-Wear
Xanen-Sail
Xeema-Island
Xellt-All
Xetiane-Shadows
Xetian-Shadow
Xeyna-Justice
Xul-January
Xuten-Fire

Y-

Yaloon-Monday
Yanae-Pages
Yana-Page
Yardos-Garden
Yayenaen-Loving
Yayena-Love
Yayenasa-Loved
Yayenas-Lover
Yayeni-Loveliest

Yayen-Lovely
Yeeh-Lot
Yelt-Arisen
Yen-Passion
Yercht-Have
Yest-Come
Yeste-Comes
Yeste-Coming
Yestoma-Letter
Yether-Face
Yethers-Faces
Yiln-Draw
Yi-Peace
Yire-Tears
Yir-Tear
Ÿlt-Frost
Ÿltid-Frozen
Yolom-Find
Youl-Accept
Yurg-Wrong

Z-

Zaden-Teasing
Zaha-Went
Zaheun-Up
Zarouchen-Earth
Zasnuil-Build
Zaysa-Glad
Zek-Reign
Zêmbyl-Mark
Zephyr-Silver
Zercht-Doubt
Zerchte-Doubts
Zerdan-Onethousand
Zered-Heard
Zere-Hear
Zeres-Hearing
Zert-End
Zerten-Ending
Zerzordan-
Onehundredthousand
Zeyla-Dog
Zeym-Mass
Zii-Notice
Zîth-Object
Zo-High
Zonn-Once
Zor-Ten
Zsoe-Eyes
Zso-Eye
Zuana-Say
Zuanas-Says
Zunaa-Out
Zuskadi-Duty
Zuskadin-Duties

Discover other titles by A.B.B.Olson

<u>Graves of Good and Evil Trilogy</u>
*Elven Race Reborn*
*Honor of Assassins*
*Prophecy's Final Price*

*Nkayt'hei*